D0378612

KATE WELSH
Small-Town Dreams
&
The Girl Next Door

Steeple
Hill®

Published by Steeple Hill Books™

STEEPLE HILL BOOKS

Steeple
Hill®

ISBN-13: 978-0-373-65124-5
ISBN-10:   0-373-65124-4

SMALL-TOWN DREAMS AND THE GIRL NEXT DOOR

SMALL-TOWN DREAMS
Copyright © 2000 by Kate Welsh

THE GIRL NEXT DOOR
Copyright © 2001 by Kate Welsh

All rights reserved. Except for use in any review, the reproduction or utilization of this work in whole or in part in any form by any electronic, mechanical or other means, now known or hereafter invented, including xerography, photocopying and recording, or in any information storage or retrieval system, is forbidden without the written permission of the editorial office, Steeple Hill Books, 233 Broadway, New York, NY 10279 U.S.A.

This is a work of fiction. Names, characters, places and incidents are either the product of the author's imagination or are used fictitiously, and any resemblance to actual persons, living or dead, business establishments, events or locales is entirely coincidental.

This edition published by arrangement with Steeple Hill Books.

® and TM are trademarks of Steeple Hill Books, used under license. Trademarks indicated with ® are registered in the United States Patent and Trademark Office, the Canadian Trade Marks Office and in other countries.

www.SteepleHill.com

Printed in U.S.A.

CONTENTS

Books by Kate Welsh

Love Inspired

KATE WELSH

is a two-time winner of Romance Writers of America's coveted Golden Heart® Award and was a finalist for RWA's RITA® Award in 1999. Kate lives in Havertown, Pennsylvania, with her husband of over thirty years. When not at work in her home office creating stories and the characters that populate them, Kate fills her time in other creative outlets. There are few crafts she hasn't tried at least once, or a sewing project that hasn't been a delicious temptation. Those ideas she can't resist grace her home or those of friends and family.

As a child she often lost herself in creating make-believe worlds and happily-ever-after tales. Kate turned back to creating happy endings when her husband challenged her to write down the stories in her head. With Jesus so much a part of her life, Kate found it natural to incorporate Him in her writing. Her goal is to entertain her readers with wholesome stories of the love between two people the Lord has brought together, and to teach His truths while she entertains.

SMALL-TOWN DREAMS

Come unto me, all ye that labor and are heavy laden, and I will give you rest.

—*Matthew* 11:28

To Mother,

In any language there is no more loving and important word than *Mother*. Mothers love and nurture us from the day we are conceived. They teach us how to go on in life from the day we are born. They are the cornerstone of the family. When we falter, they patch up our cuts and bruises—even those that don't show—and send us back into the world to earn our place. Thanks for the years of love and support.

Chapter One

Cassidy Jamison stared at her grandfather and only one word came to her mind. *Betrayal.*

"Naming Jonathan Reed as the next vice president of Information Systems wasn't an easy task. We had several excellent candidates but…"

Cassidy saw her grandfather's mouth moving as he heaped praise on his new vice president, but the buzzing in her ears drowned out the actual words.

She was honest enough with herself to admit that Jon had worked hard, too, and that he would make a good VP. But she would have done just as good a job, and she had worked just as hard as he had. Harder, in fact! Cassidy hadn't taken a vacation since joining the company out of business school six years earlier. The Mickey Mouse ears perched atop Jon's monitor were a constant reminder that he and his family had flown off to Disney World last year while she'd worked a seventy-hour week to keep ahead of the problems that he'd been able to leave behind.

But even that didn't bother her all that much. What hurt, what felt as if it had crushed her spirit, was that her grandfather had broken his word. He had promised the promotion to her.

She heard a door shut firmly and she blinked, looking around. The meeting was apparently over, and she and the all-powerful Winston Jamison were alone in his oak-paneled office.

"You made your surprise evident," he snapped.

Cassidy stood and smoothed the straight skirt of her dress-for-success, navy power suit. At five-foot-nine she was easily able to look him in the eye without looking up—the very reason she'd stood.

"Surprise, Grandfather?" Cassidy arched an eyebrow, an action stolen directly from the man before her. "That's all I gave away? Then I did rather well, don't you think? Because what I felt was *shock!* No! Call it what it is—*betrayal.*"

Her grandfather ran his fingers through his impeccably styled hair. "This is business, Cassidy. Not betrayal. And it was the most difficult decision I've ever made."

"Business? You set me up! You told me that vice presidency was mine. I've worked practically around the clock since Harold Overton died. No one has put in more time or seen to it that their teams completed more projects on time than I have."

Winston Jamison nodded his head, his white hair

gleaming in the sunlight that streamed in his office window. "That's all true but there were other considerations."

"What other considerations? Dedication? Education?" she asked, knowing full well she was ahead in those areas, as well. She'd carried two majors trying to please him and herself at the same time.

"Jon is a family man. He's stable. Trustworthy—"

"And I'm not trustworthy?"

Her grandfather looked pained. "No, of course I trust you. It was a judgment call. That's all. You'll just have to accept that."

"Accept that my own grandfather lied to me. Accept that he played fast and loose with a solemn promise as well as the truth. You know, Grandfather, if you treated any other employee the way you have me, you'd be in court faster than a lightning strike can fry a PC."

Winston's eyes widened and his face grew red. "Are you threatening me, young lady?" His tone was one she recognized. She had heard it for twenty years, each and every time he needed to haul out the big guns to manipulate her into compliance with his will. His expression was the same.

Disapproving.

Judgmental.

"Don't try that attitude and tone with me. It won't work this time," she growled and leaned her hands on his desk, which put her practically nose to nose with her new nemesis. "Who was it you called the morning

Harold died? Who had to cancel her vacation immediately to take over his workload because—let me make sure I get the wording just right here—'Cassidy, you're the only one I can count on.' Too bad you didn't call Jon. His vacation wasn't scheduled for another two weeks. But then, he got his time off, didn't he."

Her grandfather looked down at his desk and fidgeted with his calendar. "His children were counting on that trip."

"I was counting on mine. Just as I was counting on that promotion. *And* my vacation weeks the two years before that. Vacations you begged me not to take."

"I needed you here—not gallivanting off to some uncivilized place on the globe."

"Well, you obviously don't need me around here as much as you've led me to believe all these years. And since I have six weeks' vacation coming to me, you'll see me then. *If* I decide to come back!"

Her grandfather stiffened, his bushy eyebrows drawn together, his gray eyes almost as sorrowful as she felt. "I did need you. I do. I was just trying—"

"Don't, Grandfather," Cassidy snapped, cutting him off before he could do what he did best—entice her into believing him once again. "Don't say anything else," she said, her voice suddenly—*maddeningly*—full of despair. "Please. It's too late for explanations and more promises. Way too late."

With that, angry at both herself and the old man, she turned and rushed from the room, closing the door with a definite *thump*. She made it as far as the hall to the elevator before the burning started in her stomach, before tears of pain and utter desolation dammed up in her throat, and before she felt each beat of her heart inside her head.

She'd given up her dreams. He'd said that without her he couldn't run the business he'd spent a lifetime building. And out of gratitude—out of a need to be loved—she'd tucked away her charcoal, pencils and paints and had gone to work for him.

In her little German sports car some minutes and a minor traffic jam later, Cassidy sat in the parking lot and stared up at her apartment building. She'd thought of it as a haven not five minutes earlier. Now its white facade looked cold. Empty. And she knew the inside of her own apartment would be even worse. Gray and depressing. She couldn't make herself get out of her car.

Her stomach started to burn again, so she grabbed the roll of antacids that she always had sitting on the console and popped one in her mouth. She looked at the roll. Really *looked* at it this time. She'd stopped last night on the way home to buy it. It was nearly gone. How could that be?

Rubbing the heel of her hand where her stomach constantly stung, Cassidy remembered her doctor's diagnosis of an ulcer. He'd prescribed medication just last week. Cassidy had never taken the time to fill the prescription. Apparently he was right. She really did need it.

Half an hour later, a prescription bottle and a new roll

of antacids on her passenger seat, Cassidy started her car and wondered what to do next. Her grandfather had beeped her no less than ten times since she'd left his office. Her beeper was now turned off, as was her cell phone. She picked them both up off the passenger seat and glared at them. Sometimes these well-touted modern conveniences felt more like a pair of handcuffs chaining her to Jamison Steel.

But right now she was on vacation.

Without ceremony she tossed the offending technology into the backseat and determinedly put them and the company out of her mind.

For the first time since her childhood when she woke up with her grandfather sitting at her bedside in a Colorado hospital, she had no one planning her next step in life. No. This next move was all her own to make.

Rather than feeling free, Cassidy felt suddenly very alone. With her grandfather out of the equation, she had no one to rely on. He was all she had. Her friends were really more acquaintances, and most of them, save a neighbor or two, worked at Jamison.

She looked at herself in the rearview mirror, narrowing her blue eyes. When had she gotten so drawn looking? She fussed with her short, straight, blond hair for a second and bit her full bottom lip. *What do you want, Cassidy Jamison? Where do you want to go?*

"I want to get away from the rat race," she said aloud to the near-stranger in the mirror. "I need time to just think."

A penny winked up at her from next to the nearly empty antacid roll in the console. She remembered a scene from a book she'd read several years earlier. The hero had flipped a coin—a penny—and had driven toward his uncertain future, giving the coin the power he no longer felt over his life. At each crossroad, he'd let the penny send him wherever it chose. Right then, feeling adrift, she felt an acute kinship with that character and decided her discarded penny just might know more than she did about her life's choices.

She picked it up, turned it over in her hand and stared down at old Abe Lincoln's coppery visage. Above his head were words she'd seen all her life and never really read. *In God we trust.*

Cassidy wondered suddenly if there was a God. She remembered vaguely her parents talking about Him. But God hadn't been part of her upbringing under her grandfather's rule. Recalling her father's calm, easy smile, she wondered if maybe that was part of her problem. She flipped the coin. Caught it. Slapped it down on the back of her hand. "If You're up there, God, send me where I need to go. Heads north, tails south," she called, then peeked. Honest Abe stared up at her again. "North," she said, then wondered once again if she or some higher power had control of her destiny.

Winston Jamison turned from the window that looked out over Rittenhouse Square when a sharp knock echoed through his office door. "Come," he called.

His longtime secretary walked in and as far as his desk. She stood, arms crossed, and glared at him. "She hasn't answered her pages or her cell phone. I've tried her apartment. No go there, either."

"Where could she have gone?"

"Well, I doubt she went to cry on a friend's shoulder. Thanks to her hours these last several years, she hasn't got any close friends."

Rose had been with him for years. He'd kept her with generous raises and stock options. He'd kept her because he couldn't intimidate her. But just now, he wished he'd fired her thirty years ago at the first sign of insubordination. He scowled, knowing it wouldn't cow her in the least. "I'm sure there's a saltshaker in that credenza over there. Care to throw some into the wound?"

She tapped her foot and moved her hands to her ample hips. "Don't think I'm not tempted. Why on earth did you do it?"

"I didn't have a choice. The job would have been too much for her. I did it for her own good."

"You told her the vice presidency was hers. You told *me* it was hers. Why the last-minute change? I've never known you to vacillate like this."

"I was trying to save her from herself. And from me. I love that girl, Rose. This place is dragging her down. The circles under her eyes have circles."

"So this was for her own good? That child was in tears! I've never seen her cry in all the years I've known her!"

He winced. "I was wrong to insist she come in to the business. I'm trying to right a wrong."

"Oh? Now you see it, when you managed to ignore a double major and her real talent? What, pray tell, caused this sudden revelation?"

He knew he deserved her scorn, but he felt the need to squirm and didn't like it in the least! Instead he walked to his desk and sat in his big leather chair. "I overheard a conversation she had with her doctor last week. She has an ulcer, Rose. And it's my fault."

She sat in the chair where Cassidy had been sitting just a few hours earlier. "But to pull the rug out from under her like that was cruel."

"It was a last-minute decision. I just couldn't let her take on more. But I intended to explain. I really did. But she started shouting. Then I did. I lost sight of what I wanted to say and defended my choice instead. Before I knew it, she was storming out. By the time I calmed down enough to realize what had happened, she was gone."

Rose shook her head in disgust. "For your sake, I hope she isn't gone for good."

"You know, Rose, if I knew where she was, that would be okay with me. Just so she's happy."

Dusk had just settled into darkness when the six-lane interstate Cassidy was traveling narrowed rather abruptly to one lane in each direction. She drove about ten miles farther, getting anxious about the denseness of the timberland that now surrounded her.

When the Pocono Mountains had loomed ahead of her at the Lehigh Tunnel, she'd gotten excited about the possibilities they held. She'd decided to really cut loose on this vacation and pick up a sketch pad and some charcoal. Since then, she'd seen numerous valleys and stark slopes of bare deciduous trees dotted with deep green pines that she itched to sketch.

But when that vast expanse of trees had formed a dark, oppressive tunnel with no evidence of a town or resort anywhere, the countryside had become frightening. Then, just as she decided to turn around because civilization had not made its presence known, the car that had been her stalwart companion for nearly five hours suddenly coughed and bucked as she crested a hill. It settled down again when she pressed a little harder on the accelerator, but whenever she slowed down to stop and turn around, it nearly stalled.

Cassidy was left with a dilemma: she had to continue on or risk getting stuck right there, which she feared was miles from nowhere. Just the thought of breaking down amidst the darkness and thick woodlands turned up the acidic burning in her stomach another notch. The pounding in her head seemed to turn up its volume by a hundred decibels, as well.

Several hundred yards farther down the road, a sign proclaimed that the town of Mountain View, Pennsylvania, population three hundred, was only a couple of miles ahead. Reassured, she had traveled on about a mile before the car bucked again.

Cassidy could just see the tiny town, a few lights winking in the distance, when the car stalled for the first time. She got it started, but several hundred yards farther down the road it coughed again and stalled. After several tries it did turn over, but continued to buck and cough as she lumbered down the road. She barely was able to limp the car into Earl's Car Emporium in the center of town. No sooner had she pulled to a stop than the engine died.

Cassidy would have felt more confident in Earl's had the weathered wood and faded sign looked the way they did for quaint effect rather than from years of neglect and aging. She got out to look around. Rusting and greasy car parts overflowed several fifty-five gallon drums next to the rustic building. The sound of country music, a metallic pounding and the odd grumble, floated out of a crooked doorway in what she thought was a converted barn.

The disgruntled voice was not reassuring.

"Mr. Earl?" Cassie called over the music as she gingerly pushed open the door. "Hello. Could someone help me?"

"Eh? What's that?" a gravelly voice called. "Oh, well, hey there, girly. What can I help you with? Directions to Appleton?"

"Actually, my car's acting up."

Cassidy watched as a man in a greasy hat peered over the lifted hood of a car. When the mechanic came out from behind his current project, she remembered her grandfather describing someone as a long drink of water, and knew the description fit Mister—.

"Mister Earl?" she asked, and hoped he was better at his work than he was at keeping clean. Cassidy pulled off the glasses she only wore for driving and perched them on top of her blond head.

The man's pale blue eyes crinkled at the corners in a smile that he didn't betray with his mouth. "Just Earl. Earl Pedmont," he said, and offered her his hand.

Cassidy automatically reached out to shake it. But Earl only awkwardly squeezed her fingers. When his eyes rose to look into hers, it was his look of consternation that made her realize her error. And his.

He smiled in obvious discomfort, let go and stepped back, tipping his cap in a surprisingly courtly manner. "How do, little lady."

Cassidy looked down at her now-greasy hand, then back up at Earl, trying to hide her annoyance. "I've been better," she answered truthfully. "As I said, my car is acting up. It started a few miles ago. Coughing and bucking. For a while it evened out when I accelerated. Then it started stalling, no matter what I did. I barely made it to town."

Earl nodded. "Hmm. Let's take a look," he said as he turned toward the door and made his way outside.

She followed, trying not to cringe at the idea of his coveralls coming in contact with her creamy leather interior when he climbed into her pride and joy.

After starting the car and listening to the engine run a few seconds, then stall, he pursed his lips and nodded sagely. "'Pears to me you'll be spending some time here in Mountain View, little lady. 'Less you got a husband who can come get you, that is." He gave her a friendly gap-toothed smile.

"No husband," she answered, ignoring the pang in the region of her heart. Sometimes her life seemed so empty. What good was earning tons of money with no time to spend it and no one to spend it on? Especially when you didn't earn all that money in a way that was in the least fulfilling.

"That's good. That's good," Earl replied, still grinning.

His grin suddenly made Cassidy nervous. "Why do you say that?"

"Wouldn't want him to be worrying 'bout you being stuck here so far from home. Ain't a nice world no more for young ladies. Guess since you don't have a husband, you'll be staying with us for a while."

She looked around what she could see of the town. Stay? Here? Was he crazy? When the mountains had loomed ahead, a picture of her next few weeks had flashed into her head. A luxury suite. A chic hotel shop where she could buy a sketch pad and some clothes. A four-star restaurant, or maybe even room service for her meals. Calling this a one-horse town would be kind.

Cassidy looked back at Earl's smiling face and wondered why he looked so pleased. "What's wrong with my car?" she asked, trying to ignore the thought that had rocketed into her brain. What did one do in Mountain View, PA? Watch the grass grow? The frost settle?

"Could be the fuel filter. That'd be the cheapest.

Could take a few days to get one up here. But then, it could be the pump or the carb. That'd take longer. But then, could be somethin' else altogether. Won't know till I get to workin' on it."

Cassidy blew out a breath. "How long will it be until you can look at it?"

"Hmm. Well, I got several folks in line ahead of you. Guess I could squeeze you in late day after tomorrow, or the next morning."

Cassidy's head started pounding harder. "Look, I'll pay you double your labor rate to take a look at it tomorrow."

"Sorry, little lady, but a promise is a promise. Can't put you ahead. Just wouldn't be fair. But don't you worry none. I got me a good supplier. Bet it won't take long at all to get hold of any part I'll need. And once I get going, I'm real quick."

Again Cassidy looked around at the tiny hamlet where she'd landed. "I'll pay triple," she offered.

Earl shook his shaggy head. "Nope. Late day after tomorrow at best."

Cassidy squeezed her temples. Whatever had happened to her grandfather's axiom that everyone had a price? Looking at Earl Pedmont's set features, she decided *he'd* never heard of that particular rule of life. She felt as if she'd fallen down a rabbit hole.

Earl took off his cap and scratched his head. "You'll be needin' something to eat and somewhere to stay. Maybe you ought to go on down and see Irma Tallinger. She runs the café and the Mountain View Hotel. She'll fix you right up. Her place is just there up the road a piece," he said, pointing toward a flickering sign.

Cassidy saw the old sign but she saw nothing that looked like a hotel. She gave one last glance at her traitorous car, then turned to trudge toward the café Earl had recommended.

Her head ached. Her stomach burned. At least, she consoled herself, walking down the side of a road without sidewalks put her in no danger. Traffic in the booming metropolis of Mountain View was as nonexistent as foreign car parts.

Chapter Two

Cassidy held out little hope that Irma's Café would provide a decent meal. After all, it had been Earl Pedmont who'd recommended the place, and that didn't inspire much confidence. But it seemed to be the only game in town, so she headed toward the flickering neon sign he'd pointed out. Though traffic along the country road was indeed no problem, the uneven surface was.

With the prospect of spending several days watching everywhere she put her high-heel-shod feet looming in her mind, she opened the door to Irma's Café—and almost gasped aloud. Instead she stood there gaping because inside the unassuming concrete-block structure was a perfectly preserved fifties diner, replete with shining red counter and matching stools. Sitting opposite the counter was a row of cheery red-and-white booths.

Cassidy sniffed the air appreciatively and sighed. Until that moment her surprises that day had been anything but pleasant. Maybe her luck had changed. Maybe things were looking up.

"Don't get too excited, Cassidy old girl, there was nowhere to go *but* up," she muttered to herself as she went to put her hand to her throbbing head and noticed her grease-stained fingers.

As the bell over the door tinkled, an elderly woman stopped polishing the red faux-marble countertop and looked up. "Sit wherever you want," she said with a friendly smile. "I'll be with you in no time."

Cassidy nodded gratefully and nearly staggered to the nearest booth. She sank down onto the comfortable red bench and put her clean palm against her forehead, closing her eyes, trying to decide what to do next.

Her car clearly needed more than the typical in-and-out repair she was used to having done. Should she have her grandfather send a car for her, or should she look for lodging? That was really no choice at all, since right then she didn't even want to talk to her grandfather, let alone ask for his help in any way.

"Are you all right, dear?" a female voice asked.

She looked up at the elderly woman who'd called to her from behind the counter. To Cassidy, she looked like everyone's great aunt. Round. Gray. Kindly. The fairy godmother in *Cinderella* come to life.

"My car broke down and I don't know what to do next," she confided to the woman for some unknown reason.

"You look like you could use a little repair yourself."

Cassidy felt as if someone had wrapped a blanket

around her cold spirit. Baffled by her reaction to the woman, Cassidy shrugged. "Oh, it's no big deal. Just a monster headache and an ulcer burning a hole in my stomach."

"How about a bowl of homemade vegetable soup, some crackers and a nice cup of herbal tea?"

Cassidy sighed. "Is the soup what I smelled when I came in here?"

The woman sniffed the air and chuckled. "I suppose it was. So how does that bowl sound to you?"

"Perfect. I'll have the soup and crackers." She thought for a second and added, "The tea, too."

"That'll just take a couple minutes. You need anything else, just holler for Irma."

"I need to wash up." She showed Irma her greasy hand. "Earl?"

Cassidy nodded and even managed a smile. "I'd like to believe he did it by accident. After all, he's got my car."

"Oh, I'm sure it was an accident. He's really a nice man. He's just not bursting with social graces. The ladies' room is just past the counter on the left."

Cassidy stood. "Thank you, Irma. Earl also said to ask you about the Mountain View Hotel. It looks as if I'll be in town for a while, so I'll need a suite."

"Mountain View Hotel? Is that what he said?" She chuckled. "Oh, he's a card, that Earl. We don't have a hotel here in Mountain View."

Horrified, Cassidy stared at the woman. She'd given up on reaching the mountain resort of her daydreams, but she had to stay somewhere. "Then where will I stay? Earl made it sound as if I could be stuck here for days."

"In summer I sometimes rent rooms at the parsonage. Sort of a bed-and-breakfast kind of arrangement. That must be what he meant. That tease! You're welcome to stay with us, even though I don't usually rent in fall or winter. I can adjust the regular rate for the off-season, or leave it and include three meals either here or with the family." She named what Cassidy thought sounded like a very fair rate and described a room that didn't sound like a luxury suite but at least sounded comfortable.

"That sounds fine. Can you tell me how to get to a local shop? I need to buy some clothes and personal items. This was an unplanned trip."

Irma pursed her lips. "Hmm. Well, there's The Trading Post across the road. You can stop and get personal items and underthings there, but as for clothing, there's nothing in town open in the off-season except the church thrift shop. I'm sure you could get by with what you find there."

Cassidy's heart dropped. No little designer shop? No cute little mountain boutique? "A thrift shop?"

Irma didn't seem to notice Cassidy's hesitation. "It's a little ways on up the road. Last building out of town. Our home is right next door. The shop's in back of the church building. You can't miss it. It looks like a little version of the church but a lot newer. My son built it last summer."

Cassidy was appalled, but didn't want to show it

after Irma had been so kind. She felt small and petty to balk at wearing clothes from a thrift store. But this was the complete opposite of what she'd imagined, and she didn't think she'd be able to wear something a stranger had worn and discarded. "A thrift shop," she repeated.

"There are some really nice things. You'll see."

Nodding, Cassidy said, "I'll go over after I eat. How long will it be before I can get into my room? Maybe if I sleep, this headache will go away."

"I'll call Josh and warn him that you're on your way over. He and Henry can get the room ready by the time you get there. I'll go get your soup and be back in a jiffy."

"Hello, St. Luke's Thrift," Joshua said as he put the telephone receiver to his ear.

"Josh, it's Ma."

Joshua smiled. "Hi, Ma. I was just about to close up shop here and go in to wake Henry."

"I need you to do a couple things for me. Make sure the ivory-and-lavender bedroom is all made up and sparkling. We've got a young lady coming to stay a few days. She'll be needing some things from the shop, too."

"Another lost soul?"

"Smarty," she scolded with a smile in her voice. "She's a paying guest, so, no, not lost in the usual way, but…"

Now Josh heard compassion enter Irma's tone. Here it comes, he thought, and sighed. "But what?"

"Well, I guess that having enough money to pay your way isn't everything in life. I'm not sure she's real healthy, either, but I can see she's not happy even when she smiles. You'll see. She should be there in a while. I just gave her a bowl of soup and a cup of tea."

Chuckling, Josh hung up the phone to once again help Irma give aid to a needy person. He wanted to tell her to worry about herself for a change. She worked too hard. Relaxed too little. But how could he try to curb her from bringing home her strays after all she'd done for him?

Of course, there wasn't a thing amiss in the room Irma had asked him to see to, so after waking Henry, Joshua returned to the thrift shop to await the woman.

A few minutes later the bell above the door tinkled. Joshua looked up, not knowing what to expect. Then he just stared. He might not have known what to expect, but it certainly hadn't been anyone like the young woman who entered and approached the counter. Joshua stood automatically.

"Hello," she said as she stalked toward him. "Irma from the diner sent me here. I'll be renting a room for a few days. She said I might find a few things to tide me over till my car is finished. Can you direct me to the size eights?"

Joshua couldn't seem to respond. Had Irma lost her mind? This was her lost soul? This take-charge woman in the two-thousand-dollar suit? He had no idea how he knew what her suit must have cost, but he often knew things without knowing how he knew them.

"Excuse me?" the young woman said, now standing directly in front of him.

Joshua realized he was staring straight ahead at her

navy suit, and looked quickly up into the sweetest face he'd ever seen. It was heart-shaped, and her skin looked like translucent silk. Her bottom lip was full and the top a perfect bow. She had a nose that tipped up, giving her the look of a woodland sprite. The face did not match the attitude.

Then he looked a millimeter higher into the saddest eyes he'd ever seen. They were gray-blue and shadowed with unhappiness and even a hint of physical pain, as well. Yeah. Irma was right once again. The woman could certainly pay her way but she was just as certainly a lost soul.

"May I help you?" he asked, knowing she'd asked him a question yet unable to recall it.

"The size eights. I asked where you have the eights," she said slowly as if he were deaf or too dull-witted to understand her.

Joshua felt his hackles rise. Then he looked again at the woman. Irma thought she needed help. He guessed he could show enough Christian charity to swallow his anger at being patronized.

"Everything for women is in the front of the shop. All jeans are in the middle. Men's to the left. Women's to the right. The men's clothes are behind the jeans. Kids' clothes are all the way to the rear." He pointed to the signs hanging above each section. With the Lord's help, he managed not to put voice to his anger.

Joshua watched her walk through the room as if she might catch something from clothes once worn by others, and his anger flared anew. "Ma washes everything before anything gets added to the stock," he said through gritted teeth before he could stop himself.

She pivoted toward him and her cheeks flamed. "I've never had to—" She took a deep breath, shook her head slightly and tried again, "I'm sorry. I've just never been…"

"Down on your luck? Hard up enough to wear hand-me-downs?" Joshua sat back down on the stool behind the counter and leaned his back against the wall, his arms crossed.

He could actually see her temper slip its restraints. "Not having faced tough times financially isn't a crime. I'm not used to shopping like this. So shoot me! I need some clothes and these are all that's available. I can roll with the punches as good as the next guy." Her hand came up to squeeze her forehead. "I'm sorry. Could we start over?" She returned to the counter and reached her hand out to him. "I'm Cassidy Jamison."

Joshua felt his annoyance give way to compassion. She was as much a fish out of water in the small thrift shop he and Henry had put together to serve their small congregation as he would be in the city she probably came from. She couldn't change the life she'd obviously been born into any more than he could change the circumstances of his life. His own clothes had once been as expensive as hers. A suit that reminded him of the past still hung, cleaned and pressed, in his closet. Besides, she really didn't look well.

He smiled, hoping to put her at ease, and shook her hand. But it wasn't like shaking Earl's hand or any of his father's parishioners. He frowned at the feeling that zinged through him. "Joshua Daniels," he said, hearing a bewildered husky tone in his own voice.

"Irma Tallinger sent me to see her son."

"That would be me," he explained. "Suppose I play shopkeeper." He shrugged. "That's what I am today, after all."

Her tentative return smile was surprisingly shy and sweet but still didn't overshadow the sorrow in her eyes. "Tell me," she asked, "what *are* stylishly dressed stranded motorists wearing in Mountain View this season?"

He pulled out a pair of jeans and a T-shirt in her size eight, and a flannel shirt in a men's small from the men's section. "Here you go, pretty lady—the ultimate in hiking chic."

She blinked, appearing to be surprised by something, then she looked away nervously. What had he said? Joshua wondered, concerned. But then she reached out and touched the jeans, and he forgot his worry. There was something akin to wonder in her eyes now.

Then she shook her head and looked down at her feet. "I don't think that outfit would go very well with my shoes."

Joshua followed her gaze and shook his head. "There's only one thing high heels are going to get you in Mountain View—broken ankles. But if you prefer to walk around for the next few days on eggshells, over here we have a section of dresses, skirts and the like."

She looked longingly at the things in his hand. "They do look comfortable."

He could hear the disappointment and resignation in her voice and see it in her blue-eyed gaze as she continued to stare at the clothes he held. "Jeans and shirts would really be your best bet," he added, hoping to encourage her. It was as if some invisible force held her back.

Then an idea struck. One that might give her the push she needed. He snapped his fingers. "What shoe size do you wear?"

When she told him her size, Joshua smiled and breathed a little sigh. He didn't believe in coincidence. The Lord provides, and she really wanted those jeans. "You're in luck. You're the same shoe size as Ma. She has a brand-spanking-new pair of tennis shoes that I seriously doubt she'll ever break down and wear."

"Oh, I couldn't."

"The only reason they aren't already out here in the shop is because I bought them for her. Knowing Ma, she doesn't want to hurt my feelings. You'd be doing her a favor if you took them off her hands."

"They were a gift and—"

He grimaced. "What they *were* was a bad idea. It's like I was buying them for someone else." Not for the first time he wondered who. "House dresses and sensible shoes. That's our Irma. Not tennis shoes. I must have lost my head as well as my sense in that store, but Mother's Day loomed and I'd run out of ideas."

She looked at him with a serious expression, then down at the rack near where she stood. "Oh, this is wonderful!" She grabbed a red-and-white snowflake sweater. Her blue eyes sparkled a little and even that small hint of joy did something to him. Her beauty took Joshua's breath away. "I had one like this when I was a child. I guess some styles never go out of fashion."

Joshua just stopped himself from telling her that the sweater could very well be older than she was. Instead he tried to tempt her to take the tennis shoes. "But you can't wear that with a dress. Just won't do."

Her chin firmed. "It would be fine with a skirt," she argued.

"But then there is that broken ankle to worry about," he teased. "You could wind up the woman who came to dinner."

She put a sassy hand on her hip. "Has anyone ever told you that you're stubborn?"

Joshua smiled. In the hospital they'd all told him he was too stubborn to die. He guessed that counted. "Yep, sure have. I'm told it's part of my charm. Now about those tennis shoes…"

She made a face that spoke of exasperation. "Oh, all right. But I insist on paying you what they cost."

"Not necessary," he told her, shaking his head.

She arched a delicate eyebrow, then looked around the shop. "Where did you say those skirts are?"

Joshua rolled his eyes and laughed. "And you call *me* stubborn. I'll tell you what—you can pay, but only half.

I'll put the money in the till here at the shop. Like I said, the only reason she hasn't put them in the shop already is that she's worried about hurting my feelings."

The bell over the door tinkled again, and Joshua turned to see Irma entering the shop, overburdened with a bundle. "Ma, what on earth possesses you?" he scolded as he rushed to her side. "Why didn't you call me? I'd have run down to pick this up." He took the bundle from her and dropped it on the wide counter.

Irma smacked him playfully on the arm. "Will you stop coddling me? It was more cumbersome than heavy, which you know by now since you snatched it from me! Miss Maria sent them down. There's only a fluffy bedspread and a few dresses she's worn to her shows in there. She promised there wasn't a speck of paint on any of them. Maybe Miss—" Irma turned toward her latest stray "—I'm sorry, I never got a name."

"Cassidy Jamison," she said, and put out her hand to shake Irma's. "I appreciate all your help, Irma."

Irma reached out hesitantly and shook Cassidy Jamison's hand, looking as if she'd just encountered an alien. Joshua grinned. Irma would have been more comfortable dispensing a bear hug. Most of the ladies of Mountain View hadn't really caught up with the times. He knew that businesswomen always shook hands these days, but he doubted many of the residents around there were used to the gesture.

He frowned. This was the one thing he hated about outsiders coming to town. They always brought their way of doing things with them, and he understood those little social nuances without knowing how.

"Josh, are you okay?"

He snapped out of his troubling thoughts and realized that at some point he'd sunk onto the high stool behind the counter. Irma had come around to the back and stood in front of him cupping his cheek. Obviously worried, she stared into his eyes. Anxiety and hope warred in her lined face. He shook his head. "Thinking. That's all, Ma." He shrugged. "Just knew something I shouldn't."

And Irma nodded. Her lips still pursed with apprehension, she turned to Cassidy Jamison, who was staring at them with a puzzled look on her pretty face.

Embarrassed, Joshua pretended sudden interest in the large bag Irma had carried in. Then he remembered the tennis shoes.

"Ma," he called to Irma, who had directed Cassidy's attention to a second pair of jeans, "remember those tennis shoes I bought you for Mother's Day?"

"Oh…ah…I'll wear them next summer, dear. I promise."

Joshua chuckled. "Now what would Henry say if he heard his wife tell a huge whopper like that? Ms. Jamison needs more practical footwear while she's here if she's going to survive for the next few days. And she's your size. I figure this is your big chance to get rid of them gracefully."

Irma grinned. "Oh, in that case, I'm sure I could part with them for such a worthy cause."

"No, really. It's fine," Cassidy said quickly. "I'm sure I can manage."

Irma patted her on the shoulder. "Don't you pay a bit of attention to our teasing. Much as I hate to admit it, the tennis shoes just aren't me."

"Then I insist you let me pay you for them. That way you can buy yourself something to replace them."

"Dear, there's nothing on this earth I want that I don't already have. I think that's why Josh was so desperate when he bought them. Why don't you look around some more? Take whatever you think you might want and try them on in your room. We can settle up when you pay for your stay. I know you were hoping to lie down. I'm going ahead to get dinner heated up. Joshua, will you show Ms. Jamison to her room when she's done here?"

Joshua watched for the next several minutes as Cassidy Jamison added to her growing pile with surprising enthusiasm. "Goodness," she exclaimed when the stack started to slip, "I can't believe I found so many things I like."

"Here, let me take those for you," he said, coming out from behind the counter again.

"If all this fits me, I'll need a suitcase when I leave." She laughed, turning over her burden to him. "Where do all these things come from?"

Joshua blinked. Why had her laughter made his stomach knot? And was that an electric shock that he felt when she touched his arm? He frowned. He'd been feeling funny on and off since he'd first laid eyes on her.

Supremely confused, he forced his thoughts off his reaction to her and on to her question.

"I got hold of some barrels and put them in the resort hotels and ski lodges within an hour's drive of here. You wouldn't believe the stuff people leave behind and never bother to claim. In fact, we have one or two suitcases in back if you want one. I think Henry put five- or ten-dollar price tags on them."

Cassidy nodded. "Sounds like a plan. If I need one, we can add it to the tally for the clothes. *And* the amount those tennis shoes cost you."

Joshua grinned. "Didn't we agree that you'd only pay half what I did?" he put in with a raised eyebrow.

She folded her arms across her chest. "Half, if you give me the real price. I'll know if you try to undersell."

"They were a hundred and twenty dollars. Now, aren't you sorry you asked?"

Cassidy smiled, though she looked pained. "The shoes I'm wearing cost three times that much and they have to be the most uncomfortable footwear I've ever had. I hate them. Believe me, the tennis shoes will be a bargain at twice the price."

Joshua tossed her selections into a big trash bag, then slung it over his shoulder to haul it to the Ivory Room. He flipped on the floodlights and headed out the door. She followed him, and he noted she did so with careful steps. But the uneven gravel was apparently too much for her high heels. Joshua saw her teeter, and without thinking, he dropped the big bag and reached out to help her.

He didn't know how Cassidy wound up in his arms, but somehow she did. She took a sharp breath and stiffened. Josh just held on, his mind in a whirl until he focused on her eyes. He noticed that close up she had golden flecks in widened blue eyes that he thought should sparkle instead of reflecting pain and sadness. She seemed more fragile suddenly, and he quickly helped her regain a steady footing.

Cassidy sat on the bed and watched the door close behind Joshua Daniel Tallinger. He was gorgeous. With dark-dark brown hair, saved from being black by just the hint of red highlights, huge deep-set eyes that were just as deep brown in color as his hair, a skin tone that looked permanently tanned, and shoulders that looked as if they could hold up the world. No wonder she'd been surprised when she met Henry Tallinger. She'd thought to find a man much like his son, only older. But like his wife, Henry was fair, with graying hair that had obviously once been blond. And he was nearly as short as Irma, too. In fact, the only similarity between Joshua and Henry was their dry sense of humor.

She looked around the room and tried to smile. It was a room fit for a Victorian princess. Unfortunately, she didn't feel like a princess. She felt like that last five miles of bad road she'd been on as she approached the booming metropolis of Mountain View.

The whole fiasco that had been her day seemed unreal. She'd started out thinking she was about to be named Jamison Steel's next vice president. And had wound up without a job and staying in a room in a rectory miles from civilization. Her car sat outside a run-down barn awaiting repair by a man who had probably never seen a car like hers. She'd been forced to shop in what looked like a turn-of-the-19th-century general store and a church thrift shop.

And now she was sitting in a part-time bed-and-breakfast, thinking about a country bumpkin preacher in jeans and flannel whom she found attractive. Really attractive.

Cassidy old girl, you've lost it!

She surveyed her surroundings again. She knew the difference between expensive antiques and just plain old aging furniture, and though Irma's furniture would never sell at auction at Christie's it was well cared for. She was sure the wallpaper was from an era gone by, but it still looked crisp and clean. Cassidy had a feeling that this was Irma Tallinger's version of the presidential suite. And she suddenly felt honored to be staying there. Maybe Mountain View wouldn't be so bad, after all.

The glass of water Joshua had brought her sloshed a little, reminding her she still hadn't taken her ulcer medication or anything for her somewhat faded headache. After she swallowed the pills, she flopped back down on the bed, and her thoughts returned to the enigmatic son of the house. She soon drifted off to sleep, but the events of the day and those who had peopled it followed her into the night.

Chapter Three

Light streamed in the room, disturbing Cassidy's deep dream-filled sleep. She opened her eyes, disoriented for a heartbeat. Then it all came back. The meeting. The drive. The car. She looked around the big ivory-and-lavender room. *Joshua.*

He'd brought her and her things up here. Then, after getting her a glass of water, he'd promised to call her for dinner. She fingered the quilt that had been tossed over her. Its navy, burgundy and forest-green print didn't go with the elegant room. The carefully constructed log cabin quilt was just too masculine to fit in here. She brought it to her face and knew why she'd thought of Joshua almost immediately upon waking—why she'd been dreaming of him when she woke.

The quilt carried his scent.

She remembered it from those incredible seconds she'd spent in his arms when she'd stumbled on her way across the gravel drive from the church thrift shop to the Tallingers' house. The extreme care she'd taken of her footing had been doomed to failure when her heel encountered a particularly large chunk of gravel. She'd tipped sideways, and only Joshua's quickness had saved her.

Her face flamed anew. He'd seen her at her clumsiest. Had he also seen her sleeping at her most vulnerable? Had he covered her with his quilt? Taken off her shoes? Or had his mother come in? She wished she'd locked her door. She didn't like feeling so defenseless with strangers.

She caught his scent on the quilt again and tossed it off her. She especially didn't like the mixed feelings Joshua evoked in her. He was not the kind of man she'd ever been interested in. He was too masculine. Too primitive. He fit in these mountains—unlike her with her high-heeled shoes and power suits. He was completely unlike the men she'd dated occasionally over the years. Joshua was more like a diamond in the rough than those well-polished gems in her past.

But for all his masculinity and size, he was a gentle man if not a gentleman, she reminded herself. He had a kindness in his eyes that she was sure reached all the way to his core. Which meant that she hadn't completely lost her mind with this attraction she felt for him.

She remembered the way he'd treated Irma when she'd entered the thrift shop with her unwieldy bundle. He'd seemed all gruff and impatient, while tenderness and love had flooded his gaze. In the few minutes she'd been with him, Cassidy had recognized that he was a special person. Maybe that was why she'd dreamed of him.

A knock at her door drew her from her thoughts, and as if those thoughts had beckoned him, Cassidy heard Joshua call to her through the door. She scrambled off the bed, straightening her blouse and skirt as she stumbled to the door. "Yes?" she asked as she opened it.

Joshua stood there. He looked the same. Big. Strikingly handsome. Disturbing. "Ma said to tell you breakfast should be in half an hour," he told her.

"Please, tell Irma it's kind of her to include me in your family breakfast but I usually only have coffee."

"Maybe that's why you have an ulcer."

Cassidy sucked a quick breath. "How did you…"

Joshua looked instantly uncomfortable. "You keep rubbing your stomach and flinching. I figured an ulcer or close to it." He frowned and shrugged carelessly, but there was something in his eyes. A vulnerability and uncertainty that surprised her and gave her pause. "Sorry," he continued. "Sometimes I just say what I'm thinking when I shouldn't." He flashed her a self-deprecating grin.

"It's okay. You're right. It is an ulcer," she told him, wanting to reassure him. Seeing someone so strong look so vulnerable made her feel vulnerable, too, for some reason. And Cassidy always liked to feel in control. Maybe because she'd had so little control of the decisions that had formed her life into what it had become.

"Then I'll stick my neck out again. Maybe you should see someone about it."

"Done. I just started on medication. I guess my job's been getting to me. I'll try the breakfast idea. You seem to know what you're talking about."

"I don't. Not really. It's just that when I came up to wake you for dinner, you were asleep. Which means you also missed dinner. That can't be good."

"It was you who covered me?" she asked carefully, still not sure how she felt about his having been in her room while she was sleeping.

"No. When you didn't answer your door, I got worried and called Ma. She didn't want to wake you to get you under the covers but she said you looked cold. So I grabbed the quilt off my bed so she could cover you. Did you sleep okay?"

"Yes. I did," she said, trying to ignore the memory of the disturbing dream she'd had about him. They'd been dancing—waltzing, really—in a barn. She'd been wearing a dress fit only for a remake of "Oklahoma." She shook off the thought. "Well…um, thank you for your concern. Would you tell your mother I'll be down in a few minutes?"

He nodded gravely and left.

Joshua stalked through the house and out the back door, letting the storm door flap shut with a satisfying *bang* behind him. He stood at the top of the steps, his thoughts spinning. It was clear to him that temptation had come to Mountain View, but he couldn't give in to it. Even though temptation came in a very special package named Cassidy Jamison.

When the door squeaked slowly open behind him and he felt a reassuring hand settle on his back, he sank down on the wooden back steps.

"Did Ms. Jamison insult my cooking, son?" Irma asked as she settled next to him.

He grinned ruefully at his mother and shook his head, but the smile slipped into a frown. "She'll be down for breakfast, but I think I'll give it a skip." What was wrong with him? It was a warm day for late November and the sun felt good on his face. He should be in a fine mood. But all he could think of was that dreamy look that had come into Cassidy's eyes and the way it had affected him. He wanted to get to know her. And he couldn't.

Irma arched a thin eyebrow. "Oh, so it's you who's insulting my cooking. Fine. I'll give your breakfast to Bear. At least he appreciates my efforts."

Joshua didn't look at Irma but he couldn't hold back a grin, either. "Bear would eat anything, and it isn't your cooking I'm avoiding and you know it."

"Then it's the company. Don't you like Cassidy?"

"I like her fine. But…"

"But?"

He shrugged. "She makes me…uncomfortable."

"Did she do something that triggered a memory yesterday?"

Now he did look at Irma, understanding her concern.

Understanding the reluctant hope in her gaze, as well. Joshua shook his head. "No. It was like I said. I just knew something I shouldn't. She shook your hand. You looked surprised. Women around here don't usually shake hands. But it seemed just right to me. It felt real, the way things do when I know them from before."

"And that's all?"

"That and Cassidy—" Joshua stopped in mid-thought. He didn't want to talk to Irma about what Cassidy made him feel.

This time Irma's raised eyebrow wasn't speculative but annoyingly all-knowing. He could feel his cheeks heat.

"Maybe you should talk with Henry. He took Bear for a walk. They ought to be back in no time. But you *will* come to the table. I'm not sending you off to fix the Wilsons' roof without a good meal in you."

"Ma."

Irma poked him. "Don't whine and don't 'Ma' me. You get yourself to the table."

Irma had long since gone back to cooking breakfast when a deep *woof* echoed in the woods. "Hey, Bear," Joshua called to his huge mongrel dog, as the animal lumbered into the middle of the yard.

Bear was one of those strange accidents of nature that got all the extreme traits of his ancestors. And judging from the way he'd turned out, he had very large ancestors. Joshua and Henry had gone through a book on dog breeds once and picked out Newfoundland and English sheepdog as the most likely culprits. The result was a huge dog with hair so thick it stood on end and made Bear look about twenty pounds heavier than his one hundred fifty pounds. As a puppy, he'd looked more like a bear cub than a dog.

Bear had wandered into the yard the day Joshua came to live with the Tallingers. Joshua had gotten out of the car that day, still needing a walker, and had nearly tripped over the little fellow who skidded to a stop at his feet. It had been such a frightening day, facing a world of unknowns, and then he'd looked down and seen a creature even more afraid than he was. Henry had steadied Joshua, and Irma had swept the puppy up in her arms. Joshua, still not well versed in the strange world outside the hospital, had called him a "bear." The name stuck, and Bear had lived up to it all too well.

Joshua picked up a ball and sent Bear running after it, just as Henry cleared the edge of the woods. "He tire you out?" Joshua asked as Henry settled onto the picnic bench.

"Me?" he asked, huffing and puffing. "That'll be the day. You taking him up to the Wilsons' with you?"

Joshua nodded and sat down across from Henry. "Yeah. I'll get going after I eat. I was going to skip breakfast, but Ma had a fit."

"Why'd you want to go and do a fool thing like that, boy? Irma was cooking up a storm when I left, on account of our guest."

Joshua took a moment to look around him, trying to enjoy his surroundings in the hope that it would settle him. But it didn't. There was no denying the truth. "Our guest is why I tried to get out of breakfast. I'm attracted to her. Except I'm not free to be. I just wanted to steer clear of her. Ma had other ideas."

Henry leaned forward and grabbed Joshua's hand to give it a quick squeeze. It was a father-son gesture that made him feel supported and loved.

"Josh, your memory's gone. The accident, or whatever it was that happened to you, took it. It's not going to come back."

"Doctor Bennington said it still could," Joshua protested.

"That isn't the way I heard it. I believe he said that after five years it wasn't impossible, but highly unlikely."

"True, but what if—"

"You've got to forget that woman in the picture. We don't know who she is. Even the police and a national television show couldn't find out. I wish they'd never shown it to you."

Joshua frowned. "But they did."

"And you need to forget it. She could be your sister. You have to start living for the here and now, and the future. I truly don't believe the Good Lord would have you be alone in this life He's restored to you. If you like this girl, this Cassidy, then I say you ought to spend time with her. She'll be gone by day after tomorrow. Where's the harm in a little companionship?"

Bear dropped the ball in Joshua's lap, and Joshua tossed it toward the woods. "And then what? She'll go back to the city and get back to her life and the job that gave her ulcers." Joshua sighed. "And I'll be here, maybe wishing she'd stayed. What's the point? Don't you see? Even if I did feel free to think about her in the long term, she doesn't belong here."

Henry leaned down, picked up a dead leaf and twirled it between his fingers. "Maybe you're supposed to help her figure out that she shouldn't go back to her job if it's making her sick. The Lord sends people into our lives all the time with a plan in His mind. And another thing—you took a big job on yourself when you signed on as my assistant pastor. You work for a pretty demanding boss—and I don't mean me."

"I know who I work for," Joshua snapped.

Henry fixed him with a steely, blue-eyed look. "Counseling the troubled is part of your job description. Irma says Cassidy Jamison is one unhappy young lady. Your obligation to His flock doesn't stop at members of our church. You're supposed to help any of God's children who need you."

"So *you* help her," Josh groused, and unconsciously tossed the ball for Bear again.

Henry sighed, clearly exasperated. "I didn't just take you on as an assistant because you swing a mean hammer or because you're young enough to take over for me when I'm gone. I took you on because you relate to younger people and they relate to you. They open up to you. And you get to them in a way I can't."

Joshua grimaced. "I know that, but Cassidy—"

A deep *woof* and a shriek cut off Joshua's further objection. He turned in time to see Bear rear up and settle his huge front paws on Cassidy Jamison's narrow shoulders. Woman and dog hit the ground with a *thud*.

When the shrieking continued, Bear took off for the woods like a shot. Then he saw Joshua and Henry, and turned on a dime to head for Joshua.

"No, Bear!" Josh shouted, but it was too late. Dog and man collided, and there would have been a second *thud* resounding in the yard except that the yard was still soaked from a recent rain. So this time there came instead a muddy *splat*.

Then the dog, whimpering and panicked, tried to curl up on top of Joshua. When that didn't provide enough security, he tried crawling under his now-filthy owner, rolling them both in the mud. It turned into a wrestling match as Joshua tried to subdue the frightened dog.

"Bear! Will you stop it?" Joshua shouted over the din of wild barks and whimpers. "She's a nice lady. She isn't going to hurt you."

When he was finally able to wrap his arms around the dog's neck to hold him still, Joshua heard Cassidy ask, her tone understandably and utterly incredulous, "Hurt him? He pushed *me* down."

"Bear. Sit," Joshua growled as the dog tried to backpedal away from Cassidy and Henry. "Are you all right?" he asked Cassidy, holding on to Bear and looking up from where he knelt next to the dog.

Cassidy brushed off her jeans and nodded. "Is he always so erratic? I'm not used to dogs but—"

Joshua chuckled. "Bear has two problems. He's too friendly, which is all he was trying to be when he knocked you down. And he's chicken. All it took to send him running was for you to scream. He's yellow as they come. Don't let the black coat fool you," he said, ruffling that same pitch-black fur.

Joshua let out a laugh when Bear leaned into him, forcing him to sit in the mud again. Then Bear climbed into his master's lap. A considerable amount of dog didn't fit. But he kept trying, spreading the mud farther over Joshua's clothes.

"Three. He has three problems, Josh," Henry put in, deadpan. "He weighs a hundred and fifty pounds and thinks he's a lap dog." The old pastor frowned. "Well, we have to be honest. He also eats too much, is dumb as a post about what animals it's not safe to chase, and as a guard dog he'd make a better ambassador of goodwill. Probably lick a burglar to death if one ever came 'round. Guess that makes six faults. Major ones."

"You're a real mess," Cassidy said as she reached out slowly to pet the soft black fur on the dog's ruff.

Joshua took her wrist and put her hand on Bear when the dog started whining again. "This is Cassidy," he told Bear, trying to ignore the feel of Cassidy's fine-boned wrist beneath his fingers. "She's a friend. *Friend*. But no jumping. Got it?"

Bear abandoned Joshua's lap to sit at Cassidy's feet. His tail thumping, he handed her his paw, his pink tongue lolling out the side of his mouth.

Joshua chuckled at the stupid love-struck look on the dog's face. "I think you've got a friend for life," he said, and stood, trying not to look as uncomfortable as he felt. Mud streaked his clothes while Cassidy looked as fresh as a spring rain. Bear could be a real ego buster.

Cassidy looked up at him. "Oh, you're a mess, too," she sputtered, trying not to laugh.

Joshua looked down at himself and chuckled. "Yeah, I'm a mess, all right," he admitted, shooting Bear a what-am-I-going-to-do-with-you sort of look.

"Son, you'd better run and clean up before Irma gets breakfast on," Henry told him.

Joshua almost used the mud as an escape from eating with them, but then he looked at Cassidy. She was smiling down at Bear. And this time the smile was in her eyes.

Maybe he could help her get her life back on track. "I'll see y'all at the table."

Cassidy tossed the book she was reading aside and stared up at the ceiling above the bed. She was at loose ends, with nothing but a book she'd read as a child to occupy her mind. Joshua had gone to help a family whose roof leaked. She imagined Irma was running her diner and Henry had gone to the thrift shop after breakfast. She would have gone to talk to him, but he was working on his sermon for a Wednesday evening service.

She'd really stuck her foot in her mouth when that subject had come up at breakfast. She'd remarked that she'd thought people only went to church once a week—on Sunday. Joshua explained that many churches had a second Sunday evening service, and one on Wednesday night, as well. And yes, there were those who attended all three. He'd also explained that everyone referred to Henry as "Pastor Henry," not Reverend Tallinger.

Joshua was a compelling man. He was physically a big man, yet he treated his parents with a visible gentleness that was both touching and heartwarming. He had a strength of character that he projected in everything he spoke about during the meal, yet he seemed to depend on his parents in some indefinable but very tangible way. And though he treated his parents with the utmost respect, he called his father "Henry," which was the biggest contradiction about him of all.

Cassidy sat up and stared at herself in the mirror over the dresser. "Stop thinking about him!" she ordered herself. So his touch disturbed her. So he was the handsomest man she'd ever seen. He was also a hayseed preacher who fixed roofs and had an ill-mannered dog. And since when was she so curious about an unsuitable stranger? she thought stubbornly.

She needed to do something to get her mind off him and onto the things she needed to think about. A walk. She'd take a walk. Commune with nature. That was it.

Irma was in the kitchen when she walked by, so Cassidy stuck her head in the door. "I thought I'd take a walk. Which direction would you suggest?"

"There's a nice trail through the woods out behind

the house. Joshua marked it and keeps it cleared. When you come to the fork in the trail, follow the sign that points to town. It's written right on the sign. The other way is to our cabin, and that's not a walk. It's a six-mile hike up the mountain."

"Town sounds perfect. Did Josh mark it for your summer guests?"

Irma chuckled. "Goodness, no. We don't get that many. He marked it for himself. That boy has no sense of direction whatsoever."

"Did he go to school in the south?" Cassidy asked, and could have bitten her tongue. What was wrong with her?

Irma frowned. "What's that got to do with his sense of direction?"

"Nothing. Forget I asked, please."

"But why would you think that?" Irma pressed.

Now she was really sorry she'd let her curiosity get the better of her common sense. "'Y'all.' He said 'y'all' earlier," she explained. "It's a southern expression."

Irma walked to the center island and started shelling peas, a worried and thoughtful expression on her lined face. "He does say that now and again, doesn't he? Hmm. Now there's food for thought."

"Thought about what?" Cassidy asked before she could stop herself.

"Oh, about where he's from," Irma said matter-of-factly. "He could have heard it in a movie or on TV, and it might have felt familiar on his tongue."

Now it was Cassidy's turn to frown. How could his

own mother forget where Joshua was raised? Irma was up there in years and she seemed hale and hearty, but perhaps her mind wasn't as sound as Cassidy had assumed. She walked over to Irma, leaning her elbows on the island so she could watch Irma's expression.

"Josh is from Mountain View," Cassidy replied carefully, and waited for a reaction.

Irma smiled and shook her head. "Oh, no, dear, he isn't. Joshua didn't grow up here. He isn't our blood son."

Cassidy's eyes widened. "But he calls you 'Ma.' I will admit his calling your husband 'Henry' surprised me but—"

"Joshua is the child we never had. He's become our son since he came to us, but we never laid eyes on him till almost five-and-a-half years ago."

"He came here to be your husband's assistant, and you still don't know where he grew up?"

Irma patted her hand, then pushed the bag of peas to rest between them. "No, we found him, dear. He was lying beside the road in a ditch, all broken and beaten. Henry and I—we just couldn't forget that face of his once the ambulance came and took him to the hospital. We went to see him and just kept going back. He had no identification on him, you see. We were all he had. I've never prayed as hard for anything in my life as I did that that boy would live and wake up whole. The doctors didn't give him much of a chance, but we just kept praying over him. He's a miracle, that boy of ours."

"You got your wish," Cassidy said, smiling.

Irma shook her gray head. "It wasn't a wish, child. It was a prayer. And no. I didn't get all of what I asked for. I got more and less. The Lord works in strange ways. Joshua's proof positive of that. You see, when he finally did wake from the coma six months later, he couldn't talk or walk. We all soon realized that he had no idea who he was or where he'd come from. It was gone—his whole life. The doctors guessed that between twenty-five and thirty years were just…gone. And he was completely alone in the world."

Cassidy felt as if a hand had reached into her chest and had a choke-hold on her heart. She looked down and realized that she was automatically opening the pea pods and dumping the peas in a bowl that Irma must have put in front of her. "But he doesn't seem brain damaged."

"The doctors thought that he was at first, but he re-learned language so fast that they decided he had severe amnesia."

"And his past has never come back?"

"Just little impressions and vague knowledge that he doesn't remember learning."

"But his past could still come back to him?" Cassidy asked.

Irma pursed her lips and shook her head. "After this long, that isn't likely according to his doctor. He came to live with us when he was discharged. I was a teacher and I was the most qualified to teach him all he needed to know. Besides, we loved him already."

Then his attachment to the Tallingers was almost like that of a child for his parents. "So he calls you 'Ma' because you became his mother, but why doesn't he call Henry 'Dad' or 'Pa'?"

"Joshua isn't sure. He said it doesn't feel like a compliment to him. Maybe he didn't have a good relationship with his real father. It's one of those vague feelings Joshua gets—and Henry doesn't care what Joshua calls him. He just loves his Josh the way he is and is grateful to have him with us." Irma picked up both bowls, moved toward a pot on the stove and dumped in the peas for cooking. "Besides," she continued, "he didn't start out to call me 'Ma.' He just couldn't get his tongue around 'Ir-ma' at first, and it came out 'Ma.' He laughed. I laughed. And he just kept calling me 'Ma.'"

"This is all so incredible. Like a movie of the week or something."

"No. It's a miracle is what it is," Irma said. "Those doctors didn't give him a ghost of a chance to live, let alone thrive the way he has." Irma turned back to Cassidy, her pale eyes lit with pride, though her expression was serious. "His mind's so quick, all he has to do is read something once and he knows it. I taught school for thirty years and I never had a brighter student. And there's nothing he can't fix if it's broken, either. The only two problems he's left with are the loss of memory and the fact he just says whatever pops into his mind. Of course, there's that sense of direction of his, too."

Irma laughed. "But who knows if he wasn't always like that. He's a special man, and we're proud of him."

Cassidy could see that they were, but wouldn't his real family have felt the same way? Cassidy could only imagine their suffering. "Hasn't anyone tried to find out where he belongs?"

"I've thought from the first that he belongs right here, but we did try. We had people from that TV mystery show come up here and take his picture and film an interview with him about nine or ten months after he came to live with us. They did a whole story on him." She snorted in derision. "He was terribly embarrassed, and all for nothing. Nothing ever came of it. It's like he appeared out of nowhere. I like to think that the Lord meant for us to find him and bring him into our home. And Joshua has gone on to built a satisfying life for himself in the Lord's service."

He seemed to have, but Cassidy couldn't help but wonder about the people he'd spent those first twenty-five or thirty years with. She knew what their grief felt like. She remembered back to when she was eight years old. She'd awakened in a hospital to find her grandfather by her bed, telling her that her parents were dead. A wall of snow had come crashing into their vacation home while they'd sat snuggled around the fire, and had swept them from her life. The people in Joshua's life would have felt the same tearing grief she had. That she still did feel twenty years later.

She was glad that at a time when Joshua was all

alone in the world he had found the kind of unconditional love parents give. Because though Cassidy's
grandfather had raised her, she still felt she had to earn
his love—one day at a time.

Chapter Four

Cassidy wandered aimlessly along the marked trail through the woods. She'd put off her walk until after lunch, having continued to help Irma in the kitchen. Taking the time to cook from scratch was something she rarely did, and she found it, and the time with Irma, strangely soothing.

Soon after sharing a noon meal with the older couple, she'd returned to her room and had fallen into a deep sleep. When she'd awakened, refreshed but no more settled, she'd set off for the walk she'd planned that morning.

After hearing about all Joshua had endured, she felt selfish and childish for dwelling on what were minor problems in her own life. She would eventually take over the presidency of Jamison Steel, so what did it really matter if she hadn't been given the vice presidency? Why was she so unhappy and tense? She could only hope this vacation, impetuously taken, would put her disappointment and hurt into perspective.

Irma had told her the trail would lead her to the far end of Mountain View. Though she was sure there was little to see in the small town, at least it would give her the opportunity to observe the town up close and personal. She could even check to see if Earl was closer to looking at her car.

The sharp *crack* of a breaking branch to her left stopped Cassidy in her tracks. She moved only her head, and was left breathless by the sight of a doe standing almost as still as a statue. It stared unblinkingly at her. The only sign of life the animal revealed was a quivering muscle high on its haunch.

At that moment a powerful need to recreate the scene on paper gripped Cassidy. Her fingers fairly itched to hold a sketch pad and pencil. In her mind's eye she could already see the finished picture. The doe would stand frozen in time, surrounded by the stark November woodlands—and fear. It would be in charcoal, she decided—a little sad and a little edgy.

But Cassidy shook her head and banished the vision. The dream. Her sudden movement freed the deer, who bounded away. And once again she said goodbye to her heart's desire. It was not for her. She had taken a different path. One devoid of creativity and art.

For if there was one thing she *did* know about herself, it was that she couldn't devote only half her soul to something that consumed her. And where art was concerned, she always reacted the same way. Whenever she picked up a pencil or a brush, the rest of the world simply faded away—ceased to exist. She became her talent. And her talent became her. It took all her energy. All her heart. And she'd learned it the hard way when she'd tried to split herself in two during college. She'd felt just that—split. Torn. After a near breakdown late in her senior year, she'd made her decision.

She had put away her youthful dreams and passion for an unstable, nearly unattainable success in art, and had marched into adulthood at her grandfather's side, fulfilling her destiny. She was a Jamison.

She hadn't painted since graduation. She hadn't even let herself doodle on her ink blotter. She could not open that door again. It would be ungrateful. Grandfather was counting on her.

But then the memory of yesterday in his office pierced her thoughts. Her heart. And his betrayal made her soul cry out once again. He hadn't seemed to need her at all when naming Jon Reed his vice president. Remembering her last angry words to the old man who'd been her anchor in life left Cassidy feeling at sea. As domineering and gruff as he was, Grandfather had truly been her port in a storm since she was six and that wall of snow had wiped out her world in one blinding minute.

She forced her mind from the painful past and the embarrassing scene at Jamison Steel. Hadn't she already decided that it didn't matter in the grand scheme of things? Instantly, Joshua and all she'd learned about him from Irma filled her thoughts. Aside from being kind, gentle and handsome, he was a strong, courageous person, not only to have survived but to have flourished as he had. He would laugh at her whining over the loss of her dream of a fulfilling career in the art world. At least she could *remember* the dreams she'd put aside. As misty as her memory of her parents was, she did remember her mother's soft voice soothing her and her father's big strong hands holding her.

What must Joshua's life be like? He must live only in the present. Maybe for the future, too. Because anything else would be fruitless and painful.

She recalled his low comment to Irma the day before when the older woman had noticed him stare off into space. *"Just knew something I shouldn't,"* he'd muttered. Did that mean snatches of his past came back to haunt him? An ever-present reminder of all he'd lost?

Sunshine broke through the trees, and Cassidy looked up into the sun-drenched sky. She'd arrived at the end of the trail.

The first building she came to was a large, three-story, boarded-up Victorian with a half-attached, weather-beaten sign hanging from the gatepost. Swenson's Bed and Breakfast, the faded letters declared on the sign that bobbled in the breeze. The fence the gate was attached to was a wobbly picket-type that had even less paint than it had stability.

The house fired Cassidy's imagination, though it was every bit as weather-beaten as the sign and fence. It had once been lovely. She visualized its faded, peeling colors crisp and bright again, its windows shining in the sunlight, and the fence restored to its once stalwart position of authority. The upstairs tower room with its circle of tall windows would be unbelievably perfect as a studio. There was something about the house that struck a cord deep inside that said family and security.

"Wouldn't you love to get your hands on the place?" Joshua asked from behind her. "I know I would."

Cassidy whirled around. He sat in an old beat-up truck that he'd pulled to the side of the road. She smiled. "You'd get a ticket in Philadelphia for parking facing the wrong way."

Joshua set the brake and opened the door. He chuckled. "But this is Mountain View. In a town with probably fewer than thirty cars in a ten-mile radius, with three of those in the shop, and the rest parked at job sites, it hardly matters."

Cassidy glanced away from his charming grin and looked around town, wondering how he kept his sanity in such an isolated place. "I see your point. Do you even *have* a sheriff or a policeman around here?"

"The state police patrol the area. Their barracks is out on the interstate."

So even the state police hadn't been able to find Joshua's origins. "Are you finished with that roof you were fixing?"

"For now, till it leaks again."

"Why not just put on a whole new one?"

"Because they can't afford it and they won't accept charity. Patching is neighborly. Replacing isn't. You see?"

Embarrassed, Cassidy nodded and turned back toward the house. She would never have thought of that. Grace and intuition must be inborn, she decided, because she didn't see how he could have learned that kind of insight into the delicate feelings of others in only five years, especially with all the other things he'd had to relearn. Her admiration for him grew dangerously.

"Does anyone own this?" she asked to distract herself from risky thoughts of him and his apparently stellar character.

"The Swensons still own it but they don't live here anymore. They moved to Georgia to live with their son about ten years ago. The place apparently got too much for them to handle. It's been for sale for years, but it hasn't sold."

Joshua stepped by her and inside the gate. His movement set the sign swinging. "Summer people don't usually want anything this big, and we don't get many year-round families moving into the area," he continued. "It's actually pretty stable. The roof's sound. Henry and I boarded the windows up when some summer kids thought it was funny to break them out."

"That was kind of you."

He shrugged. "Just being a good neighbor. I check on the place every now and again for the real estate people. That's what I was about to do. Want to see the inside? I'm sure no one would care if you tag along."

Cassidy stared up at the house and realized what it was that called to her. It reminded her of her home—the one in suburban Philadelphia that she'd shared with her parents until that fateful vacation when she'd lost them. She didn't think she'd really had a home since. "I'd love to see it," she said automatically. Then she remembered his ever-present companion. "Where's Bear?" She really wasn't up for another of the dog's greetings without ample warning.

"You're safe from his adoration for now. He's asleep in the back of the truck. He spent the day chasing kids, rabbits and a bunch of barn cats. He's been out like a light since I pulled away from the Wilsons'."

Joshua stepped back, holding the gate open, and swept his arm toward the front door in a gesture that reminded her of a piece of Shakespearean stage direction. "After you, fair lady," he said, doffing his baseball cap.

Cassidy laughed at the silly gesture, and Josh laughed, too. "Is there any furniture left?" she asked as they sauntered along the walk to the house.

"Almost all of it. Ma dusts the place up every now and again, hoping that if we keep it nice for the Swensons, it'll sell."

"And why don't you dust it? Not men's work?"

"No. She says I don't see the dust. I think she's being a fanatic about a few specks." He shook his head and grinned that killer grin of his. "She says I suffer from what she calls 'male blindness.' Ma's a real ego bruiser, I'll tell you."

"Oh, I've noticed how cruel she is to you."

"Hey, she can be one tough lady," he protested as he vaulted up the porch steps. "Don't let that fairy-god-mother face fool you."

Cassidy was helpless to contain the giggle that bubbled up from somewhere inside her. "That's exactly what I thought when I first met her."

"Cinderella's fairy godmother come to life. That's Irma," Josh said over his shoulder as he unlocked the door.

"All she's missing is the wand," Cassidy agreed as she followed him toward the front door. He had it unlocked and opened before she reached it. Though boarded up, there was a beautiful frosted glass panel in the door that remained undamaged. Unconsciously she ran her fingers over the expertly etched flowers. "Beautiful," she whispered to herself.

"That's just the tip of the iceberg. This place is a gem just waiting to be polished."

Cassidy stepped inside the foyer as Joshua flipped on the lights. She immediately understood the love for the old house that she'd heard in his voice. If the rest of it was as wonderful as the sweeping staircase and oak wainscot panels, this house really was a gem. "So why don't you buy it and polish it to your heart's content?"

He shook his dark head. "Because even though they aren't asking much and I could afford it on my salary, it's too big for one person. This old place deserves a family. Or at least to be turned back into a B & B so a lot of people can enjoy it. I don't have a family or the inclination to run a B & B. But I'd love the process of watching it come alive again. Can you understand that?"

"Maybe you ought to rethink your profession. You sound more like a carpenter than a country preacher."

Joshua chuckled. "Well, that's kind of appropriate, since I serve a carpenter who became a preacher. I like to build things, fix things up—but it's a hobby, not a calling like my work with Henry."

"I just meant that carpentry and cabinet-making is a more lucrative profession."

"But it wouldn't be nearly as fulfilling. I really think that has to be the most important thing in choosing your life's work."

"I suppose. It's a shame we can't all be as fortunate as you've been in finding both a profession and a hobby."

Joshua stood in front of a set of floor-to-ceiling doors with his thumbs hooked in the front belt loops of his jeans. He stood casually, but the look in his eyes was anything but. "If you're so unhappy in what you do, then why don't you look for another job that won't give you ulcers."

His comment cut a little too close to the bone for comfort, and Cassidy stiffened. "It isn't my job. I'm where I belong. I just need to find a way to cope with stress better. That's all."

"So what exactly is all the stress from? What kind of work do you do?"

"Until yesterday I was acting vice president of Jamison Steel. I've been running the Information Systems department."

Josh heard a note of hurt in her voice. He narrowed his eyes, watching for her reaction to his next question. "Why until yesterday?"

"My grandfather appointed someone to the position permanently."

"But not you," he said, "even though you've been doing the job?"

"No. I was hurt at first, but I realize now that it wasn't all that important. After all, I'll be running Jamison someday. This will just give me a chance to learn other areas of the company in more depth."

"But you still have to be deeply hurt."

"No," she snapped, needing desperately to believe that she was indeed over her hurt. "I understood. It was a business decision."

"You're still hurt. I hear it in your voice. You shouldn't deny your feelings. No wonder you have ulcers if you hold all your emotions inside you like this. I know it hurts most when it's a family member who deals the blow that—" Joshua cut off the thought, his eyes widening in what looked like shock. He looked upset, but at that moment she didn't care. She couldn't let her grandfather's decision matter because then she'd never be able to return to work. And returning to Jamison Steel was her duty.

"If I'm hurt, I'll get over it. Do I have to stand here being analyzed as payment for seeing the house?"

Joshua turned away and slid open a set of pocket doors. "This was the parlor," he said, as if neither of them had spoken of anything other than the house.

* * *

Joshua closed and locked the front door to the Swenson house as Cassidy hurried along the walkway toward the street. He wished he could help her. He didn't know why Henry thought Josh could, but Josh wanted to try. Sometimes she seemed like two different people. The nervous, tense, rich girl who'd become short with him when he'd touched a nerve. And the sentimental dreamer who'd so clearly fallen in love with the Swenson place. He'd really like to get to know that person.

The trouble was that since she'd arrived she had stirred up too many feelings inside him. Some he understood, like his attraction to her. But others were shadows and whispers of a past that seemed lost to him. And he had felt them again when she'd related her story of being passed over for the promotion by her grandfather. He'd felt her pain as if it *were,* and had once *been,* his own.

There was also the problem that most times when he said anything that called her life-style into question, she got angry. That was a huge roadblock. He shrugged. Maybe he needed to take another route with her. Maybe he could show her how the other half lived. Maybe if she saw firsthand that money and power weren't the way to true happiness, that knowledge would stay with her when she returned home to the rat race of her life in Philadelphia.

"Want a ride home?" he called after her retreating back.

Cassidy stopped and pivoted toward him. "I thought I'd stop and see how much closer Earl is to looking at my car. I honestly don't see why he can't just look at it sooner. If he'd looked at it this morning, he could have ordered the part it needs by now. I'd be that much closer to getting on the road to Mountain Top or one of the other resorts up here."

Josh could easily have offered to take her on to one of those high-priced resorts. They weren't all that far away. But he knew Henry was right. Cassidy's unhappiness was deeper than just ill health and being passed over for a promotion. She needed to recognize that she must find a new direction for her life, or she'd never really get well. Doctors would cure the ulcer…and then her tension headaches would blossom into migraines or she'd have to battle high blood pressure. Something else would buckle, and her strong will would carry her forward on what he'd begun to suspect was the wrong path for her.

"Mind if I tag along?" he asked as he caught up with her.

"I'm on foot these days, but suit yourself. You could point out the other points of interest in town. We'll call it a walking tour."

Josh grimaced. "You may as well hop into the truck. I need to stop at Earl's for gas, and you just saw our only point of interest. Everything else is closed up till summer. We don't get the ski trade here. The hunters who come through don't need more than gas at Earl's, the occasional hot meal at Irma's and the odd item at The Trading Post, so the shop owners don't bother to stay open in late fall or winter."

Joshua found his attention snagged by the look in her stormy blue eyes. He would swear he could see the wheels turning behind those arresting eyes of hers.

"Maybe you could talk Earl into looking at my car sooner."

"Earl's been known to be pretty stubborn," he warned.

She grinned. "But we've already established how stubborn each of us is. If we double-team him, we can talk him into looking at it today."

Before he could protest his unwillingness to put undue pressure on Earl, she barreled around the truck and opened the passenger door. Joshua stared at her over the hood, not knowing what to say. Sometimes she reminded him of a steamroller, and others, like when he'd seen her staring up at the Swenson house, of a sad little girl. A honk of the pickup's horn made him grin. He guessed she was a little of both.

"I'm coming. You've got to slow down, little lady," he drawled. It was a southern parody of Earl's upstate Pennsylvania twang, but it was the best he could do. "You're on Mountain View time now."

She shot him a look full of exasperation. "Hopefully not for long."

"You know, I'm starting to get real insulted on behalf of everyone in town over this hurry of yours to get out of our little burg."

"I'm sorry," she said on a sigh. "It isn't what the town *is* so much as what it *isn't*. Let's just say this isn't my idea of a vacation."

"Well then, what is?" he asked as he started the car.

"I don't know. Maybe a day or two lying by a pool and sleeping in—but then I'd want to do things. See things. Go places. Make memories to take out and remember when life drives me crazy."

"Sounds like just another variation on your everyday life. To me, a vacation would be to live in a way I don't usually live. I see your idea of a vacation as the kind *I* should take and staying in Mountain View as exactly what *you* need."

He made a left into Earl's and took the opportunity to glance at Cassidy to gauge her reaction to what he'd said. She looked thoughtful, if nothing else. A little progress, he thought, but before he could enjoy the triumph, he brought the truck to a stop and she jumped out of the car. By the time he'd set the brake, she was already off searching for Earl.

"...but this is the same car you were working on yesterday," she was saying when he came upon them inside the garage after he'd pumped his gas.

"Well, now that's mighty observant of you to notice, little lady. And I do appreciate your concern. I had a devil of a time loosening the bolts to... Oh, there I go running off at the mouth. You wouldn't know a water pump from a fuel pump, would you?"

"No, I'm sure I wouldn't," Cassidy admitted, her tone aggressive and businesslike. "And yes, I am concerned. You said you couldn't look at my car until you did the work on the other people's cars who were in line ahead of me. But now that won't be for another day longer. I need to get out of here."

Joshua noticed Earl's eyes shift to him as he stepped behind Cassidy. There was something calculating and shrewd in his expression that Josh had never noticed before.

"How's Irma and Henry today?" Earl asked as he reached out to take the money Joshua held out. "I haven't even had time to stop for lunch so I didn't get on over to the diner yet today."

"It was Molly's day to work the morning and early afternoon shift. Ma's probably there by now. You really ought to stop and rest for a while."

Earl glanced at the car he had on the lift, then back to them. "You know, I think I will. In fact, I may call it a day. You headed for the diner, too? If you wait while I wash up, I'll walk along with you."

Joshua gestured toward the money. "I've got the truck. I'm just headed back from the Wilsons'."

"I'll be seeing you there then, I suppose," Earl said, and ambled off toward his washroom.

It only took a split second for Cassidy to round on him. "You were supposed to talk him into looking at my car sooner, not get him to stop for the day!"

"Didn't you notice how tired he was? Earl's not as young as he looks. He needs to take it a little easier. Tell me, what is your big hurry to move on?"

"I told you, I want a vacation."

"So roll with the punches and make this your

vacation. What you need is time to think, not just time away from work. Everyone needs to evaluate their choices in life occasionally. Maybe you didn't land in Mountain View by accident. God may have put you here. This town and your car trouble may be His way of speaking to you. I think He's telling you to slow down and take some time to think things out. What better place to do it than here? You have to admit that there's very little to distract you."

Standing there in the center of Earl's garage, Joshua waited to hear her tell him to mind his own business. That God didn't speak to people like that. He was even prepared to hear that in her opinion God didn't exist. But none of those things happened. Cassidy nodded and walked quietly—thoughtfully—away.

At the doorway she stopped and turned to him. "'In God we trust.' It's on the penny. I told Him to send me where He wanted me to go if He really existed. I flipped it every time I needed to choose a direction. I never stopped to think that He'd actually answer me. Maybe He did send me here. Thanks, Joshua. I'd forgotten. I'll give it a few days." She started to turn away, but stopped and looked around. "Your God really has a sense of humor, doesn't he."

Confused, Josh frowned. "With a dog like mine and Him being the Creator, that's a hard one to argue, but why in particular do you think that?"

"My regular mechanic has a cappuccino bar and leather sofas in his waiting room."

Chapter Five

Cassidy heard Joshua call her name just as she passed the spot where he'd pulled his truck up to the gas pump. She needed to take time to do some of that thinking Joshua was so convinced she should do, so she planned to walk back to the parsonage through town. She stopped and reluctantly looked back. She'd agreed to try it his way for a few days even though she thought he was way off base, so what more did he want from her?

"I thought we'd eat dinner at the café," he said, as if he'd heard her silent question.

To Cassidy, dinner suddenly sounded like a gigantic commitment. She knew she was being ridiculous but there it was. "Dinner?"

"Henry and I usually walk down and eat at the café on the nights Ma handles the dinner shift. It keeps her from having to cook again at home. She was only there when you arrived last night because the regular girl came in later than usual."

Either she agreed to spend even more time with Joshua, or she'd force Irma to cook a special meal for her later. Wasn't it bad enough that she'd unwisely spent time with him at the Swenson house? This man, this…country preacher-carpenter was a menace! He'd seen through the lies she'd nearly convinced herself were true to the truths she hadn't wanted to face. And apparently that wasn't enough for him.

The fact that he was handsome, obviously intelligent, kind and sensitive didn't help matters at all. He was quite frankly, except for his inappropriate tax bracket, the man of her dreams. Why couldn't he be a corporate executive home to visit his parents rather than a man with no past, no formal education, and, therefore, in her grandfather's eyes, a man with no future?

"So, is dinner at the café okay with you?" Josh asked again, dragging Cassidy out of the fog of her confused thoughts. Well, there was no help for it. Her answer was a given.

"Of course," she snapped, completely exasperated by her suddenly out-of-control emotions and life. "I wouldn't want to cause Irma extra work."

Something akin to hurt flashed in Joshua's beautiful brown eyes. "Do you want a ride down or would you rather go on alone?" he asked in an unmistakably brusque manner.

Cassidy felt about as small as an ant at that moment.

He'd been nothing but kind and friendly to her. He'd pried into her personal life, true. But considering his calling as a minister, she truly believed he had only the best of intentions. And now that she'd pushed him away, she realized that it was the last thing she really wanted. She could use a friend just now, and it may as well be Josh. What, after all, could happen between them in the few days she'd be in town?

She hugged her thrift-store jacket to herself. "It's chilly but still looks like it should be a nice evening. We probably won't see many more like it for a while. Why don't you walk down to the café with me? We can come back for the truck later."

An eyebrow arched over one of his dark, expressive eyes. "I got the impression that I'd been royally dismissed."

Cassidy shook her head. "No. Pushed away momentarily. And I'm sorry. I'm not used to sharing my personal feelings. Nor letting anyone close enough for me to want to share them. It just spooked me for a minute there. I was feeling hemmed in, but it wasn't your fault. It was mine."

Joshua nodded his acceptance of her apology. "The walk sounds like a good idea," he agreed, and they set off toward Irma's Café.

They'd walked in silence for a minute or two when Joshua stopped. "Bear. I'd better wake him up and bring him along. Last time I left him alone in the truck, we found him cowering and shaking with his paws over his eyes. He's been afraid of the dark ever since."

Cassidy couldn't help the spurt of laughter that erupted as they turned back toward the truck. "He's afraid of the dark? Is that why Irma has all those night-lights all over the house?"

His mouth kicked up on one side. "Pitiful, huh?"

"You could get that dog on TV with that late-night talk show host who likes stupid pets."

Josh laughed. "No. That's stupid pet *tricks*. Bear's just a stupid pet. But he's lovable and loyal. And when I found him, I really needed something of my own."

Cassidy didn't know whether to reveal what Irma had told her about him or not, but lying to him even by omission seemed inherently wrong. "Irma told me how you came to live with them and about your memory. I hope you don't mind. We started talking and…"

"It's okay. It's the way my life is. Everyone in town knows. I've come to grips with most of it, and the rest will come with time and the Lord's grace."

"You have an incredible attitude."

"Not really. I've just been incredibly lucky. I don't have a clue what my real parents were like, but I can't imagine them being better people than Irma and Henry."

"I imagine you're right. They are wonderful people."

"I think the three of us being together is God's plan. Since Henry turned eighty, he's slowed down. So has Ma," he said as his beautiful mouth formed a teasing grin, "though I'd never let her hear me say that. They were there for me when I needed them. Ma taught me so much. She spent an untold number of hours teaching me how to talk, read, do math. Then Henry not only helped me forge a new life, but showed me the path to an eternity in heaven by teaching me about Jesus Christ and His saving grace. In the beginning, I relied on them pretty heavily, and now they lean on me. God's been incredibly good to us by bringing us together."

"You know, Joshua, you are the most incredible person I've ever met. Would you answer a burning question for me? How did you get your name?"

"Henry hated that they called me 'John Doe' at the hospital, so one day he balanced his Bible on the spine and helped me hold it between my hands. He told me we were going to let the Lord choose a name for me. Then he pulled my hands off the book and it fell open to Joshua. He closed it and did it again, and it fell open at Daniel. So I became Joshua Daniels. I even have a Social Security card and driver's license under that name."

"So your *last* name is Daniels. I thought you were their real son and that Daniel was your middle name. I guess your Lord *was* good to you. Think of the name you could have wound up with by using that method."

They'd reached the truck where Bear was sleeping like a baby. "Bear!" Josh called out, and shook the truck bed. "Come on, boy. Wake up!"

Bear lay still as a rock.

"He's kind of a deep sleeper," Joshua explained, then clapped his hands loudly over the side of the truck bed near the dog.

The furry mound produced a paw that landed over a

floppy ear. Other than that, he showed no movement except a sigh and deepened breathing.

"Maybe you should reach in and shake him," she suggested.

Josh tried her suggestion, but to no avail. "I guess it's time to pull out the big guns. Come on, Bear. Let's go have dinner at Ma's."

A furry head popped up, followed quickly by the rest of the dog as he careened recklessly over the side of the truck, nearly knocking Joshua over. Bear was gone like a flash, running and barking down the road toward Irma's Café.

"Will she feed him?" Cassidy asked.

"Sure. She's crazy about him. But she may not feed me. I'm in for it when we get down there. He'll go charging into the place and start begging for handouts. Bear's just nuts for Ma's cooking."

"I imagine everyone in town is."

"Yeah," Josh conceded, then chuckled, "but they have lots better table manners."

Two days later, winter had really begun to make her approach known. Fending for herself in Irma's kitchen by subsisting on leftovers eaten in the privacy of her room, Cassidy had avoided Joshua like the plague. The quick dinner with him had been wonderful but, as she'd feared, dangerous. He was too compelling. Too comfortable with who he was. His grin was too charming. She just couldn't concentrate around him.

So she'd hidden away, determined to think through her problems. And now Cassidy was tired of thinking. Especially because all it did was make her more unhappy since she'd come to a monumental conclusion.

She was miserable.

Not just miserable because she'd been passed over for a promotion. But miserable with her job at Jamison itself. And with her whole life.

She worked constantly and didn't have the time to spend any of the substantial salary that she earned with all those hours she put in doing something she hated. And worst of all, Cassidy didn't have a clue what she could do about it. Despite what she'd said to her grandfather and despite what she'd thought in the days that had followed their showdown in the office, she was all the old man had in this world. She couldn't just desert him and destroy his dream of handing down his company to his descendants.

She'd call him. She'd talk to him. She'd at least let him know she was safe.

Before she could change her mind, Cassidy lifted the phone extension and dialed his office at Jamison Steel.

"Winston Jamison's office. Rose Carmichael speaking."

"Is he there?" she asked the woman who was as close to a mother as she'd had in twenty years.

"Oh, Cassidy, I'm so glad you called. He's here. I'm just not sure we shouldn't let him suffer a bit longer."

"I don't want him to suffer. At least, not any more," she added wryly.

"Then you're too generous. But then, we know that already, don't we."

Cassidy ran a hand agitatedly through her short hair. "I don't want him to worry, Rose."

"Suppose we compromise? I'll tell him you called and that you're fine but that you weren't ready to talk to him. Once he knows that you're okay, he'll be fine. How's that?"

"He's not frantic, is he? Won't he want to know where I am?"

"I wouldn't call it frantic exactly, and I'll tell him you called from Tahiti if he asks."

Remembering that one of his prized assistants recently ran off to Tahiti with his Human Resources vice president made Cassidy chuckle. "*You* are bad."

Now Rose chuckled. "And how do you think I've controlled the beast all these years? Cassidy," she said, her tone suddenly sober. "I want you to promise me that you'll kick back and think seriously about what you want out of life. Forget what your grandfather got you into here at Jamison. He's a big boy and can take care of himself. Put anything to do with Philly out of your mind, rest and think. Please promise me."

"I promise," Cassidy found herself saying.

"Good. Keep in touch. 'Bye now, sweetheart."

Cassidy dropped the receiver into the cradle and stared at it. Now where did that leave her? Thinking some more? Considering crazy ideas of where her life had gone wrong?

The *thud* of an ax in the backyard seemed to mock her. She was a grown woman and she'd been reduced— No! She'd reduced herself to cowering in a room for fear of becoming attached to a wonderful man because her grandfather wouldn't approve of him. How much, she wondered for the first time since that fateful day when her grandfather had taken charge of her life, did she owe the man who'd raised her? Surely not the rest of her life?

Joshua heard the back door close with its typical wooden *slap*. It was time to take the screen out and put the glass in for winter. In his mind, he ran a quick list of the winterizing he'd done so far and what he had yet to accomplish. He'd put up the storm windows in mid-October, but Ma liked to be able to let the heat out of the kitchen, so he'd waited for real winter weather to do the door. And Ma couldn't deny that it was cold today.

Glancing at the pile of wood for the woodstove that he'd stacked up, he mentally checked that off as almost finished. That left getting the shovels out and ready, as well as mounting the plow blade on the truck, but it was early days for that yet.

He swung the ax again, and the log split from top to bottom. A frigid blast of air ruffled his hair, and he smiled. He loved winter, he thought as he took aim at another log. Summer heat sometimes depressed him, but winter revitalized him. He was determined not to speculate on why that was.

"Oh, I hate winter," Cassidy grumbled at his back.

Startled, Joshua missed the log and buried the head of the ax six inches into the dirt. He pulled the ax out of the ground and spun to face her. "So the recluse has come out of her den. Don't you know it's dangerous to sneak up on a man who's swinging an ax?"

"I didn't think I was sneaking. That screen door slammed shut loud enough to wake the dead. And if that didn't, Bear's rather exuberant greeting would have."

Josh glanced at his traitor of a dog, who at that moment sat next to Cassidy, a huge bone sticking out the sides of his mouth and his eyes glowing with puppy-love as he stared up at her.

"Cassie, you've created a monster. Now he's going to follow you everywhere whining and hoping for more treats." Josh was shocked by the stricken look on her now-pale face. He dropped the ax and went to her. "What's wrong?" he asked as he reached out to grip her upper arms, afraid she might drop at his feet.

She blinked as if she'd just realized where she was. "Cassie," she said, her voice shaken and low. "No one calls me Cassie. Not since Cassie went on vacation and came home Cassidy."

"I'm sorry," he apologized immediately, though he still had no idea what he'd done or what her cryptic comment meant. "I didn't mean to upset you."

"It was just…I guess a blast from the past is the only way to describe it."

Josh sat back against the hip-high stump of a long-dead tree that he'd been whittling away at for the past several weeks. He took his baseball cap off and wiped his brow with the sleeve of his plaid flannel shirt, all the while considering her. "I understand how that can be," he said carefully. "I never know why it happens. But you do. Do you want to talk about why hearing a nickname turned you three shades of pale?"

"When I was a young child, my parents called me Cassie. We went to Colorado for a skiing holiday when I was six. They loved to ski and so did I. They taught me before I could ride a two-wheeler. One minute we were singing by the fire in our rented cabin, and the next there came this roar that I'll never forget. I can still see my father jump up and run to the big window that faced the mountain. My mother was right on his heels. He turned back and opened his mouth to say something. But he never got it out. I remember that the windows were black as the night, and in a split second they turned white, then burst inward behind him. The next thing I knew I was being swept away into a world that was cold and white—then everything went black."

"Avalanche?" Josh guessed, horrified for the child she'd been.

Cassidy nodded, biting her lip, her eyes full of tears. "I woke up a few times before the rescuers found me. I remember crying for my parents. Being cold. Then even the cold faded. I woke in the hospital with my grandfather sitting by my bedside. 'Cassidy,' he said, 'you're going to have to be very brave. Your parents are dead. We're all the family each other has now. We have to stick

together so we can carry on the Jamison name.' Until
that moment, I was just Cassie. After this, I was Cassidy
Jamison, heir to Jamison Steel. And you know what? I
don't mind you calling me Cassie at all because I think
I need to be her again."

"That's an awfully large burden to put on a child,"
Joshua commented, then realized that he was holding
her again, albeit loosely by her forearms. He let go
quickly and stepped back, saying a quick prayer for
strength. He was supposed to counsel her, not hug her.
He was supposed to care *about* her, not come to care *for*
her. It was a probably a fine balance, but he was sure
there was an almost physical line—and one he could not
cross. He didn't have the right.

He cleared his throat. "So while you've been playing
hermit up there in Ma's prize guest room, you've been
thinking," he quipped, hoping to sound at ease. "That's
good. But dwelling on your problems too much is as bad
as pretending they don't exist. I have an idea. I visit an
older woman who lives up the mountain. She's a shut-in.
Would you like to go along for a change of scenery? The
view of the valley from her back porch is spectacular."

Josh held his breath, waiting, hoping she'd agree. He
could see that she needed a break. Maybe if she saw how
difficult someone else's life was, she'd forget to dwell
on her own unsettled circumstances. And maybe
exposure to a woman like Maude would fan the flames
of the hunger for spiritual things that she'd given him a
glimpse of that night outside Earl's.

"Are you sure she wouldn't mind a stranger showing up out of the blue?"

"Maude loves company. She just can't get in to town much anymore." Josh decided to take her question as an indication that she wanted to tag along. "You'll see. She'll love another person to talk to. Especially a woman." He picked his watch up off a nearby log and checked the time. "I just need a little time to get washed up. Give me five minutes, and I'll meet you at the truck."

Josh left his ax where it was and rushed off before she could change her mind. He tried to put the anticipation that bubbled through him down to the thrill of victory, but he was very much afraid what he felt was excitement over the opportunity just to spend time with her.

Cassidy had already climbed inside the pickup by the time Josh returned. While they traveled, he told her several stories about Maude Herman that were steeped in local color, hoping to prevent the kind of intimacy he'd felt the last time he invited her to ride with him. He failed miserably.

When they arrived, Cassidy jumped out of the cab before he could get his door open, just as she had at Earl's after they'd look over the Swenson house. But this time she looked ill at ease when he met her at the tailgate. Did she feel the same attraction to him that he felt for her?

No. That wasn't possible. After all, what had he to offer compared to all the professional men she knew? And that was another reason he'd told Henry he didn't want to come to care for her. He had absolutely nothing to offer her. It must be that she was still uncertain of Maude's welcome, he told himself, though he thought uncertainty seemed very un-Cassidy-like.

"You're sure about this?" she asked, her gray-blue eyes endearingly shy.

"Maude will love having you. Come on." He took her arm and fought to ignore the electricity he felt flow from her.

"What exactly do you *do* when you visit her? And why is she a shut-in?" she asked, still a tentative note in her voice.

"I usually read to her and talk to her. She's crippled with arthritis, has a bad heart that's kept her from having joint replacements done, and is nearly blind. I also see to occasional repairs. In fact, she has a plumbing problem Ma promised I'd fix when she called on Maude yesterday. You two can get to know each other while I work."

Josh directed Cassidy up the steps and across the porch. He knocked on the front door and heard Maude call from somewhere in the house, "Come on in."

Josh opened the door and stopped halfway through to make sure Cassidy followed him. He was glad he had. She stood there with a shocked look on her face. "What?" he asked.

"She doesn't have her door locked."

"So?"

"It isn't safe. Didn't you say she lives up here all alone?"

"This isn't the city. No one locks their doors out here." He looked down at the knob in his hand. "I doubt this old lock even has a key anymore."

"Well, what are you standing there jawin' about, Joshua Daniels? Get on in here and stop lettin' out all my heat!" Maude yelled from the parlor.

"I'm coming, Miss Maude. I even brought you a surprise." He looked back at Cassie and grinned. "Now you've got to come in or she'll never let me hear the end of it."

Cassidy considered him seriously, her stormy-sky eyes narrowed in thought. He fought the urge to squirm. Then her lips tipped up in a wry smile.

"Your life seems to be ruled by women you act as if you're afraid of," she said, "but the truth is you just plain adore them."

"She's got your number," Maude shouted. "You comin' in or not, girl!"

"I'm coming, Miss Maude," Cassie said, chuckling as she sauntered on by him like royalty consorting with the peasants. She turned her head and looked over her shoulder at him from the doorway of the parlor. Now her smile and eyes taunted him. "Are you coming, Joshua?"

Josh chuckled ruefully when Maude let out a raucous cackle. He just might regret the day he'd tried to take Cassidy Jamison under his wing because she was capable of turning his life on its quiet ear. In fact, he very much feared she already had.

Chapter Six

Cassidy turned from taunting Joshua to the wizened old woman ensconced in a small recliner. She had a cap of snowy white, wavy hair and wore a pair of thick frameless glasses. Her snap-front housecoat, while bearing the burden of many washes, was still the brightest, cheeriest thing in the room. She made an incongruous statement sitting in an unabashed piece of modern Americana while the rest of the furniture had seen more than half a century's use.

Thin gingham curtains filtered the light, and old rag rugs dotted the wide planking of the floors. Against one wall sat a tattered old sofa covered with a patchwork quilt that was the same log cabin design as the one Joshua had lent her that first night. She wondered idly if Maude had taught Irma the pattern.

"You that new boarder at Irma's?" Maude asked.

"I've rented a room from the Tallingers, yes."

A challenging look entered the old woman's eyes. "Well, you like what you see or are you feelin' sorry for poor old Maude? If it's sorry, then go wait in the truck! Got no time for moony youngun's with more money than sense."

Cassidy was used to gruff. She'd been raised on gruff and wasn't in the least intimidated by it. In fact, after the worrisome camaraderie of the ride here, she saw the chance to spar with Maude as a welcome distraction. "I've got no problem with what I've seen of your house, Miss Maude. It's homey and clean."

"Not fancy as yours, though. That what you're thinking?"

"What I was thinking is that my apartment is about as friendly as a museum. I can guarantee you'd hate it. Actually, the day I left for this unplanned vacation, I more or less decided that I wasn't too crazy about it myself."

The old woman gave a sharp nod as if Cassidy had passed some sort of test. "Sit and tell me about yourself. Joshua, you run along and see to my water closet. So tell me, young lady, why'd you fix your home up the way you did if you don't like it?"

"I didn't, exactly. I hired a decorator because I didn't have time to do it myself."

"Did I hear you right?" Maude asked with a deep frown, and leaned forward. "You have a job that keeps you so busy you had to hire someone to spend your money for you?"

Joshua's bark of laughter echoed from the doorway. "You tell her, Miss Maude."

Cassidy scowled and shot him a look that had sent other men scurrying for cover. She'd walked into that one, but refused to let Maude score points for him. He scored enough of them for himself. "I thought you went to fix the plumbing."

Josh put his hands up as if to ward off an attack and retreated down the hall, his laughter trailing after him.

"You ain't gonna scare that boy into meekness, child. He's faced bigger challenges in his lifetime than any of God's children should ever see, and not buckled."

Cassidy turned back to face Maude and thought that the old woman was more than a little right. "It doesn't seem fair, does it," she said, giving up on the idea of using Maude as a distraction from thinking of Joshua. She felt compelled to hear all she could about his story—about him.

Maude made a dismissive gesture with her hand. "Fair's a weather forecast. Got nothin' to do with life. In my day, we were happy if we had enough to eat between wakin' with the sun and the rising of the moon. Now Joshua, he's doing fine for himself. Got a job he loves working for the Lord Almighty. No better life's work than that."

"But he's lost his whole life. All his wonderful childhood memories are gone," Cassidy said, her voice breaking. It worried her—how much she cared about his pain.

But she had no time to worry, because the old woman shrugged her thin shoulders in a way that eloquently stated *que sera sera,* and said, "Could be there aren't all that many good memories for him to recall. This could all be the Lord's plan. Maybe Joshua shouldn't remember a family who never looked for him."

"It does seem odd that they didn't, doesn't it," Cassidy conceded.

Maude pursed her lips and nodded. "Yep."

"And he does seem to have a full life."

"'Course he does. He's using the gifts the Man upstairs gave him. You should see him with the little ones crawling all over him in the nursery. And he can sit down with the ones that're just a mite bit older and make the Lord come alive for them. But it's the older ones in those hard teen years. He can sure talk to them, and, more important, he gets them talking back."

"I'd like to see that. I've only seen him with Irma and Henry."

"You didn't go to services last night?"

"No. I had some thinking to do. I'm…confused about my life."

"Can't imagine a better place to think than in the Lord's house, hearing His word preached. He's the guider of your life, child."

Cassidy shrugged, discounting that idea. "Why would He care what I do with my life? I have no desire to enter the ministry, believe me." She'd never relied on God to help her make a decision, until flipping the coin that brought her to Mountain View. A mocking voice inside her head chided, *No, you've let your grandfather run your life for you.*

"You think He doesn't care what the rest of us do? My brother Ethan prayed every morning for His guidance and wisdom to come to him throughout the day. Far as I can see, he never made a wrong step in life. So tell me, what's wrong with your life that has you confused? Besides that you hire other people to fix up your house a way you don't like, of course."

Cassidy smiled at Maude's teasing, then sobered when she really thought about how to answer the old woman. "My job is very high pressure, besides requiring long hours. And—" She hesitated, knowing that once she said it aloud, she'd have to own the truth. "And I hate it."

Maude's wrinkled face wrinkled even more. "Then, why do it?"

"I work in my grandfather's steel company. My father was supposed to take over the reins from Grandfather, but my parents were killed when I was six. Grandfather raised me after that. He always told me it was my duty to succeed him since my father was gone. I'm obligated to him. You understand obligation and family ties?"

Maude nodded, her eyes sober.

"Joshua doesn't," Cassidy continued. "He has no real family ties. He's working with Henry because he wants to, not because he has to. I *have* to. But…" She stopped mid-thought. There was wisdom in the grave murky golden eyes assessing her. And she wanted that wisdom. "Miss Maude, do I owe my grandfather the rest of my life? It doesn't seem fair, but then, you already told me the real meaning of *fair.*"

Maude only frowned, obviously deep in thought. She closed her eyes, and several silent minutes later Cassidy realized the old woman had fallen asleep. Disappointment pricked at her, but she shrugged. It was just as well, she thought. She knew the answer Maude would give her. Older people understood duty and honoring their family obligations.

So she sat thumbing through Maude's Bible and came to the book of Joshua. She remembered Josh's explanation of how he'd gotten his name, and wondered if Maude was right. Did God really do more than observe from afar? Could the distant Being she'd only thought of in passing for years really care enough about her to guide her life? To want her to be happy?

"I suppose you'll be rushing back to your grandfather and his company as soon as your car is fixed," Maude grumbled.

Cassidy fumbled the Bible. "Oh, I thought you'd drifted off!" She looked up into eyes that were shrewd and penetrating.

"Well, of course I did. I'm an old woman. I sleep all the time. Waste of time if you ask me. I don't have much left before I go home to the Lord, and here I am doing something I don't want to do but I don't have a choice. You do. It's stupid for you to waste your youth trying to be what you aren't. Now, go keep Joshua company. I'm going to take a nap. A long one this time."

* * *

Joshua looked over his shoulder as he pulled the trash out of the truck bed and tossed it into the Dumpster behind Irma's Cafe. Cassidy stood leaning against the rear fender of the pickup, looking up at the sky. She'd been quiet ever since he'd left her alone with Maude. He'd taken her up there hoping time with someone with more problems than she had would give Cassie some perspective, but she seemed even more troubled now. "Did Maude say something to upset you?"

Cassidy looked at him as he walked to her side. "Not upset. She gave me a lot to think about. At first she mostly talked about you."

"A truly terrifying subject, I can see."

She smiled for the first time in an hour. "You are such a teaser, Joshua Daniels. What I've been thinking about are the things she said about God. Her perceptions of Him, and yours and Irma and Henry's, are so different from any I've ever heard before. You all seem to think He really cares. Irma said He even cares what we do with our lives."

"I believe He does."

"I guess you must. She also told me not to waste my life doing something I don't want to do. But Josh, what about that commandment? It's something about honoring our parents. Wouldn't that extend to my grandfather, too, since he was my guardian? He wants me to work with him, and I don't think I want to. How is that honoring his wishes?"

Josh sighed. "I always thought this amnesia of mine was a burden. Maybe it isn't if pleasing family is this much trouble. I can't imagine not doing what I do. Doesn't your grandfather want you to be happy?"

"He thinks Jamison Steel will make me happy."

"Maybe you need to tell him it doesn't. It seems to me that if he loves you, he'll understand. As for God, of course He cares what you do with your life. In Luke 12:6 and 12:7, Jesus tells that even though sparrows aren't worth a lot of money, God knows about what is happening to every one of them. Now figure that if He cares that much about lowly birds, we're worth much more to Him. Is it any wonder that He cares much more what is happening to us and what we do with our lives?"

"I guess," she said almost unconsciously, and returned to her silent perusal of the sky. "Could God have a different plan for me than working at Jamison Steel?"

"I only know that we don't always understand at the time why things happen or why life takes us in another direction than the one we thought we'd go, but that eventually we understand. Then it's like this lightbulb goes on and we say, 'Oh, now I get it.'"

Cassidy crossed her arms. He could see her thinking, her eyes staring unseeingly ahead, yet alive and active. He knew a tough question was coming. She didn't disappoint him. "Then…if He's really out there directing things, why not tell us what's up somehow. And why do awful things happen, like you getting hurt so badly, if He's the one directing them?"

Josh took a deep breath and said a silent prayer for the right words. "You mean like, why do bad things happen to good people? It's an age-old question and the answer is really pretty simple. Because He gave us free will, and some people choose to use it for evil or are just careless in the case of accidents.

"I guess there are some things that happen that He could stop like tornados and such, but He doesn't. And that sort of plays into the first part of your question," he continued. "If we knew why trials come into our lives, we wouldn't need to rely on Him. And He wants us to turn to Him. In the tough times when we rely on His strength, He gives us this sweet peace about our circumstance, and we get to know His love better that way."

"So He could really want me to do something else?"

"Maybe. Or maybe He wants you at least to change your priorities." Josh dropped an arm behind her onto the wall of the pickup bed and stared off at the sky with her. He wondered if she saw the Lord's majesty in the stars the way he did.

When Cassidy turned her head and looked up at him, Josh felt as if Jerry Frank's prize mare had kicked him in the stomach.

"Why can't life be as simple as this?" she asked, her hand gesturing to the quiet forest scene before them.

"Can't imagine," he said.

He stood there staring down into her compelling gaze, at a complete loss for words. All he wanted at that moment was to feel her in his arms and her lips under his. Josh stepped back, sure she would be horrified if she knew what he'd been thinking.

As he turned away, he thought he saw a look of disappointment cross her expression. But when he looked back a split second later, he was sure he'd been wrong.

Josh looked up from the commentary on Daniel he was reading when he heard movement at the door of the study. Cassidy stood framed by the light of the parlor, curiosity written on her features. He glanced around the room with its floor-to-ceiling bookshelves and cheery fire leaping in the fireplace. He wanted to remember her here in this room he loved so dearly. "Come on in. What can I do for you?"

She shrugged. "I'm sort of at loose ends. What are you doing?"

"Henry's eyesight isn't all that good anymore. I'm looking up some references for him."

"References? You mean where something is in the Bible?"

Josh shook his head. "I've got most of that in my head. Henry, too. No, this is more like which church scholar said what. What their insights were into a certain Bible passage or a circumstance in the life of…well, like right now we're in Daniel."

She smiled. "One of your heroes if I remember correctly." Cassidy's gaze dropped to his crowded desk, then lifted to meet his eyes. "Are biblical commentaries at all like financial commentaries done by leading economists?"

"I would imagine so, except these commentaries have lasted through the centuries." He gestured with his head toward the books piled about him. "Some of these are recent, some were written hundreds of years ago. They rarely disagree on the basic tenets of faith, but they often do on other matters. Each work is one man's or men's opinion."

"Is that why you study so many different opinions?" she asked, rounding the desk. She looked over the books, then turned and leaned back against the desk.

He pushed away from the desk and rocked his chair back so he could look up at her. She looked so sweet with her oversize flannel shirt hanging to her knees and her gamine face so alive and questioning.

"That's why," he answered. "And it's why Henry taught me to search the Scriptures for myself. I never take anyone's word for what they say," he explained, then felt a little wary as he caught the probing look in her eyes.

"How long have you been writing Henry's sermons for him?"

Josh sat up straighter. "How did you—?"

"I started out doing research for Grandfather a few times when he had to give a speech to the board of directors. But he couldn't put a speech of his own together from the notes I made because they were facts *I* thought were pertinent—opinions *I* agreed with."

Josh relaxed a little, sure Cassidy wouldn't hurt Henry by mentioning what she knew. He wondered if Irma had figured it out yet. "He just can't do both sermons anymore. His eyes tire too easily. I do every other Wednesday's Bible study service myself, and write the following Sunday's message for him. By then, he's able to do the next Wednesday's by himself."

"So then you prepare his Sunday message again and Wednesday's so he can handle the following Sunday himself. Is that about the way it goes?"

"Not too much gets by you. Henry deserves any help I can give him. He and Irma saved my life as well as my sanity after I came to and had nothing to cling to but them. Henry shouldn't have to step down as pastor until he's ready to do it. He lives for his church and its parishioners."

She nodded. "I can see that. So tell me about Daniel. What's it about?"

"It's one of the hardest books other than Revelations to study, and one of the most attacked because of how accurate the prophecy is. Many people try to say it was written later than it was. His prophecy is so accurate that he foretold to the day when Jesus Christ would ride triumphant into Jerusalem."

She picked up the notes he'd finished on the third chapter of John for the following Wednesday night's service. "'For God so loved the world, that He gave His only begotten Son, that whosoever believeth in Him should not perish, but have everlasting life. For God sent not His Son into the world to condemn the world; but that the world through Him might be saved.'"

Cassie looked up, her eyes alive with hope and questions. He wanted more than to lead her to Jesus at that moment. He wanted to see that wonder and happiness every day of his life. He also knew it was impossible.

"Do you believe this?" she asked.

Josh pushed his chair back farther from where she stood so close. Too close. He was there to counsel her on life—not wish for her to become part of his. "I wouldn't be sitting here writing sermons and reading seven different commentaries if I didn't. Those two verses sort of say it all. It's one of those basic tenets I spoke of earlier. But it doesn't stop there. You can't imagine the peace believing those words brings to your life. When there was nothing but fear and trial in my life, Henry taught me those words, and Jesus brought me the peace I desperately needed. I knew that if my eternity was certain, then I could endure anything until that day came."

She had such an expressive face that he knew a question was coming. "Is everyone saved just because He came? That doesn't seem right, with all the people running around these days doing whatever they want to do. So many people commit crimes, even to the point of mass murder."

"Everyone who professes Him as savior is redeemed. Don't forget, Jesus also said the path to salvation is a narrow one. Here—" Josh rummaged in the top drawer looking for the copy of the New Testament Henry had given him in those early days when his faith was new.

He looked up and something he didn't remember feeling before slammed into him. At that moment he wanted nothing but to pull her onto his lap and just hold her. It made her nearness sheer torture to his lonely heart. Josh tried to shake off those feelings and went back to his search, moving to the next drawer down.

Finally he found what he was after, and as he handed it to her he prayed she wouldn't notice his shaking hands or see his heart's desire in his eyes. "Why don't you take this up with you and read some of it. If you have any questions, we can talk tomorrow."

Cassidy blinked, and he almost winced at the confusion that clouded her eyes.

"Sure. I'll do that," she said, backing away. "Sorry I bothered you. I can see how busy you are."

She retreated from the room in a rush before Josh could call her back and try to explain why he needed to cut their talk short. But then, he hadn't a clue what excuse he'd use anyway. All he knew was that at what he feared had been a critical moment in Cassidy's spiritual growth, he had let personal feelings intrude. He had prayed she wouldn't see into his heart but hadn't prayed that she would let Jesus into hers.

Josh knew he needed to talk to Henry. For the first time ever, he couldn't do what the pastor had asked of him. Because even though he had no intention of acting upon his feelings, he was too drawn to this woman to act as a spiritual counsel. The proof was blindingly clear. He had failed her, and yet he was afraid to follow her to try to make it right.

Chapter Seven

Cassidy sat brushing her hair at the old mahogany vanity in her room. She let the hand holding the brush drift into her lap as Joshua once again took over her thoughts. Not wanting to feel the way she did about him didn't change the truth. Cassidy Jamison, heir to a multimillion-dollar steel company, was attracted to a country preacher who, though obviously intelligent, had no education or financial prospects.

Her grandfather would hit the roof.

And she didn't care! Not about her fortune or his lack of one. Not about his lack of formal education. Not about the fact that she had only known him for four days. She only cared about him.

Of course, how she felt didn't matter, anyway. Cassidy saw little chance that anything long-lasting would evolve from their tentative friendship. And not because she thought him beneath her or because her grandfather wouldn't approve of him. The problem lay with Joshua himself. He didn't feel the same way about her. If she'd had any doubt before, the way he'd recoiled from her in the study had shown her the truth.

Cassidy had always thought she'd seen herself with impartial eyes, but now she had to wonder if there was something wrong with her that she'd never acknowledged. She had a trim figure and had been told by others that she was reasonably attractive. She didn't wear her hair in a long and flowing style, but the short cut suited her face and her busy life-style.

It was certainly true that the current condition of her clothing left something to be desired, but she couldn't imagine Joshua caring about anything as shallow as how someone dressed, as long as it was modestly. Besides, he'd pick out the particular combination she'd put on that morning, so clothes couldn't be at the root of his problem with her.

So, why did Joshua practically trip over his own feet trying to get away from her every time they were in close proximity? When she caught her reflection in the mirror trying to check her breath, Cassidy tossed the brush down.

There was nothing wrong with her!

She was a big girl and could accept that he felt none of the same attraction she did. Besides, she needed a friend more than a love interest, she told herself. She'd get over his rejection.

Always brutally honest with herself, Cassidy felt a

blush heat her face when she thought of the way he'd acted earlier. He had to suspect that she had feelings for him and was embarrassed by it. The only recourse her pride would allow was for her to get out of Dodge as soon as possible—she pursed her lips and stiffened her spine—and until then, she'd just have to hide her feelings as best she could. First thing tomorrow she'd go down to Earl's and check on her car. With any luck she'd be on the road by noon.

As she reached out to pick up the hairbrush again, she noticed the New Testament Josh had all but forced into her hands as an excuse to push her out of his vicinity. No. There had been sincerity in his voice as he'd given it to her. She had no doubt that he really and truly wanted her to read it. She shrugged. What did she have to lose?

She read the gospel of Matthew and became utterly fascinated by the unfolding of a kingdom that no one seemed to understand, even those closest to the man named Jesus of Nazareth. Then in chapter 19 she came upon a passage that troubled her.

It was the story of a rich young man who kept all the commandments already and wanted to know what else he had to do to be saved. After the young man turned away in sadness at Christ's answer, He'd told the disciples, "It is easier for a camel to go through the eye of a needle, than for a rich man to enter into the kingdom of God."

Troubled, Cassidy longed to seek Joshua out, but couldn't bear to see that same panicked look in his eyes that had sent her running earlier. An hour later, that passage still haunted and, she admitted, angered her. She heard Josh move through the hall toward his room followed by the *click* of Bear's nails on the polished wood floor. After a few minutes the house settled into silence.

Still, those words bothered her and kept her awake. She was the heir to a small fortune. Did that mean she couldn't go to heaven no matter what she did to earn it? It didn't seem to fit or to be consistent with Joshua's evenhanded approach to his faith or with the passage she'd read off his notes earlier. So what could it mean?

She remembered all the books on his desk and her conversation with Josh about how he prepared a lesson. If he could find out what others had read into the Scriptures in those commentaries, then so could she! Surely one of those scholars had answered her questions already.

Luckily, Bear's night-lights glowed softly throughout the house as Cassidy crept down the hall. She was grateful to the ridiculous dog as she moved down the stairs and into the darkened study. The floor creaked as she tiptoed across the room to the desk. "Please, God," she whispered, "don't let Josh find me sneaking around like this. A girl can take only so much humiliation in one night."

She found references in several books, and after a while she understood that this was one of those passages that the scholars agreed upon. But even so, they all seemed to see different applications in people's lives.

The first one she read seemed to say that Jesus did not really mean that it was impossible for a wealthy person to enter heaven. The rest followed suit on this, but one author continued on to explain that what Jesus meant was that heaven is impossible to earn or buy. The wealthy tend to think that everything and everyone has a price and that since they can pay that price, they think they can have anything they want. She wondered how many men in her own social circle thought they had already bought their place in heaven through charitable donations.

So, she concluded, salvation is an unearned gift. She couldn't earn it as she'd thought. No one could.

Further complicating the lives of the rich, another scholar pointed out, are the temptations money brings with it. That was easy enough for Cassidy to grasp. When a CEO friend of her grandfather's had ordered mandatory drug testing in his company because of falling revenues, it had turned out that drug abuse was rampant in the upper echelon of the company.

Yet another commentary mentioned the way money is almost worshiped in the world of the wealthy and how it is more often than not like a god to them. That was an easy idea for her to translate to her own experience. She'd learned quickly that in the world of cutthroat corporate politics, nothing was more important than the almighty dollar.

Tired of thinking and less content than ever with her life, she leaned her head back onto the big, old desk chair and let it rock back the way Josh had earlier. She closed her eyes and wondered where all this was leading her.

* * *

"Cassidy, dear, are you all right?"

Cassidy heard Irma's voice as if from afar. "What is it?" Cassidy asked, and opened her eyes, blinking in surprise, her mind still in a sleepy fog. "What's going on?"

"I saw the light on in here and came in to scold Joshua for staying up all night. Instead I found you. What on earth are you doing in here so early in the morning?"

"Doing?" Suddenly realizing where she was, Cassidy sat up. "Oh, I'm terribly sorry. I didn't mean to overstep myself by using the study without permission."

"Don't be foolish. Books are made to be read. You can't read the print off the pages. So, tell me, what were you reading?"

"Well, last night Josh shoved a New Testament at me and told me to read it in my room. I—"

"Shoved it at you?" Irma cut in and frowned. "Well now, that doesn't sound like our Josh."

"He was…um, busy, and I was asking a lot of questions."

"It still sounds as if he was rude to you."

He *had* bordered on rude but Cassidy didn't want Irma making an issue of it. She forced a smile. "Oh, I wasn't offended. Really. So, anyway, I took it upstairs and read it, and something bothered me. I didn't want to pester Joshua again so I tried to sleep on it. After a while, when I heard him go to bed, I remembered the books he'd been using to—" Cassidy halted in mid-thought, horrified that she'd almost revealed Henry and Josh's secret.

Irma smiled gently. "I know he writes Henry's sermons. He's been doing it for over six months. Everyone knows, but Henry doesn't realize the rest of us figured out how much Josh is doing."

Loyalty was a beautiful thing to behold, she thought, and let the subject drop. "Well, anyway, he had explained what the books were, so I came down here to look up the passage, hoping that I'd be able to sleep after I found the answer to my question. I certainly didn't mean to sleep here."

Irma still didn't look too happy. "Did you find your answer?"

"I think so. It was about being saved and being wealthy and how hard it is to be both. It was the story of the rich young ruler, and I think I figured out that it's okay to possess money as long as it doesn't possess you. And that you can't buy or earn your way into heaven."

Finally the older woman smiled. "I'd say you did a fine job of finding your answer. Too bad my son didn't do his as well."

"But he did. He was just tired and in the middle of the sermon he was working on. I shouldn't have invaded his privacy. I guess I'd better get upstairs. Please don't mention this to Joshua. I don't want him to be any more annoyed with me than he already is."

Cassidy didn't wait for Irma's response. She fled just as she had last night from Josh. She managed to get dressed and be on her way to Earl's in less than fifteen minutes.

The hood was up on her car, and Earl was hard at

work. "How's it coming, Mr. Pedmont?" she asked, trying to hide her anxiety.

Startled, Earl straightened and smacked his head on the hood. "Ouch! Oh, howdy. Got to your car in the middle of yesterday," he said as he wiped his hands on a rag. "Ordered up the fuel filter, but it didn't get up here till late last night. Figured, Earl, you get up at dawn and you could have the little lady back on the road by nine or ten."

Cassidy looked at her watch. An hour. She could be gone and out of Joshua's town in an hour. That was a good thing, she assured herself, and wished she didn't feel as if she were leaving home instead of heading toward it.

Then she noticed Earl's frown as he looked back down at the engine. He took his hat off and scratched his head. Then he let out a very discouraged and discouraging sigh. "Weren't the filter. That's for sure," he declared.

"It won't be done?" she asked, somehow knowing she was doomed.

"Nope. I'd suggest we let the new filter stay in, though. I'd say it was near time to replace it, anyway. Now I guess I'd best send for a fuel pump. It may be that."

"You aren't sure?"

"Can't imagine it could be anything else except maybe the carb, and we really don't want that."

"Why don't we want that?"

"A carb's an expensive piece, especially on one of these foreign jobs. Ain't a drop in the bucket on an American car, either."

No, she had to leave today. She saw the perplexed look

on Earl's lined face and suddenly he didn't seem as competent to Cassidy as he had. "Maybe I should have it towed to a bigger town. Maybe to a foreign car expert."

Earl's crestfallen expression nearly broke Cassidy's heart. "If you don't trust ol' Earl, then maybe you should do that. I'll ask my supplier to recommend some other fella in some bigger town. Just give me a minute to put her back together the rest of the way, and I'll make the call."

"It isn't that I don't trust you," she assured him, even though she didn't. She hated hurting someone who had been nothing but kind to her. After all, how much damage could he do taking out parts and putting new ones in? The money didn't matter. It was just that she'd wanted to get away from Josh before she made a bigger fool of herself than she already had. But she'd never been comfortable getting what she wanted at someone else's expense.

"So how's the car coming along?" she heard Josh call to Earl from across the garage.

"I ordered up a fuel filter hopin' it would be something cheap so it weren't too costly for the little lady. But it must be the pump itself. There wasn't really a way to tell till I got the filter up here. But the little lady was just asking about havin' herself towed to a bigger town."

"Cassie? I thought you agreed not to be in such a hurry to leave."

Cassidy stared at Josh. He looked worried. Had Irma given him a piece of her mind for being rude? She was suddenly furious with him. He *had* been rude.

"Actually, I got the feeling that I'd worn out my welcome with you. And if I have, that's too bad, Joshua Daniels, because Irma seems to like me just fine! And I like this town. It's…it's…quaint! And my stomach likes it, too!"

She turned to the elderly mechanic, ignoring Josh's bug-eyed expression. "Earl, you go right ahead and order that fuel pump, and if it needs that carb thingy, get that, too. You just tinker with that foreign job till it purrs like a kitten. No matter how long it takes. Now if you gentlemen will excuse me, my stomach and I are going to have a nice breakfast with Irma and Henry."

Josh stared after Cassidy's retreating back.

"Whew-ee, someone sure put a burr under her saddle, and I'd say that someone was you, Josh. What'd you do?"

Josh grimaced and kneaded the back of his neck to relieve a little of the tension he'd been carrying since last night. Irma's little lecture hadn't helped it, either. "Irma tells me I was rude."

Earl poked him. "Boy, are you blind? Stupid? Or just plain off your rocker? You don't act rude to a sweet girl like that when you live in a town without one single female over twenty or under fifty. Irma and Henry waited fifty years for the Lord to send them a son. And He sent you. Now how are you going to give them any grandchildren to bounce on their old knees if you chase away a find like Cassidy Jamison? You take old Earl's advice, boy, you stop at The Trading Post and see if

Pearl don't have some flowers or some trinket for you to take to that sweet child as a peace offering."

"Sweet child? She nearly took my head off."

"Served you right from what I could see. Rude, huh?" Earl turned away and ambled to the phone on the wall. He looked back after lifting the receiver. "Go on!" he ordered, and pointed toward the door.

Josh went. But he wasn't buying any peace offering!

Josh clutched at the cedar box he'd found himself buying at The Trading Post an hour earlier. He'd fought the urge to give in to Earl's suggestion—he liked to think of it as a suggestion rather than an order—but he'd realized that when somebody was right they were right. He *had* been incredibly rude last night. Especially considering that Cassidy had been seeking knowledge about the God he served—or was supposed to serve.

As he entered the parlor, Josh saw Cassidy sitting in the window seat looking out over the meadow that lay between the parsonage and the wide stream that formed the western border of the town. She seemed to be trying to memorize every rut and sleeping twig.

"That's quite a scene," he said after clearing his throat. It wasn't a comment on the landscape beyond the window. He longed to tell her so, but knew he had to keep his feelings to himself.

"It must be beautiful in spring." Cassie turned her head and looked up at him. "Josh, I'm sorry I shouted at you and that I embarrassed you in front of Earl."

"It was no less than I deserved. I should be apologizing to you. Last night I was tired and cranky, but that's no excuse." Again he found himself shoving an offering into her hands. "I got you something. It's sort of a souvenir." There was confusion in her eyes again this time, too, but no hurt at least. Instead she smiled, and he tried to ignore the kick his heart gave in answer.

"It's lovely."

He grinned. "No, it isn't. It's tourist junk. But apology gifts are few and far between in the winter around here. If I'd waited till spring or summer to be rude, you could have had wildflowers. Instead you get a cedar box with a tacky pair of earrings inside." He didn't mention that he wished with everything in him that she'd be around come spring. But praying for such a thing went against what he believed.

She opened the box and sniffed the cedar—just like a tourist. Then she laughed at the earrings. It wasn't a mocking laugh but one of delight. "Oh, they're adorable," she said, and held up a gold and rose-pink, minnow-shaped fishing lure that hung by its tail from what looked like a modified fishhook.

"Pearl's son Jamie turns lures into earrings, then she sells them for him," he told her.

"Thank you. I love them."

"Does that mean I'm forgiven?"

Her eyes narrowed a bit as she considered him for a long moment. "Are you apologizing because Irma told you to?"

He shook his head. "I'm apologizing because I was a clod."

She grinned. "In that case, you're forgiven for being a clod."

"Thanks. I think."

"You're welcome, I'm sure."

"Josh, are you taking that parcel up to Stephanie Tully?" Irma asked as she came into the room. "I think it might be for her birthday from her aunt in Wilkes-Barre. It would be so nice if she got it today."

Irma spied the box and earrings a split second later. Josh didn't like her smile one bit.

"Oh, you bought yourself a pair of those clever earrings Jamie makes."

Josh waited for the inevitable.

"Josh gave them to me as an apology for our misunderstanding," explained Cassidy.

That *I see* eyebrow of Irma's arched over one of her suddenly sparkling eyes. "Well, isn't that interesting. You know, you should take Cassidy along today. Stephanie mentioned that she wanted her and Larry to have a long talk with you soon—when I saw her after last Sunday's service. Cassidy could keep Krystal busy, while you work with her parents."

"I don't know anything about children," Cassidy protested. "I don't think I've been around a child since I was one myself."

"Don't be silly. Children are just little people with simple interests. You'd be fine," Irma said.

"It would be a big help," Josh admitted, however reluctantly. "I have a feeling that they really needed to talk out a problem." He held his breath, unwilling to hope for her answer.

"If you really think I could be of some help, then sure. I'll tag along."

"Thanks," he said, not sure he meant it. This meant hours with her. How much temptation could one man stand?

"Don't thank me till the kid lives through the experience. I'll just go get my jacket," she said, her tone a forced brand of optimism that made him feel small and petty.

It wasn't her fault he wanted things he couldn't have, he chastised himself. How had he come to feel this much so quickly?

Josh shot Irma a disgruntled look. "Ma, please stop pushing us together. It's crazy, and someone's going to get hurt. I don't want it to be Cassie." He didn't wait for a reply but stalked from the room in search of his own jacket and the package he had to deliver to Stephanie.

Josh already knew riding in the truck together would generate an intimacy he dreaded but also looked forward to. He couldn't ignore the irony of his situation. He might be uncomfortable when he was with Cassie, but he'd utterly panicked when he'd thought she was about to leave town. There seemed to be no easy solution— no solution at all from where he stood. An heiress didn't belong in Mountain View, and he was only marginally free to pursue a relationship, anyway.

Several hours later, Josh and Larry Tully walked across the fields toward Larry's small house. It had been a productive afternoon. Josh now had a carpentry project lined up for next spring and summer. It would help boost the church's dwindling treasury and would help solve the problem between Stephanie and Larry.

He'd gotten to the bottom of the issue between the couple quickly and had helped them see that it wasn't as huge a gulf as they'd thought. Stephanie's widowed mother was terribly lonely and afraid living several counties away, and had asked to move in with them. Though they wanted to help, neither really wanted to try fitting another adult into their little two-bedroom home. Unfortunately, Larry had put his foot down, and said no without asking his wife's opinion first. Stephanie had taken the opposite stand even though she wasn't exactly crazy about the idea herself.

Josh had gotten Larry to admit that he really liked his mother-in-law and wanted to help but that he felt the crowded conditions would be too much of a strain on their marriage. Stephanie had admitted that while she loved her mother dearly, she did not relish being the "daughter" in her own kitchen.

Josh had suggested that an addition to the house specifically designed as a mother-in-law apartment might be the best solution. It could have a small sitting room for television viewing or reading, a kitchenette so she could fix herself some of her own meals, and a small bedroom. He'd pointed out that it was their duty to see to their parent's needs and that having Stephanie's mother there could be beneficial. Stephanie's mother was in good health and still able to baby-sit Krystal. Stephanie had been wanting to take a part-time job at one of the nearby resorts to boost the family income, and now she'd be able to do so without paying a sitter.

Krystal shouted as she ran out the back door. Josh prepared for an armful of five-year-old as she launched herself off the top porch step. As he hugged the little girl and spun her around, he thought about Earl's comment about children. Earl couldn't know how much Josh wanted children of his own, but Josh knew it was not going to happen unless he could unlock the mystery of his past. How could he consider having children when for all he knew he already had some with the woman in the picture?

"Would you and Cassidy like to stay for cake and ice cream?" Stephanie asked as he carried Krystal into the kitchen.

Josh looked across the room to where Cassidy sat with Stephanie drinking tea. She was smiling as if she'd been having a nice time. "What did Cassidy say?"

"She says it's up to you. Daddy always says that. I think it's what married people have to say. Are you guys getting married, too?" Krystal asked.

Cassidy choked on her tea, and he almost dropped the curious child.

Larry, God bless him, came to the rescue.

He took Krystal from Josh. "Cassidy is only visiting

for a few days from Philadelphia, imp. Pastor Joshua was only being polite to his parents' guest." Larry put his daughter down and turned back to Josh. "So, you aren't going to turn down a piece of Steph's birthday cake, are you?"

Josh shrugged, trying for nonchalance when he'd have walked across hot coals to avoid being alone with Cassidy right then. "I never turn down a piece of Stephanie's cake."

"Let's open the presents first," Krystal demanded, and danced across the room to her mother with a paper sack that she'd obviously decorated herself. "This is from me. Cassie helped me wrap it. It's special."

Stephanie hugged her daughter. Then, careful not to destroy any of the bright artwork on the bag, she peeled back the tape that held the top closed. "Oh! Where on earth did you get something as wonderful as this done?" She pulled an eighteen-by-twenty piece of paper out of the sack. "Oh, Larry, thank you. It's the best gift I've ever gotten."

Larry walked over to stand behind Stephanie. "Honey, I'd love to take credit for that but I never saw it before."

Krystal laughed and beamed with pride. "Cassie drew it today. She pulled a hunk of wood out of the fireplace, and I gave her some of my drawing paper. It was like magic."

"Cassie, it's truly wonderful. I'm going to have it framed. I don't know how to thank you."

"She was upset that she didn't have anything to give you," Cassidy said. "It's just a little sketch."

Now Josh was more than a little curious. He crossed to stand next to Larry and was amazed by the "little sketch" she'd done. Her talent simply leapt from the page. Not only did it look exactly like Krystal, but Cassie had captured the child's lively character and the intelligent sparkle in her eyes.

"You're right, Krystal. It is magic," he agreed.

Chapter Eight

Josh took his eyes off the road and quickly glanced to his right. Cassie sat lost in thought on the bench seat beside him. So far neither of them had broken the silence of the ride. But he knew he had to and he didn't have much more time.

"So, have you ever heard of the expression 'hiding your light under a bushel'?"

"Yes, why?" Cassidy asked warily.

"I figured you must have, since you do such a bang-up job of it."

"I have no idea what you're talking about," she answered in that superior tone she'd taken on every time he'd gotten too close to a painful truth. He decided to ignore it.

"Yeah, you do. Just please tell me you head up the art department—or at least advertising."

She shook her head. "HR and IT."

He grinned. "Help a country preacher out here. I don't do initials unless they're books of the Bible or states of the Union."

"*IT* is Information Technology, as in computers. *HR* is Human Resources, as in personnel."

"Computers and problem employees? No wonder you have an ulcer. How can you waste yourself like that?"

"I—"

She sighed, and out of the corner of his eye Josh saw her shoulders sag.

"It wasn't supposed to be so awful. My grandfather said I'd find it rewarding. He said he needed me. That I needed to take my rightful place at his side or I'd regret it for the rest of my life."

"It was your father's rightful place if anyone's, and maybe not even his if the steel business was wrong for him. You have a talent given to you by God that you should use. How much training did your grandfather let you have?"

"Now wait a minute! However autocratic my grandfather is, he loves me. It wasn't a matter of not being allowed to pursue my art. I had art classes my whole life. I majored in Art in college."

So for the most part she was doing this to herself. Why? He decided he'd never find out if he didn't ask. "Then how did you wind up not using it?"

"I wanted to make him proud. The work ethic is very important to Grandfather. So I carried two majors. Art and business. There was little chance that I'd be able to make a living at the art. And I'm good at my job. Any money I'll inherit will be just that—an inheritance. I live off my salary."

Josh could believe that. There wasn't a lazy or spoiled bone in Cassidy Jamison's body. "That's very commendable—but you love to draw."

She dropped her head back against the headrest and closed her eyes. "Draw. Paint. I miss the smell of oils. The mess. I even miss looking in the mirror and finding charcoal smeared on my nose. I miss it all. Especially the feeling of creating something from inside myself."

"You miss it? Don't tell me you've been too busy to even have it as a hobby! No, don't bother. With your creativity, you paid to have your place decorated. And you've lived with it even though you admit to hating the way it turned out. You probably haven't picked up a brush in months."

Cassidy decided she had nothing to lose by being totally honest. "Not in years," she admitted as she sat up and looked around at the unfamiliar scenery. They weren't returning the way they'd come.

"Years? How many?" he asked, then added, "Just out of curiosity."

"Until today I hadn't picked up even a pencil to so much as doodle since I turned in my last projects. Art consumes me, and I couldn't just do it a little. Not and succeed at Jamison."

He threw her a disgusted look. "No wonder you have ulcers."

Cassidy squirmed beneath those occasional piercing

glances. "This isn't the way back to town," she said, wanting the attention off her. "Are we lost?"

He shook his head. "We need to make a stop. I promised I'd take the sketch you did to Maria so she could frame it."

"Maria?"

"She's a transplanted local. Has her own frame shop and a first-class mat cutter."

"What on earth is a 'transplanted local'?"

"She went away for years. Then she came back to live in her parents' home. Thus the 'transplanted.'" Josh frowned and made a turn onto another even narrower, one-lane road lined by dense growth. A plume of dust rose from the back of the truck as tires rolled across the cracked blue stone of the narrow trail.

Cassidy eyed him. He looked nervous. "Are you sure we aren't lost?"

"I see my reputation has preceded me. No, we aren't lost. In fact, we're here." He swung the truck to the right, and they suddenly cleared the trees. "And there's the woman we're here to see. She just came out of the barn."

Cassidy didn't see a shop—frame or otherwise. What she did see was a fashionably shabby farm. In short, an expensive piece of property. And a woman in a loose skirt and a heavy sweater coat, whose short auburn hair burned against the sunset.

"This is kind of far out for a business to do well. Does she do mail order or use the Internet?"

"Mostly shows. I doubt that qualifies as mail order, even though her stuff leaves here by truck."

"Shows?"

"She's an artist. Maria Prentice. I'm told she has quite a reputation in the East. Ever hear of her?"

Cassidy gaped at him. "Hear of her? I *studied* her as an up-and-coming regional artist during my first year at the university! She made an incredible splash in Philadelphia and New York while I was in high school. Hers was one of the first art shows I attended." Alarm flooded her. "You are *not* showing her that drawing. No way."

"It's wonderful," he said as he set the brake and grabbed the paper towel core that he'd tossed on the dash when he'd climbed behind the wheel.

Now she realized that the crude drawing she'd done of Krystal was rolled inside to keep it safe. She didn't want it kept safe. She wanted to burn it.

"I drew it and I say no!"

"I promised Stephanie I'd drop it off. Maria already said she'd make the frame. Remember that bushel and the light hiding under it," he quipped, and tapped her on the nose with the cardboard roll. She made a grab for it, but missed by half an inch.

Cassidy latched onto the sleeve of his jacket and made another failed attempt to snatch it, just as he slid out of the truck cab, chuckling, and switched it to his other hand. She let go of his sleeve and dived after him, scrambling across the seat.

"Joshua Daniels, I mean it. Give me that!"

"Nope." Laughing now, he held it over his head and stepped backward, negating any height advantage she garnered from standing on the running board of the pickup.

"Please," she wheedled. When he only shook his head and grinned in answer, she squinted against the setting sun and tried to gauge just how high above her head he could hold the tube. He was about four inches taller than she was and his arms were considerably longer, too.

But she was wiry.

Cassidy took off after him and tried a running leap into the air. The drawing was her target. It was there— that cardboard tube hovering only inches from her grasp. Then it was gone and she went sailing past it and him. She staggered to a stop and turned just in time to see Josh finish a smooth one-eighty, laughing like a hyena all the while.

Now she was really mad! Did he think he could use his superior height and agility against her? Make fun of her? Humiliate her by showing her amateur scribbles to her idol with impunity?

No way!

She ran at him again but ducked low at the last second and dived. She took him down into the damp November grass with a perfect flying tackle, bringing him down to her size and then some. They landed with a *thud,* both scrambling for the picture. Cassie rolled to reach it but bumped into Josh, who was crawling toward it on his hands and knees.

Still on her back, she looked up at him. And he looked down at her. Their gazes met. Held. And melded together in a silent, suspended moment bursting with possibilities.

A throat cleared loudly above them, breaking the spell. But Cassidy recovered a split second after Josh. A split second too late, because just as her mind came fully back into focus, he put the tube containing the sketch of Krystal into the hand of the auburn-haired woman with a milk-and-honey complexion that belied her age.

"That's the drawing Stephanie Tully asked you to frame. She got it for her birthday," Josh said.

"That's what she said. She sounded thrilled," she said distractedly as she pulled the sketch free of the tube. Before unrolling it she looked up. "Now would you like to introduce me to your wrestling partner?" Then she looked down at the drawing, her eyebrows arching over clear topaz eyes. "Or is she to remain as anonymous as our artist."

Cassidy knew she'd just die if her idol said something kind and patronizing. Cassidy held her breath, hoping Josh wouldn't betray her.

"Actually she and the artist are one and the same. Cassidy Jamison, Maria Prentice," Josh said, gesturing to each of them. Then he stood and reached to help her up. Cassidy wanted to ignore his hand, but didn't want to appear churlish in front of the other woman. So she took his hand and let him pull her up to stand beside him.

"Ms. Prentice."

"Maria, please. You have quite a gift for portrait. Who have you studied with?"

Cassidy opened her mouth and closed it. Had she heard right? That was the comment of one fellow artist to another—one professional to another. It was nothing to see a four- or five-figure price on a Prentice piece. She was not this woman's equal. She was not even in the league below Maria Prentice.

"Dr. Mario Dirazio, Eugenia Templeton—and Charles Kent was the last," she answered.

Maria Prentice peered down at the drawing in the fading light of twilight. "Good. Very good. I see you didn't let Kent stifle your emotional response to your subjects."

Cassie felt a moment of supreme vindication. Then her stomach dropped. Was she saying he'd been wrong? "He gave me a *C*." Her voice sounded as weak as she felt at that moment.

"The man's a fool. But then, you obviously knew that."

Cassie didn't know how to respond. She hadn't, of course. Kent had ridiculed every assignment. And at the same time, there had been her grandfather telling her that art was fine as a hobby but that she had to earn her way in the world, which she'd never do if *C* was her best.

There was a profound moment as Maria Prentice waited for some kind of confirmation. Cassie stared at the sketch Maria still held.

"That's the first thing Cassie's done since she graduated," Josh said, finally filling the silence.

Maria's sharp-eyed glance flicked from Cassie to

him and back again. "Hmm. You know, I ought to be able to find something for you to wear. Go away, Joshua. I haven't had a good discussion on artistic technique in a long time. I'll call Irma when I decide to give Cassidy back. Until then, she's mine. You, young woman, are due for some time in a studio. Don't even try to argue."

Josh thought his hearing was playing tricks on him, until Maria grabbed Cassie by the arm and started pulling her toward the house. "But what about the frame for Stephanie?" he asked, now unsure about this plan of his to divert Cassidy's attention from her job. He'd never seen Maria act like this.

Maria waved him off, then said over her shoulder, "I'll drop it over at the Tullys' when it's done. Now tell me, Cassidy, how do you earn your living if not with this incredible talent of yours?"

Cassie looked back at him with a bewildered brand of sadness glazing her eyes. She looked like a deer caught in headlights.

She'd probably never forgive him for leaving her to Maria's mercy, but maybe it was the best thing he could do for her. Something like the "tough love" concept he'd read about. Adding two and two, it wasn't a huge leap to guess that this Kent guy must have been discouraging Cassie at the same time her grandfather was busy guilting her into joining his company.

As Josh loped back to his truck, he realized there was more than one advantage to Cassie staying at Maria's for a few days. He'd have some time to deal with that one soul-searing moment when she'd looked up at him. And after he'd dealt with that, he would be able to face having a long talk with Henry about the role Josh should play with Cassidy.

He thought he'd still be able to try helping her with this career problem she faced. A friend would do that. But the more time he spent with her, the more convinced he was that he couldn't be her spiritual counselor. He was just too tempted to cross that line between friendship and something more. And while that was impossible, he couldn't deny the feelings that pushed and pulled at him.

Josh walked quietly into the parlor a couple of nights later. He'd put this off as long as he could. Cassidy's car was still ailing, and he had to drive up to Maria's to get her the next day. So she'd still be around, tempting him to make a try for a future with her. He needed to take a step back and let Henry fill in the gap.

"Henry, do you have a minute?"

"Of course, son," Henry said as he put down his magnifying glass and book. "What's troubling you?"

Josh felt humbled that this good man cared enough to know him so well. "How do you always know when something's up with me?"

Henry pursed his lips. "Never thought of it. Could be that hangdog expression you get. Or could be that trench you've worn in the hall, pacing from the kitchen to the study and back again."

A helpless grin pulled at Josh's mouth, and he ducked his head to hide it. Understated—that was Henry. "Point taken. I've been a little edgy."

"So what's up, son?"

"Cassidy Jamison."

"Now there's a surprise."

"I can't do what you asked me to, Henry. I've tried but I just can't do it."

"You two have another spat?" the older man asked.

Josh thought of the tussle by Maria's drive. He nearly laughed aloud until he remembered looking down into her eyes and feeling very *un*pastorly emotions toward her. The mood between them had gone from carefree to serious in a heartbeat.

Nothing would ever be the same again for him. He could no longer drift from day to day and pretend there wasn't something basic missing from his life. He feared that something was and would forever be Cassidy Jamison.

"Son?"

Josh felt Henry's hand settle, shaking and frail, over his and give it a squeeze that, though not full of power, did not lack strength.

"I want her to be more than a passing ship in my life—and that's why being her spiritual advisor feels wrong. It feels like a…I want to say a conflict of interest but that isn't really right. Of course I want what's best for her, and turning to the Lord certainly is. But she's vulnerable, and to advise her spiritually when I want more just *has* to be wrong. My feelings get in the way.

Like the other night," he began, and relayed what had happened between them when she'd come to the study to see him.

Henry nodded. "I think I understand. You're afraid you'll hurt her in some way."

Josh, still working out his confusing mix of worries and feelings, continued, "And then if she's turned to the Lord under my guidance, she might turn *from* him because I hurt her."

"Okay, son, I'll talk to Cassidy and let her know that if she has more questions about spiritual matters she should come to me."

"Thanks," Josh said, and started to stand.

A surprisingly strong tug on his arm pulled him back down. "You've had your say. Now it's my turn," Henry told him. "I agree that with these feelings you have for her, stepping aside on spiritual issues is in all probability a good idea. But I disagree with this obsession you have about remaining unattached. You have too much love to give, boy. You've got to give it or it's going to eat you alive. You don't have the gift of singleness. You take a good look at what Paul's saying to you in 1 Corinthians 7:7-9. Then you ask yourself if you don't *burn* when you're near Cassidy Jamison."

"But I'm not—"

"Didn't ask what you are, but what you feel. Read it. Just read it and search your heart." Henry stood slowly. "'Night, son."

Josh let his shoulders sag and his head hang as he

braced his elbows on his knees. He didn't have to read it. He already had. The trouble was, he knew married life was for him.

He was just very afraid he might already be married.

Chapter Nine

Cassidy saw Josh's pickup turn in to Maria's long drive and her heart sped up. As she stood anxiously at the studio window, she watched him jump out of his truck and turn back to Bear, who bounded out the door behind him. The dog jumped and frolicked his way across the wide expanse of grass toward the front door with Josh laughing that wonderful carefree laugh of his. He had become so dear to her in such a short span of time.

She admired how tirelessly he worked, whether it was making repairs to Maude's home or the Tallingers'. She was in awe of the ease with which he'd managed to get Stephanie and Larry Tully to talk out their problems. According to Stephanie, without his guidance and near Solomon-like wisdom, the couple might have wound up in divorce court instead of joyfully celebrating her birthday.

In the past couple of days, she had come to understand

that it was Josh's deep faith that allowed him to give hope and comfort to those in need. She'd come to understand that faith in God had given Joshua's life a solid foundation because it was built on the Rock of Jesus Christ. The success she'd sought, however, had evaporated, giving her no foundation at all because her life was built on the sands of transient worldly accomplishments.

He'd shown her that what she was running from wasn't disappointment or anger at her grandfather, but a life that was wrong for her. He'd even managed to give her back her art. But those things were also temporal and fleeting. More important was the knowledge of the Lord that he'd brought to her. It had produced in her a yearning after the Jesus of the Bible that had led to a decision to ask Him in to her heart and life.

Josh had given her a gift that was eternal.

She looked away to the painting before her, as he and Bear moved out of her line of sight. She smiled. Josh had opened the floodgates of her creativity by bringing her to meet Maria. It had happened the minute Maria opened the doors to her studio. The smell of the oils had grabbed her first, but then she'd spied a bin of watercolors, and the memory of crisp clear hues had burst in her mind and she'd wanted to use those, as well.

Maria's studio was an artist's playground and, oh, how Cassidy had played. Josh had been right. She had cut herself off from this important part of her inner self for too long. And according to Maria, who wanted her to put a portfolio together for her agent to see, Cassidy's grandfather had been wrong. Professor Kent had been wrong. Maria said she had no doubt that Cassidy could earn a decent living from her artistic talents.

Cassidy wasn't sure she believed that, but she was at least willing to give it a try. And the best part was that she could pursue a career in art from anywhere. Even a beautiful, simple place like Mountain View.

It had come like a bolt from the blue in that blinding instant on the ground when her eyes had met Josh's. In that moment, she had seen something in his eyes—a longing for more than friendship—and she had known that she wanted that, too. She knew it was too soon for such feelings. She had only met Josh a week ago, but she couldn't deny that she wanted to stay by his side and build a new and better life for both of them.

"Excuse me. I'm looking for a corporate executive named Cassidy Jamison. Have you seen her?" Josh asked as he entered the studio.

Cassidy turned from her painting and laughed. "Nope. I haven't seen her in a while and I doubt I'll ever see her again. But I'm Cassie. Will I do?"

"I see you're not letting any grass grow under your feet. You look like a real artist."

"You know what?" Cassie said as she looked down at her paint-smeared shirt and jeans. "I am a real artist, Josh. I always have been. And do you know what else I am?"

Josh raised an eyebrow. "No. What else are you?"

"I'm saved. I asked Jesus into my heart last night."

"You did?"

Josh seemed not only surprised but worried, when she'd thought he'd be elated.

She had to be wrong. This was what he'd been trying to encourage her to do, after all. "Yeah. And it was just the way you said it would be. I felt this incredible peace just fill me!"

"That's wonderful," he said, and smiled. But Cassie thought it looked like a nervous smile.

"It really was. I was a wreck. When I walked into this studio, I realized I'd made a big mistake by cutting everything artistic out of my life. By the next morning, Maria had already offered to show my work to her agent, and I'd realized that a career in art was what I wanted."

"And you were imagining your grandfather's reaction," Josh said.

Cassie nodded and smiled. "And worrying. And pacing. Then I remembered what you said about the peace giving your heart to Jesus gave you. I decided that if He could do that for you, considering the circumstances you found yourself in, then I'd be a fool not to turn to Him. And you were right. He's going to work this out with Grandfather. I know He is. But I have lots of other questions and—"

Josh frowned and cut in. "Cassidy, I really am happy about your decision for Christ, but I think you should talk to Henry if you have questions or concerns. I'm not the person to ask."

"Don't be silly. You're who I want to talk to."

"Cassie I'm not—" This time it was Josh whose thoughts were interrupted, as Maria swept into the room full of smiles and praise.

"So, Joshua, what do you think of this one? I may have spiked my own career by discovering her."

For the first time Joshua's eyes flicked toward the watercolor taped to the easel board. And stayed glued there. He whistled at the study of the faded old barn and landscape beyond it with the sun setting against a salmon and azure sky. "Oh. That's beautiful," he said, his tone full of wonder. "It looks so real. Cassie, you were hiding a searchlight under that bushel of yours. Don't you ever stop painting!"

She laughed. "Don't worry. I don't intend to. In fact, I'm going to stay in Mountain View and paint for the rest of my vacation. I already called Irma. She said it was fine with her."

Josh's eyes widened. "You're staying? How long's your vacation?"

"Five more weeks, officially, but I'm never going back to work at Jamison. I'll contact him eventually, but I'm not ready to talk to him yet."

"But isn't your grandfather worrying all this time? You said he really loves you. It doesn't seem fair for you to have disappeared the way you did."

Cassie was grateful now that she hadn't blurted out her feelings for Josh. He seemed to want to be rid of her. She felt a pain deep inside but tried to ignore it. "You're the one who's been telling me to stay here and think about what's wrong with my life. You sound as if you want me to go home."

"That isn't what I meant."

"Of course it isn't. Joshua doesn't want you to leave," Maria said, glaring at him. "Do you?"

Joshua blinked. "I don't. Really."

He'd made his denial, but Cassidy was afraid it didn't extend to his heart. "That's not the way it sounded from here," she said, trying to pretend anger rather than show her distress and expose her feelings.

"I was just concerned for your grandfather."

Cassie resisted the urge to roll her eyes at that excuse. "I contacted his secretary and she promised to tell him that I'm fine, but she won't tell him where I am. Honestly! The last time we talked, you were ready to tar and feather the man!"

"Do you two always squabble like a couple of misbehaving children?" Maria asked, her tone droll and amused at once.

"Yes!" Cassie all but shouted, exasperated beyond measure.

"No, *we* don't," Josh growled, then added sheepishly, "unless I make a simple comment and *she* takes offense."

"Oh, I can imagine your innocent comments," Maria said. "Well, kiss and make up. You're both giving me a headache. Cassie, I've packed up some supplies for you to use while your car is out of commission, and I found an old easel, as well."

"But I can't take your supplies. It's too—"

"Joshua," Maria interrupted, "load the supplies I left in the foyer into your truck. Cassidy, go back to Irma and Henry's and get started on that portfolio."

"But—"

Josh took Cassie's arm. "It's no use. I've seen her like this. You'll never win. Just say thank you, and we'll be on our way."

Cassie yanked her arm out of his hold. "Maybe I don't want to go somewhere I'm not wanted."

Something in Joshua's eyes dimmed, and he gazed over her shoulder rather than look her in the eyes.

"I didn't mean to make you feel unwelcome. I was worried. That's all. I'll go load the truck."

Staring after him, Cassie tried to analyze what had happened between them this time. There seemed to be only one answer; he felt burdened by her company.

"Now there's a man well and truly hooked," Maria said.

Cassie frowned. "Hooked. By what?"

"Not what. Who. Hooked by you. Hooked on you. How can you not see it?"

"No offense, but you're a few bricks short a load if you believe that. Since I arrived, he's been friendly one minute and short-tempered and standoffish the next."

"That's because he's fighting what he feels every step of the way. Which means you need to fight back twice as hard. He'll be worth it."

"Maybe I don't want a relationship with someone who doesn't want to be involved with me."

"Cassidy, have you ever thought how intimidating you and your family history could be to someone like Joshua? You're an heiress. An old-fashioned concept nowadays, but there it is. And you've a family history and an important career to go back to if you want it. What has Joshua to offer you?"

Cassidy was decidedly annoyed at her new friend. "A lot! He's a spiritual giant next to me. He's good and kind and he has a strong character. And he's funny and wise and wonder—"

"Okay!" Maria cut in with laughter in her voice. "So go convince him that you see all those sterling qualities in him, and that you don't care about money or social standing or what he can remember of his past. Let him know that you know what you want and that you aren't about to change your mind."

"Oh," she said, all anger gone. "I get it. He's trying to push me away because he's afraid to get hurt."

Josh honked the horn then and Cassidy impulsively hugged Maria. "I'd better go get started. Thank you. Thank you for everything."

Josh watched Cassie from the doorway of the tiny, virtually unused bedroom that Irma had given her to use as a studio. Last week he'd taken the twin bed down and stored it in the attic to make room for her to work.

Her hair shone in the sunlight from the tall northern windows as she concentrated on the painting before her. He'd been watching her paint for a while, but she had given no indication that she'd noticed his presence. Cassie seemed to lose herself in her art the way he lost himself in reading. And she was incredibly talented at the art she'd denied herself for so long.

Cassie had agreed to seek out Henry on any questions of faith and she spent quite a lot of time with the old pastor, learning about the God of the Bible. Her faith seemed to strengthen and grow every day.

She'd told them all at dinner one night that her parents had taken her to church regularly but that with their death that had stopped. Everything in her life had changed completely. A child who loved playing in the midst of nature during any season had been moved to a modern high-rise penthouse in the heart of the city. Concrete and traffic. Butlers and nannies. Boarding school. Parents whose love had been all-encompassing had been replaced by a brusque older man who'd preached duty to family and company above all else. Cassidy had confided that she'd felt the need to earn his love every day of her life. It was little wonder to Josh that she had turned so readily to a Savior who loved her just because she existed.

While she no longer asked him questions about faith, they did still spend time together. She talked a lot about her art, and her excitement and enthusiasm were catching. He waited each day to see what she would accomplish. She'd confided that money meant very little to her and that though she could have had anything she wanted growing up, she'd rarely asked for anything.

People, not things, had always mattered more to her. She was a miracle—totally unspoiled by the kind of wealth most people only dream of experiencing.

And he loved her deeply.

She wasn't working in oil paint today as she had been the last several days. Josh took a deep breath and was glad she'd switched media. Not because he liked her work in watercolor any better than in oil but because he could smell the delicate scent she wore from where he stood.

The age-worn table she'd had him set near the western window had her attention. The window was open, the breeze stirring the sheer curtains she had hung to filter the light for this particular work. On the table was an old rusted kerosene lantern and Irma's grandmother's sewing basket with a faded housedress of Irma's tossed partly over it so it flowed across the table top. He knew she'd placed and arranged every fold, but it truly looked as if a woman from a day long gone by had tossed down her sewing chore to hurry off to another task. He couldn't see the painting from where he stood, and the anticipation of seeing it finally outweighed his pleasure at silently observing Cassie at work.

"Am I allowed to see it yet?" he asked at a near whisper, not wanting to startle her.

Cassie turned to him with a smile as sunny as the bright fall day and chuckled. "Of course. I refuse to be temperamental and run around hiding my work before it's finished, especially when I'm living and working in someone else's home."

Josh stood rooted in place as love for her overwhelmed him. Her hair was all ruffled from running her hands through it as she worked, and she had a streak of sky-blue paint smeared across one cheek. And she was perfect.

He didn't remember walking toward her, but he suddenly found himself standing next to her at the easel.

He didn't spend those precious seconds admiring her work, but rather God's. Her blue eyes sparkled with happiness in the sunlight. They were alive with something he was afraid to try identifying. Instead, he reached out and stroked his thumb across her cheek where the paint was smeared. The paint stayed stubbornly there, but he forgot his mission as soon as his fingertips touched the silky texture of her skin.

Cassie's smile faded and she turned into his arms. "Josh?" she said, her voice low and questioning. "What's—"

He leaned closer and silenced her in the only way that felt right at that moment. He kissed her and knew for the first time how *right* a kiss could be. It was, of course, for him his first kiss, at least the first he remembered, and he was shocked at what he felt as every muscle in his body tensed.

But then came the feeling he knew all too well. That hollow detached knowledge. It made the hair on his arms stand on end as if a cold breeze had floated over him. A whisper of *before*.

This was not a first at all. And worse, he knew he'd felt love and need before—for some other woman.

Cassie's arms had risen to encircle his neck and she was clearly shocked when he reached up, took her wrists and all but pushed her away.

"I'm sorry," he whispered, and turned to flee the confusion in her eyes and in his heart. He made it to the door before her call stopped him.

"Josh! I'm not sorry. Please come back. I wanted you to kiss me. I love you. Can't you see that by now?"

Josh whirled back to face her, thrilled and horrified by her declaration. He'd never in a million years guessed that she could feel anything for him even close to the depth of what he'd come to feel for her. Looking into her gentle, caring eyes, he fully understood what he'd seen there earlier.

She did love him. Maybe as much as he loved her.

But it was an impossible love. A forbidden love.

"That should never have happened. None of this should. Don't love me, Cassie. I'm not all here. It just looks like I am. Don't waste another second thinking about me. Because I'll never love you back. I can't. I just can't."

This time he gave her no chance to stop him. He reached for the door and shut it behind him. Shut it on the woman he loved and needed as much as he needed air to live. Shut it on the life he wanted and couldn't have.

Because he loved someone else more, and under His laws Josh wasn't free to love this woman. Somewhere buried in his mind—in his past—was another.

Chapter Ten

Every bone in Josh's body screamed as he steered the truck into the parking lot next to Irma's Café.

He'd been avoiding the house these past three days ever since that wonderful, disastrous kiss with Cassidy. That first afternoon he'd excused his absence to Irma and Henry by hiking up the mountain to Henry's retreat cabin to ensure it was secure for winter. He'd left late in the day, so staying all night hadn't looked at all odd to the older couple.

He'd come home the next morning dreading any encounter with Cassie, to find a note from Larry Tully, who needed help repairing a pasture fence. It hadn't taken all day, but with winter coming, a home visit to see several of the parishioners who lived farther than most had kept him away till late that night.

As soon as he'd come home, he'd gone straight to bed. He hadn't slept well, but at least he'd gotten through another day.

Then yesterday morning he'd gone up to spend time with George Taylor, who was dying of cancer. Josh had found George's daughter and son-in-law exhausted and depressed when he'd arrived. They were determined that someone be with the older man when he died. So Josh had stayed and had taken the night shift so the couple could get some much-needed rest. George had gone home to the Lord just after his daughter returned to his bedside near dawn.

George's death had reminded Josh just how fragile life was and that he could lose Irma or Henry at any time. He'd realized that he couldn't stay away from home for the rest of Cassie's stay. He was through hiding, but had no idea what to do next.

He set the brake on the truck and hopped out. With any luck Ma was working this shift. He needed to spend some time with her. Then he wanted to have a talk with Henry. He missed his family. Almost as much as he missed Cassie.

But he had to stay away from her. The only way to minimize the hurt he had caused her with his carelessness was to stay in the background until she left. He hoped Ma or Henry could think of something better than he had.

Josh felt a little lighter when he pulled open the door and Irma looked up from pouring coffee for Ted MacDonald. "Want a cup? It's fresh," she asked, then her eyes narrowed. "You look terrible. Rough night?"

Josh settled his tired bones on the counter stool and nodded. "George went home to the Lord at around seven this morning. I stayed to help make arrangements."

Irma reached out and patted his hand. "That's always the hardest duty a pastor faces. I remember Henry's first deathbed vigil. Have you talked to him yet?"

Josh shook his head. "I stopped here. I'll go home and grab a few hours' sleep after I fill him in."

"Cassidy's been looking for you. For nearly three days now. She seems to think you're hiding from her."

"I've been..." Josh sighed and nodded. "Yeah, hiding from her."

Irma shook her head, her gaze shrewd. "She seemed awfully sure, but I told her you'd never be such a coward."

"I'm trying to keep her from getting hurt, Ma. She thinks she's in love with me."

"Only 'thinks'? Now, correct me if I'm wrong. We're talking about Cassidy Jamison. I'd guess she's about thirty."

"Twenty-nine," he corrected automatically, then leaned his elbow on the counter and groaned as he covered his eyes with one hand to squeeze his aching temples. He knew where this was going.

"Hmm. You're right. She's twenty-nine years old. A forthright, strong modern woman. Don't you think she deserves to have her feelings taken seriously and not discounted as if she's too dim-witted to know what she feels?"

He dropped his hand to the counter and sighed. "I have. But she can't love me."

Irma raised an eyebrow that somehow managed to change her sweet motherly face to imperious stone. "You had better not spout some self-deprecating platitude like 'I'm not good enough for her, Ma,' or I'll starch your underwear for a month."

Josh managed a little smile for her, then he dropped his eyes to his hands and fingered the slight bump on the ring finger of his left hand where his finger had been broken—where a plain band once must have rested. It was one of only two clues to the truth of his past. "I know money and social position don't mean anything to her. That's not it. She can't love me because I'll only hurt her."

Irma covered his hand with hers, and he looked up into her soft gray eyes. "Son, you wouldn't hurt a fly."

"I'm married, Ma. You know it. I know it. Most important, God knows it. I have to honor my vows even though I don't know who I made them to or where she is."

Irma took his coffee away.

"Hey!"

"There's nothing I can say to you that I haven't already. But I can tell you that you don't need caffeine. You need sleep so you can think with a clear head and not with your emotions. Then when you wake with a clearer head, I want you to have a long talk with Henry. Talk this out with him one last time, then put it to rest. You have to give it up, son. Your memory is just not coming back. Not today. Not tomorrow. Not next year. I truly believe that."

He wished he could believe it. For the first time, he really wished he could believe it. But that was only because now the future held something precious that the past did not. Cassie.

He stood and leaned over the counter to give Irma a peck on the cheek. "I guess I should go. Thanks, Ma."

Josh left, and Irma smiled at his back, adding silently, *Have a nice chat with Cassidy. If anyone can talk you out of this stubbornness, it's her. She's one determined young lady. Don't be surprised if she corners you.*

Josh stumbled up the last step to the second floor a few minutes later and could almost feel the mattress under his back. Half a second after his turning in to the hall, a small paint-flecked hand landed smack in the middle of his chest.

"We need to talk," Cassidy said, determination written on her every feature.

He was too tired for this. "No, we don't. I need sleep—and you need to get on with your life."

She stepped back, planting her fists on her hips and effectively blocking the hall to his room. "So you kissed me and it meant nothing?" she asked, her eyes flashing.

He propped his shoulder against the wall for a little help to remain standing, and if he looked like a punk the way the guy in "Rebel Without a Cause" had, then so much the better. Maybe she'd believe him capable of leading her on. "Yeah. Something like that. Let's just forget it and go back to being just friends."

Tears welled up in her eyes, and she tried to blink them back. "And that's all you ever felt for me. Friendship?"

Josh pushed away from the wall and tried to steady his breathing as he looked at her, his heart twisting in his chest, his throat aching. He blinked away a flood of tears in his own eyes. He couldn't lie to her. He just couldn't let her think he didn't care.

"No. It's not. You were right, Cassie. We need to talk." He took her arm and steered her into the room she used as a studio. He'd put an easy chair in there for her, and now he directed her toward it.

"What do you think we need to talk about?" she asked as she sank reluctantly into the old chair.

Josh grabbed an old desk chair from across the room and sat in front of her. He leaned forward and braced his forearms on his thighs. "We need to talk about a lot of things. Me. Who I am. What I feel. What you deserve."

"What do you feel?"

"I love you more than life, Cassie."

She smiled. He adored that smile, and the light of love that suddenly shone in her eyes—even knowing he'd have to extinguish it.

"Then what's the problem?" she asked.

"I can't love you more than my Lord. I have to stay faithful to Him."

Cassidy's heart nearly stopped at the desolation and determination she heard in his voice. She stared at him and wondered how he could think she wanted him to be less than he was. "Have I ever given you any hint, inkling or glimmer of an indication that I expect you to give up your commitment to the Lord, to the church or to Henry?"

"No. I'm not saying this right. I—" He stopped and looked down at the floor for a long moment, then back up.

The sadness and loss in Josh's eyes truly frightened her. "Just say it!"

"It's not that easy. Maybe if I start at the beginning."

He seemed so torn apart that Cassie reached out and laid her hand on his shoulder. "That's usually a good place to start."

He nodded and fished his wallet out of his back pocket. "After I was awake a few weeks—"

"Wait a minute. I thought you meant our beginning as in when I came to Mountain View."

"No. *My* beginning. That's the real problem. There were two clues to who I really am. One was this—it was in my suit coat pocket when Irma and Henry found me." He handed her a picture he'd pulled out of his wallet.

Cassidy didn't want to look, but he seemed to need her to. And what she saw broke her heart. It was Josh— a little younger, a lot more polished, wearing a dinner jacket—and a woman with black hair wearing a long, light blue gown. It wasn't the sight of him with another woman that broke her heart. No. What dealt the blow was the near worshipful look in his eyes as he gazed down at the dark, petite beauty who stood within his possessive embrace. "Who is she?"

"I have no idea. Well, actually I have an idea, but it's only that. A speculation. Cassie, the other clue was that a ring had been torn off my left ring finger when they found me. The police and the pathologist who examined my hand in those early days confirmed that it was a ring I'd been wearing for years."

"But pathologists are for—"

"I was on life support and there was every chance I'd die. The state police were trying to find out who I was and what had happened. As it was, almost all evidence of a ring was gone by the time I woke."

"And you think she was your wife."

Josh nodded. "I'm sure of it."

"But you said you don't remember anything."

"That's true."

"Then, how can you be sure?"

"Because this awful sadness descends on me like a dark cloud when I look at her picture."

"I don't want to sound insensitive," Cassie said, twisting her hands. She hated to hurt him, but one possibility leapt out at her. She took a breath. "What if she was with you when you were attacked? They may have killed her."

"Apparently the police thought so at first, but no body was ever found. Besides, this feeling I get is different from mourning her death. It's more like I know she's out there but I've lost her."

"You love her," Cassidy said, her heart breaking a little more each minute.

Josh blinked, and a look of utter despair settled over his features. "No. I love *you*. I don't even know her. She's a stranger to me—but I know I'm married to her."

"You don't know any of this for sure." Cassie fought

the urge to add that he could be feeling unhappy when he looked at the photo because he somehow knew she'd had a part in what had happened to him. Neither the idea that the woman had been killed nor that she'd tried to have *him* killed were pleasant thoughts, so Cassie held her tongue.

"I'm obligated to keep myself for her," Josh said. "I'm her husband. I can't go against God's law just because it isn't making me happy right now."

Cassidy grew more incredulous by the moment. "And you think God wants you to remain faithful to a picture?"

Josh nodded. "If I took vows to the woman in that picture, then, yeah, that's what I believe."

Cassidy saw the truth of his word in the pain written on his precious face. And she understood something else. Her presence here was sheer torture for him. Just as his would be for her.

He'd said they should go back to being just friends. But that wasn't possible. They couldn't be just friends. Their feelings went too deep. Their need for each other was too strong.

"Then there's not much else to say, is there?"

He shook his head and stood. "No. There really isn't. Except I'm sorry, Cassie. I wish with all my heart I could go back on my principles, but they wouldn't be principles if I ignored them when they became inconvenient, would they?"

Her heart breaking, Cassidy stood and hugged him. "No. They wouldn't."

"I'm sorry I'm hurting you. I wish—"

She silenced him with a finger against his lips. "I'm a big girl and I'll be fine." She forced a smile and choked back any evidence of tears. "Go take that nap. You look dead on your feet. Maybe I'll see you later."

He gave her a quick nod and turned away. "Yeah. Ask Irma to wake me for dinner, would you?"

"Sure. See you then." Cassie waited for the door to close before she let her face crumple into silent tears. She'd lied to him. Earl had finished with her car, and she would be gone by the time he woke.

It took her less than an hour to pack her car and write a check for Irma. But she hadn't been able to write the letter she'd started to the elderly woman. She finally gave up and decided that it was bad enough to be a coward with Josh, but she could at least say a proper goodbye to the Tallingers.

She found Henry in his study, reading a thick text with a magnifying glass. He looked up and grinned. "More questions?"

"No. A simple goodbye. I'm going home, Henry. Thanksgiving's less than a week away and I need to see what I can salvage of my relationship with Grandfather."

Henry shook his head. "Your grandfather doesn't have a thing to do with this. You've talked to Josh."

Cassie nodded. "I'm hurting him by being here. I'm not sure how much of this I understand, but I know that. And seeing him day in and day out would hurt me too much, too. I need to leave."

"But if you stayed—"

Cassidy interrupted with a shake of her head. "If there's one thing I've learned about Joshua Daniels in the nearly three weeks I've known him, it's how stubborn he is." She smiled, and knew it was a sad one. "It seems I've met my match in more ways than one."

Henry pushed himself to his feet and held out his comforting arms. "Give an old man a hug before you disappear from our lives, then, will ya?"

The goodbye to Irma was no less difficult. Cassidy walked into the café and found Irma waiting. "Henry called. We've been two very selfish people, dear. And we're sorry. Both Henry and I thought you'd pull Josh out of this determination to stay alone. I never wanted to see you hurt."

"I know that. And to tell you the truth, I wouldn't have it any other way. I wouldn't give up the experience of having known Josh for anything. And knowing him simply means loving him. It isn't your fault. It isn't anyone's. Maria has my address and I'll keep her informed where I move to. I won't be staying in my apartment long." Cassie remembered Irma's reaction to the tale of her apartment and its decor, and she smiled a little more easily this time. "It has terrible light and someone decorated it in the most ghastly style."

Irma came around the counter and hugged her. "Good for you, dear. You let us know how things are going. I've packed you some dinner so you won't have to stop anywhere after dark."

Tears filled Cassie's eyes, and she couldn't control her quivering lip. "I'm going to miss you so much. Thank you. Thank you for everything. Please, take good care of him."

"Always," Irma responded. "Now go if you're going before I blubber all over you."

Cassie nodded and ran for her car. How could it feel as if she were ripping her heart out and leaving it behind in a place she'd been for less than three weeks? As she headed out of town, she passed Earl's Car Emporium and slowed down as he walked toward the street from the old barn he called a garage.

He stopped about twenty feet away and shook his head sadly as she opened the car window. "Sorry to see you go, little girl," he said. "Real sorry." Then he waved her off and turned away.

"Sorry to be going, Earl," she whispered brokenly. "Real sorry."

Cassidy stepped on the gas and drove away from the only real home she remembered having in over twenty years.

Chapter Eleven

Josh woke, the morning sunlight streaming through his bedroom windows. His first thought was of Cassie. He knew she'd be thrilled with the strong morning light. She might even be able to finish the painting she always worked on between eight and ten.

Then he remembered.

Cassie would never be more than his friend, and she'd had tears in her eyes when he'd told her. She'd tried to hide them, but he'd seen—and her pain had tripled his. She should hate him for hurting her this way.

He hated that he'd hurt her. If only he'd told her sooner. If only he'd realized how deep her feelings for him had become. But he hadn't thought it possible for her to care for him. She was so far outside his small world that it had never occurred to him to tell her to guard her heart.

There was always the hope that she'd quickly come

to see how inappropriate he would have been for her. She might already have come to that conclusion. Then they could be friends, and he could love her from a safe distance. His love would never change for her, but he prayed hers for him would. He didn't want to think of her hurting the way he was.

Josh decided to stop by her studio some minutes later—and froze, horrified, in the doorway. Her paintings were gone and the supplies Maria lent her were packed in the box she'd sent them in. He rushed down the hall, his heart pounding as he approached her room, but he stopped abruptly before he got there. Her door was open. Cassie never left her door open.

And then he knew for sure.

He rushed forward, but the awful truth didn't change. The room was empty. Anything that spoke of Cassie's presence was gone. *She* was gone.

Josh wandered in and sank down onto the bed in a haze of pain and loss. He tried to come to terms with her total absence from his life. It was better, he told himself. A clean break was better. He knew it, but he couldn't seem to convince his aching heart.

Empty. For the first time since realizing that he had no idea who he was, he felt totally empty. She wouldn't be there to brighten up the dinner table or a slow afternoon. There would be no more impromptu art shows when something she'd attempted came out just right. He'd never again look out at the congregation and see her soaking up his Wednesday or Sunday night's teaching like a sponge. Or hear her slightly off-key voice raised in song next to him at Henry's Sunday morning service.

He'd survive. He knew that. He was a survivor. But right now, he didn't know how he'd do it. This day suddenly looked years long. And long, lonely years loomed ahead. He closed his eyes and clenched his hand in the quilt. Tears streamed down his face. *Oh please, Lord, take the pain away. Please.*

Philadelphia had been cold, damp and rainy for days since Cassie's return. The walls of her apartment and the tones of the furniture were all still just as gray as her decorator had insisted they should be. *Restful,* the woman had said. Depressing, Cassie had always thought. Her last two paintings were depressingly gray, as well. Even the sky, as she looked out her big floor-to-ceiling windows, was gray. It all matched her mood.

She'd been home a week and her heart still felt bruised and raw. She watched the clouds toss raindrops against the glass and let the sky cry for her. She was all cried out—drained.

Today was Thanksgiving, so she'd finally gotten up the strength to call her grandfather to tell him she was home. It was a family day, and he was her only family. And she *was* thankful for him. For all his faults and mistakes, he'd always loved her. She saw that now.

On hearing her voice, he'd immediately insisted on seeing her. She expected him at any minute. And she wanted to see him. She really did. She just wasn't looking forward to telling him she wouldn't be returning to Jamison. But it had to be done.

The doorbell rang, and she turned from her gray study. There was no time like the present to get it all out in the open, she thought, and headed for the door.

"Hello, Grandfather," she said as she opened it.

Her grandfather stared at her. Right then he reminded her of a hawk assessing its prey.

"You look better," he said. "About time, too! We need to talk."

"The last time someone said that to me, he cut my heart out," she told him, her thoughts once again returning to Josh.

But he misunderstood. "I'm sorry about the vice presidency. I did it for your own good." He took her by the shoulders and turned her toward the foyer mirror. "Just look at how much better you look."

Cassie stared at the woman in the mirror. He was right. Josh had inadvertently broken her heart, but he had done so many positive things for her, too. Showing her how foolish it was not to take care of her health had only been the first. He'd given her back her art. And most important of all, he had given her Jesus. It was He who had sustained her these past days.

She met her grandfather's blue eyes, so like her own, in the mirror. "Grandfather, I don't care about the vice presidency."

"Never try to fool me, young lady. I could see how

miserable you were. I was wrong to coerce you into coming to work at Jamison. I overheard you talking to your doctor about your ulcer and I watched you all week before I made the decision to give the position to Jon Reed. You weren't meant for corporate politics. You were meant to create pretty pictures. I don't care if you can't earn a living at it. You have your trust fund from your father, and I'll set up another if that isn't enough."

Cassie smiled. "Let's go sit. I'm sure you'll be relieved to know that I won't need another trust fund. And I really don't care about the promotion."

Her grandfather followed her and sat down, staring at her in stunned silence for a few seconds. "You don't?"

"I don't. I admit I feel better knowing you did what you did for my sake. My anger was really hurt. I thought you didn't appreciate my hard work. And I'll also admit that it's the best thing you ever did for me. I never would have stormed off the way I did if you hadn't. I never would have had the time to think about why I was sick and unhappy.

"I did a lot of thinking while I was away. And the reason I did was the family I met in Mountain View. They showed me what's really important in life. They don't have much, but they have each other and they have God in their lives. And they're happy. Their son got me painting again and introduced me to an artist who thinks I'm talented. Her agent wants to see my work."

"It sounds as if I was more than a little off base about your chances in the art world. I'm sorry, Cassidy. I didn't understand your talent, and I was wrong to discount it."

"Forgiven."

He graced her with one of his rare smiles. "So who is this agent? Want me to have him checked out?"

"No. But you could do something else for me. You could explain to me why you never took me to church. My parents were both churchgoers."

The old man sighed. "Your father joined that church of your mother's, and after that the company fell into third place in his life. By that point in my life I *was* Jamison Steel, so I felt more than a little abandoned. I'd been mad at God for a long time—ever since I lost Betty in childbirth. And now I felt He'd taken my son, as well.

"Gregory and the steel mill were all I'd had since your grandmother died—and I was angry. Then he and your mother were killed, and I had a chance to have you all to myself. I took it. If I was wrong, I'm sorry."

Cassidy nodded. "You were wrong for both of us, Grandfather. You need God as much as I do. And believe me, right now I need Him desperately."

Winston Jamison narrowed his eyes and examined her again. Cassie fought the urge to squirm.

"If you aren't upset anymore about the promotion, why does my granddaughter look so unhappy?"

"Because of the man who got me painting again while I was in the Poconos. I love him. But even though he loves me, he isn't free. No, that isn't accurate. He doesn't *feel* as if he's free to offer me a future. Since there's no future for us, I came home."

"Suppose you tell Grandfather why he thinks there's no future for you."

So she told him all about Joshua Daniels, who'd been named by the pages of the Bible he'd since come to love. She told him how committed Josh was to his Lord and all about how devastated he'd looked that last afternoon while he'd explained why their love was doomed. She was crying again by the time she finished.

Gruff as always, Grandfather handed her his handkerchief. "That's the most harebrained thinking I've ever heard. I realize I don't understand much about God, but I doubt He'd expect this young man to keep himself for a woman he'll never find and can't remember. Especially when there's every chance she's as dead as he almost was. And what are you thinking? You came home to sulk while the man you love sits up there all by himself? I raised you better than that."

"But he thinks it's wrong. I can't persuade him to go against his conscience," she protested.

"You said Henry Tallinger thinks Joshua's off base. Tallinger is a pastor. If he thinks this woman in the picture isn't an impediment, then what I'm telling you to do is try to convince Joshua that he's wrong. Try to get him to see that you two deserve a life together. I don't know if you'll succeed, but I know I raised you to try. Think about it!"

He smiled broadly. "Now show me these paintings that are going to make my granddaughter rich and famous. Then we have reservations at the Four Seasons for Thanksgiving dinner."

* * *

Joshua put the leash on Bear and adjusted the orange vest Irma had made for the big dog last year when a hunter took a shot at him during bear season. Then he stood, picked up his backpack and slung it over his shoulder. "I'll be home by this time day after tomorrow, Ma," he told Irma, who still looked worried. It was her concern that had driven him to go up the mountain to the cabin for a few days.

He needed space. Time alone.

"You ought to be headed to Philadelphia," Irma said, and hugged him.

He shook his head. He wasn't getting into that again. No one understood how strong the feeling was when he looked at the photo of the woman. They just didn't get it.

"Come on, Bear."

"Now you be careful," she added, as he stepped out onto the back steps.

Josh chuckled. "Ma, it's December. Deer season. Bear looks nothing like a deer, and neither do I. The land's posted. We'll be fine."

It took the better part of two-and-a-half hours to reach the cabin Henry had inherited as a boy. It was that cabin that had brought Henry to Mountain View. It was the church and Irma that had kept him there.

Josh sat on the porch and couldn't help wondering how different his life would have been if the people who'd left him by the road had stolen the photo along with everything else. Cassidy might still be in Mountain View, and he'd be in town enjoying her company.

Bear growled and stood. A rustling in the brush drew Josh's attention, as well. He stood and walked to the edge of the clearing, Bear at heel next to him. "That's why you're on a leash. It's probably another skunk to get you in trouble again."

There was no warning but Bear's whimper. Josh had just bent down to comfort the dog when the shot rang out.

Josh's left leg crumpled beneath him. Bear yelped and sagged under Josh's weight as they both fell to the ground. In a fog of pain, Josh heard a voice about thirty yards away.

"Buck, you fool, I think you just capped a dog! We'd better get out of here before his owner comes after us. I told you we shouldn't hunt on posted land."

Josh called for help, but darkness suddenly swamped him and his shout was little more than a whisper.

Cassidy threw the brush down and stepped back from the painting. It was good. But it was wrong. She'd sat for over an hour in the park across from the old man, sketching him as he'd fed the squirrels and pigeons. The colors were fine and clear. His skin tones were as near to perfect as she could get them.

She picked up the sketch she'd done and compared the two. And groaned. This had to stop! The problem with the painting was simple. The eyes were too young and hauntingly familiar.

Fixing the problem—really fixing it—wouldn't be simple at all. Because the eyes she'd given the old man were Joshua's eyes. Proof that she never got him completely out of her head. Not for one single second. Even when she prayed, it was in some way usually connected with him. *Help me forget. Help him forget. Bless Irma. Tell me if I should go back and fight for him or if he was right about his marriage.*

It was as if her life was in Philadelphia, but her heart and soul were in Mountain View.

It had been two weeks since she'd returned home and a week since her grandfather had challenged her to go after what she wanted. And she was still torn and undecided about what to do.

She looked again into the eyes she'd painted. They looked just the way his had that day in her little make-shift studio. Desolate. Hopeless. But there was something new, too. They were dark with pain.

She turned away, knowing with a certainty that he was as miserable as she was. And so stubborn. Well, she was just as stubborn! She'd match her stubbornness against his any day of the week.

Today, in fact.

And this time she'd make him listen to her. If she had to tie him up and gag him, he'd listen!

By the time Mountain View came into sight, Cassie's mood had ebbed and flowed from negative to positive more than a dozen times. The somber gray sky of Philadelphia had followed her. But she kept going. As her grandfather said when she'd called him to tell him she was leaving, she had nothing to lose.

She pulled into the parking lot in front of the café and got out before she could change her mind again. With so many emotions bombarding her, it surprised Cassie that a feeling of coming home won out over all the rest, as soon as she opened the door and saw Irma behind the counter.

She sighed. She was home.

Irma looked up and squealed. "Cassie! Oh, I can't believe you're here."

Cassie barreled ahead and plopped herself down at the counter in front of Irma. "Neither can I. But I had to come. I have to make him see reason. Where is he? I'd better see him before I lose my nerve again."

"He's not here. He went up to Henry's retreat cabin, and I don't think it's a good idea for you to go up there. It takes Joshua well over two hours to get up there, and he's an experienced hiker."

"Irma, I don't care if it takes me six. I have to do something. I can't stand this anymore."

"You can stand anything if you lean on the Lord. You know I don't agree with what Joshua's doing, but he believes he's doing what God would have him do."

"Believe me, I have been relying on Him. And until this morning He was sustaining me, but today it's as if He's not talking to me. I'd even started painting again. But this morning I did a painting and it had Josh's eyes.

They were so sad and in so much pain. I have to make him see reason. I know I can do it."

"Even if you could follow the trail and hike in that far, by the time you get there you'd have to stay the night. It just wouldn't be right. Why not stay with us tonight and start out in the morning?"

"First of all, it would probably take me all night just to get him to see my perspective on this. Irma, I have to see him. Please, just tell me how to get there."

"Cassie, it feels like snow. They're only calling for flurries, and we don't usually get more than a few inches at most this early on, but it could make for slippery trails."

Snow. Until Joshua had told her there was no hope for them, she'd thought nothing could strike fear into her heart the way that white menace could. Cassie sucked up her courage. "If I slip, I'll just get up. I'm going. I know where the trail starts, but it would make it easier if I had some idea where I'm going and where to look for his markers."

"And I thought *he* was stubborn. You two are a pair." Irma shook her head and grabbed a paper place mat. She slapped it on the counter, blank side up, then pinned Cassie with a sharp look. "You make him listen to reason. You hear me?"

Cassie smiled. "Yes, ma'am."

Then Irma started to draw a crude map.

Twenty minutes later, wearing a bright orange vest, a pair of warmer socks and Irma's hiking boots, Cassie was off. She moved upward following the meandering trail that wound left, then right, and occasionally even backtracked to avoid a deep section of a stream or steep-sided gully.

For the first hour, she managed to enjoy nature in its most stark season, while she rehearsed what she hoped were the right words to say to Josh. She prayed for those words, as well.

Then the flurries started, and in minutes the trail did get slippery. Cassie was surprised and a little frightened by the density of the flurries. In Philadelphia, snow of this magnitude would have been called a snowstorm.

She thought she'd gone about a mile or two farther when the wind picked up, blowing the wet snowflakes against the trees. Half an hour later, Cassie stopped short and dusted off an arrow-shaped sign that she'd almost missed because it was obscured by the thick coating of white.

Then the unthinkable happened. A wind gust tore the map from her hand, and the paper disappeared into a sea of white. She tried to find it off the trail, but it was gone.

Her heart began to pound with fear rather than exertion, and Cassie stopped, took a deep breath and sought strength in her newly found faith. *Dear Lord, keep me safe and show me the way. Hold me in the palm of Your hand and give me Your peace.*

Cassie felt that peace even as she looked around and realized that, if anything, the snow was coming down harder. She found the trail again and pushed on, picking up her pace even though she slipped more often. It didn't take a genius to figure out that the forecasted flurries had gone from storm to blizzard.

She was in the middle of her worst nightmare. It had been snowing steadily for nearly two hours, and if she didn't hurry, the next signpost could be totally obscured.

When she came to a deep ravine some time later, she realized she must, indeed, have missed a marker. So she backtracked, praying all the while for guidance, and found the sign she'd missed. The nearly obliterated trail lead straight up from there.

It was rough going, but she grabbed for branches and shrubs and scrambled upward. The steep trail lead to a meadow, but there was no cabin in sight. Cassie looked around again, trying to peer through the snow and dense woodlands for any evidence of a structure. A gust of wind almost knocked her over, but then the wind calmed. She was near the cabin. She had to be.

"Joshua!" she called out, hoping against hope that he'd hear her. But only the howling wind called back. She called Josh's name several more times, then stopped to listen. She thought she heard the deep *woof* of a dog. "Bear? Bear! Come on, boy! Where are you?"

Cassie shielded her eyes, trying to peer through the blowing snow. Suddenly she saw a huge black animal wearing what looked like an orange saddle burst into the clearing. He was running toward her at full clip, and she was so glad to see him that she didn't care if he knocked her down when he reached her.

But instead, he jerked to a stop almost immediately

and yelped. Cassie ran for him, realizing that his bright green leash had caught on a stump at the edge of the woods. The fear that came over her made no sense. She had to be close to the cabin—so she was safe, right? But Bear's frantic barking as he strained against his confining tether only cranked up her feeling of dread.

Where was Josh?

"Hey there, boy, what are you doing running around in the woods like this?" she asked as she bent down and freed the leash from its anchor on a small stump. A second later Cassie was glad she hadn't simply taken the leash off him—he immediately took off into the woods with her in tow.

It was tough going since Bear didn't bother with a trail, and Cassie's sense of urgency grew with the dog's. They were at the rustic cabin in minutes. And still, for all Bear's noise, Josh didn't emerge from the open door of the cabin.

She dropped the leash, and Bear exploded across the clearing and into the cabin. Then he came tearing back out and ran toward her. Cassie knew for sure then that something was wrong.

She found the trail of blood as she crossed the porch. But still, she never thought she'd find what she did. She thought that at worst he'd cut himself on a knife or an ax. She never thought she'd find him crumpled just inside the door in a pool of blood.

"Josh," Cassie gasped, and dropped to the floor next to him. She bit her lip. He was so still. He lay on his side, his hair falling over his eyes. There was so much blood, she couldn't tell where he was injured. Afraid to touch him—afraid not to—she reached a shaking hand out and gently pushed the thick wave of black hair off his forehead. "Josh. Can you hear me? Come on. Wake up. Please," she begged.

Chapter Twelve

Josh heard the miracle of Cassie's voice and felt the pain of her tears—tears he'd caused her to shed by letting her fall in love with him. Then the meaning of her words crystallized, but still made no sense.

Through an ocean of pain, questions bombarded him. Why was he sleeping? Why was the bed so hard? Why was he so cold? He couldn't come up with any answers without forcing his eyelids open.

It took a few seconds to focus on the wooden floor inches from his nose. Then reality crashed in on him. The sound of the gunshot. Crawling across the clearing. Pain. Bear all but dragging him up the steps and across the porch. Now he was on the floor of the cabin, lying on his side, using his arm and shoulder as a pillow.

He looked up and saw Cassie bent over him. Josh blinked—but she was still there. He hadn't been dreaming this time. How could Cassie be here? "Cassie? Is that really you?"

She nodded. "It's me, Josh."

"How?"

"Never mind about that now. Where's all the blood coming from? I haven't had the courage to look."

"Left leg." He reached out and gripped the hand she caressed his shoulder with. He was as weak as a kitten. He forced himself to take slow, deep breaths, praying for strength and deliverance from the torture in his leg. He didn't want to pass out when Cassie already looked so frightened and he had an even scarier truth to tell her. "It's a gunshot wound, sweetheart."

She went positively pale. "Who would shoot you?"

A gust of wind blew cold and snow into the cabin before he could answer. Josh shivered and his muscles tightened. Pain sliced through him and left him gasping for breath and grasping at consciousness. His mind began to dim, and he squeezed her hand. Forcing his breathing to stay even, he stared up at her beloved features. Bear pushed by Cassie then and tried to lick his face, but with surprising strength she pushed the huge dog back and sharply ordered him to sit. He whimpered but obeyed.

Josh didn't even realize he'd betrayed the agony that blast of cold had caused until her soft fingertips tried to smooth the grimace from his face.

"I know you're in terrible pain, but you have to move so we can get that door closed," she told him, and he could hear the fear in her voice.

"I crawled here from the edge of the woods. I don't think I can get any farther," he explained, then shivered again. "I'm so cold."

Cassie took his chin in her hand, her gaze strong and determined. He could see that the smile she tried to give him was forced, but it was also incredibly brave.

"We'll figure it out." She looked around, then pushed herself to her feet.

Josh lay there, his back to the room, listening to a lot of rustling and scuffing. He tried to look over his shoulder, but the hot jolt of pain even that small movement caused in his leg wasn't worth it. He lay his spinning head back down on his arm and prayed for help. And he wasn't fussy. He'd take any kind the good Lord wanted to send. Somehow He'd already sent Cassie.

A few minutes later, she dragged the big braided rug from in front of the fireplace over next to him. His clouded brain just couldn't figure out what she planned to do with it, but he didn't need to wonder long.

"I need you to help me get you onto the rug," she told him. "Just far enough so I can drag you over in front of the fireplace."

Move again? He really didn't think so. Not and stay conscious. "Uh, Cassie...I left out one small problem with moving. I think the bullet broke my thigh bone."

"Then I'd better find a way to splint it, hadn't I?" Her smile was gentle, but again he saw anxiety in her eyes.

Josh nodded.

She was back with a pair of old ski poles that had

been crossed over the bedroom door and some strips of material. She worked fast, first measuring the poles against his leg. "I hope these aren't antiques," she said, then anchored one end under her boot and snapped it off before he could muster the strength to answer.

He knew the way she felt about antiques after giving her the tour of the Swenson place. He actually felt a smile tip his lips. He loved teasing her. After she broke the second one, he said with what he considered impeccable timing, "Bamboo poles are probably considered antiques."

"Now he tells me," she muttered as she worked. First she wrapped adhesive tape around the splintered ends, then she carefully lashed the poles to his calf and ankle. "I'm going to have to move your leg to straighten your knee a little. I'm sorry."

The last thought he had before waking in front of a crackling fire was that he'd been wrong while pulling himself across the porch. The pain actually could get worse!

Cassie was the first thing he saw when he opened his eyes.

"Hi," she said. Her eyes were the color the sky had been that morning—an almost smoky blue-gray.

He glanced at the fire. "You had to get me here all on your own? I was no help at all, was I?"

"My back may never be the same," she joked, then she sobered and squeezed his hand.

He hadn't even realized she was holding it. "The leg *is* broken. I think badly. It looks awful. I tried to clean the wound and I managed somehow to get the bleeding stopped, but you need real medical attention. They don't show the kind of damage a bullet does on the news or in movies." Her hand tightened in his. "I'm scared for you, Josh."

"I'm fine. It isn't so bad," he lied. The pain had subsided a little, and he fought to control the rest. It was nothing he couldn't handle—with the help of the Lord.

"No, you aren't fine. And we're miles from help. I'm going to have to leave you alone with Bear and walk down the mountain."

Josh listened to the wind howling and the snow hitting against the windowpanes. The thought of her out there battling nature—and her fear—was more than he could stand. "Not till morning. It's too dangerous now." He reached up and touched her cheek. "After being in that avalanche with your parents when they were killed, you must have been terrified coming up here."

"I thought I was. Then I walked into this cabin and found you bleeding all over the floor. That was true terror."

"Whatever possessed you to hike up here in this kind of snow?"

"This, my dear man, is only supposed to be flurries. And *snow* is too tame a word for horizontal snow. Where I come from this is a *blizzard.*"

"It's a blizzard here, too. Too bad it didn't start an hour sooner. You'd have been safe at Irma's, and I might not have been shot."

Her gaze flicked to his leg, then back to his face. "Who shot you, Josh?"

"A hunter named Buck." He took a deep breath. "That's all I know." He told her about the man whose voice he'd heard. "So I assume he thought the dog was a bear. It's not the first time some over-anxious idiot has taken a shot at Bear. I was standing next to him, or he'd probably be dead." He shivered and glanced at the roaring fire she'd built. How could he still be so cold? "Could you get me another blanket from the chest at the bottom of the bed?"

Cassie frowned and put her hand on his forehead. It felt soft and cool. He closed his eyes and tried to memorize the feel of her, the smell of her so close. He knew it was wrong, but he loved her. And right then he was just too weak to fight her and his feelings.

"Why, Cassie?" he asked, needing to know she was there because of him. "Why are you here?"

"I came here to convince you that you were wrong about us. We belong together, Josh."

He frowned and opened his eyes. "I tried to explain."

"And I say your explanation is off. Your thinking is off." She wiped his face with a cool, damp cloth, her gentle touch belying the intensity of her voice.

"I never meant to hurt you, but I have to do what's right."

"But you're wrong about what's right, Josh. Your exact situation might not be in the Bible, but the spirit of it is. If you took a vow to that woman, it was till death do you part. You were right about that. But what you don't seem to grasp is that the man you once were died on that road where Irma and Henry found you. You've as much as said that yourself. You were born the day you woke up in the hospital. Your mind was almost a clean slate, just like a baby's. You were a new person."

"I—" He stopped. Looking into her beloved face, he couldn't seem to come up with a rebuttal. His mind had been nearly blank. Maybe he *had* been wrong, or maybe he was just tired of the loneliness. All he knew was that if he never saw another day, he'd die happy because Cassie was with him now.

He shook his head. "I don't know what's right and what's wrong anymore. All I know is that I love you so much it hurts. And that I'm confused. That's why I came up here. To think. Henry and Irma think my past was taken by God to give me a new life. I don't know. Maybe that woman in the photo was killed. Losing any memory of her would take away my grief."

"That makes sense."

"But what if she's not dead? And we make a life together. She could find me. Or I could remember her. Someone would be hurt. Maybe both of you."

Cassie shook her head. "Okay. Suppose she did find you but you still don't remember her. Do you think she'd want you back? I can tell you, I'd never continue living with a man who had no clue who I was. Who was a completely different person from the one I married. Frankly, I'd find living under those conditions impossible."

He had no comment at first. He wasn't a woman so he couldn't begin to address how a woman would feel. But then he considered how *he'd* feel. And then all he could do was stare at her—this wise woman he loved. He couldn't give her much, but he could give her the truth. "Truth be told, I'd find it pretty uncomfortable, too."

She looked away, twisting her hands the way he'd seen her do once before when they talked about this—when she'd brought up a theory she thought might hurt him. He reached over and covered those anxious hands, hoping to reassure her. "Say anything you think needs saying. I love you. Just you. That hasn't changed. I don't think it ever will."

Cassie nodded and bit her lip. "Josh, she hasn't looked for you. To me that means that there was something wrong between you before you disappeared from her life. What makes you think she'd even talk to you if you found her, let alone pick up the marriage—if there was one—where it left off?"

"Yeah. There is that." He wondered what she'd make of his other worry. The one he hadn't shared with anyone. "Suppose I did something unforgivable, and He took away my life as punishment?"

"That doesn't sound like the God you introduced to me at all."

He wondered how she'd come to understand so much about the nature of God so quickly. "No. No, it doesn't."

"Then we have to go on the supposition that Irma and Henry are right. You're no longer bound by your old life.

You can spend this life with whomever you choose. I'd like that person to be me."

"Me, too," Josh agreed. Then exhaustion seemed to descend upon him like a blanket. He shook, cold again in spite of the extra quilt Cassie had gotten him. "Cold," he said, and was surprised at how weak his voice sounded.

His whole body suddenly felt like lead.

Cassie was afraid. Not of the wind that had not stopped, nor of the snow that continued to fall as day became night. She was terrified of losing Josh. She'd come to realize that he was right. It would be suicide to try reaching town in the storm. But that didn't change the fact that he needed help.

Losing him to principles—misguided or not—had been one thing. She'd have known he was out there somewhere with his quick smile and big brown eyes, living a life of service to God. But she didn't think she'd survive if he died in her arms before morning.

At first he'd been suffering hypothermia, his temperature shockingly low, but she'd managed to get him warm. Now, however, she fought a foe she couldn't conquer with warm fires and blankets. She fought infection, and she was powerless against it. So she battled the symptom—a fever that raged in his body. But it was a fever that all her cool cloths didn't calm and that aspirin didn't lower.

"You should get some sleep," Josh said, awake again, his throat dry, his voice scratchy and weak.

In the past several hours, he'd drifted in and out, sometimes making sense and other times rambling about his early days in a hospital where everything and everyone was frightening and strange. She decided, in the few moments when the present did not consume her thoughts, that this above all else proved his past had been erased forever by God's hand.

The Lord in his infinite wisdom had given Josh a new life. Now all she had to do was convince him to live it to its fullest, because she refused to consider the possibility that his new life was at an end.

"Sleep?" she asked as she bathed his handsome face. "That would waste this opportunity to get in practice."

"Practice for what?"

She smiled and leaned forward to kiss his parched lips. "For all those nights when I won't be able to sleep later on."

"What nights?" he asked.

He looked so endearingly confused that she almost relented, wondering briefly if it was fair to outthink a man whose brain was on fire. What was the old saying? *All's fair in love and war.* Well, she was at war for their love. "The nights when our babies keep us awake. Little Throckmorton with his colic. Tiny Upsadelia when she's teething."

"Upsa*who?*"

"Our daughter and son. Upsadelia and Throckmorton. Those were the names of my dolls. But if you have an objection to those names, I'll certainly consider your input."

His smile was weak. His next words were a dream come true.

"How about Rachel and Daniel?"

She smiled back, tears welling up in her eyes. "Daniel Daniels? I don't think so. But Joshua Daniels Junior has a nice ring to it. I'd strongly consider that. Especially," she added softly as she trailed a finger lightly down his warm cheek, "if he has his father's beautiful face and big brown eyes. Sometimes when you look at me, I feel as if I could just fall into those eyes and live happily ever after."

"I love you, Cassie."

"Then promise me you'll take the Lord's gift and live the life He's given you."

"If only I could be sure."

"How much surer do you need to be? He sent me to Mountain View. And I believe He sent me here for you. I told you about the penny and how it brought me to town. And then when I would have driven right on through, because I had my mind set on staying at a big fancy resort, He made my car act up. Then when I would have left, Earl couldn't find out what was wrong with it. The Lord gave us time, Josh. Time for us to get to know one another. Time for you to tell me about Him. Time for us to fall in love.

"It's been His hand directing all of it. And then this morning I was painting a picture of an old man from a sketch I'd done. But it was wrong. When I tried to decide what was wrong, I realized that it didn't match the sketch. Do you know why?"

Josh shook his head, those brown-black eyes of his intent on her face though they were glazed with pain and fever.

"Because I'd given the old man the eyes of a much younger man. Dark eyes. Your eyes, Josh. I thought they looked the way yours had that last morning. All sad and hopeless and in terrible pain. But now, looking at you, I know that the eyes I painted looked a way I'd never seen your eyes look. I thought at the time the pain I saw was sadness because you thought we could never be more than friends. I was wrong. What I saw was physical pain. He sent me back here today so I'd be here to help you. I'd been wrestling with the idea of returning since Thanksgiving when my grandfather told me to come back and fight for what I wanted. I couldn't make myself come back until today. Then today I couldn't stop myself."

"Why couldn't you come back sooner?"

"Because I had to be sure it was the right thing to do—and I wasn't. I prayed and prayed for His guidance. I asked Him to send me a sign that He wanted us to be together. And this morning he sent it when I looked at the painting.

"This is in *His* will, Josh. He sent me here this morning to help you before you ever left Irma's." Cassie took his hand in hers—his big well-muscled hand that was so weak right now that he couldn't lift it himself— and showed him their clasped hands. "He gave us this and it would be *wrong* not to accept it. Promise me,

Joshua Daniels, that you'll accept the gift of love that the Lord sent to you."

A tear leaked out of the corner of his eye and ran into his hair. "Will you marry me, Cassie?"

Chapter Thirteen

"You'd better believe it," she whispered, and kissed his hand.

He narrowed his eyes, trying to concentrate. "Your grandfather told you to fight for me? I thought he'd be against the idea of you marrying a penniless mountain preacher. I have nothing to offer you."

"Your love is all I need. But I thought he'd object, too. I was so wrong about him. He wants me to be happy. He thought working at Jamison Steel would make me as happy as it did him. Then he heard me discussing my job and its effect on my stomach with my doctor. He decided that the vice presidency was the last thing I needed. It all went wrong for him when we started to argue and I stormed off before he could explain why he did what he did."

"Then you still have him." He looked around the cabin, his fevered gaze falling on a picture of a much younger Irma and Henry. "Cassie, if something…if for some reason I don't make it out of this mess…"

"No. Josh. Don't say that."

"Take care of them," he demanded. "Please. Henry's going downhill fast, and Irma's not as tough as she acts. They were so good to me. So patient. And Bear. He's—" His voice broke.

As she had done once before, she silenced him with a finger on his lips. "Shh. Everyone is going to be fine. You included. We haven't come this far to lose each other now. At dawn, blizzard or no, I'm going for help. In no time at all they'll be landing a rescue chopper in that meadow below the cabin. All I have to do is head downhill. Downhill leads to town."

"You have to be careful, anyway. If you take a wrong path, it'll lead you right to a dead end. It isn't much of a cliff by some standards but a thirty-foot drop can kill. That's why I marked the trail."

"I'll be careful. But I *am* going."

"But you're so afraid of this kind of weather," Josh protested.

Cassie arched her eyebrow the way she'd seen Irma do. "You have to agree that with all these trees an avalanche isn't likely. In fact, I think it's unheard of in the Poconos."

He nodded, his eyes unfocused. "Tell me about when you were growing up. And about Philadelphia," he said, and his heavy eyelids closed.

She talked to him for a while until she was sure he was asleep. Then she settled in for a long night.

Cassie dozed off but woke often. She stayed by his side and prayed for him—and with him in his more lucid moments. Those became fewer and farther between as the hours marched on toward morning. Out of desperation she cut him out of his shirt, hoping that by sponging the larger area of his chest and arms she'd control the fever. It didn't work. By dawn his fever had risen to one hundred and five.

Dangerous by anyone's standards.

And Cassie knew she had no choice but to leave. Josh needed help and he needed it immediately. In a last-ditch effort to bring down the fever or at least keep it from getting worse while she was gone, Cassie packed plastic bags of snow around him. He never woke.

She got her coat and boots on and stood looking down at him. At his side, Bear whined and looked up at her with sad eyes. Even he seemed to know how serious the situation was. She reached down and ruffled his fur. "You take good care of him," she ordered.

"Take him," Josh whispered, his throat rough, his voice weak.

She went down on her knees next to him. "I don't want to leave you here alone."

"And I don't want my wife-to-be falling off a cliff or being afraid. He can't help me, but he can help you."

"But the hunters," she protested.

"Put the leash and his vest on him. You wear mine. It's bigger than yours. More noticeable. I'll be fine here." He grinned weakly. "Probably sleep till you get back," he said, and closed his eyes.

Fear suddenly swamped her. Fear of leaving him. Fear of getting lost and not getting him help in time. Fear that she'd never again hear his laughter or see his eyes sparkle with mirth. Cassie took his hand and closed her eyes. *Protect him, Lord. Calm this infection. Keep him alive till I can get help. And give me strength to face this task.*

Cassie stood and did as Josh asked, knowing that the dog would increase her chances of getting help more quickly. She looked around the room and took a deep breath before taking Bear's leash and heading out into the storm.

Josh had been right. Bear never let her go astray. Each time she would have made a wrong turn, the big dog would whimper and scamper in the right direction. She always followed because to her every tree and path looked the same and all seemed to lead downhill. Though the snow had slowed, the wind still howled, blowing the falling snow and stirring up what had already fallen into treacherous drifts and a swirling curtain of white. She found a few of Josh's markers but most must have been covered over by the heavy wet snow that had blown horizontally all night.

An hour into her trek the snow stopped, the wind stilled, and the sun came out. Within minutes the sun turned the wet snow even wetter, soaking her to the skin by the time she struggled the last quarter mile.

When they broke through the trees, Bear lunged forward, breaking the hold Cassie's freezing fingers had on the leash. He lumbered through the deep snow, dragging his leash behind him and barking wildly to announce their arrival.

Tears of relief and worry tracked down Cassie's face as she slogged across Irma and Henry's backyard and up the wooden back steps where Bear stood on his hind legs, pawing at the door. The dog fell inside when Irma pulled the door open, and Cassie made nearly the same entrance.

"What on earth?" Irma gasped as she steadied her.

Cassie gripped Irma's forearm with a shaking hand, too breathless to speak.

"Child, what's happened?"

Cassie sank into a chair Irma almost dragged her to, as Bear continued to raise a ruckus, his paws slipping and sliding on the linoleum floor. She'd made it, she thought as she sucked in a deep breath and looked up at the clock. Though her legs trembled so much that they no longer supported her, she'd made the trek in under three hours.

"It's Josh," she croaked, her throat raw. "A hunter shot him yesterday. I had to leave him alone at the cabin. He needs help."

The next hours were long periods of tense waiting punctuated by moments of intense activity. The hospital chopper pilot landed in the meadow to pick up a map to the cabin, then he and two paramedics took off to rescue Josh. The pilot suggested that Cassie and the Tallingers start out and meet them at the hospital.

Though the Tallingers and Cassie rushed, they still

arrived after Josh, and were told that he was already in surgery. Barring complications and resistant infections he would be fine, according to a resident who came to speak to them.

Mike Howard, one of the state policemen assigned to the area around Mountain View, arrived next, but there was nothing Cassie could tell him other than what Josh had told her. There were two men. The hunter who shot him had been addressed as Buck by another man, and they'd known they were on posted land.

Then the media, hot on the trail of a story, descended upon the waiting room. Irma slid smoothly into her schoolteacher mode and controlled the mob scene. She also played the reporters like an expert, telling them of Josh's earlier accident and resulting amnesia. It made a wonderful human-interest story, and before she was done, Josh once again had the kind of media exposure he needed to uncover the mystery of his past.

It was seven in the evening when a tall blond man cleared his throat from the doorway of the waiting room. He wore faded scrubs and a weary expression. "Reverend and Mrs. Tallinger?"

Henry pushed himself to his feet, shaking his head. "It's just Henry. This is Irma and Cassie. So tell us about our boy. How's he doing?"

The doctor smiled. "Sit. Please. I'm Doctor West. I'm chief of orthopedics here. Dr. Bennington called me in on this. Joshua is very special to him. I wanted to stop by and advise you on his condition.

"He's doing very well. He responded well to the anesthesia and to a broad-spectrum antibiotic we had the paramedics start intravenously on the chopper. I had to use a plate to repair the bone because the bullet shattered it. That's why the surgery took so long. In the long run, he'll be just fine, but he'll need time to heal and extensive physical therapy. I understand he's used to that. He should be in his room within the hour, and then all of you can visit for a while."

Half an hour after that, while they still waited anxiously to see Josh, the state policeman returned. This time he had another man with him. The stranger fit the old movie image of tall, dark and handsome—as close to a version of Agent 007 as she had ever seen in the flesh. But this man wore jeans and a flannel shirt, which lead Cassie to assume he wasn't another policeman. He wasn't.

"Folks, this is Pastor Jim Dillon from down near Philadelphia. He thinks he has some information about Josh."

"You know who shot our son?" Irma asked.

"No, ma'am," he said, sounding confused as he turned to Officer Howard. "I was under the impression that he had no family and was suffering amnesia. Maybe I have the wrong man."

Mike Howard shook his head. "This is Irma and Henry Tallinger. They sort of adopted Josh when we couldn't find his family. And this is Cassidy Jamison."

Cassie felt her heart start to pound. Had Irma's little gambit with the reporters actually paid off? Could this man know Josh from before he arrived in Mountain

View? A sudden feeling of dread settled over her as Henry asked that very question.

"I think I may know him, sir. I had a friend in the Navy who would have to be his twin not to be the man you call Joshua Daniels. We stayed in touch after getting out of the service, but I lost contact with him a few years ago."

"Where was this man from?" Irma asked, and Cassie wondered why she'd ask that and not his name, or whether he had family—a wife.

"He was from the South. Florida."

Cassie couldn't keep quiet for another second. "What was this man's name?"

"Dave. Lieutenant David Chernak. I drove up here after seeing his picture on the noon news. Officer Howard tells me he's going to be all right. A phone call didn't seem right, especially with him hurt and all alone."

"Josh hasn't been alone for over five years," Cassie felt compelled to inform him. "Irma and Henry found him hurt and nearly dead. They saved his life and have been there for him every day since."

His hazel eyes softened when he looked at Irma and Henry. Cassie wanted to hate him, but he made that impossible because he projected a sense of caring and genuine compassion with every word.

"I'm glad he's had you. I'd hate to think of such a nice guy not having people to care about him. Of course, I can't be sure Joshua is my old friend. But if I see him, talk to him, I'll know."

"I'd hate to see him get all hopeful, then get let down," Henry said. "What can you tell us about this David Chernak?"

Cassie didn't like the way Jim Dillon's eyes darted to her and narrowed before he answered. "We were in the CBs. That's the Naval Construction Batallions. The man could design and build anything. And loved animals. We'd arrive somewhere to build temporary housing and before you knew it he had every stray dog in the vicinity trailing after him."

"That sounds so much like Josh," Irma said, her tone hopeful. "And Cassie, remember right after you met him, you mentioned that he says 'y'all.' You remarked that it was a Southern expression."

"That doesn't mean…" Cassie let her objection trail off. She felt selfish, but she was terribly afraid that this man was about to destroy all her hopes and dreams for a life with Josh.

A nurse stuck her head in the room. "Mr. Daniels is in his room now and awake. You can have some time with him. Two at a time."

Cassie wanted desperately to see him, but Irma and Henry had waited long enough. "You two go ahead. I was with him all last night."

Grasping Cassie's hands, Irma leaned forward and said, "Thank you, dear. We won't stay long. I just need to see that he's okay. Oh! What am I thinking? In all the upset I forgot to ask." The older woman's pale blue eyes twinkled now. "How goes the battle?"

Irma's lighthearted mood was contagious. Cassie smirked. "City girl—one. Mountain man—zero."

"He finally listened to reason! Well, hallelujah!" Irma exclaimed. "Oh, now I really am excited. You two didn't happen to decide on a date for the wedding, did you?"

Cassie chuckled and shook her head, but noticed Jim Dillon whisper something to Mike Howard. Her spirits plummeted. There was something about the stranger's presence that just stole her joy.

"If you don't mind," Mike said, standing and checking his watch, "I really have to get my report filed and I need to get Joshua's statement. I also have to make sure this really was an accident. He was violently attacked before, and that's still an open file."

"But I told you he heard the other hunter," Cassie protested.

"I still need to get a statement directly from the victim," he explained, then turned to Jim Dillon. "And on the off chance that you could jar his memory and help solve the mystery of the first case surrounding him, I'd really like you to come in with me. I think that would be the easiest way for him in the long run, anyway," he said, directing this comment to Irma and Henry. "If Mr. Dillon doesn't think Josh is his Navy friend, Josh won't have gotten his hopes up. I know how much his lost identity bothers him."

"But—" Cassie started to protest.

"Sounds like a good idea," Henry said, interrupting Cassie. "You ladies don't mind waiting so this young fella can get home to his wife, do you?"

Irma settled back in her seat. "Oh, not at all. Just see that you don't tire him out. We still want to see him. We have something to celebrate."

What could Cassie do but smile graciously and say, "Go ahead. Josh and I have the rest of our lives to be together."

Please, Lord, let it be true, she prayed, as the men left the waiting room.

Chapter Fourteen

When he heard footsteps echo through his doorway, Josh turned his head from a study of the view out his hospital room window. He knew it was Cassie. For the first time he dreaded seeing her. For the first time, he didn't want to know anything about his past.

"Hi. How's the patient?" she asked as she peeked in. She looked unsure, and his heart ached for what he had to do to her.

"I've been better." He wasn't talking about physical pain. He supposed that was beyond him. His heart hurt too much for anything else to register. Causing Cassie the same kind of pain that he felt was the last thing Josh wanted to do. But he had no choice.

She walked to the bed and gently pushed his hair off his forehead as she had done so many times last night when fever had racked his body. "Are you in much pain?" she asked, and leaned down to feather a kiss on his cheek.

He blinked away tears that had nothing to do with physical pain and everything to do with what he was about to lose. "Pain seems to be one of those relative things. The leg's nothing."

Cassie looked puzzled by his answer, but asked, "So what does Mike Howard think?"

"That there's a good possibility he can track down the idiot who shot me. I don't care for me, but that fool shouldn't be allowed within fifty feet of anything more dangerous than a cap gun. It's hunters like him who give them all a bad name."

"Dr. West said the bullet shattered your bone and that he had to fix the damage with a plate."

She took his hand and he closed his eyes, trying to capture the feel of her for the lonely days ahead.

"But he seemed hopeful for a full recovery. I'll help all I can while you're getting back on your feet," she added. He could hear her anxiety and knew he had to end it right then. A clean break.

"I understand you met Jim Dillon," he said. She nodded, apprehension darkening her eyes.

"He knows me, Cassie. He knows a lot about where I came from and what was going on in my life when I disappeared. He knows where I was living, the names of my parents and—" He broke off, his stomach tightening. That was the wrong way to say it. He tried again. "There's no easy way to say this. We can't get married, sweetheart. I'm already married."

She blinked and her back stiffened a bit. "Oh?" she

said, and other than that quick reflexive flinch, she showed no other sign of distress.

"I'm sorry," he rushed on, afraid if he paused he'd lose his resolve. "I remember what you said about how I've probably changed, and how she's probably changed but I still have to find her and try to work it out with her. It's the right thing to do. It's what I have to do."

"Does Jim Dillon know why she never looked for you? Why your parents never looked, either?"

She wasn't acting as he'd expected, but then Cassie never had been like the other women he'd met in his limited experience. "He said that the last time he talked to David—" He stopped. The name felt foreign on his tongue. Josh wasn't sure he'd ever be David Chernak again, but that was who he'd been. He started again. "The last time he talked to *me* there was trouble with the corporation I helped run. It was a construction firm. I was their architect. I guess building things is a talent that survived the head injury.

"Anyway, there was a problem with the company, and I was trying to find out who was responsible for it. Apparently, many of the homes we'd built had been destroyed by a hurricane and substandard materials were to blame. Jim said it was in all the Florida papers and even as far north as Philadelphia at first. He tried to call me at my home a few weeks after the last time we'd talked, but my wi—" Again, he stopped. He couldn't hurt Cassie by saying the word *wife* in her presence. Not when it was a place in his life that he'd already asked her to take.

"But when he called he was told," he continued, "that I had left Florida and no one knew where to find me. He got the same answer a week later. He called back about a month later and the number was disconnected."

It boggled Josh's mind that according to Jim Dillon he'd once adored the woman whose existence he couldn't even remember now.

"So you'll go to Florida," Cassie said, her tone studiously even.

He nodded. "Jim Dillon didn't know how to get in touch with my parents and felt a little strange even trying since he didn't know them. So he followed the story as best he could from so far away, figuring I'd get in touch when I was ready. It turned out that my brother was apparently responsible and has gone to prison over it. That's all he knows, except that an old paper he managed to get hold of said my father and I had a falling-out over the problems. Mike Howard promised to get their address and phone number for me."

"Will you contact them right away?"

"No. I don't want them showing up here. I'll go there to see them when I'm well enough to travel and I'm ready. As you said, they haven't looked for me."

"You're sure this is the way you want it?" she asked, her eyes and voice flat, her face expressionless.

He could have been talking to a computer for all the emotion she showed. Josh just couldn't figure her out. "It isn't what I *want,* Cassie. It's what has to be. It kills me to hurt you like this."

"I'm fine. Really. I don't want you to feel guilty. You aren't hurting me as badly as you obviously think." She bit her lip and her eyes rose to stare at something just over his shoulder. He almost looked to see what had her rapt attention but her knotted fingers drew him, then she started talking again.

"On the hike back out from the cabin, I've never known such terror. I realized that I can't live up here so far from civilization where weather like that is a common occurrence all winter. And what do all of you *do* all year? There's only so much green a person can take—and we won't even discuss white! Josh, what I'm trying to explain is that even if you were free, I couldn't marry you. You belong here, and I belong in the city where I can see a movie without planning the excursion, and where there are plays, the opera and art museums."

She bent down and kissed his forehead. "So the Lord worked it out, after all. Thank you for helping me find Him. I'd like it if we remained friends. Perhaps write and keep up with what we're doing. And of course, if you or Irma and Henry ever need anything, just call."

She backed away and looked down at her watch. "Goodness, I'd better get going before I tire you out. I'll be by to see you tomorrow unless the roads are clear to Philly tonight. My grandfather's expecting me as soon as I can get there."

Josh stared at her. This just didn't add up. "Cassie—"

"Goodbye, Joshua Daniels. Be happy." She gave him

a sad smile and turned away. She was out the door before he had a chance to say another word.

And he knew he'd never see her again.

Josh dropped his head back on his pillows and gave in to the tears and pain she apparently did not feel. Nothing had ever hurt like this. At least, nothing that he could remember. And the worst part was that he didn't know what hurt more—losing her or knowing she hadn't really cared to begin with. Then he realized that he was glad she hadn't cared as much as he had. He didn't want to think of her hurting the way he now was.

He closed his eyes and prayed for the pain to ease and for peace and the assurance that he was doing what was right. Long minutes passed before the truth about the scene with Cassie struck him.

She had lied.

That morning she'd gone back out into the blizzard to save him with resolve and a quiet bravery only she could show. She'd made light of any fears, saying that it was the possibility of an avalanche that frightened her—not the snow itself.

Everything she'd said made perfect sense in a new context. She'd wanted to set him free. To ease his guilt for hurting her. And he loved her more than ever for hiding her pain for his sake. But now he could only lie here with a hole in his life where she should have been, and imagine her pain and how she would hold it in until she was alone where she would let it spill forth and consume her.

* * *

Cassie walked down the hall, counting her steps, hoping her shaking legs would carry her out of the building, hoping to keep the tears at bay until she reached the privacy of her car. But she realized she'd failed when several people looked at her as she passed them with sympathy in their eyes.

When Cassie saw an exit sign over the stairway door, it looked like a haven. She threw it open just in time, because at that moment the clawing pain in her chest overwhelmed her. She pushed the door shut behind her and leaned her back against the cold plaster wall. Her shaking legs gave out then and she sank to the cement floor, simply drowning in an agony beyond measure.

She huddled there, muffling her tears to keep them private until a hand settled on her head. She looked up and blinked, sure her eyes were playing tricks on her. But her grandfather's image only grew clearer.

"Grandfather?"

"Come home now, Cassidy. You tried your best. That's all you can do."

"How did you know?"

"I heard about the shooting on the news and came immediately. When I got here, I met Irma and Henry. They told me everything that's happened. I know you two planned to be married, and that Joshua's old friend arrived with information about his past. I admit I don't understand what Joshua feels he has to do with the information, but I can certainly see what it has done to you."

Cassie heard the edge of anger in his voice. She didn't want him thinking ill of Josh. His memory was too precious to her. She pushed herself to her feet. "Believe me, he's hurting just as much I am. Maybe more. He felt so guilty, so I told him it was no big deal because I didn't want to marry him, after all. Then he looked... Oh, Grandfather, I didn't mean to hurt him worse. I love him so much."

Her grandfather stepped forward and put his arms around her. "So tell him why you said what you did. He'll understand. And maybe if he sees how badly he's hurt you, he'll change his mind about finding this other woman."

Cassie shook her head. "No. I can't do that and neither can he. I said what I did to free him, and it has to stay that way. Josh has to follow his conscience. And I have to accept that our not being together is the Lord's will. Henry would say He's trying to teach us something. I just wish I knew what. It would make it all so much easier."

"But—"

"No, Grandfather. You were right. Let's go home."

And they did. Cassie didn't return to her cold high-rise but to a rented carriage house on a Main Line estate. She finished her portfolio, and her talent impressed Maria Prentice's agent, who then became Cassie's agent, as well. Within months she'd have her first show. But it was hard to care about anything when her heart had been shattered. She was able to lose herself in her painting, which passed the time and made her agent happy, at least.

Portraits continued to trouble her, though. Joshua's big, long-lashed, brown eyes continued to show up in each and every one. Sometimes they were merry. Other pictures showed them sad and haunted. But they were always there. Her agent thought it might be an interesting gimmick. For Cassie, who was trying not to think of those eyes, it was downright frustrating.

She started attending services at The Tabernacle, the church Jim Dillon pastored. She made some friends among the congregation and found comfort in the Lord. Jim tried to comfort her, as well, and he kept her up on Joshua's progress. But he obviously felt responsible for a measure of her pain so Cassie put up a brave front for his sake. It was not his fault, after all, that he'd tried to be the bearer of glad tidings and had become a messenger of doom instead.

He approached her after the service three months after she'd left Mountain View to tell her that he was going to accompany Joshua to Florida in a week. She decided that with Josh gone she could visit Irma, Henry and Maria, and not run the risk of seeing him. She left for the Poconos the day Josh and Jim flew out of LVI for Fort Myers.

Josh stood alone outside his parents' home after Jim Dillon drove away, wondering what they were like. The house was a huge one-story dwelling built of gray brick and trimmed with dramatic accents of black and white. It had arched windows, a peaked slate roof, and an imposing set of stained-glass front doors, and it sat atop the gentle rise on a lushly landscaped two-acre lot. The home was grander than anything in Mountain View, and the neighborhood was as upscale as the most luxurious Pocono resort. The extent of their wealth was evident in every square inch of the property.

But money had never meant anything to him. Nothing meant much to him lately. The pain of losing Cassie had even overshadowed the torture of the intense therapy sessions he'd had to undergo to get on his feet again.

Jim Dillon, who he'd learned was a fellow pastor, had offered to accompany Josh to Florida, and Josh had taken him up on the offer. On the trip south, Jim had shared a multitude of stories from their mutual past. Some were funny, but several were tragic and heartbreaking. Jim's own past, which included the breakup of a brief marriage to a young New Zealander, was perhaps the saddest of all.

Jim had suffered from a drinking problem and it had caused the couple to clash, and then Jim had shipped out to the South Pole. The assignment had taken six months, and he'd lost his wife and his son as a result. He'd returned to civilization to find divorce papers and an address for her that was no longer current. They had disappeared and he'd been searching for them whenever he could afford it.

According to Jim, David Chernak's marriage had been the stuff of fairy tales. Jim told him that David had worshiped his wife and success, in that order, and that, like Jim, he hadn't been a Christian in that old life he'd lost on a lonely mountain road.

Another thing he'd learned was that David had resented the way his parents doted on his younger brother. In fact, he'd gone into the Navy so he could gain experience under the tutelage of someone other than his own father.

All of this made Josh wonder again what kind of people his parents were. Well, he told himself, he was about to find out. Then he chuckled. All he'd had for five years was his present. And with all the information he'd been given, it was still all he had.

Chapter Fifteen

Josh forced himself to put one foot in front of the other as he made his way up the long path to the front door. The walk to the door seemed to take forever, but before he knew it, he was watching as if from afar as his finger pressed on the doorbell.

The woman who answered the door was his mother. Josh knew who she was but not because he remembered her. Jim had found a picture of his parents, in a back issue of a newspaper, taken as they'd entered the courthouse for his brother's trial.

Nancy Chernak didn't say a thing. She just stared. She stood around five-foot-five, had hair that was nearly as dark as his but slightly streaked with white strands. Her face was unlined and her figure that of a woman thirty years younger. She was as opposite Irma as was humanly possible, but there was something in her dark eyes when she looked at him that was the same, as well.

She loved him.

And he didn't even know her.

"David! Oh, David!" she cried at last as tears turned her dark gaze liquid. She threw her arms around him and hugged him.

His hands came up and hovered at her back, and he forced himself to hug her—this stranger who was his mother.

She stepped back. "Oh. Let me look at you! Why, you look positively rustic. Where have you been? Hiding in the woods?"

"You could say that, I suppose," he replied, uncertain and embarrassed.

"Oh, I should be so angry at you for staying away for so long and not even calling. But I'm just so glad to see you."

"We…ah, we'd better talk. There's a lot I need to tell you. To explain. And questions I need answered. Could we go inside?"

She giggled like a schoolgirl and stepped back and into the house. "Oh, of course. How silly of me to keep you standing on the front steps. You go on into the family room, and I'll go get us something to drink."

For a second he was tempted to go along with her suggestion and prolong her happiness, but he realized it was impossible. He'd never be able to guess where the family room was in so large a house.

A house he didn't remember at all.

"I'd rather you didn't. We need to talk. Right away."

Nancy Chernak stiffened, and he realized that he'd sounded cross. "I had hoped you'd been able to put the past behind you," she said, her bubble clearly broken. Frowning now, she gestured to a wide doorway at the end of a long wide hall. "Very well, we'll talk now."

He followed her into a huge room with an oversize fireplace and a French door that led to a deck. A pair of short couches sat perpendicular to the fireplace toward one end of the large space. The room, though it appeared comfortable, looked unlived in. He remembered Cassie and her decorator story, and nearly flinched at the sudden flash of pain and loneliness that shot through him over the loss of her in his life.

Nancy Chernak—he just couldn't think of her as his mother—led him to the fireplace area, but he didn't feel comfortable enough to sit. Instead he leaned an elbow on the mantel and waited for her to choose a seat.

"You asked why I never called," he began after she settled on one of the small couches. "And why I never came…home."

"That can wait. We should talk over what happened before your father gets home."

He shook his head. "No, ma'am, it can't wait. You see, I didn't call, or write, or come here because I didn't know where to go."

Obviously misunderstanding, she said, "I know things were terrible when you left and I'm sure you felt adrift."

"But I don't know the way it was!" Josh blurted out. "I don't know a thing about when I left. I only knew to come here because a Pennsylvania state policeman gave me this address."

"I don't understand," she said, staring at him as if he'd lost his mind. Little did she know that he literally had.

"Ma'am, I don't know you. I don't know the David Chernak of five years ago. I was in an accident that wiped out my memory. My name has been Joshua Daniels ever since. Three months ago I was accidentally shot by a hunter and that's when I found out about the life of a man named David Chernak. Someone he'd— *I'd* been in the Navy with saw the news report on the shooting and found me."

Now she looked positively stricken. Her voice shook. "You have amnesia?"

He nodded and resisted the urge to go to her. The pastor in him demanded he offer comfort, but the unlooked-for son in him held him in place.

"That's what it's called—but it's not a temporary problem. Since I learned who I am, since I saw pictures of my family, I've come to accept what the doctors have been telling me for a while. I'll never regain my memory. I have to believe that this was God's plan for me. The pastor who took me in believes that there's something in my past the Lord wants me to be free of."

Now tears filled her dark eyes and flowed down her cheek. "You've become a Christian." She pursed her lips as if gathering her strength, and nodded sharply. "He answered one of my petitions for you, at least. I've been praying that my children would accept Jesus since I found Him in the midst of the unholy mess that sent you out of our lives. Tell me how. What brought you to Him?"

Josh understood the bond he'd been feeling for this stranger who was his mother. It was more than that she loved him. It was that she was his sister in the Lord. For the first time, he felt comforted. Felt that he'd done the right thing in seeking his past. But one of his biggest questions remained. Why had no one tried to find him? Not sure he was even ready for her reasons, he answered her question about his salvation experience instead of asking his.

"When I woke up with an almost total void in my brain, Henry, the pastor I spoke of, and his wife Irma were all I had. They were the ones who found me when I was hurt. They stayed by me and gave me more than a family. They gave me one more person to hold on to. Jesus. And He's been the most important person in my life ever since."

Josh left out the second most important person and the fact that he wouldn't be sitting here were it not for his belief in God. He'd be back in Pennsylvania, with Cassie.

"You said these people found you hurt. What happened to you?"

He told her the whole story of his last nearly six years, what he knew about what had happened to take his memory—which was very little—and about the shooting that had sent him in search of his past.

"You mentioned that you knew why I was in Pennsylvania. Jim Dillon said I had some sort of falling out with your husband over business problems. Could you tell me about it? Could you tell me why my family never tried to find me?"

She sighed and closed her eyes. When she opened them seconds later there was a quiet resolve in her gaze that had not been there before. "Lies and keeping secrets from you sent you out of our lives, and if the truth does the same, then so be it. Do you know about Regina?"

"I know I'm married to someone named Regina and that I was very much in love with her, but that's all. We couldn't find an address for her, or I would have gone to see her first."

"No, that wouldn't have been a good idea, David."

She stopped, and he knew she'd seen him flinch at the use of a name that had no meaning to him.

"Would you rather I try to remember to call you Joshua?" she asked. "This must be even more difficult for you than it is for me. At least I *know* you."

Josh nodded and silently acknowledged the truth of what she'd said. This was harder than he'd thought it would be. "About Regina?" he prodded.

"You *were* very much in love with her. So much in love that you had as great a blind spot about her as we did about your brother. Which made what happened all the worse for you."

She sighed and put a shaking hand to her forehead. "There is no easy way to say this."

Josh remembered saying those exact words to Cassie. Something bad was coming. He knew it. She stared at him, her eyes seeming to drink in his image, obviously afraid to continue.

Josh finally gave in to the urge to go to her, but he sat across from her on the couch. "Whatever it is, it can't hurt me. I don't know any of you. Remember?"

Nancy Chernak nodded and pursed her lips. "Regina and your brother had an affair."

Josh was stunned and glad he'd decided to sit. Not because of any emotion he felt. What rocked him to his core was the betrayal. How could a man perpetrate such a betrayal on his brother? And how could a woman betray her husband with her husband's brother? "How could they do that?"

"Oh, it gets worse, I assure you. Will has always disregarded rules. We'd tried to protect him from the consequences of his actions since the first time he got into trouble at age five. I've come to understand that the more we did, the worse his problems got. This was one of those occasions.

"Your father and I knew about the affair for quite some time. We told them it had to stop, but when it didn't—no, that isn't right—when they *chose* not to end the affair, we covered for them. I told myself I was doing it to keep you from being hurt. And I was, but I was also protecting Will.

"But this time there was no protecting Will. What we didn't know was the lengths he'd gone to over Regina. He bought substandard material and pocketed the difference. He finally admitted to you and your father that he'd done it so he and Regina could start over together somewhere else."

"But the hurricane Jim Dillon told me about exposed him first," Josh said.

Nancy nodded. "And it put him in prison. Which I am happy to say was the best thing that ever happened to him. He accepted Jesus while he was there, and it's changed his life."

"But why did none of you look for me when I disappeared?"

"Because you learned of their betrayal, and, quite frankly, ours, in the worst possible way. From Will. You had reached a conclusion about who was at fault for the collapsed houses before the state investigators did. When you confronted Will, he told you about him and Regina—and that we had known. You left the office, and no one heard from you for nearly a week. When you showed up here, you told us you were leaving Florida to settle elsewhere. You said that when you came to a place where you could forgive us, you'd contact us. But, of course, you never did.

"Your father grew bitter in the months that followed over what he feels was your desertion of us and the business. As for me, I didn't think you'd ever forgive us."

Feeling a little better about why his parents had abandoned him, he knew it was time to ask his next question. More than ever he didn't want to know the answer, but it was the reason he was here—the reason he'd given up a life of happiness with Cassie. "What happened to Regina?"

"You signed the house over to her and left your lawyer with power of attorney to handle the divorce. Of course, she couldn't keep up the mortgage payments so she sold it, divorced you and…" She sighed. "I'm sorry. She and Will were married before he went to prison. She had their first child while he was still in there. After the baby was born, he accepted the Lord and eventually led Regina to Him. They wanted to look for you to tell you how sorry they were, but your father controls the purse strings and refused to let them. As I said, he's rather angry that you left him to save the business on his own."

That struck Josh as terribly amusing. "About that time I was learning to walk and talk again. I couldn't even read." He chuckled. "I wouldn't have been any help except through prayer."

Suddenly Nancy Chernak's face crumpled. "Oh, my poor boy. You've been through such an ordeal because of us, and all the time we were angry at you for staying away so long. I'm so sorry."

He leaned forward to take her hand, but a huge voice pierced the moment. "How dare you return here after all these years and reduce your mother to tears?"

Josh looked up as a tall, gray-haired man stalked toward him. Ronald Chernak looked very much like his photo and was a formidable-looking man. It was easy for Joshua to see where he got his own height and build.

He stood, uncomfortable with the fury radiating from the older man. "I'm sorry, sir, but—"

"Ronald, calm down." Nancy sniffled. "You need to listen to what David has to say."

But Chernak wasn't willing to listen to anyone. "Get out!" he shouted at Joshua. "I don't want you near my family. We've hung on in spite of your callous disregard for our feelings and needs. I don't want the traitor who sent his own brother to prison in my house."

"Ronald, we don't know that," Nancy cried. "The police denied it. The district attorney denied it. David wasn't even on the witness list, and you know he would have been if he'd told them what he'd discovered. They merely reached the same conclusion he did."

Shock rooted Josh to the floor as the man charged toward him, his limited experience leaving him unprepared to deal with such hostility. Chernak grabbed Josh by his shirt. "You told them," he screamed into Josh's face, "didn't you? You went to the investigators and told them what Will had done. You broke your mother's heart because you were jealous of your brother. You saw a chance to hurt him and you took it. We had to visit our child in prison!" He pushed Josh back a step and let go of him. "I won't have you in my house, do you hear me?"

"Ronald! Stop this right this moment!" Nancy shouted. "You don't understand what happened."

The shove luckily broke the logjam in Joshua's brain just as Ronald Chernak took a roundhouse swing at him. Josh caught Chernak's fist with his open hand and held on. "I won't raise a hand to you, sir," he said. "I don't know if I did what you say or not, but I will tell you that it would have been the right thing to do. I've read the newspaper reports on what happened to those homes. Will did a lot of people a great deal of harm, and from what I hear he deserved to be punished for it. I assume he feels the same way, since your wife tells me he's accepted Jesus into his heart." Chernak was staring at him in stunned silence. Josh dropped the man's hand, and turned to Nancy.

His heart twisted in his chest and tears burned at the back of his throat. Because of this he'd lost Cassie?

"Ma'am, it *has* been good to meet you. I'll contact you before I leave Florida. Perhaps we can write each other."

"Please don't go. We have so much to settle," she begged.

"Not according to your husband. Good day, ma'am."

Josh turned and left, fighting the urge to run. Pride kept his pace quick but steady. He did start running, though, when he got outside, but when he reached the street he stopped in his tracks. Which way should he go? Jim had reluctantly dropped him off and wouldn't return until Josh paged him. So what he needed was a phone. He looked left, then right. Which direction had he and Jim come from, and had he seen a store or a payphone in that direction?

"Son. I'm told I owe you an apology," Ronald Chernak said from behind him.

He whirled to face a man much changed from the

furious person he'd faced only moments ago, but an un-characteristic anger took hold of Josh, anyway. "Don't call me 'son.' I suddenly understand why I was never able to call Henry Tallinger 'Father.' It never felt like a compliment. I just never understood why. Until today. I came here looking for roots, my wife and answers. I got the answers. I apparently never really had the wife—and suddenly I don't want the roots.

"You never looked for me," he accused, the torment of years of uncertainty and haunting feelings spilling out. "Your wife admitted that they all wanted to look but that *you* wouldn't allow it. Can you imagine looking in a mirror and not knowing the person looking back at you? Have you ever heard a song for the first time but felt a sick sadness descend on you for no reason you can remember? Have you ever pushed a woman you love out of your life because a picture of some other woman haunts you and you're afraid she's your wife?"

"I'm sorry, David. I had no idea."

"Because you didn't bother to find out. You chose one son—the one who hurt everyone in your family—over the victim of his deceit. Jim Dillon told me the first person suspected of wrongdoing was David. If he went to the police, he had every right to clear his name. Was he supposed to go to prison for Will, too?"

"You're David," Ronald Chernak told him.

"No. My name is Joshua Daniels. I don't know who David was, and the more I learn, the less I want to know."

"There were good times. And maybe if we try there

can be again." He paused and looked at the ground before looking back at Josh. "I know it was mostly my fault. I'd accepted that already. But then I came in and she was crying and it sounded as if you were playing on her sympathy. I have a short fuse where seeing my wife hurt is concerned, as I guess you noticed. I am sorry. Please. She's been so hurt by all of this. Come back inside and let's talk. Really talk. I'd like to try to make the past up to you."

Josh looked back up at the house, and the sight of Nancy Chernak standing in the window watching them softened his heart. "I'll come back, but there's nothing to make up except that reception I just got in there. Your son is dead, Mr. Chernak, as surely as if I never woke from that coma."

Ronald Chernak smiled, and Josh knew where he'd gotten his smile, as well. "That's the first time you've referred to yourself as 'I' in relation to our son. And just so you know, you might not remember being David, but you're not all that different than I remember you. Do you still like sweet iced tea?"

The wind whispered by and Josh shivered. He loved sweet tea.

Chapter Sixteen

Cassie sat staring at the woods out of the Tallingers' kitchen window. She looked away and down at the bag of green beans Irma plopped down on the counter between them. She automatically reached out and began popping the beans.

"Now explain to me what the problem is with your painting, dear," Irma urged.

"I've done four portraits since I came here. And I did five back in Philly. They all look like Josh. Oh, not the features, the age or even the gender of the people. It's their eyes. Actually, they're *his* eyes. No matter what mood a subject is in when I do the sketch, the eyes become his when I translate the drawing to paint. I've always tended to lose myself when I'm painting, and that's when it happens. My subconscious takes over—and there they are, staring back at me."

Irma reached into the bag but her hand came away

empty. She had a pensive look on her face when she glanced over at Cassie. "You've been here three weeks now and you're no closer to finding peace with the situation than you were when you arrived. I have to wonder if Henry's and my anxiety about Joshua isn't being projected onto you. Even Bear mopes around here as if he's lost his best friend."

Cassie smiled and looked over at the depressed dog lying by the back door. "I have to admit, he does mope. We all do. I try not to think about Josh and I do a pretty good job of it most times, but it's obvious from the portraits that it isn't working as well as I thought."

"He'll be back. I truly believe it. But that still leaves you hurting and missing him."

Reaching into the paper bag, Cassie took a fistful of beans and dropped them in front of her. She made short work of them, while trying to sort out her thoughts. "I'll never stop missing him. I don't know how he made himself a part of my existence in so short a time, but he did." She bit her bottom lip and willed away the tears gathering at the back of her eyes.

"Have you ever tried just painting *him?*"

Cassie broke another bean and shook her head. "No. I've thought about it, but I would never be able to sell it, and then his image would be there staring at me twenty-four hours a day. His eyes are bad enough."

Irma reached over and stilled Cassie's nervous fingers with both of her hands. Cassie looked up.

"You have to get on with your life, Cassidy Jamison.

You said you've tried not thinking of him. Well, I have an idea. Why don't I get Larry to take you and Bear up to the cabin. And when you get there, I want you to do nothing but think about Joshua. Pack in there with your art supplies and paint him. Put into that picture all the love you feel and all the pain, too. Get it all out of you and onto paper. I'll keep it for you until you want it, but *do it*. It can't make you feel worse than you do right now. The weather looks good for tomorrow. What do you say?"

Cassie considered the idea and knew she had no choice. She had nothing to lose—and she had to do something. Her heart was already broken, and every time she found Josh's eyes staring back at her from the face of a child or an old woman or a laughing teen she wasn't so sure how much longer her mind would remain intact. Irma was right: something had to give.

"Call Larry. But you have to promise me that if Josh calls and says he's coming back, you'll send somebody up to get me so I can leave before he arrives. I don't want to meet Regina."

Irma nodded. "If he calls and tells me he's coming, I'll warn you. I won't expose you to his wife. I wouldn't let you be hurt that way. Seeing you like this, I wish I'd just asked Josh to take you to one of the resorts instead of giving you a room."

It was Cassie's turn to grip Irma's hand. "Don't. I wouldn't have missed knowing Josh for anything. Loving him is a precious gift I'll always treasure."

"And I'm sure he'll always treasure having known

and loved you. Never doubt that he loves you. He does. He just feels he has to do this."

Cassie nodded and stood. "Call Larry while I start packing up some supplies."

When Josh heard someone behind him push open the sliding glass door from the family room, he closed his eyes and shut out the sight of the rippling water below his feet. His stomach knotted at the imminent presence of someone who wanted more from him than he could manage to give. Being on stage once again shattered the relative peace of the spring day.

Sometimes he felt like a seal being taught to perform to the wishes of a bunch of animal trainers. His mother—in his heart the title still belonged to Irma— wanted affection from him and she wanted him to feel a sense of connection with her that he just didn't.

Regina wanted forgiveness from someone who no longer existed, her pretty clear blue eyes reflecting a contrition that was palpable. Ronald wanted the impossible. He constantly pushed Josh to remember a past that was gone forever. Will was the only one who gave him the space he needed, but Josh had a feeling that he acted the way he did more out of guilt and embarrassment than anything else.

"Enjoying one of our perfect spring days?"

Josh's stomach unknotted a little. He straightened and turned from his study of the blue Fort Myers water to face Will. Younger by a couple of years, he was about three inches shorter than Josh and thinner. He looked more like his mother than his father but with the same coloring as Ronald. "It *is* a beautiful day," Josh agreed. "Especially on the water. The day I arrived I had no idea the house was so close to the bay."

Will chuckled. "I'm surprised you didn't run headlong into it and swim north when Dad tossed you out of the house that day."

"It still doesn't sound like a bad idea," Josh muttered, accidentally changing the tone of the exchange.

"The old man isn't letting up on you at all, is he?"

Josh shook his head. He felt uncomfortable talking about the man with his brother, but sometimes he felt that if he didn't talk out a little of his frustration, he'd explode. "Ronald took me into his office this morning. He told me I designed this house and he said he thought I'd get a charge out of the model I did on it first. I went along, but it didn't sound like anything all that exciting. Before I knew it, he had me in front of a computer trying to get me to design something. I couldn't even make the thing draw a box. I could see how disappointed he was, so I tried harder. All I got for my efforts was a monster of a headache. He gave up then and dropped me off here."

"Mom said you came home with another bad headache. Joshua, you don't belong here. Look, this was never an ideal family. It's come a long way since my arrest, but for you it's like a minefield. Maybe you should go home."

"There's something I still have to do here. I don't know what it is. It's there just out of reach—but it is there."

"Maybe you need to make a decision. I haven't wanted to pressure you but I think it's time we talk seriously. I've tried to stay in the background for your sake, but I can't anymore. Gina's a nervous wreck about what you want to do, and our son's sensing the tension. I just can't let this go on any longer."

Josh frowned, confused. "About what I want to do? About what? Going home?"

Will shook his head. "About your marriage to Regina. And in the long run, my marriage. I spoke to my minister. He said he believes that marriages that are contracted between believers before they accept the Lord are subject to the same laws as those contracted after they come to Jesus. In other words, it becomes as binding as if they were Christians when they said their vows."

"That's about the size of it," Josh concurred, still not sure where this was going.

"Unfortunately, he didn't help me figure out what we're supposed to do now with all three of us being Christians. Gina was your wife first, but we have a child who needs us. I don't know what's the right thing to do."

Now Josh understood. Will was struggling with the same question he was. "How do you feel about her?"

"Regina? I love her," Will answered vehemently.

Josh nodded, understanding Will's fierce answer. He loved someone that passionately, too. He fought off the nearly crippling pain that thoughts of Cassie always caused him. He missed her so much some days that he thought he'd die of the loneliness.

"And I don't even know her so how could I love her enough to be married to her? And as you said, you two have a child. You're married now. You were married when you accepted Jesus. I wasn't. I don't think I'm entitled to step into that and ask you two to tear apart your home and your child's life. What it comes right down to is that you have to follow your conscience. Just as I do."

Will looked away and down at the water. "I haven't been very good about that in the past. And I'm still pretty new at it. I'm not even sure I had a conscience before. If I did, I never listened to it. I couldn't have and have done the things I did." He looked back, resolve in his hazel gaze, his blond hair ruffling in the breeze. "I did some pretty terrible things. I paid my debt to the state, but I don't know how to make reparations with you. Or even if I can. But I'd like to try, Joshua."

Will Chernak had come a long way in his walk with the Lord. It was good to see. "I can easily tell you that I forgive you," Josh told him. "And I can do it easily because my emotions aren't involved. I'm not the man in the picture that I carried for so long. I'm not the man you wronged. That man's dead. He died on a mountain road. When he woke, he was me, and I'll never be him again. Will, the bottom line is that I can't help you with the guilt. You're forgiven, but not only by me. Jesus has forgiven you by virtue of your contrition and His blood.

Accept His forgiveness and go on with your life with Regina and your son."

Will gave him a relieved nod, then grinned. "Now we just have to figure out what to do with you. Mom says you mentioned having given up a woman because you thought you were still married to Regina. Will you marry her now?"

"That's what I meant about me having to follow my conscience. I don't know yet. There are several problems I have to think about. There's the divorce thing. And she said she hated Mountain View before she left. I know I could never live in Philadelphia. Cities make me crazy after a day. Nice places to visit and all that. I thought she might have been trying to set me free without a load of guilt, but I can't be sure. Then there's her money…"

"Having money's a problem? It's usually the other way around, isn't it?" Will joked.

"Yeah." Josh smiled sadly. "And that's part of it, too. I'm the one without and she's the one with. What have I got to offer her?"

"Plenty."

"Have you ever heard of Jamison Steel?"

"Show me somebody who's been in construction that hasn't," Will said, grinning.

Josh chuckled ruefully and raised his hand. "I didn't have a clue. The woman I'm in love with is Cassidy Jamison. Heir to Winston Jamison's entire estate."

His brother let out a long, slow whistle. "I get your

point, but look at it this way—unlike most women who have to consider what kind of provider their future husband will be, Cassidy Jamison is free to pick the man she wants. If it turns out that she was only trying to set you free and you're the one she wants, then where's the problem?"

Josh sighed. "Well, that's one way of looking at it."

Will slapped his hand on the railing. "And a sound one at that. Now that we have that settled, we have to talk about one more thing." He indicated with his thumb over his shoulder toward the house behind them. "They're driving you crazy, Joshua. Both of them are trying to make you into David again. Dad's making you feel guilty for who you are. Mom's pleased as punch about your work in the ministry, but she still wants you to be someone you aren't." He gestured to the house again. "You don't belong in there. You're miserable here."

Josh knew what his brother said was true. And then he was struck by a thought. In the last several minutes, Will *had* become his brother, and had somehow freed Josh to go home. He was going to an uncertain future, but it was home nonetheless.

"Will, could you drive me to the airport? I want to be on the next flight out of here."

Josh put his duffel bag down and pulled out his key, but before he unlocked the door to the parsonage, he turned away from the house and took a deep breath of cool mountain air. He looked up at the black night sky and smiled at the thousands of stars on display. He thought he knew how Dorothy felt when she woke up in Kansas with Auntie Em by her bedside.

He hadn't made the next flight out but he'd been in the air within in a few hours of his decision. And now here he was.

"Ma! Henry!" he shouted when he got into the foyer, knowing he'd get a warm reception.

He wasn't disappointed when his name resounded from the parlor. An incredibly warm feeling engulfed him.

Home. He was home.

"Is that my Josh?" Henry called from his study.

The elderly couple hurried to him from their respective rooms and engulfed him in a hug that said *family*. His throat ached as he held on to these two people who had come to mean so much to him. They'd proven that biology had little to do with parenthood.

"Why didn't you call and tell us you were coming?" Irma scolded as she broke the embrace.

Josh shrugged. "It was a spur-of-the-moment decision. Will talked me into leaving. I was staying there out of guilt." He sighed. "I just can't be what they want. I can't be David. I'm me—Joshua Daniels."

"Well, good for Will," Henry said. "But weren't your parents upset with you for leaving so suddenly?"

"Actually, one of the problems between us is that I can't seem to see them as my parents. They're strangers. I thought they'd be upset, but I think they realized that we had nothing left to say to each other. I promised to keep in touch and that seemed to satisfy them. In fact, I think they were a little relieved. Things started out strained between Ronald and me, and stayed that way."

Henry clapped Josh on the shoulder. "We missed you, son. How'd you get from the airport?"

"I was so close to home when I arrived that I decided to surprise you, so I called Larry Tully and asked him to come get me."

Irma frowned. "Larry? What'd he have to say?"

Josh wondered if the Tullys were having problems again, but he was sure Larry would have said something. He'd thought it fair to give the Chernaks a fair shot at being his family by not staying in touch with Irma and Henry while he was in Florida, but now he wondered if that had been a mistake.

"Larry didn't say much of anything. Mostly he asked me questions about how Florida was, and we talked about the addition. Why? Is something wrong that I should know about ?"

Irma blinked as if his question surprised her. "Wrong?" she asked. "What could be wrong? Our son's come home and all's right with the world! Did they feed you on the plane?"

"We had a snack but I'm not very hungry. Actually, I'd like to talk. About the Chernaks and Regina." He smiled ruefully. "I guess you noticed I arrived alone."

"Noticed that right off," Henry quipped. "Let's all get settled, and you can tell us everything."

And he did. It felt good to unburden himself. Josh

talked for what felt like hours, reliving his last few weeks, explaining the past as it had been told to him and revealing his confusion about his future because of his brother's marriage to Regina.

"Well, son, I don't see the problem," Henry said. "Right in Corinthians, Paul lays out the only allowable reason for divorce. Adultery. It's an ugly word and an even uglier deed. I believe as you do that your brother and ex-wife are forgiven, but that doesn't change the facts. She was an adulteress who divorced you. You're free."

"I want so desperately to believe that," Josh admitted. "But I keep thinking that maybe I want it too desperately. Maybe I love Cassie so much that I'm willing to sacrifice my principles for the chance of a life with her."

"Hmm," Henry said, stroking his chin and pursing his lips. "That's one theory. But here's another. Would you agree that God is our Father?"

Josh nodded.

"Now, I know I'm not your father but I'd like to think I've filled that role for you these last years."

"You know you have," Josh said immediately.

"Well, I'm pleased you think so. Would I tell you to do anything I thought would hurt you?"

"Of course not," he answered without hesitation.

"Hmm. Okay. Suppose you came to me wanting something that would make you happy, and it was within my power to grant whatever it was you asked of me, would I tell you no?"

"I doubt it."

"Well, I doubt it, too!" Henry exclaimed, and shook his head. "It never ceases to amaze me why folks think our heavenly Father is up there trying to find ways to make us miserable. Would you tell me why you think He is less apt to want you to be happy than I am?"

Josh blinked and had no answer, having never thought in those terms before. Henry certainly had a point.

"Well, now." The old pastor sighed and stood. "It's late and we all need a good night's rest. You pray on that question and then you sleep on it. I'll see you in the morning." He left, his steps slower these days, even though his mind was obviously as quick as ever.

Irma smiled and stood to leave. "He's a sneaky one, that Henry. Has you thinking, doesn't he."

Josh nodded.

Irma bent over and kissed his cheek. "What you need is to take time to reflect and pray. Why not go to the cabin tomorrow morning and think things over up there? Just you and God and plenty of peace and quiet."

"That's a good idea. I think I'll do just that. By the way, where's Bear? I ought to take him with me."

Irma's eyes widened. "Bear? Oh…Bear…uh, didn't Larry tell you? He took him along with him about a week ago. He got to be too much for us. I'll call and see if Larry could bring him back tomorrow when he has time. But in the meantime, you get that good night's sleep Henry ordered up, so you can start fresh in the morning."

"Yeah, I'll do that. Going up to the cabin is a good idea, Ma."

"Glad you think so. Pleasant dreams," she said, and left.

As she was walking out, Josh thought he heard her mutter something that sounded like *I hope you still think so tomorrow night*.

Why would she think he'd change his mind? he wondered, as he turned off the lights and headed for his room.

Chapter Seventeen

"Okay. One last time!" Cassidy said as she opened the cabin door for Bear. He'd been restless all morning, wanting in, then out. She'd been able to contend with that, but the sound of his raucous barking bounced off the cabin walls and straight through her head. "Go find a nice safe rabbit to chase. No skunks. There's no more tomato juice left after the last one you cornered. Oh, no, now I'm talking to the dog as if he's a person."

"Would it be impertinent of me to add that you're also talking to yourself?"

There was a slight Southern drawl that hadn't been there before, but she knew the sound of Josh's voice. And it tipped Cassie's world off its axis.

She stepped onto the porch and found him at the foot of the porch steps, fending off Bear, who barked and jumped excitedly about him. Josh went down on one knee and looped an arm over Bear's shoulders to calm him. He smiled as he looked up, and her heart tripped.

"I guess he missed me," he said, and laughed when Bear gave him a sloppy doggy kiss.

She wanted to tell him that the dog wasn't the only one who'd missed him—who wanted to kiss his beloved face. And even though Irma had promised not to let this happen, Cassie couldn't regret seeing him again. He looked so much better than he had the last time she'd seen him, pale and weak in a hospital bed.

He looked wonderful. Tall, tanned and terrific.

And tough to resist.

But she had to. There was no choice. He belonged to another woman now. She'd long since accepted that there wasn't a chance Regina Chernak would reject someone as wonderful as Josh. What woman in her right mind would be so foolish?

Now all she had to do was hide her joy and stick to her story. "I—I, uh…" She cleared her suddenly tight throat. "I'm surprised to see you."

"And I'm surprised to see you, too. Ma didn't tell me you were in town." He frowned. "In fact, no one did." He looked wounded, and she couldn't blame him. Didn't Irma and Henry understand that this was as hard for him as it was for her?

"I'm sorry. I'll pack up and be out of your hair in no time," she told him.

"I'd never toss a woman out in the cold." Josh looked around and took in the beautiful spring day. He shrugged. "Of course, it isn't very cold, but I was only coming up here to think. I can do that anywhere on a day like this."

He smiled that sweet, open smile of his, and Cassie's resolve almost melted. She stiffened. "But you should be able to do that here. Just the way you planned," she replied in her most no-nonsense corporate tone. "As I said, I can be gone in no time. I'd already decided to head back soon, anyway. I was only here to paint and I've accomplished what I came to do."

"Getting back to the wilds of nature for the sake of your art?"

Cassie nodded. She didn't like the edge of sarcasm that had crept into his tone, but she understood it. After all, she'd disparaged what he had come to see as his birthplace. Only she knew it had only been an excuse to bow out of his life gracefully. Josh didn't know that.

"I've been back to nature for as long as I can stand. And I have to admit, this place has a certain rustic charm," she added, and gestured toward the cabin, "but it does wear thin after a while."

When his eyes narrowed in obvious annoyance, Cassie fought to remember that she'd already set him free and that maintaining the pretense she'd used that evening in the hospital was of prime importance. She didn't want him feeling so guilty that he might subconsciously sabotage any hope for happiness with Regina. Josh deserved a happy life.

"And my agent likes the work I did while I was

staying at Irma and Henry's," she continued, congratulating herself on her acting ability. "I thought I'd provide him with the ultimate in rustic charm by hiking up here and immersing myself in all this bucolic splendor. And I have to admit that I've been able to produce exactly what he's been begging for."

Josh grabbed the stick Bear had proudly brought to him, and stood. He tossed it high into the air and far from the porch. Bear took off after it gleefully. "I hear you have another show coming up," he said, his tone stiff. "Jim said you did so well at that first small one that the gallery opted for a major event this time. Congratulations."

"Thank you," she answered, and then, at a loss for words, added, "Would you like to come in while I pack up?"

Josh nodded and started toward the steps. "I'd love to see what you've painted since you came up here."

Cassie had turned to walk inside, but froze in the doorway as the full import of her invitation hit her. The oil she'd almost finished of him still sat on the easel by the far window. And two other watercolors of him were in with the landscapes.

How was she going to keep him from seeing those? The landscapes, painted with all the love she felt for the lush spring countryside, were perfectly within the realm of her excuse for being there, but she'd never pass off the portraits as studies of rustic charm.

"Something wrong?" he all but purred into her ear from just behind her.

She whirled to face him, barring the door with a hand on each doorjamb. "I don't like to show anyone my work before it's matted and framed," she blurted out, then nearly winced.

She just wasn't a good liar. That's all there was to it. Never before had a virtue felt more like a vice. They'd lived in the same house. Chatted while he watched her paint. He'd never swallow that!

Josh confirmed her fear with a chuckle. "Since when? You always let me see what you were working on while it was in progress."

He put his hands on her shoulders, and her knees turned to water.

"Is that agent of yours making you shy about your work—or are you getting uppity again?"

His grin set a match to her well-laid fire. "I am not being uppity! I've never been uppity."

Outraged and unsettled by his nearness, she stepped back, needing the distance, then realized her error. Josh followed and was inside the cabin in a heartbeat—pretty quick moving, considering the speed at which her heart was pounding. She needed a diversion, and anger would do just fine!

"How dare you call me uppity?" she charged, hoping to keep his attention focused on her. She stalked over to the easel that was thankfully turned so the painting wasn't visible, and, as casually as she could, flipped the cover over it. "And what kind of stupid word is *uppity*, anyway? You sound like a hillbilly, and I know Irma taught you to speak better than that."

He just grinned again, and she knew she was doomed to failure. He was not about to be deterred. There was something about the way he sauntered across the room to the stack of paintings. Something new about the way he leafed through them, tilting his head this way and that, setting one then another in front to step back and study them. That something new was arrogance. A trait she'd never seen in him before. What did he have to be arrogant about? He hadn't yet gotten to the portraits.

"You're very talented," he said after looking at several landscapes. "But then, I'm sure you believe that by now."

"Thank you," she replied through gritted teeth, wanting to slap that insolent smirk right off his face.

He turned away again and kept going through them, one after another. Slowly. As if he knew what he was about to find but wanted to prolong her torture. There was no way he could know about her paintings of him, and he had no reason to want to make her squirm. He'd called off their marriage. He'd called her in to his hospital room to say goodbye to her. He'd been determined to go to Florida to find Regina.

Could she have made him so angry with her story of hating the area that he wanted to see her hurt in some way? That just didn't fit the Joshua Daniels she knew.

The sound of yet another painting being moved to the back of the pile dragged her from her thoughts. There was only one more landscape in the stack, then the two pictures she'd done of him. If her memory served her right, the first one he'd come to was of him laughing as Bear licked his face in Irma's garden. It was her favorite. Sometimes she'd close her eyes and see him that morning, trying to control that huge frightened dog, all the while laughing so hard tears rolled down his face.

The other was an opposite study. It was the way she remembered him in her little makeshift studio at Irma's as he explained that first time why any relationship between them was impossible. It was a portrait of heartbreak, his big, nearly black eyes so anguished that they transmitted every emotion he'd laid bare to her that night.

She had to get him out of here before he got that far or moved to the oil. That would unravel her story completely. Because anyone could see the oil for what it was. A portrait of her love. Every brush stroke exposed her feelings for her subject. For him.

But Josh didn't go on. He turned, and she almost gasped at the hurt in his eyes. "It wasn't really the snow that sent you running. Do you really expect me to look at these and believe you hate it up here? It was one of two other things. Either you realized that I have nothing to offer you, or you were hoping to ease my guilt for the way I treated you."

Oh, she just couldn't let him go on thinking he wasn't good enough for her. Cassie forced herself to smile past her pain. She looked him square in the eye, as difficult as that was for her, and said, "You have plenty to offer the right woman, Josh. I just don't happen to be that woman. Regina is a lucky lady. As for the paintings, you said it yourself, I'm talented."

"But you make it all come alive. You have feeling for this place. It seems to me that you could live here the way Maria does and still have an incredible career."

"You should see the one I did of a bum sleeping in a park. He wasn't a particularly attractive subject, but my agent says he nearly breathes. Not that I like that aspect of city life. No one likes to be faced with the plight of the homeless in American cities. But being back in Philly really expanded my range and opened incredible career opportunities for me."

"Oh." He turned back to the stack, and Cassie panicked.

"Look, Joshua, I'm in a hurry here." She charged over. She just couldn't let him see those watercolors of him. He was too close to the truth. "Come to the show if you want to admire my work. They'll be matted and framed by then and look even better." She scooped up the pile of paintings and hurried back across the room to shove them into her portfolio.

Josh watched Cassie hurry away clutching the watercolors. She was such a bad liar, it was laughable. And something about those paintings made her nervous; he just couldn't figure out what. Then he remembered her not so casually stalking over to cover the oil on the easel by the window, and the way her hands shook when she did it. Cassie's hands were always a dead giveaway that she was upset. Maybe that painting would reveal her secrets.

As soundlessly as he could, Josh moved to the easel and uncovered the painting. A second later he prayed that he was staring at his future. She'd never convince him that she loved a pile of brick and stone, albeit a huge city-size pile, more than she loved the man she'd painted.

He let the cover fall and grinned. Let her keep her secret a little while longer. She really shouldn't have lied to him. If Irma hadn't tricked him into coming up to the cabin, they could have lost each other forever.

"So you really hate it here?" he called across the cabin to her as he moved away from the easel.

"The silence drives me crazy."

"And the stars at night?" he asked as he stepped behind her. Her beautiful, capable, paint-smeared hands started to shake, and her breath whispered out unevenly. He grinned, then fought to put on a neutral expression.

"They...uh, make me feel too insignificant."

"It *is* a big universe. Funny how we found each other in it," he said, his lips inches from her ear.

She whirled to face him and pushed him back a step with surprising strength. "Will you just leave me alone—!" she shouted, her voice cracking on the last word.

"Nope." He stood looking down at her and wanted to scoop her into his embrace so badly that he had to fight his own body.

She stepped back and retreated several steps. "Nope? You aren't acting at all like yourself! What on earth did they do to you down there?"

"Helped open my eyes, for one thing. And by the way, there is no Mrs. David Chernak. Not anymore."

Cassie's eyes widened. "She divorced you? Is she willing to try again?"

Josh heard the hope in her voice. "Yeah. Apparently she is."

"Well, I hope you two will be very happy," she replied, her voice betraying what her expression didn't. "Now, if you'll excuse me," she snapped, "I'll just go pack my clothes and be out of your hair."

"Nope," he said again, but this time he couldn't fight the grin. But that was okay because it made Cassie even more angry. He loved it when she got mad like this. She dropped all that society pretense that had been hammered into her all her life and acted like his Cassie. Feisty but unable to hide her emotions.

And that was why he was baiting her. He had to get at the truth.

"Stop saying 'nope'!" she shouted.

"Why?"

She clenched her jaw. "Because as with *uppity,* it's not good speech."

He laughed. "I'll make a deal with you. You stop lying to me, and I'll watch the way I talk in the future."

"I do not lie!"

"Then you still contend that you simply can't live in Mountain View. We're too rustic. Too isolated. Don't have enough cultural opportunities to suit you. Or as many career opportunities."

She straightened her shoulders, which he'd have thought was impossible considering her spine-stiff stance.

"That's about the size of it. Yes. I'm sorry if that hurts your feelings, but frankly I don't see why it should. It isn't as if I'd be with you even if I wanted to stay here. Which I can't—don't," she was quick to add.

Something in him twisted, and the game came to a crashing end. Either she was lying or he'd badly misjudged yet another woman he loved. He had to know. Now. He grabbed her hand, propelled her over to the easel and flipped back the cloth with which she'd so carefully hidden the painting.

"And you don't love that man enough to give up your plays and stores and snowplows?" he demanded, then felt lower than a bug when a tear leaked out of the corner of her eye.

"I love him. I love him enough to give up the home I found here in Mountain View. Enough to give up the thousands of stars that tell me God is watching me. Enough never to look at another tree coming into leaf and not to remember the promise of a love that was doomed years before it began." She looked at him then, her tears flowing freely.

His heart broke and rejoiced all at once. She *did* love him enough to move to Mountain View. "Cassie, I—"

"No! You wanted to hear how I feel! Do you want to know how long it takes before I cry myself to sleep every night, too?"

He could resist no longer. He engulfed her in his

embrace and held on for dear life. "Shh. It's going to be okay," he promised in a whisper, his lips against her hair. He silently vowed never to let her go and prayed he'd never have to.

Irma, God bless her, had known that all he needed was to see Cassie again to realize that she was God's gift to him. Now he couldn't understand why he'd thought God would have allowed her to enter his life only to let circumstances snatch her away again.

Once he'd seen her he *had* known. He just hadn't been a hundred percent certain that Cassie had been trying to set him free of his guilt when she'd told him she had changed her mind about their marriage. He also hadn't really been certain he had enough to offer her. This was the rest of their lives he was talking about.

But what he'd forgotten was that nothing had ever been in short supply in Cassie's life except the one thing he *could* give her. His unconditional love.

"I'm sorry, sweetheart," he whispered into her hair. "I hate it that you've been so unhappy. And I didn't mean to make it worse or make you cry. But I had to know for sure that you lied to me in December. I didn't want you with me if you had to sacrifice the kind of life you need to have to be truly happy."

She tried to move away, and he loosened his hold enough so she could look up at him. "You big dope. *You're* what makes me happy. But what about Regina? You said she was willing to try to work it out with you."

He kissed her on the nose before letting her go. He

wouldn't hold her against her will, either literally or figuratively. "But I didn't say I was willing to let her try."

She sniffled and dabbed at her eyes with her paint-splattered cuffs. "But you have to. Don't you?"

He shook his head. "Not when our marriage ended because of adultery."

She smacked him on the shoulder. "Why didn't you say so?"

He grinned. "I thought I just did."

"Is that why she never looked for you?"

"Actually, she eventually wanted to. It was Ronald Chernak who vetoed the idea. He was angry that his son pulled a disappearing act when he needed him."

Cassie frowned. "Why the disappearing act?"

Josh was suddenly struck by the fact that Cassie had automatically assumed the transgression had been on Regina's part. "Because it was worse than a wife having an affair and a brother nearly destroying a business. David took off after learning that Regina's affair was with his brother."

"That snake!"

Josh smiled at her outrage. "Actually, he's not so bad. Neither is Regina, for that matter. Just before I left, he finally explained why she turned to him. I don't condone what she did, but I can understand a little."

"How can you forgive them?"

"Come on, let's sit down and I'll tell you all about it." He put his arm around her and guided her to the couch, keeping her in a loose embrace as they sat. "As

I told them, I don't *know* them, so forgiveness is easy for me. I never felt the pain of their betrayal. David Chernak did. Apparently it devastated him. But I'm Joshua Daniels."

"Then you'll keep the name Henry helped you pick out?"

Josh nodded. "Much to Ronald Chernak's annoyance."

"You still don't call him 'Dad' or 'Father.'"

"Maybe someday, but not yet. Nancy—maybe a little sooner. I feel closer to her than to him but they are both largely strangers who just spent a month trying to force memories on me that just aren't there. And after hearing about the last weeks of David Chernak's life, I think I understand why the Lord let those memories be wiped out."

He told her all about those weeks, when a decent man searched for evidence to prove his innocence and found betrayal of the highest form in the midst of his own family.

"Even your mother knew?"

"Yeah. Since all this happened, she has become a Christian and has come to see the mistakes she made. Actually, so have Will and Regina. That made my decision about the validity of their marriage a little easier. I think their present Christ-based marriage, even though it took place before they accepted Him, is the one that has to stand, especially because of Devon, their son. Will's pastor and Henry both agree."

"You said you understand what happened between

Will and Regina. Care to share that one?" she asked, a perfect eyebrow arched in enquiry.

"According to everyone I talked to, David was more than just in love with Regina. He was obsessed with her and every bit as formidable as Ronald. Which I gather caused many a clash between David and his father. Regina is sort of timid, believe it or not, and was totally overwhelmed by him. She started talking to Will, asking advice about how to construct a life of her own within her marriage. One problem was that she had nothing to do with her time. She wanted a baby, but David didn't want to share her even with their own children."

"I can see why you still can't reconcile yourself to the person you used to be. But Josh, you have to try. Apparently you weren't entirely blameless in the failure of that marriage. I think you need to force yourself to refer to David as *me* and *I*. And to your parents as your *mother* and *father*."

Josh nodded, accepting the reason he kept the truth of his origins at a distance. Everyone had mentioned it, but Cassie had gotten to the core of the matter. He was in denial about who he had been.

"I'm so different from that other person, but in a lot of ways Will and Jim Dillon say I'm the same. I guess that's what worries me. Ronald—" He broke off and sighed. "My father," he forced himself to say, "thinks I turned Will in to the authorities. When he accused me of it, I said it was the right thing to do if *I* did it. But I wasn't looking at it the way he was. He saw it as the act of a jealous sibling striking out. I saw it as turning in a felon."

Cassie turned to face him and put her hand on his shoulder. "That doesn't matter. You can't start feeling guilty for having done things that the person you are now would never do. It is probably all a matter of environment. You aren't possessive or obsessive now. It was probably something in your upbringing that made you that way. You've readily forgiven unforgivable acts on the part of your family, which proves you aren't a vindictive person. You didn't want children back then. You love them now. How do you feel about having some of your own someday?"

He grinned. Leave it to Cassie. "Well, I guess that's up to you. Are you still willing to marry a mountain preacher and itinerant carpenter?"

She pulled his face down to hers. "Just try getting out of it this time, buster," she warned, and kissed him.

Epilogue

It was a day to acknowledge miracles, Winston Jamison mused as he looked on while his only grandchild took her vows to Joshua Daniels. That was miracle number one, considering the different worlds the two hailed from.

The second miracle was that a year ago he would never have welcomed a man like Joshua into the family. The Lord had certainly been working on his heart since last Thanksgiving when he'd encouraged Cassie to return to Mountain View and fight for their love.

Because Joshua Daniels was in their lives, Winston's own faith had been restored, after years of ignoring the God he'd been raised to honor. That was a big miracle number three.

He glanced next to him at Irma, who was dabbing her eyes, and at Henry, who looked just plain pleased as punch. These folks were miracles all on their own. Loving, giving, wonderful people who had changed more lives with their faith and kindness than he bet you could count.

Across the aisle were Joshua's real parents, and his brother's wife and son, who occupied the pew behind them. Will was Joshua's best man, which as far as Winston was concerned was a pretty big miracle too.

Another was that from what he gathered, Ronald Chernak had done a complete about-face after Joshua's abrupt departure from Florida. If he understood correctly, something Joshua had said to the man had finally penetrated his armor and had gone straight to his heart. Now he was proud of the progress his older son had made toward building a new life. And maybe he hadn't yet turned his heart to Jesus, but the Lord had time to work plenty more on him.

Winston looked back to the front of the church where Pastor Jim Dillon was officiating over this important day in so many lives. Cassie smiled as Joshua repeated the solemn words Pastor Jim gave him and slipped the ring on her finger. It was the ring that Winston himself had given his own beloved wife nearly fifty years ago. He hoped Josh was as accepting of his wedding gift to them as he had been about presenting Cassie with her grandmother's wedding set.

Cassie had told Winston about the old Swenson place last Thanksgiving when she'd been so full of stories about Mountain View and so brokenhearted over losing the young man she loved. From that conversation, he knew that Joshua longed to renovate the bed-and-breakfast back into a family home—and Josh was about to get his chance.

His eyes once again drank in the sight of his beautiful granddaughter, as Josh leaned forward and gave his new wife their first kiss as a married couple. Then they turned, he in an impeccable blue suit left over from his old life and she in silk and pearls.

When you got right down to it, love was the greatest miracle of all.

* * * * *

Dear Reader,

Why is it that we so often think God is up in heaven trying to spoil our fun and that He wouldn't send things or people into our lives to make us happy? How often do you look at something and say, that can't be good for me, it's what I want.

Maybe it's the fault of how we were taught the Commandments—or the GREAT SHALL NOTs— as I once heard them called. True, there are a lot of prohibitions listed there. But if you really look at them, He gave them to us as a guideline for our lives. Keeping them keeps us from getting hurt as much as possible by the world. He is a loving God. Our Father. As Pastor Henry explained to Joshua, God wants His children to be happy.

So don't shy away from the good things this life has to offer. Just do as Joshua and Cassidy did. Pray. Seek His guidance with an open mind and heart. And accept His answer no matter what it is. He's the only one who knows if what you're asking will really bring you lasting happiness or not.

Be happy until next time,

Kate Welsh

THE GIRL NEXT DOOR

Blessed is the man who listens to me,
Watching daily at my gates, Waiting at the posts
of my doors. For whoever finds me finds life,
And obtains favor from the Lord.
—*Proverbs* 8:34–35

To my critique group:
These books are books of my heart
and as such are part of each of you, for each of you
holds a special place in my heart. I would not have
come so far were it not for the talents and counsel
you have all so willingly shared over the years.
Thanks for the laughter, the tears and the good
times. May we have many more to share.

Chapter One

Hope Taggert stared at her brother, wondering if during all those years Cole had been away he'd gone mad. "Why would I want to cut my hair?" she asked, thinking of the two-foot-long sable braid that lay heavily against her back. "I've always worn my hair like this."

"That's my point. It looked exactly like that when I left twelve years ago. You said you want Jeff to see you in a different light. That you don't want him thinking of you as my pain-in-the-neck little sister, Laurel Glen's trainer or—what was that you called yourself—the voice of his conscience?"

"Honestly, he has the worst taste in friends. Someone had to try to warn him," Hope said, grousing. "You don't know him the way I do anymore. We just had another argument about that crowd before he jetted off to California for this latest round of competitions."

"So there's tension between you. That's good, believe

it or not." Cole's grin reminded her of days gone by. "What you need to do is something drastically different physically. Wouldn't waking him up be worth it?"

"I happen to like your sister's hair exactly as it is," Ross Taggert all but growled as he entered the sunny breakfast room.

Hope watched with dismay as the grin slid off Cole's face. Somehow when her father's penetrating voice announced his arrival, the bright and airy room became dark and stifling. And her dismay turned to anger when her father continued.

"Jeffrey Carrington isn't worthy of her time, let alone cutting her hair. And I don't want her encouraging him in that way. It's bad enough that he's around when he thinks of her as just a friend."

Hope felt her hackles rise. She loved her father. She tried to honor him at all times, as the Lord commanded. But he no longer had a right to a say in her life. Before she could form an intelligent, adult response, though, Cole picked up the usual pattern of his relationship with their father.

"You just don't want to share her," Cole challenged.

"That isn't it at all," Ross snapped. "He isn't worthy of her, and she's safer if he sees her only as an occasional friend."

"No one's good enough for your princess, isn't that it?" Cole sneered, sarcasm and irritation rife in his voice.

"She's too naive to handle a man like Carrington."

"Would you take a look at her? She isn't your little

girl anymore. There's a beautiful woman hiding behind those jeans and chambray shirts. And she could do a lot worse than attracting Jeff Carrington's attention."

Ross's eyes turned frosty. "Your recommendation isn't a plus considering your track record with women, or with the rest of life for that matter."

"How would you know anything about me or my life? You haven't cared about me for years. I have a degree in veterinary medicine, but you still can't see past a few indiscretions in my adolescence. As far as you're concerned, I'm still a disgrace to the family name," Cole said.

"A few indiscretions? You were arrested for felony car theft. You didn't choose to become a solid citizen around here. Until you prove yourself to the people who knew you when, your bad record will stand with this community."

Typical, Hope thought, tuning out yet another spate of cross words. Within seconds of being in the same room, her father and brother were once again at each other's throats. Be careful what you wish for, Aunt Meg always said.

Hope had wanted her brother to come back to Laurel Glen, and now, after years away, he had. But nothing had changed. Ross and Cole's animosity toward each other hadn't faded with time as she'd hoped. Since Cole arrived home two weeks ago, being in the company of father and son was like walking through a mine field. Any subject was likely to spark an explosion. It was tiring, to say the least.

She glanced at Aunt Meg, who had lost interest in her hot cereal. The older woman's disgusted expression seemed to say, "Run for the hills. They're at it again."

Both her aunt and Hope had been through all this before. After Hope and Cole's mother was killed in a tragic accident, Aunt Meg had come back to Laurel Glen to live with them. Hope had been thirteen and Cole fifteen at the time. After Marley Taggert's death, the relationship between Ross and his son had disintegrated, and it had apparently continued along the same road in the last thirteen years since Cole left for military school at sixteen. Absence had not made their hearts grow fonder. Theirs no longer even looked like the love-hate relationship it had been back then.

Now it was all hate.

Hope stood. Cole had given her a lot to think about, and she wasn't about to get dragged into yet another argument. "Dad, since you didn't invite Jeff to the Valentine's Day party, I did," she interrupted, facing her father as he glared at Cole. "Jeff's coming as my date."

Ross's gaze swung to her. He was clearly stunned at first. "What? You know how I feel about that wastrel."

"He's *my* date. Not yours. I'm twenty-seven years old. Stop trying to pick my friends. *And* my clothes. *And* my hair style." Suddenly she didn't want to think about Cole's suggestion. She wanted to act on it and then some. "I've decided to buy a different dress than the one I wore last year. I'm going shopping."

Ross Taggert suddenly looked confused. "I helped

you pick out that nice blue dress. You always look so charming in it."

"I've worn it, what…three or four years running? And that's exactly why I want a new one." She looked from her father to Cole then back. "Please don't argue all day while I'm gone." Then on impulse she turned to Cole and leaned down to kiss his cheek. "Thanks. I'll think about the hair. Who knows, maybe a whole new me will come home."

She rushed out, trying not to think about Cole's chuckle and her father's strident tone rebuking her brother as a troublemaker. Aunt Meg was in for yet another tension-filled day. Hope wanted nothing more at that moment than to knock their heads together!

It was six o'clock when Hope crept up the back stairs. She entered her room and stared at the woman—the stranger—who stared back at her from the mirror over her dresser. She looked…

Panic invaded her heart. How could she have let them cut off her hair? Even though she'd donated her hair to Locks of Love, an organization that supplied wigs to juvenile cancer patients, she'd still cut it more to spite her father than to attract Jeff.

She sighed, knowing that she'd fallen once again into the same trap Cole had lived in for years. It had been happening more and more since Ross had refused her the job as head trainer three years ago. She'd taken a job with a competitor because her father had told her that no daughter of his was going to continue hanging around the stables with rough-and-tumble handlers for the rest of her life. To her, he'd been saying she would never be able to cut it in the job.

So she had taken the job at Lithum Creek Farm and had brought the mediocre stables up to and past the standards Ross Taggert had set for his own place. It had taken a year and a half, but one fine day Ross Taggert had come to her hat in hand. He'd begged her to leave her job and to come home. The job was hers—at an increased rate over what her current job paid. She'd agreed, but it took six months to hire and train a replacement. She'd been back home a year, and while he hadn't contradicted her in front of the men, they battled often about her decisions.

"Oh, excuse me, I was looking for Hope. Are you a friend of hers?" Hope heard Aunt Meg ask from behind.

Hope forced a smile and pivoted to face her aunt, who stood uncertainly in the doorway. "Hi, Aunt Meg."

"Oh, goodness gracious! Hope, what have you— "Oh, look at you!"

Hope's stomach rolled as she turned to do just that. She couldn't meet her aunt's eyes in the mirror. "You hate it. I look stupid, don't I? Go ahead. Tell me." Hope braced herself for the awful truth. "I saw an all-day spa and threw caution to the wind. I told them to create a whole new me. They took me at my word." She gestured to her outfit and the piles of bags on the bed. "They, uh, have a boutique. I look like I'm playing dress-up. Jeff's probably going to laugh at me."

"Laugh? My dear, you are going to knock Jeffrey Carrington's socks off! Cole certainly knew what he was talking about. You are simply gorgeous."

Hope turned quickly to face Aunt Meg and was momentarily startled by the hair that swung across her cheek before it settled into its new bouncy do. She caught her reflection in the full-length cheval mirror across the room and walked to stand in front of it.

"He was right?" Hope examined each feature of the woman in the mirror. "Cole was right," she repeated, but this time she was certain that the woman in the mirror was her—part of her that she'd always denied.

"You can never say your brother doesn't know women," Meg said sardonically.

"I was hiding, wasn't I?"

"I'd say so. Do you know why you were?" Aunt Meg asked.

"I was about to ask myself the same thing. Dad. He was so convinced a woman couldn't do my job, so I buried this part of me. I see why Cole thinks I've tried to take his place. I've been so busy trying to earn Dad's respect that I haven't been all I can be for me. I like looking like this. Dressing like this."

"Well, now, that's a start. It's okay to be beautiful, Hope. The Lord gave you your beauty."

"Mom was beautiful. Do you think Dad sees her in me? Does this hurt him?"

"I don't know what's in his heart. I wasn't here much during his marriage to your mother. And he won't talk about her even now, but I can tell you that you don't look at all like your mother. You look like my mother. Ross may have forgotten you're a woman, since you've always done work he considers traditionally male, but I don't see how he won't see it now. I'm sure he'll be proud of the lovely woman who is his daughter. And now that you see how much fun it can be, maybe I can drag you away to go shopping once in a while."

Hope grinned at her tall, willowy aunt. "I didn't get the new dress, after all. How about one night this week?"

Meg grinned in answer. "So show me all you *did* buy."

Hope got excited all over again. There was a bag full of all the things the makeup technician used to give Hope's face the look of classic beauty. She'd bought bath salts and body cream and perfume all in the same scent. She couldn't wait to soak in a nice tub instead of her usual hurried shower. According to the consultant who'd guided her through her startling remake, nothing makes you feel like a woman more than soaking in acres of bubbles and gallons of scented water. And Hope had put off womanhood long enough.

Two weeks later, Hope put the finishing touches on her makeup. Then she slipped on and buckled her new sandals. She stood in the three-inch heels then walked to the mirror and pirouetted in the middle of the floor, laughing and thinking of Jeff.

Tall and golden, Jeffrey Carrington had been the object of her love in one capacity or another from her earliest memories. Oh, sometimes when they were younger his teasing and pat-her-on-the-head mentality had pushed her to find ways to torture him as only a best friend's little sister can. But it had always been because, deep in her heart, she adored him.

A knock on her door interrupted her thoughts. "Hope, the guests are nearly all here," her father called through the door.

"Oh. Sorry. I'll be right down," she called back and checked herself one last time in the mirror. Unnecessarily, she smoothed the floor-length emerald silk sheath that she and Aunt Meg had found at a boutique, then she reached up to finger the emerald and diamond choker, a family heirloom left to Aunt Meg. She'd insisted Hope wear it the moment she'd seen Hope in the dress.

Please, Lord. Let him see me. Really see me this time.

Hope took one last deep breath and stepped into the hall. Strains of an old love song drifted up the gracefully curved stairs of the central foyer. She had just about reached the middle of the sweeping staircase when Cole opened the front door to admit a golden couple.

The man, tall and heart-stoppingly handsome, turned toward her, and Hope gasped. Jeff had arrived. With a date. Before she could retreat, Jeff glanced up at her and stared.

Hope sought out Cole with her gaze as tears stung the back of her throat. When she found him, she mentally begged him to rescue her from her frozen stance on the stairs. She blinked away telltale moisture collecting in her eyes. She refused to cry in front of Elizabeth Boyer and Jeffrey Carrington.

Unfortunately, Jeff was two steps ahead of Cole in reaching the bottom of the stairs.

"Hope?" he said, looking at her, his voice sounding a bit odd. "You— You're—"

"I'm Hope. You got it in one, sport," she said just a tad too sharply. She took the next step and then the next till she stood gazing into his darkened gray eyes. She forced a smile, determined to brazen her way through this. "You remember me, Carrington. Bane of your existence. Oft times voice of your unused conscience. Pick your chin up off the floor. You're staring."

"And drooling," Cole growled and stepped to her side. "Come dance with me, sister mine, before everyone tries to steal you away."

Cole directed her toward the band and the nearly empty dance floor. A few years earlier the caterer had come up with an ingenious way to temporarily cover and heat the stone terraces. The candle- and moonlit dance floor was now a Valentine's Day tradition in the area. On the air was the perfume of hundreds of flowers that had been placed about the perimeter of the room, twined around the myriad candelabra and arranged in beribboned clusters that surrounded the stage.

"Are you all right?" Cole whispered.

"Other than feeling like an utter fool, you mean? I'll live. I'm tough. Hasn't Daddy told you how strong and unshakable I am?"

"Sorry to destroy the legend, but right now you're quaking like a California fault line."

"Don't let the watery eyes fool you. That's pure rage you're feeling."

"Nice try, kitten, but I saw your face when you realized he wasn't here alone."

She dropped her forehead into the hollow of Cole's shoulder. "Oh, no. Tell me he didn't see."

"No. And don't worry. He isn't leaving here tonight without the imprint of my fist somewhere on his aristocratic person."

Hope looked up, and her startled gaze locked with his. "Don't you dare! I probably wasn't clear about my invitation. I was really nervous. I shouldn't have been so vague. I should have remembered how totally dense he is about me. I don't need you to fight my battles for me. Besides, if he doesn't already know what he's done, I certainly don't want him to."

"I'll make a deal with you. You don't tell me how to be a big brother, and I won't tell you how to be a little sister. There are some perks that come with each position." He wagged his straight eyebrows at her comically, making Hope laugh aloud. "Don't spoil my fun. I've missed a lot of brothering over the years. You okay now?"

Hope nodded. "Thanks for the rescue, big brother. I'm fine."

"Good, because the first in a horde of men is about to sweep you away. Hi, there, Hal. You here to ask permission to horn in on my date with this beautiful creature?"

"I certainly am. Hello, Hope."

Hope nearly groaned. Harold Pendergrass had been following her around like a puppy since junior high. Why couldn't she fall in love with him instead of a man who saw her as a sister?

What have I been thinking all these years? Jeff Carrington asked himself as he absently guided Elizabeth through the gallery toward the heated terrace where the band had set up.

He'd always insisted that Hope was the little sister his busy parents had never gotten around to providing him. And then he'd stepped inside Laurel House's foyer tonight, and his illusions had dissolved like mist in the sunshine.

As Jeff stepped through the French doors, he caught sight of Hope laughing at Cole and was relieved to see that she was only dancing with her brother. Why he felt relief he wasn't sure, and the bigger mystery was why he felt even more tense at the same time. It was the kind of tension you feel when you realize your life is about to change and you're powerless to stop it.

What he felt when he looked at Hope bore no resemblance to anything he'd feel for a sibling. His feelings were most unbrotherly and troubling.

"Am I imagining something or did something monumental just happen back there?" Elizabeth asked, dragging Jeff back from his dizzying thoughts.

Jeff shook his head and grinned. "Don't be silly."

"So Hope Taggert's new look didn't just knock you

for a loop?" She grinned knowingly. "And you aren't silently thanking your lucky stars that I came here on a mission of mercy to rescue Cole from the old biddies we both know are lining up to pick him apart?"

"You're as big a pain in the neck as Hope. You know that?"

"Ah, but when I emerged from the chrysalis several years ago, you never looked at me the way you did Hope just now in the foyer."

Jeff swallowed. Had he been that obvious? "I was...surprised."

"You always were a master of understatement. She didn't look happy to see me. You did tell her I was coming along, didn't you?"

Jeff shook his head, wondering what difference it made. "Not with my flight getting canceled yesterday. I barely got in the house in time to shower and dress. Besides, Hope wants what's best for Cole, and having you at his side will make tonight easier for him. You play along, and I'll charm us into being with the right partners. Cole won't have any idea we're taking pity on him."

Jeff watched as Cole turned Hope over to Hal Pendergrass, and from the moon-eyed expression on the other man's face, his feeling for Hope hadn't changed a bit. Jeff grinned, wondering if Hope would wind up kicking her perpetual admirer in the shins the way she had in eighth grade. The grin faded when Hope smiled and slid easily into the other man's arms.

Jeff mentally catalogued the feeling that arrowed

through him. Jealousy. He didn't want Hope dancing. At least not with anyone but him.

"Tell your lady friend you'll be right back. We're about to have a little talk," Cole said as he stepped up behind Jeff.

Jeff excused himself to Elizabeth and followed Cole. He hated scenes, and Cole looked annoyed. And because Cole had once been his best friend before the distance between Pennsylvania and California had thinned the bonds. They'd managed to meet up from time to time over the thirteen years since Cole left. Whenever Jeff was competing near where Cole lived, they made a point to get together, but it wasn't the same. As they turned the corner of the stone terrace, moving between one heated tent room to the next, Cole rounded on him and drove the breath out of him with a solid punch to his midsection.

"Oof." He gasped, then drew in a breath that was a great deal more painful than the previous one.

"Ouch," Cole said, shaking his hand in the air. "What are you doing, working out every day?"

"The Summer Olympics are this summer. Of course I am. Before I return the favor, you mind telling me what that was for?"

"It was for being a dense idiot and hurting my sister. There's more where that came from if you do it again. If you don't care about her, the least you could have done was let her down easily. You didn't have to tell her how little you care by showing up with Miss Moneybags back there."

Jeff blinked, rubbing his sore ribs. "What are you talking about?"

"Hope asked you here as *her* date, nitwit. Do you know how much trouble she's gone through for you? She even cut her hair!"

Jeff stared at Cole in horror and thought back to the phone call. In spite of feeling lower than a snake, Jeff was oddly buoyed suddenly. "She cut her hair for me?"

"Yeah. Wipe that stupid grin off your face, or have you forgotten that you showed up with a date?"

Jeff lost the grin and groaned. He'd never meant to hurt Hope. He'd not only been dense about his feelings, but hers, as well. When he'd come in and looked at her, he'd instantly wished he'd come alone. But that had been before he'd realized who the vision was who stood staring at him from above. Hope was his friend, his confidante, his touchstone. And she was lovely.

And he'd been a blind fool.

"She called me at my hotel in L.A. and asked if I'd be back in time for the party since she hadn't gotten my RSVP. I said that as far as I knew I hadn't been invited. Nothing's changed, by the way. Ross still doesn't like me. I said as much when she asked me to come tonight. She said I'd be her special guest. I swear, Cole, I had no idea she meant as her date. I don't even know what I'd have said back then if I'd realized what she was asking."

"How about now?"

"Now I'd have been the one asking. I'm an idiot. No wonder I haven't been able to find the woman for me.

I couldn't see the forest for the trees. She's been right in front of me all along."

"And when did you have this great epiphany?" Cole asked.

Jeff heard Cole's skepticism. "When I looked up and I realized my best friend and baby sister wasn't my sister at all."

"Then it might be a good idea if you asked her to dance *before* you dance with—what's her name?"

"Her name is Elizabeth Boyer. She's Reggie Boyer's daughter. You know, my coach. Don't you remember her?"

Cole frowned, and Jeff knew a mental image of Elizabeth as his friend had last seen her must have sharpened in Cole's mind. "The pudgy carrottop with the freckles and teeth? No way."

"Yes, way."

"She was a sixteen-year-old boy's worst nightmare." Cole searched out the woman in question. "And she's every twenty-nine-year-old's fantasy."

"Then you'd be interested in keeping her company? In fact, why not take over for me tonight? I'll tell Hope I brought her along for you and that you both misunderstood my intentions."

Cole nodded. "I think I could make the sacrifice for my sister. But what about Elizabeth? I've hurt enough women in the last few years. Her heart isn't engaged, is it?"

Jeff shook his head. As she said earlier, he'd never seen her as more than his coach's daughter. But he couldn't tell Cole the truth of why he'd brought Elizabeth. He had to be more subtle than that. If Cole had one failing it was that he had too much pride. "We're just friends. Her father's my coach, remember? Explain to her what's going on and she'll understand."

Cole arched an eyebrow and grinned. "I'll consider that your blessing, in that case." Then the smile faded and his eyes turned cold. "Hurt my sister again, Carrington, and you'll wish you'd never been born."

He'd never seen Cole more deadly serious. "You don't have to worry," Jeff assured him, and turned away. Just then, he caught sight of Hope whirling in someone's arms and his thoughts turned back to her and the evening ahead. He knew he was grinning like an idiot and he didn't care who saw.

She'd cut her hair for him.

Chapter Two

Jeff stopped short. Hope was dancing with Ross Taggert. If he asked her now, Ross might cause a scene and embarrass both him and Hope.

"If you're going to let my father stop you, you may as well collect Elizabeth now and step out of my sister's life," Cole murmured from behind him.

"He hates me, and I've never known why."

"I think you remind him of my mother's social set, and he wants to keep you away from his precious little girl."

"That can't be right. Your father adored your mother. Everyone knows how he still grieves for her."

"You think so?" Cole snapped. "Believe me, appearances can be deceiving. The song's just about over. Go on. Go claim your date. Think of it as really getting his goat if it helps."

Jeff turned to Cole. When they'd talked last, Hope had said the bitterness between Cole and Ross was even worse. It was sad, but Jeff understood more than most. His relationship with his own late father hadn't been the best.

"I'll try not to hurt Hope, Cole, but don't you hurt her, either. You have no idea how responsible she's always felt for the rift between you and Ross. Stop using her. You did it before, and you're still doing it now. So is your father."

Leaving Cole gaping, Jeff pivoted and approached Hope and Ross. They stepped away from each other as the song ended, but Ross kept hold of her hand.

"I hate to admit it, but Cole was right about cutting your hair. You're beautiful. I never realized how much you look like my mother," Ross was saying as Jeff stepped next to him.

"For once we agree on something, Ross," Jeff said. Though he spoke to the father, Jeff's couldn't take his eyes off the daughter. "She certainly is a beautiful woman. I was hoping I could have the next dance. There's a misunderstanding we need to clear up."

Hope smiled but, in her bottomless blue eyes, Jeff saw how deep a hurt he'd caused her.

"What about Elizabeth?" she asked. "You haven't even danced with her."

So she'd noticed. "Elizabeth *is* the misunderstanding," he told Hope, taking her hand. He turned her away from her father and into his arms, where Jeff was beginning to believe she just might belong. Now that she stood in his embrace, he wondered why he'd never noticed the way her nearness affected him. The only time he was ever truly happy when he was with her, he realized. And even Cole hadn't been as good a friend as she was. There was almost nothing he could not or would not share with her. He felt a helpless grin tip his lips up at the corners. He even loved arguing with her. Her mind was quick, her heart fierce and her spirit pure. And he vowed at that moment that she would be his.

"What's this about a misunderstanding?" Hope asked.

Her question yanked him out of his thoughts. "Oh. Elizabeth is Cole's date, not mine. I thought it might make tonight easier for him if he had a lovely woman on his arm. One who's also well accepted in the community. When he left, he wasn't high on everyone's list."

Hope blinked, then gave Jeff a sad smile. "I never thought of you as dishonest. It's always been one of your more redeeming qualities."

Jeff winced. "I'm sorry. That was a half truth. I also misunderstood your invitation," he admitted. "But I really did bring her for Cole. When she came to L.A. to visit her father last week, we got to talking about tonight and Cole. It really will be better for him if Elizabeth is with him. This community isn't going to let him off the hook too easily." Jeff hesitated and grinned at Hope. It was something that had been getting him out of hot water with women since he noticed they were a different gender. He only wished he knew why. "You aren't going to desert me now that I gave away my dance partner, are you?"

Hope arched one of her delicately defined eyebrows,

as if to say, Haven't you learned not to try that with me yet? She said, "I'll think about it."

Jeff felt an unfamiliar jolt. "You don't believe me."

"Take it or leave it, Carrington."

Jeff forced himself to relax. It would be fine. He would just have to charm her into forgiving him. Piece of cake. Undaunted, he grinned at Hope. "Then I guess the night's mine."

But when she brought her gaze to his, with a knowing look in her eyes, he realized two things. He was probably in love, and if he was then he was in big trouble. Hope was one tough cookie under the soft new look, and nothing where she was concerned would ever be a piece of cake.

The flowers arrived just as Hope and Aunt Meg came downstairs on their way to church the next morning. "Where on earth did he find a florist to deliver on a Sunday?" Aunt Meg asked as Hope closed the door after the delivery boy.

"He who? We don't even know who they're from. They could be from Harold Pendergrass."

Aunt Meg arched one thin eyebrow. "My dear, I know a besotted fool from a besotted man. Those are from Jeffrey, believe me."

Hope opened the card and chuckled at the inscription.

"Don't torture your auntie this early in the morning. Read it. Unless it's too personal, that is."

"It isn't all that personal. Just a little embarrassing.

'Sorry we got our wires crossed. Thanks for a wonderful night. Lunkhead Carrington.'"

"See, I told you. What kind of flowers? Come on. Open. Open," Aunt Meg urged.

Hope untied the satin ribbon to uncover a dozen white roses. "Oh. They're so delicate," Hope whispered, carefully touching the fragrant blooms.

"*And* out of the ordinary. Harold would have done red and sent them tomorrow. You see the difference? I think you picked a winner."

"Last night Jeff took pity on two very hard up friends."

"Let me tell you, the look on Jeffrey Carrington's face when he looked at you all night had nothing to do with pity and everything to do with possession. Didn't you notice an immediate lack of dance partners after he whisked you away from your father, when before that there was a steady stream of them?"

"Well, yes." Hope smiled. "You think he really wanted to be with me, after all?"

Aunt Meg took the flowers and handed Hope her coat, then she gave the roses to the housekeeper, who crossed the foyer at that moment. "Sally, please put these in that Waterford vase I picked up at auction last month, then put them in Hope's room."

"Good idea," Hope said. "That way Daddy won't see them. May as well avoid one argument." She sighed. "Remember when it was quiet and peaceful around here?"

Aunt Meg stared at her for a long moment. "Not since you set your sights on Howard Sothsbie's position when he was approaching retirement. Cole's livened things up more than is comfortable, but peaceful? Before? You should be on the sidelines." She flipped her cape over her shoulders in a typical dramatic Meg Taggert move. "We're off to church now, Sally dear. Thank you for taking care of the flowers." She turned and strode through the front door, her cape flying in the winter breeze.

Hope shrugged and followed her aunt outside. She finally caught up with the fifty-year-old dynamo as Meg slid behind the wheel of her silver BMW.

"We need to have a chat, my darling," Aunt Meg said as she turned the key in the ignition, then put the car in gear. "I sent those flowers to your room so you would have them to dream on. You cannot retreat to the old Hope. You took a stand with Ross and you have to hold your ground."

"You make this sound like a battle."

Meg grinned. "It is. As you learned when you quit Laurel Glen and started working for Lithum Creek Farm, peace at any price isn't worth it."

Hope turned in her seat to face Meg. "But there's so much tension already right now. You're getting a case of indigestion with every meal."

Meg chuckled, her marvelous voice dipping low. She sometimes reminded Hope of a Christian Auntie Mame. "Let me worry about my digestion. I could stand to lose a few pounds. I'll let it be known when I've had enough. My point is...well, look at this thing between Cole and

Ross. Yes, it has been relatively peaceful around here these past thirteen years but the bitterness between them has gone way beyond where it was when Cole left to finish high school at sixteen. You see? Our peace wasn't worth the price of the hatred they show each other now."

"You're saying by avoiding a clash over Jeff now, it could make it worse later. But I'm still not even sure there will be a later. He could very well have been being kind."

"Let me tell you about men staking out their territory when a woman catches their eye. It's an unmistakable expression that few men miss when it's aimed at them. And your Jeff wore it all night after he claimed that first dance. Are you going to hide your relationship from Ross?"

"I don't want to, but I don't want to cause more friction right now. You saw him shooting daggers at Jeff all night. Can you imagine the arguments Cole and Dad will get into if I toss another thing for them to disagree about into the mix? You saw what my stupid haircut caused."

"I understand, but if you start sneaking around, Jeff will soon see that he isn't first in your heart. He's never been first with anyone in his whole life but Emily Roberts, and she's been on the payroll since before he was born. You have the power to change that young man's life and touch his soul. Use that power carefully. And don't make this too easy on him. A little groveling will be just as good for his soul. He has to work to get you."

Meg flipped down the vanity mirror in front of Hope and tapped it to draw her attention to the new woman reflected there. It still surprised Hope after two weeks when she caught sight of herself in a mirror.

"And the reason he has to work to get you is that you, my dear, are a prize worthy of a bit of questing!"

Friday dawned as one of those rare February days that teases the senses with its promise of spring. It was a warm sunny fifty-five degrees, and since there'd been little rain or snow, the fields weren't muddy. It was the perfect day for a ride, which was only one of the reasons Hope was so elated.

Jeff had once again sent flowers and had once again apologized for their mix-up. He'd called every day to ask her to do something with him. Taking Meg's advice, she'd made excuses that she knew he was bright enough to figure out were just that. But this time he'd begged her to go riding with him. He'd sounded desperate, and she couldn't hold out the full week Meg had suggested. She'd invited him to come over to ride with her. He'd agreed in a heartbeat but had sounded surprised that she invited him to come there. Meg was apparently right about letting Jeff know she'd stand up to her father over him.

A shoo-in for the United States Olympic Equestrian team and a possible gold medalist, Jeff had already ridden his mount early that morning in the practice ring, so he'd agreed to ride one of Laurel Glen's mounts that needed exercise. She had both horses saddled and ready to go by the time she saw the roof of Jeff's black four-by-four gleaming in the sun as it moved quickly along the drive toward the stables.

Dressed in tan riding pants and a hunter green jacket, he jumped out of the four-by-four and reached in for his riding helmet. Hope felt at ease in the riding outfit Meg had found for her. For once she wasn't hideously under-dressed in jeans and an old tweed blazer. Jeff, his eyes sparkling in the sunlight, didn't comment on the change in her normal dress.

"What a day!" he called to her.

Hope jumped off the fence where she'd perched to wait for him, trying to look casual but feeling anything but.

"I know it's just an aberration but I swear there's spring in the air," she said, praying she sounded as if this were just a day like any other.

"So, who did you give me?" he asked as she fell in step next to him.

As they made their way toward the stone stables and the paddock where she'd left the saddled horses, he settled his arm across her shoulders and tucked her against his side. Hope felt her heart pick up its already too quick beat. She knew in that moment that this was anything but just another ride with a friend. It was the beginning of something wonderful.

"Golden Boy or Ross's Prize," she answered around the lump in her throat.

Jeff stopped in his tracks, then stepped in front of her, taking her shoulders in his strong, gentle hands. Her heart was pounding by the time she gathered her composure enough to look into his silvery eyes. They were narrowed and grave as he spoke. "Hope, your father would have a fit if I rode Prize, and you know it."

"He said both of them needed exercise. Which one would you rather ride?"

"Prize," Jeff admitted and grinned, however reluctantly.

She took his hand and pulled him along, and a carefree excitement seemed to shimmer in the air. "Then let's mount up and get at it. We're wasting the warmth of the day. This weather won't last long."

They were on their way in seconds, and Hope lost most of her nervousness. This was Jeff. Her pal. Her friend. His laughter rang out as they put the horses through their paces, taking fences and hedgerows and riding rings around each other.

Hope made it a practice to sit back and watch him ride. He thought she was helping him perfect his form, but often she just watched the beauty of him in motion, so attuned to his mount—even a strange one—that they moved as one. She pulled Golden Boy to a halt at the top of a hill that afforded a view of both Laurel Glen and Lavender Hill, Jeff's estate and breeding farm.

He and Prize took the last hedge and charged up the hill after her. "How was that?" he called on his way up.

"Perfect. You're really ready this time."

"I hope so. I don't know if I want to be doing this in another four years."

Hope nodded and looked around. "I love this view.

Have you thought any more about getting Lavender Hill up and running again as a full-service farm?"

Jeff's smile turned sad. "You mean other than that Father and Mother are already spinning in their graves because I'm breeding stock?"

"How long are you going to go on trying to please them? You went to the college you did because it was what they expected. You joined that stupid snooty fraternity because it was the right one to join. Sometimes I think the only reason you're working so hard for the Olympics is that it gives you a blue-blooded excuse to ride. They're gone, Jeff. You don't have to win their notice by living your life in their *right way* any more."

Jeff narrowed his gray eyes beneath the velvet peak of his helmet. "Well, you're back at home again."

Hope nodded. "But I made Dad come after me and beg me to come back. And he had to give me a raise. I've always been faithful to the Lord, much to my father's annoyance. And I did invite you to the Valentine's Party." She grinned. "And you're on his favorite horse right now."

"Prize is incredible, by the way. I wish Ross had sold him to me. I'd be a shoo-in at the trials with him."

"You're a shoo-in anyway. Mr. March is a wonderfully trained animal."

Jeff grimaced comically. "I still can't believe I let you talk me into naming him that."

Hope laughed. "It'll keep you humble when you're on the podium wearing that gold medal. They'll be playing the national anthem and you'll be thinking about how to explain his name to the reporters."

Jeff stared at her, suddenly serious. "Why am I riding Ross's Prize, Hope?"

Hope knew what he was asking. Her heart pounded. Jeff had always wanted a chance to ride Prize, and saddling him had been a conscious decision on her part. The answer he sought was a telling one. She took a deep breath and plunged ahead. "Because this was a good way to show my father who I'd choose if I'm forced to make a choice between you and him. Considering your parents, I thought maybe you needed to know that."

"I did need to know that because—" he began, but Hope was suddenly nervous. If Jeff felt as she did, their relationship would change forever and there would be no going back. She wheeled Golden Boy away and downhill.

Hope would never know what Jeff had intended to say. As he followed her over the first hedge, the world went instantly insane. She watched it happen as if it were in slow motion while recognizing that time was moving full speed ahead. Prize left the ground with Jeff in perfect position, but then, in the next split second, the saddle broke loose and Jeff was falling backward. A look of surprise and consternation crossed his features, but that quickly changed. He landed on his back on the hard-packed soil, and his face contorted in pain. Then he went slack and still.

Hope was at his side without remembering her dismount or falling to her knees. "Jeff!" she shouted, but he didn't respond. She looked toward the cluster of buildings half a mile away then at him lying broken on the ground. She had no choice but to leave him there. He needed help. And he needed it now.

Ross's Prize had bolted as soon as Jeff hit the ground, but he wasn't headed for the stables, so no one would know there was a problem. Harry Donovan was about to mount up when Hope galloped into the main yard. There were several other workers standing around "Call nine-one-one," she shouted to no one in particular. "Jeff was thrown. He's unconscious. Send the ambulance to the first rise above the eastern paddocks."

The farm foreman frowned as he pulled out a cell phone. "You let Jeffrey Carrington ride Ross's Prize?"

"And he's running loose. I have to get back to Jeff." Hope wheeled away and thundered up the hill, Donovan bringing up the rear. She didn't want Jeff coming to alone and trying to get up. It would be up to the paramedics to say if it was safe for him to move.

But that didn't turn out to be a problem, because he didn't come to at all. Not when the paramedics arrived, sirens screaming. Not when they carefully rolled him so they could strap him to a back board. Not when they called for the rescue helicopter, nor by the time it took off, leaving her to watch him fly off alone in the care of strangers.

His whole life, Jeff had been alone.

No one was up at Laurel House, so Hope left a message with Sally and drove to the hospital. Later she would realize that she didn't remember starting the car, or leaving Laurel Glen, or running into the emergency ward. The first thing she recalled was making a call to her church's prayer chain after being told Jeff was still unconscious. She asked the chain leader to find someone to go break the news and to stay with Mrs. Roberts, Lavender Hill's longtime housekeeper and the only real mother Jeff had ever known.

Then Hope had time to think. And to place blame. And that blame was all hers. When the paramedics had arrived, she'd picked up the saddle to get it out of their way and had been appalled by the condition of the girth. She'd stared in horror at the cracked and broken leather and the buckles still attached to the saddle. How, she asked herself over and over, had she missed such a danger when she'd saddled Prize for Jeff?

She paced and paced, going over and over that morning in her mind. But she'd been so excited by the flowers and his eagerness to ride with her. And nervous. She'd been keyed up and distracted. Had she been so distracted that she hadn't obeyed safety rules? How could she have let herself forget to check the condition of the tack?

She just didn't know.

At some point, Hope realized she had her fist so tightly clenched that her nails had scraped her palm raw. She went to wash her hands, fully aware of the danger of abrasions when working around animals. The burning sensation subsided some, but that left her with only her fears for Jeff and her guilt to haunt and consume her once again.

She found herself at a bank of windows staring at the sky. *Lord, please watch over Jeff and keep him safe. I love him. I know You would rather I love another believer, but that isn't going to happen. I've tried to put my feelings for him aside, but I guess I've loved Jeff too long to stop. My dream has always been to show him Your salvation, but I can't do that if You let him die. Please give him back to me.*

"Hope?" Cole called as he strode into the waiting room. "What happened?" he asked as he gathered her in his arms. "Manuel said Jeff fell off Prize. That's ridiculous. Jeff rides like he's glued to the saddle."

"The saddle came off and Jeff with it. I still can't believe it. We were up on the rise between the two properties standing still and talking. Then we rode downhill, and when he took the first hedgerow, Jeff was suddenly flying backward and so was the saddle. He hit hard and he's been out since, as far as I know. They won't tell me anything because I'm not family. But Cole, he hasn't got any family, and I need to know. Someone should be with him."

Cole squeezed her shoulders. "Sit down and try to relax. I'll see what I can do."

Cole sauntered up to the young nurse at the desk and leaned on the tall counter, curling his ringless left hand over the edge about two feet in front of her face. "Hi, there. I wonder if you could help me." He beamed his best lady-killer smile at her.

She sent back what he was sure was her best come-hither grin and leaned a bit forward trying to show off her considerable cleavage. Cole was immune to the whole dating game, but she couldn't know that.

"I can sure try." She all but purred the words. "What can I do for you?"

"I understand you have Jeffrey Carrington here. I'd like a report on his condition. I'm Dr. Cole Taggert."

He could have sworn dollar signs flashed in her eyes. "Certainly, Doctor. Meet me at those double doors. I'll let you in."

Cole turned and winked at Hope, then approached the doors behind which he was sure Jeff was being treated. They swung open, and he followed the nurse to a big central desk where an Asian man in a lab coat and scrubs scribbled in an illegible script in a steel chart.

"Dr. Chin, this is Dr. Cole Taggert," the nurse said. "He's here about Mr. Carrington. Dr. Taggert, this is Dr. Chin, chief of neurology here at Paoli Memorial."

The man stood and stretched out his hand. "Pleasure to meet you, Doctor."

Nothing like a little professional courtesy, Cole thought as he accepted the chart. He'd never understand why medical doctors couldn't master simple penmanship. He'd have been drummed out of veterinary school for handwriting like this. He handed it back. "Uh, I'm afraid I flunked illegible scrawl one-oh-one. Could you catch me up on my friend's condition? He has no family but is about to become engaged to my sister."

"Ah. This is personal for you, then. All right. We've ruled out brain injury. He was conscious for a while but we had to sedate him rather heavily when he became agitated over his condition. From what I can see from my exam and the MRI, there is some compression of the spinal cord at L-five S-one, which has produced paralysis, loss of some feeling and weakness of the lower extremities."

Cole was instantly glad he hadn't pretended to be Jeff's doctor. He'd never have been able to hide his reaction. He could feel the blood drain from his head. "He's paralyzed?"

Chin pursed his lips, then nodded and went on clinically describing what in effect was the end of all Jeff's Olympic dreams and then some. "As you know, there have been considerable breakthroughs in the treatment of spinal cord injury. His condition could improve quickly or with time and work, but he didn't seem to hear me say that. What function he has in six months will tell us how well he'll recover. We've given him a corticosteroid to reduce the swelling and minimize further damage."

"So we wait and see?"

Dr. Chin frowned. "He'll need extensive therapy, of course."

"I'd appreciate it if my sister could be with him. As I said, Jeff's all alone but for her and his staff. Also it might help to realize that until today Jeff was a shoo-in for not only a spot on the U.S. Olympic Equestrian team but for a gold medal, as well."

Chin nodded. "I can understand why he was so devastated. I'll see that your sister has liberal access to him. He'll be sent upstairs at any minute to the fourth floor. Room four-oh-eight. You might want to take your sister up there to wait for him." The doctor smiled. "So what is your speciality, or are you in general practice?"

Cole grimaced. Granny Taggert's training was inconvenient at the worst times. "My speciality? Equine surgery, actually. I'd better get back to my sister. Thanks for your help."

The doctor's soft laughter didn't lighten Cole's heart in the least as he made his way to the automatic doors at the end of the corridor. This wasn't going to be easy. He didn't know where he'd find the words to destroy Hope's world.

She ran toward him when he exited the treatment area. "How is he?"

"Come on. Let's sit down." Cole took her by the arm and directed her to a chair in the waiting room. She sank bonelessly into it and looked at him, her blue eyes awash with tears.

"He's dead, isn't he?"

Cole squatted and took her hands. "No, kitten, but he's got some big problems."

Her voice shook. "What kind of problems?"

There was no easy way to say it. "He's paralyzed."

"No. Oh, no. I can't believe I did this to him. It's all my fault. I invited him. I missed the damaged girth."

"Don't, Hope. It could just as easily have been a car accident."

"But it wasn't."

Cole's cell phone rang and he reached for it. "Hold on a second, kitten. This is from Laurel Glen." He pushed the talk button. "Hello?"

"It's me," his father said. "Where are you and what's all this about that boneheaded Carrington riding Prize and getting dumped off? Some Olympic contender."

Cole gritted his teeth. "I'm with Hope at the hospital. Jeff's not good. It looks as if he's paralyzed. We don't know how permanent that is yet." Cole's eyes widened at his father's language. "Dad!"

"Sorry. Tell Hope I'm sorry he was hurt."

That didn't sound as if he intended to come to the hospital. Cole looked at Hope, who sat staring ahead, tears rolling down her cheeks. She needed her father, not a brother who'd been gone for thirteen years. "What time do you expect to get here?"

"I don't," Ross Taggert snapped. "Something's wrong with Prize and I need you to look at him. He's hurt and in considerable pain."

"It's probably because he was balanced for a hundred and ninety pounds of rider and tack that suddenly went airborne before he landed. I hate to leave Hope here alone."

"Well, don't expect me to go there," Ross Taggert snapped. "If she hadn't let him ride my horse without my permission, none of this would have happened."

Cole gripped the phone tighter, annoyed by his

father's attitude and worried about Hope and Jeff. He felt torn. "I'll come home, but I'm heading back here as soon as I get a look at Prize." He disconnected, not waiting for a reply, and hunkered down in front of Hope. "Listen, when they found Prize, he was hurt. I'll be back as soon as I get a look at him and take care of whatever's wrong."

"Isn't Daddy coming?" Hope asked Cole as he clipped the cell phone to his belt.

Cole glanced at his watch. "Uh, no. He said he's sorry Jeff's hurt."

"He's not sorry. He hates Jeff. I'd like you to give him a message for me. Tell him what I told Jeff earlier today. If Dad forces me to choose between him and Jeff, Dad loses."

Chapter Three

The first thing Jeff saw when the fog in his brain lifted was Hope's lovely face. She was staring at him as if trying to will him awake. He was glad to grant her wish. "Hi, there," he said, then frowned. Why did he sound so woozy?

"Hi, yourself. You gave us all a terrible scare. But it's all going to be fine now. We'll get you well."

He remembered then. He'd been about to tell Hope how he felt about her when she'd gotten all skittish and taken Golden Boy downhill. He'd followed, but then during a perfectly routine jump, the world had dropped out from beneath him. He didn't even remember hitting the ground. Just a feeling of dizziness as he slid backward when he should have been flying over the jump on Prize's back.

And he remembered Hope screaming his name.

How, he wondered, could life change so drastically in a few seconds? His life was gone—over. He might as well be dead.

"What happened?" he asked, nearly desperate to hear it confirmed by the person who'd shared so life-ending an event.

"Prize took the hedge and the saddle broke away. I can't remember it being at all damaged when I tightened the girth." Hope bit her lip, clearly fighting tears. "I'm so sorry," she whispered brokenly.

He wanted to tell her not to feel responsible. That accidents happened. He wanted to tell her to go home and get on with her life, but his eyes grew heavy again, and soon he was floating away from her to a place where he could still fly over the fields and laugh with her as they rode.

Jeff opened his eyes some time later and stared at the green ceiling. Who on earth had had the poor taste to paint a bedroom institutional green? The clatter of a cart drew his attention and he watched, detached from his body, as a young woman walked to his bed. Without ceremony she stuck a needle in an IV tube.

He frowned, remembering. He was in the hospital. In some sort of weird bed with rings at the bottom and top attached to some sort of framework that surrounded him. He couldn't move his legs, and some fool had kept him alive. "Too much," he told the nurse, though his lips and tongue felt numb.

"This is just a muscle relaxer to keep your back from going into spasms again. Don't worry. It won't hurt you and it shouldn't knock you out."

"No. You don't get it. Give me too much. Kill me. Got it?"

He heard a gasp from the foot of the bed and found Hope staring at him in horror. His heart constricted. She was still there. She'd heard.

He'd drag her down with him. His life was clearly over, and he couldn't stand to let this thing destroy Hope the way it had him.

"Go away, Hope. There's no need for you to sit there and watch me lying here. From what Dr. Chin said, this is about as exciting as I'm ever going to get."

"Of course, it isn't."

Hope hurried to his side and took his hand. He wanted to feel her touch into eternity. It was such a temptation to tie her to him, but he couldn't do that to the free spirit that was Hope. She'd been crying. It was blatantly obvious. He hated the thought of her tears almost as much as the forced smile she tried to hide them with.

"And you say *I'm* a poor liar," he challenged.

"I'm serious. You're going to be out of that bed in no time. There's no way yet to know how much you'll improve when the swelling decreases. I'm not leaving you. And Cole was here earlier, too, but there was some sort of emergency at home. He'll be back as soon as he can get here."

"Tell him not to bother. He has better things to do than waste his time on me."

"Don't be silly. Cole is your friend. Where else would he be when you need him? Where else would *I* be?"

"I'd prefer you be anywhere else." Remembering how badly he'd done at lying to her on Saturday night, he turned his head. "Look, Hope, when the horse reared, I was about to tell you that you were barking up the wrong tree with your feelings for me. You're the little sister I never had. And a friend. But you'll never be more. I shouldn't have led you on at the Valentine's dance. But handing Elizabeth off to Cole was too big a break to pass up. I was doing him a favor getting them together, but Cole wouldn't have appreciated the gesture. Telling Cole I wanted to spend time with you was a good way not to give Elizabeth's intentions away."

"Oh."

The hollow hurt in her voice nearly killed him, but he had to let it stand. He had to make her get out of there. But before he could go further, Cole stepped into the doorway. He looked as bad as Hope.

"How's it going, buddy?" Cole asked, quietly.

Jeff responded in what was undoubtedly the least chivalrous comment he'd ever made in front of a lady in his entire life.

"That's pretty bad," Cole said lightly, clearly trying to lessen the impact of the ugly phrase, but then he sobered. "I got back here as soon as I could."

"That's good. You can get Hope to leave. I told her not to blame herself. Accidents happen."

Cole shook his head. "I don't think she's about to desert a friend like that."

Hope. He knew her. She'd stay glued to his side

whether he ever got out of this crazy contraption of a bed again or not. She was blaming herself. Jeff looked from Cole to Hope. There was one way to make sure he didn't drag Hope down with him. "I'm not up to company of any kind." He studiously ignored her hurt and confusion. This was for the best. "I don't want you back here again. Leave me alone."

"Jeff?" Hope's voice sounded small and wounded. "It isn't hopeless."

He gritted his teeth. That's exactly what his life was about to become. "If we were ever friends, we aren't anymore. You're smothering me, and there's nothing I hate more. Get out, Hope." Jeff turned his head away, and when he looked back minutes later, he was alone.

Now he could let his tears fall. Now he really *had* lost everything. Now he'd lost his Hope.

Two weeks later, time hadn't improved his paralysis and the doctors continued to lie, saying he could still see improvement at any time. They sent therapists and more doctors. But he knew it was hopeless.

Just like his life. Hopeless.

He'd banned Hope from his room. He wasn't proud of hurting her, but he knew it was for her own good, and he even thought Cole more or less understood that he couldn't let her sacrifice even an hour on him.

In the past two weeks, he'd lost all dignity. He was grateful his parents hadn't lived to see this. There'd been no room in their lives for imperfection, and he was about as imperfect as you could get. They would have been appalled by his helpless condition.

He was appalled.

He was going home today, but the doctors wanted him to go to some sort of rehabilitation facility. Jeff just wanted to go home and hide where no one could see him. He'd had it with visitors.

In the last two weeks they'd arrived as a steady flow at first and had thankfully dwindled to an annoying few. Either they treated him with an embarrassing kind of pity, asked humiliating questions about how much of his body still functioned or shot subtle little barbs at him about his lack of mobility. These were the people he'd considered friends, but Hope had been telling him for years they were no more than opportunists and social climbers.

He'd always known she was right, but he'd never needed anyone before, so it hadn't mattered. They'd filled his idle time, and he'd thought they would again. But now, when it did matter, he had no one. Which, he told himself, was just as well.

He wanted to crawl into a hole and pull it in after him. But he couldn't even crawl anymore.

"I'm sorry you feel that way, Mrs. Larchmont. Butternut and Stephanie are working well together," Hope told the pushy mother. Then listened as the woman, who didn't know which end of a horse to feed, told Hope that her Steffie needed an animal with spirit and that as her parents it was their duty to see she had what she needed. The couple had bought the perfect stallion that morning, and he would be arriving any day. Butternut was up for sale.

"Fine, we'll await his arrival and see how well Stephanie takes to him. See you Tuesday." Hope dropped the phone in the cradle and buried her face in her hands.

Lord give me strength.

Another nitwit. In the four weeks since Jeff's accident, they'd lost more than fifty percent of their business due to rumors of carelessness at Laurel Glen. Now Mildred Larchmont was insisting her ninety-pound skittish child could control a stallion named Demon.

Hope dropped her hands, flipped her month-at-a-glance calendar back a page and stared at the twenty-first of February. One month ago to the day. The date of Jeff's accident sat there in its little box unmarked, unchecked. She needed no reminder. She'd never forget that date if she lived to be a thousand. It was the day she'd lost not only her best friend but the love of her life, as well.

A month. She couldn't remember a month in her whole life when she hadn't seen Jeff at least once if he was in town. But he wouldn't see her. Two years older than Cole, Jeff had always been in her life because their mothers were friends. The boys had played together since Cole was a toddler. So Jeff had been around from her earliest memory. He used to tell her she'd pulled his hair from her crib and she was still yanking his chain.

And now Jeff had summarily cut her from his life. He'd gone so far as to have a guard put on the gate to turn her away. Her brother went to see him several times a week, but he always shook his head when he returned. Jeff still refused to see her.

She was nearly positive that he'd lied about his feelings for her. Jeff didn't have a cruel bone in his body, and it would have been cruel to send her flowers, beg to see her, stroll along the drive with his arm around her and then plan to tell her she was nothing more than a substitute for the sister he'd never had. Either he blamed her for what had happened even though he'd said he didn't or he was trying to save her from his daily struggle.

Whatever his reasons, guilt weighed on her. He was alone and hurt because of her, no matter how she looked at the situation. She prayed about it, and for Jeff, but nothing had changed. She still had to rely on progress reports from Emily Roberts when she saw Lavender Hill's housekeeper on Sundays and Wednesdays at church and on what Cole told her, which was very little. Emily's reports, however, were so depressing that Hope understood Cole's reluctance to go into detail.

From what Emily said, Jeff wasn't trying to get better. Cole said the doctor in the E.R. mentioned that Jeff had a six-month window of opportunity to regain full use of his legs. But Emily said he'd fired everyone who'd tried to push him toward exercise and therapy. Hope stared at the date. March twenty-first. One sixth of his time was gone.

Hope looked up when her father walked into the

office. Relations between them were better, but Hope knew it had nothing to do with any attitude adjustment on his part. Any improvement was due to the absence of Jeff from her life and her own determination to forgive her father's lack of support the day of the accident. She prayed daily to feel the forgiveness she'd decided to grant.

"Sorry, Daddy. Mrs. Larchmont won't budge. Want to buy Butternut? A stallion named Demon arrives before Tuesday. I hope that child doesn't get hurt. I don't know what else to do."

"See if Cole gets any bad vibes before you put her up on the stallion."

His sarcasm wasn't lost on Hope. She slapped her hand on her scarred oak desk. "That crack was unnecessary. Cole really does have an incredible rapport with the horses."

"I don't know Cole anymore, but that's what I hear."

"You know, if you'd stop trying to find fault with him all the time, and if you'd stop baiting him, maybe you would know him. He came home to try working things out with you. If you look, you might find out what a wonderful man your son really is."

"He has an attitude with me that just sets my teeth on edge. Always has."

"Always, Daddy? Or just since Mother was killed?" Hope asked. She saw the anger leap in his eyes, but she pushed on. Living and working at Laurel Glen had become intolerable, and things had to change. Aunt

Meg was right. How long were they going to tiptoe around the tragedy that had split their family?

"And your point is?" he asked, suddenly tight-lipped and tense, his hands fisted on his jeans-clad hips.

"My point is that you two have to work through Mother's death or neither of you will ever get past your grief. It keeps you both mired in the past. You have to admit that maybe he did sense something in the horse that day. And he has to admit that you made a mistake. An honest one. You have to accept it, too."

Hope's heart softened. She knew how much it hurt to love as deeply as her father had only to lose that love. "When she died, all this started. She wouldn't have wanted to come between the two of you."

"You don't know—" Her father stopped short and frowned. Then he nodded stiffly. "I'll try if he will."

"He *is* trying. He came home. Imagine how hard that had to be for him. He left here in disgrace. Military school or juvenile hall. Some choice. He's a respected man away from here. Don't rise to the bait if he baits you. Don't bait him or criticize every word that comes out of his mouth. Don't question his judgment where the stock is concerned. He's the one with the degree, remember?"

Ross smiled. "I guess we're driving you and your aunt crazy."

"You guess? Aunt Meg has a permanent case of in-digestion. You two have ruined every meal we've tried to eat as a family in the eight weeks he's been back."

The phone rang, and Hope said a quick prayer that

it wasn't another customer canceling lessons or making plans to retrieve a horse. Rumors of a poor safety record were deadly in their world.

It wasn't. It was Emily Roberts, Jeff's housekeeper. "Hope, you have to come over here," she said without preamble. "I'm at my wits' end with him and this place."

Hope looked up. Her father looked at her expectantly. She covered the mouthpiece. "It's personal—not a customer. Why don't you go on up to the house for lunch? And could you tell Aunt Meg I've already grabbed something on the fly?"

"Jeff doesn't want to see me," she reminded Mrs. Roberts when her father had left the office.

"Just please get here."

"What's so wrong all of a sudden?"

"More of the same except…he's deeply depressed and he's been drinking. And the hands in the stables aren't doing their jobs. I just had a horse on the breakfast room terrace."

Hope had to pause a moment to get a handle on that piece of information. "A horse on the terrace? And what do you mean he's drinking? Jeff's parents were killed by a drunk driver. He doesn't drink. Ever. Not even to be sociable."

"Tell him that. This has been going on for about a week. He gets that guard he hired to bring it to him. But today Reginald Boyer is here. Jeff got one of the men to bring him downstairs. I think Boyer's angling to buy Mr. March. He was in a nasty mood with me then all sweetness and light with Jeff. I'm afraid of what's going to happen if Boyer convinces Jeff. He needs the dream, at least. And I'm afraid of what Mr. Boyer will say if Jeff continues to refuse."

Hope's heart froze as she recalled Jeff telling the nurse to give him an overdose. Jeff was alone and vulnerable. No matter how angry he was at her, Hope knew she couldn't let that man take away Jeff's last vestige of hope. "Make sure the gates are open," she told Mrs. Roberts as she stood.

She made a grab for her jacket as she hung up the phone, then barreled out of her office and right into her father's chest.

"Hope, you can't go over there," he said, a mutinous expression on his face.

"Listening at doors now, Dad?" she asked, trying to tamp down her annoyance.

"I'm only trying to protect you from making a huge mistake."

"Who asked you to? And Jeff is not a mistake!"

He sighed. "Hope, he's not worth it. He'll only cause you heartache. All he cares about is having fun and spending money."

Hope stared at her father. Where did he get these ideas? "You have no idea what Jeff's really like because you've never given him a chance. I doubt you've had a civil word to say about him or to him since Cole was arrested."

"This has nothing to do with Cole. It has to do with

you being in love with a bored playboy who'll do nothing but cause you grief and waste your life!"

"Jeff isn't spoiled or lazy."

"No? Then why does he just sit over there on that estate? Why has he refused to even try getting better? Because he's always just drifted along and done the easiest thing."

"You don't know him! Now get out of my way. He needs me."

Ross grabbed her arm when she tried to sidestep him. "I'm not letting you go over there to waste your time on him."

Hope shook him off. "It's my time to waste. I am not a child and I'm not letting you pick my friends for me. It's none of your business."

"It *is* my business if you go over there during working hours. I don't pay you to play nursemaid to a spoiled cripple."

That did it! She started forward, throwing her reply over her shoulder. "I'll be back before lunch hour's over, and if not, you can dock my pay!"

Chapter Four

Pale and visibly upset, Mrs. Roberts opened the front door of Jeff's imposing neoclassical home. Hope's temper, which had already been flowing at full throttle, shot to an all-time high. She'd struggled long and hard with her temper and with the Lord's help had mostly mastered it, but seeing how upset Emily Roberts was undid a lot of work.

Mrs. Roberts dragged Hope across the marble foyer with a forceful grip, leading her toward the front parlor. "That Mr. Boyer's getting nasty, just as I feared. He hid his mood with Jeff till just a few minutes ago, but he was vicious about our boy. He said he'd been careless or he'd never have been hurt."

Hope felt a fierce stab of guilt pierce her heart. It hadn't been Jeff's carelessness but her own.

"He was vile about it when he first arrived. Luckily, Jeff was still upstairs. Please don't let him say anything too upsetting to Jeffrey's face. It'll break what's left of his spirit. I just know it."

Hope took a few calming breaths. It wouldn't do to charge in like a half-crazed mare. "Take it easy, Mrs. R," she said. "I'll see if I can divert things a bit. If Jeff doesn't toss me out first, that is."

Hope rushed ahead, determined to be as civil and pleasant as possible, but she felt her blood pressure rise when she heard Boyer's cutting voice emanate from the room ahead. She reached one of the columns that stood sentinel in the doorway of the front parlor. She gripped the cool marble, her fingertips turning white as she tried to tone down her temper.

"Honestly, Jeffrey. You're being childish," Reginald Boyer said. "Mr. March does not belong rusticating in the country or serving as a stud. He lives for competition. Gary Johnson has a shot at moving up in the standings with a better animal. You're useless to the team now, but you could make this one last contribution. Don't be so selfish. You're no good to the animal anymore. Really, when was the last time you exercised him?"

"I can't walk, Reggie," Jeff replied, his tone flat. "Obviously I'm not the one caring for him. Or exercising him."

"He's worthless to anyone out here eating grass and wasting away. As worthless as—"

"Don't you dare finish that, Mr. Boyer." Hope burst in, unable to contain her anger a second longer. She stood at the entrance to the room, anger pulsing through her. After letting go of the column beneath her fingers, she moved forward and down the two steps into the sitting area.

"What kind of man are you to come here and purposely demoralize Jeff just to get your way? Talk about selfish. Mr. March is not for sale. Take your poison personality and get out. Jeff doesn't need you coming around to make him feel worse."

"On what authority are you telling me to leave?" Reginald Boyer asked, his back stiff, his tone pompous and superior.

Hope glanced at Jeff for the first time. His handsome face looked haggard, and his beautifully sculpted jaw and chin were covered by a scraggly beard that had to represent weeks of growth. He stared straight ahead, his eyes clearly seeing nothing but his own thoughts—and those were obviously dark ones. Hope wasn't sure he even knew she was there. He was a remnant of his former self. And it was all her fault.

She looked away, the sight too painful to deal with just then. Instead she turned her attention to Jeff's former coach. "On the authority of someone who cares about Jeff. On the authority of someone who loves him and won't allow you to destroy what's left of him. He certainly isn't protesting my interference, is he?"

Boyer shook his shoulders as if straightening his jacket but said nothing, so Hope continued. "Jeff doesn't deserve to have you come here and try to take away the last of his pride and hope. He'll ride Mr. March again and he can't do that if the horse is gone.

Go find your new rising star his own mount. He can't have Jeff's."

Boyer gave her a cold-eyed stare and tried to walk closer to where Jeff sat. But Hope had given ground for the last time where Jeff's best interests were concerned. She should never have stayed away. She boldly stepped to the side and blocked Boyer's way.

She stared into his cold black eyes. "I asked you to leave," she said, her voice as cold as her temper was hot. "Get out before I call Cole to come throw you out."

"I do not like to be threatened, Ms. Taggert."

Hope smiled coolly. "I'm appalled that you think I'd threaten you. I was actually making you a promise. Mrs. Roberts, will you see the gentleman out? Good day, Mr. Boyer."

Boyer stared at her for several long moments, and Hope stared right back. Only when he'd turned away and stomped out did Hope approach Jeff. She prayed for the wisdom and words to reach him.

"Jeff, why would you let him talk to you that way?" she demanded, sitting in a chair near him.

He blinked then looked at her, but his eyes took on no more life than when he'd been staring at nothing. "Ever hear the expression about not shooting the messenger?" he asked, his tone as flat as when he'd spoken to Boyer. "I couldn't very well refute what he said. Or what he was about to say. I *am* worthless, after all."

"That isn't true!"

"To Mr. March I am. I want you to take him to Laurel Glen. Bring over a boarding agreement."

"Jeff, why? You have exercise boys and stable hands, too."

"Because I don't want to see him out there standing around bored or pacing like a nervous chicken. It'll ruin him."

"You're giving up. You worked so hard to get on the Olympic team. And to develop a name in breeding. Why can't you work as hard to get back on your feet again?"

"Been there. Done that," he said flippantly. "Do me a favor before you go, get me a beer."

Hope stood and fisted her hands on her hips. "No. I will not get you a beer. What on earth are you doing to yourself? You don't drink. I've always respected that you took that stand about alcohol after your parents were killed by that drunk driver."

"Come on, Hope. I'm not exactly driving these days, am I? Unless…do you want to count the chair?" His grin was insolent as he pushed the control switch on the chair forward and came at her—full throttle. Hope was momentarily stunned and pivoted just in time to avoid him running in to her. Jeff quickly spun the chair and laughed as he came after her again. It wasn't a happy sound.

"I'm not playing your game, Jeff Carrington!" she shouted and stomped up the steps. "Come and get me here," she challenged.

* * *

Furious Jeff gave chase and let the chair smack into the bottom step of living room just below Hope's booted feet. The room spun when he looked at her—a blurred figure in denim and suede. He was thankful he couldn't see her face clearly. There was only so much a man could take. He didn't want to see disillusionment on her face even though he was trying to chase her away.

"Why are you here?" he asked and hated the slight slur in his voice. "I told you I don't want you smothering me. Poor Jeff. Let's cheer up poor Jeff. Let's smile for poor Jeff. Let's lie to poor Jeff if we have to, but we have to keep his spirits up. Here's a news flash for you, Hope. I don't want your sympathy, your patience or your fake smile. I don't need smothering! I want to be left alone."

For just a moment her face came into focus and she smiled a real true smile. For just a moment he felt a shred of happiness.

"You're right," she said. "You don't need smothering, and I'm sorry if that's all you felt from me. I'm going to give you what you say you need. I'll be back with that agreement."

He frowned and watched her go. "That was too easy," he told Mrs. Roberts. "Much too easy."

"You should be careful or you might find out that you've managed to send away all the best people in your life."

He stared at the older woman with the round figure and

graying hair. He didn't think she'd changed a bit in all the years she'd been with him. "Get me a beer, will you?"

Mrs. Roberts frowned. "Please don't make me feed my boy that mind poison."

"I'll get Billy to handle it for me." Jeff laughed. "Mind poison? Where do you get this stuff? No wonder I keep you around. You're a regular laugh riot, Mrs. R."

"You keep me around because no one else loves you the way I do. You remember that when you're calling yourself worthless and useless. You're my sweetheart. Have been ever since the day you toddled into my kitchen looking for cookies. You remember that!" she ordered.

Jeff grimaced. Everyone who opened their mouth near him today reminded him. "I can't toddle anymore, Mrs. R."

"It wasn't the toddling that won my heart. It was that smile. I'm off to get a start on dinner. Be good."

She smiled that gentle smile of hers and went off to do what he paid her to do. Jeff found himself fighting tears. He'd always wished she was family and not paid to be with him. Growing up, his greatest fear was that she would leave him. She was all he had left.

Hope knew she had to do something. What Jeff said was true. She hadn't responded to any of his barbs as she normally would, and she'd done it right from the first. She and Cole had left when Jeff had asked rather than risk upsetting him the evening of the accident. She should have stood her ground and dared him to do his worst. She knew what she'd done wrong but hadn't a clue how to fix it.

She pulled the Jeep next to the barn where she kept her office. She longed for the warmth of the rich old knotty pine paneling and the smell of the wood fire simmering in the cast-iron stove in the corner. She wanted to hide. To curl up on the worn hunter-green leather sofa with a warm woolen blanket and just let the atmosphere chase away the chill of Jeff's marble edifice.

Entering, she found her brother on the phone behind her desk. He looked up and quickly got off the phone.

"So how was it?" he asked. "Dad was bouncing off the walls because you went over there. I gather you had quite a confrontation."

Hope tried to choke back the tears that had been threatening since she saw Jeff's dissipated condition. "He looks awful. Why didn't you tell me?" she asked, and then she lost it. She felt her face crumple along with her composure. Cole was at her side in seconds, and she was soaking his shirt just as quickly.

"Oh, sweetheart, I didn't want to hurt you," he murmured, then tightened his hold on her and let her cry.

"I knew no good would come of her going over there," Ross growled from the doorway. "I told her he'd only hurt her."

Nothing had ever stopped Hope's tears faster than anger. She pushed out of Cole's embrace and rounded on her father. "He didn't do anything to hurt me. It's the way he is that hurts. That and knowing I did it to him.

You're so wrapped up in your little prejudices that you can't see the truth. This was all my fault. I feel responsible. I *am* responsible. And I have to help him."

"Hope, you can't make Jeff care," Cole said. "I've talked till I'm blue in the face, but he won't listen."

"Have you tried to *make* him listen?"

Cole held out his hands helplessly. "What do you want me to do? Scream at a man in a wheelchair?"

She could hear Jeff's words. *I don't need smothering.* "Maybe," she said thoughtfully. "Maybe that's what he needs."

"What he needs," Ross said, as if Hope hadn't spoken, "is a good swift kick."

"Exactly, Daddy," Hope said with a sudden smile. "And I'm going to figure out how to give it to him."

"I've had it. I want you to stay away from him!" Ross ordered.

"I told you earlier." She paused and glared at her father. "What I do with my life is my business. I refuse to let you tell me who I can and who I can't care for. This is *my* decision. My life. And I'm going to do what I have to do to wake Jeff up to the possibilities that are still open to him."

"You're a fool!" Ross shouted, stalking away.

The room fell silent, and Hope stared through the glass between her office and the rest of the barn, wondering what she could do.

"That went well," Cole quipped as he leaned against the desk, his hands negligently stuffed in the front pockets of his khakis. He shook his head. "I can't believe I thought you let him run your life. I was so jealous of your relationship with him. And now I find out that you two really go at it."

Hope arched one eyebrow. "Yes, but unlike you, I've learned to pick my battles. And this is one of those issues I can't back down on."

"So what are you up to?" Cole asked. "I remember that look."

Hope shook her head. "I don't know yet. Jeff wants to board Mr. March here, so I have to go over to Lavender Hill with an agreement."

"Why is March coming here?"

Walking to the filing cabinet, Hope thought of all she'd learned today. "Because Jeff doesn't want to look at him. Besides, since Jeff's fired anyone who'd care if he got better, no animal is really safe there. I imagine you've seen the crew he's hired as replacements. Mrs. Roberts probably has to count the silver after any of them are in the house, and today one of the mares wandered as far as the back terrace."

As Hope looked for the standard boarding agreement, she noticed a power of attorney that she often had clients sign if they were leaving on a trip. If anything happened to a horse, Laurel Glen needed to be able to act as agent of the owners to get treatment.

"I wish I had power of attorney for Jeff's care. I'd toss half that crew of his out the door and get things back to normal over there," she grumbled, hooking a thick lock of hair behind her ear. She stared at the agreements. They looked nearly identical.

Could it be this easy?

"A word changed here," she murmured, "a word there."

"Hope, you've really got that look now," Cole said from his slouched seat on the old sofa. "And every time you've ever had it, you've done something outlandish."

"He needs someone riding him twenty-four seven. And it has to be someone who wants what's best for him. Someone strong enough to do what needs to be done and not bow to his will. Someone who wants him to get better as much, if not more, than he does right now. And someone who can run a farm."

She turned and reached for the phone. "Mrs. R, it's Hope. Is the homestead house unoccupied?"

Hope glanced in her rearview mirror at Laurel Glen. She still couldn't believe her father had fired her. Hope knew he'd regret it and the harsh things he'd said. She was sorry she'd driven him to act so rashly, but she had to do this.

She loved Jeff and she had to get him to help himself. Even if she had no feelings beyond friendship, she'd still have to help. It was her fault he was in the condition he was in and therefore her fault his animals were endangered. She had to make things better.

Her plan was a bold one and sure to get as strong a reaction from Jeff as it had from her father. She had warned her father not to ask her to choose between the man she loved and him. And she would just as readily explain to him another truth she'd learned lately. Peace at any price is not worth it. Jeff might hate her by the time she left, but as sure as her name was Hope Taggert, he would at least care about life again!

Chapter Five

Hope stood for a second outside Jeff's room. She looked at the piece of paper in her hand and closed her eyes. *Please forgive this deception, Lord. I won't lie but I can't tell him the truth, either. This is for his own good. I have to get him to take a good hard look at what he's doing to himself.*

Hope took a deep breath and knocked. When no answer came, she knocked again—harder this time.

"What?" Jeff's voice snapped from within.

"It's Hope. I have the agreement," she called, then entered when he told her to come in. She nearly gasped when she saw the room—smelled the room. It was worse than a locker room. She'd smelled stables that were fresher and was sure there were trash dumps that were more orderly. As she approached the bed, Hope realized that it wasn't only the room in need of a good scrubbing.

She looked at Jeff. He lay on the bed, still wearing the

T-shirt he'd had on earlier in the day. From the looks of things, it was the same one he'd had on all week. He was haphazardly covered to the waist by a wrinkled sheet. His hair was matted and needed a good washing, and the scraggly beard still hid much of his handsome face.

Mrs. R had warned her that the room was as much a mess as Jeff, but she hadn't believed it. Now she did. She'd wondered where to start. Well, she had her answer.

But there were preparations for the campaign to get him to straighten up and fly right that she and Cole had mapped out. And getting the agreement signed was the first step. Holding her breath, Hope handed Jeff the contract and a pen.

He blinked his eyes, leafed through the pages and sighed. "How much a year?" he asked, annoyed.

She named the standard boarding fee at Laurel Glen. She hadn't lied. Not yet. But Mr. March wouldn't be making a move. Because Hope already had. Into Lavender Hill's quaint little homestead house.

Jeff scribbled his name on the last page and handed it to her. "That's it then?" he asked.

Hope nodded. She'd file the papers in the morning. But today she intended to clean house. Not literally, she thought, looking around at the room's early American trash dump decor. Literal cleaning would come soon enough.

"I'll be seeing you," she told him after examining his signature.

"What, no comment?" Jeff demanded and took a

swig from a beer someone obviously had brought him. She doubted it had been Mrs. Roberts. Enjoy it, Hope thought, looking at the amber-colored bottle in his hand. It'll be your last.

Hope put her hand on her hip. "You expect a comment? About this?" She gestured to the room. "It just confirms what I've heard. You've decided to not only wallow in self-pity but to do it in a pigsty while you're at it. I'll see you tomorrow."

Tempted to make an unwise comment about what he could expect tomorrow to be like, Hope turned on her heels and left. Out in the hall, she leaned against the wall. Billy, the guard who had been toting and fetching for Jeff as well as screening his visitors, was the first on her list of things to go.

Jeff closed his eyes and let his head drop back against the headboard. Does the torture never end? Just when he'd thought he'd figured out how to get from one day to the next, he had to go and have a day like this. First Reggie stopped by and brought home just how worthless he was and made him remember all the yesterdays that were gone. Then, when he was about to really lose it, Hope had to go and ride to the rescue. Not only had it been humiliating, but seeing her again had reminded him of all the tomorrows he'd lost, too.

He glanced at the bottle in his hand, then tipped it to his lips, draining it. If only this stuff didn't taste so lousy, his new life master plan wouldn't be so bad. He reached next to the bed and pulled another amber-colored bottle out of the little refrigerator he'd had Billy fill that morning. By dark, or a little after, he ought to be able to sleep. The alcohol numbed not only his mind to the past and future but the knotted muscles in his legs and back. And when the numbness came, one more day would be over.

Just like his life.

"Well, look who's up bright and early this morning," Mrs. R said with a pleasant smile the next morning as Hope walked through the back door into the Italian country kitchen. The kitchen and breakfast room were a homey enclave from the cold starkness of the rest of the house.

"What do you plan to do today?" Mrs. R continued as she poured a cup of coffee and walked with it to the table. "Are you going to replace the staff you gave the axe yesterday?"

Hope shook her head. "I already called the agency my aunt Meg uses. I gave them the names and numbers of everyone you thought we should hire back if we can. They're going to handle the rest of that. Unfortunately when I called Gus Peoples, he said he was already working and feels he can't break his contract, so I guess I'm running the stables now. They sent temps for us till we get everything back to normal. At least today you won't have Sally's Fortune stomping around the back door.

"The next thing on my agenda is to get rid of that gorilla at the front gate. I'm looking forward to it. I took a look at the petty cash ledger last night. His math is inventive, I'll give him that much. After that happy task is over, I'll tackle the really tough job."

Mrs. R's eyebrows rose, wrinkling her brow. "Oh. What would that be?"

Hope took a deep breath. "Mrs. R, I—"

Mrs. R put her hand on Hope's shoulder. "Dear, if you're going to be living here helping my Jeffrey find himself again, don't you think we could dispense with the Mrs. R? It's Emily. Please."

Hope nodded. "Emily it is, then. I do want to help Jeff. But Jeff has to want to help himself, too. First thing this morning, I called Curtis Madden from church. I was hoping he'd be free and, praise the Lord, he is. He's looking for a long-term assignment. I gave him one. Jeff. Curt's a good nurse and an even better physical therapist. This is the type of work he trained for. He'll be here at nine and ready for a challenge."

"Challenge? You aren't going to upset Jeff, are you?" Emily asked and sank to a chair at the table. Hope saw that her hands shook. She sat across from Emily and took one of her increasingly frail hands in her own. This had to be so painful for her. She loved Jeff like a son, yet she had no say in how he went about his life.

Hope checked her watch. She had promised Emily that she'd get Jeff moving ahead in life again. But she hadn't outlined her tough-love idea yet. Without Emily's help and cooperation, this plan would fail. While Hope hated to see the older woman upset, she hated to see Jeff waste the gift of his life more. A lot more.

"Yesterday," she began, "I got Jeff's signature on a power of attorney, but he thinks he signed a Laurel Glen boarding agreement for Mr. March."

Emily's wrinkled brow scrunched with her worried frown. "I don't understand, dear."

"Jeff needs help whether he wants it or not. And he doesn't want it. You know it. I know it. He's given up. It's our job to make him want to get better. Being nice and giving him room and time to come to grips with the accident isn't working. He's gaining weight and losing muscle mass every day. There's no time to tiptoe around this. The most important month of his recovery is already wasted. That's why we're changing the staff back to people who care about him. He doesn't know what I've done. When everything is in place, he will. Are you ready for the explosion?"

"He'll be furious. Oh, Hope, I don't know about this."

"Mrs. R, Emily, do you trust me? Do you believe I love Jeff too much to take advantage of the power of attorney?"

The housekeeper looked surprised. "Of course, I do. That isn't an issue."

"Good, because the president of First Nation will be here any minute."

"The president of Jeff's bank?"

Hope nodded as the back door opened.

"Hey, what are you doing here?" Billy Dever, the soon-to-be unemployed security guard, asked. "You aren't on the *A* list."

Hope stood and smiled. "There have been a few changes in the *A* list since you left yesterday, Mr. Dever. Would you come to the study with me? We need to have a chat. Emily, if the gentleman I mentioned arrives, please show him to the front parlor and tell him I'll be with him any minute."

Moments later Hope took a seat behind the ebony desk in Jeff's study and motioned Billy Dever to the chair facing her. "I won't beat around the bush with you, Mr. Dever. Your services are no longer required at Lavender Hill. Here is a check for two months' wages. I'm sorry for the abruptness of this dismissal, but I'm sure someone as conscientious as you will be able to find employment in that amount of time."

"I'm fired? You can't do that! Carrington hired me."

"I beg to differ." Hope handed him a copy of the power of attorney Jeff had mistakenly signed the evening before. "As you can see, Mr. Carrington has placed his welfare and Lavender Hill's in my hands. And having you here, sir, is *not* in his best interests. As for unemployment compensation, I think your creative accounting speaks for itself. I wouldn't try to file a claim. If you do I may be forced to speak to the district attorney about the discrepancies I found in the petty cash account." Hope stood. "Have a nice day."

Dever glanced at the agreement in stunned silence, then at her with narrowed eyes. "I knew you were trouble."

"It's my middle name, Mr. Dever." Hope stood, fighting a smile. It was a clear dismissal. Even someone of Billy Dever's ilk knew that.

Having heard the door chimes ring just after she gave Dever his walking papers, Hope headed for the front parlor. After a short visit to Jeff's room, the banker was only too happy to help his old friends' grandson any way he could. Tough love, he'd said, was clearly better than the status quo.

"What's next?" Emily asked.

"Jeff." Hope took a deep breath. "Curt should be here any minute. Send him up, will you? Oh, and where do you keep the trash bags?"

"Rise and shine, lazybones!"

Jeff found himself blasted out of sleep. A voice—Hope's voice—reverberated in his head like a gong. Then light flooded the room and thrust a thousand knives into his skull.

"What the—" The curse word froze on his lips when he opened his eyes and saw Hope, her hair bouncing with every movement, throw open the terrace doors. Then she moved to the windows across from his bed and opened them, too. The icy fingers of March followed. He closed his eyes. His head was pounding. "Go away and let a man die in peace. What are you doing? Are you trying to torture me?"

"What I am doing is shaping you up, Carrington. And first things first." She walked to the terrace. "You all set down there, Manny?"

"All set, Ms. Taggert," Lavender Hill's gardener, jack-of-all-trades and helper of all—whether they wanted help or not—shouted.

Jeff frowned, keeping his eyes closed against the sunlight, and tried to order his thoughts. There was more wrong with this scene than Hope being in his room, opening windows and trying to blast the head off his shoulders. Oh, if only beer didn't leave him so fuzzy and achy headed after a couple six-packs. What was he saying? Fuzzy-headed mornings—a fuzzy-headed life—were what he was looking for.

"Manny. I fired Manny," he said, figuring out one inconsistency. Manny had been the first one he'd let go. His cheer and enthusiasm had been too much to bear.

"And I rehired him." Hope chirped the words gleefully, then turned back to Manny. "I'll toss the trash left and the clothes right. Just stuff it all in the plastic bags. Mrs. Roberts will see to the clothes, and you can handle the trash."

"I gave him six months' severance. And hey, why are you tossing my stuff out the window? I like my room just the way it is."

"Honestly, Jeff, I've smelled stables more pleasant than this room," Hope complained. "I didn't intend to subject anyone else to this. It can be sorted in the fresh air just as easily."

"No one invited you in here. Get out. And hey! What do you mean, you rehired him? You don't have the right to hire and fire people around here. You're fired, Manny," Jeff shouted.

"*Si*, Mr. Carrington. Whatever you say, Mr. Carrington," Manny called, sounding entirely too happy to have just lost his income.

Jeff watched in impotent fury as Hope gathered more of his clothes.

"Actually," she said as she heaved the pile over the balcony into the fresh air she seemed to crave, "I do have the right to hire and fire around here. You gave it to me yesterday when you signed the power of attorney I brought over."

"What power of attorney? The only thing I signed was a boarding agreement."

"You really shouldn't drink. Not only is it an unappealing trait but it impairs your faculties." Hope grinned and walked toward the side of the bed where Billy had replaced the nightstand with a neat little dorm fridge. She eyed it suspiciously.

Jeff glanced at the fridge that still contained a six-pack. "Where's Billy? Billy!" he bellowed.

"Billy is probably off celebrating his good fortune. You see, rather than being arrested for petty theft, he got two months' severance pay."

"You fired him? I need him. He helps me. You think I can get dressed on my own? Get into the bathroom on my own?"

Hope gave him a sour look. "It's clear that even with Mr. Dever's help you've been unable to get as far as the tub. Today all that will change."

Jeff spat out a foul oath and reached for the phone. Hope was faster. He watched in horror as she yanked on the cord and pulled it out of the wall then tossed the phone over the terrace railing.

"Heads up, Manny!" she shouted as his only means of rescue sailed off for points unknown.

"This is kidnapping," Jeff charged.

Hope raised that infernal eyebrow that always made her look so imperious and stared at him. "So far I haven't had you moved even an inch."

"I'll have you tossed in prison. Your father would just love it if you followed in big brother's footsteps. I'll tell the police I'm being held against my will and that you misrepresented that agreement. That's fraud!"

She folded her arms. "Prove it," she challenged. "Emily signed as a witness. Are you going to toss her in jail, too? Just for caring about your welfare?"

Okay, indignant didn't work. Maybe pitiful would. "Hope, you can't do this. How can you take advantage of me like this?" he asked, pitifully. He could have sworn twin flames replaced Hope's blue eyes. He stared at her, his eyes still not quite focusing correctly.

"I can do this because I care about you, Jeff. I'm *not* letting you go on this way."

Jeff watched in helpless dread as she bent, opened the

fridge and scowled. As if having her yank the phone out wasn't bad enough. "No!"

Hope bent over him till they were nose to nose. His sweet Hope had turned into the drill instructor from his worst nightmares. "Oh, yes. You want to stop me? Get out of that bed and make me."

"You know I can't do that!" To his humiliation, his voice broke. To cover the emotions Jeff fought on a daily basis, he flopped back in the bed and looked away.

"What I know is that you're not *trying* to get out of that bed. You're wallowing. In grimy sheets. In trash and dirty clothes. In filth! And worst of all, in self-pity. And it ends. Here! Now!"

Oh, he was really mad. Who did she think she was standing there—*standing* there—telling him he was wallowing in self-pity? So what if he was? He had a right. If she couldn't see that, it was her problem.

"And how do you think you're going to get me to do what you want? Are you going to haul my carcass out of this bed? Are you going to change the sheets? Give me a bath?" he taunted, expecting her to blush and run from the room.

But he was wrong. Again. A tap on the door drew their attention, but not before Hope glared at him instead of cowering, her expression annoyingly determined. Her complexion hadn't darkened even a shade, either.

"Come in, Curt. Join the party. This is your patient, Jeffrey Carrington. Jeff, this is Curtis Madden. He prefers to be called Curt."

Jeff watched in horror as a large man with muscles on his muscles, wearing navy surgical scrubs, strode into the room. On his pleasant face was a warm smile. Jeff scowled at the man.

"Do me a favor, will you, Curt?" Hope said. "Haul that nice little fridge out to my cottage. I could use something to keep soft drinks by my bed. It'll make those middle-of-the-night refrigerator raids much easier."

Jeff watched in amazement as the big hulking blond strode in and removed his lifeline to oblivion. He wouldn't miss the lousy taste, just its mind- and body-numbing effects. Just as Madden stepped into the hall, what she'd said cut through the rest of the fog in his brain. Her cottage? He narrowed his eyes.

"What cottage?"

"The cottage out back. Lavender Hill's homestead house. It was your grandparents' home, if memory serves."

"You aren't moving in there."

"Too late. Already have," she quipped.

"Then move out. Ross'll be furious. He's liable to fire you."

"Too late. Already is. Already has."

He groaned. If Ross hadn't been able to stop her, nothing he said would dissuade her from this campaign of hers. But he could still do plenty. Like resist. Like make her life miserable. The only problem was he'd cut off his association with her to keep himself from making her miserable. Well, what was the old saying? Sometimes you have to be cruel to be kind.

"You're pathetic. How desperate are you for a man if you'll go this far to get one—even one who's worthless? Didn't your aunt Meg teach you that it's gauche to throw yourself at someone?"

Jeff congratulated himself when anger flared in her blue eyes. But his triumph withered and died as soon as she gave words to her fury—disappointing words.

"I won't listen to you calling yourself worthless. You say that one more time and I swear I'll put pepper on your tongue."

"You and what army?" he replied, then looked up as the hulk—Kirk, was it?—strode into the room. "You going to get the captain here to hold me down?"

"He's here to help you. I don't need help. Now I imagine it's bath time. I'll see you boys later."

Jeff growled as she left then turned his gaze on Madden. "So, how much am I paying you to humiliate me?"

The young man in the surgical scrubs stood at the foot of the bed and crossed his meaty arms. "I'm not here to humiliate you, Mr. Carrington."

"Come on, Captain Kirk, you're apparently going to see me in my altogether. Make it Jeff. Why stand on ceremony?"

Madden nodded. "All right. Jeff it is then. And I'm Curt, or Curtis, or nurse. Not Captain Kirk—unless *you're* trying to embarrass *me*. You asked why I'm here. I'm here to either help you get better or to help you learn to cope with your disability. I'm an RN and I have a degree in physical therapy. And I specialize in cases like yours."

Jeff frowned. What kind of life was that for a twenty-something, good-looking guy? "Helping cripples learn to go on in the world? Is that your thing?" Jeff asked, pulling sarcasm around him like a shield. Madden's blue eyes seemed to see too much, though, and it made Jeff decidedly uncomfortable.

"No. I specialize in tough cases, Jeff."

"Ah. Now I see. Cases that don't have a snowball's chance at the equator of getting better. Like me."

Madden leaned down and braced his hands on the footboard of Jeff's sleigh bed. "No, Jeff. Cases where the patient won't try and can't seem to care enough to see what their self-pity is doing to those around them. You ready for your bath?" he asked. "I'm told you don't get fed till you're clean and smelling fresh as a daisy." He sniffed the air. "I'd say we have a lot of work in that area."

Hope waited till Curt let her know he had Jeff in the tub before she stripped the bed. She had finished clearing the debris from the bureau and chest and making the bed with clean linens when the therapist came in looking for a clean towel and clothes. Luckily there were plenty of both.

Half an hour later, Jeff had still not appeared in the breakfast room. Mrs. Roberts, excited that he'd be eating downstairs, had gone all out with his favorites—an omelette, fruit salad and fresh coffee cake. Not knowing whether to be worried or annoyed, Hope returned to his clean inner sanctum, and all thoughts of worry fled when she overheard him talking to Curt.

"I eat in my room. I told you. I'm not well enough to be dragged up and down the stairs all the time. Just go get me a tray. I'm hungry. And I haven't had my coffee."

Hope turned on her heels and went to the kitchen. How could he care so little about Emily? Jeff had never treated her like anything other than a grandmother, and suddenly he'd begun treating her like his parents had. Like the help.

Well, fine. If he wanted to be treated like an invalid, she'd feed him like an invalid. Maybe that would wake him up!

She stalked into the kitchen and pulled out a pot. Next she hunted up the oatmeal she knew had to be there. Not because Emily would ever serve it for breakfast but because she made the best oatmeal cookies in two counties. And they weren't nearly as good as her omelettes. Jeff didn't know what he was missing.

But he soon would.

"What on earth are you up to now?" Emily Roberts asked, worry evident in her voice.

"He says he's not well enough to come down. With a little change in the menu I'm going to demonstrate the difference between being well and being so sick you're confined to bed."

Luckily, Emily stocked quick-cooking oatmeal, so Jeff's breakfast was ready in less than five minutes. Hope loaded a tray and carried it upstairs and into his room.

"You're not up to coming down yet, I hear," she said, her voice full of sympathy. "So I brought up some breakfast fit for an invalid. I think you'll enjoy it. I brought mine along so we could visit."

Hope made a great production of settling the tray across his lap then she lifted the plate with her omelette and handed Jeff his spoon.

He frowned, dipped into the oatmeal and lifted the spoon, tilting it to the side and letting the contents plop into the bowl. "What's this? And what am I supposed to do with it? Hire a paperhanger?"

Hope chuckled. At least some of his sense of humor was still intact. "It's oatmeal. Not wallpaper paste. Aunt Meg always says hot cereal really sticks to your ribs. And I added some nice stewed prunes. And tea with a drop of milk. Just what your delicate constitution needs."

Jeff's frown turned to a full-fledged scowl. "But you have one of Mrs. R's omelettes."

"Yes, I do. But then I'm not the one too weak to go to the breakfast room."

His eyes lit with fury. "Torture! You're trying to torture me. That's it! Admit it!"

A sadness so profound fell like a shadow over Hope, and she nearly burst into tears. No one ever warned her that tough love hurt the one on the administering side more than the receiver. Jeff was genuinely angry and, from his point of view, rightly so. She was the usurper, never mind that she was only trying to help, and to his mind he was doing just fine.

Hope took a deep breath and stood. "I'm trying to

show you that there are things you can do to lead a productive, useful life and that you aren't doing them."

"Whose idea of a productive life? Yours? What do you know about what I'm capable of doing? I'm not *able* to do a thing on my own! Nothing. And you know nothing whatever about me or my capabilities."

She shook her head and walked to the bed, carrying the untouched omelette. She put it on the tray and picked up the cereal bowl. "Here's your breakfast, Jeff. I was just trying to make a point about how *well* you really are. And there's another point to eating downstairs. Do you think it's easy for Mrs. Roberts to schlep your trays up and down that flight and a half of stairs three times a day? Why don't you take the rest of the day to sulk up here? Curt can work on beginning your therapy today."

Hope took a deep breath and stiffened her resolve. Hard or easy, she couldn't back down yet. He was worth every second of her own pain and discomfort. "But it's a one-day reprieve," she continued. "Tomorrow you find a way to get downstairs or I'll know the reason why not!"

Chapter Six

On her way to convince Jeff to eat the evening meal downstairs, Hope heard Curt's voice float into the hall outside the room.

"Come on, Jeff," he urged. "Try one more time."

Jeff expelled a quick breath seconds later, and she heard the crisp sheets rustle. "I can't do it. My arms feel like jelly. I can't even get myself into a wheelchair." Jeff laughed, but it was once again sadly a bitter sound. "How worthless is that? I even fail at being a cripple."

Hope closed her eyes and blocked out Curt offering to lift him into the chair and Jeff's sharp negative retort. *Lord,* she prayed, *it hurts to hear him sound so down and discouraged, but he has to keep trying. Giving up on life isn't an option. What do I do to show him the way?*

What she really wanted to do was to go in there and hug him. To offer comfort. But that was what *she* wanted. One by one scenes from earlier in the day replayed themselves and she stiffened her resolved. Comfort wasn't what he needed. She'd done what she'd done so far to help him. And help him she would.

Turning on her heel, Hope followed the wonderful scent of Emily's cooking to the kitchen. She'd warned him, she told herself. He wouldn't be able to say she hadn't.

"Yum. That smells wonderful," Hope said as she lifted a pot lid and sniffed the gumbo Emily had been preparing for hours. "I don't think Jeff's going to be down for dinner tonight, either. But don't worry. I'll take it up to him."

"That's nice, dear," Emily said as she bent, pot holder in hand, to peer into the oven. "I'll have the baguettes out of the oven in two shakes of a lamb's tail. If you put a little butter on a bread plate, they'll be ready to go."

Hope took care of the butter and the bread plate then dished up a serving of Emily's famous gumbo. With the full dish, she walked calmly to the spice cabinet. She wouldn't need to have Curt hold Jeff down at all. He was about to dole out his own consequences all by himself. She felt her lips twitch.

"What are you doing?" Emily asked.

"Keeping a promise," Hope explained and shook out a few healthy splashes of jalapeño hot sauce onto the top of Jeff's dinner. She stirred it in only enough to disguise its presence, then picked up the tray as Emily settled the plate holding the fresh baguette and a pat of butter. "I'd have a big glass of milk ready. But don't bring it up right away. His object lesson shouldn't end too soon."

Hope sighed. The older woman's frown and worried eyes gave her pause. Maybe she shouldn't. She looked at the laced gumbo. "He said it again. Called himself worthless. It hurts hearing him so down on himself, especially when I caused the accident. I just want him to stop and think before he says something so untrue about himself. Maybe if he isn't saying it, he'll stop believing it."

"Jeffrey doesn't blame you in the least. As for the hot sauce, maybe he does need shaking up. He can't keep repeating and believing his father's criticisms or he'll waste away in that bed. Hearing him call himself worthless is like an old nightmare come back to haunt me. I thought he'd gotten far beyond all those childhood hurts, but I guess children never lose the scars of their early years."

Hope silently denounced Addison Carrington for his cruelty. The man hadn't been a father to Jeff, but a scourge, and his negligent mother hadn't been much better. Glancing at the doctored gumbo, Hope grew more comfortable with the course of action.

She wasn't being cruel. She was trying to make him see how very much he *was* worth. They called it tough love. Just as military school had broken Cole out of his destructive behavior, she hoped and prayed her version would do the same for Jeff's brand of the same malignant pattern her brother had once engaged in. Her resolve strengthened, Hope carried the bed tray upstairs and pasted a smile on her face.

"Dinner," she called as she entered the room. Jeff was

still in the bed, and Curt sat next to him in a chair. Both men looked up.

"See? Even Hope doesn't expect me to make it downstairs for dinner."

She settled the tray across his still legs. "Tomorrow's another day. Unless you want oatmeal," she said and stood back, waiting for him to take that first bite of fire. There would be no guessing when he would realize he'd truly bitten off more than he could chew. He'd challenged her to do her worst that morning, and Jeff Carrington was about to learn how bad her worst could be.

"Oh, Emily, you darling lady," he said. "The woman puts the best Cajun chef to shame." He scooped up a fork full and plunged in.

The reaction came quickly and definitively.

"Aah!" Jeff shrieked and searched frantically for something to put out the fire. Something she'd purposely left off the tray. "Water! Milk! Help!"

Hope leaned down and put her nose about two inches from his. "Next time you're tempted to call yourself worthless, Carrington, remember the walls have ears." She lifted the bowl of gumbo off his tray and turned away. "I'll send Emily up with some milk. Notice you put pepper on your own tongue. No one held you down."

"You're dangerous!" Jeff shouted at her retreating back. "And I'm adding attempted murder to the list. You'll be so deep in a prison they'll have to pump daylight to the lot of you!"

Hope passed Emily Roberts on the stairs. Far from

feeling the triumph she'd shown Jeff, she felt awful. "I'll be along with a new plate for him and one for Curt. But I don't feel much like eating tonight."

Emily nodded gravely. "I had to spank him once when he was about five or six for going into a pasture with an untamed stallion. I know how you feel, but you've reminded me that his welfare is more important than his immediate comfort."

"Don't just stand there," they heard Jeff yell, she supposed at Curt. "Get me something to drink."

"And as I'm holding a bit of relief, I'd best run along. The native seems to be restless," Emily quipped and chuckled. "This could actually be good for morale around here. You bellowed, sir," Hope heard the house-keeper say as she entered Jeff's room.

Jeff grabbed the milk like a lifeline. Hope was out of control. He gulped it down and swished it around his burning mouth, hoping all the while that it would quench the fire in his stomach, too. He looked at Emily and tried for his most pitiful expression.

"You have to get rid of her, Mrs. R. She's dangerous. This is a side of her I've never really seen before. You're the only one I can trust now. Help me?"

Mrs. Roberts stood a little straighter, and Jeff felt a rush of satisfaction. She was going to help! He could see her stiffening her resolve. But then she frowned and sat next to him on the bed. Jeff felt his heart sink into despair at the expression on her face. She hadn't worn that look since he was eighteen. But he remembered it well. He was about to get a lecture.

"Now you listen to me, young man. I've kept my mouth shut, but I see that my silence wasn't helping you at all. Hope Taggert *is* helping you." She took his chin in her papery hand and captured his gaze with her own. "That young woman is the best thing to ever happen to you. She cares about you. *You,* not your bank balance. Appreciate it. Appreciate her. She's got more moxie in her little finger than any of those so-called women you've dated over the years. Where are they now, I ask you?"

Jeff looked into the milk glass he still held. He had no answer for that. At least not one she didn't already know. They were off playing at life. He was too much work now.

"Hmm. That's about what I thought," she said of his silent reply. "And that's all I have to say on the subject."

Mrs. Roberts stood and was gone.

Jeff looked at Madden. "I guess you think that whole incident was funny?"

He shrugged. "I think you're a lucky man."

"Lucky? How can you say that? I can't walk. My career is over. My friends have deserted me. I need to pay a stranger to help me take a bath!" He swore. "Oh, that's real lucky."

"Maybe what you need to do is think about all the things you *do* have. The glass half-full instead of half-empty theory. You have Hope and Mrs. Roberts and Manny, who all care about you. You have a roof over your head—and not a shabby one, at that. You have the money to pay someone like me to come in here and help you get better. And you have your health. You're injured but not sick. There are guys your age all over this country dying of crippling diseases. Pardon me if I can't scare up too much sympathy for someone with an eight-figure bank account who had a riding accident when I've worked with kids who never got to walk let alone ride a horse."

Jeff felt ashamed for the first time in years. How had he gotten so selfish? "I don't know where to start," he admitted. "My life's fallen apart and I just don't know how to live this way."

"You do it one day at a time. You learn to rely on God. You become as independent as you can. Maybe that means having a chairlift put on the stairs. Building your upper body strength so you can get in and out and around in your chair. But maybe it means learning to walk again. Maybe…"

"I don't know if I can live life confined to a wheel-chair. At least in bed I feel sick."

"But you aren't sick and you may not have to learn how to live that way. One day at a time you'll either get better or you'll learn how to live with not walking. But one thing's for sure, sitting in bed isn't an option. It's giving up."

Curt's words stayed with Jeff long into the night. He hadn't spoken to Hope at all when she came in with more gumbo. She'd played a nasty trick on him, and it hadn't been funny. At least not to him. It hurt to think she might have thought so.

What it *had* done was illustrate to him more clearly than ever how helpless he was. And that she knew how helpless he was.

He hated that she saw him that way, he thought, as he looked at his useless legs. He had nothing to offer her. He'd always felt a woman needed someone she could respect—someone to be strong for her—women's lib or no. And he could no longer be relied upon. He was handicapped. Crippled. Useless. Worthless. And the woman he loved had seen him as just that.

Her presence was torture. Every minute she was here she reminded him of all he'd lost. Since she knew he was no longer the man she needed, she had to be here out of a sense of guilt. Curt was right when he said not trying was giving up. That's all he wanted to do. He wanted to crawl in a hole and pull it in after him, and maybe even be allowed to die in peace. That was the biggest problem with having Hope there. She made him feel alive again. And with life came pain. And that was something he didn't want any more of.

"Good morning." The object of his thoughts spoke as she sailed in with a bright smile on her face and what smelled like a mug of coffee in her hand. She wore crisp indigo jeans and a baby blue sweater. The color of the sweater made her eyes shine like sapphires.

"Did you sleep well?" she asked cheerily. "Curt said he gave you a massage to relax your muscles at bedtime."

Jeff tensed. Right. Rub it in. Curt has to put me to bed like a two-year-old. "Yeah. I slept like a baby," he sneered.

Hope put the mug on the bedside table and stepped back. The message in her eyes was clear. She'd obviously thought he'd be more cooperative this morning.

"Uh. I brought you coffee," she said, pointing to the rich brown liquid filling the room with its tempting aroma. She opened the terrace curtains then turned to him. "Curt will be up in a minute," she continued, undaunted. "He's having his first cup at the breakfast bar. If you think you aren't any good before a couple cups, you should see him."

"You two are certainly getting all nice and cozy in my house."

Hope's eyebrow climbed her forehead. "I've known Curtis Madden for years. There's no need for us to get cozy. We went to school together. We've attended the same church since I was twelve when Aunt Meg moved home and started taking me. We were in youth group, summer Bible school and Christian camp together."

"Hiring him sounds a little like nepotism, don't you think?"

Hope pivoted and stalked toward the door. She turned back when she was halfway there. "I hired him to help *you!*" she snapped. "You are the most ungrateful, spoiled *baby* I've ever had the misfortune to meet."

Baby? He was a baby, was he? People didn't really see red. It was an old stupid saying. Or so he'd thought. "Get out!" he screamed. But she just stood there. Stood there looking down her superior nose at him, thinking he was a baby. On instinct alone Jeff grabbed the plastic tumbler of water Curt had put next to his bed and threw it at her. The water sloshed all over him, but he didn't care. How dare she rub his nose in his helplessness?

She caught the tumbler easily and threw it at him. It bounced harmlessly to the floor after he let it smack into his chest, just to prove she couldn't hurt him. Down deep he'd known she would catch it and toss it back, but short of pounding his fist into the mattress and really looking juvenile, throwing it at her was his only option. He was, after all, powerless against someone who could storm out and leave him screaming at the air.

Hope's next reaction, however, was so uncharacteristic and unexpected that it took his breath. Tears welled in her big blue eyes, making them sparkle like precious gems. Her chin wobbled when she opened her mouth to speak, and she put her shaking hand up as if to hold off a further attack. And then she ran.

Through the terrace doors a few moments later, Jeff heard Manny call to her, but he couldn't decipher what was said. Nor did he hear a reply. She'd left the draperies open, so he could see her when she got a few hundred feet from the house.

And she was still running.

He felt tears sting his eyes. He hadn't meant to hurt her. Or maybe he had, but it didn't feel anywhere near as good as he'd thought it would. Why were people nasty to one another if it made them feel this awful? How had his parents looked at themselves in the mirror every day?

Jeff kept watching Hope, wanting her to turn and come back so he could apologize, but she kept running. When she reached the pasture fence, he knew she was seeing what he was, his half-wild horse, Mr. March. But that sight meant something different to each of them. She saw in the stallion possibilities for the future ripe for the picking, and he saw his past hopes languishing on the vine.

The stallion he'd raised from a yearling and trained with Hope's help prowled the pasture, clearly unhappy and tense from lack of exercise. Mr. March's head stilled. He turned toward her, then thundered over to where she'd climbed the fence, tossing his head. He paced away restively, then back to her.

Suddenly, recklessly, considering Mr. March's temperament, Hope grabbed the horse's mane and leaped onto his bare back. Jeff's heart pounded as the two flew across the field—a study in fury and freedom. And the heart he'd thought had hardened to stone cracked a little. Because there in that one scene were represented all his wishes and desires—past and present. Lost and yet to be achieved.

Mr. March represented the Olympic dream that had turned to dust, but he also stood for a more distant past when it was Jeff himself riding recklessly across the field, fleeing pain and seeking the joy and the freedom it gave him. Ironic to recognize that what he'd lost in the accident he'd really lost long ago. Joy. And now, as he discovered what he'd truly lost physically, he sat watching the treasure he'd lost that made everything else pale in comparison. For riding away and out of his life was Hope, his heart's desire.

He hadn't meant to hurt her. Just to make her want to go home—for her own good as well as his. Having her near was too painful for him. He would drag her into a world of disabilities where she didn't belong. But he hadn't wanted to make her cry.

"Sticks and stones, Hope. I guess we both forgot," he whispered brokenly.

He'd forgotten how tender her heart was. He'd forgotten how words could injure. Just as he'd forgotten the way it felt to fly with the wind, not to perfect a technique or test his mount's stamina, but to run from pain. To forget hurtful words. And to be free.

Free.

Hope needed to be free. Free of him. Free of the guilt he was sure tied her to him. Only then would she once again be able to go on with her life. But he'd tried cutting her out of his life, and that hadn't done it. She'd moved in and taken over, saying she was going to make him get better. And in trying to get her to give up on him, he'd hurt her. He wasn't strong enough to do that again. She was too precious to him.

Curt walked in, and Jeff looked up, remembering the things the younger man had said to him the evening before. There was only one way to free her. He had to do what she wanted him to do. He had to cooperate and try to make as much progress as he could. Then she'd see that he didn't need her. What would a few exercises hurt, after all? It would at least relieve some of the boredom.

He'd do as Curt had said. He'd try—at least for today.

Chapter Seven

An hour after leaping on the stallion's back, Hope slowed Mr. March as they approached the rose-brick stable. Manny pushed open the big arch-topped door and waved as she dropped to the ground off Mr. March's back.

The purpose of the wild ride had been simple—to run from the hurt of the nasty scene in Jeff's room. But once she'd managed to block out most of the pain and disillusionment of seeing Jeff become someone she scarcely recognized, she'd realized that he'd been pushing her buttons. And that she'd reacted just as he'd wanted. His rancor had been as much an act to drive her away as her tough stand was an attempt to make him care, and she'd let him get a rise out of her. That had been a mistake—a huge mistake.

But act or not, twice now she'd forced him to be cruel, something he'd never been to another person as long as she'd known him. When they were children, it had always been Cole telling her to bug off and Jeff saying he didn't mind her tagging along. He'd lived his life with cruel, snide remarks flying between his parents and directed at him from both Carringtons. He'd never channeled his pain toward the people in his life. She could never remember him being mean to another person, let alone cruel.

The realization had her wondering if she'd misread the Lord's will. Could her whole approach to helping Jeff be wrong? He wasn't fighting her challenges with that I'll-show-you attitude he'd always had when going after something he wanted. Instead, he was sinking further and further into a mean-spirited kind of existence that was poison to his soul and no life at all for someone like him. She knew Jeff's heart, and he was hurting himself far more than he was hurting her. She had known from the start that her tough love stand could mean that even if she won her battle to get Jeff back on his feet she might lose him in the end. While she didn't believe his claim that he felt only friendship for her, she was very much afraid she may have already pushed him too far and destroyed any possible future for them.

Trying not to show how at odds her thoughts were, Hope turned Mr. March over to one of the handlers for a nice rubdown and washing. It was the one part of being civilized the still half-wild animal loved.

With a heavy heart and the smell of straw and horse sweat filling her nostrils and clinging to her clothes, Hope turned toward the big house on the hill. She was surprised to find Emily Roberts singing happily as she scooted around the kitchen.

"Hope! You're an absolute miracle worker," Emily cried, rushing toward her, a happy grin wreathing her face. "He's coming down for breakfast, and Curt said he's going to start therapy this morning. And it was Jeffrey's idea. It's wonderful. I just know he's going to be fine now."

Surprised by the sudden change, Hope prayed Emily was right.

The clatter of the wheelchair drew her attention and confirmed Emily's claim. Jeff tried twice to negotiate the doorway, but the width of the chair made the task difficult for a beginner. She could see how frustrated he was but didn't know if she should offer help.

"I've got you," Curt said from behind before she decided what to do.

Jeff dropped his fisted hands in his lap. "How's anyone supposed to get around in one of these contraptions?" he complained.

"There are more compact chairs. Once you get stronger, one of those will give you better mobility. After all, you don't need the battery pack or the full arms to keep your seat. Hope, I'll write down some model numbers for the kind I'm talking about and for some additional equipment I think Jeff would benefit from. Could you see about it? And maybe do something about a chairlift on the back stairs?" Curt asked.

Hope nodded and looked at Jeff, but he refused to

meet her eyes. The sudden silence in the room was deafening, and the tension between them was clearly uncomfortable to the others. Thankfully, Hope had an excuse to leave.

"Uh, Emily, I was riding and I really need to shower and change. I'll just grab something for myself later."

"You'll do no such thing. No one gets to skip meals in this house as long as I'm around. Go have your shower, and I'll keep your breakfast warm."

Hope blinked and stared at the usually docile Emily. Heavens, she'd created a second monster! Then she heard Jeff snicker and wiped the shocked expression off her face. Instead of protesting, she nodded to Emily, shot Jeff a killing glance and fled his presence for the second time that day.

But there was no fleeing when she returned half an hour later and found Jeff alone in the breakfast room. He was clearly waiting for her. She skidded to a halt two steps into the warm sunny room as he looked up from his nearly empty plate.

"Oh, uh, hi," Jeff said and grimaced. He looked at his plate then at her. His gray eyes were wary and somber. He was dressed in a black sweat suit. He usually looked good in black, but it seemed to exaggerate how pale his skin had grown since February. He stared at her for a long uncomfortable minute, his apology already in his eyes before he said, "I'm sorry for the things I said."

She shrugged. "'S okay."

"No. No, it isn't. I was way out of line."

Hope stared at him. This was the old Jeff. Or at least a glimpse of him. "And I forgive you," she told him.

He raked his hand through his hair and sighed. "I hate this. I feel so powerless. Helpless. Hopeless. And at the risk of another spiked dinner, worthless. I'm not good for anything anymore."

Hope dropped into a chair near him. "Look, Jeff, God doesn't make junk. Believe that. You've never been worthless a day in your life. That's your father and your coach talking."

"And it turns out they were right, after all. What can I do now?"

Hope was clueless for an answer. She knew what he was talking about, and it wasn't what it would be with most men. What he didn't mean was how did he go about making money? For Jeff that had never been a goal, or a problem, for that matter. He'd followed his father's footsteps into trading on the stock market, but that was only to finance his Olympic aspirations and not for the money's sake. Money was merely a means to an end, not an end result. So what he'd really asked was what was he supposed to replace the dream of a gold medal with? What was he supposed to strive for?

Because Hope had always believed that once he'd achieved his goal of Olympic gold, he would suddenly find his life empty, she had an answer ready. And it was an answer he wouldn't want to hear. She put her hand over his where it lay fisted on the table between them. "Seek the Lord, Jeff. He knows what you need to do. Ask Him."

Jeff shook his head. "You know how I feel about all that hocus-pocus."

Hope rolled her eyes. "I have never said faith was magic. You don't even try to understand."

"No. I don't. Because I don't believe it. Come on, Hope. What kind of merciful God would let me get crippled this way? And what about my parents? And yours? Mine are dead. Your mother was killed by a crazed horse with your father and brother watching. Your father's never recovered. Neither has Cole. It's torn your family apart for years. And your aunt Meg? She's still grieving for a guy who went off to war and never came home."

"Because we have free will. And we make mistakes. You were hurt because I was careless." She held up her hand to stop his protest. "No. I missed a badly worn girth. I still can't believe I did something so stupid, but I did it. I finally know how my father felt all those years ago for not listening to Cole about that horse. But he didn't listen, did he? It was his choice to ignore his son's protests in the interest of getting Cole back in the saddle after the horse threw him. Unfortunately Dad set the incident that killed my mother into motion.

"Another person who was wrong was my mother. She didn't have to step in between Cole and Dad that day. She didn't have to prove the horse was safe.

"Then there's Cole," she continued, ticking off the people he'd cited. "Cole could have reached out to my father sometime in the last fourteen years. And vice versa. Your parents didn't have to leave that party with a friend who'd been drinking and let him drive.

"And Aunt Meg could have looked for love again after her fiancé was killed in Vietnam. She chose to stay alone."

Hope covered his hand again. "All those things happened because we have free will. Because God gave us free will. What we do with our free will can bring joy or heartache into our lives or the lives of others."

Jeff was shaking his head. "I'm not buying it. You're just rationalizing."

"You are so stubborn!"

He pulled his hand from hers. "No more so than you!"

They looked at each other. It was such a typical debate between them. The kind she missed. He smiled. She chuckled.

"Some things never change, do they?" he asked, still smiling.

"No. They don't," she replied and reached for what she assumed was the list of exercise equipment Curt had promised to leave for her.

Jeff practically snatched it out of her hand.

"Isn't that the list Curt left for me?"

"I don't need all this."

"You heard Curt. He says you do."

"I'm paying him enough. He can just improvise and earn his salary."

Hope crossed her arms. "He'll earn his salary by getting you on the road to recovery. What's the real problem here? You aren't lazy, Jeff. So it isn't the work involved. You've never been cheap or stingy, so it isn't the money that stuff will cost. What are you afraid of?"

"I'm not afraid! I—I..." He slapped the list down between them. "Fine. Go spend my money. You're right. I don't care."

Hope stood and smiled, then, on impulse, she leaned down and kissed his cheek. "Thanks. I will. How about we go see how that exercise room is coming?"

Jeff took a deep breath. Then fought to take another. Therapy? Why not just call it what is was?

Torture.

The inquisition.

He took another breath. Or tried. But the bunching muscles in his back and legs tightened, robbing him of what felt like his last thread of sanity. For the first time in his entire life, Jeffrey Carrington let someone else know he was in pain. He let out a howl loud enough to wake the dead.

And Curt Madden.

The supposedly hard-to-wake, four-cup-a-jump-start therapist arrived wide awake at his side in a nanosecond. "Spasms?" Madden asked.

In the grip of an even worse cramp than the previous one, Jeff managed to nod, then he buried his face in his pillow, letting it absorb the cold sweat and his humiliating tears. Then breathing seemed to lose its involuntary status. Jeff found himself fighting to suck air in around the pain and expel it to make room for the next breath. Then he felt Madden's hands on his back and tensed even more.

"Try to relax," Curt ordered. "Do you want medication?"

"Anything. My abs are starting to cramp now. I'm going to get sick. Do something. Lethal injection couldn't be worse than this."

Somehow the RN managed to get the medication into him, and Jeff managed to keep it down. He couldn't remember when his mind started to clear of the excruciating agony that had awakened him out of the depth of sleep. Though it was now on a level he could handle, Jeff was still in considerable pain. Almost on cue, embarrassment crept into its place as Curt manipulated the protesting muscles.

"Try to relax and go with the pain. Let it wash over you like a wave but try not to react to it. Let sleep come back and…"

Jeff closed his eyes and listened to the hypnotic rhythm of Curt's voice. It reminded him of the way Hope's voice sounded when she was working with a particularly skittish horse. Calm. Reassuring. Restful. A voice you could trust, he thought some minutes later as he slipped into exhausted sleep.

The next thing he knew, a cool breeze flowed across his skin and soft sunlight kissed the air. He was still facedown on the bed. And it was morning. He'd made it through the night.

Jeff didn't know how he was going to face therapy

again that day knowing what the increased activity would do to him in the night. He'd noticed it early on. The more they moved him around for tests in the hospital, the worse his muscles had cramped in the night. The therapy wasn't worth it. Why couldn't they leave him alone?

He opened his eyes and saw Hope sitting on the floor by his bed. She wore a soft peach sweater and a matching skirt that draped over bent knees and flowed onto the floor covering all but the tips of her shoes. Her head rested on her arms which were wrapped around her upraised knees. Her position didn't look very comfortable.

Guilt struck him.

He was about to disappoint her, but it couldn't be helped. This wasn't going to work. He'd rather die than suffer the shame again of screaming out in the night. He was thankful that with Hope sleeping in the homestead house, she couldn't have heard him, but Curt had, and, no doubt, Mrs. R.

Hope must have felt him watching her because her eyes flew open and she blushed. "Oh. You're awake! Hi."

"Ditto," he replied, his voice rough as sandpaper. Probably from that guttural scream he'd let out when the spasms had awakened him to a world of darkness and pain.

He tried to clear his throat. "Where's super nurse this morning?" he asked.

"Curt should be right back. They needed him to check out the equipment that's being delivered. And there's a mirror installer down there putting mirrors on a couple walls. I heard you had a bad night."

"You could say that."

"I'm sorry. Curt was able to help you, though. Right?"

With some difficulty, Jeff rolled over then pulled himself up in the bed while he considered how to answer her question without giving away too much about the night before. "Sure," he said with a careless shrug. "He beat the pain into submission after about an hour."

"I'd heard he was good at what he does. That's why I wanted him here to help you. You don't have any problem with moving out of this room for a while, do you?"

Was she trying to keep him constantly off balance? "Why would I move out? This has always been my room."

"Because Curt thought the ground floor of the guest wing would be better for you two. He's setting up an exercise room in a room near the hot tub and whirlpool. He also thought since there are ground-floor bedrooms in the guest wing you could both move into a couple of them and we could avoid the expense and mess of the chairlift on the back stairs."

Jeff cleared his throat again and looked away. "Forget it. He's wasting his time, Hope. So are you. The more I try, the worse I am. Look at last night."

"It's my business how I spend my time, and Curt's being paid for his. And before you say it's your money that's being wasted, you know you don't care. Try to be positive. Maybe the pain will get better. Maybe you'll get better. Can you risk not trying? Really?"

Jeff stared at her earnest face. It was the face he longed to kiss. The face that always faded away before their lips met in his dreams. Maybe he could hang in there for a little while just to show her that he had tried but that it was hopeless. Then she'd have to give up and go home to her family and leave him to his broken life and his even more painfully broken heart.

That afternoon Jeff rolled into the room Hope and Curt had set aside as his bedroom and looked around with a disgusted sigh. Like many of the rooms in the house, it was eternally white and stark. All the comforts of home, Jeff thought sarcastically. It was even more impersonal than his hospital room had been. His mother would have loved it.

He may as well have gone to that rehab the doctors had tried to stick him in. He'd lost just as much control over his life here as he would have in an impersonal institution. Next thing they'd probably do was hand him a schedule to live by. At least at the rehab some decorator would have carefully chosen colors to cheer the poor invalid.

This, Hope had told him, was all for his benefit. She probably believed it, too. Hope would never do anything to hurt him, but it was a little hard to feel grateful. It didn't seem to matter to anyone that he wanted his space. His own bed. His own furniture. His own carefully painted walls surrounding him.

He was to sleep in a hospital bed which, though he

hated to admit it, would probably make him a lot more comfortable than his own bed. There was a trapeze bar suspended by a frame that hung over the bed to help him sit up, turn over and get in the chair. The mattress was topped with an air bladder like the one in the hospital. It was made up with institutional looking sheets. White, of course. But comfortable and convenient though it might be, it was still the bed of a cripple. He wouldn't even be able to pretend to be normal in bed anymore.

"So, what do you think?" Hope asked from behind him.

Jeff refused to looked at her. She sounded nervous. He was sure she was perceptive enough of his moods to know that this change wasn't one he was happy with. And he knew she wasn't trying to hurt him. But even her limited presence in his life did that. Why couldn't she go home and leave him alone?

"Does my opinion matter?" he snapped.

He had the luxury of not seeing her face and was grateful when he heard the hurt in her answer. "This is all for your own good, Jeff. Of course your opinion matters."

"Then tell me. Did you sterilize the walls, too? It's about as personal! I like my room. It was the one thing I was allowed to pick when my father had this mausoleum built. I was only three, but I remember walking from room to room and trying to decide which one was mine. I remember it seemed impossible to choose because it all looked the same. Then I walked into my room. Maybe it was the terrace that looked out over the pastures. Or the tree that used to be outside the window. It was summer and the tree was bright green against the white walls. It was the first color I'd seen since I arrived. I don't know for sure what it was, but the room felt like home."

Her heart hitched at the sadness in his voice. "I'm sorry. This is only temporary. Pretty soon you'll be able to walk into your room and feel at home again."

He wheeled around to face her. "And what if all your optimism is off the mark?"

"Then we'll put in the chairlift and you can move back up there. Either way, this is just temporary. I promise."

Jeff looked away. He hated seeing her hurting, and almost as much, he hated the guilt he heard in her voice. It reminded him that guilt was the only reason she was here, now that he'd told her there was no future for them.

"Tell you what," Hope said after a few silent moments. "Suppose I call in some men to move the armoire and bureau down here. And maybe hanging some of your paintings would make it feel less impersonal. If you still hate it too much, we'll get an elevator chairlift put in and move you back upstairs. How does that sound?" she asked.

In the interest of cooperation, maybe he could stand the white walls with his paintings hanging and his things around him. At least this way there wouldn't be all the problems with getting him up to his room, and if he really did hate it he could still have the elevator installed.

"All right. But only if I decide I want to stay down here. Deal?"

She smiled, and the room brightened as surely as if the sun had suddenly risen right there. "Deal. I should have thought of transferring your stuff with you. I'm sorry. I'll get right on it."

Hope pivoted and rushed out before he recovered from the effects of that smile. He hadn't told her he'd once again decided to give up on the idea of therapy. Mrs. Roberts seemed to understand that the pain it caused was too unbearable. Now he wasn't sure he *could* tell Hope. If he stopped trying to work with Curt, he'd never set her free. And much as he wanted to keep her with him forever, he knew he couldn't tie her to him the way he was—half a man.

"Did you convince him to keep working at it?" Curt asked as Hope entered the kitchen. Emily turned anxious eyes toward her, as well.

Hope sat and grabbed one of Emily's cookies. "He just complained about the room." She chuckled. "Actually he demanded to know if we'd sterilized the walls. It's obvious his tastes don't run parallel to his mother's." She told them about the compromise she and Jeff had reached over the room.

"But he didn't tell you he didn't want to do his therapy because of last night?" Emily took a seat at the table with Hope and Curt. "He seemed so determined to quit earlier."

"I'm afraid Jeff feels his life isn't his to control any more," Curt added. "And screaming last night bothered him a lot."

Hope agreed. "Jeff's always been about control. I guess losing control enough to scream the way he did would have felt like the ultimate loss of control. I've always thought that's why he enjoyed riding and why he took on that half-wild animal out there in the pasture. That way he could control the seemingly uncontrollable. It's probably the same with his investments and the breeding program."

"At least he didn't give up again," Emily said, the worry clearing from her lined face.

"He must have rethought his decision after the pain faded," Hope ventured.

"It's more likely that he doesn't want to disappoint you, dear," Emily replied.

Curt nodded his agreement.

Hope couldn't deny or confirm it, so she shrugged and stood. "Well, it's time this girl hits the books. Do me a favor, drag me out of there for lunch before I OD on finance. This really isn't my forte but there's not much left to do around the stables today, and from the depth of the mail on that desk, I'd say my work's cut out for me."

Making her way to Jeff's office, Hope thought of the room where Jeff used to work. The walls, lined with shelf after shelf of books both new and old, gave her the same warm feeling her office at Laurel Glen did. She was tempted to build a fire in the fireplace but knew she'd probably fall asleep. She hadn't let Jeff know but she'd been in the kitchen in the early morning hours heating some milk to help her sleep when Jeff screamed. Only knowing that he wouldn't want her there had kept her out of his room. But she'd stood in the hall until Curt's massage and the drugs let him rest comfortably.

It was easy to see why he'd gotten so discouraged and why it would be such a temptation to quit trying. If her presence kept him working toward a goal, even if that goal was not disappointing her, she'd stay till she was old and gray, Hope thought, and settled behind the big desk.

She glanced at the stack of bills and financial statements she'd sorted into piles and groaned. There were, however, plenty of other reasons for her to stay. Jeff apparently hadn't been taking care of the household's finances, the stable feed bills or his stocks since the accident. Right now, working at his therapy would be all he could handle, so she would have to fill in for him as best she could.

Hope wished she'd paid more attention in her finance classes. She'd been able to figure out the discrepancies Billy Dever had caused in Emily's petty cash account, and with care yesterday she'd balanced Jeff's several checking accounts. She was perfectly able to write checks to pay utility, grocery and feed bills, and she did that first. Two hours later all bills were paid and she'd mastered the payroll software. Since the next day was Friday and payday at Lavender Hill, she wrote those checks, as well.

She had lunch then, for the rest of the afternoon, answered inquiries about stud fees and possible purchases of Lavender Hill's yearlings. Then she sat, staring at the last pile. What did she do with all this stuff about the stock market? The whole concept escaped her, from how to trade stocks right down to what good it was in the first place. Hope was never so grateful as when she heard Emily's sweet grandmotherly voice accompany a knock on the door. Saved by dinner!

Chapter Eight

Jeff crossed his arms and shot Hope and Curt a mutinous stare. "I said I'm on strike! For one solid month all I've done is what you two tell me to do. Including taking naps! I'm sick of it."

"Can you honestly sit there and tell me you're not doing better?" Curt asked.

"The operative word is *sit!*"

"Jeff," Hope cajoled, "you knew going in it would take a while. You lost your first month and a lot of ground with it. First you had to get back to square one. But as Curt said, you're better. The cramps are coming less and less. You sleep for less time during those horrible naps, but you do sleep. You can get yourself into your chair and into the tub and back out. You've lost all the fat you put on and gained muscle. You're moving forward now."

"I'm *rolling* forward," he retorted. And that was the

real problem. He'd wanted to believe that this wasn't all there was going to be in his life. He'd begun to believe Curt could really help him. He'd begun to believe in miracles. Then last night he'd dreamed of dancing with Hope in his arms, but when he'd awakened this morning, he'd found himself still unable to stand. It was a bitter pill to swallow to have to sit there and look up into her eyes when she should have been gazing up into his.

At the time of the accident, he'd thought he might be in love with her, and he'd wanted to explore the possibility. But now, when he couldn't, he knew there was no speculation about it. It was a simple fact. He loved her. And he would lose her.

The sooner the better.

A quick pain was better than this drawn-out cycle of agony—dreams of a glowing future in the night and the realization of the truth as day dawned.

"Why don't you both go home and leave me in peace? Go torture someone you can help," he said to Curt, then pinned Hope with a virulent look. "Go home and train horses and stop trying to train me. Why are you here, anyway? I don't need either of you. I can take care of myself for the most part now. I'll hire someone else to help me with what I can't do alone."

Jeff looked away from the wounded expression on Hope's face. He'd hurt her. He tried to make himself ignore the deep shame that came over him, but he couldn't. "I'm sorry," he said, not even waiting for Hope's response.

"Curt, would you leave us alone for a few minutes?" Hope asked. When Curt nodded and left after a long assessing look at both of them, Hope silently moved a chair in front of Jeff and sat facing him. "Want to talk about it?" she asked calmly. Kindly.

Jeff blinked. She was supposed to be angry. She was supposed to leave. He deserved an irate set down, not sweet understanding. "There's nothing to talk about. I'm an ungrateful louse who doesn't deserve a friend like you."

She shook her head. "Not good enough. Something happened between last night and this morning. What has you so discouraged today?"

Jeff wondered how she knew him so well and fought the urge to reach out and touch her. It was the same every time she was near. He looked away—and straight into his own face reflected in the mirrored wall of the exercise room.

He turned his head, unable to look at himself. He wanted her here as much if not more than he wanted her to leave. And it shamed him almost as much as hurting her had. To cover his nearly overwhelming need and to distract himself from her nearness, Jeff decided to admit to half the truth.

"I had a dream that I could walk. Then I woke up and I couldn't. Nothing mysterious. Just a cold dip in life's pool of miserable reality."

Hope reached out and gripped his hand where it lay fisted on his useless legs. "But that's only the reality of the moment," she told him, her voice rife with deep conviction. "It's not the reality of the future. The future is fluid. Always moving. Always changing and shifting. Your situation can turn around at any time."

Jeff looked into her beautiful eyes and knew the answer to his next question even before he asked it. The truth of her incredible faith in him was there in the depths of those eyes he loved so much. But there was something else there, too, and it hurt. "Do you really believe that, or is it your guilt talking? You know, wishful thinking to get you off the hook? I told you I don't blame you for the accident. I should have checked my own tack."

Hope shook her head. "No. I made the mistake. I am guilty. I feel guilty. There's no point denying it. But I also really believe you'll walk again."

Jeff closed his eyes and dropped his head back, then, taking a deep breath and drawing in her unique scent, he gazed at her again, his heart as heavy with the weight of her belief in him as his body was with his need of her. "You have more faith in me than I deserve."

"You don't give yourself enough credit," Hope said as she smiled and stood. "You never have. I wish you could forget every negative word you heard about yourself from your parents."

"Mother wasn't so bad. At least she was too busy with committees and her tennis to have much time left for criticism. Unfortunately, my father was such a genius that he only had to spend half his days making his fortune. That left him the rest of the time for me and all my faults."

Hope looked into his eyes. "I wish you could see what I see in you. And I wish you knew what I know. You have another Father, Jeff, and He wouldn't see anything but His perfect child if you'd put your faith in His Son."

Jeff blew a sharp breath through his lips. "You never give up, do you?"

"Wouldn't I be an awfully selfish person if I kept His good news to myself when it's given me such joy and peace of mind? I want you to share in His joy, Jeff. He could give you that and so much more."

Jeff had to admit, even if just to himself, that he'd never really looked at it in that way. He'd always thought she wanted to drag him to church and make his life as boring as hers. A misery-likes-company sort of scenario.

"You know what you need?" Hope continued. "You need a day off and a change of scene. We need to get you out and about in the world again."

Jeff's stomach turned to rock. "No. I'm fine. I don't need to get out. I don't want to get out. I like it here just fine."

"You can't stay cooped up here. Pretty soon you won't be able to face going off the property. My great-aunt was like that, and she didn't go out of her house for years before her death."

"I'm not your aunt." Jeff gritted his teeth. He was sick to death of feeling like a weakling around her. "I don't want people pointing at me and wondering what happened to me. I don't want to look *up* at a bunch of strangers from a chair, or sit in the handicapped section at the movies, or have waiters trying to figure out where to stick me so I won't be in their way. Don't tell me it won't happen because I've seen it happening to other people. I was probably one of the insensitive clods gawking."

"Jeff—"

"No! I don't want to go anywhere. Drop it!" he snarled and pivoted the chair so he could stare out the window. Seconds later he heard her withdraw quietly from the room. Hands fisted, Jeff pounded again and again on his useless legs, satisfied that at least they still felt pain.

When a week had passed with no indication that Jeff was ready to face the world, Hope decided to talk about it with Curt. She found him seated at the wrought-iron table on the stone patio off the breakfast room. He'd begun to brave the cool spring air to sit with his coffee, reading the Word before breakfast.

After bringing up the subject of Jeff's increasing avoidance of the outside world, she asked, "Do you think I should just force him to go somewhere?"

While Curt considered her question, Hope said a quick prayer that Curt would have a better suggestion. Even though Jeff was improving physically, she knew that every time she pushed him she tested the love she prayed he still felt for her. The possibility that he'd meant what he'd said that day when he called her pathetic haunted her sleep.

Hope's heart fell when Curt shook his head. "I doubt that would do more than make him hopping mad along with making him feel he's lost control of another aspect of his life. I don't think it's a good idea, but I confess I don't have another one. Maybe we should just let it ride a while longer."

Hope frowned and gazed over the evenly mowed fields that by summer would be tall with alfalfa. The fields were crisscrossed with sparkling white fences, as they had been when Jeff's grandfather ran Lavender Hill as a horse farm. Along the knee-high stone wall that surrounded the terrace, lined up like soldiers awaiting battle, sat several verdigris planters resplendent with purple and yellow crocuses. Rather than cheer her, the beautiful scene saddened her. The world was bursting with life and change, and Jeff was missing it all.

There had to be a way to get him out and about without driving a wedge between them, she thought. But what if she did get him out and his worst fears came true? What if people did stare? What if someone openly showed pity for him?

The only safe place she could think to take him was her church. She was sure the people at the Tabernacle would accept him as her friend and take him at face value. Of course, getting Jeff to go to a church service would be even harder than getting him to go to a dinner or movie.

Obviously seeing her distress, Curt took her hand and gave it a comforting squeeze. "Hope, he's not going to agree yet. And you can't force the man to do everything you want."

Hope sighed. "I know. I wouldn't love him if I could."

"Let's give it to the Lord and ask Him to show us the way."

Nodding, Hope joined hands with Curt and closed her eyes as he prayed for guidance and patience with Jeff. Curt's prayers for patience were less desperate these days than they once had been. It was proof positive that Jeff's attitude toward therapy had improved as much as his muscle tone. She tried to be grateful, but she wanted so much more for him than to be called cooperative by two of the few people in his life.

"Hey, you two," Emily called out the back door. "Breakfast in a few minutes. I've called Jeff."

"Thanks, Mrs. R," Curt called and let go of Hope's hand, his prayer concluded. "You better be ready for a hungry man. I could eat a horse this morning."

"Ouch, Madden. I've told you that's not an expression to use around horse people," Jeff called, laughter in his voice. He sat behind Emily in the doorway.

Curt chuckled. "With all the developments going up and all the executives moving in along the main roads, I keep forgetting that there are still so many horse farms out here on the side roads."

"That's sad, Madden. Look out there. You're living on a horse farm. And over yonder is Laurel Glen, one of the biggest in the state!"

With Jeff's words, Hope's thoughts winged their way to Laurel Glen. She was still too tied to her home to forget the reality of what all those starter castles sprouting up meant financially for her father and the farm that had been in the Taggert family for centuries. She turned and looked toward home.

"If we can't find a way to hold the line against rising property taxes, this part of Chester County is going to be as built up as the northern part of the county," she mused sadly.

"Is Laurel Glen having problems?" Jeff asked from behind her. She'd missed the sound of the wheels in her musings and turned to face him.

How could she tell him that rumor about his accident had caused her father more setbacks than the rising taxes that plagued nearly every farm in the county? Especially when the rumors were true. He *had* been crippled by a careless worker and poorly maintained tack. Her carelessness. Her father's tack. Each mistake had been inconsistent with both of them. But the result was still Jeff in a wheelchair and her at Lavender Hill searching for ways to help him venture into the world.

The snap of Jeff's fingers in front of her face jolted Hope to the matter at hand. "Hey, space cadet, I'm still waiting. Is your dad in trouble?" he asked when her eyes locked with his.

She looked away and grimaced. "Let's just say profits are down." Way down. And she felt guilty about that, as well. The farm's downhill slide had begun with her mistake. Should she be there helping? Was her insistence on helping Jeff dishonoring her father? He was probably doing the job of two, and without her there, Aunt Meg was stuck refereeing between Cole and Ross.

Hope told herself that part of the situation had been caused by her father's decisions and by his stubbornness. Unfortunately, that didn't ease her guilt a whit. She kept giving it to the Lord, along with her guilt over Jeff's injuries, but both loads of guilt kept coming back. That had never happened to her before when she'd asked Him to carry a burden for her. She needed to talk to Pastor Jim about it. Maybe he could figure out what she was doing wrong.

"Ross should get the other farm and stable owners together to see that their tax structure…"

Hope stared at Jeff, letting his words and ideas fly over her head like brilliantly crafted paper airplanes. He had such a fine mind, and she had a feeling he also had every bit of his father's financial genius.

"Would you talk to my father about all that?" she asked, thinking that maybe that was a way to show her father how much substance there was to Jeff. "I'm afraid having their wills in order and working like men possessed are the limits of Taggert family financial planning. It was about all my grandfather did, and I'll bet that's all Dad's done."

Jeff shook his head. "He'd never listen to me."

Hope smiled. "Then we'll have to work on that, won't we?"

"Are you two going to come in and eat this before it gets cold?" Emily called.

"Uh-oh. We better get in there," Jeff joked. "Mrs. R on the warpath isn't a pretty sight. I'm telling you, you created a monster."

"You just have your nose out of joint because you can't wrap her around your little finger anymore."

"I've noticed a certain amount of steel in her spine toward you these days. Like when you try to skip meals. You get away with less than I do." He smiled that smile she saw rarely lately, and her heart turned over.

There was something about Jeff that she had learned over the years. It was a simple truth that he'd never understood his power over women. He used it unconsciously and never really knew what he did that attracted them. It was that unconscious artlessness that she'd fallen in love with first.

Since his accident, he'd obviously tried to analyze what used to have women flocking to his side and giving him his way. He'd tried arrogance. Tried carelessness. Even tried looking pathetic. But none of those things had anything to do with his real charm.

His charm was in the air of naïveté his smile showed. It gave away his obliviousness to the very thing women couldn't resist. He projected that charm by the boatload with his hopeful smile and the mischief glimmering in his eyes.

And that gave her a sudden brilliant idea. *Let this be from you, Lord,* she prayed. *Please don't let me make a mistake and destroy whatever Jeff feels for me.*

They had all discussed Jeff's needs and what he had

to learn to do on his own in case he never walked again. At first Hope hadn't wanted Curt to spend time on anything but helping him walk. It smacked of giving up. But Curt Madden knew his stuff, so she'd backed off. Next on the agenda was for Jeff to learn to survive in the kitchen. But Curt hadn't yet told Jeff that today was the day they'd start working in Emily's domain. And Jeff hadn't a clue how to manipulate Emily these days because he was trying too hard and she saw right through his efforts.

Hope arched an eyebrow and smirked at him.

"What's that look about?" he demanded, taking up Hope's challenge as if on cue.

"She's just fussing over my eating habits. She feeds me wherever she can find me. But who was it who had to come to the lunch table yesterday when he wanted to eat in the whirlpool? It's your number Emily's got." She could almost see that wonderful competitive streak rise in him.

"At breakfast we'll see who she pays more attention to," Jeff challenged.

Hope added another smirk, just to egg him on. "Okay, hotshot. If she pays more attention to you than me, I have to do something you want me to do. And the same goes for you."

"Anything?" he asked with a strange gleam in his eyes.

Hope glared, wondering what was going on in his mind. "Anything as long it isn't immoral or dangerous," she added, to be certain all her bases were covered.

Jeff nodded and pivoted the chair toward the breakfast room door, and she sailed in behind him, dropping into one of the fruitwood chairs. Sunshine glinted though the crisp curtains and shone on the copper sugar bowl and creamer on the table. She loved this room. The homeliness of it. Like Jeff's room—his real room upstairs—the kitchen and breakfast nook area no longer suffered the cold brush of his mother's stark taste. This was one of the few rooms Jeff had bothered to redecorate after her death.

"I have a lot on my list for today, Emily. I really just want coffee," Hope said.

"You will do no such thing!"

"Then would you mind if I ate in the study?"

"Oh, not at all dear," Emily replied with a sweet smile. "I'll just fix you up a nice tray."

Hope sent a smirk Jeff's way as Emily fussed. Trying to cause as little work for her as possible, Hope got out the tray and grabbed a place setting of flatware off the table.

As the older woman set a plate on the tray, Jeff said, "You know, that looks like a good idea. Would you bring mine into my room?"

"No, I will not. You just get yourself right up to that table and eat like a gentleman. Honestly, as if a body hasn't got more to do than wait on you hand and foot."

Jeff stared at Emily in amazement, then he looked toward Hope, his eyes narrowed. "You set me up."

Hope shook her head. "You set yourself up, pal. We leave at six-thirty."

"Leave?"

"We're going out tonight. Dress casual. Or are you going to welsh on our bet?"

A muscle in his jaw pulsed as he gritted his teeth. "I'll be ready."

Jeff pushed his way toward the door to the hall feeling like a man on his way to his own execution. He stopped and glanced at his watch. Six twenty-five. At least he was right on time. Hope thought she was going to teach him something about human nature tonight, but it was Hope who was in for the lesson. Unfortunately, it would mean his own humiliation.

Muscles knotting and dinner lying like a rock in his nervous stomach, Jeff forced himself to roll forward. Hope and Curt stood in the foyer. "Coming to help or watch?" he asked Madden.

Curt stepped forward. "Jeff, if you don't want to go—"

"No, I don't want to go, but I let her push me and I lost. If I was stupid enough to fall into her trap, then I guess I ought to be man enough to pay the piper."

"Jeff—" Hope began.

"I don't want or need your backpedaling," he cut in. "Let's get this over with. I assume the answer to my earlier question was help," he told Madden. "So how do we go about getting the invalid into the car?"

"It's a van and it's equipped with a chairlift," Hope told him.

"Think of everything, don't you?" he grumbled.

It took a little longer than he liked, but Jeff soon found himself ensconced inside the van. Curt climbed behind the wheel and Hope climbed in next to him.

"So, where are we going?" Jeff asked.

"The Tabernacle."

Incredulous, he stared at her for a long moment. Jeff could have sworn he felt his blood pressure skyrocket. She wouldn't! "I am not going to your church. You know how I feel about that!"

"You said anything. If you had won, what were you going to ask me to do?"

He felt like a volcano overdue to blow. She was too much! "I was going to make you go home," he snapped.

"And I want you to go out. No one at the Tabernacle will stare or point or ask embarrassing questions. I know these people. They're good and decent and kind. This will be the perfect place for you to start getting out into the world again. I'm not demanding you listen to Pastor Dillon. Sit and twiddle your thumbs. I don't care."

"Take me home," he demanded.

"You promised! What are you afraid of?"

Jeff gritted his teeth. Why did she always make him feel like a coward? "I'm not afraid! Fine. I'll go to your stupid church."

Chapter Nine

It didn't take nearly enough time to get to the church, Hope thought. Jeff was still silently brooding. The sight of the big converted barn usually washed a sense of peace over her. Not so tonight. She looked at Jeff, his expression forbidding as the lift carried him to the ground and he sank from her view. Her nervous stomach flipped. She thought he'd relax a little on the ride. Lose the scowl, at least.

"Maybe we should leave," she whispered to Curt Madden as Jeff rolled forward and off the lift a few seconds later.

"Not on your life," Curt told her as he closed and locked her door. "He's here, and right now, I don't care to tempt fate by suggesting that this is too much for him. Jeff's lost enough pride."

"That's my fault. I think he hates me to see him fail."

Curt nodded. "Yeah. He does. But that's also an advantage because he works harder to keep you from seeing him fall flat on his face."

"Are you two going to stand there and whisper about me all night or are we going to get this over with?" Jeff snarled.

"Sorry," Curt said. "You think you can handle getting in yourself? I'm on stage tonight."

"Go. I'll handle it," he told Curt, then looked at the rustic building. "This isn't the church you used to go to. I thought you said you've known Curt since you two were kids."

"This isn't where we met. By coincidence we both come here now. Aunt Meg found the Tabernacle just after they started meeting at the firehouse. Curt was already a member with his parents."

"What kind of crazy church meets in a firehouse then moves to a barn?"

"It's my kind of church." Hope grinned. The Tabernacle was a little unconventional. That's why she loved it. "You go in the front door and the love of the Lord is just in there. Pastor Jim and some of the original members helped rebuild the building from the framing out with their own two hands. He says he just couldn't tear it down even though that was the original plan. That smaller building next to the barn is for our youth ministry. Pastor Jim moved it up here from the back of the property a couple years ago. He did the finish work on it almost single-handedly. That was just before he re-married his wife."

"Your pastor was divorced?"

After a chuckle, she added, "He's also recovering alcoholic. The church actually started as an Alcoholics Anonymous Bible study. He still runs AA meetings out of the church. Quite a colorful bunch around here. We're all sinners, Jeff. No one considers themself better than anyone else at the Tabernacle. If you'd give us a chance, you might find you even like us."

Jeff looked at her, his expression inscrutable. "I like you just fine. It's all the holier-than-thou strangers in there that I'm not too sure of." He looked at himself. "You said dress casual. Are you sure I don't clash with the chair or their dress code?"

Hope spread her arms and turned so he could inspect her denim skirt and casual top. "Does it look as if I dressed up? Believe me, in chinos and a golf shirt you're overdressed, if anything. And how could black clash with a mostly black chair?"

Jeff didn't crack a smile but pivoted and pushed toward the ramp and the front doors. He stopped and pointed down the hill at the new construction toward the back of the property. "What's that?"

"A house for Pastor Jim and his family. It still needs a lot of work. Since his wife just found out she's expecting their second child, we're going to be working pretty hard to get it done now that spring's here."

"Evening, Hope," Pastor Jim Dillon called as they approached the front door. A tall, dark and handsome

James Bond look-alike, he reached out and shook Jeff's hand. "A new face," the pastor said.

"Jeff Carrington. Pastor Jim Dillon," she said, introducing the men.

Jim Dillon was probably the same height as Jeff, but he somehow managed to shake Jeff's hand while not seeming to stoop to do it. "Welcome," the young pastor said. "It's always nice to see someone new."

"Well, don't get used to seeing me. She all but twisted my arm to get me here," Jeff growled.

Hope felt her face flame.

Pastor Jim chuckled. "Kidnapped another one, did you, Hope? Well, don't worry, Jeff. She's harmless most of the time, and I'm sure that she'll take you back where she found you after I get a shot at boring you for an hour or so." He looked past them and waved as a van pulled into a nearby parking spot. "You two may want to move to a safe place. Here comes the Osborne tribe."

Hope looked across the parking lot and smiled. "Come on. He's not kidding. Five kids, two parents and two grandmothers are about to pour out of that van."

They moved on, and Jeff, a bit less angry but still sullen, kept his eyes on the floor ahead of him. Hope sighed and silently prayed that the message would touch him.

As they entered the sanctuary, the praise and worship team, including Curt on bass, started playing. One of the ushers smoothly removed a chair as Hope moved into a row. "I'll just get this thing out of your way," he said to Jeff with a sheepish smile, as if it were the seat that was out of place and not Jeff's chair. A fervent prayer that hearts would be touched by the study that night followed the first song.

Pastor Jim, who taught verse by verse through each book of the Bible, was in Exodus that night. "You know when I read this section of Exodus I start to feel really sorry for poor old Moses," he began. "You have to look at what this guy's been through up to this point and remember that he's no spring chicken. This is an eighty-year-old guy who's tromping around in the desert. And these Israelites are a tough bunch to play to. He must be exhausted by this time.

"I mean, here he is—God's spokesman back in Egypt. He helped God get the Chosen People out of there after hundreds of years of slavery. He was the instrument of God's wrath and called down all sorts of privation on the people of Egypt. Then when they were being chased, he parted the Red Sea and drowned the army pursuing them.

"Remember when the Israelites were thirsty and they came to poor old Moses to complain? He cried out to the Lord for them, and the Lord answered by turning the waters of Marah sweet so they could drink. Then they came to him grousing because they were hungry. So God sent them manna.

"Now how hard is this? Go to sleep, wake up and pick up the food that's laying all over the ground. They're told to take only what they could eat in one day.

For a while it was okay. They had ba-manna bread. Manna-cotti. Marsh-mannas. But did this bunch stay content? Nope, some of them had to test God and keep more than they could eat in a day."

Hope was gratified to see Jeff relax enough to laugh with the rest of the congregation.

"I know what you're all thinking," Pastor Jim went on. "If God was doing miracles like that in my life, I'd honor Him. I'd trust Him. I'd take what He gave and be happy for it. But would you? How many of us have been given everything we need to live and we're still not happy? How many of us are out there Monday through Saturday trying to finagle a way to get more? And how many of us get what we're after only to find that it's all wrong for us, that it makes us miserable?

"How about those of us who really do need something? Do we remember to pray for it? Nope. We try to get it ourselves. And we usually mess things up more."

Then, as was his way, Jim Dillon used his own foibles as a lesson for his congregation. He related how, during his courtship of his wife, he'd had trouble fully trusting God and that by trying to "help God" win her back for him, he'd nearly driven her away.

The study went on, but Hope kept going over the beginning in her mind. Was she doing the same thing? Was she refusing to put Jeff in God's hands? She wasn't sure, but she intended to pray for him a lot more and to stop trying to manipulate him. As Pastor Jim had once said, "We can't drag our loved ones kicking and screaming into the kingdom. They have to choose to walk in hand and hand with the Lord."

"So, what did you think?" she asked Jeff at the end of the sermon.

Jeff shrugged. "The guy can sure make an hour fly by. I remember being bored to death in church. At least he's entertaining, and it has to be the first time I've ever seen a preacher in denim."

Hope's heart fell in spite of Jeff's lighthearted comments. Were the jokes and levity all he'd heard? "Yeah," she said, her heart saddened. "He's a nice guy. Listen, I have an appointment to talk with him for a few minutes. Would you mind waiting here while Curt and the band practice and I have my meeting?"

"Sure. It's not like I have a whole lot to do with my time these days. If you and Curt don't have plans for me, I'm pretty unoccupied."

Hope felt like crying. Was she that demanding? That controlling? She smiled, put her hand on Jeff's shoulder and gave it a reassuring squeeze. "That'll change, I promise. Well, thanks for your patience." She backed away. "I shouldn't be too long."

Jeff watched Hope leave, wondering at her sadness. He'd been serious. It really hadn't been too bad. He looked at the rafters over his head, recognizing aged timber framing. No wonder Dillon hadn't wanted to tear it down. Glancing around, Jeff felt the peace Hope had mentioned. At first he'd thought using a barn for a church was incongruous, at best. Crazed, at worst. But it worked. There was an earthy grassroots feel to the place he'd never felt in the marble and gilt-edged church his parents had attended on holidays.

"That is one cool chair," a young voice said, calling Jeff back to the present. He stiffened. He'd known it was too good to be true.

"You think so?" he replied tightly, taking in the auburn-haired teen lounging in a chair across the aisle from him.

"Oh, yeah. Mine was clunky and had a mean rattle in the wheels. It was impossible to sneak out of the ward to the toy room without getting caught. Sometimes I think they loosened a bolt or two just so they could keep track of me."

"You were in a wheelchair?" Jeff asked, incredulous, the tension flowing out of him.

The young redhead nodded. "When I was a kid my parents were killed in an car accident. It left me so I couldn't walk. I hurt my back in the crash and had to spend a lot of time at Shriner's Hospital. But the doctors said I had a good chance to walk again and they were right. Is there any chance for you?"

Was there? Jeff wondered. It was hard to remember exactly what had been said before his release, but Curt and Hope seemed to think so. He watched Curt. The therapist was going over chords with the others in the band. He didn't seem the type to pass out false hope.

"There's supposed to be," he answered the boy. "I'm in therapy working on it. Curt up there in the band on bass is my therapist."

"Boy, are you lucky. My therapist was a lady. She was nice, but I'd rather have had a guy. You know?"

Jeff, noticing a blush heating the kid's cheeks, nodded his agreement. Just then a high-pitched squeal rent the air, and the thunder of small feet resounded in the sanctuary. A tiny-curly haired dynamo barreled toward them. "Mic. Mic," she called, her chubby little arms held out to the teen. She ran full tilt into the boy, whom Jeff assumed must be the sought after Mic.

The teen rolled his eyes. "I'd better find our parents. She has a way of giving Dad the slip. He'll be frantic. You'd think he'd be better at this after our four-year-old sister's terrible twos."

Jeff watched as boy and toddler left the sanctuary and smiled. Would he walk that aimlessly—that unthinkingly—again? If he did, he wouldn't take a single step for granted.

"I see you encountered part of the Osborne clan anyway," Jim Dillon said with a chuckle as he sat where young Mic had been. "That was the youngest and the oldest. Mickey and Leigh."

"He says he was in a chair, too. And that his parents were killed when he was hurt. How can God do that to a kid?"

A shadow passed over the young pastor's face. "A trucker drove too many hours, fell asleep and hit Mickey's family's van. It was the trucker's choice to disobey the law—not God's. Mike and Sarah left four children. Thank the Lord the other three weren't hurt as bad as Mickey. Mike's brother and his wife have raised the four of them since. The little mop top he just carted out of here is their only biological child."

"So you don't blame God for the bad stuff in life, but you thank Him for the good. Pardon me, Pastor, but how do you justify that? I've got to tell you, I'm not sure I even believe in God." He shrugged. "But then I'm not sure I don't, either. He seems to be the only theory that makes sense. I mean, the world can't be an accident. It seems too complex for that, but if He exists, how can He be so unfair?"

Jim Dillon didn't seem to have a canned response. He thought for a few minutes, his brow crinkled, before he spoke. "God is all goodness. Therefore, good things must come from Him. Man has been corrupt since Adam and Eve fell from grace, so the bad came from man's sin. God uses our mistakes to teach us, but they are our mistakes."

"You make it sound so simple. What about an accident like mine? How'd that happen?"

The pastor pursed his lips. "That's hard to say. I know Hope blames herself, yet there's never been a kinder, gentler woman. She wouldn't hurt a fly. She says she must have been distracted and missed what looked like heavy wear. She's deeply burdened by guilt over it. We just had a chat about it, in fact."

"I can't get her to believe that I don't blame her," Jeff said, worried for Hope. She was wasting so much time on him.

"She knows you don't blame her, Jeff, but guilt is difficult to get over."

"What can I do for her? She shouldn't be wasting her time on me like this. I keep trying to get her to give up."

"You could accept her help graciously. Let her work through her guilt. If making restitution is her way to do that, then let her. She needs you right now as much as I think you need her."

"You ready to head home?" Hope called as she walked up the aisle from where the band had begun to pack their instruments. Jeff had been so engrossed in his conversation with Jim Dillon he hadn't seen her enter the sanctuary. That rarely happened to him. He was usually so in tune to her presence. It seemed to light a room for him when she entered.

Jim Dillon stood and reached out to shake hands, startling Jeff out of his thoughts. "I enjoyed our talk, Jeff. Come again. You ask thoughtful questions. It keeps a guy on his toes."

Oddly, Jeff thought he might return. The people of the Tabernacle were warm and friendly, and not once, even when questioned by the Osborne kid, had he felt like a side-show freak. Or that he'd been labeled an infidel even after questioning their pastor's sacred beliefs. It was an odd place, this Tabernacle. "I just may do that," Jeff said, as surprised as Hope obviously was by his answer.

It had been a night of surprises. Jeff had thought the man would act all puritanical and be horribly scandalized by his and Hope's living situation, even though she wasn't staying in the house. But instead, Hope's pastor thought she should stay at Lavender Hill and work though her guilt. And even more monumental was the surprising fact that tonight Jeffrey Carrington had come to the realization that he did believe there was a God. What His role was in the universe beyond a detached creator, though, Jeff had yet to decide. But he'd think about it.

He'd definitely think about it.

Chapter Ten

Hope answered the door to the main house the next afternoon and was surprised to find her father standing
there. She had missed him terribly, and instinctively a
smile bloomed on her face. It was so good to see him.
They might argue, but he'd always been a great presence
and strong influence in her life. As he wrapped his solid
arms around her in an affectionate hug, she tiptoed to kiss
his cheek and remembered what she'd always known—
they might not agree on everything, but he loved her.

"Dad! Oh, it's so good to see you. I missed you
Sunday when I was over for dinner."

"I was busy," he replied, his tone gruff.

"Cole said." He'd also said that her father was busy
filling in for her because he'd yet to even try to replace
her. It hurt to know she was needed but that Ross
wouldn't take her help. She could help Jeff stay on track
and keep Lavender Hill running smoothly and still do

the more specialized parts of her job for Laurel Glen if only Ross hadn't fired her. It would have been hard, but she could have done it.

"Do you want to come in? I have time right now, but Jeff's working with his therapist."

Ross scowled. "I didn't come to socialize with Carrington."

"Then you came to see me?" she asked, sorry that Jeff was still a sore spot between them. She'd hoped time and distance would soften his attitude and that he had come to see how Jeff was progressing.

Ross stepped inside. "You're the only thing over here that I care about, Hope," he replied, and followed her into the too-bright parlor of Lavender Hill's main house.

"Kat Carrington could have decorated the Parthenon," he grumbled. "This place always reminded me of a mausoleum."

Hope looked at the white, rough-coat walls and marble columns and floors. She chuckled as she walked down the marble steps into the conversation pit in the center of the room. "She did overdo the marble, didn't she? Jeff calls it early Roman hotel lobby."

"That's one thing we agree on," Ross said.

Hope ignored the gibe and tried for a little more small talk. "This room and the formal dining room are the worst. Jeff can't conveniently use this room anymore, of course, which is one of the few inconveniences of his paralysis that he doesn't mind. He just skirts the upper perimeter on his way to the family wing.

It has a lovely Italian country kitchen and breakfast nook plus a wonderfully cozy family room. I can give you the grand tour if you want."

Her father's left eyebrow arched. Hope nearly smiled seeing the exact expression she'd inherited from her father. It drove Jeff crazy. She braced herself, though, knowing any accord between them was quite possibly at an end.

"You've certainly settled in here. I don't approve of you living in residence with two bachelors."

Any remaining levity fled, and Hope's heart fell. Agitated, she hooked a stray lock of hair behind her left ear. "Oh, Dad. I thought you knew me better than that," she said sadly. "I haven't settled in. I'm staying in the homestead house around back. And, believe me, when Emily Roberts isn't acting like our mother, she's a bulldog of a chaperone. She even took over a room near Curt and Jeff when we moved them downstairs into the guest wing."

Hope didn't add that the older woman had moved mainly in case Jeff woke screaming in pain in the night and Curt didn't hear him. She, at least, trusted Hope's integrity.

On the off chance that if Ross knew her presence was doing some good and Jeff was coming out of his depression, Hope added, "By the way, I'm not sure you care, but Jeff's doing much better."

"I care. I care that you're wasting your life on a worthless, selfish cripple. If he was any kind of man, he'd be able to keep going without you sacrificing your career."

Angry tears sprung to Hope's eyes. "I had hoped your coming here like this represented a change of heart, but I see you're as closed-minded as always."

Ross shoved his hands into the back pockets of his jeans. "I am *not* closed-minded! Think about what you're doing. What's that saying? 'How far do you have to open your mind before your brains fall out?' I happen to know what I'm talking about where Carrington is concerned. I watched that kid grow up. He drove Addison crazy with his irresponsibility. That boy's faults were all he could talk about."

"Jeff is far from irresponsible, Dad. Did it ever occur to you that Addison might have been a lousy father? Or that his opinion was colored by unrealistic expectations? Believe me, they were. He was hypercritical, unbending and controlling. Think about it. As disgusted as you've been with Cole, did you ever talk about him that way to a mere acquaintance?

"And Jeff's mother was so involved in her clubs and charities and tennis games that she scarcely noticed her child past his toddler years. Mrs. Roberts was more Jeff's mother than Katrina Carrington was. Have you ever stopped to think how hard Jeff worked to get where he was? To get on the Olympic team you have to be the best of the best, and his place on the team wasn't even in question when he had the accident."

"So what? He was just after glory. Glory that costs a fortune and gives no return. He was spending every penny Addison ever made, and probably still is. When it's gone, he's not going to know what hit him. I don't want him to pull you down any more than he already has. Look at you. He's turned you into his personal cheerleader and social secretary."

"Jeff is a good and decent man who had his whole world destroyed in one fell swoop. He was lost for a while, but even then he tried to send me on my way. I didn't budge then and I'm still not going to."

"Then you're a fool."

Hope anchored her hands on her hips, trying not to lose her temper. "No, I'm not. That's not the first time you've said that to me. What I am is his friend. When I'm convinced that he's the best he's going to be mentally as well as physically and I know he can run Lavender Hill, then I'll consider leaving, but not before. I think you'd understand how I feel. You share responsibility for his accident. But instead of feeling guilty for the condition of your tack, all you've done is criticize him. Is that how you justify your guilt?"

Ross Taggert stared at her for a long minute. She could see him trying to get hold of his rather formidable temper. "Get this straight, Hope," he said, his teeth gritted. "I am not responsible, nor are you. A rider of Jeffrey Carrington's caliber should have checked his own girth. Besides which, the last time I used that saddle the girth was in perfect condition."

"So it just magically wore out in one ride? Come on, Dad."

Her father turned away, anchoring his fisted hands on

his lean hips, then he dropped them to his sides and pivoted to face her. "I came by to tell you that your job is waiting."

"Then I'll be back to work in the morning."

Ross shook his head. "No. I won't condone you living here at his beck and call, but I won't destroy your career the way Carrington is willing to do, either. Officially, you're on a leave of absence. When he shows his true, spoiled colors, you'll be welcome home. We miss you. I'll see myself out."

Hope watched her father's stiff back as he moved into the hall that led to the foyer. The faint squeak of Jeff's wheelchair on the marble tiles alerted her to his presence. She wondered how much he'd heard. She didn't have to wait long.

"So I guess I can lay your father's animosity toward me partially at Addison's feet. I always wondered why Ross had developed such a bad opinion of me."

"His opinion is wrong. He doesn't know you at all."

"But his heart *is* in the right place. He loves you, Hope. Don't throw away something I've always wanted. He's just looking after you. Maybe you should do what he says."

"Are you trying to throw me out again?"

Jeff shook his head and stared at her for a long, charged moment. Was that longing she saw in his eyes? And if it was, longing for what?

"I should toss you out," he said at last, his voice an octave deeper and a bit strained. "If I was half the man your father is, I would, but I don't want you to leave till you know it's time for you to go."

Hope was startled. What did that mean? That he wanted her there? She had no idea and wasn't sure she wanted to know, so she decided to ignore the comment.

"Well, it isn't time," she replied. "You promised me help on the investment stuff and to tell me what in the world a pick is."

"A pick?" Jeff's forehead crinkled, confusion clouding his expression, then light seemed to dawn in his eyes. He laughed. "Hope, that's a put."

She grinned. "Well, whatever you financial moguls call it. See? Who else is going to teach a lunkhead like me about the stock market if you won't? And you have to tell me what to do with that bill that came for a bunch of AFG stock you bought back in the beginning of February."

"Nothing. I had money in my brokerage account already. It was probably just a notice of withdrawal from the account."

"A brokerage account is different from a bank account? How much time do you have to teach me?" she asked, even more unsure of herself.

"My Viking taskmaster Curt the slave driver had to fix a piece of equipment, so I guess I'm free till he rounds me up." Jeff grew serious again. "I'm sorry, Hope. I hate that I've come between you and your father."

"*You* haven't. *He* has."

Jeff pursed his lips and nodded. "Yeah. Sure," he said, but his disgusted tone made it clear he didn't agree.

"Let's get at that investment lesson," she said, swiftly changing the subject. And wasn't it a shame, she thought as she followed Jeff to the study, that she was more comfortable discussing investments than she was her current relationship with her own father? She had to find a way to show Ross how wrong Jeff's father had been about his wonderful son.

Jeff stared in dismay at the big ebony desk a few minutes later when he moved next to Hope after she settled in the leather desk chair. He'd had no idea he'd left so many things undone since the accident. Shame washed away any feelings her nearness churned up in him. Then, as Hope quickly ran through a summary of all the business she had handled for him, the magnitude of his negligence hit him.

What had he been thinking? Mrs. R and all the other people who worked at Lavender Hill deserved to be paid for their services. Plus there were the suppliers who had gone unpaid, as well. This was a terrible burden to foist on Hope. Her father had been right about him. He'd been incredibly selfish.

He glanced at her serious face as she finished telling him about the household account. Selfish though it might be, he couldn't help being incredibly grateful that Hope had strong-armed her way into his world. She had dragged him, albeit kicking and screaming, from a pit of despair and kept his whole world from caving in around him. He looked away, tempted to take her in his arms and show her all he felt for her. But that would blow his brotherly cover and increase the daily torture of her nearness.

It was then that, in a pile of new mail, he spied the return address of the neurologist who'd handled his case. His thoughts did an abrupt one-eighty. He reached for the envelope at the same time Hope did.

"It's probably another misdirected bill. The right hand sure doesn't tell the left who to bill around that hospital," she quipped, and tore into the envelope, then pulled out a sheet of paper. "Oh, it's a letter from Dr. Chin."

"Here, I'll take care of it," Jeff said quickly. But not quickly enough. He winced when he saw the storm gathering in Hope's eyes. Uh-oh. Busted.

"You missed your checkup right before I came here to stay and you refused the call when they phoned to make a new appointment. Jeff, why?"

"It's too much trouble to go there and sit for hours just to find out nothing's changed."

"What about since then? You're stronger. Maybe the doctor will give us a better idea of what we can expect of your recovery."

Jeff heard the unconscious way Hope made them a team—a couple. It buoyed his heart for all of two seconds before reality set in. They weren't a team or a couple and wouldn't be, either, unless he managed to stand on his own two feet again. He had to stop kidding himself about his chances, and so did she.

"I still don't want to go. I'm an adult, Hope, and I can decide to see my doctor or not. I decided not to. Simple."

Hope continued to glare. "I'll agree with that. It is simple. And stupid. Why doesn't Curt know about this? I would have thought he'd need to be in touch with your doctor."

Annoyingly, he felt his face heat. "Curt knows. I told him I'd stop cooperating if he blew the whistle. I think he's been talking to the doctor, though."

Hope stared at him for a long moment before asking, "I still don't understand why you refuse to go."

Jeff fisted his hand. "Why? Because I don't want to go," he said, and hated the petulant sound of his voice. Well, too bad! He couldn't go. He just wasn't ready to hear that he'd never walk again. That any idea of a future with Hope was over. He knew it in his heart, but to hear it? No. Not yet. He wasn't prepared to hear the words. He might never be ready. At least now he had hope, and after that talk with the kid at her church his outlook seemed a little brighter. He couldn't give that up. Ridiculously optimistic or not, that was it.

"Of course you're going," Hope said and picked up the phone, evading his attempt to grab it before she could. "Honestly, you can be such an idiot sometimes," she snapped, then her voice turned pleasant and impersonal. "Hi, there. I'd like to make an appointment for Jeffrey Carrington. When? As soon as possible." She glared at him again, her blue eyes dark and stormy. "Not until then? Okay. It'll have to do. Thank you. He'll be there."

"You aren't my mother," he shouted when she put down the phone.

Hope jerked to her feet, looking more upset than angry. "No. I'm not your mother. I, at least, *care* about you. I want you to have the future you deserve, not the one I choose for you. I'd never care what school you went to or what profession you picked. I'll still care about you if you never walk or ride again. The you inside of you is all I've ever cared about. Do you get the difference between me and Kat Carrington?"

Jeff watched Hope across the cozy room working the remote control for the VCR. She had been distant since storming out of the office on Thursday afternoon. It was Saturday night and Mrs. Roberts, seemingly oblivious to the tension between them, had rented a new musical comedy that just came out on video. It was a remake of a 1940s classic. She'd insisted they settle in the family room after dinner, and they'd just finished watching the old classic version.

"Dear, before you start the new one," Emily said to Hope, "I think I'll go out to the kitchen and pop us some popcorn. What's a new movie without popcorn and a soda?"

"Want any help?" Jeff asked, grinning.

Mrs. R glared and huffed out of the room.

Jeff chuckled. She wasn't too happy with him after he messed up her clean kitchen floor. He'd been clowning around, trying to prove he didn't need anyone to teach him how to handle himself in the kitchen. The guy in the video Curt had shown him had made it look so easy. As with everything else in his life since the accident, it wasn't as easy as it looked. In fact, it was really hard. Which is why he'd dropped a jar of spaghetti sauce while trying to get it from the cabinet with the aid of a hand-controlled claw on the end of an extension pole.

He'd thought of having a small handicap-equipped kitchen put in the guest wing near the exercise room. Would it mean he was spoiled if he spent the money to put in a kitchen just for himself? He couldn't forget all the things Ross Taggert had said about him. Selfish. Worthless. Cripple. Did those descriptions fit?

Cripple certainly did, though it was a vicious word. Paraplegic sounded so much less cruel. But a rose by any other name…

He wanted to talk to Hope about his feelings. But if she found out how much he'd heard, it would only make matters that much more strained between her and Ross. It would be the same thing with Cole. With Cole the explosion would be worse. It wasn't Ross's fault, anyway. Jeff's father had poisoned the well years ago, and it had to have been out of jealousy. Jeff would keep his own counsel with both Hope and Cole, but that left him with no one to talk to.

"Would you come to church with us tomorrow?" Hope asked, taking him completely by surprise. They might very well be the first voluntary words she'd spoken to him in days.

Jeff snapped out of his musings. If he agreed, he might get a chance to talk to Hope's pastor. He needed what she called a reality check and he couldn't think of anyone better to turn to than the honest man he'd met Wednesday night.

It was certainly odd that Hope would ask him to go with her just as he'd been wishing for someone impartial to talk with, especially the way things had been between them. He had to fight a grin. He knew how Hope thought. She'd say God was working in his life if he told her what had already been on his mind.

"Okay," he said cautiously, keeping any enthusiasm out of his tone. He didn't want Hope thinking he was suddenly going to go wheeling forward for some sort of altar call or something. "These four walls get pretty boring," he added. "At least it'll be a change of scenery."

Hope nodded, her expression neutral. "That's what I thought, too. Since Curt is scheduled to play at the eleven o'clock service, I thought we'd all go then."

"I'll be ready at what? Ten-thirty?"

"Sharp," she said as Mrs. R came in with a big ceramic bowl of popcorn and a smaller one.

His housekeeper handed the small one to him. It was golden and buttery. Just the way he liked it.

"All for me?" he asked and sent her a grateful smile.

Mrs. R smiled back and tousled his hair the way she used to when he was a kid. It gave him a warm, loved feeling. He guessed he was at least forgiven for the mess he'd made. Whether Hope had forgiven him for manipulating Curt was another thing altogether. Sometimes Emily Roberts made him forget he paid her to take care of him. Sometimes she made him wish she was there just because she wanted to be. He wished the same of Hope. But Emily was there to earn a living, and Hope was only trying to work through her guilt.

Chapter Eleven

Hope watched Jeff and Pastor Jim where they sat toward the back of the sanctuary. They'd been talking only a few minutes when the pastor stood and moved away. Hope's heart fell. She'd prayed constantly since realizing that she'd been trying to help Jeff without divine assistance. But even now, after all that prayer, Jeff had listened once again to one of Jim Dillon's moving messages and hadn't accepted the Lord. She didn't understand how anyone could miss seeing God's perfect salvation as the gift it was, especially when Pastor Jim presented it the way he did. She shook her head. She'd just have to pray longer and harder.

Rome wasn't built in a day. Be patient. He's not ready yet.

He'd apologized for deceiving her and taking advantage of Curt's desire to help him. That had been a major breakthrough for someone raised to believe that he was perfectly within his rights to do whatever he needed to do to get his own way. But there was a new reserve between them that she hoped and prayed would fade.

"So, having a nice time visiting your friends?" Jeff asked as she approached him. The royal blue shirt brought out the healthy glow his skin had taken on in the last few weeks, and his eyes were a clear, sparkling silver today. He might not be ready to accept the Lord, but in his own careful way, he was seeking Him, Hope felt. There was no question that besides the obvious improvement in his general health, Jeff was mentally and emotionally better.

But what were his feelings toward her? He clearly didn't hate her. He'd said he liked her. But did he love her? Only Jeff knew, and he wasn't talking.

She took a deep breath before speaking, tired of weighing every word but afraid not to. "I ran into the pastor's wife. She's such a sweetheart and so excited about the new baby."

"Jim's excited, too. I gather he wasn't around when his son was born. But I got the sense that he's worried about money, too. I had an idea we both may benefit from, so I asked him to stop by Lavender Hill. After the disaster I made of Mrs. R's kitchen, I started thinking about adding a little handicap-equipped kitchenette in the corner of the exercise room. That way if Mrs. R ever has to be gone or is ill, I can handle meals. I remembered you saying Jim did a lot of the work around here, and Curt said Jim used to earn extra money by doing renovation projects on the side. I figured a chance to earn some extra cash might ease his mind."

"Oh. That's such a good idea and it was thoughtful of you to think of it. I can tell you he does beautiful finish work. He made that cross up on the altar out of two old, discarded beams."

Eyes fixed on the cross, Jeff rolled forward to get a closer look. Hope blinked her suddenly moist eyes and prayed that one day she would see him standing up there looking with love rather than curiosity at the cross.

Jeff pivoted and sent her a rueful smile, making Hope's heart do a quick flip. "I think I just hired the right guy," he told her. "Think he could do anything with my early Roman hotel lobby?"

Hope laughed. "I don't know. You don't happen to have a jackhammer in the toolshed, do you?"

Later that afternoon, Hope finished cleaning the bathroom and was about to start dusting the antique Shaker furniture in the bedroom when the pounding of hoofbeats vibrated through the little homestead house that was beginning to feel like home to her. She loved the old wainscoting that covered most of the walls and the high-beamed ceilings overhead.

After setting her dust cloth on the high stone hearth, Hope went to look out the window. She was just in time to see Cole dismount from the back of a horse she'd never seen before. She chuckled. Leave it to Cole to color-coordinate his mount. The horse's gleaming coat was the exact same shade of sable brown as her brother's hair. The mane and tail of his new horse, however, were an astonishing shade of golden-white.

Hope pushed away from the window and zipped through the little cottage to greet her brother.

"And who is this fine young man?" she asked Cole after a hug and peck on the cheek. Automatically she checked the gelding's lines and took hold of the throat latch of his halter. She stroked the white blaze on his forehead, and in the way her father had taught her years ago, she blew a greeting into the horse's nostrils. The big gelding whinnied then butted his head into her chest, knocking her back a step. Hope laughed.

"Don't encourage him. He's bad," Cole growled. "His name is Mischief, and I can't think of a more apt label. It should have warned me, but he was on his best behavior. Till I got him settled in. Or tried to."

"Which is what brings you to my door."

"Guilty."

"So what pushed you over the edge?"

"He pushed Elizabeth into a mud puddle." He scowled at the horse. "And I'm here to tell you it was deliberate."

"Then maybe he's just a smart horse," she quipped.

Cole didn't laugh. He glared. "Not funny, Hope. Your claws are showing. She assures me Jeff is the big brother she never had."

Oh, dear. Not only was she suddenly aware that she was terribly jealous of Elizabeth Boyer, but it also looked as if Cole was getting serious about her. Hope really didn't want to think about having Reginald Boyer as part of her brother's family. The two would mix like oil and water. And after what Reginald had tried to do to Jeff, she wasn't sure she'd ever be able to be civil to the man. "Sorry. I'm still royally ticked at her father."

"Elizabeth isn't too happy with him right now. That's why she hasn't been by to see Jeff. She's embarrassed by what her father did and isn't too sure about her welcome."

With great effort Hope did the right thing. "It was her father not her who nearly pushed Jeff's head under for the third time," she assured her brother. "Jeff wouldn't hold a grudge. His own father wasn't exactly Mr. Congeniality."

She turned to the horse. "So what other habits do we have to break this bad boy of besides knocking your latest fling into a mud puddle?"

Cole rolled his eyes. "We're just friends, little sister. And as for Laurel Glen's delinquent here," he said, his voice full of affection for his bad-boy mount, "want a list?"

Hope listened to a variety of complaints, all of which she thought were symptomatic of the fear, loneliness and boredom his early life had wrought. Her kindhearted brother had apparently been part of a rescue of the beautiful gelding and taken him on, faults and all.

"Why don't I get this big guy settled as best I can and we'll see what we can do with him in the next few weeks."

* * *

Jeff heard someone walk into the exercise room but he was bench pressing two hundred and fifty pounds of iron at that moment and didn't dare let himself lose concentration. Curt helped him guide the bar into its rest above the weight bench.

"First class, Jeff," Curt said. "Let's take a break. I'll go get us something to drink. Can I get you something?" he asked Cole who stood framed in the doorway behind Jeff. Jeff gave his friend a wave in the mirror.

Cole shook his head. "That's okay. I just had a glass of tea with Mrs. R."

After a deep breath, Jeff tensed his stomach muscles and curled forward, sitting up without the aid of the bar that hung overhead. It was a new ability he'd mastered only that morning. He didn't use a typical weight bench, of course, but one designed for someone with no power in their legs. But still, Curt said the ability to do a sit-up even on the specialized bench proved that his thigh and calf muscles were strengthening and that his gluteus muscles were responding to his brain's commands again. Jeff hoped so because the doctor's appointment he was dreading loomed ahead. And he really needed good news.

Cole smiled, clearly surprised by the sit-up. "Looking good, dude."

Jeff nodded. "Yeah. I'm doing better. What brings the busy new vet by?"

Cole hopped up to sit on the massage table in the middle of the room. "I shouldn't need a reason, but as it stands I had one. I bought a horse. Rescued, really. He's a beauty. Arabian mixed with who knows what. His past owner's too busy defending himself against animal cruelty charges to be too forthcoming with lineage information. Mischief was up to his haunches in manure when the humane society found him in his stall. He has a few bad habits. Not letting himself be stabled is just one of them."

He related the story of Elizabeth and the mud puddle and was clearly fighting laughter by the time he finished. Jeff had given up the fight long ago and wiped his eyes of gleeful tears. Just thinking of the elegant Elizabeth Boyer dripping with mud, trying to look as stately as she'd been taught to, all the while apparently defending her attacker, gave him the best laugh he'd had in months.

Jeff forced himself to stop howling when Cole started looking a little perturbed. "Come on. Admit it had to be funny. If the queen of England had been dunked in mud it couldn't be funnier. If this hadn't pushed you over the edge, who knows how long you would have gone on getting your rear end nipped and chasing him. So now you brought him to Hope, who's the best person in the county to work with him."

"So Donovan says. He tells me my little sister has a knack with hard cases. Seeing the improvement in you, I'd say it's true."

Jeff grinned. His Hope was one terrific lady. No wonder he loved her with all his heart, even though he didn't dare admit it aloud.

"You and my sister getting serious?" Cole asked, eyes narrowed.

But it didn't come across exactly as a question, and Jeff was taken aback by the warning tone in Cole's voice as much as the accuracy of the question. "What makes you say that?" Jeff asked, frantically trying to remember what he'd said that would have tipped Cole off to his secret feelings.

"Because your smile just went all gaga at the mere mention of her name."

Jeff frowned. "Don't be stupid. Hope's my friend."

"She'd better be if your face lights up like that when she's not even around. Serious relationships based on less are doomed. I should know. I'm the king of accidentally breaking women's hearts. I don't want to see her hurt that way."

Jeff realized it would be stupid to lie. He'd clearly been found out. When they were kids, Cole had always seen through him any time he'd tried to disguise his feelings. As he'd said to Hope recently, some things never changed. "Okay. I love her. But she hasn't got a clue and she won't if I have anything to say about it."

"If you get that stupid look on your face when she's around, she knows."

Jeff shook his head, his thoughts in panic mode. "She doesn't know and she can't. I can't *let* her know. If she figures out how I feel, she'll never give up on me. She'll never be free. She needs a whole man, and I'm still not sure how much better I'll get. I won't tie her to a cripple."

"Don't call yourself that!" Cole snapped, fire in his eyes.

"Why not? Your father does." Jeff barked right back then winced. He couldn't believe he'd let that slip. And to Cole, of all people.

Cole jumped from the table. "When did he say that to you?" he demanded. The fury on his face wasn't a pretty sight, even if it did mean their friendship was still intact.

Jeff raked a hand through his sweat-dampened hair. "When he came by last Thursday. And he said it *about* me, not *to* me. He was arguing with Hope. Please, whatever you do, don't say anything to either your father or Hope. I don't want him hating me more than he already does just in case there does turn out to be a future for Hope and me. And if Hope finds out that I heard Ross, it'll just make matters worse between them."

Cole subsided and leaned against the massage table. "All right. It stays here between us."

"Good. But if it's going to stay our secret then you'd better try schooling your own features. You look mad enough to chew steel, and somebody's coming down the hall. It could be Hope."

"Is this Carrington's health spa? I have an order here for a new kitchen," Jim Dillon called.

Dillon didn't look much different than he had when they first met. His jeans were a little more worn and his T-shirt wore the slogan Ask For Directions under the picture of a Bible, but the package was the same. He was a preacher who looked like he belonged in a barn. But then again, Jim's church *was* a barn.

"Jim, come in," Jeff said and reached out to shake his hand. "This is the place, all right. I didn't think you'd get here this fast."

"Are you kidding? And pass up an opportunity like this? Not on your life."

Pastor Dillon looked toward Cole expectantly.

"Haven't you two met?" Jeff asked. "Cole, this is Jim Dillon. Jim, this is Cole, Hope's older brother and my best friend back when we were kids."

Both men shook hands and exchanged polite greetings.

"So do you own your own construction company or just do this on the side?" Cole asked after they'd talked a while about the idea of putting handicap-equipped kitchen facilities in one corner of the exercise room.

"Oh, it's definitely on the side," Jim Dillon answered with a chuckle in his voice.

"Jim's the pastor of Hope's church," Jeff explained when Cole looked confused.

"Oh," Cole said stiffly. His face could have turned to stone for all the animation it had suddenly. He stood. "Well, you two have a lot of planning to do, and I'd better go check on Hope. I imagine she's having trouble with Mischief. Nice to meet you, Pastor. See ya, Jeff. Keep up the good work. And don't try to decide Hope's future for her. She's a big girl. It's her decision who she loves. Not yours." With that Cole fled. Jeff watched him in stupefied silence, wondering if Jim noticed Cole's odd behavior.

"Is it my breath or do I need a shower?" Jim Dillon asked with a crooked grin.

Jeff chuckled. "I'd say it was more your profession. Cole has a real mad on about God. He has since his mother was killed. He blames Him and his father for her death, but I really think he blames himself more."

"Ah. The prodigal son. I'd forgotten about him. Meg's been praying for him for years. I'm sorry if my arrival chased him off. Do you still need to talk or was Cole's parting advice enough help? It sounded right on the mark to me."

Jeff raked his hair off his forehead again. "I can't take his advice. It's more than my not wanting to burden Hope with half a man."

"What exactly is the extent of your injury? Are you saying you couldn't be a real husband to her?"

Jeff thought of the effect her nearness had on him. "No. That's not the problem. I just can't continue to be a burden on her. I may never be whole. Never be someone she can lean on."

"People have all different strengths and we all need different things from others."

"There are other problems. Her father, to be exact. The man can't stand the sight of me."

Jim frowned. "Is it your disability or her living on your estate that's causing the problem?"

Jeff sighed. "Neither, really. In defense of the man, he didn't want me near Hope before I got hurt. I don't even know if the chair has made it worse or not. He was here on Thursday. I heard the doorbell and by the time I got to the living room they were deep in conversation. At first I didn't want to intrude. Then, before I knew it, I was the subject of heated words between them. The wheels sometimes squeak on the marble so I was trapped in the hall, listening."

Jim shook his head, a rueful expression on his face. "They say you never overhear good about yourself."

"True. He called me selfish and worthless. Selfish I'll own up to, or Hope wouldn't still be here."

"We talked about Hope's guilt and her need to work through it being one of her reasons for wanting to be here helping you, Jeff."

Jeff didn't know whether he wanted that to be the only reason she was there so she wouldn't be hurt if a deeper relationship between them became impossible, or if he wanted her to love him too much to leave.

"Jim, what you may not realize is how much I needed her when she came here. I'm not going to kid you. I was seriously contemplating suicide. That's when Hope forced her way in here and saved my life."

He couldn't fight the sudden helpless grin memories of her throwing his things out his window brought to his face. "I think she was determined to either shape me up or kill me."

Jim looked around at the exercise equipment. "Well, you aren't dead yet, and she seems to have inspired you to take on life again."

Jeff stared at the floor, and his seesaw emotions

plummeted. "But am I still worthless? For a lot of my life my father told me exactly that. Hope's tried to disabuse me of the notion but it's always in the back of my mind. What good am I like this?"

"God doesn't make junk, Jeff."

"So Hope claims."

"Well, here's another truism. People don't get tossed on the scrap heap when they get broken. If Hope's father wants to relegate you to one, you can't let him. You have a lot of things to offer. There are things you can't do. Sure. But there are just as many things you could share with Hope. You can probably even ride again with a special saddle and a horse trained to obey a different set of commands if those are necessary. Besides which, Curt says you're getting better. Who's to say you won't be running rings around her father in a year?"

"He'd still hate me," Jeff replied.

"Let me ask you something. Were you going to let his feelings stop you before the accident?"

Jeff thought back to the night of the Valentine's Day dance and Cole standing behind him on the edge of the dance floor urging him to make up his mind whether he was going to let Ross stop him or not.

"No, I wasn't. But I had more things in the plus column then. Here's a question for *you*. The night I realized I had feelings for Hope, did God know this would happen to me?"

Jim didn't blink. "The Bible says He did. I don't know why He chose not to stop it but I'm sure He could have. That's something between you and Him. And quite frankly that's the only thing I see standing between you and Hope. It's not the weakness of your legs that'll make you less than Hope needs, but the weakness of your faith—of your spirit. That's the strength she'll need you to have. You fell apart when this happened to you. And that's because you had nothing to grab hold of when your body failed you."

"It was better when I wasn't sure He even existed. Hope says God never fails us, but it feels like He failed me."

Jim pursed his lips and nodded. "Right now I bet it does. I can *tell* you He didn't. But that's something you need to believe for yourself. That He didn't is something He has to *show* you. And He will if you give Him a chance. Think about it."

Jeff promised himself he would think about it later, and they got on the subject of the kitchenette. Then he helped Jim measure the area they decided would make a nice-size kitchenette, and they settled on a counter height that would work for someone in a wheelchair. Jim promised to bring drawings back with a variety of wheelchair-accessible configurations within a week. Jeff had only one stipulation. Nothing colored white unless it couldn't be avoided.

After Jim left, Jeff thought about all they had talked about but he couldn't understand what kind of chance God could possibly need from him. If God could create the world, it seemed to Jeff that He could just wave His hand and fix it all. He should be able to perform a miracle and wipe the last two and a half months off the face of time. But then he remembered a conversation he'd had with Hope about blaming God for the world's ills, and that pesky free will thing got in the way of his theory.

Logic told him it was all double-talk, but his heart—his heart told him the answers lay in the pages of the book Jim had silently left behind on the massage table. And that book was a Bible.

Chapter Twelve

Hope heard the wonderful sound of Jeff's laughter mingled with that of several other men a couple of weeks after Cole dropped Mischief off. She followed the sounds of male camaraderie and good humor down the first floor hall to the exercise room and found Jim, Curt and, surprisingly, Cole with Jeff. They were gathered around some drawings and a catalogue.

Jim had done a preliminary set of drawings and had given them to Jeff at church on the Sunday after he'd been over to look at the room. He'd asked Jeff to think about any changes he might want, and they'd worked on them together later in the week. Jim had painted the walls a muted parchment color in preparation for the rest of the work.

"So you can put these components into cabinets and countertops?" Jeff was saying as he examined the catalogue.

"It's a little more expensive, but I think you'll be happier with the versatility. I wish you'd come down to the kitchen place with me in the morning."

"You don't need to be carting me around with you, and you'd have to drive the big clunky van or I would."

Jim shook his head. "Bad attitude. I won't be carting you anywhere. We'll take my wife's car instead of my truck or your van. You can get in and out of your chair easily enough in here. Why can't you get into the front seat of a car as easily? Just roll up next to it and transfer in. I'll stow the chair in the trunk. No problem. I'd really feel better if you came along to order all this."

"I told you to get anything—as long as it isn't white, I don't care."

"You can't tell me that you don't care," Jim said with a sigh of exasperation in his voice. "Emily told me you worked very closely with the decorator on the kitchen and breakfast room and that most of the ideas came from you. Come on, Jeff. Ask anyone. I'm uncomfortable spending other people's money."

Jeff sighed. "All right. I'll come. But don't say I didn't warn you how much of a production this is going to be."

"Don't worry. So what was this question you wanted to ask me? Something about the Gospel of John?"

Hope tiptoed away from the door, not wanting to intrude. She'd seen the Bible Jim had left for Jeff but hadn't been sure he was reading it. Her heart was gladdened that he apparently was. Jeff had been quiet and a bit withdrawn with her since she'd made the appointment for him with his doctor. And it hurt, but knowing he was questioning and studying helped ease the ache in her heart.

Later that night she saw a light gleaming under his door and wondered if he was all right or if he was suffering from cramped muscles again. She was reluctant to disturb Curt. When she peeked, Hope was surprised to find him sitting up, reading. She could tell from across the room that he held a Bible. About to back out rather than intrude or disturb him, Hope gasped when Jeff looked up.

"What brings you out at this hour?" he asked. He was dressed in sweat clothes, and his hair was mussed as if he'd been asleep but had awakened.

Hope shrugged. "I guess the same thing that has you up and reading. I couldn't sleep. I was passing on my way to the kitchen and noticed your light. I thought maybe you were in pain and being too brave again."

"Nope, chicken to the core."

Curious about what he was reading, she nodded toward the book in his lap. "A little light reading?"

Jeff held up a notepad and grinned. "Hardly. I have a million questions for Jim tomorrow."

"What kind of questions?"

Jeff chuckled, sounding a little mysterious. "This and that. Jim says I keep him on his toes. So far he has an answer for everything," he confided then poked the pad with his pen, "but I've got him this time."

Hope quirked her eyebrow. Jim Dillon knew the Bible inside out and backward. "You think so? He's pretty quick," she warned, grinning. "And speaking of quick, I understand he was here today about the kitchen plans. What did you think?"

Jeff chuckled. "I think you should have just come in and seen them when you were lurking in the hall."

"I didn't want to interrupt the male bonding."

He narrowed his eyes. "Hope, are you avoiding me?"

She shrugged and bit her lip, fighting the tears that sprang too readily these days. He'd been so distant, as if he'd thrown up a wall between them. "I thought it was the other way around," she said as she moved to sit in the chair by the bed.

Guilt flickered in his eyes. "I've been doing a lot of thinking. Maybe I'm just preoccupied."

"No. You've been angry about the doctor's appointment I made for the day after tomorrow. I just want what's best for you."

"I know how that feels," he said cryptically and rushed on as if he'd said too much. Unfortunately, Hope had no idea what he meant.

"I'm not angry," he continued. "Dreading bad news but not angry. If I ever was, it was because you held a mirror up to my own monumental cowardice and it wasn't easy to look at. Sorry I shot the messenger."

Hope chuckled. "It's okay. I'll recover. In fact, I just did." A yawn grabbed hold of her, and she covered her mouth.

"Oh, stop that," he ordered, smothering his own expansive yawn. They looked at each other and laughed.

"I think maybe I can skip the warm milk. How about you?" she asked sleepily and yawned again. "Ready for bed?"

Any sleepiness that had been there vanished from Jeff's gaze in a nanosecond. The look in his eyes turned suddenly hot. He looked away and snapped his Bible shut. "Go to bed, Hope," he ordered, his voice husky and strained.

Hope stood and retreated to the peace of the homestead house. Unfortunately, her tiredness had fled and her heart pounded even as she pondered the full meaning of what she was nearly sure had been desire in Jeff's gaze.

Did he want her or had she just put them in a compromising situation that would have caused him to react to any woman? A long time later she fell into satisfied sleep, thinking that a sister of any kind would never garner that sort of reaction in Jeff. Jeff seemed to forget she had a brother to compare him with. And this was like comparing apples and oranges.

Two days later Hope pulled up in front of the medical building and glanced at Jeff. He was nervous. Silent and nervous. Wondering exactly what had him so unsettled about this trip, she turned off the engine and pivoted in her seat.

"Want to talk about it? Are you nervous about going out? I thought yesterday's trip with Jim went fine."

"It did, and no, I don't want to talk about it. Why bother? It won't change whatever they're about to find."

Hope was sorry she'd had to force him to do this, but she'd had no choice. She loved him. How could she live with herself if she let him destroy his chance for a normal life?

She had been truthful with herself all along. She knew that by stepping in and taking over, there was a huge chance she could destroy any feelings Jeff had begun to have for her. She no longer thought that had happened. Not after the last couple of days.

A jumpy nervous feeling was her constant companion every time she was in his presence. His gaze on her, shining with desire and tenderness, followed her constantly. But she still had to wonder how long he could withstand the anger she had felt radiating from those same stormy gray eyes all too often before they'd spoken in his room.

"I'm still sorry I had to force you into this," she said. "It's been hard prodding you along, Jeff. But there's no choice for me. Could you stand by and let someone you care about hurt themselves?"

Jeff looked annoyed. "Why do you think I—"

"Why do I think you what?" Hope asked when he abruptly cut off his thought.

He sighed and rubbed the back of his neck. "Forget it. Let's just get this over with."

Hope nodded and turned to open her door as Jeff pushed the side door open and set the lift into motion. She got out and busied herself locking the front door while trying to hide a smile. Had he been going to say,

"Why do you think I tried to get you to go home?" She didn't know for sure but she prayed that was what he'd been about to blurt out.

Jeff looked around the waiting room. It was decorated with comfortable sofas and chairs and there were paintings on the walls by a local watercolorist. A kid sat across the room, his arm in a cast. He was busy asking his mother if she thought he'd be able to pitch that season. An older woman with a walker sat reading a magazine, and a young guy with his crutches propped against the wall glanced around the room, clearly impatient to be on his way. Once Jeff would have thought all of them unfortunate to have had their lives interrupted by injury, but now he saw how lucky they were.

Hope put her hand on his shoulder as she walked around him on her way to the reception desk. Her touch startled him and dragged him from his musings. He looked into her concerned gaze. It seemed as though whatever he did hurt or worried her. He tried to smile to put her mind at ease.

When she'd come to his room the other night, he'd been surprised that she'd noticed the reserve he'd tried to hold her in ever since Cole noticed the feelings Jeff couldn't hide. But she had noticed, and worse, she'd misinterpreted his actions and clearly had been hurt, thinking he was angry with her. So he'd dropped the wall he'd been trying to build. He couldn't stand to hurt her.

A memory surfaced of her sitting by his bed during

the small hours of the night wearing a pair of old worn hospital scrubs, her eyes suddenly wide and alert as she became aware of the way he'd been looking at her. Jeff fought a grin, remembering how she'd scurried away the moment she'd understood what was in his thoughts.

He wondered who she'd been more afraid of— herself or him. It didn't matter. He liked that he could still make her feel the hidden danger of desire and that her attraction to him could worry her, as well.

I have to get better, Father. You have to help me. I don't think I can stand to cut her out of my life and hurt both of us that way. I will if I have to, but seeing her hurt that way will kill me. I love her so much. Please help me walk again so I can be the man she needs.

"Jeff, are you all right?" Hope asked.

His vision cleared, and Hope's beloved features, tight with concern, came into focus. Jeff realized he'd been praying while staring into space. Which had to mean he believed God listened to prayer and that He must touch the lives of those who call on Him. He grinned at Hope, his heart feeling light in his chest. Jim was right. There probably weren't any atheists in foxholes.

"What are you so happy about all of a sudden?" she asked. "I thought this visit had you nervous."

"I just realized that he can't tell me anything worse than what I've believed all along. And he may have some encouraging news for me instead."

The wait seemed like a year but was really only ten minutes. It seemed as if a whole team of doctors and technicians had something they needed from him, then finally, an hour later, he sat in Dr. Chin's office waiting for the verdict. And verdict really wasn't too strong a word, because whatever the doctor said would affect the rest of Jeff's life. He wished Hope were there, but she hadn't wanted to intrude, saying she'd done enough of that already. He no longer felt that way but she did so he didn't push her. He wished he had.

The doctor walked into the bright office and sat behind his chart-strewn desk. After polite greetings he got right down to business. "I was surprised when I saw your name on the patient list today. I thought you'd given up on me."

"No, I'd given up on me," Jeff replied honestly. "I'm not going to kid you, I really need good news."

"Then I hope I can give it. The prognosis is still about the same."

Jeff felt his heart stutter in his chest then fall still. But wait—he'd said he hoped he would be giving good news. That made no sense, and Jeff said so.

Doctor Chin smiled. "I wondered if you'd even heard me when you were in the hospital. Now I know you didn't. I told you improvement could be slow but as long as there was improvement and as long as you don't plateau at any stage for too long, there's every chance for you to regain full use of your legs."

"It didn't sound like that."

"No. I don't imagine to a young vital man at the top of his sport that it would have sounded encouraging, but that's what I said and it was meant to be encouraging."

"I felt as if I wasn't getting better when I was released."

"That's because nowadays hospitals are to save lives. Often people go home to mend and do it much faster away from the hospital environment. The rehab we recommended would have been such a place. I have to agree that though, when I look at your progress at home with a private therapist, yours was a better course of action. So now for further encouragement. Thus far you haven't stopped progression. The muscles in your legs are strong. The swelling in the spinal cord is slowly reducing. I would have liked it if it had gone down sooner as it does in others, but it was pretty bad and every individual is different. You have much better sensitivity and reflexes in your legs and feet, as well. The gluteus muscles are responding, as Curt Madden mentioned in his report. You just need to keep going with your therapy. Try not to get discouraged. Curt wants to have you fitted for braces to get you up using parallel bars, and now that I've seen your progress, I agree that it's nearly time. Keep your eye on the prize, Jeff, the way you must have with the gold medal, and you'll win this battle."

Jeff thought of the prize—his prize—and it was nothing so transient as glory and a medal. His prize would be Hope. His shining goal was a love to last a lifetime. But now he had something more solid than his own strength to call on for courage and perseverance. He had a Father to turn to in moments of discouragement. He had a Savior to lean on when failure made him feel worthless. He had the Spirit of God to strengthen him in the coming weeks.

And, he realized with a sudden flash, he had real friends. Hope. Curt. Cole. Jim. And Emily Roberts. He'd always had Mrs. R, who loved him with a mother's love, even if she did draw a salary. For weeks she'd stayed without one. He'd discovered that when he'd checked the payroll figures for Hope. Emily had written checks for others on the account in those first weeks after the accident before Hope came, but she'd written none for herself. He was a little ashamed for not seeing her as more than a housekeeper and for keeping her on the outskirts of his life.

Later that night in the quiet of his new room Jeff gave his heart and his life to the God of the Bible that Jim had given him. As peace and love wrapped around him, he realized that, even if he never walked again, the accident was the best thing that ever happened to him. Because, as Jesus said, *For what will it profit a man if he gains the whole world, and loses his own soul?*

He couldn't wait to tell Hope.

Chapter Thirteen

At the end of that Sunday's service, Jim gave his usual altar call, and Hope said a quick prayer that Jeff would one day heed the call of the Lord. As the congregation began singing the final song there was a stirring next to her and the sound of Jeff releasing the brake on his wheelchair. She turned in time to be on the receiving end of one of his heart-stopping grins, then he pushed forward toward the altar. Tears of joy fell unbidden as Hope turned the other way into the arms of her aunt Meg, who was sitting with them. The two women hugged then watched Pastor Jim lead the four who'd gone forward in a prayer while the rest of the congregation continued to sing.

"Why didn't you tell me?" Hope asked Jeff after hugging the daylights out of him a few minutes later.

"I was going to but I decided to make a public profession first. I didn't tell Jim, either. He was as surprised as you probably were." Jeff reached up and dried her tears. "He didn't blubber all over me, though."

"Oh," she said, embarrassed, wiping her tears. "Sorry. I'm just so happy for you."

"I'm pretty happy for me, too." He took her hand and gave it a quick squeeze. "Let's celebrate. Brunch at the Hotel Dupont. What do you say?"

Hope nodded, and they were on their way. Jeff drove, having practiced using the hand controls around the property that week. He started a discussion on current events and, taking her cue from him, she stayed away from personal topics. They teased each other about childhood and adolescent escapades, then moved on to solving the problems of Cole and her father and Aunt Meg. Jeff's solution was to lock her brother and father in a room with Jim Dillon as referee until they kissed and made up. He also wanted to find a nice old guy for Aunt Meg. Hope laughed, saying she liked Pastor Jim too much to make him suffer like that and that Aunt Meg wasn't old at fifty. Jeff conceded the point and revised his prescription to a guy in his prime but said Jim was tougher than he looked.

Laughing and talking, they moved to the entrance of the exclusive restaurant and waited to be seated. After several minutes a man approached from the back of the restaurant.

"Mr. Carrington, how good it is to see you."

Jeff looked up and smiled as if greeting an old friend. "Thanks, Malcolm. It's good to be out and about. How have you been?"

"Fine, Mr. Carrington. Business is as good as ever." The tall thin maître d' looked concerned and pensive for a moment. "I'd heard about your injuries. I hope everything turns out all right."

"So far, so good. Do you have a table available that will help me impress the lady?"

Malcolm laughed. "But of course," he replied in a terrible French accent. "Jez follow moi."

Hope laughed, as well, but she *was* impressed by the beautiful room. The chandeliers glowed, and the tablecloths gleamed a bright snowy white and set off the brilliant colors in the fragrant, fresh flowers that graced the tables.

"So tell me when you made your decision," Hope asked as soon Malcolm had seated her and they were alone. "I know you well enough to know it didn't come suddenly this morning."

"No. There wasn't any blinding moment of total discovery. At first I was just curious about what made a man like Jim Dillon become a pastor. It's clear that he could run his own construction firm and make a mint. I couldn't understand why he'd give up a chance to do something he clearly loves to be a pastor. So I started asking questions to see what it was that attracted both of you to religion. As we talked, though, I came to realize that it wasn't religion but faith in God Himself that was the driving force.

"Then, when I was in the doctor's office, I found myself praying that the news would be good. I had already come to the place where I realized that I did believe in God, but I thought of Him as this great overseer in the sky who sat up there watching us and shaking His head at the messes we made of our lives. If there was any one moment, suddenly finding myself praying was it. Once I faced the fact that He would involve Himself in our lives, it all made sense—His plan for salvation, right down to my accident."

Hope reached across the space between them and took his hand where it lay on the table. She forced herself to ignore the little frisson touching him always gave her. This was about something more lasting than earthly needs and wants.

"Jeff," she said seriously, "the accident was my fault. Not God's. He doesn't hurt us."

"I know, but Jim says that sometimes God will let us get hurt and use the evil for good. So I got to thinking that this accident may have been the best thing that ever happened to me. I'd never have taken the time to really look at my life and what was missing if I hadn't been forced to. God certainly knew if no one else did how hard you've tried over the past few years to get me to see where I was headed. But I'm not headed there any longer."

Hope smiled, albeit bittersweetly. "I'm glad you're not, but I still feel guilty about causing you to get hurt."

"I don't want you to stay at Lavender Hill because you feel guilty for the accident."

"I stayed because you needed me." *And you don't now.*

"And I did. I can't believe how wrong I was." Jeff

shook his head and grinned sheepishly. "Why you didn't smother me in my sleep, I'll never know. And I'll never be able to repay you for all you've done."

"This wasn't about repayment. It was about…" She hesitated, unable to bring herself to declare her love after he'd claimed she was only a sister to him. She still doubted that he'd meant it, but she had her Taggert pride and she was terribly afraid it was all she would have left after this brunch was over. Jeff didn't need her anymore. He had the Lord to lean on. She really had no more reason to stay.

Unless he gave her one, and she didn't think he'd come that far. To cover what any second would be an uncomfortable pause, Hope coughed then continued. "It was about friendship."

Jeff felt a cold sweat coat his body. Did it sound as if she meant to leave Lavender Hill? That was what he'd been trying to achieve all along, wasn't it? He should be relieved, but instead a cold dread filled him. He didn't need her for emotional support or to kick his rear into gear the way she had. And it wasn't as if he'd never see her again or she wouldn't visit. Hope was too strong to let her father influence her to stay away. So why was he in this sudden panic?

Maybe, he decided, it was the potential of losing the closeness of sharing duties at Lavender Hill. She'd settled into overseeing the breeding operation and the care of the horses, and he'd taken over handling his investments and the bookkeeping during the hours he wasn't working on his therapy.

No. Wonderful as sharing his life and work with her was, it wasn't what he would miss. He would miss seeing her arrive still sleepy-eyed for breakfast. He would miss the intimacy of knowing she was near. It was Hope, the pure, shining essence of the woman he loved, that he would miss for the rest of his life. Hope. Just Hope.

The waiter's arrival at that moment was a welcome distraction. After listening to the day's specials, they ordered. Jeff noticed Hope assessing him with that bright blue gaze of hers. "What?" he asked.

"Why have you resisted going to a full-service farm? With the renewed interest in equestrian competition and just plain weekend pleasure riding, why did you decide to limit yourself to breeding and sales with all those stalls just sitting vacant?"

"Because I had a dream. I wanted to start a top-quality Olympic training facility. But I wanted to be able to offer scholarships. That's where the breeding came in. That was supposed to provide for the scholarships and the seed money to get the facility started without filling the stables with other people's mounts and my taking the time to hire a lot of people I'd just have to supervise."

Hope frowned, confusion clouding her gaze. "Where'd this idea for a training facility come from?"

Jeff understood her surprise. He hadn't shared his idea with anyone. Not even Hope. She'd thought he was aimless, but he hadn't been. Not totally. He'd just been rudderless, running through life without God's grace to show him the way. Now he wanted to share it with her, the way he wanted to share everything in his life with her.

"The idea's been kicking around in my head for a while," he said. "It started a few years back with a girl several years younger than me whom I'd seen in local competitions. She was the most naturally talented rider I've ever seen and she was moving up quickly in the rankings. She had incredible presence on horseback. You just knew that animal would do anything she asked of it. She had such potential. Then she vanished from the scene. I later learned that her parents had been killed. She and Grandfather couldn't keep up with the family's horse farm and certainly not the expense of keeping her in competition. They eventually lost everything. It's always bothered me." He shook his head in disgust. "What an incredible waste of talent."

"So poor kids would get scholarships?"

"If they had the talent and drive to make it. And if that drive came from themselves and not pushy parents. Also, the scholarships would include competition expenses."

"So others like the girl you remember wouldn't be lost. It sounds wonderful."

Jeff wanted it so badly he could taste it. It was the same way he wanted her in his life. Neither seemed possible right then. Not if he couldn't get on his feet again.

Unless he had help.

Jeff's heartbeat picked up and doubled its beats. Unless Hope wanted to help…

He knew he should encourage her to go back to her job at Laurel Glen. He almost held his tongue, but then he looked at her animated expression, and his resolve melted. It was a chance to keep her close. It would be torture, but so would not seeing her every day. And now that it was apparent that her time at Lavender Hill was coming to an end he didn't think she looked particularly happy about it. Maybe a partnership was all they'd ever have. Maybe it would be enough for both of them.

Jeff took a deep breath and plunged ahead. "Hope, would you be interested in a partnership? I can't very well teach riding from a chair."

"Work at your training facility?"

"Our facility," he corrected. "I wouldn't be able to do it without you."

A smile bloomed on her face but just as quickly vanished. "But you'd be putting up all the capital."

Jeff pursed his lips, thinking. "What was your father paying you?"

Hope named a figure, and Jeff felt his eyebrows climb his forehead in surprise. Ross really had needed to beg in order to get his daughter back on the payroll. "That much?" He smiled, loving the irony of it. "Well, I hear you're worth it. Suppose you draw twenty-five percent less than that and put that twenty-five percent up against what I put into the project to get us started. Before you know it, you'll be a full partner."

Hope bit her lip, a frown still making a little crease between her eyebrows. "I'm not trying to discourage you, but what if we fall flat on our faces? You're taking all the risk."

"I don't think so. What will your father's reaction be to this?"

"Ever see the footage of Old Faithful going off?" Hope gave him a sardonic grin, but he saw worry in the set of her jaw and in the depth of her blue eyes.

"So you *will* be taking a chance. Ross won't hold your job if you sign on to work on this with me. And I imagine living at home will be more than a little difficult. You're welcome to stay on in the homestead house, of course.

"I had planned to move in there if I ever got this off the ground, but it's impossible with the chair. I won't destroy the historical value of that house with all the alterations I'd need to live there. With God's grace it would be a waste, anyway, because I'll be walking before we're ready for students. If He has a different plan for me, I'll just take over the bottom floor of the guest wing as an apartment. The kitchen's almost done, anyway." He shrugged carelessly but felt anything but careless while considering the possibility that he would never walk again—that Hope would never be more than a friend and a business partner.

She reached out and squeezed his hand again. His heart stuttered then took off like a runaway horse, reminding him how much he wanted this to be so much more than a meal shared by friends and partners.

He looked up from their hands to be snared by her keen sapphire gaze. "You won't be less of a man than you were if you don't walk again. You know that, right?" Hope demanded.

Jeff smiled wryly. Leave it to Hope to key in on his fears and not see the desire he felt for her. "But my life would be limited, Hope. I guess we'll just have to wait and see."

"And pray. Don't forget about that." She put her other hand over the one she already held. "And, Jeff, there's something else you need to pray about."

"The success of the school."

She shook her head, and her gaze snagged his. "You have to pray for the grace to live your life the way God wants you to live it, not the way you think you need to live it.

"The same goes for me," she continued. "I have to do what God wants me to do. I have to live the plan that He wants me to live. To honor Him, I can't do anything that even smacks of immoral behavior. I appreciate the offer of the homestead house, but I can't go on living there, Jeff. I came to get you working toward life again, and you're well on your way. It wouldn't look right if I stay, with you regaining your health."

Jeff stared at her. She was right. The only reason there wasn't talk yet was that most of the community considered him an invalid. Even in this modern age of people living together, sleeping together before marriage, Hope's reputation, unlike his, had always been above reproach. Her air of innocence and the sheer purity of her beauty had drawn him to her in ways none of the sophisticated women he'd been involved with over the years had. He knew that about her, but others didn't, and Jeff didn't want Hope subjected to even a hint of scandal.

"Where has my head been? I'm so sorry. I never even considered that anyone would think— I—I guess you'll be going back to Laurel Glen."

"No. You're right about my father. I refuse to go back home and fight with him every waking moment I'm there. I'd wind up with the sort of relationship with him that Cole has. There have been enough harsh words said between us already. I'll start looking for a place of my own but I'd like to stay on till then."

"You're welcome, of course," he said, but he hated the idea of her finding an apartment or a house. He hated the idea of her losing Laurel Glen. But more, he hated that he'd caused a rift so severe between her and Ross that she felt she had to live elsewhere.

"Maybe you could talk to Ross again," he suggested. "Maybe if he sees that I've got real plans for a future, he'll object less to our partnership. And if you're not living there…"

Hope shrugged. "I'll try, of course, but Dad is nothing if not stubborn."

"Well, you're certainly welcome to the homestead house for as long as you want to use it. I wish you were staying, or at least going back home, but I understand your feelings."

What Jeff didn't understand was what had turned Ross against him. That had been the worst year of his life. First Marley Taggert had been killed and Cole had gone off the deep end. Jeff had tried to keep him from doing anything too crazy, hoping to hold the only real family he'd ever known together.

Next his father had refused to fund his equestrian competitions unless Jeff went to Penn. He'd gone to Ross for advice, as he often did. Ross had said an Ivy League degree certainly wouldn't hurt him, and he'd advised Jeff to buckle down and try to get the grades he'd need to get in to Addison's alma mater. Jeff had, but then it had all fallen apart anyway.

One night during semester break, Cole had come over after an argument with Ross. Jeff had usually been able to calm his younger friend down, but Jeff had an appointment with a tutor that night, and Jeff's mother had insisted Cole leave. Cole had gone looking for trouble and found it in the guise of a police cruiser with its motor running. He'd gone on a joy ride, been caught, arrested and given the dubious choice of military school or juvenile detention with the possibility of being charged as an adult.

Jeff hadn't known why, when he came home that spring, he was no longer welcome at Laurel Glen. Now he knew that once Cole was gone Addison must have started poisoning Ross's mind. Jeff supposed Ross might have thought Jeff had been a bad influence on Cole and therefore was the author of all the family troubles.

Whatever the cause, Ross's cold anger toward Jeff had been uncomfortably evident, so he'd withdrawn from Laurel Glen except for riding occasionally with Hope when they'd meet at the border of the two properties. At least with Hope as his partner, he wouldn't finally lose it all.

Chapter Fourteen

No you don't, Hope thought. You don't have a clue why I'm leaving!

And at that moment she knew beyond a doubt that she'd made the right decision. Perhaps it was only a matter of time until Jeff saw that she didn't find him wanting because his legs no longer worked. Perhaps he'd even walk again. But she also had to accept that his new faith in God didn't guarantee that he'd come to see himself the way she did.

If she had to settle for being his partner, she would. Seeing him every day, working with him, most certainly would be better than only the occasional visit. And she couldn't go on living at Lavender Hill in the hope that he would regain his ability to walk or that he would come to a place about his paralysis where he could truthfully finish the conversation he'd begun on the hilltop just before his accident.

To wait around, living in his pocket while he kept her at a distance, would have been emotional suicide. He had God in his life now and could lean on Him for strength in difficult times. So it was time for her to leave.

Maybe she could repair her relationship with her father. And maybe—just maybe—if she wasn't quite so convenient to Jeff and if he had the chance to miss her when she was gone, he just might wake up. Maybe then he'd look past his pride and move fully into the future whether he was walking or rolling forward.

Late for dinner, Hope stopped dead in her tracks the second Jeff looked up from his plate. His right eye was on its way to a classic shiner, and his cheekbone wasn't far behind on the color scale. "What on earth happened to you?"

Jeff and Curt exchanged twin guilty looks.

"Did you two have a fight or something like that?"

Jeff was instantly indignant. "Of course not! Do we look that juvenile?"

Hope put a hand on her hip. "Actually you look like a couple seven-year-olds caught with their grimy little hands in the cookie jar. What do you think you look like?"

"I think you're too nosy," Jeff complained. "If you must know, I fell. Okay? Could we drop it at that? It's embarrassing."

Hope nodded, hating that she'd upset him, but then she caught another odd look between the men. What were they up to?

"How goes the apartment hunt?" Emily asked as she set a warmed plate of food at Hope's usual seat.

Hope sat and said a quick silent grace before answering. It was a depressing topic. "It isn't. Two weeks and all I've seen are a ton of uninspiring boxes the builders stacked along hallways and on top of one another. I've come to the conclusion that apartment complexes are just not my cup of tea. Then there were the three cottages she took me to today. They turned out to be nothing more than falling down shacks sitting at the edge of three equally dilapidated farms. Anything else the real estate agent found so far is either way out of my price range or too far from Lavender Hill."

"We could up your salary draw," Jeff suggested. "It would take a little longer for you to be a fully vested partner but—"

"No. I'll find something. You're risking too much on your own with this as it is."

"Are you sure you don't want to go back to Laurel Glen?" Jeff asked.

Hope shook her head. "After Ross's reaction to my decision to work with you on the training facility there's just no way I'm going to move back home and continue to argue with him every time we run into each other. Even short visits are getting more and more strained."

Ruby, her personal horse, felt Hope's restlessness when Hope went over a couple times a week to ride her. She should bring the mare over and stable her at Lavender Hill, but that felt so much like cutting her ties to home that she couldn't bring herself to seriously consider it.

Though she resisted the idea, Hope knew she should do it. The last time she'd seen her father had been anything but pleasant....

"You're actually going to work for him?" Ross had demanded when she'd told him about the training facility. "Hope, this is insane. Jeffrey Carrington opening a school? I know what the equestrian world is like. Between events those people have affairs and change partners the way the rest of us change clothes. Carrington running a training facility is like asking a fox to guard a henhouse."

Hope fisted her hands at her sides. Her father was the only person other than Jeff who could make her this mad. Maybe because she loved them both so much. "That's beyond insulting! Jeff would never take advantage of a young girl. That isn't the kind of person he is. If he was ever as promiscuous as you say, then he's changed. I told you that he'd accepted the Lord and that he's going to church with me now. He's become friends with Pastor Jim. You're wrong and you're too stubborn to give him a chance."

"And you're blind. This whole thing is just too convenient. He decided to open this facility right about the time you say he stopped slipping back into his so-called depressions. Don't you see? He's using this facility to hold on to you."

Hope had smiled. "Forget it, Dad. If that were true, it would mean that my fondest wish had been granted."

Emily put a drink to the right of Hope's plate and called her back to the present. "No, I won't move back there," she told Jeff. "Aunt Meg doesn't need my presence adding more tension to that house."

Jeff grimaced. "I'm sorry. I should never have asked you to work on this with me."

"I'm not a child, and my father has no right to pick my friends."

"He loves you. It's a gift some of us never got. Don't waste it, Hope."

She gave an unladylike snort. "Why tell me? Tell him. He's the one who won't even consider changing his mind."

Jeff lifted the receiver of the phone then dropped it in its cradle. He sighed. What was that? The tenth time in as many minutes that he'd chickened out on making the call?

This was ridiculous. He'd known Ross Taggert his entire life. Because Addison had gotten rid of all the animals when he'd inherited Lavender Hill, it had been Ross who'd put Jeff on a horse for the first time. It had been Ross he'd run to for advice in the confusing teen years when Jeff had been pulled in so many directions at once by his own needs and wants and those of his father, which had been diametrically opposed to his own. And now the man he'd grown up thinking was the ideal father hated the very sight of him.

But that wasn't Jeff's fault. He'd done nothing to deserve it. Somehow he had to convince Hope's father of that, then reach some kind of accord with him. Jeff couldn't let her lose what he had craved over a lifetime. He couldn't let her be hurt that way and not try to make things better.

Before he could change his mind, Jeff lifted the receiver and dialed Ross's office number.

"This is Ross Taggert. I'm busy on another line. Leave a message and I'll get back to you."

Jeff ground his teeth. He hated answering machines. "Ross, it's Jeff Carrington," he said into the mouthpiece. "It's about Hope. Could you call me right back?"

Ten minutes later Ross Taggert charged into Jeff's office. "Is Hope all right?" he barked, then stopped in his tracks, his gaze riveted on Jeff's bruised face. "Were you two in an accident? Where is she?"

Jeff fought a smile. Yeah, Ross was a real tough guy. His voice was shaking as much as his hands. Jeff wondered what it must be like to have a parent care about you like that.

"Relax. Hope's just fine," he told her father. "She isn't even here. I'm sorry I worried you. The bruises have nothing to do with Hope except that I got them in therapy and she's the one who got all that started."

Ross heaved a deep sigh and sank into the green leather wing chair opposite Jeff. He raked a trembling hand through his hair then braced his elbows tiredly on his thighs. His shoulders sagged as he let out another deep breath.

"If she's fine then why the call?" he asked, sitting back in the chair and pinning Jeff with his arresting blue eyes, so much like his daughter's.

"Physically she's fine but she misses her family. Specifically her father, since Cole visits here and she sees Meg at church all the time. I'll get right to the point. We have something in common, you and I. Hope. You love your daughter, and it might surprise you to know that I do, too."

"You don't know the meaning of love." Ross sneered.

"That was once all too true," Jeff conceded, trying to be polite. "Love is something I never had, which is probably why I didn't recognize it until it may have been too late."

"What do you mean, it may have been too late?" Ross asked, his face fixed in a deep frown.

"We have something else in common. You don't want Hope tied to a cripple. Well, neither do I. And if I can't get myself on my feet, she'll never know how I feel."

"You heard my argument with Hope about you," Ross said, looking uncomfortable and embarrassed. "I spoke in anger."

"I am a cripple, though I prefer paraplegic. But I'm not content to stay this way. I'm not giving up. If there's any way I can walk again, I will. Then, and only then, will I tell your daughter how I feel. And I'll ask her to marry me at the same time. I'd like your blessing."

"That's not going to happen," Ross growled.

"Then you'd be the loser. And Hope would lose, too. I'm sorry, Ross. You also called me selfish that day, and I guess I am. I'm not giving up the only person who's ever loved me because you want to believe things my father said about me. You never really respected his opinion about anything else. I don't know why you chose to about me."

"Because he was your father. Why would he lie? And how can you say your parents never loved you? They gave you every advantage. You went to the best schools. Had the best of everything."

"No. I didn't have the best of everything. Maybe from the outside looking in I did, but I didn't. Hope and Cole—*they* had the best. They had parents who loved them for who they were. Kids don't care about money. They care about love. They care about acceptance. They care about respecting their parents. If you couldn't respect Addison, what makes you think I could?"

Ross nodded but he didn't look as if he'd changed his mind about anything. "Is that all you had to say?" he asked, the forbidding frown still on his face.

"No. It's not. I never meant to come between you and Hope but I have. I wanted to try to show you that your worries are unfounded. I love her. I promise not to ever intentionally hurt her and I don't want to see her hurt by anything any more than I think you do. But you *are* hurting her. You've all but lost Cole. Please, Ross, don't make the same mistake with Hope. I wanted you to know how far this has gone with her. She's moving off

Lavender Hill, but she won't even consider moving home to Laurel Glen because of the tension between you."

Ross stood. He looked both thoughtful and confused. "I appreciate your honesty and your concern for Hope. I guess you've given me a lot to think about. As for Hope moving off on her own, it may be for the best. Things aren't very good at Laurel Glen right now."

"If it's financial—"

"I'll handle it," Ross said, shaking his head. He hesitated, then reached over the desk and offered his hand. "For what it's worth, I'm sorry about the accident. If any of us contributed—"

"Don't." He took Ross Taggert's hand and said a quick prayer as he shook it that this meant a new accord between them. "I should have checked the girth myself, Ross. You were right about that. I've tried to tell Hope from the beginning but she's as stubborn as her father."

Jeff grinned and added, "And maybe this talk should stay between us. Hope doesn't know how much I heard that day. Better to let sleeping dogs lie."

Ross nodded. "I'll be in touch," he said with a small smile and left.

Jeff was struck by how young the man looked when he smiled. He couldn't help wondering why so nice-looking a man had remained alone for fourteen years. Jeff imagined Ross Taggert could have had any woman he wanted. Which meant he still wasn't interested. How long could grief last?

Then Jeff thought of the very real possibility of losing

Hope, and he realized he had one more thing other than love for Hope in common with Ross. He, too, would love only one woman in his lifetime.

Chapter Fifteen

Hope heard Curt's shout of joy as she came in the back door for breakfast, then Manny's distinctive accent rang out, though she couldn't understand what he'd yelled.

"What's going on?" she asked Emily as the housekeeper stomped into the kitchen, an annoyed expression tightening her face. "They're really whooping it up down there."

"I'm beginning to think they've turned into mad scientists. Yesterday a parcel arrived addressed to Jeff, and I took it down to the exercise room. 'What is it you've ordered now?' I asked, just moderately curious. 'A secret,' said Jeffrey, and then he snickered, wheeled away and handed the package off to Curtis. Then Curtis proceeded to open it, but he stopped when he noticed me still standing there. He closed the box and pretty as you please said, 'Was there something you needed, Mrs. Roberts?' Dismissed from the room like a gossipy servant. As if I'd pry into my Jeff's private business. I know my place."

Hope didn't think it was the exact time to point out that she'd referred to Jeff as hers.

Emily anchored her work-worn hands on her ample hips. "It was just natural curiosity. I've never been a nosy sort. I just wondered if it was some newfangled thing or another for that little kitchen of his. Or if maybe it was something for his therapy. Really, I just can't—"

"Emily! Calm down," Hope demanded but took the sting out of the order with a bright smile. Hope had never seen the elderly woman so flustered. "You're going on at a mile a minute. I'm sure they're not up to anything nefarious. This is Curt and Jeff we're talking about."

"But the door was locked just now. And Manny is in there."

"They wouldn't open it to you? Maybe Jeff wasn't dressed."

Hope had to fight a grin when Emily's lower lip pouted and she slammed a pot onto the stove top. "They told me to go away! Well, let me tell you, if I'm not wanted, then far be it from me to insinuate myself. I should let them cook their own breakfasts. That's what I should do."

"Well, now *I'm* curious," Hope said. "And I *will* insinuate myself. I going to investigate. I'll warn them their future meals are in jeopardy. That ought to straighten them out."

Hope left Emily still banging pots and headed for the

exercise room. Expecting to find it locked, she was surprised when the knob turned smoothly under her hand.

"Hello, the laboratory," she called, pushing open the door. Curt and Jeff were seated at a table working on a three-dimensional puzzle of a medieval castle that Curt had started several nights before. An odd activity for the time before breakfast when they usually worked on a little therapy.

"Since when is this a laboratory?" Jeff asked, confused.

"Since you two started being so secretive. Emily thinks you have Frankenstein's monster hiding in the bathroom."

Jeff's gray eyes widened, sparkling with humor. "Secretive? Curt, have we been secretive?" he asked.

"Not that I'm aware of," Curt answered as he fitted another puzzle piece into the developing structure.

There'd been something conspiratorial about the tone of both men's voices. Hope shot them a narrow-eyed glare. "Then why was the door locked?"

Jeff frowned, but there was a teasing lilt to his voice when he asked, "Was the door locked when you came in?"

"No, Jeff, the door was not locked when I came in," Hope answered tightly. She saw why Emily was so upset. They were double-teaming her and they definitely were hiding something. And Hope didn't like it any more than Emily had.

Jeff scratched his head in what Hope felt to be feigned bewilderment. "Then why'd you say it was locked?"

"You two—no, I heard Manny, so there are three of you—have hurt poor Emily's feelings both yesterday and today. She's ready to go on strike. I want to know what you're up to."

"Should we show her?" Curt asked.

Jeff looked suddenly worried. "Maybe not yet."

"You did it before," Curt argued in answer to some silent communication between them.

"I also fell flat on my face the first time." Jeff looked at her. Hope didn't know what he saw, but he nodded and spun away from the table toward the parallel bars.

"Manny!" he called. "You can come out now. The cat's out of the bag."

The bathroom door opened and a dark head peered around the door. "Cat? Bag?"

"Old expression," Curt told him. "It means the secret's out. Come on. Jeff's about to put on a show for Hope. Just do what you did last time."

Jeff looked at Hope and gave her a nervous smile. "Now don't go getting your hopes up. This isn't as big a deal as it looks. It's mostly arm strength and braces."

For the first time Hope noticed that there were heavy braces strapped over his gray sweatpants.

"But it's the first step onto the next part of the road," Curt said encouragingly as he stood between the bars in front of Jeff. Manny took up a position at the back of the wheelchair.

Jeff was going to try to stand! The moment the saddle separated from Prize's back suddenly flashed across her mind's eye. Once again, as if in slow motion, she watched Jeff impact with the hard winter ground. She saw him grimace in pain. She saw him go slack.

Hope was suddenly horribly nervous. Not because she didn't want Jeff to walk again. Of course that wasn't it. But he was safe in his wheelchair. What if he fell? What if he did more injury to his back?

He'd said he'd already fallen! The bruises made so much sense now. Her stomach dropped, and she watched in silence as Jeff grabbed the bars. Hope instinctively closed her eyes, unable to watch when she saw his muscles bunch with the effort.

Please, Lord, don't let him get hurt.

"Hope, open your eyes before you miss the show," she heard Curt say.

She did as ordered and found herself drawn to Jeff's side, her gaze instantly locked in place by his. "You're standing," she said unnecessarily.

"On my hands," he said a little breathlessly as he looked down at her. "I'm not sure it counts exactly...but it's more than I could do a month ago."

"You're so tall," Hope told him, then felt a little foolish, but it had been so long since she'd looked up into his handsome face. She wanted so badly to touch him that she had to clench her hands behind her back to stop herself.

"Nah. You're just short. I can't believe I let a shrimp like you...bully me into all this work." Though he was breathless, Jeff's silver-gray eyes shone with a good humor that quickly faded as he searched her face. His gaze, stormy and intent, seemed to ask an unvoiced question. But his expression was so enigmatic that it left Hope at a loss for an answer.

"What?" she asked finally when he continued to stare at her.

He gave her a sad little smile before looking at Curt. "I've about had it."

"I know. Did you get dizzy this time?"

Jeff shook his head, sweat dripping from his collar-length hair.

"Good," Curt said, moving closer to his patient. "Let the braces hold you for just a second. Ease up on your grip. We're trying for balance here."

Hope watched Jeff concentrate as if trying to remember something he'd forgotten. The sweat ran in rivulets down his cheeks. He carefully eased some of the tension out of the muscles of his arms. A grin broke across his face but then he swayed a little. Curt was there just as Jeff's grip tightened on the bars.

"You did good," Curt said. "Before you know it you'll remember how to keep balanced. Now let's get you back in the chair."

"Oh!" Emily cried from the doorway. "Jeffrey, you bad boy. Keeping a secret like this. I didn't spank you enough. That's all there is to it. Breakfast is ready," she said finally, then a sob broke from her throat and she turned and scurried away.

"I'd better see to her. She loves you so much, Jeff. I hope you realize that," Hope told him, and ran after Emily.

* * *

"Hope," Jeff said when he found her on the stone breakfast terrace several minutes later. "You didn't act the way I thought you would. You looked more afraid than happy."

She shrugged. "Of course I was happy. I was worried. That's all. You're already all banged up. You said you fell on your first attempt. You're safe in the chair. You could get hurt worse than you are now."

"Or I could learn how to put one foot in front of the other again."

Hope smiled and took his hand. As always, a tiny thrill went through him at her touch. "That'll be great. You will. I know it. How tired are you from all that new activity?"

"Only a little. Why?"

"Because I wanted to bring Ruby over today, but she's a nightmare to trailer. I wondered if you'd do me a favor. Would you drive me over to Laurel Glen so I can ride her back? That way I can toss her blanket and some other equipment in the back of the van and not have to trailer her."

Jeff wished she'd put this off a few days. He wondered if it was too soon after his talk yesterday with her father. Had Ross had enough time to think?

"I don't know, Hope," Jeff said, stalling. He hoped to put her off at least a few days. "Maybe that's not such a good idea."

"I know it might be awkward for you, but you could stay in the van. We'd be in and out inside of half an hour. I doubt my father will even see you."

"Well, all right," he agreed hesitantly, thinking he should call ahead and warn Ross that the timetable had been moved up.

"Thanks. And will you make sure I don't forget to get my address book? I've gone so far as writing myself a note on my hand and I still forget to get it every time I go over there!"

Jeff nodded, thinking how odd it would be for Hope to have moved all of her stuff out of Laurel House. He couldn't imagine Laurel Glen without Hope. It had surprised him that Ross thought she should go elsewhere.

"Things aren't very good at Laurel Glen right now," Ross had said yesterday. Were tensions that high between Cole and his father? It was the only explanation. And all the more reason Hope and her father needed to patch things up. Even Meg Taggert had had enough and had left to take a cruise "to soothe her shattered nerves." Of course, Hope thought her aunt was trying to force the two men to deal with each other even if was only to say pass the salt at the dinner table.

Three hours later Jeff got himself situated behind the wheel of the van as Hope climbed in beside him. He could feel the tension coming off her in waves. "Hope, this is your home we're heading to. Has it been that bad when you've stopped by?"

Hope shrugged. "I'm worried about you and Dad. I don't want him to hurt you if he sees us."

"He won't hurt me. I promise you. The only reason

I hesitated when you asked me to drive was that I still think you should be moving home."

"I'm twenty-seven years old. It's time I moved out on my own."

"You may be right about that but I hate to see you do it with this rift between you and Ross. That's the only part of this I object to. It isn't my place to object in the first place, though. It's just that Cole left with things unsettled between them and not only has their relationship gotten worse but Cole has real problems because of it."

Hope smiled. "I promise to work on it. Okay?"

Jeff nodded and took her hand where it lay fisted in her lap. "There's my little peacemaker," he teased and started the van.

As they reached the border of the two farms, the white vinyl fencing he'd had installed earlier in the year ended, and traditional whitewashed, wooden fencing began, signaling the change of ownership. Otherwise all else remained the same. Hills continued to roll one into the next, and sleek horses trotted across the green fields and tossed their heads, looking majestic and regal with shining manes and tails flowing in their wake.

As they drove under the wrought iron archway at Laurel Glen's main entrance, Jeff fought the urge to stop to admire the artistry of a bygone era. He'd always loved the spectacular archway with its graceful renderings of the state flower that gave Laurel Glen its name. The artisan had made the laurel appear as if it twined its way through a network of delicate iron latticework.

Rarely was this one site left out of a pictorial done of the county. Especially now with the pink and white mountain laurel, still partially in bloom, bordering the drive on both sides.

Once the wealthiest farm in the area, Laurel Glen had nearly gone into bankruptcy because of estate taxes after Ross's father died. In his early twenties at the time, with two small children to support, Ross Taggert had fought to hold hearth and home together while rebuilding Laurel Glen's reputation and fortune from nearly the ground up. It was now the top horse farm in the tristate area, and it was all due to Hope's father.

And the man deserved the chance to repair his relationship with his daughter. While Addison Carrington had never earned Jeff's respect because of his shallow values, Ross had. His entire life whenever Jeff had to make a hard decision, he'd asked himself one question—what would Ross Taggert do?

If Jeff had one regret, it was that Addison had seen Jeff's feelings for Ross and had apparently set out to destroy any relationship the two had ever and would ever have.

The van topped a rise that hid all but the main house from view of the road. Laid out before them was the heart of Laurel Glen. On this farm, unlike his own, the barn and low stables fanned out before the house. They were nestled in the valley between the hill they'd just crested and an even higher rise where Laurel House sat. The stone facade of Laurel House rose from that farther mound like an elegant outcropping of nature. It seemed to keep guard over what it held most dear.

Four pristine brick and stone stable buildings formed an X with a competition-size ring at their apex. The original historical stone barn sat off to the left, in a clear position of honor. And from that precious cluster of buildings ran the fences, pastures and trails that completed all that was Laurel Glen.

He couldn't let Hope lose this.

Jeff pulled in next to the stable Hope indicated and set the parking brake. No sooner had he turned off the engine than the stable door opened and Ross and Cole stepped into the midday sunshine. Hope let out an agonized groan.

"Hey, don't assume the worst," Jeff admonished, watching the two men round the front of the van. Cole got to Hope's door first, and she put the window down. Ross stood behind his son, hanging back and looking as uncertain as Hope did.

Help me repair it, Lord, Jeff prayed.

"Hi, kitten. What brings you here?" Cole asked, though he knew, because Jeff had called and warned him of their visit.

"I…uh…I came to get Ruby," Hope stammered. "I thought I'd get more chance to ride her…you know…if she was at Lavender Hill."

Ross nodded. "Probably."

"We were just headed to the house," Cole said.

Ross pulled at the back of his neck as if the

muscles were suddenly tight. "Uh…you two have lunch yet?" he asked.

"No," Jeff replied quickly before Hope could make excuses to shorten her visit. If this was an overture, he wasn't about to pass it up. Then a thought struck him. The main house sat high, surrounded by stone terraces that fell away down the hill in a series of three sets of stone stairs. He couldn't think of a way to get himself inside that didn't include someone dragging his chair up those graceful but numerous steps.

He felt suddenly like a wounded knight staring at an impenetrable castle and wondered if Ross had invited them knowing Jeff would be excluded by virtue of the layout of the house.

Hope was way ahead of him, though, and it was clear from her tone that she thought exactly that. "Laurel House isn't exactly handicap friendly, Dad." She all but growled the words.

"It's okay, Hope." Jeff jumped in. He was not going to let her throw away this overture for his sake—not again. "You can toss the equipment you were going to pick up in the van now and ride home on Ruby after your lunch settles a little. I'm sure Mrs. R will have something ready anyway."

"Dad already figured out how to get you inside," Cole said. "Drive around the side of the house and into the garage. There are only three steps into the house from there, and if the two of us can't hustle you in that way we're ready for a rest home."

Cole opened Hope's door and turned to Ross. "It's all settled. They're staying. Walk with Dad, kitten," he said as he handily slipped Hope from the car. "I'll get the garage door for Jeff. We'll see you two in there."

Hope looked at him, and Jeff nearly laughed at the deer-in-the-spotlight look on her face. She stepped away from the door, and Cole climbed in.

"So, old son," Cole said with a grin as he slammed the door and slouched in the seat. "You think my father has finally slipped a cog or what?"

Jeff laughed and started the van. In minutes he was pulling into the garage, then Cole hauled him backward up the three steps that led to a mudroom off the kitchen. If Ross had slipped a cog, Jeff hoped it stayed out of sync. Because Hope's father had looked very much like a tongue-tied male trying to find a way to apologize while maintaining his pride. Jeff knew the look. He'd been wearing it often enough of late.

Chapter Sixteen

Hope and Ross had a pleasant stroll up to the house, but she was aware of a certain restraint between them as if each feared treading on dangerous territory. Her father talked a bit about Laurel Glen's business and his upcoming search for a new trainer. Hope offered to fill in as much as possible and help with interviews and such whenever her duties at Lavender Hill allowed. Ross accepted with alacrity, though he didn't ask how much time she could give him.

They walked into Laurel House's sunny breakfast room just as Cole pushed Jeff in from the kitchen. Hope felt Ross tense next to her.

"I could have helped," he said, and Hope nearly cringed at his sharp tone. She said a quick prayer that he and Cole could get through at least one meal with a little peace between them. Their arguments were like a malignant force that seemed to infect everyone present, drawing bystanders into the fray with incredible efficiency. She'd seen it time and time again from the day after her mother was buried to the day she'd left Laurel Glen only weeks ago.

"No need," Cole said lightly. Hope was taken aback by the determination she saw in her brother's deep brown eyes. For her sake and Jeff's he didn't intend to let himself be baited. If only he could find that kind of restraint for himself and their father, she thought sadly. "Jeff's so good with this chair he nearly did all the work himself," Cole continued, boosting Jeff's chin up and examining his bruised face with all the concern of a dedicated healer. "I did wonder if you needed seat belts, though, bud. What did you do? Fall out on your head?"

"He fell trying to stand," Hope said, proud of Jeff's determination.

As he playfully batted Cole's hand away, Jeff shot them all a self-deprecating grin. "It wasn't supposed to turn out the way it did."

"Was that wise?" her father asked. The real concern in his voice had Hope staring in awe at the father she thought she knew.

Jeff shrugged. "They say you've got to crawl before you walk, but what you really have to be able to do is stand. I won't take a first step sitting in my chair."

Cole shook his head and took a seat at the table. "Well, be careful. If you need two people to spot for you, I'll run by and help Curt out. Just name the time."

"That's a great idea," Hope said. "Manny helped this

morning, but it occurred to me that if Jeff fell backward, he'd squash the poor little guy flat."

"Consider me drafted then. That wouldn't be good for either of you. You need all the help around there you can get if you're going to get this idea of yours up and running."

"So how *are* the plans coming along for the training facility?" Ross asked, sitting next to Cole and reaching for the pitcher of iced tea in the middle of the table. "You talk to the Olympic committee yet?"

Jeff outlined what they'd done so far and explained that they probably wouldn't get the facility up and running for nine months to a year. There was a lot more red tape than they'd originally thought and so many other arrangements that had to be made that they'd decided not to rush. Jeff had also decided that he wanted the school to have a strong Christian influence. Both Cole and her father looked bewildered by what that meant.

"And the house needs work, too," Hope told them. "It'll house twenty kids easily with two in each room. Since each bedroom has a bath, that's one thing we don't have to worry about as far as renovations. But the marble has to go and the dining room has to be enlarged."

"But, Jeff, your mother loved that marble," Ross teased.

"And, Hope, you always said it looks like an upscale hotel lobby," Cole added, pointing a teasing finger at her.

She felt a blush heat her face, and Jeff's deep chuckle sent shivers up Hope's spine.

"My sentiments exactly. We want the kids to feel at home. Not like they're at a hotel," Jeff joked.

The teasing and camaraderie transported Hope to another time, back to when Jeff ate nearly every other meal at Laurel Glen. Back before the accident that killed her mother. Before her father and brother couldn't be in the same room and not snipe at each other. Back when Jeff would ask her father about things his own father should have been available to answer for his son.

Once again conversation flowed, and the old pattern of teasing picked up nearly where it had left off the day before Cole was sent away. It wasn't as relaxed as it had been the day before their mother died and Cole had become increasingly hostile and angry, but it felt right for the first time in years. She didn't even mind that she was the brunt of her brother's witty tongue because, as always, Jeff was there to take the sting out of any mocking remark Cole could make.

She glanced at her father and noticed he looked angry but also that he had a faraway look in his eyes. She reached over and covered his hand with hers, hoping to pour oil on troubled waters while Jeff and Cole laughed and relived some wild escapade they'd all shared.

Ross's vision cleared. "Jeff," he said when a moment of silence gave him an opening. "Were you with Cole the night he stole the police car?"

All the good feelings in the room evaporated in an instant. "Dad," Cole snapped, his face cold and rigid. He was clearly about to continue when Jeff held his hand up and stopped him.

"It's all right. No. I wasn't with him. Cole did come

over that night, but Mother sent him away. I had an appointment with my Calc tutor that she wouldn't let me put it off."

"I told you I wasn't with Jeff," Cole said, his teeth all but bared.

"Well, you were with someone. Chief Johnson saw someone running away. You would never say who it was."

"But I did tell you it wasn't Jeff."

Ross nodded. "I know. But Addison told me it was. At least he strongly implied that you were there," Ross explained, directing his comment to Jeff. "He apologized for not having the guts to turn you in. He begged me to understand all you'd lose if I said anything. Because you weren't a minor, you would have been instantly charged with a felony. I was furious but I didn't want that for you, either. If you weren't there why would he say you were?"

Cole looked utterly shocked but Jeff, while clearly shaken, nodded. His voice when he spoke, however, held a touch of bitterness. "I take it Addison had quite a lot to say to you about me over the years. I think I finally figured out why. He was jealous of you and my feelings for you. I can only guess, of course, but I think he set out to destroy our relationship. He hated that I respected you and all you stood for. Heritage meant nothing to him. He thought you were a fool to work so hard at building up the farm when you could have sold the land to a developer for millions. And he hated that I went to you for advice and took it."

Her father looked physically ill. "You think he actually lied so I'd turn against you?"

"It's all I can come up with. He liked manipulating people."

"But he was—" Ross cut off what he'd been about to say and shook his head.

"My father," Jeff finished for him.

"Yeah…what can I say, Jeff? I've misjudged you for years. I guess I should have realized you couldn't change that much that quickly, but…" Everyone knew what he'd left unsaid. Cole had changed. Cole had changed overnight.

Jeff shrugged and spoke into the silence. Shaken and unmistakably sad, he said, "Addison was my father. Why would you doubt him? Why would anyone?"

"I'm so sorry. For the things I've said. For the way I acted when you got hurt. I don't know if you can understand what I felt. Here you were, the golden boy. Rolling in horse dung and coming up smelling like Chanel. You'd gotten an Ivy League degree and were headed for Olympic gold and I'd lost years with my son when we might have settled our differences. He got military school and you got college. I honestly thought that this time you'd been careless and had gotten what you deserved for a change. Then my daughter tells me to all but shove her position here and she runs off to play nursemaid. I've been furious and helpless to do anything with the anger. Every time I opened my mouth, I looked like a coldhearted so-and-so. If I had

the man here right now I'd be tempted to throttle him.
I believe he lied, but all this because he was jealous of
me? You're sure?"

Jeff nodded. "Jealousy is the only thing I can come
up with as an explanation for why he'd lie."

And indeed no one else could venture a different
guess as to why Addison's version of that night should
have been so different from Cole and Jeff's. Blessedly,
the conversation veered off from there to talk of county
politics then back to Jeff's training facility.

"I've been thinking, you two," Ross said. "You said
you were going to be shut down during summers except
for arranging for competitions for the scholarship
students. Have you given any thought to changing your
focus during those months? Maybe running day camps?"

Hope thought the idea was brilliant. "Jeff, that would
solve your question about how to spot talent in under-
privileged kids when they're not usually exposed to the
equestrian world."

"Actually I was thinking of another kind of under-
privileged kid," her father said. "Like the kids in the
Special Olympics. Or the Sunshine camps. I understand
handicapped kids really benefit from contact with
horses. And I imagine Jeff could relate to handicapped
kids the way no one else I know of who works with
horses could. You'd be the perfect trainer for them even
if you don't manage to get walking again. You could do
a lot of good with this whole project, Jeff."

"Dad, that's a great idea," Hope said, feeling her

father had retracted his remark about Jeff being a worthless cripple.

Jeff was not as enthusiastic. He nodded, his thoughts clearly turned inward. "I'll give it some thought," he said and looked at her, his gaze riveted and riveting.

What are you thinking? she wondered, unable to look away. Did he understand her father's remark as a symbol of trust and value? She prayed he did, then caught sight of the clock.

"Good heavens, will you look at the time? What a bunch of chatterboxes we are. Listen, I'm going to go down to the stable and start getting things together. Jeff, why don't you follow with the van? I don't have much to load. I'll see you all in a few minutes."

"Hope, there are some things of your mother's that I think it's time you have. And Cole, didn't you mention getting Jeff's opinion on that little filly you picked up last week? You kids go on ahead and leave the van here. I'll load the boxes up and bring the van down to stable four."

Everyone agreed, but Hope wanted to run ahead and leave Cole and Jeff some time together. She noticed some of her men walking toward the stone barn. She wanted to be the one to tell them she wouldn't be returning except to fill in every once in a while, so she trotted after them.

"Tony. Maurice. Joseph!"

The men turned toward her, as did several others who stood around a pallet of hay they apparently intended to hoist into the loft. It wasn't the way she would have recommended doing it but guessed it could work to their advantage timewise.

"Listen up, guys. I wanted to let you all know I won't be back except to help out sometimes. I'm staying on at Lavender Hill as a partner and trainer of an Olympic facility Jeff wants to get up and running."

"Hey, way to go!" Maurice called.

At the same time Tony said, "Yeah, our loss is Carrington's gain."

Joseph, who rarely strung more than two words together in an hour, said, "We miss you already, boss lady."

A chorus of others added like sentiments, causing tears to dam up in Hope's throat. She was about to thank them all for their support when a strident voice echoed from inside the barn. "You lazy clowns want to stop flirting with the boss's daughter and get it in gear?"

"Uh-oh. Sorry, Ms. Taggert. Donovan's on the warpath again. The man's been a bear for months," Tony said. "Come on, boys. Let's give this crazy idea a try."

Hope stepped to the side and watched the men hoist the heavy load off the ground. For the life of her she didn't see how it was going to fit through the loft door, though. She walked forward, trying to get a better prospective.

Just as he and Cole made it to stable four, Jeff remembered he was supposed to remind Hope to get her address book. He left Cole and pushed himself toward where he saw Hope standing. She was laughing and talking with some men who were hoisting a pallet of hay. It looked like a bad way to handle so clumsy a load to him. He was sure it must be the angle he was at that made it look as if Hope was standing under the loft door, but his heart suddenly began to pound. He squinted against the glare of the sun, trying to see better. The height of the stack looked off, as if it was too tall to fit inside the opening. He pushed ahead faster.

Afraid for her, Jeff called Hope's name, but the men were all shouting as they pulled on the straining ropes. As he pumped his arms on the big rubber wheels, he looked up, and the top bale hit the header, causing the stack to list to one side.

"Hope!" he screamed, and she turned, surprise on her face. "The stack!" he yelled.

But she couldn't see what he saw from her vantage point, and rather than move, Hope look up in confusion, a frown creasing her brow.

A few feet from her, Jeff reached out to grab her as the pallet shifted above them and the bales tumbled free. Just as his hands gripped her arms and he pulled her to keep her from being crushed, Jeff felt the impact of a bale vibrate through Hope's body. She slumped forward into his arms.

The bales were tumbling amid the shouts of the men as they ran for cover. Jeff did the only thing he could think to do. He pulled her toward his chest and lurched out of the chair and over the side, causing it to overturn as they fell toward the ground. Bracing his arms around her like a safety cage, he hovered over Hope, protecting her beneath his body as the weight of the bales bore down on him.

Then it was over, and silence reigned.

"Jeff!" He heard Cole call from what sounded like a great distance. He was aware of the weight of several hundred pounds of hay on his shoulders and back. Thanks to all his exercise and probably gallons of adrenaline pumping through his veins, Jeff was able to stay on his forearms while the men pulled the bales off him. Fortunately, the overturned chair somehow kept the load off his legs.

Jeff blinked, trying to clear away the gritty hay dust and tears. Finally his vision cleared, and to his horror he saw that Hope lay still and pale beneath him.

"What nitwit thought this up?" Ross bellowed from above them. Jeff heard several voices answer at once as the men clamored to get through the hay to him and Hope.

It all seemed to be happening at a great distance, though, as Jeff's concentration remained fixed on Hope's motionless form. He could feel her shallow breathing but it did little to calm his thundering heart. He braced her head between his palms and talked to her, encouraging her to open her eyes, but she didn't respond.

One single horrifying thought paralyzed him as no fall from a horse ever could. What would he do if he lost her? He'd been facing a similar loss for months, but at least he'd have known she was alive though out of reach. And wouldn't that be a stupid waste? a quiet voice whispered.

"Are you all right?" Ross asked as the weight of the last bale was lifted off his back.

"It's Hope," Jeff said, not taking his eyes off her still features. "She's unconscious. A bale hit her before I could pull her out of the way. Somebody call nine-one-one."

Jeff saw his tears fall onto Hope's face and realized he was crying. But for the first time in his life he didn't care who saw his pain. What good was pride in an empty life? He'd been so absolutely stupid about everything. Suppose that bale injured her spine? What if she wound up like him? Would he love her less? Think less of her or need her inner strength and gentleness any less? Would *he* hesitate to marry *her* because she was physically limited? Of course, he wouldn't! Then why had he thought she should feel differently toward him?

Pride. He'd never let anyone see his pain. He'd presented facades to the world lest someone else find him wanting. Only with Hope and occasionally Cole had he shown his real self, and even then he'd hidden his most private feelings. He'd been a fool. Pride was an empty emotion full of self-pity and ultimately loneliness.

"Oh, please, dear God, don't let her be hurt!" he cried. Ross and Cole hunkered down next to them then. Cole reached over to check her pulse, and Ross put a hand on Jeff's back as if trying to brace him for bad news. "Don't take her from me," Jeff begged the Lord whom he'd known so short a time.

"Her pulse is fine," Cole assured him. "She's probably just taking a little snooze to scare us all."

"And there's an ambulance on the way. Let's get you back in your chair so Cole can take a better look at her," Ross suggested.

He knew her father was right, but he couldn't make himself move. Fear held him paralyzed more than his injured spine ever had. "I was so stupid," he sobbed, looking at Cole. "I told her we were only ever going to be friends. I didn't want to tie her to me while I was like this. Why was I so stupid?"

"Because you're a man and I'm told by my sister that we're all stupid," Cole explained patiently. "Now come on and let's get you up."

About to acquiesce, Jeff saw Hope's lashes flicker. "Hope, sweetheart, can you hear me?" he whispered, his throat tight with fear and raw with tears.

"Of course I can hear you. You're two inches from my ear," she muttered.

Jeff breathed a sigh of relief and, still holding her head between his hands, dropped his forehead onto hers for a long moment and closed his eyes in a quick prayer of gratitude.

Cole reacted to Hope's smart remark and snickered, dropping his head onto his arm where it was braced on the ground, his shoulders shaking in relieved laughter.

Ross chuckled, too, and smacked Jeff on the shoulder. "Come on, let's get you back in your chair before she slugs you for hovering. Hope hates it when people hover."

Jeff still couldn't let go of his precious burden, nor

could he drag his gaze from hers. Instead he balanced his weight on one forearm and brushed some hay off her cheek. He tried to smile, afraid his somber mood might frighten her, but he couldn't get the sight of that tilting pallet out of his head. Of the bales tumbling. Of her standing so vulnerable beneath them.

He could have lost her so easily, and still might. He'd been so stubborn, telling himself it was okay to break her heart with a lie about his feelings for her because she was better off without him. He'd been wrong, and now he didn't know how she felt about him anymore.

He'd been so awful in those first days. Had she seen a side of him that had killed her love? Was she still at Lavender Hill because of guilt? Mere friendship? Or love?

Because of his pride, he didn't know.

But then Hope answered Ross's banter. "That depends on who's doing the hovering," she whispered and reached up to caress Jeff's cheek, a loving smile brightening her face.

Jeff leaned down and gave into the wants and needs he'd denied for months. He cupped her cheek and brushed her lips with his once, twice, then he kissed her with all the love he felt in his heart.

Why had he fought this for so long? Where was the loss of pride in this? Where was the selfishness he feared would take over his soul if he took what she offered? This was all about beauty and need and desire. This was life at its most pure. This communion of spirit could be nothing less than a love sent by God.

Chapter Seventeen

Hope put her feet up on the sofa and stared at the lights of the main house. She thought over the day, hardly able to take it all in. It had started with Jeff and his incredible surprise in the exercise room and had ended with him kissing her, as Cole said, "Before God and everyone."

Then the paramedics had arrived, and she hadn't spoken to Jeff again. After checking both of them over for injuries, the technicians had decided they should both be taken to the E.R. because she had lost consciousness and because of Jeff's previous serious back injury.

It was a precaution, they had assured Jeff, and his protests to the contrary that he was fine, they had insisted on transporting both of them. Her last glimpse of him being strapped onto a backboard and loaded into an ambulance felt frighteningly like a rerun rather than a simple case of déjà vu.

That was the last time she'd seen him. Cole had

brought her home, relaying the message that Jeff's shoulders and back were badly bruised but so far nothing else had turned up. Though he'd apparently protested that he had suffered no other ill effects from his heroic actions, they'd still insisted he wait till his neurologist could see him. Dr. Chin had arrived and decided that to be on the safe side he'd like to do a CAT scan, so Jeff and her father were still at the hospital.

It frightened her to think of Jeff putting himself between her and hundreds of pounds of falling hay bales. He could so easily have been injured all over again. And it would have been her fault for wandering where she hadn't belonged.

She closed her eyes and lay her aching head back, listening to Cole rattle around in her kitchen. She had only a slight concussion, but Cole wouldn't go home. She wanted him to. Desperately. When Jeff got home, she didn't want her sardonic brother there teasing him about that kiss. It had been too special to make light of.

That kiss had been a moment out of time that she would revisit and cherish to her dying day. She'd awakened to Cole's voice, then Jeff's had come from a mere inches away. She'd thrown the wisecrack back in answer to his question before she'd identified what it was about his voice that sounded odd. She'd forced her eyes open then, her concern for Jeff overriding her foggy state. It had been an utter shock to have the tears she'd thought she heard in his voice confirmed.

Jeff had breathed a deep sigh then and dropped his

forehead onto hers, his eyes closed. He'd held her so gently. So protectively. Then Cole and her father tried to get him to let her go. He'd pulled back a little but then his gaze caught on hers and held them both suspended in a place and time of their own for long moments. She'd watched in fascination as he'd battled some inner demon while her father and brother tried to lighten the moment with teasing banter. Nervous suddenly about what was going on inside Jeff's head, she'd chimed in, too. In doing so, however, she'd given away her feelings for Jeff to anyone who'd cared to listen.

And Jeff had apparently listened, responding to her confession in a surprisingly wonderful way. He'd kissed her. And what a kiss it had been! Hope no longer doubted his love but she had no idea what he planned to do about it. It was like his effort at standing that morning. A first step on a new branch of a long road with no guarantee that he'd ever make it to that ephemeral final destination.

Cole preached cautious optimism, and she agreed in principle. A simple kiss couldn't be as monumental as it felt to her. Jeff had probably kissed hundreds of women. But for some reason Hope was still elated out of all proportion or sense.

And she wanted to see him. She wanted to find out if that kiss had been one in a million or just one of hundreds. If it had meant as much to him as it had to her. If it had opened the floodgates to the affection and chemistry she'd felt flow from him to her the night of the Valentine's dance party and that day before his accident.

Memories of those hours had sustained her all these lonely months, and now she had one more memory to tuck away for her dreams.

Cole tiptoed into the quaint little parlor and stood watching his little sister sleep the sleep of the innocent. Jeff was a lucky man. Cole hoped that kiss meant Jeff was ready to reach out and grab the brass ring. Women like his sister didn't come into a man's life every day.

In fact, Cole was nearly sure women like Hope were an endangered species. Though he hoped he'd be smart enough to run the other way if he ever ran across one, Jeff had better not try it. The truth was that Cole didn't even really know who *he* was, so there was no way he could commit himself to another person. But Jeff Carrington had better be good and ready, because slugging a man in a wheelchair was going to go against one of Cole's basic rules of life. If, however, Jeff had raised Hope's expectations only to send her into crash-and-burn mode, as her brother, that was exactly what he intended to do to his best friend.

Cole turned as the front door opened and his father came quietly in. His stomach instinctively tightened.

"How is she?" Ross whispered.

"A little headachy. I gave her something for it." At his father's sharp look Cole gritted his teeth. "Acetaminophen, Dad. I know she isn't a horse."

A look of chagrin crossed his father's face, which was progress, in a way. "Sorry. Jeff checked out fine. He'll be doing therapy in technicolor for a while but, considering the alternative, I'm mighty grateful he put himself in harm's way. You think it's okay to leave her alone?"

Cole nodded, trying not to show his surprise that Ross had actually solicited his medical opinion. "They said her concussion was extremely mild, so yeah. I asked Curt to stop and check on her every once in a while tonight."

Ross nodded and stared at Hope. "So you think I'm going to have to punch out Carrington or is he going to come up to scratch?"

Cole chuckled and opened the door, reveling in the moment of camaraderie. "You'll have to stand in line if he doesn't. He may be tough to catch, though. I'll bet he had that chair going twenty-five miles an hour this afternoon."

Jeff watched Cole and Ross drive past on their way home. He swung the chair away from the window and rolled across the hardwood floor to the mirrors, then wheeled away and back to the window. He stopped in the middle of the room on the fourth pass and chuckled. Pacing was certainly easier in a chair.

He should just go to her, tell her he loved her and ask her to marry him. But he'd promised both Cole and Ross that, unless he could walk, he wouldn't tell her how he felt. Of course, now he knew he'd been wrong and they hadn't asked for his promise in the first place. In fact, unless he'd misread Ross, he was going to be pretty annoyed if there wasn't a wedding in the offing. And soon.

So what was holding him back? He'd admitted to himself it had been pride that had held him back till now. Jim Dillon had been right. Hope didn't need physical strength in a husband. Jeff was still the same man he'd been before his accident and before he saved her this afternoon. He was still physically limited. He still wanted her.

But does she still want you? What if you misread her response to Cole? Her smile? Her part in that kiss?

Jeff heard the questions and knew immediately what the tightening in his gut meant. He was afraid she felt only pity for him. No. He was afraid he'd killed her love months ago acting like such a jerk. But if he let that fear stop him, what was really stopping him was his pride again.

His mind made up, Jeff showered, dressed in khakis and a sports shirt then headed to his office. It took some doing to pull himself up so he could open the safe, but he was determined to do at least this on his own. It wasn't pride, though. He just didn't want anyone else to know before Hope what he intended.

He made a grab for the jewel case and dropped backward into his chair when his hand closed around the velvet box. Heart pounding, he let out a tired but elated breath. Then he opened the box he'd stuffed in the safe years ago after his parents' funerals. He rooted through the gold and platinum, bypassed a string of pearls, a sapphire and diamond tennis bracelet and ignored scores of other high-priced baubles that his mother had favored. He was looking for his grandmother's engagement ring, a simple one-carat solitaire that had been in his family for generations.

He found it, and a helpless smile tugged at the corners of his mouth. It was perfect for Hope. Simple. Delicate. Elegant. Now if she would only accept it. And him.

He was halfway through the house when it struck him that his stomach was jumpy with nerves. It reminded him of his first date. He smiled, unable to remember the face of that long-ago young girl. The only face he could recall at that moment was Hope's.

His stomach did a flip, and he remembered another date—another day he'd been nervous. He'd been headed over to go riding with Hope—the ride that had shattered his world. *Please, Lord, let this turn out better than that date.*

Date!

He'd never even taken her on a real date. The brunch at the Dupont had started out as one but he'd turned it into a business luncheon by asking her to be his partner, so Jeff figured it didn't count. Here he was about to ask Hope to marry him and he'd never even taken her on a date.

Jeff looked at the ring. It couldn't wait. He couldn't wait. *He* grinned. Today was June third. If she agreed to marry him, he'd take her on an official date every June third for the rest of their lives to make up for the oversight.

Just let her say yes, Lord. I don't want to live without her.

He was at the door to the homestead house in minutes, the ring on his pinky and a bunch of flowers he'd swiped off the breakfast room table in his lap. The lights were on in the parlor, and he could see Hope curled up and asleep on the sofa. He turned away, disappointed. He hated the idea of waking her. Halfway back to the house, he stopped.

This couldn't wait. He turned back.

"Wake up, sleepyhead," he called through the open window before he could change his mind.

Hope sat up like a bolt of lightning had struck nearby and looked around, confused.

"I'm outside," he told her. "Are you up to coming out here so we can talk? It's a nice night. We could sit in the rose arbor."

Hope agreed and arrived not long after he did. She'd changed into a soft peach-colored lounging set that wasn't quite pajamas and not street wear, either. She looked like peaches and cream and good enough to eat in the low exterior lighting. Jeff swallowed—hard.

"It's a pretty night," she remarked as she drew nearer.

"Not half as pretty as you. These are for you." He handed her the flowers, the stems wrapped in paper towel. "How's your head?"

Hope looked at the flowers, puzzled. "Thanks. My head's fine." She smiled. "How's my hero?"

He grinned at that appellation then sobered. "Nervous," he said truthfully.

Hope sat heavily on the stone bench. Clearly alarmed, she reached for his hand. "The CAT scan showed more damage?" she cried.

Jeff shook his head and took her hand in his, fighting the urge to yank her into his arms. "My back's fine," he said. "It's my heart."

"Your heart!" she yelped.

Fighting a grin, he nodded solemnly. "Uh-huh. I lost it. It happened months ago, but I lied so no one would find out. So *you* wouldn't find out. I can't hide it anymore, though." He could almost see the truth dawn on her sweet features.

"You can't?"

"Nope." His heart contracted at the longing in her eyes. He couldn't draw this out any further. "I love you, Hope."

"You love me?"

"With all my heart. And I don't want you to leave. Not permanently, anyway. Just till after the wedding."

Beginning to regain her composure, Hope raised that adorable imperious eyebrow. "Wedding?"

Jeff pulled the ring off his pinky. "Will you marry me, sweetheart? Will you come be my love as well as my partner?"

Hope was tempted to pinch herself. Could she still be in the homestead house, asleep, dreaming her heart's desire? She looked around the flagstone garden and at the latticework archways of the rose arbor that surrounded them. She felt the stone bench beneath her. The cool late spring air. This definitely didn't feel like a dream. Jeff was sitting there looking hopeful with the most compelling look in his eyes.

"You love me?" she asked, checking her facts. "You want to marry me?"

"If you love me. And if you'll have me. Is that so hard to believe?"

"You said I was like a sister to you."

Even in the low light of the garden lanterns, Hope could see his silvery eyes glitter. "I'd get arrested in nearly every civilized country in the world for feeling this way about a sister."

Still holding her hand, he pulled her to her feet and into his lap. Then he kissed each of her fingers, holding her gaze captive. Warmth spread through her from her fingers to her toes.

"I thought for a long time I was hiding my feelings for your sake. But today, you could have been hurt as badly or worse than I was in February, and I'd still have loved you. Why did I think your feelings should work any differently? Because I'm supposed to be this big strong guy? I told myself when I walked—if I walked— then I'd tell you how I feel. Today I realized that was my pride talking. And I was wrong. I could have lost you today and I'd never have told you how I feel. I do love you, Hope."

"And I love you," she said simply. Finally.

A smile brightened Jeff's eyes, though his mouth remained solemn. "Will you marry me, Hope? Will you make me the happiest, luckiest guy in the world?" He pulled a pretty, old-fashioned diamond solitaire off his finger and held it out for her to accept.

Funny, she thought, looking down on his golden head as he slid the ring on her finger. He'd been the one seeking the gold and she'd been the one to win it in the end.

Epilogue

Ross jumped from the family's carefully preserved antique open carriage. Thanks to a cool sunny day he'd been able to bring Hope to the church the way every Taggert bride had arrived at her wedding for the last hundred and fifty years. Hope had insisted on it.

She'd always been a funny kid, clinging to some traditions while busting others wide open. So today his horse-training daughter planned to marry the boy next door in a church that used to be a barn while wearing her grandmother's veil and the latest in wedding dresses.

And she was a vision in the simple sleeveless dress his sister had said was made of something called tissue taffeta. The yards of material were gathered at her waist to form a full skirt, and made her look like the princess he'd always considered her.

Ross tied the horses to an ornamental piece of split rail fence, then went to escort his princess to meet her prince. He squinted as he looked up. The midsummer sun and the bright white dress combined to temporarily blind him. "You're beautiful, princess," he said and lifted her to the ground. She weighed less than a feather, but mistaking her delicate stature for fragility was a mistake he didn't make anymore. That error had gotten him in more hot water over the years than he cared to think about on such a happy day.

"You haven't called me that in years," she said, looking at him with her deep blue eyes shining with happiness.

Ross chuckled. "I was afraid of having my head handed to me."

"Was I that bad?"

"No worse than I was," he admitted. "It's hard for a father to let go and stop trying to protect his little girl." He hesitated. "Hope, if you ever need anything, remember I'm here."

Hope reached up and put her hand on his shoulder. "We'll be just fine. I know you worry because he's still in a chair—"

"No, that's not it. It's just that it seems like yesterday that your mother and I brought a fragile little bundle of nothing home and called her Hope Taggert. Now it feels like I blinked my eyes and she's about to change her name. It's a lot for a father to take in. But if you have to take another name, I'm glad it's Jeff's. He's a good man. I just wish I hadn't been so stubborn about him all these years. I let Addison's lies cheat us out of a lot of good years."

"Well, we have lots of years ahead to make up lost time."

"Time!" he all but yelped, checking his watch. "We'd better stop yammering and get you in there before your groom paces all the rubber off his wheels."

Jim Dillon greeted them at the door. Ross's problems with God always made him a little uncomfortable with the easygoing preacher, but today it was tough to resist the younger man's congenial smile.

"Oh, good. You're here," Dillon said, offering Ross his hand. "Give me a minute to get down front. I'll signal Holly to start playing the wedding march, then you two come on ahead. Meg and Cole are down there already, the way we decided last night."

"Okay. Good to go," Ross said then turned to Hope. "Ready to become a Carrington?"

Her happy smile lit his heart. "More than ready."

The first strains of the wedding march floated to the back of the sanctuary. "Good thing, 'cause we're on."

Jeff's two ushers, Curt Madden—tall, muscular and blond—and Manny Hernandez—short, slight and dark—opened the doors. With his eyes, Ross traced the white runner down the length of the aisle to the raised platform. On it sat a flower-bedecked replica of the Laurel Glen entrance archway. Jeff had commissioned it for the wedding as a symbol that Hope might be taking *his* name but he was joining *her* family.

Ross looked to the right and saw something he knew Hope from her lower vantage point could not. Jeff wasn't sitting in his wheelchair. Ross could see the top of his blond head peeking over the crowd. He couldn't imagine how desperately Jeff must have wanted to greet Hope at the altar standing on his own two feet if he was willing to risk this. The braces that allowed him to stand were heavy and uncomfortable, and there was always the risk of falling.

Ross started them walking toward the man who was his only daughter's future, then he squeezed Hope's hand and leaned sideways a bit to whisper, "Jeff's standing, princess."

"I thought he might try something like this," she whispered back. "He's been working almost nonstop at his therapy."

When they got about three-quarters of the way down the aisle the congregation suddenly sat, giving them a complete view of Jeff.

And a wonderful gift.

He stood straight and tall, no wheelchair, braces or walker in sight. Hope gasped then let out a little squeak of a sob. Jeff held out his hand and walked forward a few steps as if he'd been born on those two feet and sturdy legs.

Ross let go of Hope when she strained forward. "Go ahead, princess," he whispered, "there's your future standing there on his own two feet."

Hope looked at him, tears making her sapphire eyes glitter. Then she turned and walked forward toward a golden future....

* * * * *

Dear Reader,

I hope you've enjoyed the first book of my new LAUREL GLEN series and the updates on the congregation at the Tabernacle.

Hope and Jeff's story came to me as I watched a film of a three-day event on television. Due to an injury in my twenties that prevented me from riding, I could relate to never again flying over trails with the wind in my hair. But it was only recreation for me. I could only imagine what it would be like to be at the top of the sport and lose the complete use of my legs.

And so Jeff, the golden boy of the equestrian world, was born—fully grown. What would he do without God to give him strength? He'd need someone who loved him already, since he would, no doubt, be angry and not very lovable. She'd need to be caring but strong. And she'd need to be well centered in the Lord so she could show him what he really needed in his life. And so Hope, voice of Jeff's conscience, came to be.

Sometimes the Lord just has to knock out all the props to get us to listen to Him and His plan for our lives. Jeff finally listened and found in that golden moment that he didn't have to be alone ever again because he had a Father watching over him. In books two and three of LAUREL GLEN, Hope's father and brother will both learn the same lesson and then some.

I love hearing from my readers and can be reached at c/o VFRW, P.O. Box 350, Wayne, PA 19087-0350.

Sincerely,

Kate Welsh

REQUEST YOUR FREE BOOKS!

2 FREE INSPIRATIONAL NOVELS
PLUS 2
FREE
MYSTERY GIFTS

LoveInspired

YES! Please send me 2 FREE Love Inspired® novels and my 2 FREE mystery gifts (gifts are worth about $10). After receiving them, if I don't wish to receive any more books, I can return the shipping statement marked "cancel". If I don't cancel, I will receive 4 brand-new novels every month and be billed just $4.24 per book in the U.S. or $4.74 per book in Canada, plus 25¢ shipping and handling per book and applicable taxes, if any*. That's a savings of over 20% off the cover price! I understand that accepting the 2 free books and gifts places me under no obligation to buy anything. I can always return a shipment and cancel at any time. Even if I never buy another book, the two free books and gifts are mine to keep forever.

113 IDN ERXA   313 IDN ERWX

Name	(PLEASE PRINT)	

Address		Apt. #

City	State/Prov.	Zip/Postal Code

Signature (if under 18, a parent or guardian must sign)

Order online at www.LoveInspiredBooks.com

Or mail to Steeple Hill Reader Service:

IN U.S.A.: P.O. Box 1867, Buffalo, NY 14240-1867
IN CANADA: P.O. Box 609, Fort Erie, Ontario L2A 5X3

Not valid to current subscribers of Love Inspired books.

Want to try two free books from another series?
Call 1-800-873-8635 or visit www.morefreebooks.com

* Terms and prices subject to change without notice. N.Y. residents add applicable sales tax. Canadian residents will be charged applicable provincial taxes and GST. Offer not valid in Quebec. This offer is limited to one order per household. All orders subject to approval. Credit or debit balances in a customer's account(s) may be offset by any other outstanding balance owed by or to the customer. Please allow 4 to 6 weeks for delivery. Offer available while quantities last.

Your Privacy: Steeple Hill Books is committed to protecting your privacy. Our Privacy Policy is available online at www.SteepleHill.com or upon request from the Reader Service. From time to time we make our lists of customers available to reputable third parties who may have a product or service of interest to you. If you would prefer we not share your name and address, please check here. ☐

LIREG08R

Love Inspired.
HISTORICAL
INSPIRATIONAL HISTORICAL ROMANCE

Overnight, Delia Keller
went from penniless
preacher's granddaughter
to rich young heiress.
Determined to use the
money to give herself
the security she'd never
had, building a house
by Christmas is her
first priority. That is
until former Civil War
chaplain Jude Tucker starts
challenging her plans—
and her heart.

Look for

Hill Country Christmas
by
LAURIE KINGERY

Available October
wherever books are sold.

**Steeple
Hill®**

www.SteepleHill.com

LIH82798

beek, *Freud and America*, pp. 123–142; Lasch, *The Culture of Narcissism*, pp. 162–165 (quote from p. 162).

136. Bettelheim and Janowitz, *The Dynamics of Prejudice*, p. 177.

137. Ibid., p. 174.

2. *Propaganda Against Prejudice*

1. "Community Relations Agency Involvement in Intergroup Education," March 1953, pp. 1–2, in AJC records, box 160, "IGE 42, 44–60." For more on this "immigrant gifts approach," see chapter 3.

2. For a social scientist's contemporary description of the various techniques that comprised the propaganda approach, see Williams, *The Reduction of Intergroup Tensions*, pp. 20–21.

3. *ADL Bulletin*, 7,2 (March 1950) pp. 1, 4; Benjamin R. Epstein, "The Educational Approach to Better Intergroup Relations," paper delivered at NCRAC Fifth Plenary Session, Atlantic City, N.J., March 15–17, 1947, p. 24, copy in Nearprint files, "Slawson, John," *AJA*. On the OWI and the federal government's use of propaganda during World War II, see Polenberg, *War and Society*, pp. 51–54, 136; Blum, *V Was for Victory*, pp. 21–52.

4. Benjamin R. Epstein, "The Educational Approach to Better Intergroup Relations," paper delivered at NCRAC Fifth Plenary Session, Atlantic City, N.J., March 15–17, 1947, p. 24, copy in Nearprint files, "Slawson, John," *AJA*; "Intergroup Relations in the Entertainment Media: Trends in 1951," January 7, 1952, p. 2, in AJC records, box 168, "Mass Media—Articles and Editorials 51–62." For a detailed analysis of the Jewish agencies' domestic anticommunist programs, see chapters 5, 6, and 7.

5. "Memorandum on Special Areas," February 1, 1949, p. 1, in AJC records, box 163, "Agencies, Intergroup Rel. 49–62." Interestingly, Jewish participation in the advertising industry—as well as the ability of Jews in advertising to express their ethnicity in their work—increased precipitously in the years after 1945. See Pope and Toll, "We Tried Harder."

6. Flowerman and Jahoda, "Can We Fight Prejudice Scientifically?" p. 584. In another context, however, Flowerman argued that the analogy between commercial advertising and pro-tolerance propaganda was a poor one. See Flowerman, "Mass Propaganda in the War Against Bigotry," p. 430 n.

7. AJC-ADL Joint Memoranda, April 12, 1948 and March 3, 1948, in AJC records, box 224, "Advertisements AJC Mass Media 46–49"; ADL National Commission minutes, May 16, 1947, p. 4, in ADL records. The slogans are quoted in *ADL Bulletin*, 5,4 (May 1948), p. 3.

8. Copies of intergroup relations advertisements placed by AJC in late 1940s can be found in AJC records, box 224, "Mass Media Advertisements AJC 1946–1949."

9. Benjamin R. Epstein Oral Memoir, in Cohen and Wexler, "*Not the Work of a Day*," 1:vii, 81; Kirman, "Major Programs of the B'nai B'rith Anti-Defamation League," pp. 119–120; *ADL Bulletin*, 7,2 (March 1950), p. 4; Report of National Program Director, ADL National Commission minutes, May 16, 1947, p. 4; Report of National Program Committee, ADL National Commission meeting, November 20–22, 1953, p. 11; Draft of Report by IAD to National Program Committee, ADL National Program Committee minutes, May 1950, in ADL records.

10. IAD carcards, in Anti-Semitism, 4, "Labor and Laboring Classes, Post-World War II posters decrying bigotry and prejudice, 1944–1945," *AJA*; *ADL Bulletin*, 9,8 (October 1952), p. 7; Lester J. Waldman Oral Memoir, in Cohen and Wexler, *"Not the Work of a Day,"* 5:40; ADL National Commission minutes, December 4–7, 1958, p. 20; Report of the National Program Committee to the National Commission, p. 1, attached to National Commission minutes, November 24–27, 1956; ADL National Executive Committee minutes, October 26–27, 1957, p. 6, in ADL records. While drafting this chapter during 1993 and 1994, I repeatedly observed antiprejudice "carcards," with messages strikingly similar to those used by the IAD nearly fifty years earlier, on New York City buses.

11. IAD carcard [1947?], in author's possession; IAD carcard (1944), in Anti-Semitism, 4, "Labor and Laboring Classes, Post-World War II posters decrying bigotry and prejudice, 1944–1945," *AJA*.

12. Kazin, *The Populist Persuasion*, p. 115.

13. On the use of radio by Coughlin, Long, Roosevelt, and others during the 1930s, see Brinkley, *Voices of Protest*, pp. 26, 62, 71, 83, 91–92, 97–101, 109, 119–120, 159, 169, 193; Kazin, *The Populist Persuasion*, pp. 110, 113–115, 140–141, 155; Leuchtenburg, *Franklin D. Roosevelt and the New Deal*, pp. 330–331. On the radio programs of the Office of Facts and Figures and the Voice of America, see Blum, *V Was for Victory*, pp. 25–28, 42–43. On the programs of the OWI's Radio Bureau, see Lazarsfeld and Stanton, *Radio Research, 1942–1943*, pp. 111–150. AJC staff members were familiar with the work being conducted by Paul Lazarsfeld's Office of Radio Research, which was established by a grant from the Rockefeller Foundation in 1937 and affiliated successively with Princeton and Columbia Universities. See Lazarsfeld, *Radio and the Printed Page*.

14. Bryson and Rowden, "Radio as an Agency of National Unity," p. 137. Dorothy Rowden had been a staff member of the CBS Department of Education and of the Institute for Adult Education at Columbia University Teachers College. Lyman Bryson was a professor of education at Teachers College and director of education at CBS. He also served as secretary to the Conference on Science, Philosophy, and Religion (CSPR), part of the intergroup relations program of the Jewish Theological Seminary of America. The seminary had its own media programs, including the popular *Eternal Light* radio series, which were partly aimed at improving interreligious relations through the dissemination of information about Jews and Judaism. Milton Krents, who headed the AJC's Radio and Television Division, also directed the seminary's radio and television efforts. For more on the seminary's media programs, see Jeffrey Shandler and Elihu Katz, "Broadcasting American Judaism: The Radio and Television Department of the Jewish Theological Seminary," in Jack Wertheimer, ed., *Tradition Renewed: A History of the Jewish Theological Seminary* (New York: Jewish Theological Seminary, 1997). The seminary's radio and television programs shared certain common themes and objectives with the AJC and ADL programs described in this chapter. My thanks to Jeff Shandler for sharing a copy of this excellent article with me before its publication.

15. Form letters from John Slawson, January 3, 1944, and George Hexter, February 10, 1944, in AJC records, box 168, "Mass Media—Radio-TV 44–55"; AJC memorandum, "Press Coverage and Comment on AJC Four-Point Pledge to Combat Racial Disunity. Endorsed by Archbishop Spellman and Bishop Tucker," [1944], in AJC records, box

256, "AJC Race Relations." On the NCCJ "tolerance trios," see Pitt, *Adventures in Brotherhood*, pp. 40–62; Steele, "The War on Intolerance," p. 17. For other examples of early AJC radio programs, see Dollinger, "The Politics of Acculturation," p. 90.

16. S. H. Flowerman and Marie Jahoda, "Quandary in Combatting Intergroup Tensions: Action vs. Research," 1946, p. 9, in AJC records, box 168, "Research." A revised version of this report was published in *Commentary* magazine as Flowerman and Jahoda, "Can We Fight Prejudice Scientifically?" While the *Commentary* piece stated that Flowerman and Jahoda were writing "in their individual capacities rather than officially, and their views are not necessarily those of the American Jewish Committee," the published version closely followed the text of the authors' AJC memorandum.

17. AJC memorandum, George Mintzer to Nathan Weisman, December 1, 1948, in AJC records, box 224, "Mass Media, [1938–1960]." ADL representatives also claimed to have influenced the "Superman" show. AJC memorandum, from Milton E. Krents to Richard C. Rothschild, November 24, 1948, in AJC records, box 224, "Mass Media, [1938–1960]."

18. In this effort the AJC made use of techniques such as "social bookkeeping," developed by Paul Lazarsfeld, and "content analysis." S. H. Flowerman and Marie Jahoda, "Quandary in Combatting Intergroup Tensions: Action vs. Research," 1946, p. 9, in AJC records, box 168, "Research"; Flowerman and Jahoda, "Can We Fight Prejudice Scientifically?" p. 586.

19. For a detailed analysis of the "Americans All — Immigrants All" series and the support it received from the AJC, see Montalto, *A History of the Intercultural Education Movement*, pp. 149–170. Montalto advances the intriguing argument that AJC leaders may have supported the series partly in the hope that it would build public support for liberalization of the government's policy on admitting war refugees.

20. AJC 51st Annual Meeting, "Background Memorandum for Mass Media Education Committee — Use of AJC's Name on Programmatic Material," April 25, 1958, pp. 1–2, in AJC records, box 224, "Mass Media 48–59 AJC." See also Dinnerstein, *Antisemitism in America*, p. 147.

21. ADL Executive Committee minutes, January 4, 1940, p. 3; ADL Executive Committee minutes, February 23, 1946, p. 1, in ADL records; Lester J. Waldman Oral Memoir, in Cohen and Wexler, "*Not the Work of a Day*," 6:38–39; interview with Arnold Forster by author, June 11, 1996.

22. Benjamin R. Epstein Oral Memoir, in Cohen and Wexler, "*Not the Work of a Day*," 1:vii–viii, 80; ADL microfilm records, reel labeled "Yellows 1943 — Radio (Lest We Forget) to War (7/10/43)," in ADL records; Sigmund Livingston, "We Have Nothing to Fear from the Truth," Address to ADL Conference, September 21–23, 1940, p. 12, in Nearprint files, "Anti-Defamation League of B'nai B'rith, Special Topics," AJA.

23. ADL National Commission minutes, May 16, 1947, p. 4, in ADL records. See also Belth, *A Promise to Keep*, p. 184.

24. *ADL Bulletin*, 7,2 (March 1950), p. 4.

25. *ADL Bulletin*, 5,2 (February-March 1948), p. 1.

26. A memorandum found in the records of the AJC offered the hypothesis that "audio-visual mass media appear to be the most effective in communication. Thus TV is more effective than radio." "General Principles of Intergroup Relations," n.d., p. 2, in AJC records, box 163, "Intergroup Rel. 1950–1962." An article in the *ADL Bulletin*,

written by *New York Post* television columnist Jay Nelson Tuck, stated, "Perhaps no institution has so quickly, so deeply and so broadly penetrated American life as television. No medium more powerfully influences the thoughts, attitudes and actions of millions of us." *ADL Bulletin*, 13,7 (September 1958), p. 4.

27. Michael Kazin noted that the percentage of American homes with television sets increased from 9 percent in 1950 to over 50 percent four years later. Kazin, *The Populist Persuasion*, p. 335 n. 70.

28. AJC press release, [1951], "American Jewish Committee Produces First Human Relations 'Spots' for Television: Animated Ballad-Cartoons, with Songs by Tom Glazer, Released for Brotherhood Week"; "Television Cartoons for Better Human Relations" [August, 1954], in AJC records, box 168, "Mass Media—Radio-TV."

29. Ibid.

30. Ibid.; AJC memoranda on cartoons, dated August 19, 1954, and April 14, 1952, in AJC records, box 168 "Mass Media—Radio-TV."

31. Report of National Program Committee, ADL National Commission minutes, November 20–22, 1953, p. 11; ADL National Executive Committee minutes, September 10–11, 1955, pp. 4–5; ADL National Commission minutes, December 4–7, 1958, p. 5, in ADL records.

32. ADL National Commission minutes, December 4–7, 1958, p. 5, in ADL records; Benjamin R. Epstein Oral Memoir, in Cohen and Wexler, *"Not the Work of a Day,"* 1:104–106, 165; Nathan C. Belth Oral Memoir, in ibid., 5:113; Belth, *A Promise to Keep*, pp. 207–210.

33. *ADL Bulletin*, 14,6 (June 1957), p. 5.

34. Benjamin R. Epstein Oral Memoir, in Cohen and Wexler, *"Not the Work of a Day,"* 1:104–106; Nathan C. Belth Oral Memoir, in ibid., 5:xi–xii, 113.

35. AJC Press Release, "American Jewish Committee Commends Networks for Promoting Intergroup Unity," May 15, 1955, in AJC records, box 168, "Mass Media Radio-TV 44–55." On the mass media and the American Jewish tercentenary, see Goren, "A 'Golden Decade' for American Jews," pp. 11–12.

36. "Adventures in Human Relations," October 1955, in AJC records, box 168.

37. AJC memorandum, George Mintzer to Nathan Weisman, December 1, 1948, in AJC records, box 224, "Mass Media [1938–1960]"; *Committee Reporter*, 4,10 (October 1947), p. 5.

38. AJC Community Service Department memorandum, November 29, 1950, in AJC records, box 168. In the mid-1950s the AJC cooperated with the New York, Connecticut, New Jersey, Massachusetts, and Rhode Island State Commissions Against Discrimination to excerpt short antiprejudice presentations from commercial feature films such as *A Medal for Benny* and *The Lawless*. See documents in AJC records, box 168, "Mass Media—Film—AJC."

39. Brochure from "Brotherhood 4: Fourth Annual Brotherhood Week Film Forum" at the Public Library of Cincinnati and Hamilton County, n.d., in AJC records, box 168, "Mass Media—Films 46–61."

40. *ADL Bulletin*, 6,3 (March 1949), p. 6; *ADL Bulletin*, 7,2 (March 1950), pp. 4, 8.

41. National Program Committee report, ADL National Commission minutes, November 20–22, 1953, p. 11, in ADL records; *ADL Bulletin*, 7,2 (March 1950), p. 4; *ADL Bulletin*, 14,6 (June 1957), p. 3; "Adventures in Human Relations," October 1955, in AJC

records, box 168. Some of the ADL films, including *Heritage*, are preserved in the collection of the American Jewish Archives.

42. Jewish intergroup relations officials were aware of the main conclusions of the Studies in Prejudice before the volumes were published in 1949 and 1950. This was partly the result of the publication of initial findings in article form in the period between 1945 and 1950. In addition, the AJC had the benefit of early, unpublished studies of anti-Semitism completed by the ISR in 1944. See list of references at the end of Adorno et al., *The Authoritarian Personality*, pp. 977–982, especially numbers 30, 31, 32, 38, 53a, 57a, 70, 71. Finally, there were the findings of the AJC's Department of Scientific Research during the immediate postwar years, which are examined below.

43. AJC Department of Program Resources, "AJC's Mass Media Program — Unrealized Potentials," October 23, 1958, pp. 1–2, in AJC records, box 224, "Mass Media — AJC, 48–59."

44. ADL National Commission minutes, December 3–6, 1959, p. 10, in ADL records.

45. Richard S. Salant to Sol Satinsky, December 17, 1957, pp. 1–4 (quotes from pp. 2, 4), in AJC records, box 224, "Mass Media 57–58 AJC Program Analysis"; AJC Department of Program Resources, "AJC's Mass Media Program — Unrealized Potentials," October 23, 1958, pp. 2, 5, 9 (quote from p. 9), in AJC records, box 224, "Mass Media — AJC, 48–59." On Salant, see Whitfield, "From Publick Occurrences to Pseudo-Events," p. 56; *Current Biography Yearbook 1961*, s.v. "Salant, Richard S."

46. "Consultation Re: Mass Media program," by Ethel C. Phillips, July 15, 1957; Richard S. Salant to Ora J. Sievers, [April 1958?] and Ora J. Sievers to Richard S. Salant, March 7, 1958, in AJC records, box 224, "Mass Media AJC Program Analysis 57–58."

47. AJC Department of Program Resources, "AJC's Mass Media Program — Unrealized Potentials," October 23, 1958, p. 6 in AJC records, box 224, "Mass Media — AJC, 48–59."

48. Ibid., p. 10.

49. AJC, "Memo on Mass Media for Evaluation of AJC Program," May 5, 1958, p. 1, in AJC records, box 224, "Mass Media AJC Program Analysis 57–58."

50. Press release, "American Jewish Committee Commends Networks for Promoting Intergroup Unity," May 16, 1955, pp. 1–2, in AJC records, box 168, "Mass Media Radio-TV 44–55"; Richard S. Salant to Sol Satinsky, December 17, 1957, in AJC records, box 224, "Mass Media 57–58 AJC Program Analysis"; ADL National Commission minutes, December 4–7, 1958, p. 20; ADL National Commission minutes, December 3–6, 1959, p. 10; ADL National Executive Committee minutes, March 1–3, 1958, p. 7; ADL National Executive Committee minutes, October 26–27, 1957, p. 6; Report of the National Program Committee to the National Commission, p. 1, attached to National Commission minutes, November 24–27, 1956, in ADL records.

51. "Report of Program Committee Activities to the National Executive Committee, Delivered by Hon. Henry Epstein, September 10, 1955," pp. 4–5, attached to ADL National Executive Committee minutes, September 10–11, 1955, in ADL records.

52. Lester J. Waldman Oral Memoir, in Cohen and Wexler, "*Not the Work of a Day*," 6:40.

53. Report of National Program Committee, ADL National Commission minutes, January 11–15, 1961, p. 9, in ADL records.

54. Report of Program Committee, ADL National Commission minutes, December 4–7, 1958, p. 20; ADL National Commission minutes, December 3–6, 1959, p. 10; Report of National Program Committee, ADL National Commission minutes, January 11–15, 1961, p. 9, in ADL records.

55. This shift of priorities can be clearly seen in the Report of the Program Committee, ADL National Executive Committee minutes, October 26–27, 1957. For an analysis of the ADL's expanded educational program during the 1950s, see chapter 3.

56. ADL Bulletin, 6,2 (February 1949), p. 2; Minutes of Joint Meeting of National and NY Administrative Committees, March 29, 1948, p. 3, in ADL records.

57. ADL National Commission minutes, December 3–6, 1959, pp. 10–11, in ADL records.

58. For a discussion of the role of these and other veterans' organizations in the domestic cold war, see Kazin, The Populist Persuasion, pp. 178–183.

59. ADL memorandum, "The Attacks on Films," April 2, 1954, Civil Rights Committee bound volume, January 1953 to May 1954; ADL National Executive Committee minutes, May 1–2, 1954, pp. 3–4, in ADL records. The quote is from "STATEMENT OF THE NUTLEY HUMAN RELATIONS COUNCIL," December 9, 1953, in AJC records, box 168, "Mass Media Films."

60. Benedict and Weltfish, The Races of Mankind. The Public Affairs Committee, which published this pamphlet as part of an ongoing series, included Jewish intergroup relations professionals such as Samuel H. Flowerman and Edwin J. Lukas, both of the AJC.

61. "STATEMENT OF THE NUTLEY HUMAN RELATIONS COUNCIL," December 9, 1953, p. 1, in AJC records, box 168, "Mass Media Films."

62. The film was recommended by the United States Office of Education, the Audio-Visual Section of the American Library Association, the National Conference of Christians and Jews, and many other organizations. It was used by the General Brotherhood of Lutherans, the NAACP, the Urban League, the New York State Commission Against Discrimination, the Connecticut State Commission Against Discrimination, the public libraries of Cleveland, Detroit, and Chicago, the New York City YMCA, the Board of Education of Dade County, Florida, the University of North Carolina, Syracuse University, the University of Maine, Brigham Young University, the Board of Foreign Missions of the Congregational Church, the United States National Committee for UNESCO, and the War Department's Re-Orientation Program in Occupied Areas. See AJC memorandum, "BROTHERHOOD OF MAN," [1948]; and "STATEMENT OF THE NUTLEY HUMAN RELATIONS COUNCIL," December 9, 1953, pp. 1–2, in AJC records, box 168, "Mass Media Films."

63. After Weltfish publicized allegations that United Nations forces in Korea were practicing "germ warfare," Columbia University failed to renew her contract. Columbia officials denied that the decision was based on political considerations. AJC memorandum, "BROTHERHOOD OF MAN," [1948]; and AJC, "MEMO OF A CONVERSATION HELD BETWEEN HARRY FLEISCHMAN AND BRENDON SEXTON," July 7, 1953, in AJC records, box 168, "Mass Media Films"; Caute, The Great Fear, pp. 415, 491–520, 553; National Guardian, June 19, 1952, p. 3. On the "Hollywood Ten" and the anticommunist campaign in Hollywood, see Navasky, Naming Names; Adler, "The Politics of Culture."

64. Benedict and Weltfish, The Races of Mankind, pp. 1–3, 14, 18, 25–26; Bob Joffe

to Solomon A. Fineberg, April 3, 1951; Rex Stout to unknown, March 14, 1944; cartoon version of *The Races of Mankind*, in AJC records, box 256, "Mass Media—Publications—'The Races of Mankind.' "

65. Clipping from the *Cincinnati Enquirer*, February 22, 1959, "Legion Unit Objects to Film Shown at Brotherhood Weeks' Forum as 'Pro-Communist' "; Brochure from "Brotherhood 4—Fourth Annual Brotherhood Week Film Forum," Public Library of Cincinnati, n.d., in AJC records, box 168, "Mass Media Films."

66. AJC, "MEMO OF A CONVERSATION HELD BETWEEN HARRY FLEIS-CHMAN AND BRENDON SEXTON," July 7, 1953, in AJC records, box 168, "Mass Media Films." In a letter to Frank N. Trager of ADL, the AJC's Dorothy M. Nathan noted that the ADL was promoting *In Henry's Backyard*, another intergroup relations film based on material written by Gene Weltfish and Ruth Benedict. Nathan recalled that the ADL had previously refused to promote any film, article, or book "in which Communists, or presumed Communists, have had a hand." She questioned whether the ADL's decision to promote this film signified a switch to the AJC's policy, which she described as "we will promote movies, books, articles, etc. on their merit if the Communism of the author, magazine, or producer had no influence on the nature or quality of the production itself." Dorothy M. Nathan to Frank N. Trager, January 8, 1948, in AJC records, box 242, "Mass Media AJC 48–59."

67. "STATEMENT OF THE NUTLEY HUMAN RELATIONS COUNCIL," December 9, 1953, p. 3, in AJC records, box 168, "Mass Media Films."

68. The AJC was simultaneously collaborating with the American Legion under the auspices of the All-American Conference to Combat Communism, and therefore sought to avoid controversy with the legion over the *Brotherhood of Man* film. AJC memorandum, from Ira Gissen to Joe Woolfson, February 26, 1959, in AJC records, box 168, "Mass Media—Films 46–61." The AJC's participation in the All-American Conference to Combat Communism is discussed in detail in chapter 7.

69. In addition to the studies and reports cited below, see Lazarsfeld, "Some Remarks on the Role of the Mass Media," p. 17. Arnold M. Rose, a sociologist who participated in the 1946 "Public Relations Workshop" attended by Flowerman and Jahoda and who later advised the ADL, provided a somewhat more optimistic evaluation of the potential effectiveness of antiprejudice propaganda in Rose, "The Use of Propaganda to Reduce Prejudice." See Flowerman's response to Rose in Flowerman, "The Use of Propaganda to Reduce Prejudice: A Refutation."

70. AJC, "Memorandum on Scientific Studies," December 20, 1949, p. 1, in AJC records, box 17, "Big and Prej Studies in Prej 49–62."

71. S. H. Flowerman and Marie Jahoda, "Quandary in Combatting Intergroup Tensions: Action vs. Research," 1946, p. 8, in AJC records, box 168, "Research."

72. Ibid., pp. 2–9 passim; Flowerman and Jahoda, "Can We Fight Prejudice Scientifically?" pp. 584–585. The notion that residents of rural areas were more likely than city dwellers to be anti-Semitic was reflected in arguments, made by sociologists and historians, that American anti-Semitism was rooted in populist animosity toward cities and "Wall Street." See Rose, "Anti-Semitism's Root in City-Hatred"; Hofstadter, *The Age of Reform*.

73. John Slawson, "Programming Community Relations in the Present Period," paper delivered at NCRAC Fifth Plenary Session, Atlantic City, N.J., March 15–17, 1947, p. 7, in Nearprint files, "Slawson, John," AJA.

74. Flowerman, "Mass Propaganda in the War Against Bigotry," pp. 429–438 (quotes from pp. 434, 430). A similar point about saturation is made in Flowerman and Jahoda, "Can We Fight Prejudice Scientifically?" p. 584. Paul Lazarsfeld helped to develop the notion that antiprejudice propaganda in the mass media could have a "boomerang effect." See Lazarsfeld, "Some Remarks On the Role of the Mass Media," pp. 19, 25.

75. Cooper and Jahoda, "The Evasion of Propaganda," pp. 15–25. Paul Lazarsfeld, whose work on mass media was important to the evolution of the AJC's antiprejudice program, was particularly concerned with the problems of "evasion" and "preaching to the converted." See Lazarsfeld, *Radio and the Printed Page*; Lazarsfeld, "Some Remarks On the Role of the Mass Media," pp. 18–19; Lazarsfeld and Merton, "Studies in Radio and Film Propaganda."

76. Cooper and Jahoda, "The Evasion of Propaganda," p. 21.

77. Flowerman, "Mass Propaganda in the War Against Bigotry," p. 434. See also Flowerman, "The Use of Propaganda to Reduce Prejudice: A Refutation," especially pp. 106–107.

78. Ackerman and Jahoda, *Anti-Semitism and Emotional Disorder*, pp. 4–6.

79. The authors did suggest, however, that the mass media could influence the ways in which individuals translated their attitudes into behavior. Bettelheim and Janowitz, *Dynamics of Prejudice*, pp. 32–33, 54 (quote from p. 32).

80. Adorno et al., *The Authoritarian Personality*, pp. ix, 93, 973.

81. This critique of "Americans All—Immigrants All" was shared by the program's cosponsor, the United States Office of Education, and other analysts. See Montalto, *A History of the Intercultural Education Movement*, pp. 166–168. See also Lazarsfeld, *Radio and the Printed Page*, pp. 133–134; Lazarsfeld, "Some Remarks On the Role of the Mass Media," p. 19.

82. Marc Vosk, "Assessing Techniques for Change: Mass Media, Group Processes, and Intergroup Contact," paper given at Second NAIRO Conference on Research in Intergroup Relations, December 30, 1953, pp. 3–8 (quote on p. 4), in AJC records, box 165, "Research (NAIRO) 'Assessing Techniques for Change' (Vosk) 53–54."

83. Ibid., pp. 4, 8–10.

84. Robert B. Johnson, "A Review of More and Less Effective Actions in Intergroup Relations," January 1956, pp. 2–3, 8 (quote from p. 2), in AJC records, box 163, "Intergroup Relations 1950–1962." See also MacIver, *The More Perfect Union*.

85. Allport was pessimistic about the potential of mass media to reduce prejudice, although he noted some studies that suggested the possibility for attitude change, especially among those whose prejudices were not deeply rooted. Allport, *The Nature of Prejudice*, pp. 493–495.

86. Dean and Rosen, *A Manual of Intergroup Relations*, p. 113.

87. On the role of Jews in the film industry more generally, a separate question from the one explored here, see May and May, "Why Jewish Movie Moguls"; Gabler, *An Empire of Their Own*; Feingold, *A Time for Searching*, pp. 84–87, 129–132. On the changing image of Jews in Hollywood films during this period, see Shapiro, *A Time for Healing*, pp. 17–20.

88. Jules Cohen, "Promoting Better Human Relations via Hollywood and Vine," *Community Relations Papers Issued by the Association of Jewish Community Relations Workers* 3 (November 1950), in SAF papers, box 4, AJA; AJCongress and NAACP, *Civil*

Rights in the United States in 1950, p. 91; McManus and Kronenberger, "Motion Pictures, the Theater, and Race Relations," pp. 152–158; McCoy and Ruetten, *Quest and Response*, pp. 164–170. According to McCoy and Ruetten, this shift in Hollywood's depiction of minorities stemmed from a variety of factors, including the reaction to the Nazi's policy of mass extermination, the civil rights rhetoric of the Truman administration, pressures by civil rights agencies, fear of a black boycott of the movies, competition with television for an audience, and the personal convictions of some filmmakers.

89. "Intergroup Relations in the Entertainment Media: Trends in 1951," January 7, 1952, p. 2, in AJC records, box 168, "Mass Media—Articles and Editorials 51–62"; Dinnerstein, *Antisemitism in America*, pp. 130, 152–153.

90. For an analysis of the treatment of Jews and anti-Semitism in commercial films of this period, see Short, "Hollywood Fights Anti-Semitism," pp. 157–189.

91. *Crossfire* (RKO, 1947). *Crossfire* was based on Richard Brooks's novel *The Brick Foxhole* (New York: Harper, 1945), in which the protagonist was a homosexual. In the film treatment the murder victim was changed to a Jew. Short, "Hollywood Fights Anti-Semitism," pp. 167, 169–171; Raths and Trager, "Public Opinion and *Crossfire*," pp. 345–346, 350–351 (quote from p. 346).

92. "Crossfire: A Discussion Among Experts" (1947), in AJC records, box 7, "Anti-Semitism Mass Media Films 'Crossfire' Meetings 47."

93. Ibid., p. 2. This view, which became conventional wisdom by the 1950s, was later presented by Gordon Allport, who wrote that "People who see a pro-tolerance film will view it as a specific episode and not allow it to threaten the foundations of the system they live in." Allport, *The Nature of Prejudice*, p. 504.

94. Cohen, "Letter to the Movie-Makers," pp. 112–113. In fact, the Samuels character was supposed to have been a wounded war hero. See Short, "Hollywood Fights Anti-Semitism," p. 170; Shapiro, *A Time for Healing*, p. 19.

95. Cohen, "Letter to the Movie-Makers," pp. 113–114, 116. According to K. R. M. Short, AJC representatives met with Dore Schary at his RKO office to request that "he cancel production of the film [*Crossfire*] because of their fear that such an amateurish attempt to improve the problems of race relations could have the opposite effect." See Short, "Hollywood Fights Anti-Semitism," pp. 167–169.

96. Cohen, "Letter to the Movie-Makers," p. 115.

97. Ibid. Social scientific opinion on the effectiveness of Hollywood's "problem films" was by no means uniform. A year after Cohen's "Letter to the Movie-Makers," Irwin C. Rosen of the Department of Psychology at the University of Pittsburgh published the results of an experiment that found that viewing *Gentleman's Agreement* had a positive effect on a group of university students' attitudes toward Jews. See Rosen, "The Effect of the Motion Picture 'Gentleman's Agreement' on Attitudes Toward Jews."

98. Cohen, "Letter to the Movie-Makers," p. 118. K. R. M. Short characterized Cohen's tone in this article as "dismissive" and sarcastic. See Short, "Hollywood Fights Anti-Semitism," p. 172. The AJC's Richard Rothschild claimed that he and his colleagues had difficulty obtaining the cooperation of the commercial film industry and that Hollywood "producers, directors and writers, we found, were usually in the know-it-all category." Richard C. Rothschild, "The American Jewish Committee's Fight Against Anti-Semitism, 1938–1950," 1985, p. 22, in Small Collections files, AJA.

99. Schary, "Letter From a Movie-Maker," pp. 346–347. The Cohen-Schary exchange may well have reflected organizational rivalry between the AJC and the ADL. K. R. M. Short has argued that Schary arranged a pre-release screening of *Crossfire* for the ADL and sought the ADL's "stamp of approval" for the final version of the film. See Short, "Hollywood Fights Anti-Semitism," pp. 169, 177.

100. AJC memorandum, re: "September 30th meeting about 'Crossfire,' " Dorothy M. Nathan to John Slawson, October 1, 1947, pp. 1–2, in AJC records, box 7, "Anti-Semitism Mass Media Films 'Crossfire' Meetings 47."

101. Elliot Cohen offered a more positive assessment of the way that the issue of anti-Semitism was handled in *Gentleman's Agreement*, which he characterized as "a moving, thought-provoking film, which dramatically brings home the question of anti-Semitism to precisely those people whose insight is most needed—decent, average Americans." Even in this article, however, Cohen noted the limitations and potential hazards of propaganda against prejudice and advocated education within the Jewish community and work with religious, educational, labor, and business leaders as more effective means. Cohen, "Mr. Zanuck's 'Gentleman's Agreement,' " pp. 51–56 (quote is from p. 51).

102. Wolfenstein and Leites, "Two Social Scientists View 'No Way Out,' " pp. 388–391 (quoted phrases are from pp. 389 and 390). Wolfenstein and Leites were the authors of *Movies: A Psychological Study* (New York: Atheneum, 1970 [1950]). For another discussion of "No Way Out" that questioned its effectiveness as an antiprejudice tool, see Clurman, "Training Film for Democrats," pp. 181–183.

103. Jules Cohen, "Promoting Better Human Relations via Hollywood and Vine," *Community Relations Papers Issued by the Association of Jewish Community Relations Workers* 3 (November 1950), p. 3; "List of Members of the Association of Jewish Community Relations Workers," September 1952, in SAF papers, box 4, *AJA*. McManus and Kronenberger argued that "the white, Southern film audience, totaling at the most one-eighth of the total American film audience, is responsible for Hollywood's wary policy on treatment of the Negro in films." McManus and Kronenberger, "Motion Pictures, the Theater, and Race Relations," p. 156. On censorship of these race relations movies in the South during 1949, see AJCongress and NAACP, *Civil Rights in the United States in 1949*, pp. 67–68.

104. The ADL committee of "experts" included Louis E. Raths, director of Research at the New York University (NYU) School of Education, Avrum Ben-Avi, a clinical psychologist affiliated with NYU, Lloyd Allen Cook, professor of Educational Sociology at Wayne University, Elaine Forsythe, professor of social psychology at Albany State Teachers College, Charles Siepmann, director of NYU's Center for Communications, and Frank N. Trager, ADL research director. Raths and Trager, "Public Opinion and *Crossfire*," pp. 347–348 (quote from p. 348).

105. Ibid., pp. 349–368 passim (quote from p. 368).

106. AJC memorandum, re: "September 30th meeting about 'Crossfire,' " Dorothy M. Nathan to John Slawson, October 1, 1947, pp. 1–2, in AJC records, box 7, "Anti-Semitism Mass Media Films 'Crossfire' Meetings 47." According to K. R. M. Short, "a group of the wealthy Hollywood Jewish elite" met with Darryl Zanuck while he was producing *Gentleman's Agreement* in an attempt to "convince him that anti-Semitism would be fanned into life by raising the issue in a film." Short, "Hollywood Fights Anti-Semitism," p. 174. See also Shapiro, *A Time for Healing*, p. 19.

107. Minutes of Joint Meeting of National and NY Administrative Committees, March 29, 1948, p. 1; ADL National Commission minutes, May 5–8, 1948, p. 11, in ADL records; Benjamin R. Epstein Oral Memoir, in Cohen and Wexler, "Not the Work of a Day," 1:132; Nathan C. Belth Oral Memoir, in ibid., 5:31. This award came shortly after Schary, who was a liberal critic of HUAC and of blacklisting, was assigned to inform the Screen Writers Guild that a group of leading film industry executives had accepted the practice of refusing employment to communists. Schary's position reflected a liberal anticommunism similar to that espoused by the ADL and other "mainstream" Jewish agencies. See Moore, To the Golden Cities, pp. 195–196; Navasky, Naming Names, pp. 83–84. On the adoption of liberal anticommunism by the ADL and other Jewish agencies, see chapters 5, 6, and 7.

108. ADL Bulletin, 20,2 (February 1963), p. 6; Forster, Square One, pp. 90–92; Moore, To the Golden Cities, pp. 128–129, 148, 248.

109. ADL Bulletin, 7,7 (September 1950), p. 4.

3. Teaching Tolerance

1. AJC report, "The Year's Work in Intergroup Relations, July 1948–June 1949," pp. 27–28, in AJC records, box 163, "Reports 1955, 1948–1949."

2. NAIRO report, American Jewish Committee, October 8, 1954, p. 2, in AJC records, box 163, "Agencies, Intergroup Rel. 49–62."

3. "Activities of the American Jewish Committee in the Field of Intercultural Education—A Report to the National Community Relations Advisory Council," November 1, 1946, pp. 1–2; "Outline of Intercultural Education Activities of the American Jewish Committee Prepared for the NCRAC-Committee on Intercultural Education," December 24, 1948, pp. 1, 4; AJC memorandum, from David Danzig to Dorothy Nathan, October 18, 1950, in AJC records, box 160, "IGE AJC 45–60"; AJC report, "The Year's Work in Intergroup Relations, July 1948–June 1949," pp. 23–28, in AJC records, box 163, "Reports 1955; 1948–1949."

4. ADL Bulletin, 7,2 (March 1950), pp. 4, 8.

5. The organization's original name was the Service Bureau for Education in Human Relations; it was changed to the Service Bureau for Intercultural Education in 1936. The term intercultural education was coined, according to Nicholas Montalto, when the Progressive Education Association established a Committee on Intercultural Education in December 1935. Montalto, A History of the Intercultural Education Movement, pp. 110, 132.

6. Lewis, W. E. B. DuBois, p. 2. Rachel Davis DuBois was no relation to W. E. B. DuBois.

7. Montalto, A History of the Intercultural Education Movement, pp. viii–ix, 77–84.

8. ADL Executive Committee minutes, July 28, 1941, p. 2, in ADL records; "Activities of the American Jewish Committee in the Field of Intercultural Education—A Report to the National Community Relations Advisory Council," November 1, 1946, in AJC records, box 160, "IGE AJC 45–60"; Montalto, A History of the Intercultural Education Movement, pp. 114–115, 130, 153–161, 171–217, 220–221, 245–249, 250–259. The Service Bureau also received substantial assistance from the NCCJ during the 1930s, when the NCCJ functioned as "the unofficial sponsor of the Bureau." At that time the NCCJ itself was financially dependent upon the AJC and other "assimilationist elements

within the American Jewish community." See Montalto, ibid., pp. 96, 131, 188–201 (quotes from pp. 131 and 200).

9. "Community Relations Agency Involvement in Intergroup Education," March 1953, pp. 1–2, in AJC records, box 160, "IGE 42, 44–60."

10. Memorandum from Frank N. Trager to Sidney Wallach, January 29, 1940, in AJC records, box 256, "AJC — Race Relations"; Cohen, *Not Free To Desist*, pp. 176, 181. The ADL popularized anthropological findings, which debunked faulty notions of "race," in its educational materials. "A Discussion of Race," in "A Course on Intergroup Relations — Prepared for Interdenominational and Interfaith Youth Camps and Conferences," pp. 7–9, Dept. of Interreligious Cooperation, ADL of B'nai B'rith, in AJC records, box 163, "ADL"; Tumin, "Race and Intelligence." Hasia Diner has argued that Boas and his students, many of whom were Jewish, perceived a "direct link between Jewish identity and an interest in destroying the foundations of racism." See Diner, *In the Almost Promised Land*, pp. 142–149 (the quote is from p. 149). See also Friedman, *What Went Wrong?* pp. 124–127, 137. On these anthropologists' contribution to the reformulation of American identity, see Gleason, "Americans All," pp. 486–488, 514. Ruth Benedict and other anthropologists subsequently became involved in the intergroup relations movement. See the discussion of *The Races of Mankind* pamphlet in chapter 2.

11. Myrdal, *An American Dilemma*, 1:76. See also Jackson, *Gunnar Myrdal and America's Conscience*, pp. 194–196, 200–201.

12. Taba, "What Is Evaluation Up to and Up Against in Intergroup Education?" p. 21. Taba also had a professional relationship with the BIE. AJC memorandum, "Community Relations Agency Involvement In Intergroup Education," March 1953, pp. 3–4, in AJC records, box 160, "IGE 42, 44–60."

13. Montalto argued that the younger members of the AJC staff had become disillusioned with the "immigrant gifts" approach by 1940, thus undermining the AJC's relationship with Rachel Davis DuBois. On this point and the development of the "immigrant gifts" approach to intercultural education more generally, see Montalto, *A History of the Intercultural Education Movement*, pp. 85–87, 89–91, 94, 104, 216. On the development of the "immigrant gifts" approach to Americanization by settlement house workers and others during the Progressive era, see Higham, *Strangers in the Land*, pp. 251–253, 304; Lissak, *Pluralism and Progressives*.

14. Giles, "Basic Purposes and Problems in Evaluation of Intergroup Education," p. 13; BIE pamphlet, "Out of the Many — One," n.d., copy in author's possession. The transformation is analyzed in Montalto, *A History of the Intercultural Education Movement*, pp. 218–277. Social scientist Robin M. Williams, Jr., indicated this shift in intercultural education when he wrote in 1947 that "the likelihood of conflict is reduced by education and propaganda emphases upon characteristics and values *common* to various groups rather than upon intergroup *differences*" and "an effective propaganda approach in intergroup relations is that which emphasizes national symbols and common American achievements, sacrifices, destinies, etc., while unobtrusively indicating the common participation of minority group members." Williams, *The Reduction of Intergroup Tensions*, pp. 64, 67.

15. "Activities of the American Jewish Committee in the Field of Intercultural Education — A Report to the National Community Relations Advisory Council," November 1, 1946, p. 1; "Outline of Intercultural Education Activities of the American

Jewish Committee Prepared for the NCRAC-Committee on Intercultural Education,"
December 24, 1948, p. 1, in AJC records, box 160, "IGE AJC 45–60."

16. "Community Relations Agency Involvement in Intergroup Education," March
1953, pp. 1–3, in AJC records, box 160, "IGE 42, 44–60."

17. *ADL Bulletin*, 7,2 (March 1950), p. 4.

18. BIE pamphlet, "One of the Many—One," n.d. (quoted phrases are from pp. 3,
7, 12); AJC report, "The Year's Work in Intergroup Relations, July 1948–June 1949," p.
24, in AJC records, box 163, "Reports, 1955; 1948–1949"; Giles and Van Til, "School and
Community Projects," pp. 38–40; Johnson, "National Organizations in the Field of
Race Relations," p. 122. The contention that young children were innocent of prejudice until corrupted by intolerant adults was made by social psychologist Gordon W.
Allport and NCCJ president Everett R. Clinchy in Allport, "Foreword," "Controlling
Group Prejudice," p. vii; Allport, *The Person in Psychology*, p. 211; Clinchy, "The Effort
of Organized Religion," p. 129.

19. "Outline of Intercultural Education Activities of the American Jewish Committee Prepared for the NCRAC-Committee on Intercultural Education," December
24, 1948 (quote from p. 1); "Activities of the American Jewish Committee in the
Field of Intercultural Education—A Report to the National Community Relations
Advisory Council," November 1, 1946, p. 1; "Survey of Activities of Member Agencies with the Schools: American Jewish Committee," NCRAC-Committee on Intercultural Education, November 15, 1948, p. 1, in AJC records, box 160, "IGE AJC 45–
60."

20. "Activities of the American Jewish Committee in the Field of Intercultural Education—A Report to the National Community Relations Advisory Council," November 1, 1946, p. 3, in AJC records, box 160, "IGE AJC 45–60."

21. When the AJC and ADL assumed responsibility for distributing educational materials ordered from the BIE, they "use[d] Bureau stationery and Bureau labels, so that
the recipients may remain aware of the Bureau, and so that our handling of this operation does not make them feel that intercultural education has fallen into the hands of
Jewish agencies." "Outline of Intercultural Education Activities of the American Jewish Committee Prepared for the NCRAC-Committee on Intercultural Education,"
December 24, 1948, p. 3, in AJC records, box 160, "IGE AJC 45–60."

22. "Preliminary Memorandum on a Project in the Field of Education," June 15,
1945, pp. 1–2; "Activities of the American Jewish Committee in the Field of Intercultural Education—A Report to the National Community Relations Advisory Council,"
November 1, 1946, pp. 2–4; "Outline of Intercultural Education Activities of the American Jewish Committee Prepared for the NCRAC-Committee on Intercultural Education," December 14, 1948, pp. 1, 4–5, in AJC records, box 160, "IGE AJC 45–60"; "Community Relations Agency Involvement in Intergroup Education," March 1953, pp. 5–6,
in AJC records, box 160, "IGE 42, 44–60."

23. CCI Monthly Report for May 1948 (June 18, 1948), p. 6; CCI Monthly Report
(December 29, 1948), p. 5, in AJCongress records, box 19.

24. CCI Monthly Report for October 1948 (November 14, 1948), p. 1; CCI Monthly
Report for May 1948 (June 18, 1948), p. 1, in AJCongress records, box 19; "Questions
and Answers About CCI," October 16, 1952, p. 4, in AJCongress records, box 22; "Manual for CCI Chairmen," n.d., pp. 4–5, in AJCongress records, box 20.

25. John Slawson, "Some Approaches to the Problem of Anti-Semitism," paper

delivered at NCRAC Fifth Plenary Session, Atlantic City, N.J., March 15–17, 1947, p. 13, in Nearprint files, "Slawson, John," *AJA.*

26. Some of this work is summarized in Allport, *The Nature of Prejudice,* pp. 298–310. A study conducted by Marian Radke, Helen Trager, and Hadassah Davis for the Bureau for Intercultural Education in 1949 determined that children's attitudes toward minorities were shaped by the attitudes that they observed in their immediate environment. See Reimann, "How Children Become Prejudiced," pp. 88–94. See also Kluger, *Simple Justice,* pp. 318–319, 362, for discussion of related work by Radke and Trager. The work of Mary Ellen Goodman, republished with the aid of the ADL, lent weight to the conclusion that children formed ideas about race at a very young age. See Goodman, *Race Awareness in Young Children.* See also M. Brewster Smith, "The Schools and Prejudice: Findings," pp. 114–115, 128. The classic study in the field was Lasker, *Race Attitudes in Children.*

27. Kracauer, "The Revolt Against Rationality," p. 586.

28. Clark, "Effect of Prejudice and Discrimination on Personality Development," revised and expanded as Clark, *Prejudice and Your Child; Brown v. Board of Education of Topeka,* 347 U.S. 483 (1954). On Kenneth Clark's role in the NAACP's legal battle against discrimination, see Kluger, *Simple Justice,* pp. 315–319, 321–339 passim, 353–356, 440, 495–498, 555–557, 638, 705–706, 718–720; Wilkinson, *From "Brown" to "Bakke,"* p. 32; Greenberg, *Crusaders in the Courts,* pp. 123–124, 136–137, 149–150, 164, 180, 188, 198, 203, 255.

29. Slawson, *Unequal Americans,* pp. 114–115; Irving M. Engel, Transcript of Oral Memoir, interview conducted by Murray Polner, New York, N.Y., 1969–1970, tape 4, pp. 4–5, AJA; Kaufman, *Broken Alliance,* p. 93; Friedman, *What Went Wrong?* pp. 150–152.

30. Isidor Chein, "What Are the Psychological Effects of Segregation Under Conditions of Equal Facilities?" paper presented at the Nineteenth Annual Meeting of the Eastern Psychological Association, April 16–17, 1948, Philadelphia, pp. 1–3, in AJCongress records, box 21. The paper was subsequently published under the same title in *International Journal of Opinion and Attitude Research* 3 (1949):229–234. See also Chein and Deutscher, "The Psychological Effects of Enforced Segregation." Chein served as an expert witness for the NAACP Legal Defense Fund in the Virginia school desegregation case. Kluger, *Simple Justice,* pp. 492–494, 706; Greenberg, *Crusaders in the Courts,* p. 149.

31. On the connotations of the terms *intercultural education, intergroup education,* and *human relations education,* see Montalto, *A History of the Intercultural Education Movement,* p. 274.

32. AJC memorandum, re: "The Present Status of Intergroup Education and Proposals for Future Development," from Max Birnbaum to Alan M. Stroock, February 15, 1952, p. 6, in AJC records, box 160, "IGE 42, 44–60."

33. Minutes of Joint Committee on Intercultural Education, May 25, 1953, p. 1; January 10, 1953, p. 2, in AJC records, box 161, "AJC-ADL Joint Committee IGE 52–54"; "Community Relations Agency Involvement in Intergroup Education," March 1953, p. 6, in AJC records, box 160, "IGE 42, 44–60."

34. Minutes of Joint Committee on Intercultural Education, October 19, 1953, p. 1; February 9, 1954, pp. 1–2, in AJC records, box 161, "AJC-ADL Joint Committee IGE 52–54."

35. Minutes of Joint Committee on Intercultural Education, May 25, 1953, p. 1, in AJC records, box 161, "AJC-ADL Joint Committee IGE 52–54."

36. Minutes of Joint Committee on Intercultural Education, February 9, 1954, p. 1, in AJC records, box 161, "AJC-ADL Joint Committee IGE 52–54."

37. This competition did not, however, preclude cooperation between the two agencies; the ADL continued to cosponsor intercultural education workshops with the NCCJ during the 1950s. AJC memorandum, re: "The Present Status of Intergroup Education and Proposals for Future Development," from Max Birnbaum to Alan M. Stroock, February 15, 1952, pp. 3–4, in AJC records, box 160, "IGE 42, 44–60."

38. Ibid., pp. 3–5; "Community Relations Agency Involvement in Intergroup Education," March 1953, pp. 4–5, in AJC records, box 160, "IGE 42, 44–60"; *ADL Bulletin*, 7,2 (March 1950), p. 4.

39. ADL National Commission minutes, April 29–May 1, 1955, p. 3; Report of National Director, 1955, p. 1, in ADL National Executive Committee minutes, October 22–23, 1955, in ADL records; *ADL Bulletin*, 14,2 (February 1957), pp. 6–7. Earlier, in 1949, the ADL had organized a national conference on discrimination in higher education in collaboration with the American Council on Education. The original conference, convened in Chicago, led to the organization of regional conferences across the country during the early 1950s. These conferences were part of the ADL's campaign to eliminate the quota system in college and university admissions. AJCongress and NAACP, *Civil Rights in the United States in 1949*, p. 34; Belth, *A Promise to Keep*, pp. 189–193.

40. "Report of Program Committee Activities to the National Executive Committee Delivered by Hon. Henry Epstein, September 10, 1955," p. 1, attached to ADL National Executive Committee minutes, September 10–11, 1955; Report of National Director, 1955, p. 1, ADL National Executive Committee minutes, October 22–23, 1955, in ADL records.

41. Report of Program Committee, ADL National Commission minutes, November 24–27, 1956, p. 1; Report of National Program Committee, ADL National Executive Committee minutes, October 26–27, 1957, p. 6; Report of Program Division, ADL National Executive Committee minutes, September 20–21, 1958, p. 6, in ADL records; *ADL Bulletin*, 14,2 (February 1957), pp. 6–7 (quote from p. 6.)

42. "Report of Program Committee Activities to the National Executive Committee Delivered by Hon. Henry Epstein, September 10, 1955," pp. 2–3, attached to ADL National Executive Committee minutes, September 10–11, 1955, in ADL records.

43. Report of National Director, ADL National Commission minutes, January 10–14, 1962, p. 3, in ADL records.

44. *ADL Bulletin*, 6,7 (October 1949), p. 8; *ADL Bulletin*, 7,8 (October 1950), pp. 4–5; Report of Col. M. H. Schlesinger, chairman of National Community Service Committee, ADL National Commission minutes, October 20, 1951; "Report of Program Committee Activities to the National Executive Committee Delivered by Hon. Henry Epstein, September 10, 1955," pp. 2–3, attached to ADL National Executive Committee minutes, September 10–11, 1955, in ADL records. Sol B. Kolack Oral Memoir, in Cohen and Wexler, "*Not the Work of A Day*," 6:44–49, 81–82.

45. The NCRAC's Eighth Plenary Session took a position against religious holiday services in public schools in 1950. Minutes of Combined Meeting of Interfaith and Joint Advisory Committees, NCRAC, June 20, 1950, p. 1, in AJC records, box 185.

46. "Statement of Principles on Religious Observances in the Public Schools," 1950, in "ADL Stands on Various Issues," also attached to ADL National Commission minutes, May 13–14, 1950; Meeting of Executive Committee of ADL National Commission, January 13–14, 1951, p. 2; National Executive Committee minutes, October 22–23, 1955, pp. 15–17, in ADL records; *ADL Bulletin*, 7,9 (November 1950), p. 4; *ADL Bulletin*, 11,10 (December 1954), pp. 4–7. The general phenomenon of Jewish engagement with issues of church and state is thoroughly examined in Cohen, *Jews in Christian America*. Cohen discusses holiday observances on pp. 162–163. For another discussion of American Jews and the church-state issue, especially as it related to public education in the postwar period, see Dollinger, "The Politics of Acculturation," pp. 181–193. For an analysis of the Jewish role in fighting against religious practices in public schools in Miami and Los Angeles, see Moore, *To The Golden Cities*, pp. 177–187, 216–219.

47. *ADL Bulletin*, 11,10 (December 1954), pp. 4–7; *ADL Bulletin*, 12,8 (October 1955), pp. 6–7; ADL National Executive Committee minutes, June 24–25, 1955, pp. 4–5; ADL National Executive Committee minutes, October 22–23, 1955, pp. 15–17, in ADL records.

48. "Statement of Principles on Religious Observances in the Public Schools," 1950, in "ADL Stands on Various Issues," also attached to ADL National Commission minutes, May 13–14, 1950; Meeting of Executive Committee of ADL National Commission, January 13–14, 1951, p. 2, in ADL records; Kirman, "Major Programs of the B'nai B'rith Anti-Defamation League," p. 284; Cohen, *Jews in Christian America*, p. 163. Staff members of the AJC also worried that their commitment to church-state separation would stimulate anti-Semitism. Minutes of Joint Meeting of Church-State, Interreligious, and Intergroup Education Staff Committee, August 9, 1960, pp. 3–4, in AJC records, box 179, "Committee Staff 49–60." By the late 1950s the ADL adopted a more equivocal position on religious holiday observances, distinguishing between "sectarian observances of religious holidays" (which the league strongly opposed) and nonsectarian educational holiday programs (which the league "recognized," without approving or condemning). Proposed draft, "Statement on Religion and the Public Schools," from ADL National Commission Meeting, 1958; National Commission minutes, December 3–6, 1959, pp. 15–18, in ADL records.

49. Report of National Director Epstein, ADL National Commission minutes, April 29–May 1, 1955, p. 3, in ADL records.

50. "Report of Program Committee Activities to the National Executive Committee Delivered by Hon. Henry Epstein, September 10, 1955," attached to ADL National Executive Committee minutes, September 10–11, 1955, p. 1; Report of Program Committee, ADL National Commission minutes, November 24–27, 1956, p. 5, in ADL records.

51. Report of National Director, p. 1, in ADL National Executive Committee minutes, October 22–23, 1955, in ADL records.

52. *ADL Bulletin*, 14,2 (February 1957), p. 7.

53. ADL National Executive Committee minutes, September 20–21, 1958, p. 6, in ADL records. Several recent studies have emphasized the conflict between Northern and Southern Jews over the national Jewish agencies' vocal and active support for desegregation. See Friedman, *What Went Wrong?* pp. 275–291; Dollinger, "The Politics of Acculturation," pp. 204–245.

54. "Survey of Activities of Member Agencies with the Schools: American Jewish Committee," NCRAC-Committee on Intercultural Education, November 15, 1948, p. 1, in AJC records, box 160, "IGE AJC 45–60"; "Memorandum Concerning the Organization of a Committee on Intercultural Education," June 8, 1948, pp. 1–2, in AJC records, box 160, "IGE AJC Intercultural Ed. Committee 48–52."

55. The study was published as American Jewish Committee, Department of Scientific Research, *A Brief Survey of the Major Agencies in the Field of Intercultural Education*.

56. AJC memorandum, re: "Intercultural Education Program," from Samuel H. Flowerman to John Slawson, July 7, 1950, p. 1, in AJC records, box 160, "IGE AJC 45–60."

57. Ibid.

58. Allport, *The Nature of Prejudice*, p. 511; Neill, *Summerhill*. See also Charles Silberman's discussion of "moral education" in "The Schools and the Fight Against Prejudice," pp. 143–146.

59. "Analysis of Special Areas in Relation to Evaluative Study Committee Procedure—Intergroup Education," January 15, 1952, p. 3, in AJC records, box 160, "IGE AJC 45–60"; Minutes of Joint Committee on Intercultural Education, May 25, 1953, p. 2, in AJC records, box 161, "AJC-ADL Joint Committee IGE 52–54."

60. Minutes of Joint Committee on Intercultural Education, May 25, 1953, p. 2, in AJC records, box 161, "AJC-ADL Joint Committee IGE 52–54."

61. Human relations centers were active at schools such as Columbia University Teachers College, University of Pennsylvania, San Francisco State College, University of Miami, Albany State Teachers College, University of Oklahoma, University of Michigan, the University of Detroit, Boston University, University of Pittsburgh, Rutgers University, and the University of Rochester. "AJC Work in Intergroup Education," October 1953, p. 1, in AJC records, box 160, "IGE AJC 45–60"; AJC memorandum, re: "The Present Status of Intergroup Education and Proposals for Future Development," from Max Birnbaum to Alan M. Stroock, February 15, 1952, pp. 2–3, in AJC records, box 160, "IGE 42, 44–60"; Folders labeled "Human Relations Centers 53–62" in AJC records, box 170.

62. AJC memorandum, Max Birnbaum to John Slawson, April 5, 1954, p. 1, in AJC records, box 160, "IGE AJC 45–60"; " 'Advancing Man's Understanding of His Fellow Man'—The Ways and the Means," 1961, pp. 61–62, in AJC records, box 169, "IG REL Training 59–62."

63. AJC Public Information and Education Department, Intergroup Education Division, "Abstract of 1953 Program Statement," p. 3, in AJC records, box 160, "IGE AJC 45–60"; AJC memorandum, Max Birnbaum to John Slawson, April 5, 1954, pp. 1–2, in AJC records, box 160, "IGE AJC 45–60"; NAIRO report, American Jewish Committee, October 8, 1954, in AJC records, box 163, "Agencies Intergroup Rel 49–62."

64. AJC Public Information and Education Department, Intergroup Education Division, "Abstract of 1953 Program Statement," p. 1, in AJC records, box 160, "IGE AJC 45–60."

65. Cohen, *Jews in Christian America*, pp. 123–239; Moore, *To The Golden Cities*, pp. 180–186; AJC memorandum, re: "Material for Louis Rabinowitz's Speech," Max Birnbaum to John Slawson, April 5, 1954, p. 2, in AJC records, box 160, "IGE AJC 45–60."

66. "AJC Work in Intergroup Education," October 1953, pp. 2–4 (quote from pp. 3–4), in AJC records, box 160, "IGE AJC 45–60."

67. Minutes of Joint Committee on Intercultural Education, May 25, 1953, p. 2, in AJC records, box 161, "AJC-ADL Joint Committee IGE 52–54."

68. AJC memorandum, re: "School Systems Which Have Sought AJC Advice or Materials on Intercultural Education," from Dorothy Nathan to David Danzig, April 10, 1951; AJC Public Information and Education Department, Intergroup Education Division, "Abstract of 1953 Program Statement," p. 2, in AJC records, box 160, "IGE AJC 45–60"; AJC memorandum, re: "The Present Status of Intergroup Education and Proposals for Future Development," from Max Birnbaum to Alan M. Stroock, February 15, 1952, pp. 5–6, in AJC records, box 160, "IGE 42, 44–60."

69. Minutes of Joint Committee on Intercultural Education, May 25, 1953, p. 2, in AJC records, box 161, "AJC-ADL Joint Committee IGE 52–54."

70. "Analysis of Special Areas in Relation to Evaluative Study Committee Procedure—Intergroup Education," January 15, 1952, p. 1; "AJC Work in Intergroup Education," October 1953, p. 3; Minutes of AJC Staff Policy Committee, November 14, 1951, p. 3, in AJC records, box 160, "IGE AJC 45–60."

71. "AJC Work in Intergroup Education," October 1953, pp. 1–2; "Analysis of Special Areas in Relation to Evaluative Study Committee Procedure—Intergroup Education," January 15, 1952, p. 1; Minutes of Staff Policy Committee, November 14, 1951, pp. 1–2; AJC memorandum on "Education," July 20, 1960 (quote from p. 1), in AJC records, box 160, "IGE AJC 45–60."

72. AJC memorandum on "Education," July 20, 1960, p. 2, in AJC records, box 160, "IGE AJC 45–60."

73. Other AJC-ADL coordinating committees established after the split from the NCRAC dealt with issues such as litigation, legislation, and labor. Minutes of Joint Committee on Intercultural Education, May 25, 1953, pp. 2–3; October 19, 1953, p. 2; AJC memorandum, Max Birnbaum to Members of Ad Hoc Committee on Special Areas, March 25, 1952, p. 1, in AJC records, box 161, "AJC-ADL Joint Committee IGE 52–54"; ADL National Executive Committee minutes, May 16–17, 1953, p. 9, in ADL records.

74. Minutes of Joint Committee on Intercultural Education, May 25, 1953, pp. 2–3, in AJC records, box 161, "AJC-ADL Joint Committee IGE 52–54."

75. Unpaginated offprints of Richard C. Franklin, "A Digest of an Evaluation of Workshops in Human Relations" (July 1954); Trafford P. Maher, S.J., "Human Relations Workshops: Understanding, Social Sensitivity, and Cooperation Flourish," *Social Order* (March 1953), in AJC records, box 170, "Workshops." The workshop technique is also described in Dean and Rosen, *A Manual of Intergroup Relations*, pp. 54–56.

76. Institutions hosting human relations workshops during the 1950s and early 1960s included Loyola University of Los Angeles, Marymount College, Miami University, Rutgers University, St. Louis University, Syracuse University, Villanova University, Washington University (St. Louis), and Western Reserve University. In the summer of 1952 alone, the following schools hosted workshops: Boston University, Catholic University, Denver University, Memphis State, Milwaukee State, Northwestern University, Queens College, Rutgers University, St. Louis University, San Francisco State, Southern Methodist University, Columbia University Teachers College, University of Kansas City, University of Kentucky, University of Miami, Univer-

sity of Michigan, University of Southern California, University of Texas, Washington University, Western Reserve University, Wisconsin State, and Rhode Island University. AJC records, boxes 170–173.

77. Allport, *The Nature of Prejudice*, p. 227; Albert S. Foley, S.J., "The Workshop Way," *Interracial Review* (November 1954), offprint in AJC records, box 170, "Workshops."

78. Allport, *The Dynamics of Prejudice*, pp. 491–493; Sol B. Kolack Oral Memoir, in Cohen and Wexler, "*Not the Work of A Day*," 6:45–49.

79. Trafford P. Maher, S.J., "Human Relations Workshops," *Social Order* (March 1953), offprint in AJC records, box 170, "Workshops."

80. Albert S. Foley, S.J., "The Workshop Way," *Interracial Review* (November 1954); Trafford P. Maher, S.J., "Human Relations Workshops," *Social Order* (March 1953), offprints in AJC records, box 170, "Workshops"; Dean and Rosen, *A Manual of Intergroup Relations*, p. 56; Sol B. Kolack Oral Memoir, in Cohen and Wexler, "*Not the Work of a Day*," 6:44–45. Further documentation can be found in the folders on "Workshops—AJC" in AJC records, boxes 170–173.

81. Trafford P. Maher, S.J., "Human Relations Workshops," *Social Order* (March 1953), offprint in AJC records, box 170, "Workshops."

82. Albert S. Foley, S.J., "The Workshop Way," *Interracial Review* (November 1954), offprint in AJC records, box 170, "Workshops."

83. John Slawson, "Some Approaches to the Problem of Anti-Semitism," paper at NCRAC Fifth Plenary session, Atlantic City, N.J., March 15–17, 1947, p. 11, in Nearprint files, "Slawson, John," AJA.

84. Intergroup relations experts devoted a substantial amount of energy to the debate over whether or not contact—and, more to the point, what kinds of contact— had a significant impact on prejudice. While early intergroup relations programs often reflected the assumption that contact automatically reduced prejudice, by the 1950s many (but not all) social scientists concerned with the problem had adopted a more sophisticated view that concluded that different sorts of contact had various influences—positive, negative, or negligible—on intergroup attitudes. Allport, *The Nature of Prejudice*, pp. 261–281; Bettelheim and Janowitz, *Dynamics of Prejudice*, pp. 44–45; Ackerman and Jahoda, *Anti-Semitism and Emotional Disorder*, pp. 82–83; "Evaluating Humans," in *ADL Bulletin*, 7,6 (July 1950); Williams, *The Reduction of Intergroup Tensions*, pp. 69–73; Dean and Rosen, *A Manual of Intergroup Relations*, pp. 8–22 passim; Muzafer Sherif, "Experiments in Group Conflict," in Newman, *The Hate Reader*, pp. 23–29; Quinley and Glock, *Anti-Semitism in America*, pp. 77–78, 90–92, 193–194; Robert B. Johnson, "A Tentative Analysis of the Intergroup Relations Community," [1957?], pp. 4, 6, 8, in AJC records, box 163, "Local Community Agencies"; Marc Vosk, "The Science of Human Relations and Its Practices: Social Science and Intergroup Relations—Its Contributions and Its Limitations," Fifth National Conference, U.S. National Commission for UNESCO, November 3–5, 1955, p. 7, in AJC records, box 169, "Studies"; Marc Vosk, "Assessing Techniques for Change: Mass Media, Group Processes, and Intergroup Contact," December 30, 1953, paper given at second NAIRO conference on research in intergroup relations, in AJC records, box 165, "Research (NAIRO) 'Assessing Techniques for Change' (Vosk) 53–54"; "Differences Are Opportunities: The Role of Religion and Religious Institutions in Intergroup Relations," January 1956, p. 32, in AJC records, box 163, "Intergroup Rel. 1950—1962." The ADL's par-

ticipation in interreligious camping programs is discussed in *ADL Bulletin*, 21,6 (June 1964), pp. 6–7; *ADL Bulletin*, 7,9 (November 1950), p. 8; *ADL Bulletin*, 5,6 (September 1948), p. 6; *ADL Bulletin*, 10,6 (June 1953), pp. 5–6, 8; Report to ADL National Program Committee from Department of Interreligious Cooperation, May 11–12, 1950, pp. 1–3; Report of National Program Committee, ADL National Commission minutes, October 20, 1951, pp. 4–5, in ADL records.

85. Cohen, *Encounter with Emancipation*, p. 91. The connections between education, acculturation, and social mobility have been much debated in the historical literature on Eastern European Jewish immigrants and their offspring. For an analysis that emphasizes cultural explanations (e.g., "the high regard for learning that had for centuries pervaded the Jewish culture") and portrays education as a primary explanation for the upward mobility of the "first and second American-born generations," see Dinnerstein, "Education and the Advancement of American Jews," pp. 44–60. A number of historians have dissented from the cultural explanation, arguing that the economic successes of the early generations in skilled trades and small-scale commercial activities contributed more directly to the acculturation and educational accomplishments of subsequent generations of American Jews. See, for example, Berrol, "Public Schools and Immigrants"; Berrol, "Education and Economic Mobility"; Steinberg, *The Ethnic Myth*. In his history of American Jewry from 1920 to 1945, Henry L. Feingold emphasizes macroeconomic developments, Jews' specific locations in the American economy, educational and professional training, and the importance of ethnic credit networks as factors critical to Jewish socioeconomic mobility. Feingold, *A Time for Searching*, pp. 139–140, 143–144, 153–154. For an analysis that explores the social, cultural, and political conflicts that characterized the experiences of Jewish immigrants and their children within the American educational system, see Gorelick, *City College and the Jewish Poor*.

86. AJC Public Information and Education Department, Intergroup Education Division, "Abstract of 1953 Program Statement," p. 1, in AJC records, box 160, "IGE AJC 45–60."

87. AJC memorandum on "Education," July 10, 1960, p. 1, in AJC records, box 160, "IGE AJC 45–60."

88. John Dewey, *Moral Principles in Education*, quoted in Silberman, "The Schools and the Fight Against Prejudice," p. 136. Silberman, writing in the late 1960s, provides a less optimistic analysis of the schools' power to reduce prejudice or to spur socioeconomic mobility for the disadvantaged.

89. Marc Vosk, "The Science of Human Relations and its Practices: Social Science and Intergroup Relations—Its Contributions and Its Limitations" paper presented at the Fifth National Conference, U.S. National Commission for UNESCO, November 3–5, 1955, Cincinnati, p. 7, in AJC records, box 165, "Conferences—U.N. National Commission for UNESCO (Vosk paper) 55–60."

90. Allport, *The Person in Psychology* (quote from p. 203); Irwin Katz, "Education and Anti-Semitism: A Review of Research," [1955?], in AJC records, box 10, "Anti-Semitism—studies—[illeg.]"; Allport, *The Nature of Prejudice*, pp. 432–434.

91. AJC memorandum, "VII Education" 1959, p. 1, in AJC records, box 160, "IGE AJC 45–60." p. 1. For a public opinion study that found correlation between level of education and tolerance for political or ideological nonconformity, see Stouffer, *Communism, Conformity, and Civil Liberties*, especially pp. 91–93, 119–124. During the fol-

lowing decade an ADL-sponsored study found a strong correlation between low levels of education and high levels of prejudice. See Quinley and Glock, *Anti-Semitism in America*, pp. 23–24, 33–53, 84–85, 143, 157, 186–188.

92. AJC memorandum, "VII Education" [1959], pp. 2–3, in AJC records, box 160, "IGE AJC 45–60"; Clipping entitled "Education Bias Threat," from the *Jewish Advocate*, April 25, 1957, in Clippings file, "Slawson, John," *AJA*.

93. While Jewish organizations such as the AJC, the ADL, and the AJCongress generally supported the inclusion of ethics and nonreligious moral instruction in public education, they opposed the conjunction of such values with particular religious traditions. The AJCongress was particularly vehement in its opposition to any compromise with the principle of church-state separation. Fact Sheet on Statement of New York City Board of Superintendents on "Moral and Spiritual Values in Schools," October 22, 1955, in AJCongress records, box 37; *CLSA Reports*, "The New York Regents' Prayer Case (Engel v. Vitale): Its Background, Meaning and Implications," Leo Pfeffer, June 26, 1962, pp. 1–2, in AJCongress records, box 42; Cohen, *Jews in Christian America*, pp. 163–164.

94. AJC memorandum, "VII Education" [1959], pp. 2–3 (quote from p. 3), in AJC records, box 160, "IGE AJC 45–60."

95. AJC memorandum, re: "The Present Status of Intergroup Education and Proposals for Future Development," from Max Birnbaum to Alan M. Strook, February 15, 1952, p. 6, in AJC records, box 160, "IGE 42, 44–60."

96. *ADL Bulletin*, 8,4 (May 1951), p. 6.

97. Rorty, "The Native Anti-Semite's 'New Look,' " p. 417; Overstreet and Overstreet, *The Strange Tactics of Extremism*, pp. 250–258.

98. AJC memorandum, re: "Community Relations," from David Danzig to John Slawson, November 22, 1951, p. 3, in AJC records, box 163, "Agencies, Intergroup Rel 49–62."

99. AJC memorandum, "Philosophy Underlying the Socio-Legal Approach as a Technique in Dealing with Problems of Group Adjustment," 1955, (quote is from p. 3), in AJC records, box 168, "Legal 55–57"; "General Principles of Intergroup Relations" n.d., p. 1, in AJC records, box 163, "Intergroup Rel 50–62." Both President Truman and President Eisenhower repeatedly claimed that civil rights laws that lacked broad public support would be ignored. In 1946 Truman argued that "you must have the support of the people for any law. The prohibition law proved that." Quoted in McCoy and Ruetten, *Quest and Response*, p. 35. In the aftermath of the *Brown* case, Eisenhower said, "It is difficult through law and through force to change a man's heart." Quoted in Greenberg, *Crusaders in the Courts*, p. 213. During the escalating wave of civil rights protests in the late 1950s, Eisenhower consistently took the position that "the law must fail when it is in advance of morals." See Leskes, "State Law Against Discrimination," p. 256.

100. John Slawson, "Some Approaches to the Problem of Anti-Semitism," paper given at NCRAC Fifth Plenary session, Atlantic City, N.J., March 15–17, 1947, p. 19, in Nearprint files, "Slawson, John," *AJA*.

101. Benjamin R. Epstein, "The Educational Approach to Better Intergroup Relationships," paper given at NCRAC Fifth Plenary Session, Atlantic City, N.J., March 15–17, 1947, p. 29, in Nearprint files, "Slawson, John," *AJA*.

102. *ADL Bulletin*, 7,2 (March 1950), (quote from p. 1); Presentation by Samuel

Nerlove, report of National Program Committee, in ADL National Commission meeting transcript, October 24–26, 1952, pp. 201–202, in ADL records.

103. This de facto division of labor is noted in Robison, "Organizations Promoting Civil Rights and Liberties," p. 20; Dinnerstein, *Antisemitism in America*, p. 154.

4. Law and Social Action

1. David Petegorsky, "Report of the Executive Director to the Chairman of the Executive Committee of the American Jewish Congress," May 28, 1946, p. 4, in AJCongress records, box 23.

2. Ibid.; *Law and Social Action*, 1,1 (January 1946), p. 2, in AJCongress records, box 44.

3. Pekelis, "Full Equality in a Free Society," p. 218; *Law and Social Action*, 1,1 (January 1946), p. 2, in AJCongress records, box 44.

4. Just five years later Pekelis was killed in an airplane accident while returning from a meeting of the World Zionist Congress in Switzerland. Konvitz, *Law and Social Action*, pp. v–vii, ix–x, 260–261; Will Maslow, "Alexander H. Pekelis—Some Personal Recollections"; Will Maslow, "Loose Leaves from a Busy Life," copies in author's possession. I am grateful to Mr. Maslow for providing me with copies of these and other personal papers.

5. Pekelis, "Full Equality in a Free Society," p. 225.

6. Ibid., p. 242.

7. On Wise, see Urofsky, *A Voice That Spoke for Justice*. During World War I Wise, Brandeis, and other advocates of the AJCongress movement had similarly linked progressive politics and the Jewish tradition: "The American twentieth century ideals and aspirations—democracy and social justice—are the ages-old ideals and aspirations of the Jewish people." "The Call for an American Jewish Congress, 1915," in Raphael, *Jews and Judaism in the United States*, p. 117.

8. Pekelis, "Full Equality in a Free Society," pp. 219–220, 242. On the mission idea in Reform Judaism, see Meyer, *Response to Modernity*; Philipson, *The Reform Movement in Judaism*.

9. Pekelis, "Full Equality in a Free Society," pp. 218–219, 221–223. On the ambiguity of Emancipation, see Baron, "Newer Approaches to Jewish Emancipation"; Hertzberg, *The French Enlightenment and the Jews*.

10. David Petegorsky, "Record in Review," report presented at AJCongress Biennial Convention, March 31–April 4, 1948, New York City, p. 14, in AJCongress records, box 12.

11. Pekelis, "Full Equality in a Free Society," p. 242.

12. Ibid., pp. 258–259.

13. David Petegorsky, "Record in Review," report presented at AJCongress Biennial Convention, March 31–April 4, 1948, New York City, p. 16, in AJCongress records, box 12.

14. Stephen S. Wise Statement Before Senate Sub-Committee on Labor and Public Welfare, during hearings on federal FEPC bill (S. 984), June 12, 1947, p. 2, in AJCongress records, box 36. A similar assertion was made in "Questions and Answers About CCI," October 16, 1952, p. 7, in AJCongress records, box 22.

15. Interview with Will Maslow by author, May 16, 1996; *Who's Who In America*,

47th ed., s.v. "Maslow, Will"; *Who's Who in American Law*, 2d ed., s.v. "Maslow, Will"; Will Maslow, "Loose Leaves from a Busy Life," copy in author's possession.

16. Early members of the CLSA staff included Leo Pfeffer, Phil Baum, Howard Squadron, Lois Waldman, Naomi Levine, and Joseph B. Robison. Interview with Will Maslow by author, May 16, 1996; Will Maslow, "Loose Leaves from a Busy Life," copy in author's possession; *Who's Who in American Law*, 2d ed., s.v. "Robison, Joseph B."; Robison, "Organizations Promoting Civil Rights and Liberties," p. 26.

17. On the origins and evolution of New Deal liberalism, see Brinkley, *The End of Reform*. As Brinkley's work demonstrates, many American liberals had grown "less inclined to challenge corporate behavior" and "more reconciled to the existing structure of the economy" by the end of World War II. Ibid., p. 139.

18. The work of Jerold S. Auerbach and Peter H. Irons has helped me to put the career trajectory of some of the CLSA lawyers in a broader context. Auerbach has argued, "Jewish lawyers have been conspicuous in their defense of civil liberties, civil rights, and of clients and causes that pitted the dominant interests in society against its marginal members." Irons noted that the NLRB, in particular, was a "haven" for young Jewish lawyers with distinguished credentials but limited opportunities in private practice. See Auerbach, *Unequal Justice*, pp. 29, 173, 182–190, 191–230 passim, 231–232; Auerbach, "From Rags to Robes," pp. 253, 265–273, 282–284; Irons, *The New Deal Lawyers*, pp. 237, 298–299. See also Dinnerstein, "Jews and the New Deal," p. 464; Dinnerstein, *Antisemitism in America*, pp. 108–109, 125–126, 155–156. In a recent book former NAACP legal defense and educational fund director-counsel Jack Greenberg discusses the relationship between his Jewish family background (particularly the Socialist-Zionist political culture of his parents' generation) and his strong commitment to civil rights. See Greenberg, *Crusaders in the Courts*, pp. 50–53. See also Kaufman, *Broken Alliance*, pp. 88–89, 106.

19. Maslow, "Prejudice, Discrimination, and the Law," p. 17. See also Maslow and Robison, "Civil Rights Legislation and the Fight for Equality," pp. 363–365; David Petegorsky, "Combatting Racism by Utilizing the Forces of Social Control," paper delivered at the NCRAC Fifth Plenary Session, Atlantic City, N.J., March 15–17, 1947, pp. 36–37, in Nearprint files, "Slawson, John," AJA.

20. Sumner, *Folkways*. Gunnar Myrdal observed during World War II that "the social scientists, especially the sociologists, in America have developed a defeatist attitude towards the possibility of inducing social change by means of legislation." Myrdal, *An American Dilemma*, 1:19. See also Jackson, *Gunnar Myrdal and America's Conscience*, pp. 126–127, 192, 194. Similar observations were made by Carey McWilliams in McWilliams, "Race Discrimination and the Law," pp. 1–22. Will Maslow noted in 1951 that few "authoritative" social scientists still adhered to Sumner's theory that "stateways cannot change folkways." Among "laypeople," however, this skepticism about the social utility of law was seemingly more persistent: in a Gallup poll conducted in 1948, 40 percent of respondents agreed that "people can't be forced to change deep-rooted prejudices by passing laws." Maslow, "Prejudice, Discrimination, and the Law," p. 10. Duane Lockard argued that "during the early [post-World War II] campaigns [for state civil rights legislation] it was common for newspapers to repeat the old argument that the goal was good but that laws could never solve anything and that only an educational approach would work." Lockard, *Toward Equal Opportunity*, pp. 59–60. Gordon Allport, writing in the early to mid-1950s, claimed

that the Sumnerian credo "you cannot legislate against prejudice," remained popular. Allport, *The Nature of Prejudice*, p. 469. In a new preface to an edition of John P. Dean and Alex Rosen's classic intergroup relations manual, published in 1963, Rosen and Robert B. Johnson noted, "The counterargument is still current that 'we cannot legislate morality before we change mens' hearts.' " Dean and Rosen, *A Manual of Intergroup Relations*, p. xi.

21. David Petegorsky, "Record in Review," report presented at AJCongress Biennial Convention, March 31–April 4, 1948, New York City, p. 16, in AJCongress records, box 12. CLSA Chairman Shad Polier made the same argument in "Law, Conscience, and Society," p. 491.

22. Maslow and Robison, "Civil Rights Legislation and the Fight for Equality," p. 364. In response to the *Brown* decision and other successful legal action against segregation, social scientists increasingly came to the conclusion that legal sanctions against discriminatory behavior could change prejudiced attitudes. In 1966, for example, Gordon Allport wrote: "In general, discrimination reinforces prejudices, and prejudices provide rationalizations for discrimination. The two concepts are most distinct when it comes to seeking remedies. The corrections for discrimination are legal, or lie in a direct change of social practices, whereas the remedy for prejudice lies in education and the conversion of attitudes. The best opinion today says that if we eliminate discrimination, then—as people become acquainted with one another on equal terms—attitudes are likely to change, perhaps more rapidly than through continued preaching or teaching of tolerance." Allport, *The Person in Psychology*, pp. 209–210.

23. From 1941 to 1962 the American Jewish Congress competed with the Joint Defense Appeal (JDA), the collaborative fund raising organ of the AJC and ADL, for local welfare funds. In many communities the JDA allocation was much more than twice that received by the AJCongress, and staff members of the AJCongress Welfare Department issued repeated calls for "parity." There are several factors that may help to explain the discrepancy in support. Evidence suggests that leaders of local Jewish communities were often unaware of the ideological and strategic differences that distinguished the intergroup relations programs of the AJC, ADL, and AJCongress. In the absence of direct knowledge of the national organizations, many communities with large numbers of B'nai B'rith members seem to have favored the ADL (associated with B'nai B'rith). This factor may help to explain the relative success of the JDA in securing larger allocations. It should be noted that the AJC, ADL, and AJCongress were competing for a relatively small portion of community resources; the bulk of local welfare funds went to overseas relief—especially to the United Jewish Appeal, responsible for resettling displaced persons during the late 1940s and early 1950s, and for the development of Israel—and to local institutions such as hospitals, synagogues, religious schools, and community centers. Only a small portion of local welfare funds went to support national agencies such as the AJC, ADL, and AJCongress. For a wealth of primary evidence, see reports of the AJCongress National Finance Commission, in AJCongress records, box 18. See also Elazar, *Community and Polity*, pp. 297–313 passim, for supporting evidence drawn from a somewhat later period (1969–1971).

24. For information on ADL and AJC media expenditures, see chapter 2. The figure of $100,000 for the CLSA's 1948 budget (which was approximately 8 percent of the total AJCongress budget of $1,234,000 for that year) was given in a communication from Will Maslow to *Yale Law Journal*, February 15, 1949, cited in Note, "Private Attorneys-

General," p. 596 n. This figure seems to be in accord with CLSA proposed budgets for 1949 ($125,000 out of AJCongress total of $1,257,742) and 1950 ($105,000 out of AJCongress total of $843,250), as well as with CLSA's recorded expenses for 1953 ($105,244 out of AJCongress total of $902,539) and 1954 ($108,957 out of AJCongress total of $879,630). These figures were calculated from tables and other information found in the papers of the American Jewish Congress's National Finance Commission, AJCongress records, box 18. The AJC and the ADL, working through the Joint Defense Appeal, seem to have been more successful at raising large sums of money. *Committee Reporter* 6,12 (December 1949), p. 1; Maslow, *The Structure and Functioning of the American Jewish Community*, pp. 22, 24; Clippings from the *National Jewish Post*, January 10, 1947, and the *Jewish Advocate*, April 22, 1948, in Clippings file, "Slawson, John," AJA.

25. David Petegorsky, "Report of the Executive Director to the Chairman of the Executive Committee of the AJCongress," May 28, 1946, p. 9, in AJCongress records, box 23. For other media and educational activities of the AJCongress in this period, see chapter 2. Will Maslow recalled that he and other members of the CLSA legal staff saw the social scientific program of the AJCongress's Commission on Community Interrelations as too far removed from practical social action. Interview with Will Maslow by author, May 16, 1996.

26. David Petegorsky, "Record in Review," report presented at AJCongress Biennial Convention, March 31–April 4, 1948, New York City, pp. 15–17, in AJCongress records, box 12.

27. Stephen S. Wise Statement Before Senate Sub-Committee on Labor and Public Welfare, hearings on federal FEPC bill (S. 984), June 12, 1947, p. 6, in AJCongress records, box 36.

28. David Petegorsky, "Record in Review," report presented at AJCongress Biennial Convention, March 31–April 4, 1948, New York City, p. 17, in AJCongress records, box 12. A similar evaluation of pro-tolerance "exhortation" was made by Goodwin Watson in Watson, *Action for Unity*, pp. 27–30. Watson's work was conducted under the auspices of the AJCongress's action-research division, the Commission on Community Interrelations (CCI).

29. Resolutions passed at the Biennial Convention of the American Jewish Congress, April 4, 1948, p. 3; Resolutions entitled "President's Civil Rights Program," "Resolution on Discrimination," and "Resolution on Federal Housing," adopted at National Convention of AJCongress, November 9–13, 1949; "Civil Rights and the Federal Government," resolution adopted at the Biennial Convention of the American Jewish Congress, April 15, 1956, in AJCongress records, box 12; American Jewish Congress Resolutions on Federal Aid to Education, "Integration in the North," "The Southern Sit-Ins," and "Civil Rights and Federal Responsibility," adopted at the AJCongress Biennial Convention, May 1960; American Jewish Congress Resolution on Civil Rights and Federal Responsibility, adopted at Biennial Convention, May 1960, in AJCongress records, box 13; Resolutions on "Civil Rights" and "Legislative Malapportionment" from the 1962 Biennial Convention, in AJCongress records, box 14; Resolution on "Civil Rights" adopted at the Biennial Convention, April 14–19, 1964, in AJCongress records, box 15. The AJCongress also issued recommendations for national party platforms in election years. "Statement of the American Jewish Congress in Submitting Proposed Platform Planks to the National Political Parties" and

"Proposals of the American Jewish Congress for the 1948 Platforms of the National Political Parties," n.d., in AJCongress records, box 36; AJCongress-CLSA, "Recommendations for Platform Planks on Civil Rights," submitted to Democratic National Committee Advance Platform Hearings, April 28, 1960, pp. 3–9, in AJCongress records, box 39.

30. Maslow also called for the enactment of state laws against discrimination in education and housing, measures that are discussed later in this chapter. Text of Oral Statement by Will Maslow before the President's Committee on Civil Rights, Washington, D.C., May 1, 1947, in AJCongress records, box 36; Maslow and Robison, "Civil Rights: A Program for the President's Committee." The report of the President's Committee closely followed Maslow's recommendations. See President's Committee on Civil Rights, *To Secure These Rights*. Maslow claimed that he had an influence on the report. Interview with Will Maslow by author, May 16, 1996; Friedman, *What Went Wrong?* p. 147.

31. "Testimony Given Before or Statements Submitted to Congressional Committees by the American Jewish Congress, August, 1945–August, 1955," August 1955, pp. 1–3, in AJCongress records, box 38; Statement of AJCongress before U.S. House of Representatives, Sub-Committee of House Committee on Administration, Hearings on H.R. 3044 and 3199, May 10, 1949, p. 1, in AJCongress records, box 31; "Statement of Leo Pfeffer on Behalf of the American Jewish Congress on Federal Aid to the Public Grade and High Schools, Submitted to the Committee on Education and Labor of the House of Representatives," March 29, 1961, pp. 1–2; "Statement of the American Jewish Congress on Federal Aid to Public Grade and High Schools, Submitted to the Senate Committee on Labor and Public Welfare," March 10, 1961, in AJCongress records, box 39; *Law and Social Action*, 3,1 (January-February 1948); *Law and Social Action*, 3,2 (March-April 1948), p. 75, *Law and Social Action*, 5,1 (January-February 1950), in AJCongress records, box 44; Maslow and Robison, "Civil Rights Legislation and the Fight for Equality," pp. 380–382.

32. As a direct result of the practice of filibustering—by which obstructionist senators could prolong debate indefinitely, thus preventing a vote—the Congress failed to pass a civil rights law any time between 1875 and 1957. AJCongress and NAACP, *Civil Rights in the United States in 1948*, p. 6; AJCongress and NAACP, *Civil Rights in the United States in 1949*, pp. 5–7; AJCongress and NAACP, *Civil Rights in the United States in 1950*, pp. 6–7, 30–31; AJCongress and NAACP, *Civil Rights in the United States in 1951*, pp. 5, 7–9; AJCongress and NAACP, *Civil Rights in the United States 1952*, p. 7; AJCongress and NAACP, *Civil Rights in the United States 1953*, pp. 6–8; Konvitz, *A Century of Civil Rights*, pp. 72–74, 84; McCoy and Ruetten, *Quest and Response*, pp. 26, 31–33, 35, 70, 132–133, 149, 171–178, 186–187, 190–195, 197–199, 204, 281–287, 300, 312–313; Nieman, *Promises to Keep*, pp. 125, 133, 142, 235 n. 7; Greenberg, *Crusaders in the Courts*, pp. 16–17.

33. Resolution on "The President's Civil Rights Program," adopted at the National Convention of the American Jewish Congress, November 9–13, 1949, p. 1; "Civil Rights and the Federal Government," resolution adopted at the Biennial Convention of the American Jewish Congress, April 15, 1956, pp. 2–3, in AJCongress records, box 12; American Jewish Congress Resolution on Civil Rights and Federal Responsibility, adopted at Biennial Convention, May, 1960, pp. 2–4, in AJCongress records, box 13; Convention Resolution on "Civil Rights," as adopted by the Resolutions Committee,

April 12, 1962, p. 2, in AJCongress records, box 14; Shannon, "Political Obstacles to Civil Rights Legislation," pp. 56–57; McCoy and Ruetten, *Quest and Response*, pp. 171–178, 199, 282, 286, 288; Maslow and Robison, "Civil Rights Legislation and the Fight for Equality," pp. 399–404 (quote from p. 404).

34. McCoy and Ruetten, *Quest and Response*, pp. 29, 178, 196, 199, 269–273, 285, 313.

35. Bilbo is quoted in Dinnerstein, *Antisemitism in America*, p. 136.

36. Quoted in McCoy and Ruetten, *Quest and Response*, p. 136.

37. For more on the confluence of civil rights and anticommunism, see chapters 5, 6, and 7.

38. The quoted phrase is from "Civil Rights and the Federal Government," resolution adopted at the Biennial Convention of the American Jewish Congress, April 15, 1956, New York City, in AJCongress records, box 12. See also clippings from *New York Times*, May 15, 1958; *New York Herald-Tribune*, May 19, 1958, in "Prinz, Joachim," Nearprint files, Biographies, *AJA*.

39. AJCongress representatives characterized the 1957 and 1960 Civil Rights Acts as "very limited advance[s]" that "exercise only a small portion of the constitutional power of the federal government to secure equality." American Jewish Congress Resolution on Civil Rights and Federal Responsibility, adopted at Biennial Convention, May 1960, pp. 2–3, in AJCongress records, box 13; *CLSA Reports*, "Report of Activities," April-June, 1963, p. 5; *CLSA Reports*, "The Federal Fair Employment Law: A Summary and Analysis of Title VII of the 1964 Civil Rights Act," July 31, 1964, p. 1, in AJCongress records, box 42; "Statement of the American Jewish Congress Submitted to the Large City Budgeting Conference," November 11, 1964, St. Louis, Mo., p. 1, in AJCongress records, box 18; clipping of Rabbi Joachim Prinz's obituary, from the *New York Times*, October 1, 1988; clipping from the *Jewish Exponent*, October 7, 1966; typescript "Biographical Sketch," Rabbi Joachim Prinz, September 1963, in "Prinz, Joachim," Nearprint files, Biographies, *AJA*; *Congress Bi-Weekly*, May 23, 1966, p. 4; Maslow, "Loose Leaves from a Busy Life," copy in author's possession; Friedman, *What Went Wrong?* pp. 199–200.

40. In addition, AJCongress President Joachim Prinz and Howard Metzenbaum, who at that time was a national vice president of the AJCongress, both served on the National Citizens' Committee for Community Relations created by the 1964 Civil Rights Act. "Civil Rights Chronology of Will Maslow," in author's possession; "Statement of the American Jewish Congress Submitted to the Large City Budgeting Conference," November 11, 1964, p. 5, in AJCongress records, box 18; Report of AJCongress Executive Director, July-September 1964, p. 1, in AJCongress records, box 17.

41. AJCongress and NAACP, *Civil Rights in the United States in 1949*, p. 5; Will Maslow, "The Enforcement of Northern Civil Rights Laws," address before the Fisk Institute on Race Relations, Nashville, Tenn., June 28, 1950, p. 1, in collection of Columbia University Law Library; Lockard, *Toward Equal Opportunity*, pp. 26–27, 41–42.

42. The quote is from AJCongress memorandum, from CLSA to Jewish Community Leaders and Workers (cover letter dated February 7, 1946), p. 3, in AJCongress records, box 33. See also Maslow, "Prejudice, Discrimination, and the Law," pp. 16–17.

43. McCoy and Ruetten, *Quest and Response*, p. 62.

44. Lockard, *Toward Equal Opportunity*, pp. 28, 61–63. On the opposition of white homeowners and homeowners' associations to residential integration, see Hirsch, "Massive Resistance in the Urban North"; Sugrue, "Crabgrass-Roots Politics."

45. Lockard, *Toward Equal Opportunity*, p. 41. See also Dinnerstein, *Antisemitism in America*, pp. 153–154.

46. My decision to focus on the legal efforts of the AJCongress-CLSA, which reflects my judgment that the AJCongress had the most innovative legal program in the Jewish community, should in no way be taken to suggest that the AJC, ADL, and other Jewish organizations were not active in promoting civil rights legislation and litigation. In some cases, the efforts of the other Jewish agencies paralleled the efforts of the CLSA discussed in this chapter.

47. The role played by Jewish groups in initiating civil rights legislation sometimes resulted in anti-Semitic attacks by the enemies of civil rights. During the debate over a state fair employment practices law in Massachusetts, a legislator denounced the bill as being "of Jewish origin." See Lockard, *Toward Equal Opportunity*, pp. 41–42.

48. Handwritten statement [by Justine Wise Polier?], "The Role of the Women's Division since 1948," in AJCongress records, box 134.

49. In *An American Dilemma* Gunnar Myrdal posited a "rank order of discrimination," in which whites objected least to equality in employment and blacks most desired equal job opportunity. Thus, as Myrdal and other social scientists observed, the employment field was a particularly "strategic" arena in which to fight for civil rights. Myrdal, *An American Dilemma*, 1:60–61. See also Allport, *The Nature of Prejudice*, p. 467; AJCongress and NAACP, *Civil Rights in the United States in 1949*, p. 21.

50. "Bills Drafted By the American Jewish Congress and Introduced in Various Legislatures, 1945–1955," August 1955, p. 1, in AJCongress records, box 37; *Law and Social Action*, 2,3 (March-April 1947), p. 55; *Law and Social Action*, 3,2 (March-April 1948) p. 76; *Law and Social Action*, 4,1 (January-February 1949), p. 95; *Law and Social Action*, 4,2 (March-April 1949) p. 98, in AJCongress records, box 44; *CLSA Reports* (November-December 1946), p. 2; *CLSA Reports*, "Report of Activities," January-March 1948, p. 1; *CLSA Reports*, "Report of Activity," March 1949, p. 1; *CLSA Reports*, Report of Activities 1950, (January 29, 1951), pp. 10–11, in AJCongress records, box 40; AJCongress and NAACP, *Civil Rights in the United States in 1949*, pp. 21–22; AJCongress and NAACP, *Civil Rights in the United States in 1950*, p. 31; AJCongress and NAACP, *Civil Rights in the United States in 1951*, pp. 39–43; AJCongress and NAACP, *Civil Rights in the United States 1952*, pp. 46, 50; AJCongress and NAACP, *Civil Rights in the United States 1953*, p. 8; Commission on Law and Social Action of the American Jewish Congress, "Report on State Anti-Discrimination Agencies and the Laws They Administer," (1957); Commission on Law and Social Action of the American Jewish Congress, "Check List of State Anti-Discrimination and Anti-Bias Laws," 1953; Maslow and Robison, "Civil Rights Legislation and the Fight for Equality," pp. 397–399; Maslow, "Prejudice, Discrimination, and the Law," p. 9; Nieman, *Promises to Keep*, p. 141; Lockard, *Toward Equal Opportunity*, pp. 20–24; Leskes, "State Law Against Discrimination," pp. 199–202; Morroe Berger, "Fair Employment Practices Legislation," pp. 34, 38. On the ADL's contribution to the New York State FEPC bill, see Benjamin R. Epstein Oral Memoir, in Cohen and Wexler, "*Not the Work of a Day*," 1:x, 77.

51. *Law and Social Action*, 4,1 (January-February 1949), in AJCongress records, box 44; AJCongress and NAACP, *Civil Rights in the United States in 1949*, pp. 42–43; Caro, *The Power Broker*, pp. 961–962; Schwartz, *The New York Approach*, p. 111. Schwartz discusses the AJC and ADL's efforts to promote affordable and nondiscriminatory housing in New York City on pp. 161–163, 167, 190–195, 198–202.

52. *CLSA Reports*, "Report of Activities 1950," January 29, 1950, p. 8; *CLSA Reports*, "Report of Activities," April, 1950, p. 1, in AJCongress records, box 40; *Law and Social Action*, 5,3 (May-June 1950) in AJCongress records, box 44; AJCongress memorandum, Leo Pfeffer to CRCs, April 5, 1950, in AJCongress records, box 40; AJCongress and NAACP, *Civil Rights in the United States in 1950*, pp. 8, 53–55; Will Maslow, "The Enforcement of Northern Civil Rights Laws," address before the Fisk Institute on Race Relations, Nashville, Tenn., June 28, 1950, p. 2, in collection of Columbia University Law Library; Commission on Law and Social Action of the American Jewish Congress, "Check List of State Anti-Discrimination and Anti-Bias Laws"; Schwartz, *The New York Approach*, p. 111. By 1951 similar measures were passed in Indiana, Minnesota, Pennsylvania, and Wisconsin. Maslow, "Prejudice, Discrimination, and the Law," p. 9.

53. Various other states outlawed discrimination in public housing after 1945. See Lockard, *Toward Equal Opportunity*, p. 117; Leskes, "State Law Against Discrimination," p. 198.

54. Although New York City passed an ordinance banning discrimination in tax exempt projects in 1944, the law was not applied retroactively and therefore failed to effect the legal battle over racial discrimination in Stuyvesant Town, discussed below. "Bills Drafted By the American Jewish Congress and Introduced in Various Legislatures, 1945–1955," August 1955, pp. 2, 3, in AJCongress records, box 37; *Law and Social Action*, 2,4 (May-June, 1947); *Dorsey v. Stuyvesant Town Corp.*, 87 N.E.2d 541 (1949); AJCongress and NAACP, *Civil Rights in the United States in 1949*, p. 38; Schwartz, *The New York Approach*, p. 111. The 1944 measure against discrimination in tax-exempt developments is included in the appendix to the Petition for a Writ of Certiorari to the Court of Appeals of the State of New York, submitted by Maslow, Abrams, Marshall, Polier, and Robison on October 14, 1949, p. 43, in AJCongress records, box 189.

55. The 1954 New York City Council measure was the Sharkey-Brown-Isaacs ordinance (1954). In 1955 one of the two Metcalf-Baker laws applied the provisions of the Sharkey-Brown-Isaacs ordinance to all of New York State. Similar measures were passed in Colorado, Rhode Island, Massachusetts, New Jersey, Oregon, and Washington by 1957. "Bills Drafted by the American Jewish Congress and Introduced in Various Legislatures, 1945–1955," August 1955, pp. 2–3, in AJCongress records, box 37; "Summary of the Two Metcalf-Baker Bills on Discrimination in Housing Adopted by the 1955 New York State Legislature," in AJCongress records, box 41; Commission on Law and Social Action of the American Jewish Congress, "Summary of 1957 State Anti-Discrimination Laws," September 24, 1957, pp. 1, 4; Lockard, *Toward Equal Opportunity*, pp. 117–118; Leskes, "State Law Against Discrimination," p. 237. For more on the impact of these laws, see the discussion of Levittown below. Most of these laws applied only to multiple dwellings containing three or more apartments and to housing developments with ten or more units. Single-family, owner-occupied homes were exempted from most state and local fair housing laws.

56. See AJCongress CLSA pamphlet "Through These Portals . . . Pass Only the Selected Few" [1946?], in AJCongress records, box 36; Urofsky, *A Voice that Spoke for Justice*, p. 358; Note, "Private Attorneys-General," pp. 591 and 591 n.; interview with Will Maslow by author, May 16, 1996.

57. *Law and Social Action*, 1,9 (October 1946), p. 35; *Law and Social Action*, 3,1 (January-February 1948), in AJCongress records, box 44; *CLSA Reports* (November-

December 1946), p. 2; *CLSA Reports*, "Report of Activities January and February 1947," in AJCongress records, box 40.

58. According to Theodore Leskes, "The law of New York already contained a section prohibiting discrimination on the grounds of race, creed, color, or national origin in all public schools." Leskes, "State Law Against Discrimination," p. 227.

59. *Law and Social Action*, 3,2 (March-April 1948), in AJCongress records, box 44 (quotes from p. 75); "Bills Drafted By the American Jewish Congress and introduced in Various Legislatures, 1945–1955," August 1955, p. 2, in AJCongress records, box 37; AJCongress and NAACP, *Civil Rights in the United States in 1948*, pp. 22–23; Commission on Law and Social Action of the American Jewish Congress, "Check List of State Anti-Discrimination and Anti-Bias Laws"; Note, "Private Attorneys-General," pp. 591, 591 n.; Saveth, "Fair Educational Practices Legislation," pp. 41–43; Saveth, "Discrimination in the Colleges Dies Hard," pp. 115–121. A copy of a proposed Fair Educational Practices Act for New York State, dated August 1, 1947, is in the records of the AJCongress, box 36. For a more detailed analysis of the provisions of the Quinn-Olliffe law, see Leskes, "State Law Against Discrimination," pp. 224–226. Similar measures were passed during the following year in Massachusetts and New Jersey. "Bills Drafted By the American Jewish Congress and Introduced in Various Legislatures, 1945–1955," August 1955, p. 2, in AJCongress records, box 37; AJCongress and NAACP, *Civil Rights in the United States in 1949*, pp. 7, 29; Maslow and Robison, "Civil Rights Legislation and the Fight for Equality," p. 411; Saveth, "Fair Educational Practices Legislation," pp. 43–44; Leskes, "State Law Against Discrimination," pp. 227–229.

60. AJCongress CLSA, "Inventory of Pending CLSA Projects," September 16, 1948, p. 5, in AJCongress records, box 40; Maslow, "The Law and Race Relations," p. 81; Maslow and Robison, "Civil Rights Legislation and the Fight for Equality," pp. 404–406, 410. On the use of law to prevent discrimination in public accommodations, see Konvitz, "Legislation Guaranteeing Equality of Access to Places of Public Accommodations," pp. 47–52; Leskes, "State Law Against Discrimination," pp. 155–193.

61. *Law and Social Action*, 4,2 (March-April 1949), in AJCongress records, box 44 (quote from p. 98); *CLSA Reports*, "Report of Activity," March 1949, p. 1, in AJCongress records, box 40; Report of the Executive Director of the American Jewish Congress, June-September 1948 (dated September 7, 1948), pp. 2–3, in AJCongress records, box 17; AJCongress and NAACP, *Civil Rights in the United States in 1949*, pp. 43–44; Konvitz, "Legislation Guaranteeing Equality of Access to Places of Public Accommodations," pp. 50–52; Leskes, "State Law Against Discrimination," pp. 180–183, 227–228.

62. See the sources cited in previous note. Additional sponsors of this bill are listed in an AJCongress Press Release, September 3, 1948, in AJCongress records, box 31. The ADL helped to spearhead a similar movement to pass comprehensive antidiscrimination legislation in Massachusetts. See Sol B. Kolack Oral Memoir, in Cohen and Wexler, "Not the Work of a Day," 6:35–36, 38–39, 51–52. For more on such ad hoc groups as advocates of state and local civil rights laws, see Lockard, *Toward Equal Opportunity*, pp. 43–46.

63. Konvitz, "Legislation Guaranteeing Equality of Access to Places of Public Accommodations," pp. 48–50; Lockard, *Toward Equal Opportunity*, pp. 17, 135; Nieman, *Promises to Keep*, pp. 122–123; Leskes, "State Law Against Discrimination," pp. 155–157, 177–180; Comment, "The New York State Commission Against Discrimina-

tion," pp. 839–841; Note, "Legislative Attempts to Eliminate Racial and Religious Discrimination"; Maslow and Robison, "Civil Rights Legislation and the Fight for Equality," p. 406; AJCongress and NAACP, *Civil Rights in the United States in 1948*, p. 28; Will Maslow, "The Enforcement of Northern Civil Rights Laws," address before the Fisk Institute on Race Relations, Nashville, Tenn., June 28, 1950, pp. 3–4, in collection of Columbia University Law Library.

64. Polier, "Law, Conscience, and Society," p. 491.

65. Maslow, "The Law and Race Relations," pp. 75–81; Berger, "Fair Employment Practices Legislation," pp. 34–40 passim; Commission on Law and Social Action of the American Jewish Congress, "Report on State Anti-Discrimination Agencies and the Laws They Administer"; Nieman, *Promises to Keep*, p. 141. Model bills can be found scattered throughout the records of the AJCongress CLSA.

66. These commissions came to be known as the New York State Commission Against Discrimination, the New Jersey State Division Against Discrimination, and the Massachusetts State Commission Against Discrimination. These more inclusive names were adopted after the commissions had expanded their jurisdiction beyond the enforcement of fair employment practices legislation. The Massachusetts Fair Employment Practice Commission, for example, was renamed the Massachusetts Commission Against Discrimination in 1950, when it assumed responsibility for enforcing the state's law against discrimination in public accommodations. See Leskes, "State Law Against Discrimination," pp. 182–183.

67. In the first two years after Roosevelt issued Executive Order 8802, the FEPC was poorly funded, understaffed, and repeatedly shunted from one federal agency to the next. The committee's efforts were further hampered by the opposition of southern Democrats in Congress and the administration's overriding concern for maximizing industrial output. In May 1943 Roosevelt's Executive Order 9346 reestablished the FEPC within the executive office of the president and gave the committee broader powers, a bigger budget, and a larger staff. Even with this new authority, however, the FEPC was largely unsuccessful at getting employers to comply with its recommendations. Opponents of the committee successfully precluded the establishment of a peacetime FEPC by cutting its budget in half in 1945 and closing it down in 1946. See Polenberg, *War and Society*, pp. 117–123; Hamby, *Liberalism and Its Challengers*, p. 48; Lockard, *Toward Equal Opportunity*, pp. 18–19. For a more positive assessment of the FEPC's effectiveness, see McCoy and Ruetten, *Quest and Response*, p. 9.

68. On the powers and practices of the state antidiscrimination commissions, see Comment, "The New York State Commission Against Discrimination," pp. 837–863 (the quote is from p. 856); Will Maslow, "The Enforcement of Northern Civil Rights Laws," address before the Fisk Institute on Race Relations, Nashville, Tenn., June 28, 1950, pp. 5–6, in collection of Columbia University Law Library; Commission on Law and Social Action of the American Jewish Congress, "Report on State Anti-Discrimination Agencies and the Laws They Administer," p. 12 (appendix 3, table B); AJCongress and NAACP, *Civil Rights in the United States in 1948*, p. 20; AJCongress and NAACP, *Civil Rights in the United States in 1949*, pp. 22–24; AJCongress and NAACP, *Civil Rights in the United States in 1950*, pp. 33–37; AJCongress and NAACP, *Civil Rights in the United States in 1951*, pp. 43–50; AJCongress and NAACP, *Civil Rights in the United States 1952*, pp. 52–57, 101–103; AJCongress and NAACP, *Civil Rights in the United States 1953*, pp. 60–68, 121–124. On the enforcement powers of

the NLRB, see Irons, *The New Deal Lawyers*, pp. 213, 228–229, 240–241, 243, 254–271 passim.

69. Two other states had commissions without enforcement powers. Commission on Law and Social Action of the American Jewish Congress, "Report on State Anti-Discrimination Agencies and the Laws They Administer," p. 1. According to a CLSA analysis, by 1963, 93.9 percent of American Jews lived in states with laws banning discrimination in public accommodations, 89.7 percent lived in states with fair employment laws, and 78.4 percent lived in states with laws against housing discrimination. Report of AJCongress Executive Director, December 1963, p. 2, in AJCongress records, box 17.

70. Duane Lockard noted "the tendency for antidiscrimination laws with administrative enforcement to be passed in stages, beginning with employment, then following with public accommodations and housing." Lockard, *Toward Equal Opportunity*, p. 23. See also Leskes, "State Law Against Discrimination," pp. 180–183.

71. Figures for 1948 and 1950 NYSCAD budgets from Will Maslow, "The Enforcement of Northern Civil Rights Laws," address before the Fisk Institute on Race Relations, Nashville, Tenn., June 28, 1950, p. 9, in collection of Columbia University Law Library. Figures for the 1964 budget of NYSCAD, along with the budgets of other state commissions, can be found in Lockard, *Toward Equal Opportunity*, p. 86. The rest of the data in this paragraph is drawn from Commission on Law and Social Action of the American Jewish Congress, "Report on State Anti-Discrimination Agencies and the Laws They Administer," pp. 1, 4–8, 11–21 (especially the appendixes); Commission on Law and Social Action of the American Jewish Congress, "Summary of 1957 State Anti-Discrimination Laws," pp. 2–8 passim. By 1959 the total number of states that had antidiscrimination commissions with enforcement powers had grown to sixteen, with the addition of Alaska, California, and Ohio. Commission on Law and Social Action of the American Jewish Congress, "Summary of 1958 and 1959 State Anti-Discrimination Laws," pp. 2–5.

72. Will Maslow, "The Enforcement of Northern Civil Rights Laws," address before the Fisk Institute on Race Relations, Nashville, Tenn., June 28, 1950, p. 16, in collection of Columbia University Law Library.

73. For more information on who could lodge complaints before various state commissions, see Commission on Law and Social Action of the American Jewish Congress, "Report on State Anti-Discrimination Agencies and the Laws They Administer," p. 12 (appendix 3, table A).

74. Review note, " 'Persons Aggrieved' Under the Ives-Quinn Law," pp. 421–422 (the quote is from p. 422); Comment, "The New York State Commission Against Discrimination," pp. 839–840; Brief in Support of Jurisdiction, by Will Maslow, Alexander H. Pekelis, and Shirley Adelson, submitted to State of New York, Executive Dept., State Commission Against Discrimination, American Jewish Congress as Complainant Against Lumbermens Casualty Company of Illinois, Case no. 1189/45, dated January 31, 1946, p. 4, in AJCongress records, box 189. Organizations also had the right to file complaints under the wartime FEPC. See Comment, "The New York State Commission Against Discrimination," p. 855 n.

75. The initial NYSCAD ruling, in October of 1946, limited the CLSA's right to bring complaints before the commission to violations of the provision of the Ives-Quinn law that outlawed discriminatory advertisements and applications forms. *Law and Social*

Action, 1,9 (October 1946), in AJCongress records, box 44; AJCongress CLSA, "Inventory of Pending CLSA Projects," September 16, 1948, p. 2, in AJCongress records, box 40; Brief in Support of Jurisdiction, by Will Maslow, Alexander H. Pekelis, and Shirley Adelson, submitted to State of New York, Executive Dept., State Commission Against Discrimination, American Jewish Congress as Complainant Against Lumbermens Casualty Company of Illinois, Case No. 1189/45, dated January 31, 1946, in AJCongress records, box 189; Review note, " 'Persons Aggrieved' Under the Ives-Quinn Law," pp. 421–423.

76. Note, "Private Attorneys-General," p. 592 n.

77. *Law and Social Action*, 3,5 (September-October 1948), p. 88, in AJCongress records, box 44.

78. *CLSA Reports*, "Report of Activities 1950," January 29, 1951, p. 10, in AJCongress records, box 40.

79. *CLSA Reports*, "Annual Report 1958: Commission on Law and Social Action, American Jewish Congress," 1958 (the quote is from p. 5), in AJCongress, box 41; *CLSA Reports*, "Report of Activities," May 1957, p. 6, in AJCongress records, box 41; CLSA Summary and Analysis of the Sharkey-Brown-Isaacs Bill, December 16, 1957, pp. 1–2, in AJCongress records, box 37. The Sharkey-Brown-Isaacs measure served as a model for a large number of state and municipal laws against discrimination in private housing. In 1959 state laws banning discrimination in private housing were adopted in Colorado, Connecticut, Massachusetts, and Oregon. By 1964 seven additional states and at least fifteen cities had passed such measures. See Lockard, *Toward Equal Opportunity*, pp. 24, 118; Leskes, "State Law Against Discrimination," pp. 237–242.

80. *CLSA Reports*, "Annual Report 1958: Commission on Law and Social Action, American Jewish Congress," 1958, pp. 21–22, in AJCongress, box 41.

81. AJCongress CLSA, "Inventory of Pending CLSA Projects," September 16, 1948, p. 1, in AJCongress records, box 40.

82. *CLSA Reports*, "Report of Activities 1950," pp. 4–5; *CLSA Reports*, "Report of Activities," July-August 1950, p. 3, in AJCongress records, box 40. Jewish agencies were particularly dissatisfied with the enforcement of the Quinn-Olliffe Law. A joint analysis made by the AJC and ADL and investigations conducted by the AJCongress and the NAACP all concluded that the enactment of the law had not appreciably reduced discriminatory practices by the early 1950s. See Saveth, "Fair Educational Practices Legislation," p. 45; AJCongress and NAACP, *Civil Rights in the United States in 1949*, pp. 29–30; AJCongress and NAACP, *Civil Rights in the United States in 1950*, pp. 42, 46–47; AJCongress and NAACP, *Civil Rights in the United States in 1951*, pp. 57, 59–60, 66; AJCongress and NAACP, *Civil Rights in the United States 1952*, pp. 66–67; AJCongress and NAACP, *Civil Rights in the United States 1953*, pp. 79–80, 92–93; Will Maslow, "The Enforcement of Northern Civil Rights Laws," address before the Fisk Institute on Race Relations, Nashville, Tenn., June 28, 1950, pp. 13–14, in collection of Columbia University Law Library.

83. The NAACP Legal Defense and Educational Fund, Inc., was established as a separate entity, for reasons related to tax exemption, in 1939. See Tushnet, *The NAACP's Legal Strategy Against Segregated Education*, p. 100; Greenberg, *Crusaders in the Courts*, pp. xvii, 30; Kaufman, *Broken Alliance*, p. 91.

84. AJCongress memorandum, from CLSA to Jewish Community Leaders and Workers (cover letter dated February 7, 1946), p. 2, in AJCongress records, box 33.

85. Maslow and Robison, "Civil Rights Legislation and the Fight For Equality," p. 363.

86. 83 U.S. 36 (1873).

87. 92 U.S. 542 (1876).

88. 109 U.S. 3 (1883).

89. 163 U.S. 537 (1896).

90. Nieman, *Promises to Keep*, pp. 87–113; Wilkinson, *From "Brown" to "Bakke,"* pp. 12–23; Konvitz, *A Century of Civil Rights*, pp. 102–105, 114–121, 125–130.

91. The NAACP's central role in prompting this "Constitutional revolution" is recounted in Nieman, *Promises to Keep*, pp. 125–139 passim, 144–145. On the NAACP's fight against segregated schools, see Tushnet, *The NAACP's Legal Strategy Against Segregated Education*; Kluger, *Simple Justice*. The early campaign against restrictive covenants is examined in Vose, *Caucasians Only*, chapters 1–3. On the reorientation of the Supreme Court and the federal bench generally after 1937, see Domino, *Civil Rights and Liberties*, pp. 5–6; Vose, *Caucasians Only*, pp. 177–183; Walker, "The Growth of Civil Liberties, 1900–1945," pp. 36–51; Irons, *The New Deal Lawyers*, pp. 4, 14, 277–298 passim; Brinkley, *The End of Reform*, pp. 19–20. For contemporary analyses of the expansion of the doctrine of "state action," see Note, "The Disintegration of a Concept," pp. 402–414; Note, "Applicability of the Fourteenth Amendment to Private Organizations," pp. 344–352; Marshall, "The Supreme Court as Protector of Civil Rights," pp. 101–110.

92. *Shelley v. Kraemer*, 334 U.S. 1 (1948); *Hurd v. Hodge*, 334 U.S. 24 (1948). See Vose, *Caucasians Only*, pp. 151–211.

93. Note, "The Disintegration of a Concept," pp. 402–414 (the quotes are from p. 405); Note, "Applicability of the Fourteenth Amendment to Private Organizations," pp. 344–352; Konvitz, *A Century of Civil Rights*, p. 149. For a recent study of the NAACP Legal Defense and Educational Fund's postwar campaign against discrimination by its former director-counsel, see Greenberg, *Crusaders in the Courts*. Greenberg deals with the issue of state action in the white primary, transportation, and restrictive covenant cases on pp. 108–112.

94. Pekelis, "Full Equality in a Free Society," pp. 226–230 passim. See also Pekelis's essay on "Private Governments and the Federal Constitution," in Konvitz, *Law and Social Action*, pp. 91–127.

95. Maslow, "The Law and Race Relations," p. 75.

96. Pekelis, "Full Equality in a Free Society," p. 229; interview with Will Maslow by author, May 16, 1996. I have borrowed the phrase "private attorneys general" from the title of Note, "Private Attoneys-General." The note's author, Norman Redlich, applied the term to the CLSA, the ACLU, and the NAACP-LDF.

97. AJCongress and NAACP, *Civil Rights in the United States 1952*, pp. 80–81; Lockard, *Toward Equal Opportunity*, p. 63. On white resistance to residential integration in Chicago and Detroit, see Hirsch, "Massive Resistance in the Urban North"; Sugrue, "Crabgrass-Roots Politics."

98. AJCongress and NAACP, *Civil Rights in the United States 1952*, pp. 80–81; AJCongress and NAACP, *Civil Rights in the United States in 1948*, p. 26; AJCongress and NAACP, *Civil Rights in the United States in 1949*, pp. 36–37; AJCongress and NAACP, *Civil Rights in the United States in 1951*, pp. 70–71. For a contemporary review of the social scientific evidence that indicated that integrated housing contributed to the

reduction of racial prejudice, see Allport, *The Nature of Prejudice*, pp. 268–274. See also Deutsch and Collins, *Interracial Housing*.

99. See Jackson, *Crabgrass Frontier*; Caro, *The Power Broker*; Schwartz, *The New York Approach*, p. 86. In a statement before the Senate Committee on Banking and Currency in 1947, one senator claimed that "in order to put the housing plant of the United States in reasonable shape there should be built in 10 years about 12,000,000 houses." Quoted in Groner and Helfeld, "Race Discrimination in Housing," p. 426 n.

100. The relevant cases, from which many of the details in the subsequent analysis are drawn, are *Dorsey v. Stuyvesant Town Corp.*, 74 N.Y.S.2d 220 (1947), *aff'd*, 85 N.Y.S.2d 313 (1948), *aff'd in part*, 87 N.E.2d 541 (1949), *cert. denied*, 339 U.S. 981 (1950). The quoted phrase is from 87 N.E.2d at 543. The facts and legal issues in the case were also discussed in contemporary law review articles, including "Exclusion of Negroes from Subsidized Housing Project," pp. 745–756; Note, "Applicability of the Fourteenth Amendment to Private Organizations," pp. 349–352; Groner and Helfeld, "Race Discrimination in Housing," pp. 438–444. Additional analysis was provided in journalistic treatments such as Abrams, "The Walls of Stuyvesant Town," pp. 328–330; "Metropolitan Life Makes Housing Pay," pp. 133–136, 209–216; Abrams, "Race Bias in Housing," pp. 67–69. In his recent study of slum clearance in New York City, Joel Schwartz provides an excellent analysis of the planning and politics of Stuyvesant Town. He also demonstrates that the project was the main precedent for the city's wave of postwar redevelopment. Schwartz, *The New York Approach*, pp. 84–107.

101. "Metropolitan Makes Housing Pay," p. 133.

102. *Dorsey v. Stuyvesant Town Corp.*, 74 N.Y.S.2d 220; *Dorsey v. Stuyvesant Town Corp.*, 87 N.E.2d 541; Petition for Writ of Certiorari to the Court of Appeals of the State of New York, submitted by Maslow, Abrams, Marshall, Polier, and Robison on October 14, 1949, in AJCongress records, box 189; *CLSA Reports*, "Analysis of the Stuyvesant Town Case" [1950], p. 1; *CLSA Reports*, "Analysis of the New York Court of Appeals Decision in the Stuyvesant Town Case," July 22, 1949, pp. 1–2, in AJCongress records, box 40; *Law and Social Action*, 4,5 (September-October 1949), p. 110, in AJCongress records, box 44; "Metropolitan Life Makes Housing Pay," p. 136; Schwartz, *The New York Approach*, p. 84.

103. Petition for Writ of Certiorari to the Court of Appeals of the State of New York, submitted by Maslow, Abrams, Marshall, Polier, and Robison on October 14, 1949, pp. 4–5, in AJCongress records, box 189; Groner and Helfeld, "Race Discrimination in Housing," p. 438 n. According to Joel Schwartz, efforts to relocate the former residents of the gas-house district were generally ineffective. Few of the working-class people who had lived in the area found new housing through the relocation bureau sponsored by Metropolitan Life, and few were absorbed into public housing projects. Schwartz, *The New York Approach*, pp. xix, 84, 93, 98–99, 104–105, 106, 300. Schwartz's analysis confirms arguments made during the 1940s by housing reformer Charles Abrams, who claimed that the project would force the area's original inhabitants into other, more expensive, substandard housing. According to Abrams, the city was simultaneously "subsidizing Stuyvesant Town to clear a single slum and . . . perpetuating slums all over the city which it had hoped eventually to clear away." Abrams, "The Walls of Stuyvesant Town," p. 329. By contrast, *Fortune* magazine's laudatory evaluation of Metropolitan Life's housing program provided a more positive portrayal of the process of relocation. See "Metropolitan Life Makes Housing Pay," p. 209.

104. Quoted from *Dorsey v. Stuyvesant Town Corp.*, 74 N.Y.S.2d at 221.

105. Article 18 of the New York State Constitution (1938) and the Redevelopment Companies Law of New York State (Laws 1942, Ch. 845, as amended by Laws 1943, Ch. 234, McKinney's Unconsolidated Laws, Sections 3401–3426) are included in the appendixes to Petition for a Writ of Certiorari to the Court of Appeals of the State of New York, submitted by Maslow, Abrams, Marshall, Polier, and Robison on October 14, 1949, pp. 29–43, in AJCongress records, box 189. See also Schwartz, *The New York Approach*, pp. 50, 61, 81, 90–93, 299.

106. Ecker is quoted in the Petition for a Writ of Certiorari to the Court of Appeals of the State of New York, submitted by Maslow, Abrams, Marshall, Polier, and Robison on October 14, 1949, p. 7, in AJCongress records, box 189; Abrams, "The Walls of Stuyvesant Town," p. 328. According to the petition, Ecker "refrained from either admitting or denying the existence of the policy" of racial exclusion when he appeared as a witness at the Board of Estimate hearing. Ibid., p. 7. See also Schwartz, *The New York Approach*, pp. 96–97. For Ecker's role as the commanding force behind Metropolitan's housing projects, see "Metropolitan Life Makes Housing Pay," pp. 133–136, 209–216. Metropolitan Life was simultaneously constructing another housing project, known as Riverton, near the Madison Avenue Bridge in Harlem. Riverton was to be occupied exclusively by black tenants, although this policy was in violation of the 1944 law against discrimination in tax-exempt projects. See "Exclusion of Negroes from Subsidized Housing Project," p. 752; Abrams, "The Walls of Stuyvesant Town," p. 328; Abrams, "Race Bias in Housing," p. 68.

107. Quoted from *Dorsey v. Stuyvesant Town Corp.*, 87 N.E.2d at 555. See also *Dorsey v. Stuyvesant Town Corp.*, 74 N.Y.S.2d 220; *CLSA Reports*, "Analysis of the Stuyvesant Town Case" [1950], p. 1, in AJCongress records, box 40; Walter White, Roger N. Baldwin, and David Petegorsky, "Text of Letter to Mayor O'Dwyer," [1949?] p. 1, in AJCongress records, box 31; *Law and Social Action*, 2,4 (May–June 1947), in AJCongress records, box 44; Groner and Helfeld, "Race Discrimination in Housing," pp. 438 n., 443, 443 n.; Schwartz, *The New York Approach*, p. 97.

108. *Law and Social Action*, 2,4 (May–June 1947); *Law and Social Action*, 5,3 (May–June 1950), in AJCongress records, box 44. The quote is from the 1944 measure against discrimination in tax-exempt developments (Admin. Code of the City of New York J. 41–1.2, July 1944), which is included in the appendix to the Petition for a Writ of Certiorari to the Court of Appeals of the State of New York, submitted by Maslow, Abrams, Marshall, Polier, and Robison on October 14, 1949, p. 43, in AJCongress records, box 189.

109. Quoted in *Dorsey v. Stuyvesant Town Corp.*, 87 N.E.2d at 547. See also Groner and Helfeld, "Race Discrimination in Housing," p. 443 n. Charles Abrams, who labeled Moses the "author of Stuyvesant Town," also claimed that Moses had "tailored" the Redevelopment Companies Law to requirements set by Metropolitan Life. Abrams, "The Walls of Stuyvesant Town," pp. 328–329. Joel Schwartz's study makes it clear that Moses played the central role in shaping the Redevelopment Companies Law and the plan for Stuyvesant Town to suit the needs of Metropolitan Life. Schwartz, *The New York Approach*, pp. 86–87, 92–93, 106, 108.

110. An earlier lawsuit against Metropolitan Life's announced policy of racial exclusion was dismissed as premature, since the project was not yet open for occupancy. See *Pratt v. La Guardia*, 47 N.Y.S.2d 359 (1944), *aff'd*, 52 N.Y.S.2d 569 (1944), *app. granted*, 62 N.E.2d 394 (1945).

111. *Dorsey v. Stuyvesant Town Corp.*, 74 N.Y.S.2d 220; *Dorsey v. Stuyvesant Town Corp.*, 85 N.Y.S.2d 313; *Dorsey v. Stuyvesant Town Corp.*, 87 N.E.2d 541; Petition for Writ of Certiorari to the Court of Appeals of the State of New York, submitted by Maslow, Abrams, Marshall, Polier, and Robison on October 14, 1949, in AJCongress records, box 189; *CLSA Reports*, "Analysis of the Stuyvesant Town Case" [1950], pp. 1–2; *CLSA Reports*, "Report of Activity," April 1949, p. 1, in AJCongress records, box 40; *Law and Social Action*, 3,6 (November–December 1948); *Law and Social Action*, 4,5, p. 110, in AJCongress records, box 44. Abrams was formerly general counsel to the New York City Housing Authority and subsequently served as the chairman of the New York State Commission Against Discrimination. Abrams, "Race Bias in Housing," p. 67; *CLSA Reports*, "Report of Activities," September–October 1957, pp. 6–7, in AJCongress records, box 41; Schwartz, *The New York Approach*, pp. 38–39, 270, 297.

112. Abrams, "The Walls of Stuyvesant Town," pp. 329–330.

113. Groner and Helfeld, "Race Discrimination in Housing," p. 430.

114. See Schwartz, *The New York Approach*, pp. xxi, 95, 101–104 (quote from p. 95).

115. These statutes are given in Petition for a Writ of Certiorari to the Court of Appeals of the State of New York, submitted by Maslow, Abrams, Marshall, Polier, and Robison on October 14, 1949, pp. 23–25 n., in AJCongress records, box 189. See also "Exclusion of Negroes from Subsidized Housing Project," pp. 755–756. Redevelopment laws in Pennsylvania, Illinois, Indiana, and Wisconsin, unlike most of these statutes, barred racial discrimination in such projects. Groner and Helfeld, "Race Discrimination in Housing," p. 444; Maslow and Robison, "Civil Rights Legislation and the Fight for Equality," p. 409 n.

116. Abrams, "The Walls of Stuyvesant Town," p. 328.

117. Abrams, "Race Bias in Housing," p. 68.

118. "Exclusion of Negroes from Subsidized Housing Project," p. 756 n.; "Metropolitan Makes Housing Pay," pp. 134–135, 209–210. The *Fortune* article reported that Parkchester, Metropolitan's biggest housing project, was "the best-paying item in Metropolitan's entire investment portfolio." Ibid., p. 134.

119. "Exclusion of Negroes from Subsidized Housing Project," pp. 755–756 n.; Groner and Helfeld, "Race Discrimination in Housing," p. 430 n.; "Metropolitan Life Makes Housing Pay," pp. 133–134, 215.

120. Petition for a Writ of Certiorari to the Court of Appeals of the State of New York, submitted by Maslow, Abrams, Marshall, Polier, and Robison on October 14, 1949, p. 26, in AJCongress records, box 189.

121. Lockard, *Toward Equal Opportunity*, p. 108. Results of the 1940 census and statistical evidence compiled by the Federal Housing Administration are presented in Groner and Helfeld, "Race Discrimination in Housing," pp. 427–428, 432 n.; AJCongress and NAACP, *Civil Rights in the United States 1953*, pp. 99–100, 105.

122. See figures for 1947, derived from United States Housing and Home Finance Agency, *Housing of the Nonwhite Population, 1940–1947* (Washington, D.C., 1948), cited in McCoy and Ruetten, *Quest and Response*, p. 61.

123. Schwartz, *The New York Approach*, pp. 104, 106; Sugrue, "Crabgrass-Roots Politics," p. 563.

124. McCoy and Ruetten, *Quest and Response*, p. 217.

125. AJCongress and NAACP, *Civil Rights in the United States 1953*, p. 105; Abrams, "The Walls of Stuyvesant Town," pp. 328–330.

126. The New York Supreme Court also dismissed Shad Polier's suit. *Dorsey v. Stuyvesant Town Corp.*, 74 N.Y.S.2d 220; *Dorsey v. Stuyvesant Town Corp.* and *Polier v. O'Dwyer*, 85 N.Y.S.2d 313. The decisions are also summarized in the Petition for Writ of Certiorari to the Court of Appeals of the State of New York, submitted by Maslow, Abrams, Marshall, Polier, and Robison on October 14, 1949, in AJCongress records, box 189. This last document notes that the city itself accepted the characterization of Stuyvesant Town as "quasi public housing" in an August 1949 report of the New York City Housing Authority. Ibid., p. 21.

127. The quotes are from *Dorsey v. Stuyvesant Town Corp.*, 87 N.E.2d at 551. See also *CLSA Reports*, "Analysis of Stuyvesant Town Case" [1950], p. 2; *CLSA Reports*, "Analysis of the New York Court of Appeals Decision in the Stuyvesant Town Case," July 22, 1949, pp. 1–5, in AJCongress records, box 40; *Law and Social Action*, 3,6 (November-December 1948); *Law and Social Action*, 4,4 (July-August 1949), p. 107, in AJCongress records, box 44.

128. Quoted from *Dorsey v. Stuyvesant Town Corp.*, 87 N.E.2d at 553, 555.

129. *Dorsey v. Stuyvesant Town Corp.*, 339 U.S. 981; Petition for a Writ of Certiorari to the Court of Appeals of the State of New York, submitted by Maslow, Abrams, Marshall, Polier, and Robison, October 14, 1949, in AJCongress records, box 189; *CLSA Reports*, "Analysis of the Stuyvesant Town Case" [1950], pp. 1–3, in AJCongress records, box 40; *Law and Social Action*, 4,5 (September-October 1949), p. 10; *Law and Social Action*, 5,3 (May-June 1950) in AJCongress records, box 44.

130. Note, "Private Attorneys-General," p. 592. Tenants who had been active in the movement to end discrimination in Stuyvesant Town and other developments owned by Metropolitan Life alleged that the corporation refused to renew their leases. After litigation and "widespread public protest" Metropolitan ultimately "announced that the families would not be evicted." AJCongress and NAACP, *Civil Rights in the United States in 1951*, pp. 76–77.

131. *CLSA Reports*, "Report of Activities 1950," January 29, 1951, pp. 7–8, in AJCongress records, box 40; *Law and Social Action*, 5,3 (May-June 1950) in AJCongress records, box 44; AJCongress and NAACP, *Civil Rights in the United States in 1950*, p. 56; Schwartz, *The New York Approach*, p. 111.

132. *CLSA Reports*, "Report of Activities 1950," January 29, 1951, p. 8, in AJCongress records, box 40.

133. AJCongress and NAACP, *Civil Rights in the United States in 1950* (quote from p. 53); AJCongress and NAACP, *Civil Rights in the United States in 1951*, pp. 71–73; AJCongress and NAACP, *Civil Rights in the United States 1952*, pp. 91–92; "CLSA Manual for Committee Chairmen," n.d., p. 7, in AJCongress records, box 33.

134. Herbert J. Gans reported that the New Jersey Division Against Discrimination and "pro-integrationist groups" targeted Levittown because it was the largest new suburban development in the state and because "they felt if Levitt would integrate, other builders would follow suit." He also argued that Levittown had become "a national symbol of suburbia" and thus its integration would attract "considerable" publicity. Gans, *The Levittowners*, p. 373.

135. On Levittown, Long Island, see Jackson, *Crabgrass Frontier*, pp. 234–238, 241, 244–245.

136. *CLSA Reports*, "Report of Activity," March 1949, p. 3, in AJCongress records, box 40; AJCongress and NAACP, *Civil Rights in the United States in 1949*, p. 42.

137. *CLSA Reports*, "Report of Activities 1950," January 29, 1951, p. 9, in AJCongress records, box 40; AJCongress and NAACP, *Civil Rights in the United States in 1950*, p. 57. The NAACP Legal Defense and Educational Fund's case against racial discrimination in the Long Island Levittown was unsuccessful, because the court ruled that there was no state action involved. See Greenberg, *Crusaders in the Courts*, p. 81.

138. An AJCongress analysis of the Metcalf-Baker Act noted that "the importance of this new law can be indicated by saying that there cannot now be another Levittown in New York State." "Summary of the Two Metcalf-Baker Bills on Discrimination in Housing Adopted by the 1955 New York State Legislature," p. 3, in AJCongress records, box 41.

139. Jackson, *Crabgrass Frontier*, p. 241.

140. AJCongress and NAACP, *Civil Rights in the United States 1952*, pp. 82, 91 (the quote is from p. 82); AJCongress and NAACP, *Civil Rights in the United States in 1951*, p. 77.

141. Gans argued that this characterization was greatly exaggerated, and that "there was no violence and only two stones were thrown." Nonetheless, he indicated that the desire to avoid the perception of racial unrest was instrumental in the more tranquil resolution of the New Jersey situation. *CLSA Reports*, "Report of Activities," July-August 1957, p. 7, in AJCongress records, box 41; Gans, *The Levittowners*, pp. 371–372, 375; Lockard, *Toward Equal Opportunity*, p. 115.

142. Quoted from *CLSA Reports*, "Annual Report 1958: Commission on Law and Social Action, American Jewish Congress," p. 5, in AJCongress records, box 41; Gans, *The Levittowners*, p. 371.

143. *CLSA Reports*, "Report of Activities," May-June 1958, p. 7, in AJCongress records, box 41; *CLSA Reports*, "Report of Activities," January-February, 1960, p. 8, in AJCongress records, box 42.

144. Gans, *The Levittowners*, p. 372.

145. *Levitt & Sons, Inc. v. Div. Against Discrimination in State Dept. of Educ.*, 153 A.2d 700 (1959), *aff'd*, 158 A.2d 177 (1960), *app. dismissed*, 363 U.S. 418 (1960); *CLSA Reports*, "Annual Report 1958: Commission on Law and Social Action, American Jewish Congress," 1958, p. 20, in AJCongress records, box 41; Gans, *The Levittowners*, p. 372; Leskes, "State Law Against Discrimination," pp. 246–248. As seen above, New Jersey had passed a law (known as the Clapp Law) against discrimination in "publicly-assisted" housing in 1950. A 1957 measure extended the ban on discrimination to housing built with the assistance of FHA or Veterans' Administration mortgage insurance. CLSA, "Summary of 1957 State Anti-Discrimination Laws," pp. 1, 4; CLSA, "Report on State Anti-Discrimination Agencies and the Laws They Administer," pp. 6, 13–14, 18. The FHA contributed to residential segregation by its reluctance or refusal to insure mortgages in interracial neighborhoods, by granting mortgage insurance to "white only" developments, and (before the 1948 Supreme Court decisions banning judicial enforcement of restrictive covenants) by providing a model restrictive covenant that proscribed members of racial minority groups from occupying many homes with FHA-insured mortgages. The agency, along with the Veterans Administration, made some limited steps to "liberalize" its procedures during the late 1940s, such as adopting a policy against restrictive covenants, effective in February 1950. The FHA continued to effectively sanction discrimination, however, especially in private housing. McCoy and Ruetten characterized the change in federal housing policy during the Truman

years as "a pathetic improvement . . . a step from misery to slightly less misery." McCoy and Ruetten, *Quest and Response*, pp. 210, 213–217; Abrams, "Race Bias in Housing," p. 69; AJCongress and NAACP, *Civil Rights in the United States in 1949*, pp. 37–38; AJCongress and NAACP, *Civil Rights in the United States 1952*, pp. 89–90; Jackson, *Crabgrass Frontier*, pp. 190–230; Lipsitz, "The Possessive Investment in Whiteness," pp. 372–373; Sugrue, "Crabgrass-Roots Politics," p. 564.

146. *CLSA Reports*, "Annual Report 1958: Commission on Law and Social Action, American Jewish Congress" (quote is from p. 21); *CLSA Reports*, "Report of Activities," May-June, 1960, p. 6, in AJCongress records, box 41; *CLSA Reports*, "Report of Activities," January-February 1960, p. 8; *CLSA Reports*, "Report of Activities," July-August, 1960, pp. 7–8, in AJCongress records, box 42; AJCongress-CLSA letter to "Dear Colleague," re: Levitt case, dated June 17, 1960, in AJCongress records, box 31. Franklin Todd, one of the men who alleged racial discrimination by Levittown, was individually represented by Jerome C. Eisenberg, a former chairman of the New Jersey CLSA, and Herbert H. Tate, who was affiliated with the NAACP.

147. *Levitt & Sons, Inc. v. Div. Against Discrimination in State Dept. of Educ.*, 153 A.2d 700, *aff'd*, 158 A.2d 177, *app. dismissed*, 363 U.S. 418.

148. The desegregation plan is described in Gans, *The Levittowners*, pp. 375–379. Gans also noted that Levitt "attempted to obtain postponements from the lower courts, hoping to sell an all-white community to as many people as possible before a higher court finally ruled for integration." Ibid., p. 374. *CLSA Reports*, "Report of Activities," July-August 1960, pp. 7–8; *CLSA Reports*, "Report of Activities," September-October, 1960, p. 6, in AJCongress records, box 42. According to Theodore Leskes, "Levitt and Green Fields had signed a stipulation agreeing to cease and desist from discrimination in the sale of their houses if the New Jersey Supreme Court dismissed their petition. That stipulation, among other things, required the developers to sign contracts for homes with the Negro complainants if they still wished to purchase homes in the developments." Leskes, "State Law Against Discrimination," p. 248.

149. Gans, *The Levittowners*, p. 379.

150. Lockard, *Toward Equal Opportunity*, p. 114; Gans, *The Levittowners*, pp. 380, 406 n. 27.

151. The phrase is quoted from AJCongress memorandum, from CLSA to Jewish Community Leaders and Workers (cover letter dated February 7, 1946), p. 4, in AJCongress records, box 33.

152. Pekelis, "Full Equality in a Free Society," p. 232.

153. AJCongress memorandum, from CLSA to Jewish Community Leaders and Workers, (cover letter dated February 7, 1946), p. 4, in AJCongress records, box 33.

154. See Cohen, *Not Free to Desist*, pp. 411–428. The AJC's Solomon Andhil Fineberg recalled that the AJCongress tended to attract less well-off Jews who were still relatively close to their Eastern European heritage, while the AJC and ADL drew many of their supporters from wealthier, more established Jews "who had made it." S. Andhil Fineberg Oral History Interview, conducted by Isaiah Terman, 1974, pp. 2:100 to 2:101, in SAF papers, box 5, AJA.

155. Pekelis, "Full Equality in a Free Society," p. 160.

156. Franklin Delano Roosevelt, "Economic Bill of Rights," (1944), in Levy, *100 Key Documents*, pp. 356–359.

157. Text of Oral Statement of Will Maslow before the President's Committee on Civil Rights, Washington, D.C., May 1, 1947, pp. 1–2, in AJCongress records, box 36. See also Maslow and Robison, "Civil Rights: A Program for the President's Committee," p. 113, for the same argument in slightly different language.

158. Pekelis, "Full Equality in a Free Society," p. 244 (emphasis in original).

159. CCI, "Working Together," November 11, 1947, "The Congress Chapter's Role in Initiating and Supporting Projects of Community-Wide Interest" (cover letter by David W. Petegorsky, executive director of AJCongress), p. 1, in AJCongress records, box 12.

160. In his recent study of New Deal liberalism, Alan Brinkley notes that by the end of World War II most labor leaders and other liberal reformers were in the process of abandoning a dedication to the redistribution of wealth in favor of "the emerging liberal belief that the key to a successful society was economic growth through high levels of consumption." By the end of the war, according to Brinkley, the "liberal agenda" included "a belief in the capacity of American abundance to smooth over questions of class and power by creating a nation of consumers." Brinkley argues that the guarantee of full employment was the cornerstone of this new consumption-oriented liberal ideology. See Brinkley, *The End of Reform*, pp. 226–264, 268 (quoted phrases from p. 226). In her study of Eleanor Roosevelt's postwar political career, Allida M. Black argues, "Throughout the 1940s ER emphasized economic opportunity as a key component of racial justice." See Black, *Casting Her Own Shadow*, p. 89.

161. For an example, see Allport, *The Nature of Prejudice*, p. 55.

162. Myrdal, *An American Dilemma*, 1:78.

163. See President's Committee on Civil Rights, *To Secure These Rights*, pp. 141–146.

164. Elmo Roper, "The High Cost of Prejudice," *ADL Bulletin*, 5,9 (December 1948), p. 8.

165. Quoted in "Public Statements on Intergroup Relations by Christian Businessmen," [1957], in AJC records, box 256, "Religious Position—Race Relations." See also Samuels, "Prejudice in the Marketplace," pp. 150 n., 153–155 passim; Jackson, *Gunnar Myrdal and America's Conscience*, p. 276.

166. Kellogg, "Civil Rights Consciousness in the 1940s," p. 41. See also Brinkley, *The End of Reform*, pp. 9–10, 165–170.

167. Gans, *The Levittowners*, p. 380.

168. Duane Lockard credits the Stuyvesant Town case with inspiring not only the 1951 Brown-Isaacs ordinance against discrimination in publicly assisted housing, but also with stimulating the subsequent enactment of the 1958 Sharkey-Brown-Isaacs law which banned discrimination in private housing in New York City. Lockard, *Toward Equal Opportunity*, p. 64.

169. Gans, *The Levittowners*, p. 384.

170. Lockard, *Toward Equal Opportunity*, pp. 13–14, 73–74, 95–96; McCoy and Ruetten, *Quest and Response*, pp. 289, 349–350.

171. Will Maslow, "The Enforcement of Northern Civil Rights Laws," address before the Fisk Institute on Race Relations, Nashville, Tenn., June 28, 1950, p. 8, in collection of Columbia University Law Library; Lockard, *Toward Equal Opportunity*, pp. 10, 137–138; Dinnerstein, *Antisemitism in America*, pp. 154–158.

172. AJCongress and NAACP, *Civil Rights in the United States in 1951*, pp. 10–11, 40; AJCongress and NAACP, *Civil Rights in the United States 1952*, pp. 9, 45; AJCongress

and NAACP, *Civil Rights in the United States 1953*, p. 12; Commission on Law and Social Action of the American Jewish Congress, "Report on State Anti-Discrimination Agencies and the Laws They Administer," p. 9; Will Maslow, "The Enforcement of Northern Civil Rights Laws," address before the Fisk Institute on Race Relations, Nashville, Tenn., June 28, 1950, pp. 7–8, in collection of Columbia University Law Library; Lockard, *Toward Equal Opportunity*, pp. 13, 81, 96, 130.

173. Lockard, *Toward Equal Opportunity*, pp. 13–14, 83–86; interview with Will Maslow by author, May 16, 1996.

174. The study is summarized in Lockard, *Toward Equal Opportunity*, p. 93. Gordon Allport noted that few New Yorkers were aware of the state's fair employment law in the early 1950s, and that even those who knew about the law were reluctant to use it. Allport, *The Nature of Prejudice*, p. 470.

175. Leskes, "State Law Against Discrimination," pp. 216–218; Lockard, *Toward Equal Opportunity*, pp. 78, 92–93, 123, 146–147.

176. For critiques of the "case-complaint" system, see Lockard, *Toward Equal Opportunity*, pp. 78–79, 82–83, 89–91, 98, 101, 121–125, 139–140, 142, 147, 149, 150; Will Maslow, "The Enforcement of Northern Civil Rights Laws," address before the Fisk Institute on Race Relations, Nashville, Tenn., June 28, 1950, pp. 9–12, in collection of Columbia University Law Library. At least some state antidiscrimination commissions had the power to initiate investigations and charges on their own initiative, although civil rights advocates claimed that this power was not adequately exercised.

177. Lockard called this alternative the "pattern-centered" approach. Lockard, *Toward Equal Opportunity*, pp. 98, 125–127, 139–140, 147, 150.

178. Will Maslow, "The Enforcement of Northern Civil Rights Laws," address before the Fisk Institute on Race Relations, Nashville, Tenn., June 28, 1950, p. 12, in collection of Columbia University Law Library.

179. Lockard, *Toward Equal Opportunity*, pp. 12, 142.

180. Ibid., pp. 130–131.

5. *The Adoption of Liberal Anticommunism*

1. On the confrontation of the ACLU, ADA, CIO, and other liberal organizations with the politics of domestic anticommunism after World War II, see McAuliffe, *Crisis on the Left*; Walker, *In Defense of American Liberties*, pp. 173–214; McAuliffe, "The Politics of Civil Liberties"; Oshinsky, "Labor's Cold War"; Theoharis, "The Politics of Scholarship," pp. 267–269. A recent discussion of the debate over anticommunism and civil liberties within the American Committee for Cultural Freedom, which has important parallels with the AJC and ADL, can be found in Bloch, "The Emergence of Neoconservatism in the United States," pp. 36–63.

2. Wistrich, *Antisemitism*, pp. 107, 140, 242, 282 n. 17; Heale, *American Anticomunism*, pp. 106, 108–109, 118–119; Dinnerstein, *Antisemitism in America*, pp. 77, 79–82, 115–117, 135–136, 163; *Facts*, 13,4 (October-November, 1958), pp. 127–128, 130 (quote from p. 130). On Father Coughlin and the political anti-Semitism of the 1930s, see chapter 1. Rankin's remarks, made in a speech in the House of Representatives, were quoted in AJCongress and NAACP, *Civil Rights in the United States in 1951*, p. 119.

3. Schlesinger, *The Vital Center*. On the evolution of liberalism of the "vital center" in the postwar period, especially as manifested in the Truman administration, see

Hamby, *Liberalism and Its Challengers*, pp. 52–70, 86–93; Hamby, *Beyond the New Deal*, pp. 277–292.

4. Liebman, "The Ties That Bind," pp. 305–306; AJC Background Memorandum no. 2, "The Communist Problem as It Affects American Jews," revised September 8, 1949, p. 1, in AJC records, box 246, "1949 Communism"; Feingold, *A Time for Searching*, pp. 222–223; Teller, *Strangers and Natives*, p. 178; Transcript of an Oral Interview with Morris U. Schappes, New York, N.Y., March 9, 1968, p. 50, in Biographies, "Schappes, Morris," *AJA* (conducted as part of Cornell Program in Oral History).

5. AJC Staff Committee on Communism minutes, March 23, 1954, p. 1; October 6, 1954, p. 1, in AJC records, box 247, "AJC Committee on Communism Minutes 1950–56"; "First Report of Coordinator of Staff Activities in Reference to Communism," S. Andhil Fineberg to John Slawson, October 6, 1950, p. 3; "Fourth Report of the Coordinator of the AJC Program on Communism," S. Andhil Fineberg to John Slawson, December 28, 1951, pp. 2–3, in AJC records, box 248, "Polit Phil Communism Program Activities 50–55"; AJC memorandum, from S. Andhil Fineberg to Eleanor Ashman, August 1, 1956, p. 1; AJC memorandum, from S. Andhil Fineberg to John Slawson, "AJC Activities Re: Communism Since January 21, 1953," August 25, 1953, pp. 1–3, 5–6, in AJC records, box 248, "Polit Phil Communism Program 53–57"; AJC Background Memorandum no. 2, "The Communist Problem as It Affects American Jews," revised September 8, 1949, pp. 1–5, in AJC records, box 246, "1949 Communism"; AJC memorandum, to Domestic Affairs Committee, August 11, 1950, p. 4, in AJC records, box 246, "Polit Phil Communism June-August 1950"; "PI&E Work on Communism, 1951," p. 2, in AJC records, box 246, "Polit Phil Communism 51–53."

6. The phrase, from a speech Slawson made before the Essex County chapter of the AJC, is quoted in an AJC press release, "Struggle to Expand Civil Rights Means All-Out Battle Against Communism," November 29, 1950, in AJC records, box 246, "Polit Phil Communism Sept-Dec 1950."

7. ADL memorandum, "Varying Recommendations from New York and Chicago Sub-Committees of National Civil Rights Committee: Decisions Arrived At," 1950, p. 100, in ADL records; AJC memorandum, "Communist Views on Arms Shipments and Arab-Israel Tensions," November 17, 1955, in AJC records, box 246, "Polit Phil Communism 54–57"; AJC press release, "Struggle to Expand Civil Rights Means All-Out Battle Against Communism," November 29, 1950, in AJC records, box 246, "Polit Phil Communism Sept-Dec 1950"; Untitled memorandum on communism, February 2, 1948, p. 1, in AJC records, box 246, "Polit Phil Communism 36–48"; AJC Staff Committee on Communism minutes, November 25, 1952, p. 1; March 23, 1954, p. 1, in AJC records, box 247, "Committee on Communism Minutes 1950–56." In December 1952 John Slawson wrote, "We believe that what happened in Prague only recently is the beginning of a genocidal venture for the purpose of uniting the reactionary—fascist and communist—forces in Germany, in all of Europe, in the middle East, in Asia, against the free Western world." John Slawson to Isaac Toubin, December 9, 1952, p. 2, in AJC records, box 248, "Polit Phil Communism AJC-ADL-AJCongress 50–52." An AJC memorandum written several weeks earlier warned that the Slansky trial was "laying the groundwork for a pogrom of genocidal proportions. If not aided in time by massive protests all over the free world, the Jews behind the Iron Curtain will be exterminated in slave labor camps." AJC memorandum, from Joseph Gordon to Staff Committee on Communism, November 24, 1952, p. 3, in SAF papers, box 1, *AJA*.

8. Liebman, "The Ties That Bind," pp. 319–320; Shapiro, *A Time for Healing*, p. 38.

9. *AJYB* 49 (1947–48), pp. 188–189; *AJYB* 51 (1950), p. 110; *AJYB* 52 (1951), pp. 65–67; *AJYB* 53 (1952), p. 135; *AJYB* 54 (1953), p. 90; interview with Arnold Forster by author, June 11, 1996. Leonard Dinnerstein notes and affirms the contemporary perception that anti-Semitism went "underground" after 1945 in Dinnerstein, *Antisemitism in America*, pp. 165, 170–171. See also Forster, *Square One*, pp. 83, 85, 87–88; Rorty, "The Native Anti-Semite's 'New Look' "; clipping from *JTA News*, "Organized Anti-Semitism Still Seen as Threat to U.S. Jewry," May 26, 1954, in Nearprint files, "Slawson, John," *AJA*.

10. The quote is from Rorty, "The Native Anti-Semite's 'New Look,' " p. 413. On the use of anticommunist rhetoric to undermine liberal civil rights measures such as the federal FEPC, see chapter 4.

11. "Political and Social Factors (to be considered in planning AJC's 1954 program)," November 18, 1953, p. 1, in AJC records, box 246, "Political Philosophies 46–54."

12. ADL National Commission meeting transcript, October 24–26, 1952, pp. 298–299, in ADL records; "Racist Pitch in Politics," *ADL Bulletin*, 9,6 (June 1952); *ADL Bulletin*, 11,6 (June 1954), pp. 7–8; "Political and Social Factors (to be considered in planning AJC's 1954 program)," November 18, 1953, pp. 1–2; Minnesota Jewish Council memorandum, from Executive Director Samuel L. Scheiner to CRC offices, August 24, 1950, in AJC records, box 246, "Political Philosophies 46–54"; *AJYB* 54 (1953), p. 90; *AJYB* 55 (1954), p. 75; Forster, *Square One*, pp. 112–113; Caute, *The Great Fear*, pp. 77–78. On the Tenney committee and the anticommunist campaign in Hollywood, see Adler, "The Politics of Culture," pp. 245–247. On the confluence of anticommunism and anti-Semitism in the Tenney committee's campaign, see Moore, *To the Golden Cities*, pp. 201–202, 211.

13. "Pro-McCarthy Petition entitled TEN MILLION AMERICANS MOBILIZE FOR JUSTICE," November 23, 1954, p. 6, in AJC records, box 246, "Polit Phil Communism 54–57"; Lipset, "The Sources of the 'Radical Right,' " p. 357 n.; Rorty, "The Native Anti-Semite's 'New Look,' " pp. 414–415; Rorty, "What Price McCarthy Now?" pp. 31, 33 n., 35; Oshinsky, *A Conspiracy So Immense*, p. 486; Heale, *American Anticommunism*, p. 104; Lipset and Raab, *The Politics of Unreason*, p. 244.

14. Flowerman, "Portrait of the Authoritarian Man," p. 28. Philip Gleason noted that McCarthyism "seemed to confirm" the psychological diagnosis presented in *The Authoritarian Personality*. See Gleason, "Americans All," p. 510.

15. The results of Srole's study are summarized in Stember et al., *Jews in the Mind of America*, pp. 165–167. See also ADL National Commission meeting transcript, October 24–26, 1952, pp. 58–59, in ADL records.

16. "Are Jews Widely Regarded as Communists and Atom Spies? Highlights of an Analysis of the 'Communist' Survey," May 8, 1951, p. 1, in AJC records, box 249, "Polit Phil Communism Jews 50–59"; AJC memorandum, from Samuel H. Flowerman to John Slawson, May 4, 1951, re: "Poll Rider Questions on Julius and Ethel Rosenberg, and Criticism of Jews," in AJC records, RG 347.17 Gen-12, box 139, "Rosenberg Case 50–52"; AJC Annual Report, "Studies on Jews and Communism," in *AJYB* 54 (1953), p. 574; Stember et al., *Jews in the Mind of America*, pp. 156–165, 168–169; Report of Program Committee Director Harold Lachman, ADL National Commission minutes, 1951, p. 2, in ADL records. On the general infrequency of the association of Jews with communists see Stouffer, *Communism, Conformity, and Civil Liberties*, pp. 172, 174, 184, 277 n. 16.

17. Oshinsky, *A Conspiracy So Immense*, p. 205 n. Several of the contributors to *The New American Right* argued that overt anti-Semitism, and ethnic intolerance more generally, was decreasing during the 1950s, even as ideological intolerance was increasing. See Bell, *The Radical Right*, pp. 168, 226, 356–357, 361–362, 364. This volume is an updated and expanded edition of *The New American Right* (New York: Criterion Books, 1955). James Rorty reported a "rather surprising" decline in anti-Semitism during the 1950s, despite the prominence of Jewish names in the anticommunist investigations. Rorty, "The Native Anti-Semite's 'New Look,' " p. 419. Historians have similarly noted the apparent divergence between demagogic anticommunism and anti-Semitism during this period. See Higham, *Send These to Me*, pp. 171–172; Shapiro, *A Time for Healing*, pp. 34–35; Kazin, *The Populist Persuasion*, pp. 167, 328 n. 5. See also the discussion in Lipset and Raab, *The Politics of Unreason*, pp. 240–244.

18. Dawidowicz and Goldstein, "The American Jewish Liberal Tradition," p. 299.

19. Nathan C. Belth Oral Memoir, in Cohen and Wexler, "*Not the Work of a Day*," 5:33. Belth attributes these statements to ADL National Chairman Henry E. Schultz in Belth, *A Promise to Keep*, p. 206.

20. Bell, *The Radical Right*. Most of the analyses advanced in this collection were strongly influenced by the "authoritarian" model. For direct references to the findings of the Studies in Prejudice, especially *The Authoritarian Personality*, see pp. 76–77, 85 n., 88–89, 91, 110, 111 n., 118, 344 n., 358–359 n., 411–413. In a study of political extremism conducted during the 1960s for the Anti-Defamation League, Seymour Martin Lipset and Earl Raab also noted the correspondence between support for McCarthyism and authoritarianism. See Lipset and Raab, *The Politics of Unreason*, pp. 234–235. By the late 1960s and early 1970s revisionist historians argued that the contributors to *The Radical Right* had misapprehended the nature of the postwar anticommunist crusade, which the revisionists saw as a product of partisan politics, not pathology. See, for example, the essays collected in *The Specter*, especially Theoharis, "The Politics of Scholarship."

21. Hofstadter, "The Pseudo-Conservative Revolt," p. 91.

22. Job Dittberner, "Interview with Daniel Bell," quoted in Bloch, "The Emergence of Neoconservatism," p. 70 n. See Michael Kazin's discussion of "The Great Liberal Fear" in Kazin, *The Populist Persuasion*, pp. 190–193 (the quote is from p. 191). Seymour Martin Lipset and Earl Raab noted "the liberal intellectual's belief that McCarthyites were generally intolerant people" in Lipset and Raab, *The Politics of Unreason*, p. 241.

23. Allport, *The Nature of Prejudice*, pp. 404–405; Stouffer, *Communism, Conformity, and Civil Liberties*, pp. 94–107.

24. Much of the information in the following analysis is drawn from the transcript of the confirmation hearings on Anna M. Rosenberg's nomination, held before the Senate Committee on Armed Forces, cited herein as Senate Committee, *Nomination of Anna M. Rosenberg*. A brief biographical sketch of Rosenberg can be found in Rayner, *Wise Women*, pp. 197–207. For a contemporary analysis of the controversy over Rosenberg's nomination by two ADL leaders, see Forster and Epstein, *The Troublemakers*, pp. 25–60.

25. Senate Committee, *Nomination of Anna M. Rosenberg*, pp. 1–4, 24; Rayner, *Wise Women*, pp. 198–199, 206; *Who's Who in America, 1964–1965*, s.v. "Rosenberg, Anna M."; *Who's Who of American Women, 1958–1959*, s.v. "Rosenberg, Anna M."

26. Senate Committee, *Nomination of Anna M. Rosenberg*, pp. 7–9; Rayner, *Wise Women*, pp. 200–201, 203, 206; *Who's Who in America, 1964–1965*, s.v. "Rosenberg, Anna M."; *Who's Who of American Women, 1958–1959*, s.v. "Rosenberg, Anna M."

27. Senate Committee, *Nomination of Anna M. Rosenberg*, pp. 9, 24; Rayner, *Wise Women*, p. 206.

28. Senate Committee, *Nomination of Anna M. Rosenberg*, pp. 10–11, 13, 16–17, 19, 20–21, 26–27, 37–93 passim, 117–122, 128, 145–201 passim, 362–366; Forster and Epstein, *The Troublemakers*, p. 28.

29. Senate Committee, *Nomination of Anna M. Rosenberg*, pp. 26–27, 38–39, 42, 66, 79, 92–93, 115–122. See also Oral History of Anna M. Rosenberg, June 7, 1957, p. 9, Herbert Lehman project, Columbia University Oral History Archives.

30. Oshinsky, *A Conspiracy So Immense*, p. 205.

31. According to his own testimony, De Sola was Jewish (the name is apparently Sephardic) on his father's side. Senate Committee, *Nomination of Anna M. Rosenberg*, pp. 55–56, 105.

32. Ibid., pp. 26, 48, 63, 154, 224–228; House Committee on Un-American Activities, *Preliminary Report on Neo-Fascist and Hate Groups*, pp. 17–18.

33. *ADL Bulletin*, 7,10 (December 1950), pp. 4–6; *Facts*, 6,1 (January 1951); *AJYB* 53 (1952), p. 135; Louis J. Segel to S. Andhil Fineberg, December 9, 1950, in AJC records, RG 347.17 Gen-12, box 139, "Rosenberg Anna"; Forster and Epstein, *The Troublemakers*, p. 29; Senate Committee, *Nomination of Anna M. Rosenberg*, pp. 129, 149–150, 152, 159, 162.

34. Senate Committee, *Nomination of Anna M. Rosenberg*, pp. 26, 149–150, 180, 192, 222, 224–228, 307–308, 371; Forster and Epstein, *The Troublemakers*, pp. 27, 30, 35, 40–41, 46–49, 50–54; Forster, *Square One*, p. 121; Kazin, *The Populist Persuasion*, p. 330 n. 26. On the anti-Semitism of Gerald L. K. Smith and John Rankin, see Dinnerstein, *Antisemitism in America*, pp. 134, 136; Shapiro, *A Time for Healing*, pp. 40–41, 108. On McCarthy's role in the Anna Rosenberg affair, see Oshinsky, *A Conspiracy So Immense*, pp. 203–205. J. B. Matthews, the former staff director of the Dies Committee, went on to become the staff director of Senator McCarthy's Senate Subcommittee on Investigations. He was forced to resign the latter position after writing a article charging that the "largest single group supporting the Communist apparatus in the United States today is composed of Protestant clergymen." Heale, *American Anticommunism*, pp. 179, 188; Oshinsky, *A Conspiracy So Immense*, pp. 118, 318–320; Clipping from *New York Times*, July 11, 1953, in Nearprint files, "Blaustein, Jacob," AJA.

35. "Williams' Intelligence Summary," put out by the West Coast-based anti-Semitic propagandist Robert H. Williams, warned: "If Congress approves the Rosenberg appointment, we may presently see an order issued by the President or perhaps the Rosenberg office itself requiring factories to abnegate their priceless God-given right to discriminate in employment, forcing them to open our gates to all the motley hordes of incoming races or else go without war contracts." Quoted in *Facts*, 6,1 (January 1951), p. 1. On Williams and his anti-Semitic activities, see House Committee on Un-American Activities, *Preliminary Report on Neo-Fascist and Hate Groups*, p. 14. A large number of individuals who wrote letters urging the Senate Armed Services Committee to reject Rosenberg's nomination were doctors, who were apparently concerned about Rosenberg's views on health insurance. Senate Committee, *Nomination of Anna M. Rosenberg*, pp. 10–11, 18, 20, 232–268 passim.

36. *ADL Bulletin*, 8,1 (January 1951), p. 2.

37. *ADL Bulletin*, 7,10 (December 1950), pp. 4–5.

38. *Facts*, 6,1 (January 1951), p. 1. See also Forster and Epstein, *The Troublemakers*, pp. 25–60.

39. *ADL Bulletin*, 7,10 (December 1950), pp. 4–5.

40. *Facts*, 6,1, (January 1951), p. 1.

41. Senate Committee, *Nomination of Anna M. Rosenberg*, p. 20; *ADL Bulletin*, 7,10 (December 1950), p. 5; Forster and Epstein, *The Troublemakers*, pp. 27–28, 51; ADL, "Personally Yours, An Intimate Report from the Regional Director, Wisconsin," 1,3 (January 1951), p. 1, in Nearprint files, "Anti-Defamation League of B'nai B'rith, Special Topics," *AJA*.

42. The anti-Semitic hate sheets are quoted in *Facts*, 6,1 (January 1951), p. 2. On the question of the Jewish role in the "atom spy" cases and the response of American Jewish organizations, see chapter 6.

43. Quoted in *Facts*, 6,1 (January 1951), p. 4. See also Forster and Epstein, *The Troublemakers*, pp. 54, 56.

44. Cohen, *Not Free to Desist*, pp. 360–361; *Committee Reporter*, 8,3 (February-March 1951), p. 4; Minutes of the Executive Committee of ADL National Commission, January 13–14, 1951, p. 3, in ADL records; interview with Arnold Forster by author, June 11, 1996.

45. Other expressions of support for Rosenberg's nomination came from prominent liberals and former New Dealers, including Bernard Baruch, James F. Byrnes, Everett R. Clinchy, Thomas J. Concoran, David Dubinsky, Samuel I. Rosenman, Nathan Straus, and Robert F. Wagner, Jr., as well as from General Dwight D. Eisenhower. Senate Committee, *Nomination of Anna M. Rosenberg*, pp. 113–114, 335–362. See also Oral History of Anna M. Rosenberg, June 7, 1957, Herbert H. Lehman project, Columbia University Oral History Archives; *The Committee Reporter*, 7,7 (October 1950), p. 6.

46. Senate Committee, *Nomination of Anna M. Rosenberg*, pp. 333–335, 381; Forster and Epstein, *The Troublemakers*, p. 60; Payment authorization to Julius Goldstein, February 5, 1951; AJC memorandum from Edwin Lukas to Marcus Cohn, December 26, 1950, in AJC records, RG 347.17 Gen-12, box 139, "Anna Rosenberg 50–56."

47. Memorandum from Edwin J. Lukas to Marcus Cohn, December 26, 1950, AJC records, RG 347.17 Gen-12, box 139, "Anna Rosenberg 50–56."

48. Heale, *American Anticommunism*, pp. 164, 177; Cain, "Security of the Republic," p. 7.

49. *ADL Bulletin*, 12,4 (April 1955), p. 2.

50. McCarthy claimed that there was a connection between convicted spy Julius Rosenberg and alleged communist infiltration at Fort Monmouth. Rosenberg had been employed by the Army Signal Corps during World War II, several of the suspended employees had known Julius Rosenberg at City College, and there was speculation that a "Rosenberg spy ring" may have operated at the Fort Monmouth site. S. Andhil Fineberg of the AJC, who was "reasonably certain that all of those suspended persons are innocent," believed that Rosenberg had engaged in espionage at Fort Monmouth during and immediately following the war. S. Andhil Fineberg to Albert L. Arenberg, January 25, 1954, p. 1, in AJC records, box 246, "Polit Phil Communism

54–57." On the "Julius Rosenberg connection" at Fort Monmouth, see Caute, *The Great Fear*, pp. 63, 180–182; Oshinsky, *A Conspiracy So Immense*, pp. 330, 335, 339, 341; Marker, "The Jewish Community and the Case of Julius and Ethel Rosenberg," p. 118. A report sponsored by the Federation of American Scientists and prepared by the Scientists' Committee on Loyalty and Security contended that there was little evidence of a Rosenberg espionage group active at Fort Monmouth after 1947–1948, although it maintained that "there may have been serious espionage at Monmouth during World War II." See Federation of American Scientists, Scientists' Committee on Loyalty and Security, "The Fort Monmouth Security Investigation, August 1953–1954" (mimeographed, issued April 25, 1954), pp. 4–3, 4–4, 4–8, 4–9; Scientists' Committee on Loyalty and Security, "Fort Monmouth One Year Later" in *Bulletin of Atomic Scientists*, 11,4 (April 1955). I am indebted to historian Jessica Wang for sharing copies of these reports with me.

51. The exact number of suspended employees and employees whose security clearance was revoked but who remained employed is difficult to determine, partly because some employees were suspended, reinstated, and suspended once again. *ADL Bulletin*, 12,4 (April 1955), p. 1; *ADL Bulletin*, 11,7 (September 1954), p. 7; AJCongress, "Fact Sheet V: The Federal Employee Security Program," n.d., in AJCongress records, box 31; Caute, *The Great Fear*, pp. 273–274, 479–484; Cohen, *Not Free to Desist*, p. 358; Oshinsky, *A Conspiracy So Immense*, pp. 330–344; Federation of American Scientists, "The Fort Monmouth Security Investigation, August 1953–1954," 4–15 to 4–32, 5–4, 6–7.

52. *ADL Bulletin*, 11,7 (September 1954), pp. 7–8; *ADL Bulletin*, 12,4 (April 1955), p. 1; Benjamin R. Epstein Oral Memoir, in Cohen and Wexler, "Not the Work of a Day," 1:145.

53. *ADL Bulletin*, 11,7 (September 1954), p. 8; Oshinsky, *A Conspiracy So Immense*, pp. 331–332.

54. AJCongress, "Fact Sheet V: The Federal Employee Security Program," n.d., in AJCongress records, box 31; Cohen, *Not Free to Desist*, p. 358; Caute, *The Great Fear*, p. 484.

55. *ADL Bulletin*, 11,7 (September 1954), pp. 7–8; Forster, *Square One*, pp. 120–121, 124–125, 150–151, 160; interview with Arnold Forster by author, June 11, 1996. Benjamin R. Epstein later recalled that the ADL rejected an attempt by Roy Cohn, McCarthy's associate, to join the ADL National Commission because "we rejected Mr. Cohn's methods, and the methods of Mr. McCarthy." Benjamin R. Epstein Oral Memoir, in Cohen and Wexler, "Not the Work of a Day," 1:133–134, 147–148. On the reluctance of liberal anticommunists and anticommunist socialists to publicly criticize McCarthy before 1954, see Bloch, "The Emergence of Neoconservatism," pp. 50–52, 55, 57.

56. Quoted from AJCongress, "Fact Sheet V: The Federal Employee Security Program," n.d., in AJCongress records, box 31.

57. Quoted from Walker, *In Defense of American Liberties*, p. 178; *ADL Bulletin*, 12,4 (April 1955), p. 1.

58. AJCongress, "Fact Sheet V: The Federal Employee Security Program," n.d., in AJCongress records, box 31; Caute, *The Great Fear*, p. 278; *ADL Bulletin*, 12,4 (April 1955), p. 1.

59. Rorty, "The Dossier of Wolf Ladejinsky," pp. 326–334 (the quote is from p. 326); Cohen, *Not Free to Desist*, pp. 359–360. The letter, written by George M. Vitt and

released by the Department of Agriculture's Milan D. Smith, is quoted by Rorty on pp. 327–328. The fact that Ladejinsky had worked briefly during the early 1930s as an interpreter for Amtorg, the Soviet trading company, was also used to impugn his loyalty.

60. *Committee Reporter*, 12,2 (March 1955), p. 4; Cohen, *Not Free to Desist*, pp. 359–360; Rorty, "The Dossier of Wolf Ladejinsky," pp. 326, 333–334; Caute, *The Great Fear*, p. 308.

61. Cain, "Security of the Republic," p. 8. Cain's remarks were originally made in a speech delivered on January 15, 1955.

62. Cohen, *Not Free to Desist*, pp. 359–360; Caute, *The Great Fear*, p. 308; Rorty, "The Dossier of Wolf Ladejinsky," p. 328.

63. *ADL Bulletin*, 12,4 (April 1955), p. 1.

64. ADL National Commission minutes, November 20–22, 1953, pp. 10–11, in ADL records.

65. AJCongress, "Fact Sheet V: The Federal Employee Security Program," n.d., pp. 1–2, in AJCongress records, box 31; "Bills Drafted by the American Jewish Congress and Introduced in Various Legislatures, 1945–1955," August 1955, p. 4, in AJCongress records, box 37. AJCongress general counsel Will Maslow joined ADA national chairman Joseph L. Rauh, Jr., in testimony before a Senate subcommittee investigating the federal security program in August 1955. Rauh and Maslow both urged the Security Subcommittee of the Senate Post Office and Civil Service Committee to implement a variety of reforms designed to prevent infringements of individuals' civil liberties by the federal security program. *New York Times*, August 31, 1955, pp. 1, 12.

66. See Schlesinger, *The Vital Center*, pp. 213–218, for a concise formulation of the liberal anticommunist recommendations for the federal employee loyalty program.

67. ADL National Commission minutes, November 20–22, 1953, p. 6, in ADL records.

68. On the federal loyalty and security program see Caute, *The Great Fear*, pp. 267–293; McAuliffe, *Crisis on the Left*, pp. 77–83; Heale, *American Anticommunism*, pp. 137–138; Hamby, *Beyond the New Deal*, pp. 170–171, 387–388, 393–395, 397, 468.

69. Amendment of Minutes, ADL National Commission meeting, May 14–15, 1949, in ADL records. For evidence that the Truman loyalty program unfairly targeted African Americans, especially those involved in civil rights activities, see McCoy and Ruetten, *Quest and Response*, pp. 263–265. For a subsequent, more extensive ADL resolution on the need to introduce specific civil libertarian reforms into the federal loyalty program, see ADL National Commission minutes, November 20–22, 1953, pp. 10–11.

70. "The Year in Retrospect," excerpts from address by Irving M. Engel, in *Committee Reporter*, 8,3 (February-March 1951), p. 4. Engel served as president of the AJC from 1954 to 1959.

71. "Statement of Aaron Lewittes on behalf of AJCongress on Mundt and Ferguson Bill (S. 1194 and 1196) before Sub-Committee of Senate Committee on Judiciary," pp. 1, 6, June 8, 1949, in AJCongress records, box 36. See also resolution against Mundt-Ferguson Bill adopted at the National Convention of the American Jewish Congress, November 9–13, 1949, in AJCongress records, box 12.

72. Resolution Against the Mundt-Ferguson-Johnston and Nixon Bills, March 24, 1950, appended to Background Memorandum no. 1, "The Problem of Civil Liberties," AJC National Executive Committee Meeting, April 29–30, 1950, in AJC records, box

246, "Polit Phil/Communism Jan-May 1950." See also "Joint Statement on the Mundt-Ferguson-Johnston and Nixon bills (S. 2311 and H.R. 7595)," March 31, 1950, in AJCongress records, box 33; *AJYB* 52 (1951), p. 84; George J. Hexter to Alfred Kohlberg, August 31, 1950, pp. 1–2, in AJC records, box 246, "Polit Phil Communism Sept-Dec 1950." On the legislative history of the Mundt-Nixon bills, see Tanner and Griffith, "Legislative Politics and 'McCarthyism,' " pp. 176–178.

73. The measure in question was introduced by Senator Warren G. Magnuson and Representative Emmanuel Celler. Louis Breier to William Katz, August 31, 1950 (note pencil inscription: "same letter sent to all field reps") in AJC records, box 246, "Polit Phil Communism June-August 1950." The quoted phrase is from a statement issued by the National Civil Liberties Clearing House, whose signatories included all the constituent organizations of the NCRAC. "News from NCRAC" press release, stamped received August 28, 1950, in Nearprint files, "Slawson, John," *AJA*. The Jewish community's opposition to the McCarran Act, the Mundt-Nixon bills, and related measures is also discussed in Dollinger, "The Politics of Acculturation," pp. 164–168.

74. Typescript of telegram from NCRAC to Truman, September 1950, in AJC records, box 246, "Polit Phil Communism Sept-Dec 1950."

75. CLSA report, "The Internal Security Act of 1950 (The McCarran Act): An Evaluation and Analysis," 1950, in AJCongress records, box 36; AJCongress-CLSA, "Report of Activities 1950," p. 15, in AJCongress records, box 40; *AJYB* 52 (1951), p. 84; Resolution Adopted by the National Administrative Committee of the American Jewish Congress, November 19, 1950, in AJC records, box 251, "NCRAC—Polit Phil/Communism." On the provisions and implementation of the McCarran Act, see Tanner and Griffith, "Legislative Politics and 'McCarthyism,' " pp. 172–189; Heale, *American Anticommunism*, p. 156.

76. Transcript of ADL National Commission meeting, October 24–26, 1952, pp. 61, 207; ADL National Commission minutes, October 24–26, 1952, pp. 11–12, in ADL records; David Petegorsky, "Progress and Prospect—A Report on the American Jewish Congress," Submitted by the Executive Director to the Biennial National Convention, November 17–19, 1951, pp. 26–27, in AJCongress records, box 20. On the general liberal reaction to the McCarran Act, see Tanner and Griffith, "Legislative Politics and 'McCarthyism,' " pp. 181–182.

77. Allport, *The Nature of Prejudice*, p. 503.

78. Resolution Adopted by the National Administrative Committee of the American Jewish Congress, November 19, 1950 (quote is from p. 1), in AJC records, box 251, "NCRAC—Polit Phil/Communism"; Resolutions on Civil Liberties Adopted at the National Convention of the American Jewish Congress, November 9–13, 1949, in AJCongress records, box 12; ADL National Executive Committee minutes, October 1955; Resolution on Communism and Civil Liberties, attached to ADL National Executive Committee minutes, May 16–17, 1953, in ADL records; "Proposed Memorandum for Guidance on Certain Problems Related to Communism," Approved by the Ad Hoc Committee on Problems Related to Communism, January 27, 1951, p. 1, in AJC records, box 247, "AJC—Ad Hoc Committee on Problems Related to Communism"; Memorandum re: report on civil liberties and communism, from Morris Fine to John Slawson, January 15, 1953, in AJC records, box 248, "Communism, Program"; *Committee Reporter*, 12,2 (March 1955), p. 4.

79. The lawyers at the NAACP Legal Defense and Educational Fund asked themselves similar questions and determined, like the AJC and ADL, to avoid becoming involved in civil liberties cases that were not directly connected with their civil rights mandate. Greenberg, *Crusaders in the Courts*, p. 351.

80. Quoted from "General Jurisdiction of ADL in Matters Effecting Civil Rights and Civil Liberties (Authority: Proceedings of the National Commission, October 22, 1950)," in folder entitled "ADL Stands on Various Issues." Other accounts and confirmations of the 1950 policy were given in ADL National Commission minutes, 1951, pp. 12, 14; Transcript of ADL National Commission meeting, October 24–26, 1952, pp. 57–58; ADL National Commission minutes, October 24–26, 1952, p. 12; Memorandum from Arnold Forster to Monroe R. Sheinberg, July 30, 1953, p. 1, and Memorandum from Benjamin R. Epstein to National Executive Committee, July 28, 1953 (both in Civil Rights Committee bound volume, January 1952 to May 1954); Report of the National Director, ADL National Commission minutes, April 29–May 1, 1955, pp. 23–25, in ADL records.

81. Report of the National Director, ADL National Commission minutes, April 29–May 1, 1955, p. 24, in ADL records.

82. "ADL Policy and Civil Liberties," memorandum from Arnold Forster and Lester J. Waldman to National Civil Rights Committee and National Program Committee, October 1952, pp. 1–2, in National Civil Rights Committee binder, ADL records.

83. Ibid., p. 2.

84. Ibid., p. 3. Transcript of ADL National Commission meeting, October 24–26, 1952, pp. 60–61; ADL National Commission minutes, October 24–26, 1952, pp. 11–12 (quote from p. 12), in ADL records.

85. Background Memorandum no. 1, "The Problem of Civil Liberties," AJC National Executive Committee Meeting, April 29–30, 1950, pp. 2–3, in AJC records, box 246, "Polit Phil Communism Jan-May 1950."

86. Ibid.

87. *Law and Social Action*, 4,5 (September-October 1949), p. 110, in AJCongress records, box 44. The Supreme Court refused to hear the case. See Navasky, *Naming Names*, p. 84; Caute, *The Great Fear*, p. 498.

88. Navasky, *Naming Names*, pp. 112–113, 123–127 (quote from p. 113); John Slawson to Edmund Waterman, November 22, 1950, re: AJC opposition to "Red Channels," in AJC records, box 246, "Polit Phil Communism Sept-Dec 1950"; Forster, *Square One*, pp. 145–147; Adler, "The Politics of Culture," pp. 242–260. Deborah Dash Moore, in her analysis of the reaction of the Los Angeles Jewish community to anticommunism, argues that "creation of the blacklist pitted Jews against each other." Moore, like Navasky, notes that Jewish entertainment lawyers such as Martin Gang, a leader of the Los Angeles AJC chapter, similarly served as "clearance" lawyers. See Moore, *To the Golden Cities*, pp. 195–196, 200–201; Navasky, *Naming Names*, pp. 98–100.

89. The AJCongress opposed loyalty oath measures "dealing with an individual's political beliefs other than his allegiance to the Constitution" in a number of states, including New Jersey, New York, and Michigan. See David Petegorsky, "Progress and Prospect—A Report on the American Jewish Congress," Submitted by the Executive Director to the Biennial National Convention, November 17–19, 1951, p. 27, in AJCongress records, box 20; *Law and Social Action*, 4,5 (September-October 1949), p. 110, in AJCongress records, box 44; Resolution on Civil Liberties, adopted at the

National Convention of the American Jewish Congress, November 9–13, 1949, in AJCongress records, box 12.

90. ADL National Commission minutes, 1951, pp. 12–15, in ADL records.

91. ADL National Executive Commission minutes, May 1–2, 1953, p. 2, in ADL records.

92. The Feinberg Law (Chapter 360 of the Laws of 1949) was designed to fortify existing statutes, passed in 1917 and 1939, which banned those advocating sedition or the overthrow of the government by violent or unlawful means from employment in the public school system. See Brief of American Jewish Congress as Amicus Curiae, by Will Maslow and Shad Polier, in the case of *Thompson v. Wallin*, Supreme Court of the State of New York, County of Albany, October 6, 1949, pp. 1–2, in AJCongress records, box 189; *Thompson v. Wallin* and *L'Hommedieu v. Board of Regents*, 93 N.Y.S.2d 274 (1949); Heale, *American Anticommunism*, pp. 185–186.

93. The AJC's failure to take a strong stand against the Feinberg Law seems to have reflected the divide within the committee's staff, which is explored further in chapter 7, over the proper balance between the demands of anticommunism and civil liberties. In June 1950 members of the AJC Staff Civil Rights Committee, who tended to emphasize civil liberties, discussed the case of eight New York City school teachers who had been dismissed under the Feinberg Law and determined that "it shall be the position of the American Jewish Committee that membership in the Communist party alone should not be considered adequate grounds for dismissal from employment." Minutes of AJC Staff Civil Rights Committee, June 6, 1950, p. 1, in AJC records, box 246, "Polit Phil Communism June-August 1950." In August of the same year the New York chapter AJC Civil Rights Department discussed the possibility of joining the ACLU and AJCongress in an *amicus* brief challenging the constitutionality of the Feinberg Law in the consolidated cases of *Thompson v. Wallin* and *L'Hommedieu v. Board of Regents*, 95 N.E.2d 806 (1950), before the Court of Appeals of New York. Civil Rights Dept. memorandum, August 29, 1950, pp. 2–3, in AJC records, box 246, "Polit Phil Communism June-August 1950." Several years later, however, Morris Fine, chairman of the AJC's Committee on Communism and Civil Liberties, suggested that most of his committee agreed that "avowed" communists should be prevented from teaching in the public schools. Although members of the Fine committee contended that the Feinberg Law unfairly singled out public school teachers and was improperly enforced, "no one suggested that the AJC should take any action on the Feinberg Law at this time other than to watch the methods used to enforce it." AJC memorandum, from Morris Fine to Members of Staff Committee on the Problem of Communism and Civil Liberties, June 27, 1952, p. 3, in AJC records, box 246, "Polit Phil Communism 51–53"; AJC memorandum, from Morris Fine to John Slawson, January 15, 1953, pp. 4–5, in AJC records, box 248, "Communism Program 53–57."

94. Quoted from copy of *amicus* brief, p. 3, in AJCongress records, box 31; *Law and Social Action*, 4,5 (September-October, 1949), p. 110. While the New York State Supreme Court declared the Feinberg Law unconstitutional in 1949, the law was upheld by New York's highest court in 1950 and by the United States Supreme Court two years later. The Feinberg Law remained on the books until it was declared unconstitutional by the United States Supreme Court in 1967. AJCongress memorandum, from Leo Pfeffer, December 2, 1949, p. 1, in AJC records, box 246, "Polit Phil Communism Sept-Dec 1950"; *AJYB* 52 (1951), pp. 26–27; *AJYB* 54 (1953), p. 28; *Thompson v.*

Wallin, 93 N.Y.S.2d 274 (1949), *rev'd*, 95 N.Y.S.2d 784 (1950), *aff'd*, 95 N.E.2d 806 (1950), *aff'd sub nom, Adler v. Bd. of Educ.*, 342 U.S. 485 (1952); *Keyishian v. Bd. of Regents*, 385 U.S. 589 (1967).

95. John Paul Jones, Osmond K. Fraenkel, Roger N. Baldwin, Shad Polier, and Melvin Mandell to New York Board of Regents, April 20, 1949, in AJC records, box 246, "1949 Communism."

96. See Markowitz, *My Daughter, the Teacher*, pp. 4, 151–172 passim. Markowitz notes that all of the teachers who were dismissed during the postwar Red Scare were Jews who were active in the Teachers Union. Ibid., pp. 151, 166–170.

97. Herman L. Weisman to Hon. Chauncey W. Reed, Chairman of House Committee on Judiciary, February 25, 1954, p. 1, in AJCongress records, box 41.

98. "Annual Report 1958: Commission on Law and Social Action, American Jewish Congress," p. 6, in AJCongress records, box 41.

99. AJCongress *amicus* brief to United States Supreme Court, October 1957, in *Speiser v. Randall* and *Prince v. City and County of San Francisco*, written by Shad Polier, Will Maslow, and Leo Pfeffer, p. 2, in AJCongress records, box 190. For the disposition of the case, see *Speiser v. Randall* and *Prince v. City and County of San Francisco*, 357 U.S. 513 (1958).

100. Quoted from Resolution on Civil Liberties, adopted at the National Convention of the American Jewish Congress, November 9–13, 1949, in AJCongress records, box 12. AJCongress's leaders' forthright recognition of the threat posed to the agency (and liberalism in general) by communism is given clear expression in "Address at the Opening Session of the National Convention of the American Jewish Congress, November 9, 1949, by Hon. Justine Wise Polier, President, Women's Division," p. 2, in AJCongress records, box 19.

101. The origins, constituencies, and politics of the AJC, ADL, and AJCongress in the period before World War II are briefly considered in chapter 1. For a more lengthy discussion, see Svonkin, "Jews Against Prejudice," pp. 24–36.

102. On the ADL and AJC's cooperation with the FBI, HUAC, and other federal agencies, see AJC memorandum, from Joel D. Wolfsohn to John Slawson, May 25, 1949, in AJC records, box 249, "Polit Phil Communism Jews AJC"; "Seventh Report of Staff Coordinator of Program on Communism," S. Andhil Fineberg to John Slawson, February 1955, p. 3, in AJC records, box 247, "Polit Phil Communism 48–61"; Edwin J. Lukas to Senator Robert Morris, Senate Internal Security Subcommittee, March 30, 1956; Edwin J. Lukas to Courtney E. Owens, House Committee on Un-American Activities, October 29, 1954, in AJC records, RG 347.17 Gen-12, box 65, "Jewish Peoples Fraternal Order"; AJC Community Affairs Dept. memorandum, S. Andhil Fineberg to John Slawson, re: Fineberg's role in HUAC Investigation of Committee to Secure Justice in the Rosenberg Case, October 10, 1955; S. Andhil Fineberg memo to "AJC, CRC and ADL local directors," re: HUAC investigation of Committee to Secure Justice in the Rosenberg Case, September 1956, p. 1; AJC memorandum, Seymour Samet to Manheim Shapiro, March 27, 1953; AJC memorandum, Morris Fine to John Slawson, October 22, 1953; Seymour J. Rubin to Simon Segal, February 15, 1954, in AJC records, RG 347.17 Gen-12, box 139, "Rosenberg Case 53–57"; ADL National Commission minutes, November 20–22, 1953, p. 7, in ADL records; interview with Arnold Forster by author, June 11, 1996; Cohen, *Not Free to Desist*, pp. 354–356, 358; Navasky, *Naming Names*, pp. 118–120. See also the documents reproduced in Berkson, "The Case of Julius and Ethel Rosenberg," pp. 207–210.

103. Resolution on HUAC passed at the Biennial Convention of the American Jewish Congress, April 4, 1948, p. 4; Resolution on civil liberties adopted at the National Convention of the American Jewish Congress, November 9–13, 1949, in AJCongress records, box 12.

6. The Contradictions of Cold War Liberalism

1. ADL National Commission meeting transcript, October 24–26, 1952, pp. 20–21, in ADL records; Ross, "The Communists: Friends or Foes of Civil Liberties?" pp. 4–7.

2. This analysis of the riots draws heavily upon contemporary accounts, each of which represented—and thus helps to illuminate—a particular ideological perspective. The New York papers, including the *New York Times* and the *New York Post-Home News*, put the riots into the context of the rising tide of concern over communism, even as their editorials expressed dismay over the violence. The anticommunist view was given by James Rorty and Winifred Rauschenbush, in their *Commentary* article, "The Lessons of the Peekskill Riots." A report by the American Civil Liberties Union, entitled "Violence in Peekskill," emphasized that the riots effectively prevented Robeson and his supporters from exercising their constitutional liberties. The findings of the state's official investigation, which was strongly influenced by the politics of anticommunism, can be found in Supreme Court of the State of New York, County of Westchester, "Presentment of the October 1949 Grand Jury of Westchester County," hereafter cited as Grand Jury Presentment. A pro-Robeson interpretation was given by the Westchester Committee for a Fair Inquiry into the Peekskill Violence in a pamphlet entitled *Eyewitness: Peekskill U.S.A.* Howard Fast's version of events can be found in Fast, *Peekskill: USA: A Personal Experience* and in his memoir, *Being Red*, pp. 226–238. Robeson's own comments on the incidents can be gleaned from Foner, *Paul Robeson Speaks*, especially pp. 224, 230–233, 235, 236–241, 309, 390–393. I have also benefited from the work of several historians who have examined these incidents. For an account that places the riots in geographical and cultural context, see Shargel, "Leftist Summer Colonies," pp. 352–354. An analysis by a sympathetic Robeson biographer can be found in Duberman, *Paul Robeson*, pp. 364–374.

3. Rorty and Rauschenbush, "The Lessons of the Peekskill Riots," pp. 310, 312; ACLU, "Violence in Peekskill," pp. 5–8; Grand Jury Presentment, p. 5; Shargel, "Leftist Summer Colonies," p. 352; Fast, *Peekskill: USA*, pp. 15, 71; *New York Times*, September 4, 1949, p. 28.

4. ACLU, "Violence in Peekskill," p. 6; Rorty and Rauschenbush, "The Lessons of the Peekskill Riots," pp. 310–311; Shargel, "Leftist Summer Colonies," pp. 352, 352 n.

5. Rorty and Rauschenbush, "Lessons of the Peekskill Riots," p. 311; *AJYB*, 52 (1951), p. 62.

6. Rorty and Rauschenbush, "The Lessons of the Peekskill Riots," pp. 311–312; ACLU, "Violence in Peekskill," pp. 7–9; Grand Jury Presentment, pp. 5–7; Shargel, "Leftist Summer Colonies," pp. 338–352 passim. My use of the term *interethnic* to describe relations among Peekskill-area Protestants, Catholics, and Jews reflects my conviction that the differences and tensions among the groups were not limited to issues that can properly be considered to be matters of religion. I conceive of the term *interethnic* as a more inclusive description of these relations, one aspect of which could

be described as *interreligious*. The most useful term to describe these relations is *ethnoreligious*, but *interethnoreligious* is too awkward.

7. Liberal anticommunists avoided collaboration with the Civil Rights Congress. During the organization of the National Emergency Civil Rights Mobilization in late 1949 and early 1950, the NAACP and participating religious, labor, and civic agencies "fended off attempts of the Civil Rights Congress to infiltrate the movement." McCoy and Ruetten, *Quest and Response*, p. 190. On the NAACP Legal Defense and Educational Fund's differences with the Civil Rights Congress during the early 1950s, see Greenberg, *Crusaders in the Courts*, pp. 101–102. Arthur M. Schlesinger, Jr., characterized the Civil Rights Congress as one of "the more obvious Communist-controlled groups." Schlesinger, *The Vital Center*, p. 121.

8. Grand Jury Presentment, p. 7; Rorty and Rauschenbush, "The Lessons of the Peekskill Riots," p. 312; Duberman, *Paul Robeson*, p. 364; Fast, *Peekskill: USA*, p. 15; Kaufman, *Broken Alliance*, pp. 203–204, 206; Friedman, *What Went Wrong?* pp. 119–120, 231.

9. In 1948 Robeson was an ardent supporter of Henry Wallace's Progressive Party campaign for the presidency, a candidacy that both conservative and liberal critics attacked as communist controlled. In April 1949, at the Paris World Peace Conference, Robeson made a speech that was widely (although erroneously, according to Martin B. Duberman) reported to include the statement: "It is unthinkable that American Negroes would go to war on behalf of those who have oppressed us for generations against a country [e.g., the Soviet Union] which in one generation has raised our people to the full dignity of mankind." Robeson also took an active part in the protests against the trial of Communist Party leaders for violating the Smith Act, which was underway during the period of the riots. Robeson appeared at the trial to testify as a defense witness. Although he was unable to present his testimony in court, he publicly praised the Communist Party for its commitment to racial equality. See McCoy and Ruetten, *Quest and Response*, pp. 112, 128; Duberman, *Paul Robeson*, pp. 316–362 passim (see p. 342 for Peace Conference quote); Foner, *Paul Robeson Speaks*, pp. 3–4, 19–21, 230–233, 236–241; Dudziak, "Desegregation as a Cold War Imperative," p. 107 n.; *New York Times*, August 27, 1949, p. 6.

10. Grand Jury Presentment, p. 8.

11. Peekskill *Evening Star*, August 23, 1949, quoted in ACLU, "Violence in Peekskill," p. 12; Grand Jury Presentment, pp. 9–10; Rorty and Rauschenbush, "The Lessons of the Peekskill Riots," pp. 313–314.

12. Peekskill *Evening Star*, August 23, 1949, quoted in ACLU, "Violence in Peekskill," p. 13; Rorty and Rauschenbush, "The Lessons of the Peekskill Riots," p. 313.

13. Duberman, *Paul Robeson*, p. 364; Westchester Committee, *Eyewitness: Peekskill U.S.A.*, n.p.; Shargel, "Leftist Summer Colonies," p. 353 n.; *New York Times*, August 27, 1949, p. 6; August 28, 1949, p. 52; August 31, 1949, p. 16; September 4, 1949, p. 17; *New York Post-Home News*, August 31, 1949, p. 20.

14. In the midst of the chaos a local veteran who was part of the anti-Robeson demonstration was stabbed. There were conflicting claims as to whether the veteran was wounded before or after the rioting broke out. Those sources (including the grand jury presentment) most sympathetic to the veterans argued that the stabbing catalyzed the riot, while those most sympathetic to Robeson (especially the Westchester Committee report) argued that the stabbing occurred as a result of the riot. ACLU, "Violence

in Peekskill," pp. 17–26; Rorty and Rauschenbush, "The Lessons of the Peekskill Riots," pp. 314–315; Grand Jury Presentment, pp. 9–15; Duberman, *Paul Robeson*, pp. 364, 366; *New York Times*, August 28, 1949, pp. 1, 52. The American Legion leader is quoted in the *New York Times*, August 30, 1949, p. 28.

15. Rorty and Rauschenbush, "The Lessons of the Peekskill Riots," p. 317; ACLU, "Violence in Peekskill," pp. 31–45 passim; Grand Jury Presentment, pp. 20–25; Duberman, *Paul Robeson*, pp. 368–370; Shargel, "Leftist Summer Colonies," pp. 353–354; *New York Times*, September 4, 1949, pp. 1, 17; September 5, 1949, pp. 1, 3; September 6, 1949, pp. 1, 23, 26; September 8, 1949, p. 34; *New York Post-Home News*, September 6, 1949, pp. 2, 6, 7; Fast, *Peekskill: USA*, pp. 69–91 passim.

16. After the first riot some local residents proudly displayed placards, banners, and automobile stickers bearing the slogan, "Wake Up America—Peekskill Did!" Rorty and Rauschenbush, "The Lessons of the Peekskill Riots" (the quoted phrase in the text is from p. 309); ACLU, "Violence in Peekskill," pp. 27, 38, 46; Fast, *Peekskill: USA*, p. 73; *New York Times*, September 4, 1949, p. 17; *New York Post-Home News*, September 6, 1949, p. 7.

17. Governor Dewey's charge to the Westchester County district attorney is included in the Grand Jury Presentment, p. 2.

18. Westchester Committee, *Eyewitness: Peekskill U.S.A.*, n.p.; Grand Jury Presentment, p. 17; Fast, *Being Red*, pp. 226–238; Fast, *Peekskill: USA*, pp. 14, 18, 20–50, 57, 67–68, 69, 78–79, 80, 84, 86–89, 91, 93–94; *New York Times*, August 29, 1949, p. 19; September 5, 1949, p. 2; September 6, 1949, pp. 1, 23; September 7, 1949, p. 22; *New York Post-Home News*, August 29, 1949, pp. 2, 14; September 1, 1949, p. 1; September 6, 1949, p. 2; *National Guardian*, September 5, 1949, pp. 1, 3; September 12, 1949, p. 5. Interestingly, one of the officers of the pro-Robeson Westchester Committee was Dr. Goodwin Watson, a Columbia University social psychologist who was the author of an intergroup relations study sponsored by the American Jewish Congress. Clipping from *The Daily Argus* (Mt. Vernon, N.Y.), December 9, 1949, in SAF papers, box 4, AJA; Watson, *Action for Unity*.

19. Westchester Committee, *Eyewitness: Peekskill U.S.A.*, n.p.

20. Quoted in Foner, *Paul Robeson Speaks*, p. 224. See also Grand Jury Presentment, p. 17.

21. Robeson's remarks are quoted in Duberman, *Paul Robeson*, p. 370; Rorty and Rauschenbush, "The Lessons of the Peekskill Riots," p. 321; *New York Times*, September 6, 1949, p. 23. At a concert in Los Angeles several weeks later, Robeson similarly "thanked the Jewish people of Peekskill for having turned out in numbers to protect him in that town." Duberman, *Paul Robeson*, p. 377.

22. Quoted in Foner, *Paul Robeson Speaks*, p. 235. See also *National Guardian*, September 12, 1949, pp. 1, 4; September 26, 1949, p. 7, for explicit comparisons of the Peekskill riots with German fascism.

23. Quoted from Patterson's introduction to Fast, *Peekskill: USA*, p. 7.

24. Ibid., p. 93. The allegation that the riots presaged the advent of American fascism pervaded Fast's account.

25. The investigation was conducted by Westchester County District Attorney George M. Fanelli, who had directed the police operations during the September 4th concert. The ACLU, the ADL, the JWV, the AJCongress, the Civil Rights Congress, and other organizations protested this obvious conflict of interest and recommended, with-

out success, that a more objective person be chosen to conduct the proceedings before the grand jury. ACLU, "Statement by American Civil Liberties Union," p. 2; ACLU, "Violence in Peekskill," p. 2; *New York Times*, August 31, 1949, p. 16; September 1, 1949, p. 5; September 10, 1949, p. 8; *New York Post-Home News*, September 1, 1949, p. X2; September 2, 1949, p. 2; *ADL Bulletin*, 6,7 (October 1949), pp. 2, 8.

26. Grand Jury Presentment, pp. 2–3, 11–12, 14–15, 20–23, 25.

27. Ibid., pp. 15–16.

28. Ibid., pp. 22, 28.

29. The quote is from a memorandum from the Chicago Commission on Human Relations, [September, 1949?], p. 1, in AJC records, box 246, "1949 Communism."

30. The national leadership of the JWV had originally suggested that the protest parade, if it had to be held at all, should be held at a separate location. After the riots, the national leaders of the JWV emphasized that local JWV members who had participated in the parade were in violation of the national organization's charter. CRC minutes, September 9 and 11, 1949, New York City, p. 1, in AJC records, box 251, "Communism 49"; ACLU report, "Violence in Peekskill," p. 22; Rorty and Rauschenbush, "The Lessons of the Peekskill Riots," pp. 314–315; ACLU, "Statement by American Civil Liberties Union," p. 8; Grand Jury Presentment, p. 28; *New York Times*, August 31, 1949, p. 16; September 1, 1949, p. 5; September 2, 1949, p. 10; September 3, 1949, p. 11; September 4, 1949, p. 17; *New York Post-Home News*, August 31, 1949, p. 20.

31. On the origins and early history of *Commentary*, see Shapiro, *A Time for Healing*, pp. 23–26.

32. See Teller, *Strangers and Natives*, p. 258.

33. The AJC's S. Andhil Fineberg corresponded with Irving Kristol about the best means for battling communist influence among liberals and those "anti-anticommunists"—such as the adherents of the Emergency Civil Liberties Committee—they saw as aiding the communist cause. S. Andhil Fineberg to Irving Kristol, January 22 and 23, 1953, in SAF papers, box 1, AJA. On the anticommunism of the *Commentary* editors, see Shapiro, *A Time for Healing*, pp. 25–26. The role of *Commentary* in the AJC's anticommunist campaign is detailed in Typescript, "The Problem of Disassociating Jews and Communists in the Public Mind," [prepared by Elliot Cohen], January 7, 1948, pp. 1–4; AJC memorandum, from S. Andhil Fineberg, "Proposed Program in Reference to Communism," August 8, 1950, pp. 4–5, in SAF papers, box 1, AJA. The arrangements for reprints of the Rorty-Rauschenbush article are discussed in Second Report of the Staff Coordinator of Program on Communism, S. Andhil Fineberg to John Slawson, November 28, 1950, p. 5, in AJC records, box 248, "Polit Phil Communism Program Activities 50–55." The Rorty-Rauschenbush article is also cited as part of the AJC's anticommunist program in Third Report of the Staff Coordinator of Program on Communism, S. Andhil Fineberg to John Slawson, April 3, 1951, p. 7, in AJC records, box 248, "Polit Phil Communism Program Activities 50–55." Members of the *Commentary* editorial staff were active in the ACCF. Until he left his position with the magazine in 1953, Irving Kristol served simultaneously as a *Commentary* editor and as executive director of the ACCF. See Bloch, "The Emergence of Neoconservatism," pp. 38–41. For a discussion of the ACCF and its position on anticommunism and civil liberties, see McAuliffe, *Crisis on the Left*, pp. 108–129. Michael Kazin classifies Rorty as a conservative intellectual, whom he associates with Will Herberg, Whittaker Chambers, Max Eastman, Eugene Lyons, and other right-wing ex-Marxists, in *The Populist*

Persuasion, p. 171. See also James Rorty and Moshe Decter, *McCarthy and the Communists* (Boston: Beacon, 1954).

34. Rorty and Rauschenbush, "The Lessons of the Peekskill Riots," p. 312.

35. Ibid., pp. 315, 317–318.

36. Ibid., p. 320. Similar interpretations of the riots as part of a communist propaganda plot were printed in *Life* and *Newsweek* and are quoted in Duberman, *Paul Robeson*, pp. 370–371.

37. Rorty and Rauschenbush characterized the grand jury report as "temperate and fair in its review of the facts, intelligent and liberal in its recommendations." They saw the ACLU report, by contrast, as naive and "cavalier" in handling the facts of the riots. Rorty and Rauschenbush, "The Lessons of the Peekskill Riots," p. 320.

38. Ibid., pp. 312, 314.

39. For the development of the "quarantine strategy" and debate over its value, see Fineberg, *Overcoming Anti-Semitism*; Fineberg, *Punishment Without Crime*; Fineberg, "Checkmate for Rabble-Rousers"; Fineberg, "Deflating the Professional Bigot," reprinted in Newman, *The Hate Reader*, pp. 111–116; Glatstein and Howe, "How to Fight Rabble-Rousers?"; Riesman, "The 'Militant' Fight Against Anti-Semitism"; Allport, *The Nature of Prejudice*, pp. 468–469; Solomon Andhil Fineberg Oral History Interview, 1:42 to 1:48, 2:55, 2:70, transcript in SAF papers, box 5, AJA. Additional material on the subject can be found in SAF papers, boxes 1 and 2, AJA. On quarantine and the history of group libel law during and after World War II more generally, see Walker, *Hate Speech*, pp. 77–100. The divergent approaches of the major Jewish agencies are discussed in Moore, *To the Golden Cities*, pp. 165–166; AJC memorandum, S. Andhil Fineberg to David Danzig, October 1, 1952, re: THE TROUBLEMAKERS, p. 2; AJC memorandum, Solomon Andhil Fineberg, "Publicity for Anti-Semitism in the Responsible Press," October 31, 1958, p. 6, in SAF papers, box 2, AJA; Benjamin R. Epstein Oral Memoir, in Cohen and Wexler, "*Not the Work of a Day*," 1:59, 93. The AJCongress, which had a long history of supporting mass protest against anti-Semitism, dissented from the quarantine approach during and immediately after World War II. When the NCRAC officially endorsed the quarantine treatment in 1947, David Petegorsky of the AJCongress presented the "minority view," in which the AJCongress expressed its opinion that "counter-demonstrations against rabble-rousers" were "of utmost importance." "Unanimous Adoption of Quarantine Treatment from the Minutes of the Executive Committee of the National Community Relations Advisory Council, December 17, 1947," in SAF papers, box 2, AJA. During the 1940s and early 1950s the AJCongress favored the passage of group libel laws that would have prohibited certain expressions of racial, religious, and ethnic hatred. Later the organization rejected this strategy. See Maslow and Robison, "Civil Rights: A Program for the President's Committee," pp. 119–120; Walker, *Hate Speech*, pp. 77, 82, 83, 99, 100, 186 n. 3.

40. S. Andhil Fineberg to Noah H. Andur, December 15, 1949, in AJC records, box 246, "1949 Communism."

41. CRC minutes, September 9 and 11, 1949, New York City (the quote is from p. 1), in AJC records, box 251, "Communism 49"; Rorty and Rauschenbush, "The Lessons of the Peekskill Riots," p. 319; NCRAC memorandum, "Suggestions for the Guidance of Jewish Organizations in Connection with the Paul Robeson Tour," October 10, 1949, in AJC records, box 246, "1949 Communism"; Minutes of NCRAC Committee on Overt

Anti-Semitism, November 7, 1949, p. 1, in AJC records, RG 347.17 Gen-12, "Robeson, Paul 49"; Memorandum from Chicago Commission on Human Relations, [September 1949?], p. 1, in AJC records, box 246, "1949 Communism"; Memorandum from S. Andhil Fineberg to John Slawson, "Preventing Riot Incident to Communist Meetings," September 20, 1949, pp. 1–2, in SAF papers, box 1, AJA; ACLU, "Violence in Peekskill," p. 48; Duberman, *Paul Robeson*, pp. 375–378. After the first riot the national commander of the JWV threatened to "court martial" any JWV member who had participated in the violence. *New York Times*, August 31, 1949, p. 16; *New York Post-Home News*, August 31, 1949, p. 20; Shargel, "Leftist Summer Colonies," p. 353 n. JWV officials from Westchester County, however, "defended the Peekskill post of the JWV as having participated in a 'peaceful, orderly protest parade.'" *New York Times*, September 1, 1949, p. 5.

42. Rorty and Rauschenbush, "The Lessons of the Peekskill Riots," pp. 320–321. Randolph took a position comparable to that of the AJC and ADL. While he condemned the violence directed against Robeson and the concertgoers, Randolph's main objective was "dissociating this whole affair from the cause of the Negro and his fight for liberation." Randolph emphasized that the Peekskill violence "was not racial" and that Robeson did not represent the black community. See Duberman, *Paul Robeson*, p. 374.

43. CRC minutes, September 9 and 11, 1949, New York City, pp. 1–2, in AJC records, box 251, "Communism 49."

44. Emergency Defense Committee Meeting minutes, September 14, 1949, p. 2, in AJC records, RG 347.17 Gen-12, "Robeson, Paul 49."

45. Ibid., pp. 1–2; CRC minutes, September 9 and 11, 1949, New York City, pp. 1–2, in AJC records, box 251, "Communism 49"; Rorty and Rauschenbush, "The Lessons of the Peekskill Riots," pp. 318–319.

46. ADL and AJC staff members recognized stickers (which read "Communism Is Treason, Behind Communism Stands—the Jew! Therefore, for My Country—Against the Jews") distributed in the Peekskill area during the period of the riots as the work of professional anti-Semites. *ADL Bulletin*, 6,7 (October 1949), pp. 2, 8; *AJYB* 52 (1951), pp. 62–63; Rorty and Rauschenbush, "The Lessons of the Peekskill Riots," p. 316; ACLU, "Violence in Peekskill," p. 44; Emergency Defense Committee Meeting minutes, September 14, 1949, pp. 3–4, in AJC records, RG 347.17 Gen-12, "Robeson, Paul 49"; CRC minutes, September 9 and 11, 1949, New York City, pp. 3–4, in AJC records, box 251, "Communism 49"; Grand Jury Presentment, p. 28.

47. Minutes of NCRAC Committee on Overt Anti-Semitism, November 7, 1949, p. 1, in AJC records, RG 347.17 Gen-12, "Robeson, Paul 49."

48. CRC minutes, September 9 and 11, 1949, New York City, pp. 2–3, in AJC records, box 251 "Communism 49."

49. Quoted from "Some Major AJC Intergroup Relations Programs of Interest to Jewish Communities Abroad," June 7, 1955, p. 7, in AJC records, box 163, "Report, 1955; 1948–1949." See also Benjamin R. Epstein Oral Memoir, in Cohen and Wexler, "*Not the Work of a Day*," 1:viii–ix, 60–61; Cohen, *Not Free to Desist*, pp. 214–215; Dinnerstein, *Antisemitism in America*. pp. 45–47, 69–71, 113–122 passim; Forster, *Square One*, pp. 66–67, 72, 74, 101, 148; *AJYB* 41 (1939–1940), p. 212.

50. Many contemporary (and subsequent) observers, including ADL and AJC staff members, argued that support for "McCarthyism," or demagogic anticommunism,

was particularly strong among American Catholics. In 1955, Morris N. Kertzer, the AJC's director of interreligious affairs, wrote, "Most Roman Catholics, at least in their organizational life, regard the threat to America posed by internal security problems [as being] so real and ever-present that they seem less interested in living up to the letter of the Constitution in civil liberties matters." Morris N. Kertzer, "The Nature and Scope of Religious Issues in the Community Today," June 20, 1955, p. 3, in AJC records, box 177, "Interreligious 1955." A similar argument can be found in AJC memorandum, "Political and Social Factors (to be considered in planning AJC's 1954 program)," November 18, 1953, p. 3, in AJC records, box 246, "Political Philosophies 46–54." See also the sources cited in the previous note. For scholarly analyses linking support for McCarthyism with Catholicism, see Lipset, "The Sources of the 'Radical Right,'" pp. 350–355; Lipset and Raab, *The Politics of Unreason*, pp. 213, 220, 224, 229, 231–232; Caute, *The Great Fear*, pp. 108–110. For historical analyses that argue that the organized Catholic community contained both right-wing (i.e., pro-McCarthy) and liberal (i.e., anti-McCarthy) anticommunists, see Crosby, *God, Church, and Flag*; Crosby, "The Politics of Religion." For a recent discussion of Catholic anticommunism after 1945, see Kazin, *The Populist Persuasion*, pp. 173–178.

51. *New York Times*, September 6, 1949, p. 23. Martin B. Duberman notes that the forces mobilized against Robeson on August 27 included not only veterans' associations but also individuals associated with St. Joseph's, the local Catholic high school, who "proudly unfurled . . . [the school's] banner" at the demonstration. Duberman, *Paul Robeson*, pp. 364–365. A Jewish resident of the Peekskill area blamed the August 27 riot on a group of "hoodlums," which she identified with "the Verplanck Irish." Mrs. Henry L. Messutta to Mrs. Newton S. Arnold, August 28, 1949, in AJCongress records, box 143.

52. The quoted phrase is from [AJC], "Proposed Three-Faith Statement on Injection of Spurious Religious Issues in the Battle Against Communism," July 1953, in AJC records, box 177, "Interreligious 1953." The contention that "religion and totalitarianism are irreconcilable" was also expressed in "Statement on Interreligious Cooperation," AJC 47th Annual Meeting, January 29–31, 1954, in AJC records, box 179, "Statements and Resolutions 47–57."

53. "Differences Are Opportunities: The Role of Religion and Religious Institutions in Intergroup Relations" (January 1956), pp. 15–16, in AJC records, box 163, "Intergroup Rel. 1950–1962."

54. Quoted in the *New York Times*, September 9, 1949, p. 15; *New York Post-Home News*, September 9, 1949, p. 3.

55. *New York Times*, August 31, 1949, p. 16; September 1, 1949, p. 5; September 7, 1949, p. 22; September 10, 1949, p. 8; Duberman, *Paul Robeson*, pp. 367, 371, 695 n. 19; Westchester Committee, *Eyewitness: Peekskill U.S.A.*, n.p. This disparity between AJC and AJCongress leaders and members persisted into the 1950s. In January 1953 Rabbi Joachim Prinz, who later became president of the AJCongress, was one of the sponsors of a "Conference on the Bill of Rights," held at Carnegie Hall under the auspices of the Emergency Civil Liberties Committee. In the same month S. Andhil Fineberg, the AJC's leading anticommunist, was seeking ways to limit the influence of the ECLC, whose leaders, he believed, had "a highly tender regard for Joseph Stalin and his henchmen." Clark Foreman to S. Andhil Fineberg, January 22, 1953; S. Andhil Fineberg to Clark Foreman, January 27, 1953, in SAF papers, box 1, AJA.

56. Resolutions Adopted at the National Convention of the American Jewish Congress, November 9–13, 1949, n.p., in AJCongress records, box 12.

57. Ibid.; NCRAC memorandum, from Samuel Spiegler to NCRAC Member Agencies, November 18, 1949, in AJC records, box 251, "Polit Phil Communism NCRAC 49–54." The AJCongress's position on anticommunism and civil liberties was made especially clear in "Resolution Adopted by the National Administrative Committee of the American Jewish Congress, November 19, 1950, on Civil Liberties," copy in AJC records, box 251.

58. The Council Against Intolerance was founded in 1938 by James Waterman Wise, the son of AJCongress President Stephen S. Wise. ACLU, "Violence in Peekskill," pp. 1–3; Rorty and Rauschenbush, "The Lessons of the Peekskill Riots," p. 310; Steele, "The War on Intolerance," p. 22.

59. ACLU, "Violence in Peekskill," pp. 1, 19, 21–22, 34, 44–45, 50 (quote from p. 50.) The AJCongress-NAACP annual report on civil rights for 1949 repeated these assertions. AJCongress and NAACP, *Civil Rights in the United States in 1949*, pp. 8, 9, 11.

60. ACLU, "Violence in Peekskill," pp. 1, 13–14, 16, 22, 25–27, 31–33, 38–40, 50.

61. Ibid., pp. 11, 17, 41–43. In the aftermath of the riots ACLU representatives solicited signatures for a public statement defending freedom of expression for communists and all other Americans. See Duberman, *Paul Robeson*, pp. 374, 697–698 n. 29.

62. ACLU, "Violence in Peekskill," p. 2 (emphasis added). A group of prominent African American leaders in Washington, D.C., which included church and NAACP officials, issued a similar statement that disagreed with some of Robeson's political beliefs but defended his right to freedom of speech. See Duberman, *Paul Robeson*, p. 377.

63. ACLU, "Violence in Peekskill," pp. 1–2, 32, 49; ACLU, "Statement By American Civil Liberties Union," p. 1.

64. Rorty and Rauschenbush, "The Lessons of the Peekskill Riots," pp. 321, 323 (the quoted phrase can be found on p. 323). For social scientists' distinctions between ethnic and ideological intolerance, see Petersen, "Prejudice in American Society," pp. 347–348; Allport, *The Nature of Prejudice*, pp. 253–257, 431–432.

65. Rorty and Rauschenbush, "The Lessons of the Peekskill Riots," pp. 322–323.

66. Grand Jury Presentment, pp. 27–28.

67. Schlesinger, *The Vital Center*, pp. 38, 40, 115, 159–160.

68. Kristol, " 'Civil Liberties,' 1952," pp. 230–231, 233–236 (the quote is from p. 231). See also Westin, "Our Freedom," p. 34.

69. Kristol, " 'Civil Liberties,' 1952," pp. 229, 236; Westin, "Our Freedom," pp. 33, 35–37 (quotes are from pp. 35 and 37). See Bloch, "The Emergence of Neoconservatism," pp. 45–47, for further discussion of Kristol's views.

70. AJC memorandum, "Political and Social Factors (to be considered in planning AJC's 1954 program)," November 18, 1953, p. 4, in AJC records, box 246, "Political Philosophies 46–54."

71. Schlesinger, *The Vital Center*; McAuliffe, *Crisis on the Left*; Crosby, *God, Church, and Flag*; Crosby, "The Politics of Religion"; Greenberg, *Crusaders in the Courts*, pp. 102–106, 349–353.

72. This terminology of "The Hards and the Softs" appeared in the *New Leader*, May 20, 1950, p. 30, and was called to my attention by McAuliffe's *Crisis on the Left*, pp. 109–115 (the quote is from p. 109). See also Norman Markowitz, "A View from the Left."

73. McAuliffe, *Crisis of the Left*, pp. 7–8, 108–129. The *New Leader* was founded by the Socialist Party and supported in its early years by the Jewish labor movement—especially the ILGWU. Originally an organ of the anti-Stalinist left, it moved increasingly toward an anticommunist liberalism in the postwar era. See Liebman, "The Ties That Bind," p. 299; Markowitz, "A View from the Left," pp. 94, 101; Bloch, "The Emergence of Neoconservatism," pp. 28–29. The AJC sometimes worked with the ACCF. In 1954, for example, the AJC cooperated with the ACCF in a dispute with the Emergency Civil Liberties Committee, which both agencies viewed as "soft" on communism. AJC Staff Committee on Communism minutes, March 23, 1954, p. 2, in AJC records, box 247, "Committee on Communism minutes 1950–56."

74. McAuliffe, *Crisis on the Left*, pp. 7–8, 108–115.

75. Alan F. Westin, in his rejoinder to Irving Kristol, singled out the civil libertarianism of the AJCongress. See Westin, "Our Freedom," p. 40.

76. The quoted phrase is from Rorty and Rauschenbush, "The Lessons of the Peekskill Riots," p. 323.

77. It is noteworthy that Kristol, who later became one of the founders of neoconservativism, consistently distinguished between his own anticommunism and that of "liberals" in his 1952 *Commentary* article. For the connection between the adoption of cold war liberalism and the development of neoconservatism, see Bloch, "The Emergence of Neoconservatism," chapters 1–3.

78. Until recent years much of the secondary literature on the Rosenberg case was shaped by a long-standing debate over the guilt or innocence of the Rosenbergs, Morton Sobell, and others. That debate—which was waged in Schneir and Schneir, *Invitation to an Inquest*, Radosh and Milton, *The Rosenberg File*, and numerous other books and articles—is not integral to my analysis of the role that the case played in advancing and revealing the ideological transformation of the organized Jewish community. (Moreover, this debate has been at least partially resolved by the recent release of formerly classified documents, which have convinced even some of the Rosenbergs' most stalwart defenders that Julius Rosenberg was involved in some form of espionage. See Kazin, "The Agony and Romance of the American Left," p. 159 n. 64.) More pertinent to the present discussion are Moore, "Reconsidering the Rosenbergs"; Marker, "The Jewish Community and the Case of Julius and Ethel Rosenberg" (a shorter, revised version was published as Marker, "The Case Against the Jews"); Berkson, "The Case of Julius and Ethel Rosenberg." Edward S. Shapiro also briefly addresses the "Jewish" aspects of the case in *A Time for Healing*, pp. 36–38. Both Marker and Berkson provide detailed accounts—based primarily on published sources—of the responses of rabbis, the Jewish press, Jewish leftists, and Jewish communal organizations to the Rosenberg case. My discussion—which is more narrow, based largely on archival material, and seeks to answer different questions—follows them on a number of points.

79. AJC memorandum, Samuel Flowerman to John Slawson, "Public Relations Effects of Activities of Jewish Atom Spies," July 31, 1950, in AJC records, RG 347.17 Gen-12, box 139, "Rosenberg Case 50–52." This crucial document states that "the main reason for concern is the belief that the non-Jewish public may generalize from these activities and impute to the Jews as a group treasonable motives and activities." The British physicist Klaus Fuchs, whose arrest led the FBI to Gold, Greenglass, the Rosenbergs, and Sobell, was often incorrectly identified as a Jew by anti-Semites. Harry Gold

and David Greenglass, two of the chief prosecution witnesses in the Rosenberg-Sobell trial, were also convicted of espionage.

80. "Are Jews Widely Regarded as Communists and Atom Spies? Highlights of an Analysis of the 'Communist' Survey," May 8, 1951, p. 1, in AJC records, box 249, "Polit Phil Communism, Jews 50–59"; AJC memorandum, from Samuel H. Flowerman to John Slawson, May 4, 1951, re: "Poll Rider Questions on Julius and Ethel Rosenberg, and Criticism of Jews," in AJC records, RG 347.17 Gen-12, box 139, "Rosenberg Case 50–52"; AJC Annual Report, "Studies on Jews and Communism," in *AJYB* 54 (1953), p. 574; Stember et al., *Jews in the Mind of America*, pp. 156–165, 168–169; Report of Program Committee Director Harold Lachman, p. 2, attached to ADL National Commission minutes, 1951, in ADL records; Stouffer, *Communism, Conformity, and Civil Liberties*, pp. 172, 174, 184, 277 n. 16.

81. While I have followed the tendency of the staff members of Jewish organizations to speak mainly of "the Rosenbergs" and "the Rosenberg case," many of the same arguments apply to the case against Morton Sobell and the other Jews implicated in espionage.

82. AJC memorandum, "Public Comment on the Atom Spies," by S. Andhil Fineberg, May 1951, pp. 1–2, in AJC records, box 249, "Atom Spies" (emphasis in original). The same point is made in AJC memorandum, from S. Andhil Fineberg to Charles Posner, November 9, 1953, p. 1, in AJC records, box 246, "Polit Phil Communism 51–53."

83. AJC memorandum, S. Andhil Fineberg to John Slawson, "AJC Activities Re Communism Since January 21, 1953," August 25, 1953, p. 4, in AJC records, box 248, "Communism Program 53–57." This memorandum reported that the AJC's public relations director initially advised New York newspapers and international news services to disregard the press releases of the Rosenberg Committee. See also Solomon Andhil Fineberg to Louis Nizer, March 13, 1973, p. 1, in AJC records, RG 347.17 Gen-12, box 139, "Rosenberg Case 'Fact or Fiction' AS Fineberg."

84. Quoted from *National Guardian*, August 15, 1951, p. 1; August 22, 1951, p. 1. Rueben's articles are in the *National Guardian*, August 22, 1951, p. 3; August 29, 1951, pp. 1, 3; September 5, 1951, pp. 5–6; September 12, 1951, p. 5 (which mentions the absence of Jewish jurors); September 19, 1951, pp. 4–5; September 26, 1951, p. 5; October 3, 1951, p. 5. Both before and after Rueben's articles were published in the *National Guardian* editors of the anticommunist Jewish press—including the *Forward*, the *Day*, and various English-language papers—criticized the death sentence as exceptionally severe. AJC Library of Jewish Information, "The Defense of Julius and Ethel Rosenberg: A Communist Attempt to Inject the Jewish Issue," March, 1952, pp. 6–13, in AJC records, RG 347.17 Gen-12, box 139, "Rosenberg Case 50–52"; Dawidowicz, " 'Anti-Semitism' and the Rosenberg Case," pp. 42–43; Marker, "The Jewish Community and the Case of Julius and Ethel Rosenberg," pp. 107–111, 115; Berkson, "The Case of Julius and Ethel Rosenberg," pp. 32–33, 39–42; Radosh and Milton, *The Rosenberg File*, pp. 87, 170; Shapiro, *A Time for Healing*, p. 37. On the relationship of *Jewish Life* and the *Morning Freiheit* to the Communist Party, see Liebman, "The Ties That Bind," pp. 296–297, 302, 306 n, 307, 310; Teller, *Natives and Strangers*, pp. 43–45; Mendelsohn, *On Modern Jewish Politics*, pp. 88–89.

85. Dawidowicz, " 'Anti-Semitism' and the Rosenberg Case," pp. 42–43; Berkson, "The Case of Julius and Ethel Rosenberg," pp. 31–32. William A. Rueben briefly

served as the provisional chairman of the Rosenberg Committee, which was founded in October 1951, and made speeches on behalf of the defense campaign in various parts of the country. The Rosenberg Committee appealed for members, financial support, attendance at mass meetings, and petition signatures in the pages of the *National Guardian*. See *National Guardian*, October 10, 1951, p. 3; October 31, 1951, p. 3; November 7, 1951, p. 3; November 14, 1951, p. 3; December 19, 1951, p. 2; January 16, 1952, p. 3; February 13, 1952; February 27, 1952, p. 1; March 5, 1952, p. 1; March 19, 1952, p. 5; April 9, 1952, p. 12; May 15, 1952, p. 5; May 22, 1952, p. 3; October 16, 1952, p. 1. The "Fact Sheet" is quoted in both of the following: AJC Library of Jewish Information, "The Defense of Ethel and Julius Rosenberg: A Communist Attempt to Inject the Jewish Issue," March 1952, p. 11, in AJC records, RG 347.17 Gen-12, box 139, "Rosenberg Case 50–52"; Fineberg, *The Rosenberg Case*, p. 65.

86. Moss's letter to Kaufman is quoted in an editorial from the *Shreveport Times*, January 6, 1953, a typescript of which is in AJC records, RG 347.17 Gen-12, box 139, "Rosenberg Ethel and Julius 52–55."

87. AJC memorandum, Morris Fine to John Slawson, October 22, 1953, in AJC records, RG 347.17 Gen-12, box 139, "Rosenberg Case 53–57"; Dawidowicz, "False Friends and Dangerous Defenders," pp. 14–15; AJC Library of Jewish Information, "The Defense of Ethel and Julius Rosenberg: A Communist Attempt to Inject the Jewish Issue," March 1952, pp. 12–13, in AJC records, RG 347.17 Gen-12, box 139, "Rosenberg Case 50–52"; AJC memorandum, [Solomon Andhil Fineberg], "The Communists Find a New Opening: The Rosenberg Case as a Wedge," June 5, 1952, in AJC records, RG 347.17 Gen-12, box 139, "Rosenberg Case 50–52"; Report of Civil Rights Committee, ADL National Commission meeting transcript, October 24–26, 1952, p. 301, in ADL records; Sixth Report of Staff Coordinator of Program on Communism, S. Andhil Fineberg to John Slawson, January 21, 1953, in AJC records, box 248, "Polit Phil Communism AJC Program Activities 50–55"; Solomon Andhil Fineberg Oral History Interview, 1974, pp. 4:169–170, in SAF papers, box 5, AJA.

88. John Slawson to Joseph Roos, January 14, 1954, p. 3, in AJC records, box 246, "Polit Phil Communism 54–57"; First Report of Coordinator of Staff Activities in Reference to Communism, S. Andhil Fineberg to John Slawson, October 6, 1950, p. 2, in AJC records, box 248, "Polit Phil Communism Program Activities 50–55."

89. Information on Fineberg's life and career is drawn from Berkson, "The Case of Julius and Ethel Rosenberg," pp. 48–50; *Committee Reporter*, 6,12 (December 1949), p. 7; Typescript, "Solomon Andhil Fineberg Archives, Community Service Department of the American Jewish Committee"; "The Objectives and Procedures of the Community Service Department of the American Jewish Committee," November 5, 1947, in SAF papers, box 1, AJA; Typescript by Solomon Andhil Fineberg, "The Intra-Jewish Battle Over Methodology," August 1972, in SAF papers, box 2, AJA; American Jewish Committee, Thirty-Seventh Annual Report, 1943, Report of the Executive Committee, p. 53, in Nearprint files, "Slawson, John," AJA; Solomon Andhil Fineberg Oral History Interview, 1974, pp. 1:5–12, 30–31, 33–35, 37–39, 42, in SAF papers, box 5, AJA.

90. AJC memorandum, [Solomon Andhil Fineberg], "The Communists Find a New Opening: The Rosenberg Case as a Wedge," June 5, 1952, in AJC records, RG 347.17 Gen-12, box 139, "Rosenberg Case 50–52"; S. Andhil Fineberg Oral History Interview, 1974, pp. 4:169–170, in SAF papers, box 5, AJA; Marker, "The Jewish Com-

munity and the Case of Julius and Ethel Rosenberg," pp. 112–113; Solomon Andhil Fineberg, "They Screamed for Justice"; subsequently condensed as "Plain Facts About the Rosenberg Case"; Cohen, *Not Free To Desist*, pp. 357–358.

91. Fineberg, *The Rosenberg Case*. Radosh and Milton called Fineberg's book "a slavish endorsement of every aspect of the government's handling of the case" and "a semi-official government document" that had "quasi-official sponsorship by the Eisenhower administration." Radosh and Milton, *The Rosenberg File*, pp. 355, 479. Fineberg himself claimed that paper-bound copies of the book were "prepared for the State Department" for distribution overseas. S. Andhil Fineberg to LaVerne Perdue, December 10, 1953, in SAF papers, box 1, AJA; Edwin S. Newman to Lester W. Waldman, November 17, 1953, in SAF papers, box 5, AJA.

92. Solomon Andhil Fineberg, "The Communists Find a New Opening: The Rosenberg Case as a Wedge," June 5, 1952; AJC Library of Jewish Information, "The Defense of Ethel and Julius Rosenberg: A Communist Attempt to Inject the Jewish Issue," March 1952, pp. 12–13, in AJC records, RG 347.17 Gen-12, box 139, "Rosenberg Case 50–52"; AJC memorandum, "Plain Facts about the Rosenberg Case," by S. Andhil Fineberg, October 12, 1953, in AJC records, RG 347.17 Gen-12, box 139, "US Govt Loyalty and Security Cases Rosenberg 51–57"; Fifth Report of Staff Coordinator of the AJC Program on Communism, S. Andhil Fineberg to John Slawson, June 2, 1952, p. 3; Sixth Report of Staff Coordinator of Program on Communism, S. Andhil Fineberg to John Slawson, January 21, 1953, pp. 7–8, in AJC records, box 248, "Polit Phil Communism AJC Program Activities 50–55."

93. AJC Library of Jewish Information, "The Defense of Julius and Ethel Rosenberg: A Communist Attempt to Inject the Jewish Issue," March 1952, in AJC records, RG 347.17 Gen-12, box 139, "Rosenberg Case 50–52" (this memorandum was sent to "All [AJC] Chapter Chairmen"); AJC memorandum, from Seymour Samet to Manheim Shapiro, March 27, 1953, in AJC records, RG 347.17 Gen-12, box 139, "Rosenberg Case 53–57." After Julius and Ethel Rosenberg were executed in June 1953, the AJC and ADL continued to warn local Jewish community leaders against cooperating with the Rosenberg Committee (renamed the "National Committee to Secure Justice for Morton Sobell in the Rosenberg Case"), which was seeking public support for the transfer of Morton Sobell from Alcatraz. AJC-ADL Joint Memorandum, "Campaigns Launched By Pro-Communist Groups," May 12, 1954, in AJC records, RG 347.17 Gen-12, box 139, "Rosenberg-Sobell Case 52–61"; Seventh Report of the Staff Coordinator of Program on Communism, S. Andhil Fineberg to John Slawson, February 1955, p. 5, in AJC records, box 247, "Polit Phil Communism 48–61"; S. Andhil Fineberg to Rabbi Bernard Rosenberg, August 12, 1957, p. 1, in AJC records, RG 347.17 Gen-12, box 139, "Rosenberg Case 53–57."

94. AJC memorandum, from S. Andhil Fineberg to Will Katz, February 28, 1952, p. 1, in AJC records, RG 347.17 Gen-12, box 139, "Rosenberg Case 50–52"; "Proposed Memorandum for Guidance on Certain Problems Related to Communism," approved by the Ad Hoc Committee on Problems Related to Communism, January 27, 1951, pp. 1, 3, in AJC records, box 247, "AJC—Ad Hoc Committee on Problems Related to Communism." The Chicago office of the ADL apparently played a part in preventing a Rosenberg defense meeting from being held at Chicago's Temple Judea. *National Guardian*, February 13, 1952, p. 4; Marker, "The Jewish Community and the Case of Julius and Ethel Rosenberg," p. 110.

95. AJC memorandum, from Nathan Weisman to "All Chapter Chairmen," March 27, 1952, p. 1, in AJC records, RG 347.17 Gen-12, box 139, "Rosenberg Case 50–52." This memorandum was attached to the AJC's Library of Jewish Information memorandum, "The Defense of Ethel and Julius Rosenberg: A Communist Attempt to Inject the Jewish Issue," March 1952, in AJC records, RG 347.17 Gen-12, box 139, "Rosenberg Case 50–52."

96. Irving M. Engel to "Dear JDA Friend," April 11, 1952, in AJC records, RG 347.17 Gen-12, box 139, "Rosenberg Case 50–52."

97. NCRAC statement, May 13, 1952, quoted in Fineberg, *The Rosenberg Case*, p. 69; Fifth Report of the Coordinator of the AJC Program on Communism, S. Andhil Fineberg to John Slawson, June 2, 1952, p. 3, in AJC records, box 246, "Polit Phil Communism 51–53."

98. "Report on Rosenberg Meeting, August 19, 1953," in AJC records, RG 347.17 Gen-12, box 139, "US Govt Loyalty and Security Cases Rosenberg 51–57"; "Report on Meeting of the L.A. Committee to Secure Justice in the Rosenberg Case Held at the Park View Manor . . . April 14, 1952," April 21, 1952, in AJC records, RG 347.17 Gen-12, box 139, "Rosenberg Case 50–52"; Confidential memorandum, report of meeting held by Rosenberg Committee in Minnesota, November 13, 1952, in AJC records, RG 347.17 Gen-12, box 139, "Rosenberg Ethel and Julius 52–55"; "Meeting of Detroit Committee for Justice in the Rosenberg Case," attached to Jewish Community Council of Detroit memorandum, from Walter E. Klein to Milton Ellerin and S. Andhil Fineberg, September 9, 1953, in SAF papers, box 3, AJA; S. Andhil Fineberg to Irving Kristol, January 21, 1953, p. 1, in SAF papers, box 1, AJA; Solomon Andhil Fineberg to Louis Nizer, March 13, 1973, p. 1, in AJC records, RG 347.17 Gen-12, box 139, "Rosenberg Case 'Fact or Fiction' AS Fineberg"; Fineberg, *The Rosenberg Case*, pp. 41–44; Solomon Andhil Fineberg Oral History Interview, 1974, 5:174–175, in SAF papers, box 5, AJA. Fineberg also identified himself ("I was the anonymous heckler") in a written notation on a clipping from the *New York World-Telegram*, dated April 30, 1952, recounting the interruption of a Rosenberg defense meeting by an unidentified "well-dressed, middle-aged man," in AJC records, RG 347.17 Gen-12, box 139, "Rosenberg Case 50–52."

99. Quoted from "Report on Meeting of the L.A. Committee to Secure Justice in the Rosenberg Case Held at the Park View Manor . . . April 14, 1952," April 21, 1952, p. 3, in AJC records, RG 347.17 Gen-12, box 139, "Rosenberg Case 50–52." The summaries of the speeches at this meeting provided in the AJC report contain various allegations—phrased in the most provocative terms—that the United States government was moving toward fascism. See also Dawidowicz, " 'Anti-Semitism' and the Rosenberg Case," p. 44; Confidential Memo, Report of Meeting held by Rosenberg Committee in Minnesota, November 13, 1952, in AJC records, RG 347.17 Gen-12, box 139, "Rosenberg Ethel and Julius 52–55"; Fineberg, *The Rosenberg Case*, pp. 41–44.

100. Quoted in Dawidowicz, " 'Anti-Semitism' and the Rosenberg Case," p. 43. See also *National Guardian*, March 5, 1952, p. 5.

101. Dawidowicz, "False Friends and Dangerous Defenders," pp. 10, 13; Library of Jewish Information, "Communist Approach to Jews," October 20, 1950, p. 7–8, 17, in AJC records, box 246, "Polit Phil Communism Sept-Dec 1950"; AJC memorandum, from Morroe Berger to The Sub-Committee on Appraisal, Staff Committee on Communism, March 27, 1952, p. 2, in AJC records, box 248, "Communism Committees Staff Special Projects"; AJC memorandum, from S. Andhil Fineberg to Charles Posner,

November 9, 1953, p. 1, in AJC records, box 246, "Polit Phil Communism 51–53." For examples of the Rosenbergs' belief in the threat of American fascism, see Meeropol and Meeropol, *We Are Your Sons*, pp. 131–132, 230; *National Guardian*, March 26, 1952, p. 2; May 22, 1952, p. 3.

102. Dawidowicz, "False Friends and Dangerous Defenders"; Dawidowicz, " 'Anti-Semitism' and the Rosenberg Case"; S. Andhil Fineberg, "The Communists Find a New Opening: The Rosenberg Case As A Wedge," June 5, 1952, pp. 6–7, in AJC records, RG 347.17 Gen-12, box 139, "Rosenberg Case 50–52"; AJC Library of Jewish Information, "Communist Approach to Jews," October 20, 1950, pp. 8, 17, in AJC records, box 246, "Polit Phil Communism Sept-Dec 1950."

103. *ADL Bulletin* (March 1952), pp. 1, 7–8. This article was written by *New York Post* reporter Oliver Pilat, who covered the trial for the *Post*. Pilat published *The Atom Spies* (New York: Putnam, 1952), the earliest book on the case, in which he strongly affirmed the Rosenbergs' guilt.

104. Report of Benjamin R. Epstein, ADL National Director, in National Executive Committee minutes, March 28, 1952, p. 3; Report of Civil Rights Committee, ADL National Commission meeting transcript, October 24–26, 1952, pp. 301–302; ADL National Commission minutes, October 24–26, 1952, p. 28, in ADL records. See also Berkson, "The Case of Julius and Ethel Rosenberg," pp. 68–70.

105. ADL National Commission meeting transcript, October 24–26, 1952, pp. 20–21, in ADL records.

106. ADL National Chairman Meier Steinbrink, who was himself a respected jurist, noted Judge Kaufman's affiliation while denying that there was any taint of anti-Semitism in the government's case against the Rosenbergs. ADL National Commission meeting transcript, October 24–26, 1952, p. 21, in ADL records. United States Attorney Irving H. Saypol, who led the prosecution in the Rosenberg case, was elected a member of the AJC's Executive Committee in 1950. See Irving Spiegel, "Fight on Reds Seen Aiding Civil Rights," *New York Times*, October 16, 1950, clipping found in AJC records, box 36.

107. Radosh and Milton, *The Rosenberg File*, p. 288; NCRAC memorandum, from Albert Vorspan to Ad Hoc Committee on Communist Issue, April 23, 1951, p. 1, in AJC records, RG 347.17 Gen-12, box 139, "Rosenberg Case 50–52"; Felix Bloch to Jacob Blaustein, April 11, 1951; AJC memorandum, from S. Andhil Fineberg to John Slawson, April 18, 1951, re: Letter of Dr. Felix Bloch, in AJC records, RG 347.17 Gen-12, box 139, "US Govt Loyalty and Security Cases Rosenberg 51–57."

108. Quoted from AJC memorandum, Manheim Shapiro to Seymour Samet, March 30, 1953, in AJC records, RG 347.17 Gen-12, box 139, "Rosenberg Case 53–57." This point is also made in AJC memorandum, "Public Comment on the Atomic Spies," by S. Andhil Fineberg, May 1951, p. 2, in AJC records, box 249, "Atom Spies."

109. Jacob Blaustein to Felix Bloch, May 1, 1951 (quote from pp. 1–2), in AJC records, RG 347.17 Gen-12, box 139, "Rosenberg Case 50–52"; Bloch to Harry S. Truman, April 11, 1951; Bloch to Jacob Blaustein, April 11, 1951, in AJC records, RG 347.17 Gen-12, box 139, "US Govt Loyalty and Security Cases Rosenberg 51–57." Blaustein was not the only AJC official who entertained this notion. In a communication to AJC executive vice president John Slawson, Edwin J. Lukas, the director of the AJC's Civil Rights Division, wrote, "There probably is considerable validity in the feeling shared by many that the imposition of the death sentence was motivated by the judge's apprehension that any-

thing less than the death sentence would have been misinterpreted as a gesture of lenity by a Jewish judge toward Jewish espionage agents." Alfred L. Bernheim, the director of the Public Information and Education Department, wrote to Slawson: "I agree with Prof. Bloch's assumption that Judge Kaufman was 'leaning backward' in sentencing the Rosenbergs to death, and that this act is an indication of the Judge's acceptance of the theory of group responsibility. I also agree the sentence is, and the execution will be, inhumane and revolting." Despite their opposition to the death sentence, however, both Lukas and Bernheim opposed AJC participation in the clemency campaign. AJC memorandum, from Edwin Lukas to John Slawson, April 24, 1951; AJC memorandum, from A.L. Bernheim to John Slawson, April 19, 1951, p. 1, in AJC records, RG 347.17 Gen-12, box 139, "Rosenberg Case 50–52."

110. Fineberg, *The Rosenberg Case*, p. 137. Years later, Fineberg claimed that he never took a position either for or against the Rosenberg death sentence but that "Judge Kaufman knew what he was doing." Solomon Andhil Fineberg Oral History Interview, 1974, p. 5:185, in SAF papers, box 5, *AJA*.

111. Irving Kaufman to S. Andhil Fineberg, June 23, 1952, in SAF papers, box 3, *AJA*. The letter is reproduced in Berkson, "The Case of Julius and Ethel Rosenberg," p. 211.

112. Jesse Moss to Judge Irving Kaufman, quoted in *Shreveport Times* editorial, January 6, 1953, typescript in AJC records, RG 347.17 Gen-12, box 139, "Rosenberg Ethel and Julius 52–55."

113. AJC memorandum, Manheim S. Shapiro to Seymour Samet, March 30, 1953; AJC memorandum, Seymour Samet to Manheim Shapiro, March 27, 1953, in AJC records, RG 347.17 Gen-12, box 139, "Rosenberg Case 53–57"; AJC memorandum, from S. Andhil Fineberg to all members of the Committee on Communism, November 21, 1952, p. 4, in AJC records, box 246, "Polit Phil Communism 51–53"; Fineberg, "They Screamed for Justice," pp. 47–48. Other Jewish leaders, especially rabbis and editors from the Jewish press, did make pleas for clemency. See Marker, "The Jewish Community and the Case of Julius and Ethel Rosenberg," pp. 114–117. The AJC seems to have had no formal policy on capital punishment at the time of the Rosenberg case. However, S. Andhil Fineberg argued that the AJC was "urging capital punishment and *no less*" for Nazi war criminals and thus would be hypocritical to oppose the same punishment for the Rosenbergs. Many years later Fineberg claimed that the AJC had held no formal position on capital punishment until the early 1970s. AJC memorandum, from Edwin Lukas to John Slawson, April 24, 1951; AJC memorandum, from S. Andhil Fineberg to John Slawson, April 18, 1951, in AJC records, RG 347.17 Gen-12, box 139, "Rosenberg Case 50–52"; Solomon Andhil Fineberg to Louis Nizer, March 13, 1973, p. 2, in AJC records, RG 347.17 Gen-12, box 139, "Rosenberg Case 'Fact or Fiction' AS Fineberg"; Typescript, "Solomon Andhil Fineberg Archives, The Trial of Adolph Eichmann . . .," in SAF papers, box 1, *AJA*.

114. Fineberg, *The Rosenberg Case*, pp. x, 56–57, 109; Fineberg, "They Screamed for Justice," p. 48; Fineberg, "Plain Facts About the Rosenberg Case," p. 14; Dawidowicz, "False Friends and Dangerous Defenders," p. 14; Marker, "The Jewish Community and the Case of Julius and Ethel Rosenberg," pp. 115–116. In November 1952 the AJC issued a public statement on the Slansky trial that warned, "The trial of Rudolph Slansky, renegade Jew and his colleagues, who betrayed Judaism in serving the Communist cause, should awaken everyone to the fact that anti-Semitism has become an open instrument of Communist policy. It is ironical [*sic*] that these men

who deserted Judaism, which is inimical to Communism, are now being used as an excuse for the Communist anti-Semitic campaign. . . . The Kremlin's effort to employ anti-Semitism as an instrument of domestic policy is now clearly revealed as an integral part of its attack upon democratic nations." AJC press release, November 21, 1952, p. 1, in SAF papers, box 1, *AJA*.

115. Quoted in Fineberg, *The Rosenberg Case*, p. 57.

116. For an impassioned defense of the impartiality of the American justice system, as contrasted with the arbitrary and biased Soviet system, see the chapter of Fineberg's *The Rosenberg Case* entitled "American Justice." See also Fineberg, "They Screamed for Justice," pp. 22, 48.

117. ADL National Commission meeting transcript, October 24–26, 1952, p. 301; ADL National Commission minutes, October 24–26, 1952, p. 28, in ADL records.

118. AJC memorandum, "Plain Facts About the Rosenberg Case," by S. Andhil Fineberg, October 12, 1953, in AJC records, RG 347.17 Gen-12, box 139, "US Govt Loyalty and Security Cases Rosenberg 51–57"; AJC memorandum, from S. Andhil Fineberg to all members of the Committee on Communism, November 21, 1952, p. 2; Fifth Report of the Coordinator of the AJC Program on Communism, S. Andhil Fineberg to John Slawson, June 2, 1952, p. 3, in AJC records, box 246, "Polit Phil Communism 51–53"; Sixth Report of Staff Coordinator of Program on Communism, S. Andhil Fineberg to John Slawson, January 21, 1953, p. 8, in AJC records, box 248, "Polit Phil Communism AJC Program Activities 50–55"; Typescript of S. Andhil Fineberg's testimony, to be offered at the House Committee on Un-American Activities Hearing on the Committee to Secure Justice in the Rosenberg Case, August 1955, p. 2, in AJC records, RG 347.17 Gen-12, box 139, "Rosenberg Case 53–57." See also statement by S. Andhil Fineberg, June 26, 1961, reproduced in Berkson, "The Case of Julius and Ethel Rosenberg," p. 226. While Fineberg claimed that the AJC, the ADL, and their allies were responsible for minimizing support for the Rosenberg defense effort among American Jews, he recognized that the "Jewish issue" had found much greater credence abroad, particularly in England, France, and Italy. As a result, Fineberg and other AJC staff members corresponded and met with representatives of the United States State Department to discuss plans for counteracting the negative impression of the American justice system that the Rosenberg case had created in Europe. AJC memorandum, from Morris Fine to John Slawson, October 22, 1953; Seymour J. Rubin to Simon Segal, February 15, 1954; AJC memorandum, Eugene Hevesi to Zachariah Shuster, February 18, 1954, in AJC records, RG 347.17 Gen-12, box 139, "Rosenberg Case 53–57"; Eugene Hevesi to Zachariah Shuster, April 8, 1954, and Shuster to Hevesi, April 8, 1954, in AJC records, RG 347.17 Gen-12, box 139, "France Rosenberg Case France Reaction FC-EUR 52–54"; Sixth Report of Staff Coordinator of Program on Communism, S. Andhil Fineberg to John Slawson, January 21, 1953, pp. 8–9, in AJC records, box 248, "Polit Phil Communism AJC Program Activities 50–55"; Seventh Report of Staff Coordinator of Program on Communism, S. Andhil Fineberg to John Slawson, February 1955, p. 4, in AJC records, box 247, "Polit Phil Communism 48–61." For a more detailed account of the foreign reactions to the Rosenberg case and the AJC's efforts to influence those reactions, see Berkson, "The Case of Julius and Ethel Rosenberg," pp. 79–82, 88–89, 91–92, 102–106, 128–133, 192–200.

119. Quoted in Radosh and Milton, *The Rosenberg File*, p. 324. Deborah Dash Moore called the case "a Jewish performance with Jewish actors," in Moore, "Recon-

sidering the Rosenbergs," pp. 27–28. S. Andhil Fineberg argued that "to suggest a resemblance between the Rosenberg case and the Dreyfus case is to besmirch the memory of Captain Dreyfus." Fineberg, *The Rosenberg Case*, p. 141.

120. Radosh and Milton, *The Rosenberg File*, p. 359; Berkson, "The Case of Julius and Ethel Rosenberg," pp. 114–116, 217–221.

121. Radosh and Milton, *The Rosenberg File*, p. 240; *ADL Bulletin* (March 1952), p. 7; Meeropol and Meeropol, *We Are Your Sons*, p. 159.

122. Warshow, "The 'Idealism' of Julius and Ethel Rosenberg," p. 417; Berkson, "The Case of Julius and Ethel Rosenberg," pp. 29, 82–83. Warshow raised the possibility that the letters were not written by the Rosenbergs, and he was convinced that they had been edited for publication. Neither issue affects this analysis, since Jewish intergroup relations agencies were concerned with efforts to identify the Rosenbergs as Jews, whether these efforts were made by the Rosenbergs themselves or by their supporters. The letters were originally published as *Death House Letters of Ethel and Julius Rosenberg* (New York: Jero, 1953).

123. Quoted from Meeropol and Meeropol, *We Are Your Sons*, p. 33. See also Warshow, "The 'Idealism' of Julius and Ethel Rosenberg," p. 417.

124. Quoted in Meeropol and Meeropol, *We Are Your Sons*, p. 44. See also Warshow, "The 'Idealism' of Julius and Ethel Rosenberg," p. 417; *National Guardian*, October 10, 1951, p. 37 (where the quote appears in a slightly different form). Ethel Rosenberg similarly noted the passage of Passover in her letter of April 20, 1951, in Meeropol and Meeropol, *We Are Your Sons*, p. 46.

125. Meeropol and Meeropol, *We Are Your Sons*, pp. 66–70, 182. See also Warshow, "The 'Idealism' of Julius and Ethel Rosenberg," p. 417.

126. *ADL Bulletin* (March 1952), p. 7.

127. Fineberg, *The Rosenberg Case*, pp. 69–70.

128. Fineberg, "They Screamed for Justice," p. 44. See also Fineberg, "Plain Facts About the Rosenberg Case," p. 11.

129. S. Andhil Fineberg to Abraham Cronbach, November 6, 1952, p. 1, in AJC records, RG 347.17 Gen-12, box 139, "Rosenberg Case 50–52." Fineberg made the same argument in "The Role of Religion in Combating Communism," an address before the All-American Conference to Combat Communism, Philadelphia, March 10, 1951, in SAF papers, box 1, AJA.

130. In an analysis that focused on second-generation New York Jews, historian Deborah Dash Moore has argued: "the trial of the Rosenbergs became a definitional ceremony in which opposing versions of American Jewish identity competed for ascendancy. At stake was an understanding of what was required of a Jew in America. The antagonists in the trial articulated conflicting visions of the proper synthesis of Jewishness and Americanism." Moore, "Reconsidering the Rosenbergs," pp. 21–22.

131. Report by Jacob Blaustein to "Dear Member," re: meeting of the AJC Executive Committee, October 14–15, 1950, p. 8, in AJC records, box 246, "Polit Phil Communism Sept-Dec 1950"; AJC memorandum, to Domestic Affairs Committee, August 11, 1950, p. 6; AJC memorandum, S. Andhil Fineberg to David Danzig, re: Difficulties in local Jewish communities due to Communism, August 1, 1950, p. 3, in AJC records, box 246, "Polit Phil Communism June-August 1950"; clipping from *Baltimore Jewish Press*, August 25, 1950, in Nearprint files, "Blaustein, Jacob," AJA. In July 1950, Rabbi Irving Miller publicly pledged the AJCongress to support "the stand taken by the United

States and the United Nations on 'meeting the challenge of aggression in Korea.' "
Quoted in [Lucy S. Dawidowicz], "The American Jewish Congress Against Communism," February 2, 1951, p. 3, in AJC records, box 251, "Polit Phil Communism Other
Organizations—Jewish." During the following month AJC President Jacob Blaustein
made a similar statement, in which he argued, "If the United Nations is kept from taking proper action in Korea there will be little hope of stopping Communist aggression
elsewhere by action of the U.N." Clipping from New York *Herald-Tribune*, August 20,
1950, in Nearprint files, "Blaustein, Jacob," AJA.

132. On the weakening ties between American Jews and communism, Trotskyism,
democratic socialism, and labor Zionism, particularly after World War II, see Arthur
Liebman, "The Ties That Bind." Liebman provides a useful analysis of the transformation of American Jewish communal leadership—especially the displacement of the
Jewish "left" by the Jewish intergroup relations agencies and other anticommunist
organizations.

7. *The Anticommunist Campaign in the Jewish Community*

1. Herbert B. Ehrmann to Jacob Blaustein, May 7, 1947, pp. 1–2, in AJC records, box
246, "Polit Phil Communism 36–48."

2. Although the AJC had taken steps to counter communism in the late 1940s, its
concerted anticommunist program began in earnest at the end of 1950, when the Staff
Committee on Communism headed by S. Andhil Fineberg was revitalized. First
Report of Coordinator of Staff Activities in Reference to Communism, S. Andhil
Fineberg to John Slawson, October 6, 1950, p. 1, in AJC records, box 248, "Polit Phil
Communism Program Activities 50–55"; AJC memorandum, to Domestic Affairs Com-
mittee, re: "Alleged Association of Jews and Communism," August 11, 1950, p. 2, in AJC
records, box 246, "Polit Phil Communism June-August 1950"; Cohen, *Not Free to
Desist*, pp. 346–348.

3. "Proposed Memorandum for Guidance on Certain Problems Related to Communism," p. 1, approved by the Ad Hoc Committee on Problems Related to Communism, January 27, 1951, in AJC records, box 247, "AJC—Ad Hoc Committee on Problems
Related to Communism"; AJC Library of Jewish Information, "Communist Approach
to Jews," October 20, 1950, pp. 1–17; Report by Jacob Blaustein to "Dear Member," re:
meeting of the AJC Executive Committee, October 14–15, 1950, pp. 4, 6; AJC Library of
Jewish Information, "The National Committee of the Communist Party of the U.S.A.
on Work Among the Jews," November 1950, p. 5, in AJC records, box 246, "Polit Phil
Communism Sept-Dec 1950"; AJC memorandum, from Lucy Dawidowicz to Morris
Fine, re: "Communist Infiltration of Jewish Organizations," April 29, 1954, pp. 1–3, in
AJC records, box 246, "Polit Phil Communism 54–57." The quoted phrase is from AJC
memorandum, from Morroe Berger to the Sub-committee on Appraisal, Staff Com-
mittee on Communism, March 27, 1952, p. 1, in AJC records, box 248, "Committees
Communism Staff Special Projects." On the communists' efforts to make inroads in
the Jewish community before and during World War II, see Feingold, *A Time for
Searching*, pp. 220–223.

4. Ehrmann served as a member of the AJC's executive committee, a member of the
administrative committee, and as national vice president before he became president
of the AJC, an office he held from 1959 to 1961. Years earlier he had earned a measure

of fame as an associate defense counsel for Sacco and Vanzetti. *Committee Reporter*, 8,3 (February-March 1951), p. 1; AJC Thirty-Seventh Annual Report, 1943; clipping from *Jewish Advocate* (Boston), April 22, 1948, in Nearprint files, "Slawson, John," *AJA*; clipping from the *New York Times*, January 24, 1949, in Nearprint files, "Blaustein, Jacob," *AJA*; *Who Was Who in America With World Notables, 1974–1976*, vol. 6, s.v. "Ehrmann, Herbert B."; *The New York Times Biographical Edition*, June 18–September, 1970, p. 1403; *Who's Who in the East 1953*, s.v. "Ehrmann, Herbert Brutus."

5. Will Herberg to Edwin J. Lukas, June 12, 1951, p. 2, in AJC records, box 246, "Polit Phil Communism 51–53." For biographical information on Herberg and an analysis of his ideological metamorphosis, see David G. Dalin, "Will Herberg in Retrospect," in Dalin, *From Marxism to Judaism*, pp. xii–xviii; Dalin, "The American Element in the Thought of Will Herberg," pp. 296–308.

6. The typescript of Herberg's memorandum, entitled "Communism vs. Judaism," and documents related to the project are in AJC records, box 250, "Herberg Memorandum 48–51."

7. AJC memorandum, from S. Andhil Fineberg to David Danzig (cc: John Slawson, Edwin Lukas, George Kellman, Nathan Weisman), re: Difficulties in local Jewish communities due to Communism, August 1, 1950 (the quoted passage appears on pp. 1–2); AJC memorandum, to Domestic Affairs Committee, re: "Alleged Association of Jews and Communism," August 11, 1950, p. 11, in AJC records, box 246, "Polit Phil Communism June-August 1950."

8. Typescript, "Solomon Andhil Fineberg Archives, American Jewish Committee Committee on Communism," pp. 1–2, February 1973; Typescript, "Solomon Andhil Fineberg Archives, Files on Communism," pp. 2–3, 1972–1973; AJC memorandum, S. Andhil Fineberg, "Proposed Program in Reference to Communism," pp. 4–7, August 8, 1950, in SAF papers, box 1, *AJA*; Solomon Andhil Fineberg Oral History Interview, pp. 5:191, 6:235, 1974, in SAF papers, box 5, *AJA*; AJC memorandum, to Domestic Affairs Committee, re: "Alleged Association of Jews and Communism," August 11, 1950, pp. 7–14, in AJC records, box 246, "Polit Phil Communism June-August 1950."

9. First Report of Coordinator of Staff Activities in Reference to Communism, S. Andhil Fineberg to John Slawson, October 6, 1950 (quote from p. 2); Third Report of the Staff Coordinator of Program on Communism, S. Andhil Fineberg to John Slawson, April 3, 1951, p. 6, in AJC records, box 248, "Polit Phil Communism Program Activities 50–55."

10. Minutes of the Meeting of the Planning Committee on Communism, April 28, 1952, p. 1, in AJC records, box 246, "Polit Phil Communism 51–53."

11. AJC memorandum, from S. Andhil Fineberg to Manheim Shapiro, July 15, 1954, in SAF papers, box 1, *AJA*.

12. AJC memorandum, from Edwin Lukas to John Slawson, August 2, 1950, pp. 1–2, in AJC records, box 246, "Polit Phil Communism June-August 1950."

13. AJC Staff Civil Rights Committee minutes, June 6, 1950, pp. 1–2 (quotes from p. 1), in AJC records, box 246, "Polit Phil Communism June-August 1950"; *Committee Reporter*, 4,9 (September 1947), p. 5; Solomon Andhil Fineberg to Hon. Paul F. Meissner, August 6, 1963; AJC memorandum, from S. Andhil Fineberg to Area Directors and Executive Assistants, re: KNOW YOUR AMERICA WEEK (November 24–30, 1963), October 9, 1963, in SAF papers, box 1, *AJA*.

14. AJC memorandum, from S. Andhil Fineberg to Edwin J. Lukas, November 6, 1950, pp. 1–2, in AJC records, box 246, "Polit Phil Communism Sept-Dec 1950."

15. Cohen, *Not Free to Desist*, p. 347.

16. Members of the Staff Committee on Communism and Civil Liberties initially included Morris Fine (chairman), John Slawson (ex officio), David Danzig, Edwin Lukas, Fred Robin, and Simon Segal. Subsequent additions included Alfred Bernheim and Edwin Newman. Members of the Fine committee voiced opposition to civil liberties violations that resulted from the anticommunist campaign, including book censorship, the "undemocratic provisions of [the] McCarran-Walter Immigration Law," the Internal Security Act of 1950, "attacks on modern public education as Communist or Communist inspired," and the institution of loyalty oaths in universities and in the professions. In addition, members of the Fine committee asserted "the need to improve the practices of legislative committees of inquiry so as to protect the individual from the kind of publicity which prejudices a fair hearing of his case and results in other violations of civil liberties which have been known to occur in these inquiries." AJC memorandum, from Morris Fine to Members of Staff Committee on the Problem of Communism and Civil Liberties, June 27, 1952, pp. 1–2; AJC memorandum, from Morris Fine to Staff Committee on Communism and Civil Liberties, September 24, 1952 (the quote is from p. 1), in AJC records, box 246, "Polit Phil Communism 51–53"; AJC memorandum, from Morris Fine to John Slawson, January 15, 1953, pp. 2–3, in AJC records, box 248, "Communism Program 53–57."

17. "Statement of Policy Toward Communist Affiliated and Communist Led Organizations," adopted by AJC Domestic Affairs Committee, June 27, 1950, attached to Report by Jacob Blaustein to "Dear Member," in AJC records, box 246, "Polit Phil Communism Sept-Dec 1950"; "Proposed Memorandum for Guidance on Certain Problems Related to Communism," p. 1, approved by the Ad Hoc Committee on Problems Related to Communism, January 27, 1951, in AJC records, box 247, "AJC—Ad Hoc Committee on Problems Related to Communism"; AJC memorandum, to Domestic Affairs Committee, re: "Alleged Association of Jews and Communism," August 11, 1950, p. 5, in AJC records, box 246, "Polit Phil Communism June-August 1950"; Third Report of the Staff Coordinator of Program on Communism, S. Andhil Fineberg to John Slawson, April 3, 1951, p. 2, in AJC records, box 248, "Polit Phil Communism Program Activities 50–55."

18. Quoted from "Varying Recommendations from New York and Chicago Subcommittees on National Civil Rights Committee: Decisions Arrived At (Communism)," in "ADL Stands on Various Issues," p. 102, in ADL records. Even earlier, in 1946, the ADL National Administrative Committee adopted a policy that mandated the ADL avoid cooperation or contact with pro-communist organizations or individuals. ADL National Administrative Committee minutes, November 18, 1946, p. 3, in ADL records.

19. On the Jewish community councils, see Diner, "Jewish Self-Governance, American Style," pp. 293–295; Elazar, *Community and Polity*, pp. 181, 188; Moore, *To the Golden Cities*, pp. 61–62, 74–75, 190, 193. Moore provides an excellent analysis of the political and ideological evolution of Los Angeles Jewry after World War II in chapter 7 of her study.

20. For the case of the Los Angeles branch of the JPFO, see Moore, *To the Golden Cities*, pp. 193–194. Moore notes that Jewish representatives of the anti-Stalinist left,

especially socialists associated with the Jewish Labor Committee, were adamantly opposed to association with the JPFO.

21. AJC Staff Committee on Communism minutes, May 25, 1954, p. 1; April 20, 1956, p. 1, in AJC records, box 247, "AJC Committee on Communism minutes, 1950–56."

22. AJC memorandum, from S. Andhil Fineberg to Charles Posner, November 9, 1953, pp. 2–3, in AJC records, box 246, "Polit Phil Communism 51–53." Several decades later, while affirming that "the members of the Jewish Peoples Fraternal Order were serving Communist interests," Fineberg maintained that "most of them were non-Communists" who "belonged to the JPFO for social and cultural purposes." Typescript, "Solomon Andhil Fineberg Archives, Files on Communism" (quotes from p. 4); Typescript, "Solomon Andhil Fineberg Archives, American Jewish Committee on Communism," p. 3, in SAF papers, box 1, AJA. Victor Navasky has argued, "The JPFO had indeed been created by the Communist Party, but it was in all other respects a harmless fraternal organization where left-wing Yiddish-speaking Jews came together for mutual economic and cultural benefit." Many JPFO members were elderly Jewish immigrants, who were described by one Jewish intergroup relations worker as "a bunch of *alte cockers*." Navasky, *Naming Names*, pp. 113–114.

23. Liebman, *Jews and the Left*, pp. 310–325; Liebman, "The Ties That Bind," pp. 296–297, 307 (quoted phrases from pp. 297, 307); Caute, *The Great Fear* (quote from p. 173); Mendelsohn, *On Modern Jewish Politics*, pp. 80, 82, 94; Isserman, *Which Side Were You On?* pp. 172–174. In the mid-1950s the AJC's Edwin J. Lukas supplied members of HUAC and the Senate Internal Security Subcommittee with information about the radical schools formerly affiliated with the JPFO. These schools had become independent of the JPFO in 1950. Edwin Lukas to Senator Robert Morris, March 30, 1956; Edwin Lukas to Rep. Courtney E. Owens, October 29, 1954, in AJC records, RG 347.17 Gen-12, box 65, "Jewish Peoples Fraternal Order 48–56"; AJC Staff Committee on Communism minutes, October 29, 1954; March 30, 1956, in AJC records, box 247, "Staff Committee on Communism minutes, 50–56"; Liebman, "The Ties That Bind," pp. 296–297.

24. AJC Staff Committee on Communism minutes, January 11, 1951, p. 3; March 1, 1951, p. 1; April 5, 1951, p. 1, in AJC records, box 247, "Staff Committee on Communism minutes 1950–1956"; Abram G. Becker to John Slawson, cc: Benjamin Epstein, September 20, 1950, in AJC records, box 248, "Communism AJC-ADL-AJCongress 50–52"; First Report of Coordinator of Staff Activities in Reference to Communism, S. Andhil Fineberg to John Slawson, October 6, 1950, p. 10; Third Report of the Staff Coordinator of Program on Communism, S. Andhil Fineberg to John Slawson, April 3, 1951, p. 5, in AJC records, box 248, "Polit Phil Communism Program Activities 50–55."

25. AJC Library of Jewish Information, "The Jewish Peoples Fraternal Order of the International Workers Order," November 1950, in AJC records, box 250, "The Jewish Peoples Fraternal Order of the International Workers Order"; AJC memorandum, "Jewish Peoples Fraternal Order," August 31, 1950, pp. 1–4, in AJC records, RG 347.17 Gen-12, box 65, "Jewish Peoples Fraternal Order 48–56"; AJC memorandum, from S. Andhil Fineberg to Edwin J. Lukas, September 27, 1951, in AJC records, RG 347.17 Gen-12, box 148, "Social Service Employees Union 51–52"; Third Report of the Staff Coordinator of Program on Communism, S. Andhil Fineberg to John Slawson, April 3, 1951, p. 2, in AJC records, box 248, "Polit Phil Communism Program Activities

50–55"; George J. Hexter to Aaron Goldman, October 24, 1950; Dorothy M. Nathan to Isaac Frank, October 24, 1950; AJC memorandum, from Louis S. Breier to "Field Representatives," December 21, 1950, p. 1, in AJC records, RG 347.17 Gen-12, box 65, "Jewish Peoples Fraternal Order 48–56."

26. Dr. Jack D. Fisher to Joseph J. Woolfson, December 28, 1950, in AJC records, box 246, "Polit Phil Communism Sept-Dec 1950"; Nathan Rosenberg to Michael Freed, December 13, 1950, p. 1, in AJC records, RG 347.17 Gen-12, box 65, "Jewish Peoples Fraternal Order 48–56"; Moore, *To the Golden Cities*, p. 204.

27. John Slawson to Joseph Roos, January 14, 1954, p. 1, in AJC records, box 246, "Polit Phil Communism 54–57"; Third Report of the Staff Coordinator of Program on Communism, S. Andhil Fineberg to John Slawson, April 3, 1951, pp. 2, 9; Fourth Report of the Coordinator of the AJC Program on Communism, S. Andhil Fineberg to John Slawson, December 28, 1951, pp. 4–5, in AJC records, box 248, "Polit Phil Communism Program Activities 50–55"; Joseph Roos to Dorothy M. Nathan, December 22, 1950; George J. Hexter to Aaron Goldman, October 24, 1950; Dorothy M. Nathan to Isaac Frank, October 24, 1950, in AJC records, RG 347.17 Gen-12, box 65, "Jewish Peoples Fraternal Order 48–56"; Walter E. Kalin to Dorothy Nathan, December 5, 1951, p. 1, with attached statement by Benjamin M. Laikin, March 25, 1946, in SAF papers, box 1, *AJA*.

28. Joseph Roos to Dorothy Nathan, December 22, 1950, in AJC records, RG 347.17 Gen-12, box 65, "Jewish Peoples Fraternal Order 48–56"; L.A. City Committees Jewish Peoples Fraternal Order, Emma Lazarus Division, "The Jewish People's Fraternal Order and the Fight for Democracy in the Los Angeles Jewish Community," n.d., in AJC records, RG 347.17 Gen-12, box 65 "Jewish Peoples Fraternal Order 48–50." The expulsion of the JPFO from the Los Angeles Jewish Community Council is discussed in greater detail in Moore, *To the Golden Cities*, pp. 202–205.

29. Caute, *The Great Fear*, pp. 173–174; AJC Staff Committee on Communism minutes, March 23, 1956, p. 1, in AJC records, box 247, "Staff Committee on Communism minutes 1950–1956."

30. On the expulsion of pro-communist unions from the CIO, see Oshinsky, "Labor's Cold War," pp. 118–119, 128, 149–151, 312 n. 27; McAuliffe, *Crisis on the Left*, pp. 54–62.

31. "The Social Service Employees Union," draft of AJC Study on the Social Service Employees Union, October 15, 1951, pp. 12–13, 23–24 (quote from pp. 23–24); AJC memorandum, from S. Andhil Fineberg to Manheim Shapiro, May 5, 1951, p. 1; S. Andhil Fineberg to Arthur Greenleigh, September 27, 1951, p. 1; AJC memorandum, from S. Andhil Fineberg to Edwin J. Lukas, September 27, 1951; John Slawson to Louis L. Bennett, May 16, 1951, in AJC records, RG 347.17 Gen-12, box 148, "Social Service Employees Union 51–52"; AJC memorandum, from Lucy S. Dawidowicz to Solomon Andhil Fineberg, March 28, 1951, in AJC records, box 246, "Polit Phil Communism 51–53"; AJC Staff Committee on Communism minutes, September 13, 1951, p. 1; June 7, 1951, p. 1, in AJC records, box 247, "Staff Committee on Communism Minutes 1950–1956"; First Report of Coordinator of Staff Activities in Reference to Communism, S. Andhil Fineberg to John Slawson, October 6, 1950, p. 7; Third Report of the Staff Coordinator of Program on Communism, S. Andhil Fineberg to John Slawson, April 3, 1951, pp. 2–3; Fourth Report of the Coordinator of the AJC Program on Communism, S. Andhil Fineberg to John Slawson, December 28, 1951, p. 5, in AJC records, box 248, "Polit Phil

Communism Program Activities 50–55"; AJC memorandum, "The Stockholm Peace Petition—A Communist Ideological Weapon," August 8, 1950, p. 1, in AJC records, box 246, "Polit Phil Communism June-August 1950"; AJC Library of Jewish Information, "Communist Approach to Jews," October 20, 1950, pp. 1, 7–10, 17; Report by Jacob Blaustein to "Dear Member," re: meeting of the AJC Executive Committee, October 14–15, 1950, p. 5, in AJC records, box 246, "Polit Phil Communism Sept-Dec 1950"; clipping from *Baltimore Jewish Press*, August 25, 1950, in Nearprint files, "Blaustein, Jacob," AJA; Cohen, *Not Free to Desist*, p. 348.

32. "The Social Service Employees Union," draft of AJC Study on the Social Service Employees Union, October 15, 1951, pp. 21–30, in AJC records, RG 347.17 Gen-12, box 148, "Social Service Employees Union 51–52"; Fourth Report of the Coordinator of the AJC Program on Communism, S. Andhil Fineberg to John Slawson, December 28, 1951, p. 5, in AJC records, box 248, "Polit Phil Communism Program Activities 50–55." As early as 1946 the ADL had determined that it "would not negotiate with or recognize a Communist dominated union." "ADL Position on Staff and Clerical Union: Also Communist Dominated Unions," November 23, 1946, in "ADL Stands on Various Issues," in ADL records.

33. AJC Library of Jewish Information, "The National Jewish Youth Conference: Example of Communist United-Front Policy in Action," October 1950, p. 2, in AJC records, box 246, "Polit Phil Sept-Dec 1950."

34. Third Report of the Staff Coordinator of Program on Communism, S. Andhil Fineberg to John Slawson, April 3, 1951, p. 2, in AJC records, box 248, "Polit Phil Communism Program Activities 50–55."

35. AJC Library of Jewish Information, "The National Jewish Youth Conference: Example of Communist United-Front Policy in Action," October 1950, in AJC records, box 246, "Polit Phil Sept-Dec 1950"; AJC memorandum, from Lucy Dawidowicz to S. Andhil Fineberg, re: "Expulsion of Jewish Young Fraternalists from National Jewish Youth Conference," September 1, 1953, pp. 1–2 (the quoted phrase is from p. 1), in AJC records, box 246, "Polit Phil Communism 51–53"; AJC Staff Committee on Communism minutes, May 3, 1951, p. 1, in AJC records, box 247, "Staff Committee on Communism 1950–56"; *New York Times*, August 27, 1949, p. 14.

36. AJC Staff Committee on Communism minutes, February 13, 1956, p. 1; March 23, 1956, pp. 1–2, in AJC records, box 247, "AJC Committee on Communism minutes, 1950–56"; Moore, *To the Golden Cities*, pp. 214–215, 324 n. 68.

37. Moore, *To the Golden Cities*, pp. 175, 202.

38. "Resolution Adopted by the Board of the Jewish Family and Children's Service on June 15, 1950" (quote from p. 1); "Memorandum to AASW on Membership in the Communist Party," May 18, 1950, in AJC records, box 246, "Polit Phil Communism June-August 1950."

39. "Proposed Memorandum for Guidance on Certain Problems Related to Communism," approved by the Ad Hoc Committee on Problems Related to Communism, January 27, 1951, p. 2, in AJC records, box 247, "AJC—Ad Hoc Committee on Problems Related to Communism"; John Slawson to Louis L. Bennett, May 16, 1951, p. 5, in AJC records, RG 347.17 Gen-12, box 148, "Social Service Employees Union 51–52"; Third Report of the Staff Coordinator of Program on Communism, S. Andhil Fineberg to John Slawson, April 3, 1951, p. 1, in AJC records, box 248, "Polit Phil Communism Program Activities 50–55."

40. Minutes of Special Staff Committee on the Communist Problem, Subcommittee on Communist Appeal to Jews, October 26, 1950, p. 3, in AJC records, box 246, "Polit Phil Communism Sept-Dec 1950"; AJC Staff Committee on Communism minutes, July 9, 1953, p. 1; May 14, 1953, pp. 1–2, in AJC records, box 247, "Committee on Communism minutes 1950–56"; Berger, *Graenum*, pp. 257–258; AJC memorandum, from Lucy S. Dawidowicz to Morris Fine, February 12, 1951, p. 1, in AJC records, box 246, "Polit Phil Communism 51–53." Deborah Dash Moore provides a detailed analysis of how the conflict over whether or not communists and other political dissidents could gain access to Jewish centers played out in Los Angeles. Moore notes that "within the Los Angeles Jewish community by 1951, centers remained organizations most sympathetic to the left." According to her analysis, however, "left-wing control of centers weakened," for a variety of reasons having little to do with anticommunism, during the early 1950s. See Moore, *To the Golden Cities*, pp. 206–212.

41. Clipping from the *Washington Daily News*, November 30, 1954, in AJC records, box 246, "Polit Phil Communism 54–57"; Draft of Proposed Letter from Irving M. Engel to Chief Officers of National Jewish Organizations, June 11, 1954, in AJC records, box 251, "Polit Phil Communism Other Organizations Jewish"; "Resolution on Communism," National Community Relations Advisory Council Plenary Session, June 17–20, 1954, in AJC records, box 251, "Polit Phil Communism NCRAC 49–54"; AJC memorandum, from Lucy Dawidowicz to Morris Fine, re: "Communist Infiltration of Jewish Organizations," April 29, 1954, pp. 1–3, in AJC records, box 246, "Polit Phil Communism 54–57"; AJC Staff Committee on Communism minutes, May 25, 1954, p. 1, in AJC records, box 247, "AJC Committee on Communism minutes 1950–56."

42. [Lucy S. Dawidowicz], "The American Jewish Congress Against Communism," February 2, 1951, p. 2, in AJC records, box 251, "Polit Phil Communism Other Organizations—Jewish"; Isaac Toubin to John Slawson, November 18, 1952, p. 1, in AJC records, box 248, "Polit Phil Communism AJC-ADL-AJCongress 50–52." The AJCongress had accepted the JPFO as an affiliated organization in May 1945. See Moore, *To the Golden Cities*, p. 317 n. 12.

43. Interview with Will Maslow by author, May 16, 1996; Maslow, "Loose Leaves from a Busy Life," copy in author's possession.

44. Hon. Justine Wise Polier, "Address at the Opening Session of the National Convention of the American Jewish Congress," November 9, 1949, p. 2, in AJCongress records, box 19. At this convention the AJCongress resolved "to clean house of all Congressites who . . . manifest more loyalty to alien directives than to the needs of this country or to their own brethren." Quoted from Moore, *To the Golden Cities*, p. 206.

45. Resolution of the AJCongress National Administrative Committee, November 19, 1950, quoted in David Petegorsky, "Progress and Prospect—A Report on the American Jewish Congress," submitted by the Executive Director to the Biennial National Convention, November 17–19, 1951 (dated November 14, 1951), pp. 24–26, in AJCongress records, box 20.

46. Undated *New York Times* clipping, "Jews in U.S. Urged to Bar Communism," in AJC records, box 249, "Polit Phil Communism 46–47"; [Lucy S. Dawidowicz], "The American Jewish Congress Against Communism," February 2, 1951, pp. 1–5 (Miller's remarks are quoted on p. 3), in AJC records, box 251, "Polit Phil Communism Other Organizations—Jewish."

47. David Petegorsky, "Progress and Prospect—A Report on the American Jewish Congress," submitted by the Executive Director to the Biennial National Convention, November 17–19, 1951 (dated November 14, 1951), pp. 28–29, in AJCongress records, box 20.

48. The quote is from Isaac Toubin to John Slawson, December 2, 1952, p. 2. See also Isaac Toubin to John Slawson, November 18, 1952; John Slawson to Isaac Toubin, November 25, 1952, in AJC records, box 248, "Polit Phil Communism AJC-ADL-AJCongress 50–52."

49. John Slawson to Isaac Toubin, December 9, 1952, p. 3. See also John Slawson to Isaac Toubin, November 25, 1952, in AJC records, box 248, "Polit Phil Communism AJC-ADL-AJCongress 50–52."

50. In 1950 AJC officials claimed that "communists in the Jewish field cite as the most successful united-front activity . . . the American Jewish Congress. . . . This does not mean that the American Jewish Congress, until its expulsion of its communists, was a communist organization. It does mean that the communists were able to use the Congress for certain specific purposes of their own." Quoted from AJC Library of Jewish Information, "The National Jewish Youth Conference: Example of Communist United-Front Policy in Action," October 1950, in AJC records, box 246, "Polit Phil Communism 51–53." Similar concerns were expressed in AJC Library of Jewish Information, "The National Committee of the Communist Party of the U.S.A. on Work Among the Jews," November 1950, p. 2, in AJC records, box 246, "Polit Phil Communism Sept-Dec 1950." The AJC's Library of Jewish Information compiled evidence to show that the "American Jewish Congress has a better record than the World Jewish Congress with regard to Communism." [Lucy S. Dawidowicz], "The American Jewish Congress Against Communism," February 2, 1951, p. 1, in AJC records, box 251, "Polit Phil Communism Other Organizations—Jewish."

51. Statement, "All-American Conference to Combat Communism," n.d. (the quote is from p. 1); George N. Craig to John Slawson, December 28, 1949, in AJC records, RG 347.17 Gen-12, box 3, "All American Conference to Combat Communism 49–62." Craig convened the All-American Conference shortly after he became the legion's national commander. See the *New York Times*, September 2, 1949, p. 1.

52. The quoted phrase is from the Constitution of the All-American Conference to Combat Communism, 1953, in AJC records, RG 347.17 Gen-12, box 3, "All-American Conference to Combat Communism 49–62." Organizations affiliated with the All-American Conference at various times included the American Gold Star Mothers, the American Hotel Association, the American Hungarian Federation, the American Jewish Committee, the American Jewish League Against Communism, the American Latvian Association, the American Legion, the American Medical Association, the American Federation of Labor, the Catholic War Veterans, the Fraternal Order of Eagles, the General Federation of Women's Clubs, the Independent Order of Odd Fellows, the Jewish War Veterans, the Knights of Pythias, Lions International, the Motion Picture Association of America, the National Association of Evangelicals, the National Chiropractic Association, the National Council of Catholic Men, the National Interfraternity Conference, the National Panhellenic Conference, the Slovak League of America, the Ukrainian Congress Committee of America, the National Chamber of Commerce, the National Education Association, the Federal (later National) Council of Churches of Christ, the American Association of University Women, the Dis-

abled American Veterans, Kiwanis International, the Knights of Columbus, and the Veterans of Foreign Wars of the United States. List of Organizations Affiliated with the All-American Conference to Combat Communism, [1954?], in AJC records, RG 347.17 Gen-12, box 3, "All-American Conference to Combat Communism 49–62"; John Slawson to Joseph Roos, January 14, 1954, p. 2, in AJC records, box 246, "Polit Phil Communism 54–57"; AJC memorandum, from S. Andhil Fineberg to Eleanor Ashman, August 1, 1956, p. 2, in AJC records, box 248, "Polit Phil Communism Program 53–57."

53. George N. Craig to John Slawson, December 28, 1949; John Slawson to George N. Craig, January 4, 1950; AJC memorandum, from S. Andhil Fineberg to John Slawson, February 20, 1950, p. 1; AJC memorandum, from Joseph J. Woolfson to S. Andhil Fineberg, re: "All-American Conference," February 7, 1950, p. 1, in AJC records, RG 347.17 Gen-12, box 3, "All-American Conference to Combat Communism 49–62."

54. The B'nai B'rith's Frank Goldman subsequently minimized the role of B'nai B'rith-ADL staff members at the first All-American Conference meeting. Statement by Frank Goldman, President of B'nai B'rith, February 14, 1950; Confidential JWV memorandum, re: All-American Conference, from Jackson J. Holtz, May 19, 1950; Edwin J. Lukas to Ely Aaron, May 11, 1950, in AJC records, RG 347.17 Gen-12, box 3, "All-American Conference to Combat Communism 49–62"; Edwin J. Lukas, "The All-American Conference to Combat Communism," in the *Committee Reporter* (August-September 1950), offprint in AJC records, RG 347.17 Gen-12, box 4, "AACCC Participants AJC 50–60."

55. Although the CIO participated in the planning stages of the conference, it withdrew shortly after the January 1950 meeting. David Petegorsky, "Progress and Prospect—A Report on the American Jewish Congress," submitted by the Executive Director to the Biennial National Convention, November 17–19, 1951 (dated November 14, 1951), pp. 28–29, in AJCongress records, box 20 (quotes are from pp. 27–28); clipping from the *National Jewish Post*, October 27, 1950, entitled "AJCommittee Uncertain Whether to Stay in Legion Anti-Red Group," in AJC records, RG 347.17 Gen-12, box 4, "AACCC Participants AJC 50–60"; Statement by Frank Goldman, president of B'nai B'rith, February 14, 1950, in AJC records, RG 347.17 Gen-12, box 3, "All-American Conference to Combat Communism 49–62."

56. Quoted from "Critics of Anti-Red Conference Assailed as Jewish Isolationists," *National Jewish Post*, January 12, 1951, p. 5.

57. Edwin J. Lukas, "The All-American Conference to Combat Communism," in *Committee Reporter* (August-September 1950), offprint in AJC records, RG 347.17 Gen-12, box 4, "AACCC Participants AJC 50–60"; S. Andhil Fineberg to Sidney Hollander, September 21, 1951; AJC memorandum from Joseph J. Woolfson to S. A. Fineberg, February 7, 1950, re: "All-American Conference," p. 1, in AJC records, RG 347.17 Gen-12, box 3, "All-American Conference to Combat Communism 49–62"; S. Andhil Fineberg Oral History Interview, 1974, p. 6:231, in SAF papers, box 5, AJA.

58. AJC memorandum, re: "The All-American Conference to Combat Communism," from Edwin J. Lukas to John Slawson, November 21, 1950, p. 1, in AJC records, RG 347.17 Gen-12, box 3, "All-American Conf to Combat Communism 49–62."

59. The AJC accepted the original invitation to join the conference after "repeated and heated discussions" and very close votes of the Civil Rights Committee, the Administrative Committee, and the Domestic Affairs Committee. AJC memorandum, to Domestic Affairs Committee, re: "Alleged Association of Jews and Communism,"

August 11, 1950, p. 4, in AJC records, box 246, "Polit Phil Communism June-August 1950"; John Slawson to George N. Craig, January 4, 1950; S. Andhil Fineberg to Sidney Hollander, September 21, 1951, in AJC records, RG 347.17 Gen-12, box 3, "All-American Conference to Combat Communism 49–62"; AJC memorandum, from S. Andhil Fineberg to Eleanor Ashman, August 1, 1956, p. 2, in AJC records, box 248, "Polit Phil Communism Program 53–57."

60. Typescript, "Solomon Andhil Fineberg Archives, All-American Conference to Combat Communism," April 1973, pp. 1–2, in SAF papers, box 1, AJA. Sol Kolack, who directed the ADL's veterans' programs immediately after World War II, sought the cooperation of the American Legion, but remained suspicious that the legion was a "reactionary" "isolationist" group "out of tune" with the ADL's liberalism: "I had a sense that when they passed their motions and talked about communism, they weren't really talking about communism, they were really talking about broad concepts of democracy and liberalism, which I think so many of the leaders of the American Legion despised." Sol B. Kolack Oral Memoir, in Cohen and Wexler, "*Not the Work of a Day*," 6:14–16.

61. J. George Fredman to S. Andhil Fineberg, February 16, 1950 (the quote is from p. 1); AJC memorandum, re: All-American Conference, from Joseph J. Woolfson to S. Andhil Fineberg, February 7, 1950, p. 1, in AJC records, RG 347.17 Gen-12, box 3, "All-American Conference to Combat Communism 49–62"; Edwin J. Lukas, "The All-American Conference to Combat Communism," in *Committee Reporter* (August-September 1950), offprint in AJC records, RG 347.17 Gen-12, box 4, "AACCC Participants AJC 50–60."

62. S. Andhil Fineberg, "Merwin Hart Calls It 'Zionist' " (1950), p. 2, in AJC records, RG 347.17 Gen-12, box 3, "All-American Conference to Combat Communism 49–62."

63. Edwin J. Lukas to Robert W. Hansen, December 12, 1950, p. 2; AJC memorandum, re: "The All-American Conference to Combat Communism," from Edwin J. Lukas to John Slawson, November 21, 1950, p. 1; S. Andhil Fineberg, "Merwin Hart Calls It 'Zionist' " (1950), pp. 1, 3; AJC memorandum, re: "All-American Conference," from Joseph J. Woolfson to S. Andhil Fineberg, February 7, 1950, p. 1; AJC memorandum, from S. Andhil Fineberg to John Slawson, February 20, 1950, pp. 1, 4; Statement by Frank Goldman, president of B'nai B'rith, February 14, 1950; clipping from the *National Jewish Post*, October 27, 1950, entitled, "AJCommittee Uncertain Whether to Stay in Legion Anti-Red Group"; clipping from the *National Jewish Post*, January 12, 1951, entitled "Critics of Anti-Red Conference Assailed as Jewish Isolationists"; John Slawson to "Tom" Sawyer, March 21, 1950, pp. 1–2; Edwin J. Lukas, "The All-American Conference to Combat Communism," *Committee Reporter* (August-September 1950); Edwin J. Lukas to Ely Aaron, May 11, 1950; Confidential JWV memorandum, re: All-American Conference, from Jackson J. Holtz, May 19, 1950; J. George Fredman to Jackson Holtz, May 16, 1950, pp. 1–2, in AJC records, RG 347.17 Gen-12, box 3, "All-American Conference to Combat Communism 49–62"; Third Report of the Staff Coordinator of Program on Communism, S. Andhil Fineberg to John Slawson, April 3, 1951, p. 4; Fourth Report of the Coordinator of the AJC Program on Communism, S. Andhil Fineberg to John Slawson, December 28, 1951, p. 3, in AJC records, box 248, "Polit Phil Communism Program Activities 50–55"; Typescript, "Why the American Jewish Committee Should Remain in the All-American Conference to Combat Communism," October 8, 1964, in SAF papers, box 1, AJA; AJC Annual Report, by AJC Exec-

utive Committee Chairman Irving M. Engel, in *AJYB*, 54 (1953), p. 575; *Committee Reporter*, 8,3 (February-March 1951), p. 4; AJC Staff Committee on Communism minutes, May 19, 1952, pp. 1–2, in AJC records, box 247, "Staff Committee on Communism minutes 50–56."

64. Edwin Lukas to J. George Fredman, September 20, 1951; Edwin J. Lukas to Joseph F. Barr, June 30, 1961, in AJC records, RG 347.17 Gen-12, box 3, "All-American Conference to Combat Communism 49–62"; AJC Staff Committee on Communism minutes, September 13, 1951, pp. 1–2, AJC records, box 247, "Staff Committee on Communism 1950–1956"; Fourth Report of the Coordinator of the AJC Program on Communism, S. Andhil Fineberg to John Slawson, December 28, 1951, p. 3, in AJC records, box 248, "Polit Phil Communism Program Activities 50–55"; AJC memorandum, from S. A. Fineberg to Edwin J. Lukas and A. Harold Murray, November 5, 1962, re: The All-American Conference to Combat Communism; Minutes of Executive Council, All-American Conference to Combat Communism, May 11, 1963, Washington, D.C., p. 2, in SAF papers, box 1, AJA.

65. The AJC's Joseph Woolfson acted as chairman of "Know Your America Week" until the early 1960s, when he was replaced by S. Andhil Fineberg. AJC Staff Committee on Communism minutes, May 14, 1953, p. 1; June 5, 1953, in AJC records, box 247, "Staff Committee on Communism minutes 50–56"; W. C. "Tom" Sawyer to Herbert B. Ehrmann, January 26, 1960; Memorandum, re: meeting minutes of the Executive Council of the All-American Conference to Combat Communism, September 15, 1952, pp. 2–3; AJC memorandum, from Gustave F. Falk to Joseph S. Wolfson [*sic*], November 13, 1961, p. 1; Edwin J. Lukas to Joseph F. Barr, June 30, 1961, in AJC records, RG 347.17 Gen-12, box 3, "All-American Conference to Combat Communism 49–62"; "PI&E Work on Communism, 1951" (1951), p. 1, in AJC records, box 246, "Polit Phil Communism 51–53"; AJC press release, December 31, 1953, in AJC records, box 246, "All American Conf to Combat Communism 51–58"; S. A. Fineberg to Hon. Paul Meissner, August 6, 1963; AJC memorandum, from S. Andhil Fineberg to Edwin J. Lukas, January 24, 1964; Typescript, "Solomon Andhil Fineberg, All-American Conference to Combat Communism," April 1973, pp. 2–3; Brochure for Know Your America Week, November 22–28, 1964, in SAF papers, box 1, AJA.

66. AJC memorandum, from S. Andhil Fineberg to Area Directors and Executive Assistants, May 4, 1962, re: The American Jewish League Against Communism, p. 1, in AJC records, RG 347.17 Gen-12, box 12, "Am. Jewish League Against Communism 54–62"; Lora, "A View from the Right," pp. 45–46; Caute, *The Great Fear*, pp. 114, 310, 349, 447, 521–522; Berkson, "The Case of Julius and Ethel Rosenberg," pp. 24–25; Oshinsky, *A Conspiracy So Immense*, pp. 118–119, 205 n., 252–254, 301, 318, 473; Kazin, *The Populist Persuasion*, pp. 175–176, 331 n. 29; Heale, *American Anticommunism*, pp. 153, 155.

67. Irving M. Engel to John Slawson, September 13, 1953, p. 2; Edwin J. Lukas to Irving M. Engel, June 25, 1963, in AJC records, RG 347.17 Gen-12, box 12, "American Jewish League Against Communism 52–53"; AJC memorandum, "Rabbi Benjamin Schultz," June 1952, revised October 1954, p. 1, in AJC records, RG 347.17 Gen-12, box 144, "Schultz, Benjamin 51–52"; AJC memorandum, "The American Jewish League Against Communism," May 4, 1962, in AJC records, RG 347.17 Gen-12, box 12, "American Jewish League Against Communism 49–62"; AJC memorandum, "Rabbi Benjamin Schultz," attached to Edwin J. Lukas letter to Walter Rothchild, February 9,

1953, in AJC records, RG 347.17 Gen-12, box 12, "Am. Jewish League Against Communism"; AJC Staff Committee on Communism minutes, August 30, 1950, in AJC records, box 247, "Staff Committee on Communism Minutes 1950–1956."

68. *New York World-Telegram*, October 14, 1947, p. 6; October 15, 1947, p. 27; October 16, 1947, p. 8; AJC memorandum, "Rabbi Benjamin Schultz," June 1952, revised October 1954, p. 1, in AJC records, RG 347.17 Gen-12, box 144, "Schultz, Benjamin 51–52"; AJC memorandum, "Rabbi Benjamin Schultz," p. 1, attached to Edwin J. Lukas letter to Walter Rothchild, February 9, 1953; AJC memorandum, S. Andhil Fineberg to John Slawson, April 7, 1953, p. 1; "Rabbi Benjamin Schultz and the American Jewish League Against Communism, Inc.," p. 1, attached to AJC memorandum, from Michael Sage to Manheim Shapiro, December 8, 1954, in AJC records, RG 347.17 Gen-12, box 12, "Am. Jewish League Against Communism"; Berkson, "The Case of Julius and Ethel Rosenberg," pp. 22–23; Urofsky, *A Voice That Spoke for Justice*, pp. 359–360.

69. AJC memorandum, from S. Andhil Fineberg to John Slawson, April 17, 1953, pp. 1–2, in AJC records, RG 347.17 Gen-12, box 12, "Am. Jewish League Against Communism 52–53"; AJC Staff Committee on Communism minutes, September 14, 1950, p. 3, in AJC records, box 247, "Staff Committee on Communism Minutes 1950–56"; Berkson, "The Case of Julius and Ethel Rosenberg," pp. 23–24; Typescript, "Solomon Andhil Fineberg Archives, Communism—American Jewish League Against," November 30, 1972, in SAF papers, box 4, AJA; Solomon Andhil Fineberg Oral History Interview, 1974, pp. 5:213–215, in SAF papers, box 5, AJA. During the 1950s and 1960s Fineberg maintained contact with Rabbi Schultz and made repeated efforts to advance Schultz's rabbinical career. Solomon Andhil Fineberg to Benjamin Schultz, November 9, 1962; November 20, 1962; Benjamin Schultz to Solomon Andhil Fineberg, November 27, 1960; Solomon Andhil Fineberg to Perry Nussbaum, December 5, 1962; Solomon Andhil Fineberg to Eugene Lyons, September 24, 1951; Solomon Andhil Fineberg to Dr. Oscar Groner, July 10, 1962, in SAF papers, box 4, AJA; Solomon Andhil Fineberg Oral History Interview, 1974, pp. 6:217, 258, in SAF papers, box 5, AJA.

70. Joint Statement of the American Jewish Committee, American Jewish Congress, and Anti-Defamation League of B'nai B'rith, Re: Communism and Civil Liberties, December 26, 1950 (quote from pp. 1–2), in AJC records, box 248, "AJC-ADL-AJCong Polit Phil Communism"; AJC memorandum, from S. Andhil Fineberg to John Slawson, April 17, 1953, p. 1, in AJC records, RG 347.17 Gen-12, box 12, "Am. Jewish League Against Communism 52–53"; Third Report of the Staff Coordinator of Program on Communism, S. Andhil Fineberg to John Slawson, April 3, 1951, p. 3, in AJC records, box 248, "Polit Phil Communism Program Activities 50–55."

71. Resolution Jointly Adopted by American Jewish Committee, American Jewish Congress, Anti-Defamation League of B'nai B'rith, Jewish Labor Committee, Jewish War Veterans of the USA, National Community Relations Advisory Council, Union of American Hebrew Congregations, January 15, 1951, attached to NCRAC memorandum, from Isaiah M. Minkoff to NCRAC Membership and CJFWF Agencies, December 22, 1954, in AJC records, RG 347.17 Gen-12, box 144, "Schultz, Rabbi Benjamin 47–61."

72. First Report of Coordinator of Staff Activities in Reference to Communism, S. Andhil Fineberg to John Slawson, October 6, 1950, p. 9, in AJC records, box 248, "Polit Phil Communism Program Activities 50–55"; AJC memorandum, "Rabbi Benjamin Schultz," attached to Edwin J. Lukas letter to Walter Rothchild, February 9, 1953, in

AJC records, RG 347.17 Gen-12, box 12, "Am. Jewish League Against Communism"; "Rabbi Benjamin Schultz and the American Jewish League Against Communism, Inc.," p. 3, attached to AJC memorandum, from Michael Sage to Manheim Shapiro, December 8, 1954, in AJC records, RG 347.17 Gen-12, box 12, "Am. Jewish League Against Communism 54–62."

73. "Rabbi Benjamin Schultz and the American Jewish League Against Communism, Inc.," p. 3, attached to AJC memorandum, from Michael Sage to Manheim Shapiro, December 8, 1954; AJC memorandum, "American Jewish League Against Communism," February 16, 1955, in AJC records, RG 347.17 Gen-12, box 12, "Am. Jewish League Against Communism 54–62"; "Rabbi Benjamin Schultz," June 1952, revised October 1954, pp. 1–2, in AJC records, RG 347.17 Gen-12, box 144, "Schultz, Benjamin 51–52"; NCRAC memorandum, from Isaiah M. Minkoff to NCRAC Membership and CJFWF Agencies, December 22, 1954, p. 1, in AJC records, RG 347.17 Gen-12, box 144, "Schultz, Rabbi Benjamin 47–61"; Berkson, "The Case of Julius and Ethel Rosenberg," p. 25; Rabbi Benjamin Schultz to Frederick S. Harris, October 24, 1951, pp. 1–2, in AJC records, RG 347.17 Gen-12, box 13, "Am. Jewish League Against Communism 51"; interview with Arnold Forster by author, June 11, 1996.

74. Oshinsky, *A Conspiracy So Immense*, pp. 473, 486; Rorty, "What Price McCarthy Now?" p. 34.

75. AJC memorandum, from S. Andhil Fineberg to Area Directors and Executive Assistants, re: The American Jewish League Against Communism, May 4, 1962, p. 2, in AJC records, RG 347.17 Gen-12, box 12, "Am. Jewish League Against Communism 54–62."

76. AJC Staff Committee on Communism minutes, August 30, 1950, p. 4, in AJC records, box 247, "Staff Committee on Communism minutes 1950–56"; Edwin J. Lukas to Walter White, September 8, 1950, pp. 1–2, in AJC records, RG 347.17 Gen-12, box 13, "Am. Jewish League Against Communism 50."

77. "Rabbi Benjamin Schultz," June 1952, revised October 1954, pp. 1–2 (the quote is from p. 2), in AJC records, RG 347.17 Gen-12, box 144, "Schultz, Benjamin 51–52"; George J. Hexter to Alfred Kohlberg, August 31, 1950, pp. 1–2, in AJC records, box 246, "Polit Phil Communism Sept-Dec 1950"; AJC memorandum, from S. Andhil Fineberg to John Slawson, April 17, 1953; Irving M. Engel to John Slawson, September 13, 1953; Edwin J. Lukas to Irving M. Engel, June 25, 1953, in AJC records, RG 347.17 Gen-12, box 12, "American Jewish League Against Communism 52–53"; AJC memorandum, "The American Jewish League Against Communism," May 4, 1962, p. 2, in AJC records, RG 347.17 Gen-12, box 12, "American Jewish League Against Communism 49–62"; Resolution of the AJC, AJCongress, and ADL, December 26, 1950, attached to NCRAC memorandum, from Isaiah M. Minkoff to NCRAC Membership and CJFWF Agencies, December 22, 1954; Leon M. Birkhead to Rabbi Louis Newman, October 21, 1954, in AJC records, RG 347.17 Gen-12, box 144, "Schultz, Rabbi Benjamin 47–61"; AJC memorandum, re: The American Jewish League Against Communism, from S. Andhil Fineberg to Area Directors and Executive Assistants, May 4, 1962, p. 2, in AJC records, RG 347.17 Gen-12, box 12, "Am. Jewish League Against Communism 54–62."

78. Eugene Lyons to Jacob Blaustein, December 6, 1950; Eugene Lyons to Jacob Blaustein, November 25, 1950, in AJC records, box 246, "Polit Phil Communism Sept-Dec 1950"; "Rabbi Benjamin Schultz and the American Jewish League Against Communism, Inc.," p. 3, attached to AJC memorandum, from Michael Sage to Manheim

Shapiro, December 8, 1954, in AJC records, RG 347.17 Gen-12, box 12, "Am. Jewish League Against Communism 54–62"; Edwin Lukas to Irving M. Engel, June 25, 1953, p. 2, in AJC records, RG 347.17 Gen-12, box 12, "Am. Jewish League Against Communism 52–53"; Irving M. Engel Oral Memoir, 1969–1970, pp. 5:5–7, in AJA.

79. Edwin Lukas of the AJC reported that unseating Rabbi Schultz "entailed a good deal of behind-the-scenes maneuvering since Schultz is a rather popular person among the delegates." AJC memorandum, re: "The All-American Conference to Combat Communism," from Edwin J. Lukas to John Slawson, November 21, 1950, pp. 1–2; Report by Joseph Woolfson on the First Plenum Session of the All-American Conference, November 18–19, 1950 (dated January 1951), p. 1; [Rabbi Benjamin Schultz?], "Deterioration of So-Called 'All-American Conference to Combat Communism,' " August 1951 (quoted phrase is from p. 1), in AJC records, RG 347.17 Gen-12, box 3, "All American Conference to Combat Communism 49–62"; AJC memorandum, "Rabbi Benjamin Schultz," June 1952, revised October 1954, p. 2, in AJC records, RG 347.17 Gen-12, box 144, "Schultz, Benjamin 51–52"; Third Report of the Staff Coordinator of Program on Communism, S. Andhil Fineberg to John Slawson, April 3, 1951, p. 4, in AJC records, box 248, "Polit Phil Communism Program Activities 50–55"; *Committee Reporter*, 4,9 (September 1947), p. 5; S. A. Fineberg to Hon. Paul F. Meissner, August 6, 1963; AJC memorandum, from S. Andhil Fineberg to Area Directors and Executive Assistants, re: Know Your America Week (November 24–30, 1963), October 9, 1963, in SAF papers, box 1, AJA.

80. Liebman, "The Ties That Bind," pp. 315–316.

81. On Jewish support for New Deal social welfare measures during the 1930s, see Dollinger, "The Politics of Acculturation," pp. 24–53 passim.

8. Return and Renewal

1. "Report of the Study Committee," in ADL National Commission minutes, April 29–May 1, 1955, p. 3, in ADL records.

2. I relied most heavily on the following works to establish the broad context for this chapter: Shapiro, *A Time for Healing*, especially chapters 7–8; Elazar, *Community and Polity*; Waxman, *America's Jews in Transition*; Liebman, *The Ambivalent American Jew*; Cohen, *Not Free to Desist*; Cohen, *American Jews and the Zionist Idea*, especially chapters 7–9; Moore, *To the Golden Cities*; Auerbach, *Rabbis and Lawyers*; Bershtel and Graubard, *Saving Remnants*.

3. Rabbi Marc H. Tannenbaum, the director of interreligious affairs for the AJC, argued that the Six-Day War "appeared to most Jews as the imminent prospect of another Auschwitz for the corporate Jewish body in Israel." See Tannenbaum, "Israel's Hour of Need and the Jewish-Christian Dialogue," *Conservative Judaism* 22 (Winter 1968), p. 8, quoted in Fishman, *American Protestantism and a Jewish State*, p. 168. Other observers characterized the overwhelming American Jewish response to the Six-Day War as a delayed reaction to the Holocaust. See Dawidowicz, "American Public Opinion," pp. 203–206, 211, 214, 217. Dawidowicz's contemporary account of the American response to the Six-Day War, written for the *American Jewish Year Book*, notes the reactions of American Jews, Jewish organizations, Jewish youth, Christian churches, leftists, and black nationalists. The author describes American Jewry as "fearful of the fate of a collective Auschwitz for the Jews in Israel." Ibid., p. 205. See also Teller, *Strangers and Natives*, pp. 287–288.

4. Individual Protestant leaders did speak out in support of Israel's right to exist, but they were in the minority, and generally did not represent official denominational bodies. Fishman, *American Protestantism and a Jewish State*, pp. 166–177, 179 (the quote is from p. 167); Cohen, *American Jews and the Zionist Idea*, p. 137; Dawidowicz, "American Public Opinion," pp. 218–224.

5. Cohen, *American Jews and the Zionist Idea*, p. 136; Dawidowicz, "American Public Opinion," pp. 228–229; Carson, *In Struggle*, pp. 266–270; Weisbord and Stein, *Bittersweet Encounter*, pp. 90–110; Friedman, *What Went Wrong?*, pp. 217–221, 228–233; Kaufman, *Broken Alliance*, pp. 80–83, 200–202, 208–211, 230, 244–245.

6. On the AJC's battle against social discrimination, discrimination in the "executive suite," and related problems during the late 1950s and 1960s, see Cohen, *Not Free to Desist*, pp. 411–428.

7. ADL National Executive Committee minutes, October 21–22, 1961, pp. 4–7, in ADL records; Cohen, *Not Free to Desist*, pp. 378–382; Heale, *American Anticommunism*, p. 199; Belth, *A Promise to Keep*, pp. 210–213; "Statement of the American Jewish Congress Submitted to the Large City Budgeting Conference," November 11, 1964, pp. 2–3, 14, in AJCongress records, box 18; Reports of the Executive Director, American Jewish Congress, April, May, July-August, and September 1962, in AJCongress records, box 17. For published results of the ADL's extensive investigation of the John Birch Society and its ideological allies, see Forster and Epstein, *Danger on the Right*; Epstein and Forster, *The Radical Right*. The latter work included an updated version of the authors' *Report on the John Birch Society, 1966*. These volumes provide a wealth of information relevant to the analysis in the following paragraphs. For another contemporary study, see Overstreet and Overstreet, *The Strange Tactics of Extremism*. For results of an ADL-sponsored study of political extremism that included an analysis of the radical right, see Lipset and Raab, *The Politics of Unreason*, especially pp. 248–337.

8. ADL National Executive Committee minutes, March 25–26, 1961, pp. 2–3; ADL National Executive Committee minutes, October 21–22, 1961, p. 5, in ADL records; Westin, "The John Birch Society," pp. 240, 242 (quote from p. 240); Lipset, "Three Decades of the Radical Right," pp. 373–446 passim; Lipset and Raab, *The Politics of Unreason*, pp. 248, 250–251, 255–257; Cohen, *Not Free to Desist*, p. 379; Lipset, "Prejudice and Politics," p. 46; Epstein and Forster, *The Radical Right*, pp. 3–4, 87–88, 195–203; Epstein and Forster, *Report on the John Birch Society*, pp. 1, 6, 16–18, 43, 83–87; Forster and Epstein, *Danger on the Right*, pp. xvi, 11, 17–18; Heale, *American Anticommunism*, p. 198; Overstreet and Overstreet, *The Strange Tactics of Extremism*, pp. 25–26, 34, 63, 239, 244.

9. ADL National Executive Committee minutes, March 25–26, 1961, pp. 2–3; ADL memorandum, Arnold Forster to Civil Rights Committee, October 30, 1961, p. 1, in ADL records; Lipset, "Prejudice and Politics," pp. 44–46; Lipset and Raab, *The Politics of Unreason*, pp. 248–250, 267–269, 271, 300; "Statement of the American Jewish Congress Submitted to the Large City Budgeting Conference," November 11, 1964, pp. 1–3, in AJCongress records, box 18; Proceedings of the Annual Conference, Association of Jewish Community Relations Workers, June 3–6, 1962, Atlantic City, N.J., Panel on "The Ultra-Right: Implications for Jewish Communities," pp. 1, 5, in SAF papers, box 4, AJA; Westin, "The John Birch Society," pp. 244–245, 247–248, 259–260; Epstein and Forster, *The Radical Right*, passim; Epstein and Forster, *Report on the John Birch Society*, pp. 7–15, 39, 41–43; Forster and Epstein, *Danger on the Right*, pp. xviii, 5, 102–103,

105–106, 112, 123–124, 133, 137, 141, 143, 155, 159, 164–165, 171, 180; Overstreet and Overstreet, *The Strange Tactics of Extremism*, pp. 26–27, 57, 103, 117–118, 122, 130–133, 154.

10. ADL National Executive Committee minutes, March 25–26, 1961, in ADL records (Kolack's statement is on p. 3); Proceedings of the Annual Conference, Association of Jewish Community Relations Workers, June 3–6, 1962, Atlantic City, N.J., Panel on "The Ultra-Right: Implications for Jewish Communities," p. 2, in SAF papers, box 4, AJA; Westin, "The John Birch Society," pp. 241–242, 247–249, 261, 266–267; Epstein and Forster, *The Radical Right*, pp. 88–89, 99–100, 145, 165–173; Overstreet and Overstreet, *The Strange Tactics of Extremism*, pp. 9, 19, 28, 30–31, 36, 53; Lipset, "Prejudice and Politics," pp. 44–47; Lipset, "Three Decades of the Radical Right," p. 379; Epstein and Forster, *Report on the John Birch Society*, pp. x, 1–2, 44–49; Forster and Epstein, *Danger on the Right*, p. 19.

11. Cohen, *Not Free to Desist*, pp. 379–380 (quote from p. 379); "Statement of the American Jewish Congress Submitted to the Large City Budgeting Conference," November 11, 1964, p. 3, in AJCongress records, box 18; Reports of Executive Director, American Jewish Congress, April, July-August, 1962, in AJCongress records, box 17.

12. ADL National Executive Committee minutes, March 25–26, 1961, pp. 1–2; ADL National Executive Committee minutes, October 21–22, 1961, p. 5, in ADL records; Westin, "The John Birch Society," p. 253; Epstein and Forster, *The Radical Right*, pp. 3–4; Forster and Epstein, *Danger on the Right*, pp. 11, 21, 44; Westin, "The John Birch Society, Fundamentalism on the Right," in Newman, *The Hate Reader*, pp. 153, 154; Overstreet and Overstreet, *The Strange Tactics of Extremism*, pp. 33, 36, 39, 100–101, 119.

13. "Statement of the American Jewish Congress Submitted to the Large City Budgeting Conference," November 11, 1964 (the quoted phrase is from pp. 2–3), in AJCongress records, box 18; ADL National Executive Committee minutes, April 7–8, 1962, pp. 5–6; ADL National Executive Committee minutes, March 25–26, 1961, p. 2, in ADL records; Cohen, *Not Free to Desist*, p. 379; Epstein and Forster, *The Radical Right*, pp. 8, 10, 11, 31, 34–35, 39, 45–49, 64–66, 69–70, 93, 96–97, 98, 104, 110–114, 128–137, 214; Epstein and Forster, *Report on the John Birch Society*, pp. 8, 28–37; Forster and Epstein, *Danger on the Right*, pp. 26–37 passim; Lipset and Raab, *The Politics of Unreason*, pp. 265–267, 438. Alan Westin noted that Welch often defended himself against charges of anti-Semitism by referring to Jewish friends and supporters, including an endorsement from the American Jewish League Against Communism. Westin, "The John Birch Society," pp. 255–258; Westin, "The John Birch Society, Fundamentalism on the Right," in Newman, *The Hate Reader*, pp. 156–157.

14. ADL National Executive Committee minutes, October 21–22, 1961 (Forster's remarks are on pp. 5–6), in ADL records; Proceedings of the Annual Conference, Association of Jewish Community Relations Workers, June 3–6, 1962, Atlantic City, N.J., Panel on "The Ultra-Right: Implications for Jewish Communities," p. 1, in SAF papers, box 4, AJA; interview with Arnold Forster by author, June 11, 1996. Alan Westin similarly reported a "clear atmosphere of anti-Semitism at some of his [Welch's] public meetings and anti-Semitic questions from the floor." Westin, "The John Birch Society," p. 257.

15. Danzig, "The Radical Right and the Rise of the Fundamentalist Minority," p. 298; Westin, "The John Birch Society," pp. 240, 247, 251, 264–265; Epstein and Forster, *The Radical Right*, pp. 3–5, 27–28, 87, 89–90, 164–165, 169–171; Overstreet and Over-

street, *The Strange Tactics of Extremism*, pp. 207–221 passim; Forster and Epstein, *Danger on the Right*, pp. 75–77, 175–176; interview with Arnold Forster by author, June 11, 1996.

16. Danzig, "The Radical Right and the Rise of the Fundamentalist Minority" (quote from p. 292); ADL National Executive Committee minutes, April 7–8, 1962, pp. 5–6, in ADL records; Proceedings of the Annual Conference, Association of Jewish Community Relations Workers, June 3–6, 1962, Atlantic City, N.J., Panel on "The Ultra-Right: Implications for Jewish Communities," p. 2, in SAF papers, box 4, AJA; Cohen, *Not Free to Desist*, pp. 378–379; Epstein and Forster, *The Radical Right*, pp. 11, 23, 38, 74, 83; Heale, *American Anticommunism*, p. 199; Overstreet and Overstreet, *The Strange Tactics of Extremism*, pp. 143–203 passim. For a subsequent, more equivocal analysis of the relation between Protestant fundamentalism and the radical right, see Lipset and Raab, *The Politics of Unreason*, pp. 12, 30, 263–264, 273–276, 300, 302, 453.

17. Cohen, *Not Free to Desist*, p. 381.

18. Joachim Prinz to Barry Goldwater, March 4, 1965, p. 2; Barry Goldwater to Joachim Prinz, February 3, 1965, in "Prinz, Joachim," Correspondence file, AJA.

19. ADL National Executive Committee minutes, March 25–26, 1961, p. 3, in ADL records; Epstein and Forster, *The Radical Right*, p. 3. See also Epstein and Forster, *Report on the John Birch Society*, pp. 88, 92; Forster and Epstein, *Danger on the Right*, pp. xvi–xvii, 8–9, 69, 81, 92–94, 101, 114, 126–129, 149–150, 153, 272–280; ADL memorandum, from Benjamin R. Epstein to ADL Regional Offices, May 4, 1966, in "Anti-Semitism IV, Information on the John Birch Society and Anti-Semitism Compiled by the Anti-Defamation League of B'nai B'rith, April-May 1966," Correspondence file, AJA.

20. Lipset, "Prejudice and Politics," p. 46. See also Lipset, "Three Decades of the Radical Right," pp. 379, 436–441; Lipset and Raab, *The Politics of Unreason*, pp. 257, 295–297, 310–311.

21. ADL National Executive Committee minutes, September 17–18, 1960, pp. 6–7, 12; ADL National Executive Committee minutes, March 25–26, 1961, pp. 3–5; ADL National Commission minutes, January 11–15, 1961, pp. 5–6; ADL National Commission minutes, January 31-February 3, 1963, pp. 18–21; Memorandum of National Civil Rights Committee, entitled "Rabble-Rousers" (January 1963), pp. 1–14, in ADL records; *ADL Bulletin*, 20,4 (April 1963), pp. 6–7; "George L. Rockwell, U.S. Nazi," in *Facts*, 15,2 (October 1963), pp. 271–280; Shad Polier to "Dear Colleague," July 1, 1960, pp. 1–2, in AJCongress records, box 31.

22. A similar number of incidents occurred in West Germany during this period. *ADL Bulletin*, 17,2 (February 1960), pp. 4–5; *ADL Bulletin*, 17,1 (January 1960), p. 1; ADL National Executive Committee minutes, February 27–28, 1960, pp. 1, 5, in ADL records; Ira Guilden to Judge Philip Halpern, January 19, 1960, p. 2, in AJCongress records, box 31; Belth, *A Promise to Keep*, pp. 260–262. The incidents are described in detail in Caplovitz and Rogers, *Swastika 1960*, pp. 13–26 passim. The authors of this report, which was published by the ADL, asserted, "ADL research shows that each year there are approximately three dozen incidents of this type." Ibid., p. 13 n. Another report of the incidents, prepared for the AJC, was Ann G. Wolfe, "Why the Swastika?" (AJC, 1962), excerpted in Newman, *The Hate Reader*, pp. 8–35. See also Quinley and Glock, *Anti-Semitism in America*, p. xi. By January 13, 1960, less than two weeks after the American desecrations started, the AJC had received over one hundred incident

reports. AJC memorandum, S. Andhil Fineberg, re: "Effect of Publicity on Vandalism," no. 4, January 13, 1960, in SAF papers, box 1, AJA.

23. ADL National Executive Committee minutes, February 27–28, 1960, p. 5, in ADL records; *ADL Bulletin*, 17,1 (January 1960), pp. 1–2; Ira Guilden to Judge Philip Halpern, January 19, 1960, p. 2, in AJCongress records, box 31; Caplovitz and Rogers, *Swastika 1960*, pp. 13–26 passim, 33–34, 48; Quinley and Glock, *Anti-Semitism in America*, p. xi; Wolfe, "Why the Swastika?" in Newman, *The Hate Reader*, pp. 68, 71, 84; AJC memorandum, from S. Andhil Fineberg, re: "Current Anti-Semitic Vandalism," January 5, 1960; AJC memorandum, S. Andhil Fineberg, January 8, 1960, re: "Increased Vandalism in the United States," no. 2; AJC memorandum, S. Andhil Fineberg, re: "Effect of Publicity on Vandalism," no. 4, January 13, 1960, in SAF papers, box 1, AJA.

24. Report of Civil Rights Committee, ADL National Commission minutes, January 11–15, 1961, p. 5; ADL National Executive Committee minutes, March 25–26, 1961, p. 6; ADL National Executive Committee minutes, February 27–28, 1960, pp. 1, 5–7, in ADL records; *ADL Bulletin*, 17,1 (January 1960), pp. 1–2; Caplovitz and Rogers, *Swastika 1960*; Cohen, *Not Free to Desist*, pp. 376–377; Dinnerstein, *Antisemitism in America*, p. 163; AJC memorandum, from S. Andhil Fineberg, re: "Current Anti-Semitic Vandalism," January 5, 1960; AJC memorandum, S. Andhil Fineberg, January 8, 1960, re: "Increased Vandalism in the United States," no. 2; AJC memorandum, S. Andhil Fineberg, re: "Effect of Publicity on Vandalism," no. 4, January 13, 1960, in SAF papers, box 1, AJA.

25. Benjamin R. Epstein, foreword to Caplovitz and Rogers, *Swastika 1960*, p. 8.

26. John Slawson, "Guidelines—The Lessons of the Swastika," *Committee Reporter* (March 1960), p. 12.

27. Quoted from Ira Guilden to Judge Philip Halpern, January 19, 1960, p. 2, in AJCongress records, box 31. A similar point was made in ADL National Executive Committee minutes, February 27–28, 1960, p. 5, in ADL records.

28. As a result of the "swastika epidemic" investigations, the ADL discovered twenty-seven neo-Nazi youth gangs. Previously, the league had information on thirteen such groups. Some of these groups, Caplovitz and Rogers suggested, may have actually been formed in response to the "swastika epidemic," while others predated and played a role in the outbreak. Caplovitz and Rogers, *Swastika 1960*, pp. 9, 36–41. See also Wolfe, "Why the Swastika?" in Newman, *The Hate Reader*, pp. 69, 73, 75, 76, 78–79, 80–82; Fact-Finding Division memorandum, "Neo-Nazi Youth Groups," March 1960, in SAF papers, box 1, AJA.

29. The results of Deutsch's study are summarized in *ADL Bulletin*, 19,2 (February 1962), pp. 1–2, 8 (quotes from p. 1). See also *ADL Bulletin*, 17,2 (February 1960), p. 4; Caplovitz and Rogers, *Swastika 1960*, p. 41; Wolfe, "Why the Swastika?" in Newman, *The Hate Reader*, pp. 71–78; "Material Relating to Psychological Studies of Three Boys Involved in Defacing Jewish Homes," Augusta, Kansas, January 1960, pp. 2, 5, 7, 9, 10, in Documents file, "Anti-Semitism IV," AJA.

30. Benjamin R. Epstein, foreword to Caplovitz and Rogers, *Swastika 1960*, p. 8. The AJC conducted a similar educational program in postwar Germany. See Cohen, *Not Free to Desist*, pp. 483–495.

31. Report of Program Division, ADL National Executive Committee minutes, September 20–21, 1958, p. 6; ADL National Executive Committee minutes, October 21–22,

1961, p. 11, in ADL records. On the ADL's approach to intercultural education during the 1950s, see chapter 3.

32. Shapiro, *A Time for Healing*, pp. 213–216 (quote from p. 213); Waxman, *America's Jews in Transition*, pp. 121–123. Waxman noted that the Eichmann trial sparked "the first awakening to the Holocaust as a symbol" but maintained that "it was not until after the Six-Day War . . . that the Holocaust became incorporated into American Jewish civil religion." Ibid., p. 121.

33. AJC memorandum, " 'Advancing Man's Understanding of His Fellow Man'— The Ways and Means," (1961), pp. 65–66, in AJC records, box 169, "IG REL Training 59–62."

34. ADL National Commission minutes, January 11–15, 1961, pp. 7–8 (the quote is from p. 8), in ADL records; Typescript, "Solomon Andhil Fineberg Archives, The Trial of Adolph Eichmann . . . ," 1972; AJC press release, "How the Israelis View the Eichmann Trial," S. Andhil Fineberg, January 18, 1961, p. 1; AJC memorandum, from S. Andhil Fineberg, "The End of the Eichmann Trial—Suggestions for Programming," December 6, 1961, pp. 1–3; David Landor to S. Andhil Fineberg, January 3, 1962; Flyers from Fineberg's speeches in various cities during February and March, 1961; Typescript of speech, "Another Nazi Triumph in the Making," S. Andhil Fineberg, in SAF papers, box 1, AJA; Solomon Andhil Fineberg Oral History Interview, 1974, 5:194 to 5:200, in SAF papers, box 5, AJA; "Prinz, Joachim," *Current Biography* (February 1963), p. 33. For the efforts of the AJC and other Jewish agencies to prevent Eichmann's kidnapping and trial from sparking anti-Semitism in Argentina, see Cohen, *Not Free to Desist*, pp. 547–548.

35. AJC press release, "How the Israelis View the Eichmann Trial," S. Andhil Fineberg, January 18, 1961, p. 1, in SAF papers, box 1, AJA.

36. For Forster's own account and excerpts from many of his radio reports, see Forster, *Square One*, pp. 179–236. AJC staff member and Jewish historian Lucy S. Dawidowicz argued that American Jews' "suppressed" guilt feelings about surviving the Holocaust "began to emerge" as a result of the Eichmann trial. See Dawidowicz, "American Public Opinion," p. 203.

37. Quinley and Glock, *Anti-Semitism in America*, pp. 114–116, 123, 125–126, 127; Glock, Selznick, and Spaeth, *The Apathetic Majority*, pp. 24–28 passim; ADL National Commission minutes, January 31–February 2, 1964, p. 10, in ADL records.

38. Jewish intergroup relations officials were not the only ones who voiced such concerns. As Deborah Dash Moore recounts, in her study of Miami and Los Angeles Jews, during this period "a series of increasingly dire predictions regarding the Jewish future" began to appear in popular magazines and newspapers. Moore notes that even earlier, in the 1950s, several careful observers of American Jewish life—including sociologists Nathan Glazer and Herbert Gans—had offered "gloomy" predictions about the Jewish future. Moore, *To the Golden Cities*, pp. 272, 335 n. 17.

39. Schary's speech was printed in *ADL Bulletin*, 20,2 (February 1963), p. 6.

40. Address by Dr. Joachim Prinz, president of the American Jewish Congress, at the National Biennial Convention, Waldorf-Astoria Hotel, April 13, 1962, pp. 1–3 (quote from p. 3), in AJCongress records, box 14. Accounts of speeches in which Prinz sounded similar themes are given in clippings from the *New York Times*, September 8, 1958; June 30, 1959, in "Prinz, Joachim," Nearprint files, Biographies, AJA.

41. "Statement of the American Jewish Congress Submitted to the Large City Budgeting Conference," November 11, 1964, p. 12, in AJCongress records, box 18.

42. See Moore, *At Home in America*; Moore, *To the Golden Cities*; Shapiro, *A Time for Healing*, pp. 133–139, 143–153. For contemporary sociological works on Jewish suburbanization, see chapter 1, note 52.

43. Address by Dr. Joachim Prinz, president of the American Jewish Congress, at the National Biennial Convention, Waldorf-Astoria Hotel, April 13, 1962, pp. 4–5, in AJCongress records, box 14; AJCongress Women's Division Core Programs, "Meeting Years of Challenge" (1961–1962) and "Israel and International Jewish Concerns," (1969), in AJCongress records, box 145b; AJCongress Women's Division National Board minutes, June 10, 1957, in AJCongress records, box 133.

44. Address by Dr. Joachim Prinz, president of the American Jewish Congress, at the National Biennial Convention, Waldorf-Astoria Hotel, April 13, 1962, p. 3, in AJCongress records, box 14. See also AJCongress news release, April 15, 1962, pp. 1–2, in AJCongress records, box 14; "Prinz, Joachim," *Current Biography* (February 1963), p. 33.

45. "Statement of the American Jewish Congress Submitted to the Large City Budgeting Conference," November 11, 1964, pp. 12–13 (the quote is from p. 12), in AJCongress records, box 18; AJCongress Women's Division Executive Committee minutes, October 14, 1964, pp. 3–4; October 12, 1966, in AJCongress records, box 132; AJCongress National Women's Division Core Program for Jewish Education, "The Integrated Jew" (1958), in AJCongress records, box 145b; AJCongress Women's Division, Biennial Convention Report, 1965, p. 14, in AJCongress records, box 135. After retiring as executive vice president of the AJC in 1967, John Slawson, who characterized his own religious education as "very spotty," became involved with the Brandeis Camp Institute in Los Angeles and a number of other programs dedicated to strengthening religious and ethnic identification among young Jews. In order to stem the tide of assimilation, Slawson argued, "We need to present Judaism in a manner that will make it intellectually attractive, emotionally satisfying and esthetically enjoyable to our young." John Slawson Autobiographical Sketch, April 1, 1970, pp. 6–7, AJA. For an analysis of the Brandeis Camp Institute, see Moore, *To the Golden Cities*, pp. 140–152.

46. Quoted from AJCongress news release on Biennial Convention, April 15, 1962, p. 2, in AJCongress records, box 14.

47. Segal's comments, which appeared in *Der Tog* (The Day) on May 21, 1960, were quoted and discussed by Shad Polier in his "Dear Colleague" letter, May 26, 1960, p. 1, in AJCongress records, box 13.

48. Address by Dr. Joachim Prinz, president of the American Jewish Congress, at the National Biennial Convention, Waldorf-Astoria Hotel, April 13, 1962, p. 5, in AJCongress records, box 14.

49. Ibid.

50. Lipset, "Intergroup Relations/The Changing Situation of American Jewry," pp. 317–338 (the quote is from p. 336). Sklare's observation is quoted from his introductory comments on p. 315. This schism within the Jewish community is also discussed in Friedman, *What Went Wrong?* pp. 265–266. For an in-depth sociological analysis of this phenomenon, see Rieder, *Canarsie*.

51. For discussions of this transformation, see Bloch, "The Emergence of Neoconservatism"; Shapiro, *A Time for Healing*, pp. 221–223; Kaufman, *Broken Alliance*, pp. 107–110, 213–215, 270; Friedman, *What Went Wrong?* pp. 266–268, 317. For an elabo-

ration of the argument that liberalism is inconsistent with Jewish interests, see Wisse, *If I Am Not for Myself*.

52. Nathan Belth wrote that by the 1960s, "Jews had truly merged into the majority; they were in thought, aspirations, commitment, and status part of the majority." Belth, *A Promise to Keep*, pp. 281–282.

53. On black-Jewish relations, see Dinnerstein, *Antisemitism in America*, pp. 197–227; Weisbord and Stein, *Bittersweet Encounter*; Henthoff, *Black Anti-Semitism and Jewish Racism*; Kaufman, *The Broken Alliance*; Phillips, *An Unillustrious Alliance*; Lerner and West, *Blacks & Jews*; Friedman, *What Went Wrong?*

54. In a recent article on Jewish community relations and civil rights activist Irving M. Levine, Gerald Sorin notes that Levine concluded a new approach was needed to deal with interethnic and interracial conflict by the late 1960s. Sorin quotes Levine as saying, "We must recover from our shock at having at least for the time passed out of the brotherhood-intergroup relations-dialogue stage of racial progress and into a more difficult era of group conflict, group interest, and group identity." Sorin, "From the Brownsville Boys Club," p. 284. For a discussion that deals with the breakdown of the liberal civil rights paradigm in another context, see Jackson, *Gunnar Myrdal and America's Conscience*, pp. 297–310.

Bibliography

Abbreviations

AHR   *American Historical Review*
AJA   *American Jewish Archives*
AJH   *American Jewish History*
AJHQ   *American Jewish Historical Quarterly*
AJYB   *American Jewish Year Book*
Annals *Annals of the American Academy of Political and Social Science*
AQ   *American Quarterly*
JAEH   *Journal of American Ethnic History*
JAH   *Journal of American History*

Archival Collections

This study is based on archival records of the American Jewish Committee, the American Jewish Congress, and the Anti-Defamation League of B'nai B'rith, as well as other archival materials related to the activities of the leaders and staff members of those organizations. Specific references are recorded in the notes.

American Jewish Archives, Cincinnati, Ohio

Solomon Andhil Fineberg Papers

> *Subject files*

American Nazi Party
Anti-Semitism III and IV
Anti-Defamation League of B'nai B'rith

Biographies files, nearprint files, oral histories, and autobiographies

Jacob Blaustein
Irving M. Engel
Walter S. Hilborn
Morris Kertzer
Will Maslow
Joachim Prinz
Richard C. Rothschild
Morris U. Schappes
John Slawson
Meier Steinbrink

Anti-Defamation League films

Heritage
Toward Full Integration
Can We Immunize Against Prejudice?
A Trumpet for the Combo
As the Twig is Bent
A Tribute to the American Theater

American Jewish Committee Records, RG 347 Gen-10 and RG 347.17
Gen-12, at the YIVO Institute for Jewish Research, New York City

American Jewish Congress Records, *I-77, at the American Jewish
Historical Society, Waltham, Massachusetts

Anti-Defamation League Records, Anti-Defamation League national
headquarters, New York City

Periodicals Consulted

ADL Bulletin
American Jewish Year Book
Commentary
Committee Reporter
Congress Weekly
Facts
National Guardian
New York Post-Home News
New York Times

Published Primary Sources

Abrams, Charles. "The Walls of Stuyvesant Town." *Nation* 160 (March 24, 1945):328–330.

— "Homes For Aryans Only: The Restrictive Covenant Spreads Legal Racism in America." *Commentary* 3 (May 1947):421–427.

— "Race Bias in Housing, I. The Great Hypocrisy." *Nation* 165 (July 19, 1947):67–69.

Ackerman, Nathan. "Foreword." In Earl A. Grollman, *Judaism in Sigmund Freud's World*. New York: Bloch, 1965.

Ackerman, Nathan, and Marie Jahoda. *Anti-Semitism and Emotional Disorder: A Psychoanalytic Approach*. New York: Harper, 1950.

Adorno, T. W. "Scientific Experiences of a European Scholar in America." In Donald Fleming and Bernard Bailyn, eds., *The Intellectual Migration: Europe and America, 1930–1960*. Cambridge: Harvard University Press, 1969.

Adorno, T. W., Else Frenkel-Brunswik, Daniel J. Levison, and R. Nevitt Sanford. *The Authoritarian Personality*. New York: Harper, 1950.

Allport, Gordon W. "Foreword." In "Controlling Group Prejudice." *Annals* 244 (March 1946):vii–viii.

— *The Person in Psychology: Selected Essays*. Boston: Beacon, 1968.

— *The Nature of Prejudice*. 25th anniversary ed. Reading, Mass.: Addison-Wesley, 1979.

American Civil Liberties Union. "Violence in Peekskill, A Report of the Violations of Civil Liberties at Two Paul Robeson Concerts Near Peekskill, N.Y., August 27th and September 4th, 1949." New York: ACLU, 1949.

— "Statement by American Civil Liberties Union on Grand Jury Presentment Concerning Peekskill Disorders." New York: ACLU, 1950.

American Jewish Committee. *Report of the Conference on Group Life in America, Arden House, November 1956*. New York: AJC, 1956.

— "The People Take the Lead: A Record of Progress in Civil Rights, 1948 to 1958." New York: AJC, 1958.

American Jewish Committee, Department of Scientific Research. *A Brief Survey of the Major Agencies in the Field of Intercultural Education*. New York: AJC, 1950.

American Jewish Congress, Commission on Law and Social Action. "Check List of State Anti-Discrimination and Anti-Bias Laws." Rev. ed. New York: Commission, 1953.

— "Report on State Anti-Discrimination Agencies and the Laws They Administer." New York: American Jewish Congress, [1957].

— "Summary of 1957 State Anti-Discrimination Laws." New York: [1957].

— "Summary of 1958 and 1959 State Anti-Discrimination Laws." New York: [1959].

American Jewish Congress and National Association for the Advancement of Colored People. *Civil Rights in the United States in 1948: A Balance Sheet of Group Relations*. [New York]: American Jewish Congress and National Association for the Advancement of Colored People, [1949?].

— *Civil Rights in the United States in 1949: A Balance Sheet of Group Relations.* [New York]: American Jewish Congress and National Association for the Advancement of Colored People, 1950.

— *Civil Rights in the United States in 1950: A Balance Sheet of Group Relations.* [New York]: American Jewish Congress and National Association for the Advancement of Colored People, 1951.

— *Civil Rights in the United States in 1951: A Balance Sheet of Group Relations.* [New York]: American Jewish Congress and National Association for the Advancement of Colored People, [1952?].

— *Civil Rights in the United States 1952: A Balance Sheet of Group Relations.* [New York]: American Jewish Congress and National Association for the Advancement of Colored People, 1953.

— *Civil Rights in the United States 1953: A Balance Sheet of Group Relations.* [New York]: American Jewish Congress and National Association for the Advancement of Colored People, [1954?].

"Application of the Anti-Discrimination Law to University Employment Agencies." *Columbia Law Review* 47 (1947):674–675.

Barron, Milton L., ed. *American Minorities: A Textbook of Readings in Intergroup Relations.* New York: Knopf, 1957.

Bell, Daniel. "The Dispossessed." In Daniel Bell, ed., *The Radical Right.* Garden City, N.Y.: Doubleday, 1964.

Bell, Daniel, ed. *The Radical Right.* Garden City, N.Y.: Doubleday, 1964.

Benedict, Ruth, and Gene Weltfish. *The Races of Mankind.* Pubic Affairs Pamphlet No. 85, 1943.

Berger, Clarence Q. "Evaluating Community Acceptance of Intercultural Education." *Journal of Educational Sociology* 21 (September 1947):58–64.

Berger, Morroe. "Fair Employment Practices Legislation," *Annals* 275 (May 1951):34–40.

Bettelheim, Bruno, and Morris Janowitz. *Dynamics of Prejudice: A Psychological and Sociological Study of Veterans.* New York: Harper, 1950.

Brameld, Theodore. "An Inductive Approach to Intercultural Values." *Journal of Educational Sociology* 21 (September 1947):4–11.

Brown, Earl. *Why Race Riots? Lessons from Detroit.* Public Affairs Pamphlet No. 87, 1944.

Brown, Sterling. *Primer in Intergroup Relations.* New York: National Conference of Christians and Jews, 1949.

Broyard, Anatole. "Portrait of the Inauthentic Negro: How Prejudice Distorts the Victim's Personality." *Commentary* 10 (July 1950):56–64.

Bryson, Lyman, and Dorothy Rowden. "Radio as an Agency of National Unity." *Annals* 244 (March 1946):137–143.

Cain, Harry P. "Security of the Republic." *New Republic*, January 31, 1955, pp. 6–10.

Caplovitz, David, and Candace Rogers. *Swastika 1960: The Epidemic of Anti-Semitic Vandalism in America.* New York: Anti-Defamation League of B'nai B'rith, 1961.

Chein, Isidor. "Some Considerations in Combatting Intergroup Prejudice." *Journal of Educational Sociology* 19 (March 1946):412–419.

— "What Are the Psychological Effects of Segregation Under Conditions of Equal Facilities?" *International Journal of Opinion and Attitude Research* 3 (1949):229–234.

Chein, Isidor, and Max Deutscher. "The Psychological Effects of Enforced Segregation: A Survey of Social Science Opinion." *Journal of Psychology* 26 (1948):259–287.

Christie, Richard, and Peggy Cook. "A Guide to the Published Literature Relating to the Authoritarian Personality Through 1956." *Journal of Psychology* 45 (1958):171–191.

Clark, Kenneth B. *Prejudice and Your Child*. Boston: Beacon, 1955.

Clinchy, Everett R. "The Effort of Organized Religion." *Annals* 244 (March 1946):128–136.

Clurman, Richard M. "Training Film for Democrats." *Commentary* 8 (August 1949):181–183.

Cohen, Elliot E. "Letter to the Movie-Makers: The Film Drama as a Social Force." *Commentary* 4 (August 1947):110–118.

— "Mr. Zanuck's 'Gentleman's Agreement': Reflections on Hollywood's Second Film About Anti-Semitism." *Commentary* 5 (January 1948):51–56.

Cohen, Oscar, and Stanley Wexler, eds. *"Not the Work of a Day": Anti-Defamation League of B'nai B'rith Oral Memoirs*. 7 vols. New York: Anti-Defamation League of B'nai B'rith, 1987.

Comment. "The New York State Commission Against Discrimination: A New Technique for an Old Problem." *Yale Law Journal* 56 (1947–1948):837–863.

Cook, Lloyd Allen. "The Frame of Reference in the College Study." *Journal of Educational Sociology* 21 (September 1947):31–42.

Cooper, Eunice and Helen Dinerman. "Analysis of the Film 'Don't Be a Sucker': A Study in Communication." *Public Opinion Quarterly* 15 (Summer 1951):243–264.

Cooper, Eunice, and Marie Jahoda. "The Evasion of Propaganda: How Prejudiced People Respond to Anti-Prejudice Propaganda." *Journal of Psychology* 23 (1947):15–25.

Danzig, David. "The Radical Right and the Rise of the Fundamentalist Minority." *Commentary* 33 (April 1962):291–298.

Dawidowicz, Lucy S. " 'Anti-Semitism' and the Rosenberg Case: The Latest Communist Propaganda Trap." *Commentary* 14 (July 1952):41–45.

— "False Friends and Dangerous Defenders." *Reconstructionist* 19 (May 1, 1953):9–15.

— "American Public Opinion." *AJYB* 69 (1968):198–229.

Dawidowicz, Lucy S., and Leon J. Goldstein. "The American Jewish Liberal Tradition." In Marshall Sklare, ed., *The Jewish Community in America*. New York: Behrman House, 1974.

Dean, John P., and Alex Rosen. *A Manual of Intergroup Relations*. Chicago: University of Chicago Press, 1955.

Deutsch, Monroe E. *Our Legacy of Religious Freedom*. [New York]: National Conference of Christians and Jews, 1941.

Deutsch, Morton, and Mary Evans Collins. *Interracial Housing: A Psychological Evaluation of a Social Experiment*. New York: Russell and Russell, 1951.

Dodson, Dan W. "Is Evaluation Much Ado About Nothing?" *Journal of Educational Sociology* 21 (September 1947):53–57.

Duker, Abraham. *Jewish Community Relations: An Analysis of the MacIver Report*. New York: Jewish Reconstructionist Foundation, 1952.

Epstein, Benjamin R., and Arnold Forster. *Report on the John Birch Society, 1966*. New York: Random House, 1966.

— *The Radical Right: Report on the John Birch Society and Its Allies*. New York: Vintage, 1967.

"Exclusion of Negroes from Subsidized Housing Project." *University of Chicago Law Review* 15 (1947–1948):745–756.

Fast, Howard. *Peekskill: USA: A Personal Experience*. [New York]: Civil Rights Congress, 1951.

— *Being Red*. New York: Dell, 1990.

Fineberg, Solomon Andhil. *Overcoming Anti-Semitism*. New York: Harper, 1943.

— "Checkmate for Rabble-Rousers: What to Do When the Demagogue Comes." *Commentary* 2 (September 1946):220–226.

— *Punishment Without Crime: What You Can Do About Prejudice*. New York: Doubleday, 1949.

— "They Screamed for Justice." *American Legion Magazine* 55 (July 1953):22–23, 43–49.

— "Plain Facts About the Rosenberg Case." *Reader's Digest* 63 (September 1953):9–14.

— *The Rosenberg Case: Fact and Fiction*. New York: Oceana, 1953.

Flowerman, Samuel H. "Mass Propaganda in the War Against Bigotry." *Journal of Abnormal and Social Psychology* 42 (1947):429–439.

— "The Use of Propaganda to Reduce Prejudice: A Refutation." *International Journal of Opinion and Attitude Research* 3 (1949):99–108.

— "Portrait of the Authoritarian Man." *New York Times Magazine*, April 23, 1950, pp. 9, 28–31.

Flowerman, Samuel H., and Marie Jahoda. "Can We Fight Prejudice Scientifically? Toward a Partnership of Action and Research." *Commentary* 2 (December 1946):583–587.

Foner, Philip S., ed. *Paul Robeson Speaks: Writings, Speeches, Interviews*. New York: Brunner/Mazel, 1978.

Forster, Arnold. *Square One: A Memoir*. New York: Donald I. Fine, 1988.

Forster, Arnold, and Benjamin R. Epstein. *Danger on the Right: The Attitudes, Personnel, and Influence of the Radical Right and Extreme Conservatives*. New York: Random House, 1964.

— *The Troublemakers: An Anti-Defamation League Report*. 2d ed. Westport, Conn.: Negro Universities Press, 1970.

Fredman, J. George, and Louis A. Falk. *Jews in American Wars*. New York: Jewish War Veterans of the U.S., 1942.

Freud, Sigmund. *Moses and Monotheism.* Trans. Katherine Jones. New York: Vintage, 1967.

— *Civilization and Its Discontents.* Trans. James Strachey. Intro. Peter Gay. New York: Norton, 1989.

Fromm, Erich. *Escape from Freedom.* New York: Rinehart, 1941.

— *Man For Himself: An Inquiry Into the Psychology of Ethics.* New York: Holt, Rinehart and Winston, 1947.

— *The Sane Society.* New York: Holt, Rinehart and Winston, 1955.

Gans, Herbert J. "Park Forest: Birth of a Jewish Community." *Commentary* 11 (April 1951):330–339.

— "The Origin and Growth of a Jewish Community in the Suburbs." In Marshall Sklare, ed., *The Jews: Social Patterns of an American Group.* New York: Free, 1958.

— *The Levittowners: Ways of Life and Politics in a New Suburban Community.* New York: Columbia University Press, 1982.

Gersh, Harry. "Gentlemen's Agreement in Bronxville: The 'Holy Square Mile.' " *Commentary* 27 (February 1959):109–116.

Giles, H. H. "Basic Purposes and Problems in Evaluation of Intercultural Education." *Journal of Educational Sociology* 21 (September 1947):12–18.

Giles, H. H., and William Van Til. "School and Community Projects." *Annals* 244 (March 1946):34–41.

Glatstein, Irwin Lee, and Irving Howe. "How To Fight Rabble-Rousers? A Discussion." *Commentary* 2 (November 1946):460–466.

Glazer, Nathan. "The Authoritarian Personality in Profile: Report on a Major Study of Race Hatred." *Commentary* 9 (June 1950):573–583.

— "New Light on 'The Authoritarian Personality': A Survey of Recent Research and Criticism." *Commentary* 17 (March 1954):289–297.

Glock, Charles Y., and Rodney Stark. *Christian Beliefs and Antisemitism.* New York: Harper and Row, 1966.

Glock, Charles Y., Gertrude J. Selznick, and Joe L. Spaeth. *The Apathetic Majority: A Study Based on Public Responses to the Eichmann Trial.* New York: Harper and Row, 1966.

Glock, Charles Y., and Ellen Siegelman, eds. *Prejudice U.S.A..* New York: Praeger, 1969.

Goodman, Mary E. *Race Awareness in Young Children.* Rev. ed. New York: Collier, 1964.

Gordon, Albert I. *Jews in Suburbia.* Boston: Beacon, 1959.

Gordon, Milton M. *Assimilation in American Life: The Role of Race, Religion, and National Origins.* New York: Oxford University Press, 1964.

Graeber, Isacque, and Steuart Henderson Britt, eds. *Jews in a Gentile World: The Problem of Anti-Semitism.* New York: Macmillian, 1942.

Greeley, Andrew M. *Why Can't They Be Like Us? Facts and Fallacies About Ethnic Differences and Group Conflicts in America.* New York: Institute of Human Relations Press, 1969.

Groner, Isaac N., and David M. Helfeld. "Race Discrimination in Housing." *Yale Law Journal* 57 (1947–1948):426–456.

Gumbiner, Joseph H. "On the Horizon: Interfaith at Walla Walla." *Commentary* 9 (February 1950):176–181.

Handlin, Oscar. "Prejudice and Capitalist Exploitation: Does Economics Explain Racism?" *Commentary* 6 (July 1948):79–85.

— "Group Life Within the American Pattern: Its Scope and Limits." *Commentary* 8 (November 1949):411–417.

— "Party Maneuvers and Civil Rights Realities." *Commentary* 14 (September 1952):197–205.

— "Freedom or Authority in Group Life? Voluntary Agreements Work, Our Experiences Tell Us." *Commentary* 14 (December 1952):547–554.

Herberg, Will. "The Sectarian Conflict Over Church and State: A Divisive Threat to Our Democracy?" *Commentary* 14 (November 1952):450–462.

— "Communism, Democracy, and the Churches: Problems of 'Mobilizing the Religious Front.' " *Commentary* 19 (April 1955):386–393.

— *Protestant-Catholic-Jew: An Essay in American Religious Sociology*. New York: Doubleday, 1955.

Herrick, Arnold and Herbert Askwith, eds. *This Way to Unity*. New York: Oxford, 1945.

Himelhoch, Jerome. "Is There a Bigot Personality? A Report on Some Preliminary Studies." *Commentary* 3 (March 1947):277–284.

Himmelfarb, Milton. "Our Jewish Community and Its Critics: Why Single, Central Authority Is Not for Us." *Commentary* 16 (August 1953):115–121.

— *The Jews of Modernity*. New York: Basic, 1973.

Hobson, Laura Z. *Gentlemen's Agreement*. New York: Simon and Schuster, 1947.

Hofstadter, Richard. *The Age of Reform*. New York: Vintage, 1955.

— "The Pseudo-Conservative Revolt." In Daniel Bell, ed., *The Radical Right*. Garden City, N.Y.: Doubleday, 1964.

— "Pseudo-Conservatism Revisisted: A Postscript." In Daniel Bell, ed., *The Radical Right*. Garden City, N.Y.: Doubleday, 1964.

Horkheimer, Max, and Theodor W. Adorno. *Dialectic of Enlightenment*. Trans. John Cumming. New York: Herder and Herder, 1972.

Johnson, Charles S. "National Organizations in the Field of Race Relations." *Annals* 244 (March 1946):117–127.

Kecskemeti, Paul. "Prejudice in the Catastrophic Perspective." *Commentary* 11 (March 1951):286–292.

— "The Psychological Theory of Prejudice: Does It Underrate the Role of Social History?" *Commentary* 18 (September 1954):359–366.

Konvitz, Milton R. "The Courts Deal a Blow to Segregation: The 'Separate But Equal' Doctrine Begins to Crumble." *Commentary* 11 (February 1951):158–166.

— "Legislation Guaranteeing Equality of Access to Places of Public Accommodation." *The Annals* 275 (May 1951):47–52.

— *A Century of Civil Rights*. New York: Columbia University Press, 1961.

— *Judaism and the American Idea*. Ithaca: Cornell University Press, 1978.

Konvitz, Milton R., ed. *Law and Social Action: Selected Essays of Alexander H. Pekelis*. Ithaca: Cornell University Press, 1950.

Kracauer, Siegfried. "The Revolt Against Rationality." *Commentary* 3 (June 1947):586–587.

Kristol, Irving. " 'Civil Liberties,' 1952—A Study in Confusion." *Commentary* 13 (March 1952):228–236.

Lasker, Bruno. *Race Attitudes in Children*. New York: Henry Holt, 1929.

Lazaron, Morris S. *Common Ground: A Plea for Intelligent Americanism*. New York: Liveright, 1938.

Lazarsfeld, Paul F. *Radio and the Printed Page*. New York: Duell, Sloan and Pearce, 1940.

— "Some Remarks on the Role of the Mass Media in So-Called Tolerance Propaganda." *Journal of Social Issues* 3 (Summer 1947):17–25.

— "An Episode in the History of Social Research: A Memoir." In Donald Fleming and Bernard Bailyn, eds., *The Intellectual Migration: Europe and America, 1930–1960*. Cambridge: Harvard University Press, 1969.

Lazarsfeld, Paul, and Frank N. Stanton. *Radio Research, 1942–1943*. New York: Duell, Sloan and Pearce, 1944.

Lazarsfeld, Paul H., and Robert K. Merton, "Studies in Radio and Film Propaganda." *Transactions of the New York Academy of Science* 6 (1943):58–79.

Leskes, Theodore. "State Law Against Discrimination." In Milton R. Konvitz, ed., *A Century of Civil Rights*. New York: Columbia University Press, 1961.

Lewin, Kurt. *Resolving Social Conflicts*. New York: Harper, 1948.

Lippit, Ronald, and Marian Radke. "New Trends in the Investigation of Prejudice." *Annals* 244 (March 1946):167–176.

Lipset, Seymour Martin. "Changing Social Status and Prejudice: The Race Theories of a Pioneering American Sociologist." *Commentary* 9 (May 1950):475–479.

— "Three Decades of the Radical Right: Coughlinites, McCarthyites, and Birchers." In Daniel Bell, ed., *The Radical Right*. Garden City, N.Y.: Doubleday, 1964.

— "The Sources of the 'Radical Right.' " In Daniel Bell, ed., *The Radical Right*. Garden City, N.Y.: Doubleday, 1964.

— "Prejudice and Politics in the American Past and Present." In Charles Y. Glock and Ellen Siegelman, eds., *Prejudice U.S.A.* New York: Praeger, 1969.

— "Intergroup Relations/The Changing Situation of American Jewry." In Marshall Sklare, ed., *The Jewish Community in America*, New York: Behrman House, 1974.

Liveright, A. A. "The Community and Race Relations." *Annals* 244 (March 1946):106–116.

Lowenthal, Leo, and Norbert Guterman. *Prophets of Deceit: A Study of the Techniques of the American Agitator*. New York: Harper, 1949.

Lurie, H. L. " 'Freedom or Authority?' " Letter to the editor with response by Oscar Handlin. *Commentary* 15 (February 1953):200–203.

MacIver, Robert M. *The More Perfect Union: A Program for the Control of Intergroup Discrimination in the United States.* New York: Macmillan, 1948.

— *Report on the Jewish Community Relations Agencies.* New York: National Community Relations Advisory Committee, 1951.

— "Professor MacIver Demurs." Letter to the editor with response by Oscar Handlin. *Commentary* 15 (May 1953):513–518.

MacIver, Robert M., ed. *Group Relations and Group Antagonisms: A Series of Addresses and Discussions.* New York: Institute for Religious and Social Studies [Harper, distribution], 1944.

— *Unity and Difference in American Life: A Series of Addresses and Discussions.* New York: Institute for Religious and Social Studies [Harper, distribution], 1947.

— *Civilization and Group Relationships: A Series of Addresses and Discussions.* Port Washington, N.Y.: Kennikat Press, 1969 [1945].

McManus, John T., and Louis Kronenberger. "Motion Pictures, the Theater, and Race Relations." *Annals* 244 (March 1946):152–158.

McWilliams, Carey. "Race Discrimination and the Law." *Science and Society* 9 (Winter 1945):1–22.

— "Does Social Discrimination Really Matter? 'Exclusiveness' in a Democracy." *Commentary* 4 (November 1947):408–415.

— *A Mask for Privilege: Anti-Semitism in America.* Boston: Little, Brown, 1948.

— *Witch Hunt: The Revival of Heresy.* Boston: Little, Brown, 1950.

Marshall, Thurgood. "The Supreme Court as Protector of Civil Rights: Equal Protection of the Laws." *Annals* 275 (May 1951):101–110.

Marx, Gary T. *Protest and Prejudice: A Study of Belief in the Black Community.* New York: Harper and Row, 1967.

Maslow, Will. "The Law and Race Relations." *Annals* 244 (March 1946):75–81.

— "Prejudice, Discrimination, and the Law." *Annals* 275 (May 1951):9–17.

— *The Structure and Functioning of the American Jewish Community.* New York: American Jewish Congress and American Section of the World Jewish Congress, 1974.

Maslow, Will, and Joseph B. Robison. "Civil Rights: A Program for the President's Committee." *Lawyers Guild Review* 7 (May-June 1947):112–121.

— "Civil Rights Legislation and the Fight for Equality, 1862–1952." *University of Chicago Law Review* 20 (1953):363–413.

Massing, Paul M. *Rehearsal For Destruction: A Study of Political Anti-Semitism in Imperial Germany.* New York: Harper, 1949.

"Metropolitan Life Makes Housing Pay." *Fortune,* April 1946, pp. 133–136, 209–216.

Muelder, Walter G. "National Unity and National Ethics." *Annals* 244 (March 1946):10–18.

Myrdal, Gunnar. *An American Dilemma: The Negro Problem and American Democracy.* 2 vols. New York: Harper, 1944.

Neill, A. S. *Summerhill: A Radical Approach to Child Rearing.* New York: Hart, 1960.

Northrup, Herbert R. "Proving Ground for Fair Employment: Some Lessons from New York State's Experience." *Commentary* 4 (December 1947):552–556.

Note. "Legislative Attempts to Eliminate Racial and Religious Discrimination." *Columbia Law Review* 39 (1939):986–1003.

— "Segregation in Public Schools—A Violation of 'Equal Protection of the Laws.' " *Yale Law Journal* 56 (1946–1947):1059–1067.

— "Prevention of Discrimination in Private Educational Institutions." *Columbia Law Review* 47 (July 1947):821–827.

— "Applicability of the Fourteenth Amendment to Private Organizations." *Harvard Law Review* 61 (1947–1948):344–352.

— "The Disintegration of a Concept—State Action Under the 14th and 15th Amendments." *University of Pennsylvania Law Review* 96 (1947–1948):402–414.

— "Private Attorneys-General: Group Action in the Fight for Civil Liberties." *Yale Law Journal* 58 (March 1949):574–598.

Olson, Bernhard E. *Faith and Prejudice: Intergroup Problems in Protestant Curricula*. New Haven: Yale University Press, 1962.

Overstreet, Harry and Bonaro. *The Strange Tactics of Extremism*. New York: Norton, 1964.

Pekelis, Alexander H. "Full Equality in a Free Society: A Program for Jewish Action." In Milton R. Konvitz, ed., *Law and Social Action: Selected Essays of Alexander H. Pekelis*. Ithaca: Cornell University Press, 1950.

Petersen, William. "Prejudice in American Society: A Critique of Some Recent Formulations." *Commentary* 26 (October 1958):342–348.

Petersen, William, Herbert C. Kelman, and Thomas F. Pettigrew. "How to Understand Prejudice: An Exchange." *Commentary* 28 (November 1959):436–445.

Polier, Shad. "Law, Conscience, and Society." *Lawyers Guild Review* 6 (May-June 1946):490–491.

President's Committee on Civil Rights. *To Secure These Rights: The Report of the President's Committee on Civil Rights*. New York: Simon and Schuster, 1947.

Raphael, Marc Lee, ed. *Jews and Judaism in the United States*. New York: Behrman House, 1983.

Raths, Louis. "Evaluation in Programs of Intercultural Education." *Journal of Educational Sociology* 21 (September 1947):25–30.

Raths, Louis E., and Frank N. Trager. "Public Opinion and *Crossfire*." *Journal of Educational Sociology* 21 (January 1948):345–368.

Reimann, Miriam. "How Children Become Prejudiced: A Survey of Recent Studies." *Commentary* 11 (January 1951):88–94.

Review note. " 'Persons Aggrieved' Under the Ives-Quinn Law." *Lawyers Guild Review* 6 (January-February 1946):421–423.

Reznikoff, Charles, ed. *Louis Marshall, Champion of Liberty: Selected Papers and Addresses*. 2 vols. Philadelphia: Jewish Publication Society of America, 1957.

Riesman, David. "The 'Militant' Fight Against Anti-Semitism: Education and Democratic Discussion is the Better Way." *Commentary* 11 (January 1951):11–19.

Riesman, David, and Nathan Glazer. "The Intellectuals and the Discontented Classes." In Daniel Bell, ed., *The Radical Right*. Garden City, N.Y.: Doubleday, 1964.

Riesman, David, with Nathan Glazer and Reuel Denney. *The Lonely Crowd: A Study of the Changing American Character.* New Haven: Yale University Press, 1950.

Robison, Joseph B. "Organizations Promoting Civil Rights and Liberties." *Annals* 275 (May 1951):18–26.

Rorty, James. "The Native Anti-Semite's 'New Look': His Present 'Line' and His Prospects." *Commentary* 18 (November 1954):413–421.

— "What Price McCarthy Now? Exit Caliban?" *Commentary* 19 (January 1955), pp. 30–35.

— "The Dossier of Wolf Ladejinsky." *Commentary* 19 (April 1955):326–334.

Rorty, James, and Winifred Raushenbush. "The Lessons of the Peekskill Riots: What Happened and Why." *Commentary* 10 (October 1950):309–323.

Rose, Arnold M. "The Neurosis of Urbanization." *Commentary* 3 (June 1947):583–586.

— "Anti-Semitism's Root in City-Hatred: A Clue to the Jew's Position as Scapegoat." *Commentary* 6 (October 1948):374–378.

— "The Use of Propaganda to Reduce Prejudice." *International Journal of Opinion and Attitude Research* 2 (1948):221–229.

Rosen, Irwin C. "The Effect of the Motion Picture 'Gentleman's Agreement' on Attitudes Toward Jews." *Journal of Psychology* 26 (1948):525–536.

Rosenberg, Anna M. Oral History. Herbert Lehman project, Columbia University Oral History Archives, June 7, 1957.

Ross, Irwin. "The Communists: Friends of Foes of Civil Liberties?" New York: American Jewish Committee, 1950.

Samuels, Howard J. "Prejudice and the Marketplace." In Charles Y. Glock and Ellen Siegelman, eds., *Prejudice U.S.A.* New York: Praeger, 1969.

Sartre, Jean-Paul. *Anti-Semite and Jew.* Trans. George J. Becker. New York: Grove, 1948.

Saveth, Edward N. "Discrimination in the Colleges Dies Hard: Progress Report on an American Sore Spot." *Commentary* 9 (February 1950):115–121.

— "Fair Educational Practices Legislation." *Annals* 275 (May 1951):41–46.

Schary, Dore. "Letter from a Movie-Maker: 'Crossfire' as a Weapon Against Anti-Semitism." *Commentary* 4 (October 1947):344–349.

Schlesinger, Arthur M., Jr. *The Vital Center: The Politics of Freedom.* Boston: Houghton Mifflin, 1949.

Selznick, Gertrude J. and Stephen Steinberg. *The Tenacity of Prejudice.* New York: Harper and Row, 1969.

Shanks, Hershel. "Jewish-Gentile Intermarriage: Facts and Trends." *Commentary* 16 (October 1953):370–375.

Shannon, Joseph B. "Political Obstacles to Civil Rights Legislation." *Annals* 275 (May 1951):53–60.

Silberman, Charles E. "The Schools and the Fight Against Prejudice." In Charles Y. Glock and Ellen Siegelman, ed., *Prejudice U.S.A.* New York: Praeger, 1969.

Simmel, Ernst, ed. *Anti-Semitism, A Social Disease.* New York: International Universities Press, 1946.

Simpson, George Eaton, and J. Milton Yinger. *Racial and Cultural Minorities: An Analysis of Prejudice and Discrimination.* 4th ed. New York: Harper and Row, 1972.

Slawson, John. "Intergroup Relations in Social Work Education." In *Education for Social Work, Proceedings of the Sixth Annual Program Meeting.* New York: Council on Social Work Education, 1958.

Smith, M. Brewster. "The Schools and Prejudice: Findings." In Charles Y. Glock and Ellen Siegelman, eds., *Prejudice U.S.A..* New York: Praeger, 1969.

Stark, Rodney, and Charles Y. Glock. "Prejudice and the Churches." In Charles Y. Glock and Ellen Siegelman, eds., *Prejudice U.S.A..* New York: Praeger, 1969.

Stember, Charles H. et al. *Jews in the Mind of America.* New York: Basic, 1966.

Stouffer, Samuel A. *Communism, Conformity, and Civil Liberties: A Cross-section of the Nation Speaks Its Mind.* Garden City, N.Y.: Doubleday, 1955. Repr., Gloucester, Mass.: Peter Smith, 1963.

Sumner, William Graham. *Folkways.* Salem, Mass.: Ayer, 1992 [1906].

Supreme Court of the State of New York, County of Westchester. "Presentment of the October 1949 Grand Jury of Westchester County: The Peekskill Incidents." White Plains, N.Y., June 1950.

Taba, Hilda. "What Is Evaluation Up to and Up Against in Intergroup Education?" *Journal of Educational Sociology* 21 (September 1947):19–24.

Tumin, Melvin J. [*sic*] "The Idea of 'Race' Dies Hard." *Commentary* 8 (July 1949):80–85.

Tumin, Melvin M., ed. "Race and Intelligence: A Scientific Evaluation." New York: Anti-Defamation League of B'nai B'rith, 1963.

U.S. House Committee on Un-American Activities. *Preliminary Report on Neo-Fascist and Hate Groups.* Washington, D.C.: U.S. Government Printing Office, 1954.

U.S. Senate Committee on Armed Forces. *Nomination of Anna M. Rosenberg to Be Assistant Secretary of Defense: Hearing Before the Committee on Armed Services.* 81st Cong., 2d session. Washington, D.C.: U.S. Government Printing Office, 1950–1951.

Van Den Haag, Ernest, and Oscar Handlin. "Federal Aid to Parochial Schools: A Debate." *Commentary* 32 (July 1961):1–11.

Vorspan, Albert, and Eugene J. Lipman. *Justice and Judaism: The Work of Social Action.* New York: Union of American Hebrew Congregations, 1956.

Warshow, Robert. "The 'Idealism' of Julius and Ethel Rosenberg: 'The Kind of People We Are.'" *Commentary* 16 (November 1953):413–418.

Watson, Goodwin. "The Problem of Evaluation." *Annals* 244 (March 1946):177-182.

— *Action for Unity.* New York: Harper, 1947.

Westchester Committee for a Fair Inquiry Into the Peekskill Violence. *Eyewitness: Peekskill U.S.A. Aug. 27; Sept. 4, 1949.* White Plains, N.Y.: Committee, 1949.

Westin, Alan F. "Our Freedom—And the Rights of Communists: A Reply to Irving Kristol." *Commentary* (July 1952):33–40.

— "The John Birch Society." In Daniel Bell, ed., *The Radical Right.* Garden City, N.Y.: Doubleday, 1964.

Williams, Robin M., Jr. *The Reduction of Intergroup Tensions: A Survey of Research on*

Problems of Ethnic, Racial, and Religious Group Relations. New York: Social Science Research Council, 1947.

Wirth, Louis. "The Unfinished Business of American Democracy." *Annals* 244 (March 1946):1–9.

Wolfe, Ann G., ed. *A Reader in Jewish Community Relations.* New York: Ktav, 1975.

Wolfenstein, Martha, and Nathan Leites. "Two Social Scientists View 'No Way Out': The Unconscious vs. the 'Message' in an Anti-Bias Film." *Commentary* 10 (October 1950):388–391.

Wood, Alan. "I Sell My House: One Man's Experience with Suburban Segregation." *Commentary* 26 (November 1958):383–389.

Secondary Literature

Abrahams, Roger D. "Folklore in the Definition of Ethnicity: An American and Jewish Perspective." In Frank Talmage, ed., *Studies in Jewish Folklore: Proceedings of a Regional Conference of the Association for Jewish Studies Held at the Spertus College of Judaica, Chicago, May 1–3, 1977.* Cambridge, Mass., 1980.

Adler, Les K. "The Politics of Culture: Hollywood and the Cold War." In Robert Griffith and Athan Theoharis, ed., *The Specter: Original Essays on the Cold War and the Origins of McCarthyism.* New York: New Viewpoints, 1974.

Auerbach, Jerold. *Unequal Justice: Lawyers and Social Change in Modern America.* New York: Oxford University Press, 1976.

— "From Rags to Robes: The Legal Profession, Social Mobility and the American Jewish Experience." *AJHQ* 66 (December 1976):249–284.

— *Rabbis and Lawyers: The Journey From Torah to Constitution.* Bloomington: Indiana University Press, 1990.

Bahr, Ehrhard. "The Anti-Semitism Studies of the Frankfurt School: The Failure of Critical Theory." In Judith Marcus and Zoltán Tar, eds., *Foundations of the Frankfurt School of Social Research.* New Brunswick, N.J.: Transaction, 1984.

Baron, Salo W. "Newer Approaches to Jewish Emancipation." *Diogenes* 29 (Spring 1960):56–91.

Bayor, Ronald H. *Neighbors in Conflict: The Irish, Germans, Jews and Italians of New York City, 1929–1941.* Baltimore: Johns Hopkins University Press, 1978.

— "Historical Encounters: Intergroup Relations in a 'Nation of Nations.' " *Annals* 530 (November 1993):14–27.

Belth, Nathan C. *A Promise to Keep: A Narrative of the American Encounter with Anti-Semitism.* New York: Times, 1979.

Berger, Graenum. *Graenum.* Hoboken, N.J.: Ktav, 1987.

Berrol, Selma. "Public Schools and Immigrants: The New York City Experience." In Bernard J. Weiss, ed., *American Education and the European Immigrant, 1840–1940.* Urbana: University of Illinois Press, 1982.

— "Education and Economic Mobility: The Jewish Experience in New York City, 1880–1920." *AJHQ* 65 (March 1976):259–270.

Bershtel, Sarah, and Allen Graubard. "The Mystique of the Progressive Jew." *Working Papers* 10 (March-April 1983):18–25.

— *Saving Remnants: Feeling Jewish in America.* New York: Free, 1992.

Black, Allida M. *Casting Her Own Shadow: Eleanor Roosevelt and the Shaping of Postwar Liberalism.* New York: Columbia University Press, 1996.

Bloom, Jack M. *Class, Race, and the Civil Rights Movement.* Bloomington: Indiana University Press, 1987.

Blum, John Morton. *V Was for Victory: Politics and American Culture During World War II.* New York: Harcourt Brace Jovanovich, 1976.

Branch, Taylor. *Parting the Waters: America in the King Years, 1954–1963.* New York: Simon and Schuster, 1988.

Brinkley, Alan. *Voices of Protest: Huey Long, Father Coughlin, and the Great Depression.* New York: Vintage, 1982.

— *The End of Reform: New Deal Liberalism in Recession and War.* New York: Knopf, 1995.

Bronner, Stephen Eric, and Douglas MacKay Kellner, eds. *Critical Theory and Society: A Reader.* New York: Routledge, 1989.

Caro, Robert A. *The Power Broker: Robert Moses and the Fall of New York.* New York: Vintage, 1975.

Carson, Clayborne. *In Struggle: SNCC and the Black Awakening of the 1960s.* Cambridge: Harvard University Press, 1981.

Caute, David. *The Great Fear: The Anti-Communist Purge Under Truman and Eisenhower.* New York: Simon and Schuster, 1978.

Chyet, Stanley F. "American Jews: Notes on the Idea of a Community." *AJH* 81 (1992):331–339.

Cohen, Naomi W. *Not Free to Desist: The American Jewish Committee, 1906–1966.* Philadelphia: Jewish Publication Society of America, 1972.

— *American Jews and the Zionist Idea.* New York: Ktav, 1975.

— *Encounter with Emancipation: The German Jews in the United States, 1830–1914.* Philadelphia: Jewish Publication Society of America, 1984.

— *Jews in Christian America: The Pursuit of Religious Equality.* New York: Oxford University Press, 1992.

Cohen, Steven M. *The Dimensions of American Jewish Liberalism.* New York: American Jewish Committee, 1989.

Cohen, Steven M., and Charles S. Liebman. *The Quality of American Jewish Life—Two Views.* New York: American Jewish Committee, 1987.

Cohn, Norman. *Warrant for Genocide: The Myth of the Jewish World-Conspiracy and the Protocols of the Elders of Zion.* New York: Harper and Row, 1967.

Conzen, Kathleen Neils, David A. Gerber, Ewa Morawska, George E. Pozzetta, and Rudolph J. Vecoli. "The Invention of Ethnicity: A Perspective from the USA." With comments by Herbert J. Gans and Lawrence H. Fuchs and response. *JAEH* 12 (Fall 1992):3–63.

Cooney, Terry A. "New York Intellectuals and the Question of Jewish Identity." *AJH* 80 (Spring 1991):361–376.

Crosby, Donald F. "The Politics of Religion: American Catholics and the Anti-Communist Impulse." In Robert Griffith and Athan Theoharis, eds., *The Specter: Original Essays on the Cold War and the Origins of McCarthyism*. New York: New Viewpoints, 1974.

— *God, Church, and Flag: Senator Joseph R. McCarthy and the Catholic Church*. Chapel Hill: University of North Carolina Press, 1978.

Dalfiume, Richard M. "The Forgotten Years of the Negro Revolution." *JAH* 55 (June 1968):90–106.

Dalin, David G. "The American Element in the Thought of Will Herberg." *AJH* 81 (1992):296–308.

Dalin, David G., ed. *From Marxism to Judaism: The Collected Essays of Will Herberg*. New York: Markus Wiener, 1989.

Daniels, Roger. *Concentration Camps USA: Japanese-Americans and World War II*. New York: Holt, Rinehart and Winston, 1971.

Diner, Hasia R. *In the Almost Promised Land: American Jews and Blacks, 1915–1935*. Westport, Conn.: Greenwood, 1977.

— "Jewish Self-Governance, American Style." *AJH* 81 (1992):277–295.

Dinnerstein, Leonard. "Anti-Semitism Exposed and Attacked, 1945–1950." *AJH* 71 (September 1981):134–149.

— "Education and the Advancement of American Jews." In Bernard J. Weiss, ed., *American Education and the European Immigrant, 1840–1940*. Urbana: University of Illinois Press, 1982.

— "Jews and the New Deal." *AJH* 72 (June 1983):461–476.

— *Uneasy at Home: Antisemitism and the American Jewish Experience*. New York: Columbia University Press, 1987.

— *Antisemitism in America*. New York: Oxford University Press, 1994.

Domino, John C. *Civil Rights and Liberties: Toward the 21st Century*. New York: HarperCollins, 1994.

Dower, John W. *War Without Mercy: Race and Power in the Pacific War*. New York: Pantheon, 1986.

Duberman, Martin Bauml. *Paul Robeson*. New York: Knopf, 1988.

Dudziak, Mary L. "Desegregation as a Cold War Imperative." *Stanford Law Review* 41 (November 1988):61–120.

Elazar, Daniel J. *Community and Polity: The Organizational Dynamics of American Jewry*. Philadelphia: Jewish Publication Society of America, 1976.

Evans, Sara. *Personal Politics: The Roots of Women's Liberation in the Civil Rights Movement and the New Left*. New York: Vintage, 1980.

Feingold, Henry L. *The Politics of Rescue: The Roosevelt Administration and the Holocaust*. New York: Holocaust Library, 1970.

— "Who Shall Bear Guilt for the Holocaust: The Human Dilemma." *AJH* 68 (March 1979):261–281.

— A *Time for Searching: Entering the Mainstream, 1920–1945*. Baltimore: Johns Hopkins University Press, 1992.

Fisher, Alan. "Continuity and E...~sion of Jewish Liberalism." *AJHQ* 66 (December 1976):322–348.

Fishman, Hertzel. *American Protestantism and a Jewish State*. Detroit: Wayne State University Press, 1973.

Fleming, Donald, and Bernard Bailyn, eds. *The Intellectual Migration: Europe and America, 1930–1960*. Cambridge: Harvard University Press, 1969.

Friedman, George. *The Political Philosophy of the Frankfurt School*. Ithaca: Cornell University Press, 1981.

Friedman, Murray. *The Utopian Dilemma: American Judaism and Public Policy*. Washington, D.C.: Ethics and Public Policy Center, 1985.

— *What Went Wrong? The Creation and Collapse of the Black-Jewish Alliance*. New York: Free, 1995.

Friedman, Saul S. *No Haven for the Oppressed*. Detroit: Wayne State University Press, 1973.

Fuchs, Lawrence H. *The Political Behavior of American Jews*. Glencoe, Ill.: Free, 1956.

— "Introduction." In *Jews and American Liberalism: Studies in Political Behavior*. Special bicentennial issue of *AJHQ* 66 (December 1976):181–189.

Gabler, Neal. *An Empire of Their Own: How the Jews Invented Hollywood*. New York: Crown, 1988.

Gans, Herbert J. "Symbolic Ethnicity." In David Riesman, ed., *On the Making of Americans*. Philadelphia: University of Pennsylvania Press, 1979.

Gay, Peter. *Freud: A Life for Our Time*. New York: Norton, 1988.

Gerstle, Gary. "The Protean Character of American Liberalism." *AHR* 99 (October 1994):1043–1073.

— "Race and the Myth of the Liberal Consensus." *JAH* 82 (September 1995):579–586.

Gilbert, Arthur. *A Jew in Christian America*. New York: Sheed and Ward, 1966.

Gittelsohn, Roland G. "The Conference Stance on Social Justice and Civil Rights." In Bertram Wallace Korn, ed., *Retrospect and Prospect: Essays in Commemoration of the Seventy-fifth Anniversary of the Founding of the Central Conference of American Rabbis, 1889–1964*. New York: Central Conference of American Rabbis, 1965.

Glazer, Nathan. *American Judaism*. Rev. ed. Chicago: University of Chicago Press, 1972.

— "The New Left and the Jews." In Marshall Sklare, ed., *The Jewish Community in America*. New York: Behrman House, 1974.

Gleason, Philip. "Americans All: World War II and the Shaping of American Identity." *Review of Politics* 43 (October 1981):483–518.

Glenn, Susan A. *Daughters of the Shtetl: Life and Labor in the Immigrant Generation*. Ithaca: Cornell University Press, 1990.

Goodheart, Eugene. "The Abandoned Legacy of the New York Intellectuals." *AJH* 80 (Spring 1991):377–396.

Gorelick, Sherry. *City College and the Jewish Poor*. New Brunswick: Rutgers University Press, 1981.

Goren, Arthur A. *New York Jews and the Quest for Community: The Kehillah Experiment, 1908–1922*. New York: Columbia University Press; Philadelphia: Jewish Publication Society of America, 1970.

— *The American Jews*. Cambridge: Belknap Press of Harvard University Press, 1982.

— "The New Pluralism and the Politics of Community Relations." YIVO *Annual* 19 (1990):169–198.

— "A 'Golden Decade' for American Jews: 1945–1955." In Peter Y. Medding, ed., *A New Jewry? America Since the Second World War: Studies in Contemporary Jewry, An Annual*. Institute of Contemporary Jewry, Hebrew University of Jerusalem. No. 8. New York: Oxford University Press, 1992.

Greenberg, Jack. *Crusaders in the Courts: How a Dedicated Band of Lawyers Fought for the Civil Rights Revolution*. New York: Basic, 1994.

Griffith, Robert. "American Politics and the Origins of 'McCarthyism.' " In Robert Griffith and Athan Theoharis, ed., *The Specter: Original Essays on the Cold War and the Origins of McCarthyism*. New York: New Viewpoints, 1974.

Griffith, Robert, and Athan Theoharis, eds. *The Specter: Original Essays on the Cold War and the Origins of McCarthyism*. New York: New Viewpoints, 1974.

Grosskurth, Phyllis. *The Secret Ring: Freud's Inner Circle and the Politics of Psychoanalysis*. Reading, Mass.: Addison-Wesley, 1991.

Halperin, Samuel. *The Political World of American Zionism*. Detroit: Wayne State University Press, 1961.

Halpern, Ben. "The Roots of American Jewish Liberalism." *AJHQ* 66 (December 1976):190–214.

Hamby, Alonzo L. *Beyond the New Deal: Harry S. Truman and American Liberalism*. New York: Columbia University Press, 1973.

— *Liberalism and Its Challengers: F.D.R. to Reagan*. New York: Oxford University Press, 1985.

Heale, M. H. *American Anticommunism: Combating the Enemy Within, 1830–1970*. Baltimore: Johns Hopkins University Press, 1990.

Henthoff, Nat, ed. *Black Anti-Semitism and Jewish Racism*. New York: Richard W. Baron, 1969.

Hertzberg, Arthur. *The French Enlightenment and the Jews: The Origins of Modern Anti-Semitism*. New York: Columbia University Press, 1968.

Higham, John. *Send These To Me: Immigrants in Urban America*. Rev. ed. Baltimore: Johns Hopkins University Press, 1984.

— *Strangers in the Land: Patterns of American Nativism, 1860–1925*. 2d ed. New Brunswick: Rutgers University Press, 1988.

Hirsch, Arnold R. "Massive Resistance in the Urban North: Trumbull Park, Chicago, 1953–1966." *JAH* 82 (September 1995):522–550.

Hobsbawm, Eric. "Introduction: Inventing Traditions." In Eric Hobsbawm and Terence Range, eds., *The Invention of Tradition*. Cambridge: Cambridge University Press, 1983.

Hollinger, David A. "Ethnic Diversity, Cosmopolitanism, and the Emergence of the American Liberal Intelligentsia." AQ 27 (1975):133–151.

Howe, Irving. *World of Our Fathers: The Journey of the East European Jews to America and the Life They Found and Made*. New York: Harcourt Brace Jovanovich, 1976.

Irons, Peter H. *The New Deal Lawyers*. Princeton: Princeton University Press, 1982.

— *The Courage of Their Convictions: Sixteen Americans Who Fought Their Way to the Supreme Court*. New York: Penguin Books, 1990.

Isserman, Maurice. *Which Side Were You On? The American Communist Party During the Second World War*. Middletown, Conn.: Wesleyan University Press, 1982.

Jackson, Kenneth T. *Crabgrass Frontier: The Suburbanization of the United States*. New York: Oxford University Press, 1985.

Jackson, Walter A. *Gunnar Myrdal and America's Conscience: Social Engineering and Racial Liberalism, 1938–1987*. Chapel Hill: University of North Carolina Press, 1990.

Jay, Martin. *The Dialectical Imagination: A History of the Frankfurt School and the Institute of Social Research, 1923–1950*. Boston: Little, Brown, 1973.

— *Permanent Exiles: Essays on the Intellectual Migration from Germany to America*. New York: Columbia University Press, 1985.

Jick, Leon A. *The Americanization of the Synagogue, 1820–1870*. Hanover, N.H.: University Press of New England, 1976.

Karp, Abraham J. "Jewish Perceptions of America: From Melting Pot to Mosaic." B. G. Rudolph Lecture in Judaic Studies, Syracuse University, March 1976.

Katz, Jacob. *Out of the Ghetto: The Social Background of Jewish Emancipation, 1770–1870*. New York: Schocken, 1973.

Kaufman, Jonathan. *Broken Alliance: The Turbulent Times Between Blacks and Jews in America*. New York: Scribner's, 1988.

Kazin, Michael. *The Populist Persuasion: An American History*. New York: Basic, 1995.

— "The Agony and Romance of the American Left." AHR 100 (December 1995):1488–1512.

Kellogg, Peter J. "Civil Rights Consciousness in the 1940s." *Historian* 42 (1979):18–41.

Kluger, Richard. *Simple Justice: The History of Brown v. Board of Education and Black America's Struggle for Equality*. New York: Vintage, 1977.

Konvitz, Milton R. "Horace M. Kallen." In Carole S. Kessner, ed., *The "Other" New York Jewish Intellectuals*. New York: New York University Press, 1994.

Kramer, Judith R., and Seymour Leventman. *Children of the Gilded Ghetto: Conflict Resolutions of Three Generations of American Jews*. New Haven: Yale University Press, 1961.

Krause, P. Allen. "Rabbis and Negro Rights in the South, 1954–1967." AJA 21 (April 1969):20–47.

Kraut, Benny. "Toward the Establishment of the National Conference of Christians and Jews: The Tenuous Road to Religious Goodwill in the 1920s." *AJH* 77 (March 1988):388–412.

Lasch, Christopher. *The Culture of Narcissism: American Life in an Age of Diminishing Expectations.* New York: Norton, 1978.

Lazin, Frederick A. "The Response of the American Jewish Committee to the Crisis of German Jewry, 1933–1939." *AJH* 68 (March 1979):283–304.

Lerner, Michael, and Cornel West. *Jews and Blacks: A Dialogue on Race, Religion, and Culture in America.* New York: Plume/Penguin, 1996.

Leuchtenburg, William E. *Franklin D. Roosevelt and the New Deal, 1932–1940.* New York: Harper and Row, 1963.

— *In the Shadow of FDR: From Harry Truman to Ronald Reagan.* Ithaca: Cornell University Press, 1989.

Levy, Peter B. *One Hundred Key Documents in American Democracy.* Westport, Conn.: Greenwood, 1994.

Lewis, David Levering. *W. E. B. DuBois: Biography of a Race, 1868–1919.* New York: Henry Holt, 1993.

Liebman, Arthur. "The Ties That Bind: The Jewish Support for the Left in the United States." *AJHQ* 66 (December 1976):285–322.

— *Jews and the Left.* New York: John Wiley, 1979.

Liebman, Charles S. *The Ambivalent American Jew: Politics, Religion, and Family in American Jewish Life.* Philadelphia: Jewish Publication Society of America, 1973.

Lipset, Seymour Martin, ed. *American Pluralism and the Jewish Community.* New Brunswick, N.J.: Transaction, 1990.

Lipset, Seymour Martin, and Earl Raab. *The Politics of Unreason: Right-Wing Extremism in America, 1790–1970.* New York: Harper and Row, 1970.

Lipsitz, George. "The Possessive Investment in Whiteness: Racialized Social Democracy and the 'White' Problem in American Studies." *AQ* 47 (September 1995):369–387.

Lissak, Rivka Shpak. *Pluralism and Progressives: Hull House and the New Immigrants, 1890–1919.* Chicago: University of Chicago Press, 1989.

Lockard, Duane. *Toward Equal Opportunity: A Study of State and Local Anti-Discrimination Laws.* New York: Macmillan, 1968.

Longstaff, S. A. "Ivy League Gentiles and Inner-City Jews: Class and Ethnicity Around *Partisan Review* in the Thirties and Forties." *AJH* 80 (Spring 1991):325–343.

Lora, Ronald. "A View from the Right: Conservative Intellectuals, the Cold War, and McCarthy." In Robert Griffith and Athan Theoharis, ed., *The Specter: Original Essays on the Cold War and the Origins of McCarthyism.* New York: New Viewpoints, 1974.

McAuliffe, Mary Sperling. "The Politics of Civil Liberties: The American Civil Liberties Union During the McCarthy Years." In Robert Griffith and Athan Theoharis, ed., *The Specter: Original Essays on the Cold War and the Origins of McCarthyism.* New York: New Viewpoints, 1974.

—— *Crisis on the Left: Cold War Politics and American Liberals*. Amherst: University of Massachusetts Press, 1978.

McCoy, Donald R., and Richard T. Ruetten. *Quest and Response: Minority Rights and the Truman Administration*. Lawrence: University Press of Kansas, 1973.

Mann, Arthur. *The One and the Many: Reflections on the American Identity*. Chicago: University of Chicago Press, 1973.

Marable, Manning. *Race, Reform, and Rebellion: The Second Reconstruction in Black America, 1945–1990*. 2d ed. Jackson: University Press of Mississippi, 1991.

Marcus, Judith, and Zoltán Tar, eds. *Foundations of the Frankfurt School of Social Research*. New Brunswick, N.J.: Transaction, 1984.

Marker, Jeffrey M. "The Jewish Community and the Case of Julius and Ethel Rosenberg." *The Maryland Historian* 3 (Fall 1972):105–121.

—— "The Case Against the Jews." *Davka* 4 (Winter 1974):12–17.

Markowitz, Norman. "A View from the Left: From the Popular Front to Cold War Liberalism." In Robert Griffith and Athan Theoharis. eds., *The Specter: Original Essays on the Cold War and the Origins of McCarthyism*. New York: New Viewpoints, 1974.

Markowitz, Ruth Jacknow. *My Daughter, the Teacher: Jewish Teachers in the New York City Schools*. New Brunswick, N.J.: Rutgers University Press, 1993.

Maslow, Will. "Jewish Political Power: An Assessment." *AJHQ* 66 (December 1976):349–362.

Matusow, Allen J. *The Unraveling of America: A History of Liberalism in the 1960s*. New York: Harper and Row, 1984.

May, Lary L., and Elaine Tyler May. "Why Jewish Movie Moguls: An Exploration in American Culture." *AJH* 72 (September 1982):6–25.

Meeropol, Robert, and Michael Meeropol. *We Are Your Sons: The Legacy of Ethel and Julius Rosenberg*. Urbana: University of Illinois Press, 1975.

Mendelsohn, Ezra. *On Modern Jewish Politics*. New York: Oxford University Press, 1993.

Mendes-Flohr, Paul R., and Jehuda Reinharz, eds. *The Jew in the Modern World: A Documentary History*. New York: Oxford University Press, 1980.

Mervis, Leonard J. "The Social Justice Movement and the American Reform Rabbi." *AJA* 7 (June 1955):171–230.

Meyer, Michael A. *Response to Modernity: A History of the Reform Movement*. New York: Oxford University Press, 1988.

Miller, James. *"Democracy is in the Streets": From Port Huron to the Siege of Chicago*. New York: Simon and Schuster, 1987.

Montalto, Nicholas V. *A History of the Intercultural Education Movement, 1924–1941*. New York: Garland Publishing Inc., 1982.

Moore, Deborah Dash. *B'nai B'rith and the Challenge of Ethnic Leadership*. Albany: State University of New York Press, 1981.

—— *At Home in America: Second-Generation New York Jews*. New York: Columbia University Press, 1981.

— "Reconsidering the Rosenbergs: Symbol and Substance in Second-Generation American Jewish Consciousness." *JAEH* 8 (Fall 1988):21–37.

— *To The Golden Cities: Pursuing the American Jewish Dream in Miami and L.A.* New York: Free, 1994.

Morris, Aldon D. *The Origins of the Civil Rights Movement: Black Communities Organizing for Change.* New York: Free, 1984.

Morse, Arthur D. *While Six Million Died.* New York: Random House, 1965.

Navasky, Victor S. *Naming Names.* New York: Penguin, 1980.

Newman, Edwin S., ed. *The Hate Reader.* Dobbs Ferry, N.Y.: Oceana, 1964.

Nieman, Donald G. *Promises to Keep: African Americans and the Constitutional Order, 1776 to the Present.* New York: Oxford University Press, 1991.

Oren, Dan A. *Joining the Club: A History of Jews and Yale.* New Haven: Yale University Press, 1985.

Oshinsky, David M. "Labor's Cold War: The CIO and the Communists." In Robert Griffith and Athan Theoharis, eds., *The Specter: Original Essays on the Cold War and the Origins of McCarthyism.* New York: New Viewpoints, 1974.

— *A Conspiracy So Immense: The World of Joe McCarthy.* New York: Free, 1983.

Osofsky, Gilbert. *Harlem: The Making of a Ghetto.* 2d edition. New York: Harper and Row, 1971.

Overstreet, Harry, and Bonaro Overstreet. *The Strange Tactics of Extremism.* New York: Norton, 1964.

Penkower, Monty Noam. *The Jews Were Expendable: Free World Diplomacy and the Holocaust.* Urbana: University of Illinois Press, 1983.

— *The Holocaust and Israel Reborn: From Catastrophe to Sovereignty.* Urbana: University of Illinois Press, 1994.

Pfeffer, Leo. *Church, State, and Freedom.* Rev. ed. Boston: Beacon, 1967.

Philipson, David. *The Reform Movement in Judaism.* Rev. ed. New York: Ktav, 1967.

Phillips, William M., Jr. *An Unillustrious Alliance: The African American and Jewish American Communities.* New York: Greenwood, 1991.

Pitt, James E. *Adventures in Brotherhood.* New York: Farrar, Straus, 1955.

Polenberg, Richard. *War and Society: The United States, 1941–1945.* New York: Lippincott, 1972.

— *One Nation Divisible: Class, Race, and Ethnicity in the United States Since 1938.* New York: Penguin, 1981.

Pope, Daniel, and William Toll. "We Tried Harder: Jews in American Advertising." *AJH* 72 (September 1982):26–51.

Pozzetta, George E., ed. *Folklore, Culture, and the Immigrant Mind.* New York: Garland, 1991.

Quinley, Harold E., and Charles Y. Glock. *Anti-Semitism in America.* New York: Free, 1979.

Radosh, Ronald, and Joyce Milton. *The Rosenberg File: A Search for the Truth.* New York: Holt, Rinehart and Winston, 1983.

Rayner, William P. *Wise Women: Singular Lives that Helped Shape Our Century*. New York: St. Martin's, 1983.

Rieder, Jonathan. *Canarsie: The Jews and Italians of Brooklyn Against Liberalism*. Cambridge: Harvard University Press, 1985.

Ringer, Benjamin. *The Edge of Friendliness: A Study of Jewish-Gentile Relations*. New York: Basic, 1967.

Rischin, Moses. *The Promised City: New York's Jews, 1870–1914*. Cambridge: Harvard University Press, 1962.

Robinson, Ira. "The Invention of American Jewish History." *AJH* 81 (1992):309–320.

Rose, Peter I. *They and We: Racial and Ethnic Relations in the United States*. New York: Random House, 1964.

Rose, Peter I., ed. *The Ghetto and Beyond: Essays on Jewish Life in America*. New York: Random House, 1969.

Ruitenbeek, Hendrik M. *Freud and America*. New York: Macmillan, 1966.

St. John, Robert. *Jews, Justice, and Judaism: A Narrative of the Role Played by the Bible People in Shaping American History*. New York: Doubleday, Inc., 1969.

Sanders, Ronald. *The Downtown Jews: Portraits of an Immigrant Generation*. New York: Harper and Row, 1969.

Schneir, Walter, and Miriam Schneir. *Invitation to an Inquest*. New York: Pantheon, 1965.

Schwartz, Joel. *The New York Approach: Robert Moses, Urban Liberals, and the Redevelopment of the Inner City*. Columbus: Ohio State University Press, 1993.

Shapiro, Edward S. *A Time for Healing: American Jewry Since World War II*. Baltimore: Johns Hopkins University Press, 1992.

Shapiro, Yonathan. *Leadership of the American Zionist Organization, 1897–1930*. Urbana: University of Illinois Press, 1971.

Shargel, Bella Round. "Leftist Summer Colonies of Northern Westchester County, New York." *AJH* 83 (September 1995):337–358.

Short, K. R. M. "Hollywood Fights Anti-Semitism, 1945–1947." In *Feature Films as History*. Knoxville: University of Tennessee Press, 1981.

Sitkoff, Harvard. *A New Deal For Blacks: The Emergence of Civil Rights as a National Issue*. New York: Oxford University Press, 1978.

— *The Struggle for Black Equality, 1954–1992*. Rev. ed. New York: Hill and Wang, 1993.

Sklare, Marshall. *America's Jews*. New York: Random House, 1971.

Sklare, Marshall, ed. *The Jews: Social Patterns of an American Group*. New York: Free, 1958.

— *The Jewish Community in America*. New York: Berhrman House, 1974.

Sklare, Marshall, and Joseph Greenblum. *Jewish Identity on the Suburban Frontier: A Study of Group Survival in the Open Society*. New York: Basic, 1967.

Sklare, Marshall, and Marc Vosk. *The Riverton Study: How Jews Look at Themselves and Their Neighbors*. New York: American Jewish Committee, 1957.

Slawson, John. *Unequal Americans: Practices and Politics of Intergroup Relations*. Westport, Conn.: Greenwood, 1979.

Sorauf, Frank J. *The Wall of Separation: The Constitutional Politics of Church and State*. Princeton: Princeton University Press, 1976.

Sorin, Gerald. *The Prophetic Minority: American Jewish Immigrant Radicals, 1880–1920*. Bloomington: Indiana University Press, 1985.

— "From the Brownsville Boys Club to the Institute for American Pluralism: Irving M. Levine and the Modern Challenge to Jewish Liberalism." In Jeffrey S. Gurock and Marc Lee Raphael, eds., *An Inventory of Promises: Essays on American Jewish History in Honor of Moses Rischin*. Brooklyn, N.Y.: Carlson, 1995.

Southern, David W. *Gunnar Myrdal and Black-White Relations: The Use and Abuse of an American Dilemma, 1944–1969*. Baton Rouge: Louisiana State University Press, 1987.

Steele, Richard W. "The War on Intolerance: The Reformulation of American Nationalism, 1939–1941." *JAEH* 8 (Fall 1989):9–35.

Steinberg, Stephen. *The Ethnic Myth*. Rev. ed. Boston: Beacon, 1989.

Stern, Stephen. "Ethnic Folklore and the Folklore of Ethnicity." *Western Folklore* 36 (1977):7–32.

Sugrue, Thomas J. "Crabgrass-Roots Politics: Race, Rights, and the Reaction Against Liberalism in the Urban North, 1940–1964." *JAH* 82 (September 1995):551–578.

Sussman, Lance J. " 'Toward Better Understanding': The Rise of the Interfaith Movement in America and the Role of Rabbi Isaac Landman." *AJA* 34 (April 1982): 35–51.

Synnott, Marcia Graham. *The Half-Opened Door: Discriminations and Admissions at Harvard, Yale, and Princeton, 1900–1970*. Westport, Conn.: Greenwood, 1979.

Tanner, William R., and Robert Griffith. "Legislative Politics and 'McCarthyism': The Internal Security Act of 1950." In Robert Griffith and Athan Theoharis, eds., *The Specter: Original Essays on the Cold War and the Origins of McCarthyism*. New York: New Viewpoints, 1974.

Tar, Zoltán. *The Frankfurt School: The Critical Theories of Max Horkheimer and Theodor W. Adorno*. New York: John Wiley, 1977.

Teller, Judd L. *Strangers and Natives: The Evolution of the American Jew from 1921 to the Present*. New York: Delacorte, 1968.

Theoharis, Athan. "The Politics of Scholarship: Liberals, Anti-Communism, and McCarthyism." In Robert Griffith and Athan Theoharis, eds., *The Specter: Original Essays on the Cold War and the Origins of McCarthyism*. New York: New Viewpoints, 1974.

Tushnet, Marc V. *The NAACP's Legal Strategy Against Segregated Education, 1925–1950*. Chapel Hill: University of North Carolina Press, 1987.

Tuttle, William M., Jr. *Race Riot: Chicago in the Red Summer of 1919*. New York: Atheneum, 1970.

Urofsky, Melvin I. *American Zionism from Herzl to the Holocaust*. Garden City, N.Y.: Anchor/Doubleday, 1976.

— *We Are One! American Jewry and Israel*. Garden City, N.Y.: Anchor/Doubleday, 1978.

— A Voice That Spoke for Justice: The Life and Times of Stephen S. Wise. Albany: State University of New York Press, 1982.

Vose, Clement E. Caucasians Only: The Supreme Court, the NAACP, and the Restrictive Covenant Cases. Berkeley: University of California Press, 1967.

Wakefield, Dan. New York in the Fifties. Boston: Houghton Mifflin, 1992.

Walker, Samuel. In Defense of American Liberties: A History of the ACLU. New York: Oxford University Press, 1990.

— "The Growth of Civil Liberties, 1900–1945." In Raymond Arsenault, ed., Crucible of Liberty: 200 Years of the Bill of Rights. New York: Free, 1991.

— Hate Speech: The History of an American Controversy. Lincoln: University of Nebraska Press, 1994.

Waxman, Chaim I. America's Jews in Transition. Philadelphia: Temple University Press, 1983.

Weisbord, Robert G., and Arthur Stein. Bittersweet Encounter: The Afro-American and the American Jew. Westport, Conn.: Negro Universities Press, 1970.

Whitfield, Stephen J. "From Publick Occurrences to Pseudo-Events: Journalists and Their Critics." AJH 72 (September 1982):52–81.

Wilkinson, J. Harvie, III. From "Brown" to "Bakke": The Supreme Court and School Integration: 1954–1978. New York: Oxford University Press, 1979.

Wisse, Ruth R. If I Am Not For Myself . . . The Liberal Betrayal of the Jews. New York: Free, 1992.

Wistrich, Robert S. Antisemitism: The Longest Hatred. New York: Schocken, 1991.

Wyman, David. Paper Walls: America and the Refugee Crisis, 1938–1941. Amherst: University of Massachusetts Press, 1968.

— The Abandonment of the Jews: America and the Holocaust, 1941–1945. New York: Pantheon Books, 1984.

Yerushalmi, Yosef Hayim. Freud's Moses: Judaism Terminable and Interminable. New Haven: Yale University Press, 1991.

Zborowski, Mark, and Elizabeth Herzog. Life Is with People: The Culture of the Shtetl. New York: Schocken, 1962.

Unpublished Dissertations and Theses

Berkson, Marc E. "The Case of Julius and Ethel Rosenberg: Jewish Response to a Period of Stress." Rabbinical thesis, Hebrew Union College-Jewish Institute of Religion, 1978.

Bloch, Avital Hadassah. "The Emergence of Neoconservatism in the United States, 1960–1972." Ph.D. diss., Columbia University, 1990.

Dollinger, Marc Lindsey. "The Politics of Acculturation: American Jewish Liberalism, 1933–1975." Ph.D. diss., University of California, Los Angeles, 1993.

Frommer, Morris. "The American Jewish Congress: A History, 1914–1950." 2 vols. Ph.D. diss., Ohio State University, 1978.

Kirman, Joseph M. "Major Programs of the B'nai B'rith Anti-Defamation League: 1945–1965." Ph.D. diss., New York University School of Education, 1967.

Overmeyer, Deborah Ann. " 'Common Ground' and America's Minorities, 1940–1949: A Study in the Changing Climate of Opinion." Ph.D. diss., University of Cincinnati, 1984.

Powell, James Henry. "The Concept of Cultural Pluralism in American Social Theory, 1915–1965." Ph.D. diss., University of Notre Dame, 1971.

Sable, Jacob M. "Some American Jewish Organizational Efforts to Combat Anti-Semitism, 1900–1930." Ph.D. diss., Yeshiva University, 1964.

Svonkin, Stuart. "Jews Against Prejudice: American and the Intergroup Relations Movement from World War to Cold War." Ph.D. diss., Columbia University, 1995.

Index

Abrams, Charles, 100, 101, 249*n*103, 250*n*109, 251*n*111

Acheson, Dean, 27–28

Ackerman, Nathan:
— *Anti-Semitism and Emotional Disorder*, 35, 36; on economic factors, 39; on information dissemination, 55; ISR and, 212*n*114; welfare agency records and, 211*n*110, 214*n*132
— *Crossfire* and, 58

ADL Bulletin: on economic costs, 109; on education, 77; on government employees, 122, 124; on A. Rosenberg, 120; on J. and E. Rosenberg, 156, 159; on television, 217–18*n*26

Adler, Cyrus, 11

Adorno, Theodor W., 33, 210*nn*99, 102, 103
— *The Authoritarian Personality*: "action-research" conception of, 31; American population and, 214*n*128; *Dynamics of Prejudice* and, 213*n*125; "Elements of Anti-Semitism" and, 211*n*111; on "Genuine Liberal," 212*n*116; Hofstadter and, 213*n*126; Horkheimer and, 212*n*115; impact of,

37; on ineffective methods, 55–56; McCarthyism and, 258*n*14; methodology of, 211*n*108; misconstruction of, 212*n*112; popularization of, 115–16; on pseudo-conservatives, 38; recommendations of, 39; sample group for, 34–35; San Francisco study and, 211*n*110; Sartre and, 213–14*n*127; socioeconomic allusions in, 35–36; on status/ethnocentrism nexus, 214*n*130
— *Dialectic of Enlightenment*, 211*n*111

Advertising Council of America, 42, 43, 46

Africa, 5, 27

African Americans: antidiscrimination commissions and, 93; Bettelheim-Janowitz findings on, 37–38, 214*n*129; Clark study of, 66; communist strategy and, 142; complaints of discrimination by, 111, 112; economic inequality of, 108, 110; education of, 26, 67; Epstein on, 203*n*35; fair employment and, 88, 242*n*49; false beliefs about, 63; film industry and, 59, 223*n*88, 224*n*103; *Home of the Brave* and, 60;

ence meeting in, 32; Stuyvesant
Town issue and, 98–99, 100, 249n103,
252n126; vandalism in, 184
New York City Administrative Code, 100
New York City Board of Education, 71
New York City Board of Estimate,
99–100, 250n106
New York City Council, 103–4, 130,
243n55
New York City Department of Investiga-
tion, 83
New York City Housing Authority,
251n111, 252n126
New York City Planning Commission,
100
New York City Police Department, 16
New York City Tax Commission, 90
New York City Teachers Union, 267n96
New York City YMCA, 220n62
New York Federation of Jewish Philan-
thropies, 167
New York Jewish Board of Guardians,
210n103
New York Jewish Family and Children's
Service, 168–69
New York Joint Defense Appeal, 154
New York Medical College, 185
New York Metropolitan Council of
B'nai B'rith, 61
New York Post, 218n26, 281n103
New York Post-Home News, 268n2
New York Redevelopment Companies
Law (1942), 99, 101, 102, 250n109
New York State: anticommunism law in,
131, 150, 164, 266nn92–94; education
antidiscrimination law in, 90–91, 95,
244n58, 247n82; employment antidis-
crimination law in, 89, 94, 256n174;
housing antidiscrimination law in,
90, 99, 104–5, 110, 243n55, 253n138;
Jewish congregations in, 153; loyalty
oaths in, 265n89; neo-Nazism in,
184

New York State Appellate Division, 102
New York State Board of Charities, 32,
209n96
New York State Board of Regents, 91, 131
New York State Commission Against
Discrimination, 245n66; Abrams and,
251n111; Brotherhood of Man and,
220n62; budget of, 93; commercial
films and, 218n38; employment dis-
crimination and, 111; founding of, 92;
Ives-Quinn law and, 246n75; on "per-
sons aggrieved," 94
New York State Commission of Educa-
tion, 91
New York State Committee on Discrim-
ination in Housing, 90, 102
New York State Communist Party, 131
New York State Constitution, 99, 102,
103, 131
New York State Court of Appeals, 103,
266n93
New York State Insurance Department,
167; see also New York State Superin-
tendent of Insurance
New York State Legislature, 90, 124
New York State Public Housing Law
(1939), 90, 99
New York State Superintendent of
Insurance, 100; see also New York
State Insurance Department
New York State Supreme Court, 102,
252n126, 266n94
New York State Temporary Commission
on the Need for a State University in
New York, 90
New York Times, 268n2
New York Times Magazine, 38, 115–16
New York University, 67, 224n104
New York World-Telegram, 175
A Night of Vigil (TV program), 47
Nimitz, Chester W., 175
North Atlantic Treaty Organization
(NATO), 87